MYSTERY IN WESTMINSTER SQUARE

MYSTERY IN WESTMINSTER SQUARE

AIDEN PATTERSON

WHITE MOUNTAIN

White Mountain Books is an affiliate of
The Arcadian Group S.A., Case Postale 431, 1211 Geneva 12, Switzerland
Copyright © White Mountain Books 2017

Database right White Mountain Publications (maker)

First published 2017

All rights reserved. No part of this publication may be reproduced, stored in a retrieval system, or transmitted, in any form or by any means, without the prior permission in writing of White Mountain Books, or as expressly permitted by law, or under terms agreed with the appropriate reprographics rights organization. Enquiries concerning reproduction outside the scope of the above should be sent to White Mountain Books, at the above address.

You must not circulate this book in any other binding or cover and you must impose this same condition in any acquirer.

Copyright restrictions in favor of
The Arcadian Group S.A. apply. © 2017

ISBN 9781941634790

Designed and typeset by Megan Sheer

Printed in Great Britain by CPI UK,
141-143 Shoreditch High Street, London, E1 6JE

Typeset in Monotype Arcadian Bembo

Although based on the author's experiences, it should be noted that this book is a work of fiction presented entirely for entertainment purposes. The author and publisher are not offering professional service advice. The stories and their characters and entities are fictional. Any likeness to actual persons, whether in terms of character profiles or names, either living or dead, is strictly coincidental.

To the royals and high court judges; doctors and politicians; authors and actors who lived in the City of Westminster, and whom I had the pleasure of socialising with over the course of thirty years. This book is for you.

AUTHOR'S NOTE

Having lived in New York and Paris before moving to London in the 1960s, the first thing that struck me when settling into life in the British capital, was the number of residential squares there were. I had seen them in many movies, of course, and read about them in children's books. But on a restless Sunday evening in the balmy month of August, not long after I had arrived in the country, I took a long stroll through the borough of Westminster. It was a hot day. People were outside enjoying the sun. Everyone wore bright smiles and the sound of laughter tinkled through the air. Far from the grim, iron-grey picture many had painted when warning me about London – I found it exquisite. The grand architecture, the red phones boxes, the black cabs: it was all so charming, so quaint. And with every corner I took, I seemed to stumble upon yet more of these squares. Out of all the treasures of London, it was these that fascinated me most. Pretty green patches of tranquillity, fenced off from the rest of busy London by glossed-black iron railings and high clipped hedges. They were Eden-like. Cloaked in mystery. I would stop and peer in. Some were larger than others, and accessible to the public, but by far the most enchanting were those forbidden to all but the residents.

Over the next twenty-five years, I came to know these squares very well. Lots of my friends and acquaintances lived in Kensington, Chelsea and Mayfair. I often went to parties in some of the stucco-white houses that overhung them, tiered-high like wedding cakes. I would gaze out from the windows at them.

At other times, under full moons I took midnight strolls with girlfriends in Berkeley Square, and under high suns I enjoyed summer picnics in Grosvenor Square. I worked in trading before I became a journalist, and many of the oil-affiliated companies I was acquainted with had offices in Westminster, such as Victoria Street and Park Lane.

During these experiences, I enjoyed bumping into the residents. I walked the twisting lanes of the manicured gardens. I said hello to dukes and dames, politicians and thespians, writers and oligarchs. I overheard their stories as they muttered. Their habits and tiffs. Their likes, their dislikes; who they hated; who they would invite to their garden parties; who was a crook, and who was sleeping with whom. They drifted over the hedge tops. It was while learning about these eccentrics that I began to dream up the plots and characters that would later populate this novel. I envisioned a square, small and prestigious. And in it, faces and figures who piqued curiosity and aroused suspicion in equal measure.

Thus, I took a pen and paper into the gardens near my home and began to lay out my ideas, frenzied as they were. The first draft came together in a blur. I wrote and wrote and wrote. By the end, I was happy with the cast of characters, the figures behind the black doors of the Georgian porticos: a barrister, a policeman, a novelist and a dame – that was a start. But I wanted more razzmatazz. So I created a Hollywood actor with money problems, a Ukrainian oligarch with shady dealings, a Middle Eastern magnate with seedy obsessions, and a local gossip who could unite their stories. It was then clear that I needed to pit them against one another, and to do that I needed a crime that they could all be suspected of. Mystery was always going to be at its heart, and the murder of a beautiful young socialite seemed to complete the cast. From there, the book evolved into what it is now, and I hope the reader will be as thrilled reading it as I was writing it.

Finally, I would like to thank my editorial team for their invaluable help in assisting me with the completion of this book. In particular, I would like to offer special thanks to Amanda Block and Joe Quince for their untiring dedication.

PROLOGUE
1994

The Royal West was one of the grandest hotels in all of London. Like many of the buildings in Westminster, it was a fine example of Georgian architecture, with its pillared façade, large windows and high ceilings. When checking in, the hotel's visitors (who were always well-off, well-connected, or both) would climb a few steps to enter the opulent hallway — complete with crystal chandelier — where they would be immediately fussed over by three receptionists, who would offer them tea, coffee and juice while looking up their rooms. Then, when the booking was found, and the keys handed over, the guests' luggage would be whisked away by uniformed bellboys, and they would face the choice between stepping into the old-fashioned gilded lift, or seeing more of the Royal West's interior by climbing the wide, green-carpeted staircase, trailing their fingers along the bronze handrail as they ascended.

Rafaela, one of the hotel's cleaners, was used to seeing a very different side of the Royal West than the establishment's illustrious guests. Instead of the impressive entranceway, she was required to let herself in the back door of the hotel, which was next to the kitchen, and therefore usually retained an unpleasant waft of the previous night's dinner. She was greeted by nobody and offered nothing to drink as she hung up her jacket in a dingy hallway, put on her tabard and tied up her long dark hair in a bright red scarf. And in order to move around the building, she was forced to clamber up and down the service stairs or — if there was no-one around — sneak into the large modern lift at the back of the building, which was meant to be used exclusively for ferrying towels and bed linen between the different floors. Rafaela far preferred this second option because, at fifty-five years old, she was both a little too large and far too impatient to use the narrow, cold staircase that was once reserved for the servants of the house.

One Sunday morning in June, Rafaela was in a particularly bad mood as she arrived at work, despite the fact that, even at six o'clock, it was already a beautifully sunny day. But Rafaela didn't care about that, because the hotel's manager, a Mr Edwin Brackenwell, had requested she start her shift half an hour early, in order to ensure no evidence remained of the charity party that had been hosted by the Royal West the previous night. Rafaela had accepted Edwin's promise of extra pay, although rather ungraciously: it was bad enough she had to tidy up rich people's mess first thing on a Sunday, but losing half an hour's sleep for the privilege only added insult to injury.

The mess in the hotel's main function room, which was called the Duke Room, was as bad as Rafaela had anticipated; so bad, in fact, that she muttered some choice Italian swearwords under her breath as she surveyed the damage from the night before: empty bottles of champagne, used wine glasses and side plates, dishes of leftover canapés and half a cake littered the tabletops, while the floor was strewn with crumbs, more dirty crockery, a woman's shawl, and some potent-smelling flowers that had evidently fallen down from the elaborate arrangements on the wall. With a sigh, Rafaela reminded herself the mess wouldn't tidy itself, and so she picked up a large black bin bag and began throwing the rubbish into its depths, stopping every so often to pick at the cake as she passed.

Around ten minutes later, the door opened and Edwin Brackenwell himself bustled in. The manager of the Royal West was a fussy, pretentious man in his mid-thirties. He was tall, thin, and always looked immaculate from his head to his toes; from his neatly-combed dark hair to his Hermès shoes, which were so shiny one could almost see one's reflection in them. Rafaela disliked him immensely.

'A very good morning to you, Rafaela,' Edwin said pompously.

Rafaela, who was chewing on her third mouthful of cake, could only scowl in response. However, given this was how she usually greeted Edwin, he was unfazed.

'I see you're doing a very good job in here — a very good job indeed,' he continued in his clipped voice, despite the fact she had barely started her cleaning. 'But I think, before you continue with this, you should move onto the business conference room.'

Rafaela finally swallowed her mouthful of sponge and icing. 'What?' she demanded.

'*The — business — conference — room*,' repeated Edwin slowly, as though she hadn't understood.

'*The — party — was — in — here*,' replied Rafaela slowly, as though he were stupid.

Edwin drew his hands to his hips and looked at the ceiling, his expression long-suffering. 'Yes, Rafaela, I know that, thank you. But often these events spill out into other rooms, and given we have an important meeting starting in the business conference room at eight o'clock sharp, don't you think it might be a good idea to ensure it's clean and tidy?'

Rafaela realised he had a point, but as she would have rather given up her *nonna's* secret recipe for spaghetti Bolognese than admit this, she responded by silently slouching off in the direction of the business conference room, trailing the black bin liner behind her.

This adjoining space was a large, plush room dominated by a polished wooden conference table, although beyond that there were a trio of sofas positioned around a smaller table for coffee. To Rafaela's annoyance, it looked as though Edwin was right once again, and a little of the party had indeed spilled over into this area: there was another empty champagne bottle on the table, a plate full of half-eaten canapés on one of the chairs, and she could see a few glasses and other bits of debris on the floor beside the sofas.

With a theatrical sigh, Rafaela began to tidy, working her way down the large table until she reached the three sofas at the other end of the room. Then, as she bent down to pick up one of the two crystal tumblers from the floor, she gave a start: lying on one of the large, squashy sofas was a young woman, evidently fast asleep. She was curled up against the cushions, so all Rafaela could see of her was the back of her black evening gown, her bright blonde hair, which had come a little loose from its neat chignon, and her stiletto heels, one of which was still on her foot and one of which had fallen onto the floor.

'Big night, eh?' Rafaela murmured.

The woman didn't respond: Rafaela suspected she'd hit the champagne a little too hard at the party, and was now in a deep, alcohol-fuelled sleep. She chuckled, reminded a little of her younger sister back in Italy. *Well, let this one rest*, thought the cleaner, looking from the sleeping blonde woman to her watch. These business meetings wouldn't start for another hour, why not let the girl catch some extra kip? It made no difference to her.

Rafaela continued to tidy, making an effort to do it quietly now. What would it be like to be that rich, she wondered, replacing the stopper on a crystal decanter full of what looked like whisky, and moving it to a tray to be taken back to the bar. For from the look of her dress and shoes, there was no doubt the snoozing woman was wealthy — besides, only a person with a lot of money would have the audacity to fall asleep in the business conference room of one of the grandest hotels in London, alcohol or no alcohol. When she had left Italy as a young woman, Rafaela had had dreams of marrying an affluent Englishman and behaving in a similar way. *If only things had turned out the way I'd planned,* she thought sadly, looking down at the bin liner clutched in her dry, cracked hands.

Around ten minutes later, when she had decided the business conference room was presentable once again, it occurred to Rafaela that it might be wise to wake up the sleeper before she brought in the vacuum cleaner. Perhaps, if she explained she had let the woman have a few minutes extra slumber, she might even get a tip for her trouble.

'Excuse me, Miss,' whispered Rafaela, tiptoeing forward, anxious not to shock the woman awake. 'I think you should get up…'

Now she was almost standing above her, Rafaela had a better look at the sleeper's face. She was, the cleaner realised, a very beautiful creature, with a small nose, pink lips and a porcelain complexion. Lying there, the length of her lashes emphasised by her closed eyes, she might have been Sleeping Beauty.

'Miss!' said Rafaela, a little louder now. 'You have to wake up. You have to —'

She frowned, suddenly noticing something: at her neck and wrists, the woman's pale skin was discoloured by patches of darkness, as though something was casting odd shadows on her body. Rafaela reached out, both to gently awaken the woman and to check she was all right. But as soon as her hand found the sleeper's right shoulder, she snatched it back, as though she had been burned, although in fact the effect had been quite the opposite: the woman was completely cold.

'Miss!' cried Rafaela, urgently now. 'Please, wake up! Miss, please!'

She forced herself to touch the icy shoulder once more, shaking it, although by the time Rafaela had pulled the woman onto her back, and the pale arm had flopped uselessly towards the floor, the cleaner had realised she was not breathing. She reached her shaking fingers towards the woman's bruised throat: there was no pulse.

Rafaela staggered backwards, almost tripping over her bin liner as she did so, and a high-pitched scream escaped her mouth. Then she clapped her hands over her lips, and began to count to ten, just as she had taught herself to do when she was younger, and she had come across something unpleasant in her native Naples: *One... two... three... four...*

The door burst open.

'What on earth is going on?' Edwin demanded, from the other side of the business conference room. 'Stop that shrieking at once, Rafaela! What if the guests hear you? You'll wake up the whole hotel!'

She turned to look at him, wide-eyed. Her expression must have startled him, because the anger in his face gave way to apprehension.

'What's the matter?' he asked. 'What's going on?'

Still trembling, Rafaela pointed wordlessly towards the occupied sofa. Edwin walked forward a few paces and peered in the direction of the blonde woman.

'Ah!' he said, looking relieved. 'Oh dear! It looks like someone's had a bit too much to drink, doesn't it? Well, we'll have to wake her up, although I expect she'll be rather embarrassed about it all...'

Rafaela didn't move.

'Go on,' Edwin continued. 'Wake her up and get her out of here, Rafaela — we don't have time for this.'

Still the cleaner remained where she was. 'She's not asleep,' she said, her voice barely a whisper.

Edwin hesitated, and Rafaela thought she saw comprehension dawning on him, quickly followed by denial. 'Yes she is — of course she is! She just passed out at the party, that's all.'

'She's not asleep!' Rafaela repeated, more loudly than she had meant to.

'Shh!' Edwin looked around in panic. 'For God's sake *keep your voice down*! Think of the guests!'

But Rafaela didn't care about the guests. 'She's dead, Mr Brackenwell! She's dead and she's covered in bruises! I think' — she could feel a sob rising up in her throat — 'I think someone's killed her!'

Edwin mouthed silently at her for a few seconds, like a goldfish out of water. 'Don't be ridiculous!' he hissed at last, although his face had drained of all colour. 'That's absurd! She can't — she isn't —'

He staggered forward and collapsed into the nearest seat, a high-backed leather chair at the conference table. He then ran his hands through his neat dark hair, causing it to stand on end at the sides, which Rafaela would have found comical under other circumstances.

'She can't be,' Edwin moaned. 'Not here… I don't — she *can't* be!'

'She's dead,' repeated Rafaela, who felt a little calmer in the face of Edwin's panic. 'You should call the police.'

He looked up at her, his face a mask of horror. 'We can't!' he cried. 'There'll be a scandal! It'll be in all the papers! The reputation of the Royal West Hotel will be *ruined*! We'll forever be associated with this…'

'*The woman is dead*!' Rafaela shouted, wondering how many times she had said this now. 'Are you just going to leave her here? Are you going to let all those businessmen and women hold their meeting at eight o'clock with a dead body lying on the sofa?'

'The meeting — I forgot!' gasped Edwin.

This was not exactly the point Rafaela had been trying to make, but it did seem to bring him to his senses.

'You need to call the police,' she told him again. 'I think it's too late for the ambulance, but you need to call the police as soon as possible.'

Yet it looked as though Edwin lost the ability to move his long body. 'Can you do it?' he asked plaintively.

She rolled her eyes, although inwardly Rafaela wondered whether she could use this situation against him in the future; in her opinion, finding a dead body and dealing with the police definitely justified a conversation about a pay rise.

'Fine,' she said, looking over her shoulder at the dead girl. 'But you stay with her, all right?'

'What?' Edwin looked panicked. 'No! Why?'

'Because she shouldn't be alone,' said Rafaela, through gritted teeth. Then, when Edwin still looked as though he was going to object, she added, 'And think of what will happen if someone else finds her — think of what will happen if a guest wanders in here accidentally!'

'Oh my Lord! Oh, the guests! No, you're right, quite right indeed. Thank you, Rafaela, thank you...'

She gave him a grim nod and then began to cross the room, feeling a mixture of emotions as she went. The thought that she had been tidying up around a dead body for so long without realising it filled her with revulsion, and yet it was also an ache to walk away from the sleeping beauty. *If only I had been right*, thought Rafaela; *if only she had just had too much drink.* Somehow, the cleaner could not help but think that she herself was somehow responsible for the woman's fate, as though she would still be alive and well if Rafaela hadn't found her this morning. But of course, that was nonsense: it wasn't her fault - the woman had been here for hours — and besides, Rafaela's gut told her that someone else had had a hand in this death.

Just before she reached the door, Edwin called out to her, looking as helpless as a child.

'When you call the police, ask to speak to Boyle directly.'

'Boyle?'

'Barry Boyle, yes. He's the Chief Superintendent at the Victoria Police Station. In fact, don't tell anyone else anything, only talk to him.'

'Why?'

'*Because*, Rafaela!' Edwin looked more frustrated with her than he ever had done in all the years of their unhappy working relationship. 'Because he'll know how to handle this, how to be... *discreet*.'

Rafaela gave a click of disapproval with her tongue. Was that all Edwin Brackenwell cared about? Being discreet? Protecting the reputation of his poxy hotel? Never mind that some poor woman had probably been murdered under his roof, the important thing was to ensure the guests and the papers and the public didn't find out...

'*Rafaela*,' said Edwin, warningly.

'Barry Boyle, yes,' she snapped. 'I'll only talk to him.'

Unable to look at her spineless manager any longer, she made to exit the business conference room, reflecting that this was not how she had anticipated spending the extra half hour of her shift that morning. Then, as she walked back into the Duke Room, intending to head straight to the phone at reception, she thought she heard Edwin muttering to himself before she shut the door:

'I just can't believe something like this could happen in Westminster Square...'

CHAPTER ONE

Magnus Walterson woke early that morning, despite it being a Sunday. He hadn't set an alarm, but perhaps his body thought it was time to get up and go to work. Or maybe he had simply been roused by the sliver of bright sunlight streaming through the gap in the curtains: it looked as though it was going to be a beautiful day.

After he had decided he might as well get up and make the most of the morning, Magnus checked the clock on the bedside table: it was just after six. Then he rolled over in the four-poster bed to find that Juliana was still fast asleep. Her copper-coloured hair was spread out over the pillow, and there was an unusual aura of great contentment about her, possibly due to her calm expression and her slow, deep breathing. As contentment was not necessarily a characteristic Magnus associated with his wife, he thought it best not to disturb her, and so he extricated himself from the sheets and blankets as quietly and carefully as possible.

Once up, Magnus peeked through the gap in the curtains and confirmed that, yes, it was already a lovely day out there in Westminster Square. His and Juliana's bedroom looked right down onto the southeast of this eminent London address, and because their apartment was on the third floor, he could see right into a section of Westminster Square Gardens, the four, gated pockets of greenery that ran down the centre of the quadrant. This early on a Sunday, it was unusually quiet, for there was hardly any traffic on the main road that ran down the centre of both the square and its gardens. This peaceful atmosphere, along with the weather, decided it for Magnus: he would go for a jog.

After he had changed into a t-shirt and tracksuit bottoms, and looked in on Rosanna and Lee, who were still snoozing in their respective bedrooms, Magnus padded through to the kitchen. For although a shower could wait until he returned from his jog, a coffee and a bite to eat most certainly could not.

The kitchen was one of Magnus' favourite rooms in the flat. It was a large, airy space, featuring granite work surfaces and all the latest mod-cons, including a coffee machine, which he switched on now. It also boasted a balcony that, like the bedroom, looked down onto Westminster Square Gardens. Keen to take full advantage of the sunshine, as well as air out the old apartment, Magnus walked towards the French windows that led to this little terrace and threw them open. He then gave a startled yelp as two or three birds flew up, the beating of their wings next his face causing him to stagger backwards.

'Go on, shoo!' cried Magnus, when he had recovered from this unexpected assault, waving his arms at the birds. 'I'm not Juliana, I've nothing for you — get out of here!'

He clapped his hands a few times, and this seemed to do the trick, for the birds — which he now saw were an assortment of pigeons and doves — finally soared up into the sky and out of sight. He then walked forward to the wrought iron railings of the balcony, under which Juliana had left a little collection of seeds and nuts. With a sigh, Magnus brushed these offerings off the ledge, so they scattered onto the pavement far below.

He felt a twinge of guilt at sabotaging his wife's attempts to domesticate these wild birds, but Central Square Properties were so strict about the upkeep of the buildings in Westminster Square, he knew it would only be a matter of time before some official called round, complaining about the birds or the mess they made. Besides, Magnus thought, as he was almost poked in the eye by a swaying branch of vegetation, didn't Juliana already have enough wildlife to be getting on with? Most people on Westminster Square had a couple of neatly-trimmed shrubs on their balconies — they were pleasant splashes of greenery against the cream-coloured buildings — but the Walterson's balcony was now practically a jungle. Juliana was cultivating all sorts out here, from tropical trees to planters full of flowers, from herb boxes to a small but successful vegetable patch. Magnus had never seen anything like it, and it was almost impressive, how much she had managed to fit into this small space — although every corner of the apartment was also stuffed with palms, ferns, aloe vera and spider plants, not to mention vases overflowing with flowers. No, Magnus thought, pushing his way back through the greenery and towards the kitchen once more: the birds were a step too far.

After he had made himself a cup of coffee and a couple of pieces of toast, Magnus sat down at the round wooden table in the kitchen, trying to decide between *The Sunday Times* and *The Sunday Telegraph*, which had already been pushed through the letterbox. By the time the day was out, he would have read both newspapers from cover to cover, but for now he opened a page of *The Times* at random, telling himself not to become too engrossed, otherwise he wouldn't make it out for his jog. But no sooner had he settled down to an article on the International Olympic Committee celebrating its first centennial, than the door of the kitchen opened.

'Morning,' yawned Juliana, rubbing at her eyes. 'You're up early.'

She was wearing her dressing gown, and her bright hair was tousled from sleep. Magnus thought she looked very beautiful, and rose to kiss her on the cheek.

'I was woken up by the sun,' he told her. 'It's such a gorgeous day, I thought I might go out for a jog.'

She sighed, casting a longing look out at the balcony. 'It *is* a gorgeous day,' she said. 'If only we lived in the countryside, we could go for a walk, or to the beach. We could have a picnic. But instead we live *here*, in the middle of this dirty, ugly city.'

Magnus knew better than to engage with this, so instead he said, 'There's coffee in the pot, if you want some. It'll still be warm.'

Juliana looked a little mollified to hear this, and crossed to the counter to pour herself a cup.

'Well, I'm surprised *I* woke up so early,' she said, as though her grumble about the city hadn't happened. 'We had quite a late night.'

Magnus nodded. The previous evening, they had been in Bishop's Avenue, Hampstead, at a party hosted by one of his friends from the Royal Automobile Club. It had been an enjoyable event, full of interesting, intelligent people, and even Juliana had had a good time.

'I wonder how the party here went,' said Magnus, referring to the big fundraising bash at the Royal West Hotel, to which they had also been invited, although they had already committed to the Hampstead event.

'Oh, who cares?' said Juliana, dismissively. 'I expect it was exceptionally dull. Do you know, I can't bear any of those people? All they talk about is money, money, money. I doubt anything happened at all, other than they quaffed champagne and compared bank balances.'

Magnus thought this was a little unfair — not everyone in the area was as snobby and greedy as Juliana was implying — but he bit his tongue; there was no point getting into another argument with her about Westminster Square.

Juliana, meanwhile, put down her coffee cup and picked up a watering can instead, which she filled from the kitchen tap. Then, after adding a few drops of plant food to the water, she began to move around the room, humming as she doused the various flowers and foliage. Magnus watched her for a few moments, thinking — not for the first time — how Juliana sometimes only seemed truly happy when she was caring for her plants, her little bit of countryside in Westminster. It was saddening, but it confused him too: as far as Magnus was concerned, they were living at one of the most enviable addresses in the country, if not the world. Westminster Square was impressive to look at, safe for their children, convenient for his work, and yet Juliana often acted as though they were living on a rubbish dump.

'Don't eat too much of that toast,' she said, interrupting his thoughts. 'After your jog, I'll pop over to the bakery and buy us some pastries and some better bread. Then we can have a nice big breakfast with the children when you're back.'

'That sounds great,' said Magnus, pleased that caring for her plants seemed to have improved her mood.

Juliana smiled and, still carrying the watering can, headed towards the balcony, looking up at the sky and letting her face be bathed in the sunshine. She disappeared from sight for a few moments, during which

Magnus drained the last of his coffee, and then she returned to the kitchen, looking excited.

'They're gone!' she said.

'What's gone?'

'The seeds and nuts I put out for the birds on the balcony — I think they've eaten them all!'

'Ah,' said Magnus, feeling uncomfortable, and very much hoping she didn't look down at the pavement.

'Although, I did hope that putting out that food would tempt them to stay,' continued his wife, her expression growing melancholy. 'Still, maybe that'll take time. I'll put out some more right now.'

'Um...' Magnus began, not sure what he was going to say.

'Yes?' Juliana, who was already reaching into one of the kitchen cupboards, paused. 'What is it?'

'Um... I think I might head out for that jog now,' said Magnus. 'You know, before it gets too hot.'

'Good idea,' said Juliana absently, already arranging various packets on the granite work surface. 'I'll get the children up when you come back.'

A few minutes later, as he made his way down the stairs of the apartment building, Magnus cursed himself for being such a coward: why couldn't he just tell Juliana to stop feeding those dratted birds? Why did he seem to have absolutely no say over what she did in their shared home? And equally, why was he trying to deny her this little bit of happiness? Perhaps he should simply let her get on with turning their apartment into a botanical garden, and Central Square Properties would just have to deal with it.

'Top o' the mornin' to you, Mr Walterson!'

Magnus had been so preoccupied with thoughts of his wife that he gave a start as Patrick, the doorman of his apartment building, called out to him in greeting.

'Oh, hello there, Patrick. How are you?'

'Oh, fine, fine,' said the young Irishman, who had a shock of red hair and was as skinny as a bean pole. 'It's a grand day, don't you think? You out for a run?'

'Probably more of a jog,' Magnus admitted, for he was now approaching fifty, and he thought his running days might be behind him.

'Well, I envy you,' said Patrick, holding open the front door for him. 'I hope it's still nice when I finish my shift — do you know, at the moment, even my little flat downstairs is gettin' some sun?'

'That's great,' said Magnus. 'Well, I'll see you shortly, Patrick!'

'*Slán*, Mr Walterson!' called the doorman, which Magnus now knew meant 'goodbye' or 'be safe'

As he stepped outside, Magnus discovered the morning was just as fine as he had suspected; indeed, the concrete already felt warm beneath his trainers, and it wasn't even seven o'clock. After he had begun to jog, cajoling his stiff limbs into movement, he pondered where to go: Hyde Park and Green Park were fairly close by, but a lengthy case at work meant Magnus had not done much exercise over the past few weeks, so perhaps he should start slow. A gentle run around the perimeter of Westminster Square, and then through its four private gardens (for which, fortunately, Magnus had remembered the key) ought to cover a couple of miles, he thought. Besides, it seemed like a good idea to take advantage of the peace and quiet of his neighbourhood on this sleepy Sunday morning.

Magnus was puffed out and sweating in just a few minutes, but even his discomfort could not spoil his enjoyment of the jog: there was something so liberating about running solo, especially when he felt as though he had the whole of Westminster Square to himself.

Yet no sooner had Magnus thought this than someone came sprinting into view from the north-east corner of the quadrant. He too was exercising, but he was running far faster than Magnus, and undoubtedly looked far more impressive too. In mere seconds he had covered the entire length of Magnus' run so far, his arms and legs slicing through the air, as swift and agile as a cheetah. From the look of his familiar and famous face, he seemed to be in a world of his own — especially as he appeared to be clutching some kind of Walkman — so much so that as he came up behind Magnus, the older man had to wave at him to gain his attention.

'Good morning, Jem!'

Jem McMorran skidded to a halt and turned his bright Hollywood smile on Magnus. He was an exceptionally handsome man in his mid-thirties, with chiselled features, light brown hair and piercing blue eyes. Magnus thought of Jem as a neighbour first and foremost, and sometimes he forgot that the young man was also a very famous film star. Jem had been working since his late teens, and had found international attention about a decade ago, when he had been cast in an action-adventure picture called *Pioneer of the Past*, which chronicled the escapades of a young explorer who journeyed to the jungle of Mexico and solved an ancient Aztec mystery. The film had made a lot of money, and Jem had shot several sequels set in Egypt, Turkey and Greece respectively. They had also been box office hits, although Magnus privately thought none of them had lived up to the standard of the original, which had been a lot of fun. Still, the franchise had made Jem McMorran a household name, not to mention a lot of money, and for as long as Magnus had known him, Jem had spent far more time away on film shoots than he had done at his flat in Westminster Square.

'Hello, Magnus,' said the actor, removing his headphones from his ears but continuing to jog on the spot. 'How are you?'

'Very well, thank you — just enjoying this beautiful weather!' Then, in a somewhat hopeful tone of voice — for the actor didn't look as though he had broken a sweat — Magnus asked, 'Are you just starting your run?'

'Oh no, I've been out for ages!' smiled Jem, his feet still bouncing up and down on the concrete. 'I've already done two laps of Hyde Park, and listened to an entire album on this.'

He held up what Magnus now realised was a Discman — a personal CD player, the very height of technology.

'Really?' said Magnus, feeling a little deflated to hear this. 'You've far too much energy, Jem.'

'That's what they tell me!'

'And you seem to be in a very good mood.'

Jem spread his arms wide. 'Like you said, it's a beautiful day!'

'Weren't you out late at this big party last night? Shouldn't you be feeling a little worse for wear?'

'Oh, I know how to handle my drink. And don't forget, I was playing in the tennis tournament during the day as well, so I only started on the fizz after six.'

'The tennis tournament that I trust you won?' said Magnus, giving voice to the question he knew Jem wanted him to ask.

'Of course,' said the actor, giving him another winning smile. 'But then, I don't have much competition around here, do I?'

This, Magnus thought, was perfectly true: Westminster Square had its own tennis court, and Jem was probably one of the youngest residents who bothered to use it.

'Well, congratulations,' said Magnus, who often found himself willing to indulge the young man's egotism, simply because he was charming. 'And how was the party?'

'Oh, you know, the usual,' said Jem, noticeably losing interest. 'You didn't miss much. A lot of rich people drank a lot of expensive champagne and talked a lot of rubbish.'

Magnus chuckled at how close this description was to Juliana's assumptions.

'But I think it raised a lot of money for Dame Winifred's charities,' Jem went on, 'so that's something, I suppose…'

He trailed off, casting an eye towards his surroundings. Throughout this whole exchange, he had continued to jog on the spot, and seeing as he wasn't showing any signs of stopping, and didn't seem in the least bit tired, Magnus had the impression the actor was keen to carry on with his run.

'Well, I'll let you get on,' he said. 'What is it, another lap of Hyde Park before breakfast?'

'Maybe,' grinned Jem. 'Or maybe I'll head off to Green Park now…'

He waved and turned to leave, but then Magnus called him back.

'Actually, Jem, before you go, can I just say —?'

'Yes, yes, yes — I know. I'm sorry.'

'For what?'

'For the car. That's what you're talking about, isn't it? My car being parked in your spot again?'

'Well, yes,' said Magnus, hating that this awkwardness had spoilt their cheerful exchange but persevering nonetheless. 'Look, Jem, I know you have a lot of cars, and it wouldn't be such a problem if those wretched attendants weren't hovering around all the time, giving tickets to anyone who's parked even an inch out of their space, but…'

'Yes, yes,' interrupted the actor, 'it won't happen again.'

Magnus raised his eyebrows. Seeing as last Friday had been the seventh or eighth time he had found one of Jem McMorran's sports cars in the parking spot outside his house, he sincerely doubted this was true.

'Honestly,' said the actor, seeing Magnus' expression. 'I promise, it won't happen again.'

'Really? Because I'm thinking of charging you a beer every time you do this, Jem, and you should know you're almost into double figures…'

'Really! I promise!' Jem laughed, as carefree as ever. 'Anyway, I'm not even going to be around here for much longer.'

'Aren't you?' Magnus was surprised to hear this. After all, Westminster Square was both a convenient and secure address for an A-list actor. 'Are you moving away?'

'Maybe.'

Jem was looking up at the canopy of leaves above their head, his expression unreadable. Part of Magnus' mind — the lawyer part — thought it looked as though the young man was trying to distract from the fact that he had said too much. But then, he was smiling as he gazed upwards, so perhaps he was simply happy.

'A film shoot, you know,' continued Jem vaguely. 'And then, who can say… Anyway, I must get on, or else my muscles will seize up. I'll see you around, Magnus!'

'See you around,' he replied, although he wasn't sure the actor had heard him, for he had already replaced his headphones over his ears, crossed over the road and was now speeding towards the other end of Westminster Square.

Magnus watched him for a few moments, and then began to jog himself, although not half as energetically as the young actor. As he made his way slowly down the pavement of Westminster Square, he scolded himself for not being stricter with Jem. It was, after all, very annoying risking a parking ticket or — worse — having to find a different spot in Central London, just because the local celebrity had too many cars. And the overzealous parking attendants always had a fit if the council disk displayed in your windshield did not match up to the space your car occupied. Magnus supposed this was one negative aspect of living in Westminster Square, although perhaps he would neglect to mention it to Juliana. And no matter what Jem said, unless the actor was indeed implying he was leaving Westminster Square, Magnus doubted very much this would be the last time he would have to have this petty conversation about parking spots.

Still, Magnus told himself firmly, it was far too lovely a morning to be worrying about something so trivial, so after he had frowned one last time at the retreating form of Jem — who was now a mere speck on the horizon — he tried to put the matter from his mind. This, it turned out, was not too difficult, for now his conversation with the actor was over, he was again able to appreciate how quiet Westminster Square was, how peaceful, how —

Nee-naw, nee-naw, nee-naw!

As the sound of sirens grew louder, Magnus slowed his already leisurely pace, and by the time the three police cars had come careering into view, he had stopped entirely, his mouth hanging open at the sight.

He had never thought about it before, but one rarely saw the emergency services in Westminster Square. Once or twice, an ambulance had come to pick up some poor old dear who'd had a fall, and police sometimes patrolled the area on foot, but that was about it. To see multiple police cars come racing through the area was, Magnus now realised, a remarkable spectacle. What on earth could have happened? A burglary, perhaps? But surely that would not require so much police attention?

Their sirens still screaming, the three cars raced down the length of Westminster Square, before they vanished beyond the northern corner of the quadrant. Magnus frowned, his heart pounding, partly from the exercise, but also from the sudden, noisy appearance of the police, which had instantly and completely shattered the tranquillity of the morning.

Not long afterwards, the sirens stopped. However this did not quell Magnus' sense of unease, for rather than fading into the distance, the noise had cut out abruptly, as though the vehicles had reached their destination — and that destination was nearby. As he looked around sunny Westminster Square, which was empty and quiet once more, Magnus' brow furrowed still further.

Then, without really thinking about what he was doing, he started to jog. Only now, instead of letting himself into each of the gated gardens as he had planned, he started towards the part of the Square where the police cars had disappeared. Magnus didn't really know why he was following them — he certainly had no right or authority to do so — but as his pace increased, so did his curiosity, as well as his determination to find out what was going on.

CHAPTER TWO

Standing in the corner of the business conference room of the Royal West Hotel, Police Constable Bryn Summers felt a thrill of excitement.

He was, of course, very saddened by the sight of the dead woman, who was still curled up on one of the leather sofas at the other end of the room. It was alarming how young she was — Bryn thought she looked to be in her early thirties at most — and he could hardly bear to imagine the shock and grief her family and friends were about to experience when they found out what had happened.

But even so, if he took emotion out of the equation, there was simply no denying that this was by far the most exciting thing that had happened to him in the six months or so he had been working at the Victoria Police Station. In fact, as he stood there, watching the medical examiner, her assistant and a few of his colleagues hovering around the body, Bryn thought this might be the most exciting thing that had *ever* happened to him.

When he had dropped out of his Electrical Engineering college course to start police training, this was exactly the sort of situation he had envisioned having to deal with on a daily basis, especially when he had transferred to London. But since then, his life as a Police Constable had been disappointingly dull. Bryn tended to think of his main duties as the three Ps: patrolling, paperwork and peacekeeping, the latter of which was probably the dullest of all, given it merely involved standing around at public events and giving directions to tourists.

Whenever he moaned over the phone to his parents about this frustrating lack of excitement in his career, they always reminded him that he was young, he had only just completed his two year probationary period, and he should count himself lucky to have had such a gentle start to police work. Yet Bryn knew they were just relieved he was still in one piece: his mother and father, who lived just outside Aberystwyth, had been stunned when he had announced his intention to drop out of college, move to Cardiff and train to be a policeman, and then downright distressed when, just over half a year ago, he had been offered this job in London. So of course they were going to be happy that, apart from less serious crimes such as bike theft, shoplifting and vehicle damage, not much seemed to happen in the eminent neighbourhood of Westminster. Not much, that was, until now.

It was only seven thirty in the morning, and yet the day had already been jam-packed with activity. Because he was the newest member of the force, Bryn was always put on the early Sunday morning shift, which was reliably quiet, given that almost everyone was in bed. So it had been Bryn who had taken the phone call from the Italian cleaner that morning; the woman who had insisted so forcefully on speaking to Boyle, no matter how many times Bryn had told her he was unavailable. And it had been Bryn and a few colleagues who, along with the ambulance, had gone speeding to the Royal West Hotel, and Bryn who had been one of the first to be shown through to the business conference room, where the dead woman lay.

He gave a little shudder as he recalled the moment he had clapped eyes on her. Despite the relatively short time he had been in the force, Bryn had now seen a number of dead bodies: an old lady who had died in her sleep; a homeless man who had drunk himself to death; the horrific, bloody repercussions of a car accident back in Cardiff... It was always unpleasant, but Bryn found he had become slightly desensitised to the experience over time — it was simply part of his job. Even so, he had never seen anything quite like this before: the woman on the sofa was young and beautiful, and it had been almost eerie, looking down at her inert form, because she looked so peaceful she could have been asleep. Instead of calling the medical examiner, Bryn had been tempted to fetch a blanket to keep her warm. Although, now he thought back on it, that had all been before the cleaner had pointed out the bruises...

Lost in these memories of under an hour ago, it took Bryn a few moments to realise that someone was trying to attract his attention.

'Excuse me? Erm, hello? Might I have a word?'

Bryn turned to find the manager of the Royal West, a fussy dark-haired individual whose name he had forgotten, teetering on the spot next to him. This man had been a constant irritant ever since Bryn and his colleagues had arrived on the scene, for he had buzzed around them like an annoying fly (although never straying too close to the body, Bryn noticed), yet he had not told them anything remotely useful about the circumstances under which the woman had been found — unlike the Italian cleaner, who seemed far calmer and far more in command of the situation than her employer.

'Of course,' said Bryn, 'how can I help you, Mr —'

'Brackenwell, Edwin Brackenwell,' said the manager crisply. 'It's just, as I said before, I really was expecting Chief Superintendent Barry Boyle to be here by now…'

Bryn resisted the urge to roll his eyes. 'And as I said before, Mr Brackenwell, the Chief Superintendent is on his way.'

'But that's not good enough!' cried Edwin. 'Don't you understand? There's a —' He lowered his voice. 'There's a *body* in my hotel! I need Boyle to… smooth things over.'

'Smooth things over?' repeated Bryn, raising an eyebrow.

'You know what I mean!' said Edwin. 'I have to consider the reputation of the Royal West. I don't know where you're from, young man —'

'Aberystwyth in Wales,' said Bryn cheerfully, privately thinking this man was very bad at interpreting accents.

'Well, I don't know how they do things in Ab — in Aberwis — well, in Wales,' said the manager, 'but here, protecting the good character of Westminster is of the utmost importance, and Boyle understands this.'

'Does he indeed?' said Bryn, conversationally.

'Has he even been told about this — this *situation*?' demanded Edwin.

'He has.'

'So where on earth is he?'

Bryn hesitated. In truth, he wasn't exactly sure where Chief Superintendent Barry Boyle was, although he could make an educated guess that his superior was either still in bed or in some greasy spoon shovelling a fried breakfast into his mouth.

'The Chief Superintendent is currently indisposed on police business,' said Bryn, even though Boyle little deserved this loyalty. 'He will be here as soon as possible.'

Edwin gave a sigh of frustration, but then, to Bryn's relief, stalked away, probably to bother one of the other police officers who were standing guard around the business conference room and the rest of the Royal West.

A few minutes later, the medical examiner stopped circling the body and, to Bryn's surprise, headed straight towards him. She was a short woman with a rather severe bob of greying hair and a steely expression.

'Who's in charge here?' she asked him.

'Erm... Not really anyone at the moment,' admitted Bryn.

'Where's Boyle?'

'Indisposed.'

'I see,' she said, and it looked as though she too could guess a few places Barry Boyle might be. Then, after removing each of her latex gloves with a snap, she offered him her bare hand.

'Marlene Hardwitt, medical examiner.'

'Bryn Summers, police constable.'

He winced as they shook hands: she had a firm grip.

'Well, I can't wait around here all day, so I might as well tell you what's what, Mr Summers, and you can pass it onto Boyle or whoever bothers to show up,' said Marlene.

'Fantastic!' said Bryn, perhaps a little too enthusiastically, given the circumstances. He pulled his notebook from his utility belt. 'What can you tell me?'

'Well first of all, her name is Anne-Laure Chevalier.'

'Anne-Laure Chevalier?' repeated Bryn, as he wrote this down. 'She's French?'

'I'm afraid medical examiners are not gifted with the ability to determine nationality from corpses,' said Marlene dryly.

'Of course,' said Bryn, embarrassed. 'But then, how do you know her name?'

Marlene clicked her fingers in the direction of her assistant, who came trotting over carrying a gold designer handbag in his gloved hands.

'She was lying on this,' said the medical examiner, before adding, somewhat disapprovingly, 'It seems we're doing some of your police work for you here... I can't believe your lot didn't notice.'

Bryn flushed again: it was perhaps true that he and his colleagues had not dealt with this situation as thoroughly as they should have. But then, they were not CID, and until their Chief Superintendent arrived, it was difficult to know exactly which protocol to follow, and Boyle was bound to criticise them regardless.

'I apologise for that oversight,' Bryn said humbly. 'Did the bag contain some sort of identification?'

The medical examiner's assistant pulled out a purse, which contained a number of cards, including a driver's license, which he showed to Bryn. As Marlene had said, the woman's name was Anne-Laure Chevalier, and her address was listed as being in the Mews, the small cobbled street that ran behind Westminster Square. The photograph was small and grainy, but it was definitely her, and she was even more striking with her large eyes open.

'It's a British license,' said Bryn, more in an attempt to say something observant, than because he was particularly preoccupied with her nationality. 'What else is in there?'

The medical examiner's assistant opened the handbag wide to show Bryn its contents: some loose change, a lipstick, a chunky compact mirror, some hair grips, a small bunch of keys, a little purple book that looked as though it contained addresses... Although he was not especially familiar with the contents of women's handbags — especially not women of this class — Bryn thought this all looked fairly innocuous.

'So how did she die?' he asked.

'Well, that's the question,' said Marlene. 'To all intents and purposes, she looks perfectly fit and healthy — apart from the fact that she's dead.'

Bryn didn't know whether or not to laugh at this: the medical examiner was either very straightforward in her manner, or in possession of a rather blunt sense of humour.

'I don't think she's been dead for too long,' continued Marlene. 'She's cold, but not *that* cold, and rigor mortis hasn't set in, so I'd estimate she died around two o'clock in the morning, give or take a few hours.'

'So it's likely this charity party was over by then,' said Bryn, thinking aloud, 'which is why the cleaner was the first one to find her this morning.'

'Perhaps,' shrugged the medical examiner, who didn't seem particularly interested in the circumstances, only the body. 'But while I'm fairly sure about the time, I admit the cause of death stumped me for a good few minutes. As far as I can tell from my initial examination, there's no sign of any external injury, other than the bruising on her neck and wrists, which could be significant. But she certainly didn't bump her head or anything like that, and given her age, I thought it unlikely she'd a heart attack — although not impossible. I was just beginning to speculate it was more likely she'd had some sort of brain haemorrhage — an incredibly quick one, given she's lying there so peacefully — when I noticed her nose.'

'Her nose?' Bryn had not been expecting this.

'Yes, there's a little inflammation around the septum that caught my attention. And then we had a closer look at this.'

She gestured to her assistant, who had been standing next to her obediently throughout this exchange, and he withdrew the compact mirror from the dead woman's handbag. Very gently, he opened it with his gloved fingers, to reveal a small plastic packet of white powder enclosed within.

'I'm guessing those aren't bath salts,' said Bryn.

Marlene let out a gruff laugh. 'No, I very much doubt they are.'

'Cocaine?' he asked.

'You'll have to send it to the lab, but it seems likely, given the state of her nose.'

'And you think a dose of cocaine was enough to kill her?'

Marlene looked stern, and Bryn was reminded suddenly of a very strict headmistress he'd had in primary school. 'Cocaine is a dangerous and illegal Class A drug, Constable,' the medical examiner said.

'Yes, I know that,' Bryn assured her quickly. 'It's just, in this form, given she's so young...'

'Cocaine increases the heart rate, which can cause heart attacks, even in young people,' said Marlene. 'It also constricts blood vessels in the brain, which can lead to strokes or fatal seizures. I'd imagine it was one or the other, and we can take her in and do a few tests to find out which. But yes, in answer to your question, at this point I'm fairly certain it was an accidental death caused by her body reacting badly to the drug.'

Bryn was silent for a few moments, before he mused aloud, 'You say "accidental", but what about those bruises on her wrists and neck? And there might even have more we haven't seen...' he added, realising this for the first time. 'I mean, she can't have done that to herself, can she?'

Marlene looked a little uncomfortable. 'No, I don't think it's likely. And if you're thinking those bruises don't match up with the rest of this picture — well, you'd be right. They might not have killed her, but marks like that are suspicious, especially on a dead body. I'm also puzzled by the position in which she was found. The cleaner thought she was asleep for several minutes, and to be perfectly honest I don't blame her. Anne-Laure Chevalier looks unusually tranquil for someone who's accidentally overdosed. Drug deaths are a messy business, Mr Summers — believe me, I've seen a few. Which leads me to conclude that either the overdose *wasn't* accidental, or —'

But Bryn never heard the end of this sentence, for at that moment, to his great annoyance, Edwin Brackenwell popped up once more.

'Did I hear you say Anne-Laure Chevalier?' he gasped.

'This is the manager of the Royal West,' explained Bryn, answering Marlene's enquiring expression, while her assistant, the policeman noticed, replaced the compact of cocaine in the bag, so Edwin couldn't see it. 'Do you know Ms Chevalier?' Bryn then asked the manager.

'Everybody around here knows her!' cried Edwin. 'She works in events organisation, party-planning, that sort of thing. In fact, she was responsible for putting together the fundraising party last night — and the tennis tournament that preceded it. My God, I didn't even realise it was her!'

Considering the manager hadn't dared to go anywhere near the body, Bryn found this unsurprising.

'Anne-Laure Chevalier, dead!' exclaimed Edwin. 'It's unbelievable…'

Marlene, looking as though she had already had enough of Edwin Brackenwell, turned back to Bryn. 'We need to decide how to proceed,' she said, her tone business-like. 'I think it'd be best if I take her in for an autopsy to confirm this theory of ours regarding how she died.'

'All right,' said Bryn, ignoring Edwin, who was looking between them curiously.

'Meanwhile, if you haven't already, I'd call the CID. Get them over here to take a few pictures, just so we've covered our backs. Although unfortunately, it looks as though that cleaner has tidied up quite a bit of the evidence around the body…'

'The CID?' interrupted Edwin. 'Doesn't that stand for Criminal Investigation Department?'

'It does,' said Bryn, wishing the manager would go away.

'But — but there's been no crime here!'

'As I just said, it's a precautionary measure,' snapped Marlene. 'You can't deny that a young and healthy-looking woman suddenly dropping dead is a little unusual. And when you add to that the fact she's covered in bruises, well… I wouldn't want to miss anything.'

'And neither would I,' added Bryn quickly.

'But — but —' Against their united front, Edwin Brackenwell was virtually powerless. 'But don't you think we should wait for —?'

As if on cue, the double doors of the business conference room banged open and Police Chief Superintendent Barry Boyle lumbered over the threshold. In his late fifties, Boyle was a vast man, both in height and girth, and his belly was so big that the buttons of his shirt always looked as though they were threatening to ping open. His pudgy face was permanently red, and dominated by bushy eyebrows and a huge walrus-like moustache, in which traces of his latest meal could often be found. Today, as he entered the scene, his fat fingers were scrunching up a brown takeaway bag emblazoned with the McDonald's logo, leaving Bryn in no doubt as to why he was so late to the Royal West.

'What's going on here?' Boyle roared, causing Edwin to cower in alarm. 'Who's died and got me up so early on a Sunday morning?'

As he waited for his answer, the Chief Superintendent looked around the room, spotted the Italian cleaner, and threw the screwed-up remains of his breakfast towards her. She caught it deftly, but scowled as she deposited it into the black bin liner she was holding.

When it became apparent that nobody was going to answer Boyle's question, Bryn cleared his throat and summoned his courage.

'Um, according to her driver's license, the deceased's name is Anne-Laure Chevalier,' he began tentatively.

Under his moustache, Boyle's lip curled with dislike. 'A froggy, eh?'

'It's a British license, so we think not. According to Mr Brackenwell here, Chevalier worked in events, and was responsible for the party that took place here last night at the Royal West…'

'Get to the point, Summers!' growled Boyle. 'How did she die?'

'That's unconfirmed at the moment,' said Marlene, stepping forward.

Boyle surveyed her with his dark, piggy eyes. 'Oh, it's *you*,' he said, with evident dislike.

'It's a pleasure to see you as well, Mr Boyle,' she said, apparently completely unconcerned by his rudeness.

'Well?' he demanded. 'Are you a medical examiner or not? Why can't you tell me how she died?'

Marlene looked warningly towards Edwin and the cleaner, the two civilians on the scene. Boyle, however, didn't seem to care who was present.

'Come on — out with it, woman!'

'Given we found what looks to be cocaine in her handbag, and there are signs of damage to her nasal septum, my initial findings suggest she died of an accidental overdose.'

'Oh for goodness' sake!' cried Boyle, glaring around the room. 'You got me out of bed for *this*? Some silly French tart with a drug problem? Case closed!'

Marlene's lips thinned. 'If you inspect the body, you will notice there is substantial bruising to her wrists and neck, which I call suspicious.'

'Probably injection sites,' muttered Boyle, but he did then waddle off towards the other end of the room to peer down at Anne-Laure Chevalier. 'She's a fine-looking filly, isn't she?' he announced to the room at large. 'Still, probably a complete bimbo to have got herself into this sort of state...'

Beside him, Bryn heard Marlene make a low hissing noise. The Italian cleaner looked equally unimpressed. Edwin, however, began to edge towards Boyle, moving closer to the body than he had dared to venture thus far.

'Chief Superintendent Boyle, as you well know, this hotel has an unrivalled reputation, as does Westminster as a whole. Given that Rafaela, my cleaner here, noticed nothing out of the ordinary when she was tidying up around the — the *woman* earlier, I don't really see why this should affect the —'

'Yes, yes,' said Boyle, turning his back on the body and returning to Bryn and Marlene, pushing past Edwin as he went. 'I happen to completely agree with you. Whose idiotic idea was it to come racing to the Royal West with the sirens on?'

When it looked as though none of his colleagues were going to own up, Bryn said, 'I thought that was the correct protocol, in this situation? A dead woman had been found under suspicious circumstances...'

'But they're not suspicious circumstances!' bellowed Boyle. 'I thought we'd just covered that! And now, because of all that fuss you morons have made, everyone thinks something is afoot at the Royal West! You know, there are already people gathering outside in the street, and I bet you at least some of them are *journalists*.'

Edwin gave a low moan. Bryn, however, was unable to stop himself from exclaiming, 'But there *is* something afoot at the Royal West!'

For a moment, Boyle said nothing, but shuffled towards Bryn until they were standing inches apart, and the young police constable was completely dwarfed by his overweight superior.

'Look, you little Welsh twerp,' he said, his foul-smelling breath hot on Bryn's forehead. 'I know your big ambition is to become some sort of modern-day Sherlock Holmes, but I'm telling you now — just as I told you when I turned down your application for detective training — you don't have the brains, you don't have the stomach and, most importantly, you don't have my approval. So why don't you keep your mouth shut and spare me from having to listen to another second of that dim-witted accent?'

Bryn felt his face burn hot with shame, both at the public dressing-down and at the reminder of how brutally Boyle had thwarted his attempts to become a detective. The Chief Superintendent seemed particularly adverse to him, and Bryn suspected it had less to do with his being Welsh and more to do with him being the youngest and newest member of the local constabulary, and therefore an easy target for bullying.

'So you're saying you want to treat this death as entirely unsuspicious?' said Marlene, disapproval dripping off her every word. 'In spite of the woman's youth, in spite of her bruises?'

'That's exactly what I'm saying.'

'You're not even going to get the CID to take a few photos?'

'What would be the point? Edwin's just said this foolish foreigner already tidied up all of the evidence...'

The cleaner — Rafaela, apparently — muttered something in Italian under her breath. Boyle jabbed a stubby finger in her direction.

'I don't know what you're saying, missy, but if you speak to me like that again, I'll have you arrested. How do you feel about that, eh?'

The cleaner looked at her feet.

Boyle nodded and turned back to the medical examiner. 'Well, what are you waiting for? I want that body out of here in the next five minutes, and the room returned to normal in the next ten. Do you understand?'

'Perfectly,' said Marlene, coldly.

'Oh, thank you! Thank you!' gulped Edwin, looking giddy with relief.

'It'll cost you,' Boyle told the manager of the Royal West. 'For my trouble and discretion, I'll expect a meal at the hotel every Sunday evening for the next three months, starting tonight.'

'Of course, of course!'

'And you can throw in a few free whiskeys to wash down that grub, while you're at it.'

'Anything!'

'You can't do that, it's extortion!' cried Bryn, before he could stop himself.

This time, Boyle didn't even bother to speak. He merely grabbed Bryn by the shoulder with his large hand and began to shove him out of the business conference room, through the neighbouring function room — which was still littered with the remains of the previous night's party — and out into the reception area. Bryn, who had almost tripped over his own feet as he had been dragged through the Royal West in this manner, expected Boyle to loosen his grip once they were alone, but instead the Chief Superintendent dug his fingers deeper into the young policeman's left shoulder blade, causing him to wince.

'I think it's time you left the grown-ups to do the real work here,' growled Boyle in Bryn's ear. 'You can go outside and babysit the public and the press. And remember, Summers, if you say a word to anyone about what's going on in there — and if you ever, *ever* disrespect me like that again — you'll be back in Wales so fast you won't know what's hit you. Understand?'

'Yes,' gulped Bryn, his shoulder now throbbing with pain.

'Good — now go!' said the Chief Superintendent, thrusting Bryn through the grand entranceway of the Royal West Hotel and out onto the street beyond.

CHAPTER THREE

It did not take Magnus long to track down the police cars, even with their sirens off. Initially, he thought they had stopped outside a house, and wondered what could have happened inside. But then, with a jolt of surprise, he realised they were actually outside the Royal West Hotel, which looked very similar to the surrounding residential buildings, due to Central Square Properties' strict rules and regulations about maintaining the character of the area.

Jogging a little closer, Magnus considered what he knew about the hotel. Obviously, given he lived so close by, he had never stayed in any of its rooms, but he and Juliana had dined there on a few occasions, and it was always a slightly dissatisfying experience; the food was perfectly palatable, but there was something about the hotel's ambiance that grated on Magnus, who always felt the waiters and other members of staff were exceptionally snooty, even for Westminster. He had also attended a couple of events there over the years... And that was when Magnus remembered: the party! Dame Winifred Rye's fundraising event that he and Juliana had been invited to; that had taken place at the Royal West only last night! Was that party somehow connected to these three police cars parked outside the hotel this morning?

There was no one around to answer this question, and dressed as he was in a t-shirt and tracksuit bottoms, Magnus was not properly attired to go into the Royal West. So, for want of anything better to do, Magnus decided to jog around the block a few times, in order to continue with his exercise while at the same time keeping an eye on what was happening at the hotel.

This turned out to be an interesting way to pass the time, because Magnus soon discovered that every time he passed the Royal West, something had changed: the first time he jogged by, an ambulance had pulled up; the second time, a small crowd of people were gathering on the pavement;

and the third time, a very large and angry-looking policeman had arrived and was pushing his way into the hotel clutching a bag of McDonald's takeaway. Soon after this, Magnus developed a sharp stitch in his left side (he had been concentrating so much on what was going on at the Royal West, he had probably been running harder than he should have) and so he walked around the next block, considering everything he had just seen.

By the time he had returned to the hotel once again, there were around twelve or so people gathered outside, and Magnus was so puffed out by his exercise he thought he might as well join this small crowd and see if he could learn more about what had happened. He also noticed that another policeman had been stationed at the hotel's entrance; one far younger and about five times thinner than his colleague who had entered the Royal West about ten minutes beforehand.

For a little while, not much happened, aside from the fact that Magnus' breathing and heart-rate began to return to normal. The young policeman stared determinedly into space, his jaw set, ignoring the few questions that were being posed to him by the bolder members of the crowd. But then, just as Magnus was beginning to wonder whether he should go home for a proper breakfast and wait to hear about whatever had happened at the Royal West from the news later in the day, his patience was rewarded: out of the entranceway of the hotel came a short, stern-looking woman and a younger man who might have been her assistant, followed by two policemen who were wheeling what was unmistakably a bodybag on a stretcher.

As he watched this little group calmly begin to deposit their cargo into the back of the ambulance, Magnus felt suddenly cold, despite the warmth of the morning: someone was dead. Around him, the crowd as a whole seemed to shiver, and a few people began to murmur to each other in low, anxious voices. Then, behind them all, shattering the respectful quiet that had followed the appearance of the body bag, there was the roar of an approaching motorbike.

Magnus turned in time to see a man in a leather jacket pulling up at the side of the curb, hopping off the motorbike, and removing his helmet to reveal a greasy mop of dark hair underneath.

'Hey, what's happened here?' he shouted, his eyes on the disappearing body bag. 'Hey, you! At the ambulance! What's going on?'

He let his motorbike slump to the ground and ran towards the short woman, pulling out a card from his jacket as he did so. 'Ricky Nicholls, *The Dawn Reporter*,' he announced, thrusting his ID under her nose. 'I had a call about a disturbance at the hotel… What's happened? Was that a body? Has someone died at the Royal West?'

But the little woman turned on her heel and headed towards the front of the ambulance.

'Let's go,' she told her colleagues.

'Hey!' cried Ricky Nicholls, as her assistant and the policemen disappeared into the vehicle. 'Who was that? Hey, I've just a few questions!'

But it was no use: as soon as all of the team were inside, the ambulance pulled out and drove away. Undeterred, the journalist turned his attention to the remaining policeman, who was still stood at the entranceway of the hotel.

'Has someone died at the Royal West?' he demanded again. 'Who did that body belong to? Man or woman? Old or young? What's happened here?'

'Get back, please!' cried the policeman, for Nicholls was pushing towards him, causing some of the crowd to be shoved forward as well. 'We have no comment to make at this time. Ladies and gentlemen, please stand back!'

He had, Magnus noticed, a strong Welsh accent, and looked a little overwhelmed, as though he had never had to deal with this sort of situation before. Which made sense, when one considered that bodies didn't show up every day in Westminster hotels. Perhaps the journalist sensed weakness, because he continued to push forward.

'Have you managed to identify the body?' he cried. 'Are the police treating this death as suspicious?'

'Would you mind not shouting quite so loudly?' asked Magnus, trying to remain polite, despite the fact this man was being very irritating. It also did not help that Magnus considered *The Dawn Reporter* the worst of all tabloids, and that he was predisposed to dislike anyone even vaguely connected to that excuse for a newspaper.

Unsurprisingly, Nicholls ignored him, continuing to bear down on the policeman with his questions and cries of 'Hey, you!' Now, the young officer, faced with both the reporter and members of the public pressing towards him, looked completely overwhelmed, and sensing the situation was about to get ugly, Magnus darted forward.

'I'd do as he says and get back if I were you,' he told Nicholls, 'otherwise you might find yourself in hot water.'

'Hot water?' sneered the reporter. 'And why exactly would that be?'

'Well, from where I'm standing, you look like you're behaving in a threatening and disorderly manner, and you're therefore close to being guilty of Section 5 of the Public Order Act, 1986. At the very least, you'll be fined, and I expect it will be a hefty one, given you've been unwise enough to accost a police officer.'

Nicholls hesitated. 'Who are you?'

'Magnus Walterson. I'm a barrister at Grey's Inn, so I think I'm a least a little familiar with the law.'

The journalist looked between Magnus and the Welsh police officer and clearly decided it wasn't worth pursuing this argument, so stepped back, melting a little into the crowd. The young constable gave Magnus a look of appreciation, which Magnus returned with a nod.

There followed a few further minutes of inactivity. Ricky Nicholls, who had at last quietened down, took advantage of this lull to make frenzied notes on a pad of paper. Magnus could see the policeman's eyes flicking towards the journalist, his expression wary. Amongst the rest of the crowd there seemed to be a general feeling of restlessness, and one or two people drifted away, evidently deciding that seeing a body bag was enough excitement for a Sunday morning.

Magnus was just beginning to think along the same lines himself — especially as he remembered Juliana's offer to go and buy pastries for breakfast from the bakery — when the door of the Royal West Hotel opened once again, and the large, angry-looking policeman from earlier stood in the entranceway, sneering down at the crowd.

'What are you lot still doing here?' he demanded. Then, before anyone could answer, he rounded on his young colleague. 'Why didn't you get rid of them?'

'They're not doing any harm,' the Welshman pointed out. 'I can't very well tell them not to stand on a public pavement.'

His superior looked as though he were about to reprimand him, but then Ricky Nicholls jumped up again.

'Police Chief Boyle! Police Chief Boyle!' he cried.

'That's Police Chief *Superintendent* Boyle to you!'

The reported looked unfazed. 'I'm Ricky Nicholls from —'

'From *The Dawn Reporter,* I know,' finished Boyle, with a scowl. 'Unfortunately, I remember you from our previous encounters... Well, I've nothing to say, do you hear? *No comment.*'

'You've nothing to say about the death at the Royal West?' said Nicholls. 'You've no comment to make about the fact that these good people and I just saw a body bag being taken out of the hotel and put into an ambulance?'

Boyle swore loudly. 'Why the hell did you let them see that?' he shouted at his colleague.

'I couldn't help it!' cried the Welshman. 'I didn't know Marlene was just going to come out with her like that, nobody gave me any warning...'

'So the body belongs to a woman, does it?' Nicholls piped up.

'Damn it, Summers!' bellowed Boyle. 'Now look what you've done! Tell me, are all the Welsh idiotic, or is it just you?'

This, Magnus thought, was far below the belt, but all the fight seemed to have gone out of the young constable, who was now looking miserably at his feet.

'All right,' said Boyle, after chewing thoughtfully at the end of his bushy moustache for a few moments, 'all right.' He turned to the journalist. 'Just so you don't start making up any old rubbish like you normally do, how about I give you a statement to write in your stupid paper, and they we can all clear out of here? Deal?'

'Deal,' said Nicholls, his pen poised over his pad.

'Right,' said the Police Superintendent slowly, and Magnus could practically see the cogs whirring in his brain as he tried to work out what to say. 'Well, it's true that, at approximately six-thirty am this morning, one of the cleaners of the Royal West Hotel found the body of a female guest. The medical examiner has since declared the woman passed away from natural causes, so we are not treating the death as suspicious, and will be making no further comments on this matter. Thank you.'

While Boyle had been delivering this little speech, Magnus' eyes had strayed towards the Welsh policeman — Summers — and he could not help but notice that the younger man was frowning slightly, as though he disapproved of what his superior was saying.

'Wait, what?' cried Nicholls, when it became clear that the Chief Superintendent wasn't going to say any more. 'That's all you're giving us? We already knew someone had died and that she was a woman! And who cares if the cleaner found her? Who else is going to come across a body in a hotel at six-thirty in the morning? You haven't told us anything!'

Despite his irritating manner, it seemed Ricky Nicholls had the crowd on his side, for there was some mutinous mutterings among those gathered around the Royal West. Boyle, however, didn't seem to care.

'You stay here and get rid of these people,' he told his young colleague, before stepping down from the entranceway of the hotel.

'Hey!' cried the reporter. 'Who is she? Have you identified the body? Hey! Do you have a name?'

Yet Boyle had clearly had enough. 'Get out of my way!' he cried, shoving past Nicholls so violently that the reporter went stumbling into the road, which was fortunately devoid of traffic.

'Hey!' shouted Nicholls again, although this time his exclamation might have been due to pain and indignation than curiosity. 'Just one more question, Chief Superintendent, just —'

But it was no use. Along with another of his officers, Boyle let himself into one of the parked police cars, and moments later he was gone.

'Right, well, I think the show's over now, folks!' announced Summers, from the entranceway of the Royal West. 'So come on, now — let's all get on with our days!'

He was not a naturally authoritative man, Magnus reflected — and the accent certainly didn't help. Nevertheless the crowd began to disperse, although that probably had less to do with the young constable's manner and more to do with the fact that it now looked as though there would be no further excitement. Even Ricky Nicholls, who winced as he clutched at the place on his side where Boyle had elbowed him, soon climbed back onto his motorbike and zoomed away.

'Mr Walterson? Hello?'

Magnus, who had been heading back towards Westminster Square, stopped in his tracks to find the Welsh policeman trotting towards him.

'Yes?'

'Bryn Summers, Police Constable,' he said sticking out his hand. 'I wanted to thank you for standing up for me back there.'

'Oh,' said Magnus, gripping the young man's fingers. 'You're very welcome. I was happy to help.'

Bryn's face seemed to fall a little. 'But I'm a police officer; I shouldn't need the help.'

'Everybody needs help from time to time, even police officers,' said Magnus gently. 'And, you'll forgive me for saying so, but you seem quite young, so I expect you're fairly new to the job?'

The other man nodded.

'And not from around here either, going by your accent?'

'I'm from Aberystwyth.'

'Ah, a lovely part of the world,' said Magnus. 'It has a beautiful beach, if I remember rightly?'

The young policeman beamed, but then something seemed to occur to him, and he began to look grave.

'Mr Walterson?'

'Please, call me Magnus.'

'Magnus, then. Are you really a barrister?'

Magnus chuckled. 'Of course! I can show you my card if you like...' But as he reached for his jacket pocket, he remembered he was wearing his jogging clothes. 'Ah, another time, perhaps.'

'I believe you,' said Bryn. 'But, as a man of the law, perhaps I could ask your advice?'

In his profession, Magnus was used to being asked his opinion, although admittedly not usually by police officers. 'Of course,' he said.

For some reason, the younger man looked uncomfortable. 'If, say, in your work, you think something important has been overlooked by one of your colleagues, you should flag it up, right?'

'Well, yes, naturally,' said Magnus, already wondering whether Bryn was talking about the body at the Royal West. 'For their sake as much as yours.'

'But... but what if flagging it up isn't as easy as all that?' continued the young police officer. 'What if you think it's the right thing to do, but you're not sure whether it's the *smart* thing to do?'

Magnus scratched at his chin, which was a little stubbly, given he had not yet shaved. 'I'm not sure I quite follow you,' he said. 'I think you might need to be a little more specific.'

Bryn looked around and then, with a slight jerk of his head, indicated he and Magnus should walk a few steps away from the entrance to the Royal West, to almost the end of the road.

'Can I speak to you in complete confidence about this?' he said, when they were safely out of earshot of any of the remaining crowd.

'You have my utmost discretion,' said Magnus.

Bryn took a deep breath. 'I don't think the woman in there died from natural causes,' he said. 'She's young — really young — about the same age as me.'

Magnus raised his eyebrows: he had not been expecting this.

'We found what we think is cocaine in her handbag,' continued Bryn in a hushed voice, 'so it looks like an accidental drug overdose, but the manager of the Royal West —'

'Doesn't want it getting out that people have been using drugs in his hotel,' finished Magnus, nodding with understanding. 'I see. That's what all that "natural causes" business was about.'

'But there's more!' Bryn continued urgently. 'The position she was found in was odd. It looked like she'd curled up and gone to sleep, and the medical examiner thought this was unusual for a drug overdose. And even stranger than that, there was severe bruising to her neck and wrists, as though someone had attacked her!'

'My goodness, that's quite a puzzle.'

'It is!' said Bryn. 'Only, Barry Boyle — that's the Chief Superintendent back there — he doesn't want to investigate it. He's decided she's some silly girl with a drug problem, and he's going to leave it at that. Well, not even that, because he's already telling the press a pack of lies. The "natural causes" bit, as you just heard, and she wasn't a guest at the hotel — she lives in the Mews! Do you know, he wouldn't even let the CID come in and take a few pictures, just in case, which was the advice of the medical officer!'

Magnus frowned: this did all seem very unprofessional for a Police Chief Superintendent. 'And do you think Boyle is doing all of this to protect the reputation of the Royal West?' he asked.

'Yes,' said Bryn. 'And also... Well, Boyle's lazy. I don't know what he was like in his younger days — I've only been here six months — but people say he's only a few years from retirement, so he wants a quiet life until he can sit back and start spending his massive pension, you know? But then, if there are suspicious circumstances surrounding this body, surely it's his duty — it's all of our duties as officers of the law — to investigate this thoroughly?'

Magnus nodded, now seeing Bryn's predicament clearly: he wanted to do the right thing, but he was afraid of angering his superior, who, by the looks of things, was not an easy man to work with.

'I think it's very admirable that you want to pursue this,' he told the younger man. 'This isn't just some misfiled paperwork, this is a woman's life — or rather, her death — and it sounds as though there are complications that shouldn't just be swept under the carpet. So yes, in answer to your original question, I do think you should flag up your concerns, absolutely.'

'But—'

'But Boyle is a difficult man, I understand that. Well, if I were you, I'd try again in a day or so, when he's cooled off. It's a Sunday morning, it's a beautiful day, and he's had to get up early and look at a dead body, so no wonder he's not in good mood...'

'Oh, he's always like that,' said Bryn quickly.

'Be that as it may, perhaps you could catch him at a better time? After a big meal, perhaps? Or you could talk to another of your colleagues?'

Bryn looked a little more enthusiastic at the prospect of this latter suggestion. 'Thank you, Magnus. That's good advice.'

As their conversation seemed to be drawing to a close, Magnus realised this was his chance to ask his own questions about the body in the Royal West, if indeed he had any. Just as he was considering this, something Bryn had said a few moments previously came back to him.

'You said she lived in the Mews, this woman? Do you mean the Mews behind Westminster Square?'

'Yes.'

Magnus felt another chill run through him.

'Why, that's just behind my house,' he said. 'I don't suppose you could tell me her name? Just to put my mind at rest, because now I'm worried it's someone I know...'

Bryn seemed to understand: 'Well, again, I'd appreciate your discretion on this one. We think the body belongs to a woman named Anne-Laure Chevalier.'

Anne-Laure Chevalier, thought Magnus. He certainly had no friend called that, although he thought he might have heard of or even met this woman before, because 'Anne-Laure Chevalier' rang a vague bell in his mind, and it was too distinctive a name for him to have confused it with someone else.

But he was soon distracted from these ponderings by the sound of laughter coming from behind the wall. Frowning, Magnus took a step backwards, to see who it was just around the corner, and that was when he clapped eyes on Hilda Underpin, hobbling into view.

She was an elderly woman of at least eighty years old, with beady eyes and an overlarge nose, with which she was constantly looking down on people, despite the fact she wasn't much over five feet tall. She wore old-fashioned dresses with dropped hems, as though she hadn't changed her style since the 1920s, when she had been young, and wherever she went she carried a huge handbag, into which she always stuffed her fluffy white Chihuahua, Tam Tam.

'Ah, Hilda, good morning. How nice to see you.'

Magnus spoke without a trace of sincerity, because Hilda Underpin was one of his least favourite people in Westminster Square, if not in all of London. She was mean, rude, and the biggest busybody he had ever met: she seemed to spend most of her days sat at her window armed with binoculars and spying on her neighbours.

'Trying to lose weight are you, Magnus?' Hilda said by way of greeting, jabbing her walking stick at his trainers. 'Thank goodness for that. I've been thinking for a while you were looking a bit *porky*...'

'Well I appreciate your concern for my health,' said Magnus, through gritted teeth.

'How's Juliana?' asked the old woman.

'Very well, thank you.'

'I saw she was out in her jeans again the other day,' said Hilda, disapprovingly. 'I do think it taints the character of the area, when women dress like that.'

'I'll be sure to pass on your comments,' said Magnus, intending to do no such thing.

Juliana in particular loathed Hilda Underpin, who was constantly complaining to her about the myriad offences she thought Juliana had committed around Westminster Square. These included (but were not limited to) the noise the children made as they walked to school, the fact that she had once left the garden gate unlocked, and more or less everything she ever wore — as though Hilda were enforcing a dress-code on the entire area. In fact, Magnus feared much of his wife's animosity towards Westminster Square was actually just hatred of their cantankerous old neighbour.

'Well, I'll let you get on, Hilda,' said Magnus, turning back towards Bryn and hoping the old woman would take the hint and go away.

'Not so fast,' said Hilda, baring her crooked yellow teeth. 'I want to hear more about this body. Is it really that Anne-Laure girl?'

'Were you eavesdropping round the corner there?' Magnus sighed, not even very surprised: Hilda Underpin was always spying on someone.

Bryn, however, looked alarmed. 'Excuse me, Madam, but that was a private conversation!' he cried.

But Magnus shook his head: there was no point using the word 'private' in front of Hilda — the woman didn't know what it meant.

'I thought I was too late,' said Hilda. 'When I heard the sirens, it took me a long time to get out of the house and over here on these old legs...' She tapped at the ground with her stick. 'But it looks like I arrived just at the right moment.'

'How much did you hear?' asked Bryn, who was obviously fearing for his job.

'Not much,' said Hilda, looking interested. 'I heard you say there was a body, and it belonged to *her*. Why, is there more?' Her eyes glittered with shameless curiosity.

'No,' said Magnus and Bryn together.

'There is!' said the old woman, looking gleeful. 'What is it? How did she die? Was it drink? Drugs? Or something else? Maybe she was killed — I did see several police cars from my window.'

'Hilda, show some respect!' cried Magnus, partly because he was horrified by her elation, and partly in an attempt to deflect attention from Bryn, who was beginning to look decidedly uncomfortable. 'This isn't some game, a woman is dead!'

'Puh, not much of a woman,' said Hilda. 'And certainly not one deserving of respect. If she was murdered, I'm not surprised.'

'Hilda!'

But while Magnus blustered, Bryn looked thoughtful.

'What do you mean, you're not surprised?' the Police Constable asked. 'Do you think she was in some kind of trouble?'

'She *was* trouble!' cried Hilda.

Magnus and Bryn's surprise must have shown on their faces, for the old woman shook her head in disgust.

'You men, you're always so beguiled by a pretty face…'

Magnus thought this very unfair, considering neither he nor Bryn had ever knowingly met the woman in question, let alone been beguiled by her. But before he could tell Hilda this, she was pushing them out of the way with her walking stick and continuing along the pavement, no doubt to inspect the Royal West Hotel for herself.

'All I'm saying is this,' she muttered as she passed them: 'if Anne-Laure Chevalier *was* murdered, that girl got exactly what was coming to her.'

CHAPTER FOUR

PARTY GIRL FOUND DEAD AT THE ROYAL WEST
by Ricky Nicholls

The peace of Westminster, one of London's wealthiest neighbourhoods, was shattered during the early hours of yesterday morning, when a woman's body was discovered in a luxury hotel.

Shortly afterwards, Chief Superintendent Barry Boyle of the Victoria Police Station issued the following statement: "At approximately six-thirty am... one of the cleaners of the Royal West Hotel found the body of a female guest. The medical examiner has since declared the woman passed away from natural causes, so we are not treating the death as suspicious, and will be making no further comments on this matter."

It has since been revealed that the deceased woman was Anne-Laure Chevalier, a 28-year-old events organiser who worked in Westminster and lived in the Mews behind Westminster Square, one of London's most famous addresses. The Dawn Reporter can exclusively reveal that Ms Chevalier, a statuesque blonde, was a regular on the London party circuit. According to sources, she was a good-time girl who could often be found frequenting the kind of nightclubs favoured by celebrities, royalty and business heirs.

The Victoria Police continue to insist no foul play was involved in Ms Chevalier's death, but readers will find themselves wondering how such a young — not to mention attractive — woman could have died so suddenly. This reporter, who witnessed Ms Chevalier's body being removed from the hotel, saw a number of police on the scene. Does this indicate there is more to the tragedy than Boyle is letting on? Or did Anne-Laure Chevalier's wild lifestyle simply catch up with her in the end?

[More pictures of Anne-Laure Chevalier can be found on page 8].

Juliana Walterson sighed, closed *The Dawn Reporter,* and threw it straight into the bin. What an appalling rag it was. She had never read much of the so-called newspaper before, and had certainly never purchased it herself, but this morning, when walking through Victoria Station, she had seen a copy of the tabloid lying abandoned on one of the benches. The front cover was dominated by a full-sized picture of Anne-Laure Chevalier, evidently at one of her parties, for the striking young woman was wearing a low-cut green dress, and the photograph had evidently been chosen to appeal to *The Dawn Reporter*'s male readership — never mind if the picture's subject was now dead. Despite Juliana's disapproval of this editorial decision, and despite her disdain for the paper as a whole, upon seeing that image of her former neighbour she had been seized by so much curiosity she felt compelled to pick up the newspaper from the bench and take it to work with her.

Did tabloid editors celebrate when pretty girls died, Juliana wondered? How many more newspapers did they sell when they emblazoned their pages with pictures of deceased blonde beauties? She had no doubt Anne-Laure Chevalier would not have made the front page if she had been older, or plainer, or poorer, or male — especially as the circumstances of her death were apparently unsuspicious.

Trying to put the girl from her mind, Juliana looked up and took a deep breath, inhaling the mingling sweet scents pervading The Station Garden, the flower shop she owned. As with her and Magnus' flat, this space was stuffed with plants and freshly-cut flowers of all descriptions, as well as various seeds and bulbs for home-planting, and as with her Westminster Square home, it calmed her to be surrounded by all this greenery. So much so, in fact, that Juliana often wished she didn't have to sell any of it at all, so she could simply sit in the midst of all this foliage and pretend she was back in the Kentish countryside.

In reality, however, she was right in the middle of central London, for her flower shop was positioned in the shopping area above Victoria Station. As far as Juliana was aware, Victoria had been built in the latter half of the nineteenth century to better connect Central London to the

South, including her beloved home county of Kent. But when the station had been developed, the builders had clearly not anticipated the modern need for shops nearby, and so more recently an ugly glass structure had been created on the top of the original architecture, the garish panes and metal frames of which seriously undermined the old station's elegance, or so Juliana thought. It always reminded her of when she and Magnus had visited New York — a city she had hated even more than London — and they had been taken out to visit an American mall, one of the ghastliest places she'd ever been.

Still, when Magnus had convinced her to move to London a decade ago, so that he would be closer to his work in Grey's Inn, the rent above Victoria Station had been cheap, and its proximity to their apartment in Westminster Square made it a natural choice for the location of her flower shop.

Furthermore, Juliana liked to think she brought a little happiness to the harassed tourists and commuters who came into her shop looking for gifts for their friends, family, sweethearts or colleagues. She enjoyed the idea that everyone who came into The Station Garden, no matter how stressed they were from the daily grind of life in London, left feeling a little happier, a little bit more at peace with the world. That was the effect of being surrounded by flowers, Juliana thought, and the more she did this herself, the more she could convince herself that she could tolerate this life in the middle of the sprawling city, far away from the idyllic countryside in which she had grown up.

'Would you like a cup of tea, Mrs Walterson?' asked Daisy, her young employee, interrupting these thoughts.

'Oh, yes, if you're making one, Daisy, thank you.'

The girl nodded, and disappeared into the little kitchenette at the back of the shop. Juliana watched her go, smiling. Daisy was the daughter of her old gardener at her family home in Kent. She was a sweet girl, small and pretty with dark hair and fine features.

Although Daisy's parents had come from modest backgrounds themselves, they'd had aspirations for their daughter's future, and she had been sent to a top girls' school in Tunbridge Wells, although it had been so tough she had failed most of her A-levels, and in doing so dashed her parents' hopes of her earning a place at Oxbridge, or indeed any good university. Nevertheless, they had then pushed Daisy into moving to London, in order to get some experience temping in offices, with the hope that she would one day climb through the ranks of some company, or make enough money and connections to do some vocational training in the capital.

When Daisy had come into The Station Garden a year or so ago, Juliana had been shocked to see the change in her. Daisy's rosy complexion had gone, and she had seemed very grave and sad. Tearfully, the girl had confessed she hated London, she missed the countryside, and she couldn't bear the stuffy offices in which she worked all day. Juliana had been instantly sympathetic, and had quickly offered Daisy a job as her assistant in The Station Garden, feeling that then the girl — like her — would at least be surrounded by a little greenery.

This had turned out to be the best decision Juliana had ever made with regard to the shop. Like her father, Daisy was exceptionally green-fingered, and even better at cultivating plants and flowers than Juliana herself. Moreover, the girl had turned out to be far brighter than Juliana had realised, especially with regard to numbers — Maths, it turned out, had been the only final exam she had passed at school, and with an A grade to boot. After discovering this, Juliana had put Daisy to work on The Station Garden's accounting, and after she had excelled at that, promoted her to manager of the shop. This arrangement suited Juliana down to the ground, given she was not a particularly organised person herself; Daisy could worry about the day-to-day running of the enterprise, she could take responsibility for the more artistic side of things, such as the flower arrangements.

A few minutes later, Daisy returned with two mugs of steaming, perfectly-brewed tea, one of which she handed to Juliana. As she leaned over the counter, she caught a glimpse of Anne-Laure Chevalier's face looking up at her from the wastepaper basket, and sighed.

'It's just terrible, isn't it?' said Daisy. 'That poor woman... She was so young.'

'Yes,' said Juliana, pushing the bin further under the counter with the toe of one of her shoes: she didn't want the customers to see it.

'They're saying she lived in the Mews behind Westminster Square,' Daisy went on. 'Did you know her?'

'I don't think so, no. At least, we never met officially. I might have talked to her at a party and forgotten...' Juliana paused, and then finally articulated what had been bothering her all morning, seeing the woman's face emblazoned across every tabloid. 'I think I recognise her, though — from seeing her around Westminster Square and so on. After all, a face like that isn't easy to forget, is it? And she was always dressed to the nines...'

She frowned as she recalled the newspaper referring to Anne-Laure as a 'party girl'. Juliana was long past parties herself, and had never particularly enjoyed them before she'd had Rosanna and Lee, but she didn't like the implication in *The Dawn Reporter's* article, that Anne-Laure's love of going out was somehow to blame for her death.

'She's not much older than me,' said Daisy, who seemed a little fixated on the woman's youth. 'And yet they're saying it was "natural causes". It makes you think, doesn't it? We could any of us go at any moment!'

It *did* make Juliana think, although not about her own mortality. Yesterday, after coming back from his jog, Magnus had told her about the body in the Royal West and — after swearing her to secrecy — recounted a conversation he'd had with a young policeman. As far as she could gather, it sounded like Anne-Laure Chevalier had died of an accidental cocaine overdose, and the poor woman had been knocked about by somebody before it had happened, leaving Juliana to wonder whether it had been accidental at all... What if she had taken her own life to escape an abusive relationship? Or what if someone had taken it for her?

'It's a bit early on a Monday morning to be discussing this, Daisy,' she said, in response to her young manager's point about sudden death. 'Why don't you go and tidy up the window display? I'm going to get some sunflowers from the flower market tomorrow, so perhaps you could make room for them? I'd better pick up some more purple ribbon too...'

'Of course, Mrs Walterson.'

They set to work in a companionable silence, and Juliana tried to forget about her dead neighbour. Then, just as she was finishing her tea, the bell above the door of The Station Garden tinkled, signalling that someone was entering the shop. Juliana looked up from her arrangement, eager for distraction.

'Dame Winifred,' she said, smiling. 'How nice to see you!'

'A very good morning to you, Juliana! And to you, Daisy.'

Dame Winifred Rye was a large and exceptionally posh woman of around fifty years old. She had a round face, greying blonde hair, and would have been moderately attractive if she wasn't in the habit of caking her face in so much make-up. In fact, with her over-bronzed complexion, her eyelashes clogged with clumps of mascara, and her lipstick-covered teeth, she looked positively cartoonish. Her clothes too, although designer and no doubt very expensive, did not particularly suit her, for Dame Winifred always chose to dress in loud shades like hot pink and lime green, which completely washed her out, even with all the make-up.

Still, Juliana thought, as her eyes moved over today's outfit — which consisted of a bright orange skirt and matching jacket — it felt unkind to judge Dame Winifred on her poor styling choices. Firstly, as she lived in the north-west of Westminster Square, she was a neighbour, and Juliana felt a certain affinity with most of the people who lived around her, given that they were all stuck in this miserable part of the country together (only Hilda Underpin was excluded from Juliana's sense of neighbourly loyalty, but that was because the old bag was one of the nosiest and meanest people she had ever had the misfortune to meet).

Secondly, Juliana had a lot of sympathy for Dame Winifred because she was a widow. Lord Rye, from whom Winifred had inherited her title and money, had apparently died young, and many years before Juliana and Magnus had moved to Westminster Square. In fact, the sight of Dame Winifred bustling about on her own was so common, it was almost impossible to believe she had ever had a husband.

Then finally, and perhaps most importantly, Juliana always made an effort to be nice to Dame Winifred because the aristocrat was a very charitable person herself. Perhaps it was because she was childless and had been alone for so long, but as far as Juliana was aware, Dame Winifred was constantly throwing parties and hosting events to raise money for everything from orphans in Africa to endangered species of animals in the Amazon rainforest. Indeed, it had been for one such cause that Dame Winifred had hosted Sunday afternoon's tennis tournament, not to mention the party that had taken place at the Royal West Hotel that evening, for which The Station Garden had provided the flowers.

'I must say, as lovely as it is to see you again, I'm surprised you're back here so soon,' said Juliana, considering this party was only just behind them.

'Well, first of all, I wanted to thank you — and Daisy, of course — for your lovely arrangements. The Royal West looked simply splendid; a veritable Eden! You do have a great talent, Juliana.'

Juliana could not help but stand up a little straighter at hearing this. 'It's very kind of you to say so, Dame Winifred...'

'Not at all, not at all,' said the older woman, waving Juliana's modesty away. 'And secondly, I've come to place my next order — you see, I've already another charity event on the horizon, this time at my house, and I'll no longer consider anyone but The Station Garden for my flowers.'

'I'm very pleased to hear it,' said Juliana. 'But another event? So soon?'

'Oh, there's no rest for the wicked,' smiled Dame Winifred.

'But you must have raised a lot of money on Saturday night alone — it's very commendable!'

After Dame Winifred had given a shrug of her large shoulders, there was a moment's pause in which Juliana began to feel awkward. She wanted to ask about the party, how it had gone, but given it had ended in the death of a young woman — which Dame Winifred surely knew about by now — she wasn't sure how to broach the subject. But then, to her surprise, it was the aristocrat who first referred to the matter.

'I'm afraid that party, as smoothly as it went at the time, has now been rather tainted, considering... Well, considering what happened. I assume you've read the papers this morning?'

Juliana nodded, exceptionally grateful that she'd pushed the wastepaper basket under the desk, and Dame Winifred would not be able to see the copy of *The Dawn Reporter* she'd thrown inside.

'Such a tragedy,' said Dame Winifred. 'Such an awful, terrible —'

And then, to Juliana's great surprise, tears suddenly sprang into Dame Winifred's eyes.

'Oh my goodness, I'm so sorry!' she gasped, reaching into her handbag for a lacy handkerchief. 'Oh dear, oh dear — what must you think of me? I'm dreadfully sorry!'

'That's quite all right,' said Juliana, signalling at Daisy to bring the crying woman a chair. 'Please, don't apologise. Would you like us to make you a cup of tea or something? Daisy just made a round, so the kettle will still be hot.'

'Oh no, no, I'll be all right in a minute,' said Dame Winifred, before adding, 'Thank you, dear,' to Daisy, and slumping into the chair she had brought over.

'Take your time,' said Juliana, for there were no other customers, and she was secretly rather stunned at the aristocrat's sudden outburst of emotion; Dame Winifred was usually jolly and boisterous. 'Are you sure you wouldn't like some tea? Or a biscuit, perhaps? We have a tin of shortbread somewhere...'

'I'm fine, thank you so much,' said Dame Winifred, wiping at her eyes. Then, when she drew the handkerchief away, Juliana saw it was stained with smears of foundation, eye shadow and mascara. 'Goodness me, what a spectacle I've made of myself!' she added, with a little laugh. 'The thing is, I think I'm still in shock — it's still sinking in. You see, I knew the girl. I knew Anne-Laure... Not particularly well, of course. In fact, I'm not sure anybody was very close to her — she kept herself to herself that one, despite always being out and about.' Dame Winifred blew her nose loudly, making a sound like a trumpet, before continuing,

'But we had a little history, Anne-Laure and I. She lived in a flat I own, one in the Mews.'

'Really?' said Juliana. 'I didn't know she was renting from you...'

'Yes, she was there for years, since she arrived in London about a decade ago. Back then, I charged her a very reduced rate for her rent, because otherwise she couldn't have afforded to live here in Westminster. Perhaps that was silly and sentimental of me, but I knew she'd do well, that girl. You can see from all those dreadful photographs in the papers that she was very beautiful, but what they won't tell you is how smart she was. And how good. It was my pleasure to start her off.'

Juliana nodded. Dame Winifred had, she knew, taken a few girls under her wing over the years, rather like a fairy godmother. She liked to use her contacts to help them find work, somewhere to live, or further their education. Juliana supposed it was not so very unusual; in fact, it was almost exactly what she had done with Daisy. And of course the middle-aged woman had never had any children of her own. The fact that Anne-Laure Chevalier was one of these young protégées certainly accounted for the woman's distress.

'I read that she worked in events organisation and party-planning,' Juliana said tentatively, because she didn't want to further upset Dame Winifred. 'So I'm presuming you collaborated with her on a lot of your charity fundraisers?'

Dame Winifred gave a sigh. 'Funnily enough, not as many as you might think,' she said. 'Unfortunately, Anne-Laure's time was always taken up by that Russian chap — you know the one I mean — the man who's always having those business parties.'

'Vasyl Kosnitschev,' said Juliana, referring to another of their neighbours in Westminster Square. 'Actually, I think he might be Ukrainian...'

'Russian, Ukrainian,' said Dame Winifred, with a wave of her hand. 'Anyway, Anne-Laure was always so busy arranging all of *his* events, she hardly had any time for mine, which was a shame. Although, to be perfectly honest, I rather like organising all the bits and pieces for a party — like the flowers,' she said, nodding around The Station Garden in approval. 'And I don't want it to sound as though Anne-Laure was ungrateful for the help I'd given her when she first moved to London. She was always very apologetic. *"You have to give me more notice, Winnie,"* she'd tell me. *"I'd love to do your charity events…"'*

Juliana smiled sadly.

'And that's exactly what I did, for the tennis tournament and the party at the Royal West,' continued Dame Winifred. 'I booked her months and months in advance.'

'Anne-Laure organised it, then?' said Juliana, with a little shiver: it seemed rather sinister somehow, for her to have been responsible for the party at which she had died.

'Yes — apart from the flowers, of course — and she did a lovely job,' said Dame Winifred. 'She had such an eye for detail, and left no stone unturned when it came to organisation. But more than that, it was just a joy, spending time with her again in the run-up to Saturday. It felt like old times…'

The terrible truth seemed to wash over Dame Winifred once more, and she gripped her handkerchief to her mouth to stop a sob escaping her.

'The papers are saying she was found at the Royal West first thing in the morning,' the aristocrat said, tears beginning to leak from her eyes once more. 'That's what I can't stop thinking about. I didn't see her after the party — I wanted to thank her for her hard work in person, you see — only I couldn't find her. So I assumed she'd gone home, when in reality she was still there, somewhere. I imagine she was tidying up, or at least checking nobody had left anything behind, and she probably thought I'd swanned off and abandoned her!'

'I'm sure she didn't think that,' Juliana said reassuringly, while Dame Winifred's face crumpled with grief.

They were now close to discussing the thing that had been occupying Juliana's thoughts ever since Magnus had returned from his jog yesterday morning, and although Juliana knew it was insensitive to even consider bringing up the manner of Anne-Laure's demise, something made her ask, 'I don't suppose you know how she died?' Then, realising how blunt this sounded, she went on, 'Because she looks very young, from all the photographs...'

But Dame Winifred could only shake her head. 'I know as much as you do, dear. All the papers are saying it was "natural causes", but it seems very unnatural that someone who was so healthy and who was, as you say, so young could pass away so suddenly. I don't understand it. I suppose it must have been an aneurysm or something like that, but really, it doesn't make any sense to me...'

Juliana hesitated. 'You don't think...' she began slowly. 'You don't think Anne-Laure might have... well, *taken* something?'

Dame Winifred looked up, her tear-streaked face confused. 'What do you mean? Taken what?'

'I don't know, some kind of substance?' said Juliana, not daring to say the word 'drugs' aloud. Then, because the aristocrat was looking so aghast, she added hurriedly, 'You know what young people are like nowadays, and these things are freely available. And she might not have taken anything on *purpose*...'

But Dame Winifred was shaking her head. 'No,' she said firmly, 'absolutely not. Not Anne-Laure. She was a good girl.'

'But —'

'And she wouldn't have taken anything without realising,' said the older woman. 'She was smart and she was careful. No, I won't believe it for a second.'

Juliana nodded, seeing there was little point arguing.

'If it wasn't from "natural causes", as the police say, she must have had some sort of accident,' continued Dame Winifred. 'Maybe she bumped her head?'

'Yes, maybe,' echoed Juliana, although — from what Magnus had told her — this sounded unlikely.

Dame Winifred shuddered. 'I don't think I want to dwell on it anymore, it's just too horrible.'

'Of course,' said Juliana quickly, regretting that she had steered the conversation down this path. 'You're quite right. Let's talk about something else — let's talk about the flowers for your next party!'

'Oh yes,' said Dame Winifred, heaving herself up from her chair. 'But you get on, Juliana, dear. And I should hurry up too, I have to get to the bank after this. I'll discuss the flower arrangements with Daisy…'

'All right,' said Juliana, somewhat unnecessarily, for the aristocrat was already walking towards Daisy.

For a few moments, she watched Dame Winifred smiling down at the young manager, who was taking her through a catalogue of floral designs, and Juliana hoped, for a little while at least, Daisy's sweetness would act as a kind of balm to the older woman's grief.

* * * *

On her way home from work that afternoon, Juliana took a detour to Victoria Street, in order to pick up some groceries for the week. This was another of the many things that irritated her about living in Westminster Square: there were no shops in the immediate vicinity — or at least, no shops that could provide the relevant quality and quantity of food required to satisfy a family of four.

By the time Juliana was heading back towards her house, she was laden with shopping bags and feeling grumpy and unusually resentful of the sun, which was shining brightly on her face. Cursing Westminster Square, she put her head down to shield her eyes from the dazzling light, and marched forward, intending to get home as quickly as possible. But no sooner had she begun to walk in this determined manner than she collided into somebody coming the other way, and dropped her bags in surprise.

'Oh *no*!' she cried, as much of her shopping went spilling over the pavement. 'Oh, bother!'

'I'm sorry,' gasped the person she had crashed into, stooping to stop an orange that was in danger of rolling into the road.

'Don't apologise, it was my fault,' Juliana replied, bundling tins and packets back into her bags. 'I wasn't looking where I was — Oh, hello, Morris! I didn't realise it was you.'

She gathered up the last of the food and straightened up, blinking at Morris Springfield through the sunlight. He was a gangly man in his late twenties, who walked with a self-conscious stoop and exuded an aura of awkwardness. He had dark, receding hair, rather bulging pale eyes, and his face was a little too asymmetrical to be considered handsome.

Not that looks were particularly important in his field of work, however: Morris Springfield was a writer, and something of a literary talent — at least, according to Magnus, who was more interested in such matters. All Juliana knew was that Morris had published two novels, which had both been well-received by critics but were, for her — and, she suspected, many members of the public — completely inaccessible. Allegedly, he was working on a third book, although nowadays he seemed to spend most of his time writing letters and opinion pieces for newspapers like *The Guardian*.

'Are you taking a walk?' Juliana asked, for Morris was not far from home: Magnus had told her that the young writer lived in a small flat on Westminster Row, which was two roads behind Westminster Square.

'Yeah,' mumbled Morris, handing Juliana the last of her shopping, which consisted of some apples and a carton of milk. 'A walk, yeah.'

'Well, I'm glad you're taking a break from your writing to get outside,' she said, gesturing up at the cloudless sky. 'You can't stay cooped up in weather like this.'

'Yeah,' said Morris again.

He was so monosyllabic this afternoon that Juliana found it difficult to believe he was a wordsmith, let alone a moderately successful one. Then something occurred to her.

'Hold on, Morris — it's Monday and we haven't seen you in the shop!'

She was referring to the fact that at the beginning of every week, Morris Springfield came in to order a modest bunch of flowers for his ailing mother, who lived outside of London. Despite her reservations about the young man's social skills, Juliana thought this very sweet, especially as he always then headed off to buy chocolates or biscuits or jam to accompany his gift, and therefore never even took up her offers of free delivery on the flowers.

'The shop?' repeated Morris, blankly.

'Yes, The Station Garden,' said Juliana, wondering whether he was all right. 'I mean, you're under no obligation to buy your flowers there, of course, but we've come to rather expect you on a Monday, Morris.'

'The Station Garden, yes,' he said. 'No, I haven't bought mother's flowers today...'

'I noticed that,' laughed Juliana. Then, feeling this conversation was going nowhere, she said, 'Well, I shan't pry into your personal life any longer. I'll let you get on with your walk...'

He seemed to wake up a bit then, for he gave his head a little shake and said, 'Sorry, I think I'm miles away...'

'That's all right,' said Juliana. Then, thinking back on Dame Winifred, she added, 'I think everybody's a bit out of sorts today. You know, considering what happened at the weekend...'

'At the weekend?'

Juliana took in the sight of his confused expression. Was it possible he didn't know? Morris Springfield was certainly not the sort of person who read *The Dawn Reporter,* but the death of Anne-Laure Chevalier had been covered widely, especially in the local news, so surely even he had heard by now?

'You know, because of that poor girl who died at the Royal West,' said Juliana.

'Oh, yes,' said Morris at once. 'Yes, what a horrible thing...'

He had an odd expression on his face — he suddenly looked physically pained, as though he had developed a stomach complaint — and Juliana didn't know whether he was thinking of the young woman and her early death, or whether he disliked talking about such sensational matters in public.

'Well, there's no point thinking about it too much,' Juliana said briskly, more because she didn't want to be seen as a gossip than because she actually believed this; after all, she had been thinking about Anne-Laure Chevalier's death since yesterday morning. 'It won't bring her back, will it?'

Then, to her great surprise, Morris made an odd snorting sound, and she realised he was trying to hold back tears. Juliana could hardly believe it: this was the second time today somebody had broken down in front of her.

'Morris, I'm so sorry — did you know her?'

'What?'

'Did you know Anne-Laure Chevalier?'

'Oh —'

He shook his head, apparently unable to talk any more. Juliana rifled through her handbag for a packet of tissues, which she offered to him.

'Thanks,' he whispered, his voice rather muffled, because he had buried his whole face in the tissue he had taken. 'No, I didn't know her. I don't even recognise the pictures. It's just... It's been a difficult weekend. My mother...'

Juliana gasped. 'Oh, Morris!'

'She's alive,' he said quickly. 'But she's had to go into hospital. She's caught some sort of infection... That's why I didn't come in for the flowers, as usual.'

'Of course!'

He wiped at his face with the tissue. 'And I'm sorry about that girl, I am, but there's been so much talk of *death,* I just can't bear it...'

'Of *course,*' Juliana said again, wishing she had known about his mother before bringing up Anne-Laure Chevalier. 'Are you going to see your mother in... Where is it you're from again?'

'East Sussex. Yes, I'm going tomorrow morning. I have to finish an article this evening...'

Juliana privately felt East Sussex was close enough for Morris Springfield to have hopped on a train straight away, but she refrained from saying anything. After all, she had no idea what the life of a writer was like; Morris might be under severe pressure from several editors for all she knew.

'Well, if you have time before you go tomorrow, why don't you pop in to The Station Garden and we'll put together a really beautiful bouquet for your mother — on the house,' she added. Then, when he began to object, she said, 'No, I insist. You've given us plenty of business over the past couple of years, and we can even send it on ahead of you, if you don't want to take it on the train. To make up for all those free deliveries you've missed.'

'Thank you, Juliana,' he gulped, evidently trying to pull himself together.

It was with a little relief that, after reiterating her offer of free flowers, Juliana then said goodbye and finally managed to extricate herself from this conversation with Morris Springfield. Perhaps she would ask Magnus to call in on the young man in a few days' time and see how he was doing. Yes, that would be an idea… And in the meantime, she could start thinking about this bouquet she would make for Mrs Springfield first thing tomorrow morning.

But Juliana's pleasant imaginings of what these flowers might look like only lasted so long, for a few moments later, as she continued towards home, she crossed the Mews. It was a narrow, cobbled street behind Westminster Square where the houses had been converted from stables decades ago. And although she was trying to follow her own advice, and not dwell any longer on the morbid fate of one of her neighbours, Juliana could not help but feel very cold as she considered that one of these flats was now lying empty, its young inhabitant never to return.

CHAPTER FIVE

On Wednesday evening, four days after the death of Anne-Laure Chevalier, Magnus had finally begun to put the matter from his mind. Instead he had turned his attention to the tedious but significant struggle he was currently having with Central Square Properties, the company that managed the properties in Westminster Square, and his recent decision to call a meeting and involve his neighbours in this conflict.

This gathering was to take place at the Cosmopolitan Club, which was situated on the northern side of Westminster Square. Magnus told himself he had chosen the eminent old club as a venue because it was nearby, and for a small amount he had been able to hire a large room he hoped would house all of the neighbours who turned up. But secretly, Magnus had an ulterior motive for picking the Cosmopolitan Club that evening: although it was still in Westminster Square, it was on the opposite side to his own flat, and therefore there was less chance of Juliana getting wind of what he was up to. As he reflected on this duplicity — and on the fact that he had told her he would be working late at Grey's Inn — Magnus felt a gnawing of guilt in his stomach. He never lied to his wife, but in this case he thought he was doing the right thing: Juliana loathed living in Westminster Square enough as it was; if she found out what had prompted this meeting, she would probably book a removal van for the very next day.

Furthermore, Magnus liked the Cosmopolitan Club. Like the other architecture on the quadrant, it was a grandiose Georgian building, although unlike many of the residences nearby, which had been divided up into flats, all seventeen thousand square feet of the property belonged to the Club itself.

As he walked through the entrance hall that evening, Magnus was struck, as he always was, by the impression of faded grandeur that emanated from the Cosmopolitan Club. On the one hand, the interior possessed the impressive high ceilings of all the Westminster Square properties, a large central staircase, and the walls were lined with portraits of various international figures, which lent a certain gravitas to the setting. Yet it was also a building that felt a little as though it were going to seed. The musty old rooms smelled of stale beer and cigarette smoke, and some of the walls needed a touch-up to cover the tobacco stains and peeling paintwork. In fact, the whole establishment felt rather like an old and much-loved local pub sorely in need of a little redecoration — which was perhaps the point, now Magnus came to think about it. In any case, the Cosmopolitan Club's aesthetic shortcomings had certainly never put off its steady stream of visitors. Former Prime Ministers had been known to frequent its walls, and it was also a favourite haunt of artists and writers, especially poets.

The room where the meeting was to be held was dominated by a large wooden table, which was somewhat sticky from age and alcohol, around which a number of battered old leather chairs had been arranged. While he waited for his guests to arrive, Magnus paced up and down at the head of this table, wondering whether he had done the right thing in calling this meeting — and whether the fact he hadn't told Juliana anything of what he was about to discuss with all his neighbours would come back to haunt him.

Then, just after the grandfather clock in the corner began to chime eight, Magnus' guests began to file in. For the most part, the individuals who had turned up to his meeting were middle-aged, white and wealthy — which was also, as far as he was aware, the general profile of an average Westminster Square resident. The room seemed to be divided into those who had come from work, and so were dressed in grey or pinstripe suits, and those who were so well-off they didn't need to work, and were therefore in more casual (but still smart and expensive) attire.

As Magnus shook hands, nodded and said hello to these various neighbours, some of whom he knew well and others only by sight, he noted that there were three men who looked as though they did not quite belong in the group, given their dress, which ranged from unusual to downright eccentric.

The first and perhaps least offensive-looking of these individuals was the Ukrainian, Vasyl Kosnitschev. He was around fifty years of age, with grey hair, a hooked nose, pock-marked skin and a permanently disgruntled expression on his craggy features. Tonight, as he often did, Vasyl was wearing a khaki-coloured suit, which Magnus always thought made him look even more Soviet — more Stalin-like, in fact — than he already did.

The oligarch was famed around Westminster for his parties, which were more business-orientated than the fundraising events of someone like Dame Winifred Rye, although Magnus had always made a point of politely declining any invitations he received. Perhaps he was being judgemental, but on the basis of the few encounters he'd had with Vasyl Kosnitschev, he didn't think the Ukrainian seemed like much fun.

The second person who caught Magnus' eye for looking rather remarkable that evening was Lord Bevis Ellington. Ellington was a tall, willowy man in his early sixties with white-blond hair and a rather large mouth. Like the Cosmopolitan Club itself, he emitted an aroma of whiskey and tobacco, and he walked around with an air of extreme confidence, even arrogance. Magnus was always surprised to remember that Ellington was a Labour Lord, for his dress and manner suggested he was leaning far more to the right in his old age.

His current outfit was a perfect example of this: for some reason, Lord Bevis Ellington had come to a meeting about properties in Westminster Square in full riding regalia. Though this would have looked odd on anyone, the bright red jacket looked especially silly against his ruddy complexion, and the tight white trousers downright absurd on his long, frog-like legs. But the cherry on the cake, as far as Magnus was concerned, was the silver-handled whip; when he caught sight of this tucked into Ellington's belt, he had to turn away to hide his laughter. What a snobby old fool, Magnus thought, as Ellington strutted slowly towards his seat like a peacock.

But the award for the evening's most flamboyant outfit — or at least, the most unusual — had to go to Sheikh Hazim bin Lahab. Hazim was a short and morbidly obese man from the Arabian Gulf, who continued to wear long tribal robes and a headdress, despite the mild temperature of England in comparison to his homeland. As entitled as he was to do so, Magnus could not help but think that, on his grotesquely fat frame, it looked a little as though Hazim was dressed in a giant marquee, the sort that might be erected for a wedding or a garden party.

As the sheikh lowered himself into a chair, which creaked dangerously under his weight, Magnus reflected that it was quite a surprise he had even turned up this evening, given the meeting did not involve either food or women. These were Hazim's two great passions, and it was a common sight to see either great slabs of meat or gaggles of girls being ushered into his Westminster Square house of an evening, much to the outrage of old Hilda Underpin, who would inevitably be spying from across the road.

When everybody had finally settled into chairs, and the backroom of the Cosmopolitan Club was looking much fuller than it had done ten minutes beforehand, Magnus tapped a pen against his glass of water to call for quiet.

'A very good evening to you all,' he began, 'and thank you for taking the time to come here tonight.'

Various nods and murmurs of 'Not at all, not at all' rippled around the room.

Magnus smiled at the assortment of neighbours gathered around him. It was a good turn-out, he thought; over thirty people had shown up. There were a few noticeable absences: Jem McMorran never usually came to Westminster Square events unless they involved tennis or were purely social, and besides, Magnus thought the actor might be off on a film shoot by now. Dame Winifred Rye had alternative plans that evening, but had written ahead to send her apologies. And the nonappearance of Hilda Underpin was curious, until Magnus remembered he had been too cross with her for eavesdropping on his conversation with Police Constable

Bryn Summers to invite her in the first place. He would no doubt come to regret this pettiness in due course, however, as the old busybody was bound to find out about the meeting sooner or later, and if there was one thing Hilda hated it was being left out of the loop.

Still, the old woman's vitriol — along with keeping this meeting a secret from Juliana — was something to worry about in the future. For now, Magnus had a case to make.

'As you may or may not be aware,' he continued to the crowd in the Cosmopolitan Club, 'the reason for this meeting is to discuss the maintenance costs that we are charged for living in Westminster Square.'

Fewer people nodded and murmured their approval this time. Magnus had the impression this wasn't going to be the easiest meeting he had ever chaired. Steeling himself for a lot of talking, he decided to start as simply as possible, in order not to lose anybody along the way.

'First of all, I should say we are all incredibly lucky to be able to live where we do. An address in Westminster Square or the surrounding streets is nothing to sniff at; in fact, our properties are undoubtedly some of the most enviable in all of London — if not the world.'

'Hear, hear!' cried a man Magnus didn't know, with great enthusiasm.

'However, that is not to say that owning — or rather, leasing — a property in or around Westminster Square is without its drawbacks,' continued Magnus, before anybody else could interrupt. 'As you're all aware, because of the historic nature of this area, our houses and flats don't officially belong to us, and instead they are the property of the crown and its associates. Like me, you have all agreed upon a long-term lease of ten, twenty, or even seventy years with Central Square Properties, or CSP, who administer these residences, and this is the closest we can come to actually owning our homes here.'

Magnus paused to look around at the faces of his listeners; it seemed as though they were all following what he was saying. *So far so good*, he thought.

'With that in mind, when you all moved here, you would have signed a contract in which you agreed to pay for this long-term lease for your respective properties, and in which you also agreed to pay monthly maintenance charges for living in or around Westminster Square. Is that correct?'

Most people nodded. One rather portly man, however, raised his hand.

'Excuse me, Magnus,' he said, 'I did agree to these monthly maintenance charges, but I'm still not sure I quite understand what they're for. Perhaps you could enlighten me?'

'Ah yes,' said Magnus, 'that's an important point, thank you. According to my contract, at least, the monthly maintenance charges are meant to cover the cost of maintaining the buildings and gardens of Westminster Square to a high, almost royal standard. With this meeting in mind, I actually wrote to CSP for a more specific breakdown of these costs, and in return I was sent a list that included things like heating and power for the hallways of our buildings, insurance, management fees, ground rent, service charges, doormen, gardeners, general maintenance of the historic architecture, upkeep of the tennis court... even insurance against terrorism! And let me just say that, in principle, I have no issue with paying a monthly maintenance fee. As I've said, I feel privileged to live where I do, and I understand that having such an address comes with certain financial obligations.

'However,' continued Magnus, 'it is my opinion that, over the years, CSP have been steadily upping these charges to such a degree that I am now paying an astronomical amount each month for the so-called "maintenance" of my fairly modest three-bedroom flat. Therefore, the purpose of this meeting is first of all to find out whether we're all in the same boat on this issue, and — if we are — what we're all going to do about it.'

Magnus paused to take a sip of water; he felt as though he had been talking for some time. Over the rim of his glass, he watched his audience begin to digest what he had just said. Many of them already looked fired-up, and he thought they were muttering among themselves about the way they had also been overcharged. Others, however, looked as though they might need a little more convincing.

MYSTERY IN WESTMINSTER SQUARE

'Look,' said Magnus, 'I know the Brits among you hate talking about money, but if you'll allow me to be vulgar and discuss some figures for a moment, I can better make my case. Plus, being from Sweden originally, I am not too squeamish about money...'

Sheikh Hazim threw back his head and laughed: evidently he did not see anything wrong with discussing finances in public either. When nobody seemed to object to Magnus' suggestion, the barrister ploughed on.

'My wife Juliana and I moved here ten years ago, in 1984,' he said. 'For a twenty-year lease of our flat we paid four hundred thousand pounds. Which is quite a lot, when you consider it only has three bedrooms, but at the time we felt it was worth it for the provenance and convenience of living in Westminster. Incidentally, I dread to imagine the amount we'll be asked to pay for a new lease, when this one expires in 2004 — I expect it'll be in the millions...'

And Juliana will never agree to that, Magnus thought sadly. But then he shook his head: he was becoming distracted.

'Anyway, back in 1984, although it was a fairly expensive property, it seemed like a good deal, because the maintenance charges were only fifty pounds a month. Once the lease was paid off, fifty pounds felt like negligible amount to part with twelve times a year in exchange for living in a beautiful flat in so fine an area. However, like I said, over the past decade that monthly fee has gone up and up, until now, in 1994, I'm being charged a whopping *three thousand pounds a month.*'

There was a rushing sound, as though several people had gasped in surprise. Magnus nodded grimly.

'That's sixty times what I was paying ten years ago,' he said. 'It's absurd, and I don't know how they can justify it. Obviously, there was always going to be a little inflation, but that much? In only a decade? No! I could rent another London property for that amount — several, in fact! And I dread to think what I'll be paying by the year 2004...'

He finally seemed to have inspired some outrage in his audience, for several of them began to cry out at once:

'I'm paying at least that!'

'They're just putting it up as they want, they don't even give us any warning!'

'What do they think they're playing at?'

Only two men seemed to be unmoved by the general atmosphere of indignation. One was Vasyl Kosnitschev, who seemed jittery and distracted, and the other was Hazim, who merely laughed.

'Magnus, Magnus!' the sheikh boomed, over the noise of the crowd. 'What does it matter? Westminster Square is the best place to live in the whole world — you said so yourself!'

'Actually, I didn't say that *exactly*...' Magnus began, but Hazim waved aside his objection.

'It's not as if any of us are *poor*,' the sheikh went on. 'We all have money, that's why we live here. We are the princes of London! So what does it matter if we pay fifty pounds or three thousand? Can we not afford it?'

'Well, of course we can, but that's not the point,' spluttered Magnus. 'Sheikh Hazim, it's the principle of the thing!'

'*Principle?*' cried Hazim, as though he had never heard the word before. 'Puh, who cares about principles? I want an easy life, Magnus, not a cheap one.'

He clasped his hands over his fat belly with an air of great satisfaction, as though he thought he had put forward an excellent argument. Magnus resisted the urge to say something he would regret, and instead turned to Vasyl.

'You don't look convinced either,' he said.

The Ukrainian oligarch frowned. 'It is not that I disagree with you, Magnus. In fact, I can see exactly where you are coming from. But to be perfectly honest, regarding Central Square Properties, I currently have more pressing issues than these maintenance charges.'

'Oh?' said Magnus, feigning innocence, although he had heard on the grapevine that Vasyl Kosnitschev was having all sorts of trouble obtaining planning permission to renovate his large house.

'Yes, this CSP will not let me do a single thing with my house — the house that I have paid a lot of money for. I cannot knock down this wall,

I cannot move this fireplace, I cannot even put up a painting in a certain place! It is madness!'

'As Magnus said, if you live here, you have to respect the fact that these are historic buildings,' said Lord Ellington pompously.

'I am aware of this,' snapped Vasyl. 'But I do not have time to worry about these maintenance charges when there is so much on my mind. I need to work out how to move my house around without getting on the wrong side of these CSP people before my next party. And of course it does not help that my chief events girl has just been found *dead*.'

He glowered darkly, and Magnus had the impression he was more annoyed by the inconvenience of the situation than anything else. However, he appeared to be the only one put out by the recent tragedy; at his words, excitement seemed to spark around the room, and everybody leaned forward in their seats so as to get a better look at the oligarch.

'Oh ho!' cried Hazim, rubbing his fat hands together. 'I forgot she worked for you, Vasyl. What was her name again?'

'Anne-Laure Chevalier,' said the Ukrainian, neither his voice nor his face betraying any emotion.

'And she turned up dead at the Royal West!' continued the sheikh with relish. 'What a scandal!'

'There is nothing scandalous about it,' Vasyl told him coldly. 'Have you not read the papers? She died of natural causes.'

'That is what they *say*,' Hazim shrugged. 'Seems a bit fishy to me. Wasn't she quite young?'

'Do not pretend ignorance; you have clearly read up all about it,' said Vasyl, 'and about *her*. After all, you can never resist a pretty girl, can you, Hazim?'

'No, I cannot,' said the sheikh, without a trace of shame. 'But I am afraid I did not know about this one. If I had done, well... It is a waste, that is all I will say.'

'Anne-Laure wouldn't have touched you with a barge pole!' cried Lord Ellington, suddenly launching himself into the discussion.

Hazim, along with the rest of the room, looked at the Labour Lord with interest.

'So you knew her as well, did you, Ellington?'

'No I didn't!' cried the aristocrat, suddenly looking panicked. 'I mean, I did a little, yes. I'd seen her around at parties and suchlike. But I didn't *know* her.'

'Well, alas, I did not have the pleasure of being *intimately* acquainted with Anne-Laure Chevalier, as much as I now regret this fact,' said Hazim. 'And I do not expect you did either, did you Ellington, seeing as she is not exactly your type?'

'I beg your pardon?'

'Well, she was a little — how should I put this? — *feminine* for your tastes, was she not?'

'How dare you!' cried Ellington, leaping from his chair in what was perhaps an attempt at intimidation, although it failed completely, given he was in his ridiculous riding outfit. 'Sir, what are you implying?'

'He's not implying anything, Bevis,' said Magnus, even though this was patently untrue. 'He's just winding you up, that's all. Come on, sit down, and let's all stop talking about this poor girl like a bunch of old gossips. We're none of us Hilda Underpin, are we?'

This elicited a great deal of laughter from around the backroom of the Cosmopolitan Club; evidently, he was not the only resident of Westminster Square who'd had frequent run-ins with the old lady. Then Magnus looked down at his notes, trying to remember how many of his points he had covered, before they had become distracted by the topic of Anne-Laure Chevalier's death.

If he was being truly honest with himself, he had deliberately allowed Vasyl, Hazim and Ellington free reign to talk about Anne-Laure just now, because following his discussion with the young police constable on Sunday morning, Magnus was still curious about the strange circumstances surrounding her death. However, it did not seem as though any of the men would be able to shine much light on whether Anne-Laure had died of natural causes, or even whether her death had been an accidental one. For Vasyl, it seemed she had only existed in a work context; Ellington had probably had as much contact with her as Magnus himself — in other words, he might have bumped into her once or twice at parties; and apparently Hazim, to his obvious regret, hadn't encountered her at all.

'Right, well, let's get back to business, shall we?' suggested Magnus.

As he said this, he could feel the disappointment of every person in the room, and he knew they would all much prefer to continue discussing Anne-Laure; after all, the body of a young and beautiful woman being discovered in the Royal West Hotel was by far the most exciting thing that had happened in the area for as long as Magnus could remember. Yet given that everybody was far too polite and refined to admit to this, Magnus was able to continue without complaint.

'As I've explained, I think the way the maintenance charges keep increasing is unacceptable, and I would like to know why this is happening. Is it because, up until recently, CSP have had some fuddy-duddy old accountant in the office, and he's now been replaced by someone more modern and money-grabbing? And if we do find out the cause, what are we — as clients — going to do about it? As a lawyer, it is my professional opinion that we have a good case against Central Square Properties here and…'

He trailed off as Lord Ellington gave a loud gasp. 'A *case*?' he cried. 'You mean — you want to *sue* them?'

'Let's not get ahead of ourselves,' said Magnus, trying to sound reassuring. 'All I'm saying is, I think CSP are guilty of a breach of contract here, and I for one would like to hold them accountable for it. However, legal action should always be a last resort. What I suggest we try first is banding together and signing this.'

He held up a piece of paper that had been typed up by his solicitor. Everyone in the room looked at with curiosity, apart from Ellington, who was staring at it with undisguised fear, as though it were a bomb likely to explode at any moment.

'But — but what is it?' he stammered.

'It's a petition requesting an audit of CSP,' explained Magnus. 'It's not legally binding, but I'm hoping that if it bears all of our signatures, they will agree to give us a thorough breakdown of these so-called maintenance charges and then, if they are unreasonable — which I'm sure they will be — we can enter into negotiations.'

'And if they do not agree?' challenged Hazim. 'What are you going to do then, Magnus?'

'I'm not sure,' admitted the barrister. 'But I'm fairly certain it will at least have some effect. For one thing, this document will alert CSP to the fact that we are unhappy and united against them, which I imagine will scare them a little, and stop them fiddling about with these costs. Who knows, maybe they'll even lower them?' He gave the paper in his hand a little shake. 'So who's with me? Who's going to put their name to this? Don't forget I'm a barrister, and I charge a ridiculous amount for my time. If I were you, I'd be jumping at the chance to take advantage of this free legal advice and aid.'

More laughter followed this pronouncement, and Magnus was confident he had won them all at last. Sure enough, Vasyl Kosnitschev then stretched out a hand towards the petition.

'Give it to me,' he instructed. 'I do not think it is a secret that there is no love lost between myself and CSP. So I will sign your document, Magnus, and I will wish you luck with this. But then I must leave, for I have much to organise and, as I said, I am one party-planner down.'

True to his word, the oligarch scrawled his name at the bottom of the document and then, without another word, stood up and left the room. Hazim waggled his fingers at the closing door.

'Bye, then!' he called, with a chuckle. Then, turning back to the table, he announced, 'I will sign it next, Magnus. I do not really care about these maintenance costs — they do not seem too high to me — but it is the neighbourly thing to do, isn't it? Plus this seat is very uncomfortable — I need to get back to my *majlis*.'

Magnus watched the sheikh print his name, both in English and in Arabic. Then, like Vasyl before him, Hazim heaved himself to his feet and waddled from the room, pausing only at the threshold to figure out how best to fit his vast bulk through the doorframe.

The rest of the room seemed to be encouraged by the example set by these two foreigners — or perhaps they, like Vasyl and Hazim, had simply had enough of the meeting, wanted to leave, and this seemed the quickest way. Whatever the reason, following the sheikh's exit, Magnus' document was passed around the table and every single person signed their name to it, before making their excuses and departing the backroom of the Cosmopolitan Club.

Everyone, that was, apart from Lord Bevis Ellington.

'I'm just not sure, Magnus,' he said, when only he and the barrister remained, and he had read the entire petition through three times.

'Speaking as a lawyer, if you're not sure about something, it's probably best not to sign it,' advised Magnus. 'You're under no obligation to do anything here, Bevis.'

As much as he wanted the aristocrat's support, he wasn't going to beg for it. Plus, he wasn't particularly keen on the idea of standing here all night while Ellington ummed and ahhed; after all, Juliana would be expecting him back soon.

'I *want* to sign it,' the Labour Lord continued. 'But I don't want to — Well, I don't think... As a politician, I would hate to take sides...'

Isn't that the point of a politician, Magnus thought, but managed to bite his tongue. Instead, he said, 'Look, Bevis, if you're worried about incurring the wrath of CSP, I don't think you need to. They can't exactly kick you out over a letter.'

Ellington looked up at him fearfully. 'Couldn't they? I can't lose my home, Magnus!'

'No, they couldn't,' said Magnus firmly. 'And even if they could, this petition gives us safety in numbers — they can't kick us all out. Besides, if they're going to come after anybody, they'll come after me. I'm the ringleader, aren't I?'

Ellington nodded vaguely, although it was clear he was hardly listening to what Magnus was saying. Instead, there seemed to be an internal battle going on inside him, almost as though the old Bevis Ellington, who had fought for his principles, was trying to win over the new Bevis Ellington, who was scared of losing an intrinsic part of his luxurious lifestyle.

Magnus stifled a yawn. 'As I said, you're under no obligation…'

But at that moment, Ellington snatched up the petition, grabbed a pen, and wrote his name so fiercely Magnus was afraid he would rip a hole in the paper.

'There!' said Ellington, in the manner of a child who wanted praise from a parent. 'There, I did it.'

'Well done,' said Magnus, resisting the urge to pat the ridiculous man on the white-blond head. 'Now, if you'll excuse me, Bevis, I'll tidy up here…'

'Oh yes, and I must go riding,' said Ellington, scrambling to his feet and straightening up, so as to better show off his absurd outfit.

'Have fun,' said Magnus, trying not to laugh; he was convinced the only activity Ellington would be doing that evening would be moving his arms to refill his pipe and pour himself glasses of whiskey.

What a lot of eccentric neighbours I have, Magnus reflected, as he tucked chairs neatly under the big wooden table and collected the used glasses onto a tray for one of the bar staff, keen to remain in the good books of the Cosmopolitan Club. Still, as he turned out the lights and picked up his petition, which now featured over thirty signatures — far more than he could have hoped for — Magnus smiled. The other residents of Westminster Square might have been a little peculiar at times, but what did that matter, when they were allying with him against Central Square Properties?

CHAPTER SIX

Police Constable Bryn Summers was having a miserable week. For five whole days now, he had been cooped up in the Victoria Police Station doing the most mundane administrative tasks imaginable: alphabetising paperwork, filing paperwork, shredding paperwork... In fact, Bryn was so bored that the high point of the last few days for him had been a lengthy phone conversation with an old lady who had lost her cat.

It was difficult to believe that, just under a week ago, he had been one of the first officers on the scene after the discovery of Anne-Laure Chevalier's body. That dramatic start to Sunday morning had been one of the most exciting events of his time as a policeman, and certainly of his time as a policeman in Westminster. Bryn had even hoped it would herald the start of a new, more interesting phase of his career. After all, if he was able to gain more experience like that, and if he was given a little more responsibility by his superiors, in a year or so his application to detective training might be more successful...

Unfortunately, when he had taken a look at the rota on Monday morning, Bryn had quickly realised how wrong he had been to anticipate these improvements in his working life. He had been assigned to office duties all week, and was not even scheduled to do any patrolling to break up the time, which was especially galling in this sunny June weather. Bryn wasn't even sure it was following the rules, confining him to so many hours in the office, but he didn't dare complain, because he was fairly certain he knew who had drawn up the rota: Police Chief Superintendent Barry Boyle.

Bryn paused in the act of sticking stamps onto envelopes to scowl at the thought of his boss. He was certain that Boyle had deliberately given him the worst duties in order to punish him for challenging his authority at the Royal West on Sunday. Bryn knew he had made mistakes: he shouldn't have accidentally revealed the body's gender to that journalist, he shouldn't have disagreed with Boyle so publicly, and he certainly shouldn't have accused Boyle of extortion. Bryn had disapproved of the Police Chief Superintendent's handling of the case — and he still did.

This was the problem with putting him on paperwork, Bryn reflected. Boyle had probably expected him to go half-mad from boredom and forget about Anne-Laure Chevalier altogether, but in fact it had given the young police constable ample opportunity to go over the details of the case in his head. He repeated them now, like a puzzle he was trying to solve: a conference room in the early hours of the morning; a dead woman on the sofa, initially appearing to be peacefully asleep; no sign of fatal injury, but bruising to her wrists and neck; the damage to her nose and the cocaine in her handbag implying a drug-related death, and yet... At this point, Bryn always sighed, frustrated. What would have been discovered, if that cleaner hadn't tidied up around the body? What would have come to light if Boyle had allowed the CID in to have a look around?

As he threw another stamped envelope onto the pile, Bryn wondered whether he was looking for a mystery where there was none. But even so, he didn't like the fact that there were so many questions surrounding the death of Anne-Laure Chevalier: who had given her those bruises? Was cocaine the real cause of her death? And if so, was it an accidental overdose, was it suicide, or was it something even more sinister?

After he had pondered these points for the hundredth time, Bryn's thoughts turned to his conversation with the barrister he had met outside the Royal West, Magnus Walterson. Magnus had urged Bryn to try talking to Boyle once more about the Anne-Laure Chevalier business, because it was his duty as a police officer to flag up any concerns he had about the case. And despite the fact that Magnus couldn't know what an awful person Boyle was, Bryn thought the barrister, who had seemed fair and thoughtful, was probably right.

He glanced up at the clock: it was half past one, and Barry Boyle would be finishing his lunch. Given his boss was marginally less vile after eating, if Bryn wanted to talk to him today, now was his opportunity.

With slightly shaking legs, the young Police Constable stood up, crossed to the corner of the main office, and knocked on the door of the Chief Superintendent's lair.

'Excuse me, sir,' he said, teetering on the threshold, 'could I have a word?'

'No, I'm busy.'

This was very obviously untrue: Barry Boyle was leaning back in his chair, his clumpy boots resting on the surface of his desk, completely ensconced in the latest edition of *The Dawn Reporter*. Bryn, who was almost certain Boyle was leering at the scantily-clad girls on the first few pages of the so-called paper, told himself firmly to stand his ground.

'Sir, it'll only be a few minutes, and it's quite important.'

Boyle lowered the paper, his red, angry face rising into view over the top of the pages like some terrible sea monster emerging from the water.

'*Summers...*' he growled.

'I'll only be a few minutes,' Bryn said again.

He could practically see the cogs whirring in Boyle's mind. If the Police Chief Superintendent made him go away, Boyle could get back to enjoying his newspaper in peace. But if Boyle listened to what Bryn had to say, he would undoubtedly have the opportunity to be rude and mean, which would probably prove more enjoyable.

'*One* minute,' barked Boyle, throwing down his paper and, in doing so, revealing that he had, in fact, been more preoccupied by women than news.

Bryn edged into the office, trying not to look timid, but feeling a little like a mouse creeping into the den of a lion. Then, as he crossed the threshold, he was hit by a stench so overpowering he nearly retched: the office absolutely reeked. The stink of Boyle himself was present, of course; a mixture of unpleasant smells that usually included cigarettes, body odour and whatever he had had for breakfast. But the air was also heavy with the pong of old and possibly rotten food, presumably because there were so many half-empty boxes of takeaway lying around the room. In fact, if he closed his eyes, Bryn had the impression that Barry Boyle worked in a bin.

'Don't sit down,' Boyle snapped, just as Bryn was about to lower himself into the chair in front of the Chief Superintendent's desk. 'You're only staying for a minute. You can stand for that long, can't you?'

'Um, yes,' said Bryn, privately thinking that he doubted Barry Boyle could do the same, given his immense weight.

'Well, then,' said Boyle.

He picked up a document from his desk, apparently at random, and began to read it — or at least, pretended to read it. Bryn sighed quietly. This was one of Boyle's many intimidation techniques: telling colleagues who wanted to speak to him he only had limited time, and then using up said time by doing something he deemed more important than talking to them. It was a challenge, really, to see how his inferiors would respond, and Bryn knew better than to say a word.

While he waited, the young police constable took in the sight of Barry Boyle's office. The walls behind the Chief Superintendent were plastered with newspaper cuttings of old crimes Boyle had helped to solve, while a vast corkboard was covered with various photographs, documents and post-it notes concerning more current cases and people the police were keeping an eye on. Much of this newer paraphernalia seemed to be related to the IRA, with which Boyle was known to be particularly obsessed. In fact, it was thought that the only reason he hadn't applied for early retirement was because he was determined to bring down at least a few members of the Irish movement before he hung up his hat and truncheon for good.

The desk, above which Bryn continued to hover while Boyle ignored him, was cluttered with paperwork, empty crisp packets, and dominated by a state-of-the art computer, which Bryn longed to try out, as it was so much larger than the one he shared with his colleagues, and even had a CD-ROM drive. Also rising from the mess was a framed photograph of a much younger Boyle receiving an award for bravery. Bryn was somewhat fascinated by this picture, as the Boyle it featured was not only half the size of the man he knew, but also milder and happier-looking. What on earth had happened since to make the Chief Superintendent so unpleasant? And, if it was just the drudgery of the job, would Bryn become equally as nasty in time?

'Are you still here?'

Bryn gave a little jump. Boyle was staring at him over the top of his document.

'Um, yes,' said the young police constable. 'I haven't told you what I came to talk to you about...'

Boyle frowned, his bushy eyebrows almost obscuring his little dark eyes. Then he rooted around under the paperwork on his desk and withdrew a plate of cold sausages and pickles.

'What is it?' he demanded, stuffing a whole sausage into his mouth.

Bryn took a deep breath, reminding himself of Magnus' encouragement. 'Sir, I was wondering what was happening with the Anne-Laure Chevalier case,' he said quickly, his words coming out a little garbled.

'The *what?*'

'I was wondering whether there was any news on Anne-Laure Chevalier?'

He spoke more slowly this time, although Boyle still looked completely baffled.

'*Who?* What the hell are you talking about, Summers?' he roared, spitting bits of half-chewed sausage over the desk.

'Sir, the dead woman we found at the Royal West Hotel on Sunday morning.'

'Oh!' Boyle's eyes narrowed with dislike. '*Her.*'

'Have there been any developments?'

'Developments?'

'Has the medical examiner officially confirmed a cause of death?'

'She —' Boyle seemed to be about to answer Bryn's question, and then appeared to change his mind. 'What business is this of *yours*, Summers?' he sneered instead.

'I was one of the first officers on the scene,' said Bryn. 'I saw the body. And, as I told you at the time, I thought the bruising on her —'

But at the word 'bruising', Boyle had let out a growl.

'Shut that door!' he hissed.

Very reluctantly — for he did not want to be trapped inside this smelly room without any ventilation — Bryn closed the door to the Police Chief Superintendent's office behind him.

'Don't you dare start shouting on about "bruising" where anybody can overhear you!' roared Boyle.

Bryn refrained from pointing out that it was Boyle who was now shouting about bruising, and he himself had mentioned the matter at a perfectly reasonable volume.

'If I find out you've mentioned those bruises to *anyone...*'

'I haven't,' said Bryn quickly, hoping his trust in Magnus Walterson had not been misplaced.

Boyle picked up a cold sausage, holding it between his stubby fingers like a fat cigar. 'I can see you've become obsessed with this, Summers,' he said. 'Obviously you still need to accept you're not going to become a detective — not now, not ever.'

Bryn knew Boyle was trying to goad him into becoming angry or upset, but he refused to let the older man get to him.

'I'm simply wondering, as one of the first officers on the scene, whether the medical examiner came to any conclusions about the death.'

Boyle, looking disappointed Bryn had not risen to his bait, muttered, 'Yes, she did, as it happens.'

'And?' asked Bryn keenly.

'And what?'

'And what did she find out?'

Boyle leaned back in his chair, the material of his shirt straining against belly. 'Why should I tell *you* that, Summers?'

'Well,' Bryn said, thinking fast, 'according to your statement at the Royal West — and according to all the news reports that followed — Anne-Laure Chevalier died of natural causes. And given that there's been absolutely no mention anywhere of the cocaine found in her handbag, I assume you've kept that information back for a good reason. Sir, I just want the full picture so I can understand how these kinds of cases work, as part of my police training.'

He blinked innocently at Boyle, who looked completely unconvinced.

'You know perfectly well why I kept that information back,' snapped Boyle. 'I did it to keep what's-his-name happy, you know, that manager of the Royal West.'

'Edwin Brackenwell?' supplied Bryn.

'Yeah, him — *Edwina*,' sneered Boyle. 'You'll never understand this, Summers, because you hail from some hovel in Wales, but in England — in *London* — we have to protect the reputation of historic areas like Westminster, of illustrious establishments like the Royal West. That's why I was discreet.'

And because your discretion is going to be rewarded by free meals and whiskey, Bryn thought, but he didn't dare say it aloud, considering what had happened the last time he had accused Boyle of extortion.

'You know what the press are like,' Boyle continued. 'Those vultures are already speculating wildly about what happened to that girl, I can't imagine the fuss they'll make if they hear the medical examiner found cocaine in her system...'

'So she did!' Bryn cried.

'What?'

'The medical examiner confirmed Anne-Laure Chevalier died of a cocaine overdose?'

Boyle opened his mouth, and then shut it, apparently very annoyed with himself for accidentally revealing this information.

'But is she sure?' Bryn pressed excitedly. 'Could Chevalier have been forced into taking something? What about the bruises?'

He expected to be booted out of the office at any moment, but to his surprise, Boyle pulled out a phone from under the rubbish on his desk and jabbed his fat fingers against the number pad.

'You!' he barked, after someone had picked up on the other end. 'My office. *Now*.'

Slamming down the receiver, he looked back to Bryn. 'I'm only doing this because I'm sick of you asking these questions,' he said, 'and I'm doing it on the understanding that, after you leave my office this afternoon, you never bring up the matter of this wretched girl again, do you understand?'

Bryn hesitated.

'*Do you understand?*' repeated Boyle.

'Yes!' squeaked the Welshman, highly resentful that the Chief Superintendent was forcing such a promise from him.

A few moments later, Marlene Hardwitt, the little medical examiner that Bryn had met at the Royal West the previous Sunday, entered the room, her nose wrinkling as she too was hit by the smell. She looked between Bryn and Boyle, and her slightly confused expression gave way to comprehension.

'I assume this is about Anne-Laure Chevalier?' she said.

'Shut the door!' barked Boyle.

After a moment's hesitation, Marlene pushed the door away from her, but left it hanging slightly ajar, which allowed a merciful draught of non-toxic air to continue into the room.

'Tell Summers what you found in the girl's blood,' Boyle demanded, without preamble.

'Cocaine,' said Marlene simply.

'*And?*' prompted Boyle.

'And the blood sample we took contained a high concentration of the drug, suggesting very recent ingestion. Most likely by inhalation, going by the state of her nose.'

'There you go!' said Boyle, triumphantly.

But Bryn frowned. 'Yes, but that doesn't prove, unequivocally, that the drug killed her, does it? It only proves she took it before she died.'

'Did you see a noose around her neck?' Boyle shouted. 'A dagger sticking out of her chest? Of course it proves that's how she died — there's no other explanation!'

Marlene stepped forward. 'Sir, if you would allow me to do a thorough examination of the body — a proper autopsy — I could prove beyond reasonable doubt that her body reacted against the drug and she did die of either a heart attack or some kind of stroke. But as it stands, Mr Summers is correct: all we can say for sure is that she took the drug, not that she died from it.'

Boyle looked between them for a moment, his expression suggesting he was beginning to regret inviting Marlene to participate in this conversation.

'No,' he said firmly, 'no I won't allow you to do a full autopsy. For God's sake, woman! Give me one good reason we should waste any more police time, money or effort on this?'

'The bruises,' said Bryn at once.

'Yes, and the fact she was found curled up like a cat by a fire,' said Marlene. 'In my experience, overdose victims tend to look far less tranquil and far more messy, unless...' She looked uncomfortable. 'Well, unless she *wanted* to die.'

'That's what you think, is it?' Boyle demanded of Marlene. 'You think that a pretty, wealthy girl like that killed herself deliberately?'

'Pretty, wealthy girls have problems too,' said Marlene, 'and we already know someone was knocking her about, so she obviously wasn't having the best time of it...'

'Even if you're right, she's still dead, isn't she?' said Boyle. 'It doesn't make any difference if it's a suicide.'

'Of course it does!' said Marlene, flaring up. 'It makes a great deal of difference! What are you going to tell her family?'

'So far, none of them have bothered to show up. In fact, we're struggling to even find a next of kin... I thought we'd be crawling with weeping friends and relatives as soon as the papers got hold of her picture, but no.'

Bryn frowned: this did seem very odd. From what he had read, Anne-Laure Chevalier had been a sociable woman. He supposed, going by her name, her family could be in France, and therefore hadn't heard, but was it really possible she hadn't had any friends, even though she went to all those parties? Or was it more likely her friends were staying away from the police on purpose?

Then, following a train of thought from earlier, he said, 'What if the person responsible for her bruises was also responsible for her death?'

'You mean, they *made* her take the cocaine?' Marlene asked, looking sceptical.

'Yes... Or, I don't know, maybe the cocaine is a distraction.'

'What are you talking about, Summers?' cried Boyle.

'I mean, what if we're meant to *think* it's an overdose, but actually it's something else?'

'Like what?' asked Marlene.

'I don't know. I suppose that's why we should do a full autopsy.'

'We're not doing a full autopsy!' blustered Boyle. 'This is ridiculous! Summers, I won't sit here and listen to any more of these conspiracy theories. Why would someone kill the girl and leave her lying about in a hotel?'

'So we mistook it for a drug-related death, and they didn't need to bother with disposing the body?'

'*I said I won't listen to any more of these conspiracy theories!*' shouted Boyle, ignoring the fact that Bryn had simply answered his question. 'Summers, you've clearly been watching too many police shows on TV, you need to stop talking such rubbish and get back to working in the real world. And *you*,' he added to Marlene, whose name he didn't seem to know, 'have you issued the certificate approving the release of the body?'

'Not yet,' she said.

'Did I not tell you to do so two days ago?'

'You did, but —'

'So why haven't you done it?'

Marlene drew herself up to her full height, which was not particularly tall, although Bryn had to admire her spirit.

'If, as you say, no next of kin has yet come forward, there's no rush, is there? Why don't we take advantage of this extra time, do a proper autopsy and —'

'No!' Boyle shouted, heaving himself to his feet, his face purple with rage and the exertion of standing up. 'No! No! *No!* I've already said, multiple times, I don't want to do a full autopsy! Am I not the Chief Superintendent of this police station? Am I not in charge here? Am I not making myself clear? Or are you two even stupider than you look, and can't follow a simple instruction?'

Bryn and Marlene looked at one another, and the young police constable could see defeat in the medical examiner's eyes.

'You!' Boyle continued to Marlene. 'Issue that certificate and get rid of the body. Find a relative. Find a friend. Hell, Santa Claus can take her for all I care, just as long as he buries her and I never have to hear about her again. I'm sick to death of this idiotic druggie and her idiotic death. Am I making myself clear now?'

'Crystal,' said Marlene, her lips tight with disapproval.

'And as for *you*,' Boyle continued, glaring down at Bryn, 'as I said before, this is the last time you and I have a conversation about this girl. I don't care what little Agatha-Christie-style fantasies you have going on in your tiny Welsh brain, I'm not interested. You need to stop dreaming about a career you'll never have, and remember your place in this police station — which is right at the bottom. Do you hear that? You're the lowest of the low here, Summers, and if I ever hear you questioning my authority again — in fact, if you so much as utter that girl's name in my presence — it will be only too easy to boot you out of the door. In fact, I'll do it myself, and gladly.'

Bryn swallowed, hardly daring to breathe in case Boyle used it as an excuse to make good on his promise right here, right now.

'Now get out of my sight, the pair of you,' Boyle snapped, sinking back into his chair, which creaked loudly under his bulk, and helping himself to another cold sausage. 'I need to get back to my lunch...'

Bryn and Marlene did not need telling twice. They both hurried out of the Chief Superintendent's room as quickly as possible, inhaling great lungfuls of the relatively fresh air in the shared office beyond.

'He's a dreadful man,' Marlene said, when they were out of earshot of Barry Boyle. 'Not even a man, really — he's a dreadful *pig*.'

Bryn nodded, even though she seemed to be speaking more to herself than to him. Wordlessly, the medical examiner then headed through the office and out of the front door of the Victoria Police Station and Bryn, who was due a lunch break, followed. Marlene paused on the steps of the entranceway and produced a packet of cigarettes and a lighter from her bag. She did not seem to be surprised or annoyed to find Bryn standing next to her. On the contrary, after lighting one for herself, she offered him a cigarette.

'No thank you,' said Bryn, who was a little shocked she smoked. As a medical examiner, surely she knew the adverse effects tobacco and nicotine had on the human body?

Marlene shrugged and continued to take great gasps of her cigarette. In fairness, Bryn thought, it had to be more preferable to whatever they had been inhaling in Boyle's office. And perhaps, given the nature of her job, smoking was how she coped. For a few moments they stood there in the sunshine, each silently contemplating the way they had been vanquished and then humiliated by Boyle.

'I'm sorry I dragged you into all of that,' Bryn said eventually, more out of politeness than anything else, as his conscience prevented him from regretting bringing up the matter with Boyle.

Marlene blew out a long strand of smoke.

'That's all right,' she said. 'I happen to agree with you. Perhaps not on all of it,' she added hastily, as Bryn looked excited, 'but on the fact there's something fishy about this whole business.'

'Do you really think she died of an accidental overdose?' Bryn asked, careful not to say the woman's name, in case Boyle overheard and went ballistic again.

'Honestly? I don't think it was entirely accidental. I mean, she might not have consciously decided to die, but there was something so peaceful in her position on that sofa, and if she was looking to escape from this abusive relationship or whatever trouble she was in…' Marlene shook her head. 'It's just conjecture, but that's what I believe, given Boyle's not given me an opportunity to prove otherwise.'

'But you do think it was an overdose?' said Bryn, disappointed.

'Yes.'

The young police constable said nothing. He knew, if he continued to theorise about the death of Anne-Laure Chevalier, the conversation would just go round and round, just as it was going round and round in his head.

'Boyle is just so frustrating!' Bryn burst out. 'He can't be completely blind to the idea that this doesn't add up, but he's too interested in skipping the Happy Hour queue at the Royal West to bother getting any real answers, let alone justice, for Anne — I mean, for the woman.'

Marlene dropped the butt of her cigarette to the ground and crushed it underfoot. Then she gave Bryn an oddly pitying look.

'You're not going to let this go easily, are you?' she said.

'I — no, I don't think I am,' said Bryn, only at that moment realising this was true.

'Well might I suggest, if you do continue to ask questions about this death, you do so quietly, so Boyle doesn't hear about it?'

'Oh yes, I think that's the only way,' Bryn agreed.

'I'd also rather you didn't involve me,' Marlene continued. 'After all, given Boyle won't let me do a proper autopsy, there's nothing more I can tell you. And I'd rather not get on the wrong side of him any more than I have to.'

'Of course,' said Bryn, 'I understand. It's just... Well, it would set my mind at rest to know what happened to her, and I can't deny I'm quite keen to do a little digging. But I'm afraid I don't really know how to start...'

He trailed off, frowning. He was not really expecting Marlene to respond, let alone offer him any advice, and was therefore very surprised when she said, 'If I were you, I'd start with the doormen.'

'Excuse me?'

'The doormen of the buildings around here. They always know what's going on: *he's doing business with him*, they'll tell you, *she hates her, he's sleeping with that man's wife*... Trust me, my father was a doorman — not around here — but he ended up knowing everybody's business, whether he wanted to or not.'

'Really?' Bryn was very interested to hear this.

'It probably doesn't occur to all the snobs living around here that their doormen are real people, with real eyes and ears and brains, who will have *really* taken note of what's going on in Westminster. But that's the truth. And if *I* were investigating that young woman's death, I'd ask the doormen what they know about her, and whether they noticed anything suspicious on Saturday night.'

'That's — that's really good advice, thank you,' said Bryn, before adding, 'Maybe *you* should be a detective…'

Marlene allowed him a small smile. 'Oh no, I'm too fond of dead bodies,' she said. Then, as he laughed, she continued, 'I'm serious — I like peace and quiet.'

And with that, she gave him a curt nod and headed back into the police station.

CHAPTER SEVEN

Following the medical examiner's advice, Bryn spent the next few days questioning the doormen of Westminster Square and the surrounding streets. As he was still consigned to the police station during working hours, he went out every lunchtime to conduct these interviews, always looking over his shoulder as he did so, for the police constable had no doubt Barry Boyle would not hesitate to follow up on his threat to dismiss him. Bryn did not even dare to tell his colleagues what he was up to, even the ones he trusted or those who hated Boyle as much as he did, for fear his plans would somehow get back to the Chief Superintendent. No, this was an assignment he was undertaking both in secret and alone.

For want of any better plan, Bryn started on the northern side of the square, slowly making his way around the beautiful old Georgian properties one by one. He was usually able to talk to three or four doormen each lunch hour, and after a few days of this, Bryn was able to make several observations about the gatekeepers of Westminster Square's fine buildings.

Firstly, all the doormen, who he had learned were employed by Central Square Properties, wore identical uniforms; smart grey outfits with shiny buttons. Secondly, they all seemed to be either Irish or Portuguese. Bryn could not quite understand why men of these two nationalities in particular seemed to dominate the doorways of Westminster Square, but that was the way it was, almost without exception.

Thirdly, after the wariness of finding him on their doorstep had worn off, most of the doormen he met were exceptionally chatty (Bryn had discovered long ago that nobody was ever initially pleased to see a uniformed policeman at their door). Bryn supposed it was a rather dull job, milling around in the hallways of these grand old buildings, only being able to snatch snippets of conversations here and there, as the residents rushed by. It was probably even more boring than his own job had become in the last week, although he doubted these Irish and Portuguese men had to bother with as much paperwork as he currently did. Yet despite their willingness to alleviate their boredom in conversation with him, unfortunately none of the doormen he had spoken to so far seemed to have a clue about what had happened to Anne-Laure Chevalier.

They all knew her name, of course; Bryn doubted anybody in the area was unaware of her existence, given how much news coverage she had received since her death. Indeed, many of the doormen were keen to talk about the dead woman, hoping that Bryn could give them some insider information about the circumstances of her death. Bryn, of course, said nothing about the cocaine or the bruises — he knew he would be out of Victoria Police Station quicker than he could say 'Aberystwyth' if those particular details became public knowledge. But that did not stop the various doormen speculating about what had happened to Anne-Laure Chevalier. Somehow, perhaps because of her youth, people seemed to have picked up on the fact that her death was unusual, even suspicious. As he made his rounds, therefore, Bryn was subjected to countless theories about what had happened to her, some of which were dull, like that she had fallen and bumped her head; some of which skirted close to real life, like that she had drunk herself to death; and some of which were downright insane, like that she had been a London gangster's moll, and had known too much sordid information to be allowed to live.

However, nobody seemed to have any useful information about Anne-Laure Chevalier. A few of the doormen claimed to have known her by sight (although Bryn suspected at least two of these men were indulging in wishful thinking), but none of them had spoken to her, and she didn't seem to have come into any of their buildings. This reminded Bryn that none of Anne-Laure's friends or family had come forward to claim her body. He was starting to wonder whether this woman, despite her relatively high profile on the city's party circuit, had made a lasting impression or impact on anyone at all. He was beginning to picture her drifting through Westminster like a ghost, wispy and untouchable.

Furthermore, none of the doormen were able to report that they had seen or heard anything unusual on the Saturday night that Anne-Laure Chevalier had died. In fact, most of the men Bryn talked to took pains to tell him that Westminster Square had been very quiet that evening, due to almost everybody being over at Dame Winifred Rye's party at the Royal West Hotel. By all accounts, very few people had been coming into or going out of the various properties, and after the guests of the tennis tournament had vacated the court for the hotel, the square had been virtually empty for the rest of the night.

All in all, the doormen were so useless that Bryn was beginning to lose hope. Perhaps Boyle had a point, and boredom was leading him to imagine a mystery or conspiracy where there was none. Maybe this was all just a waste of time — and it did take up a lot of time, for all the doormen wanted to talk to him once it was clear he hadn't come to arrest them or tell them anybody had died, especially when he mentioned the magic words, *Anne-Laure Chevalier*. But was it really likely he was going to find out anything worthwhile? And even if he did, was any of this worth risking his job at the Victoria Police Station?

I'll carry on today, and that's it, thought Bryn, looking at his watch and discovering he still had half an hour of his lunch break left. Then, on a whim, he decided to abandon the northern side of the quadrant, and instead crossed the road and picked out a building entirely at random halfway down the southern side of Westminster Square.

The doorman who let him into the elegant, airy hallway looked to be another Portuguese man. He was a grizzled individual with a hangdog expression, and his smart grey uniform was not wholly successful in distracting from his untidy dark hair and general aura of scruffiness.

'My name is Police Constable Bryn Summers,' said Bryn, trying to sound cheerful, for this doorman was looking at him with undisguised fear.

'Inacio,' was all the man grunted in return.

'Good afternoon, Inacio,' continued Bryn brightly. 'I was wondering whether I could ask you a few questions?'

The other man frowned. 'About what?'

'About the events of last Saturday evening.'

Usually, this introduction to the subject of discussion calmed the doormen, who could presumably remember what they had been doing the previous week, and could reassure themselves it was all perfectly innocent. Yet, if anything, Inacio now looked more worried, which struck Bryn as a little odd.

'What about Saturday evening?' he asked slowly, his heavily-accented voice hoarse.

'As you may know from the news, a woman died in the Royal West Hotel that night...'

He trailed off, watching Inacio's eyes, which would not quite meet his own.

'I thought she died of — how you say? — *natural causes*?' asked the doorman after a pause. 'That is what I heard on the news.'

'Indeed,' said Bryn, not wanting to dwell on this point for too long, lest the doorman grow suspicious as to why he was there. 'But I've simply been dispatched to dot the "i"s and cross the "t"s, if you know what I mean?'

Inacio plainly did not know what Bryn meant, which was unsurprising, given that the police constable was being deliberately vague. However, still not looking directly at him, Inacio said, 'I know nothing about her, this Anna Laura person.'

'Anne-Laure Chevalier,' Bryn corrected, automatically. Then, trying a different tack, he said, 'Were you working here on that Saturday evening, Mr Inacio?'

'Yes.'

'And did you notice anything unusual, either in this building or out in the square?'

'No.'

'Right,' said Bryn, disappointed. 'Well then, thank you for your time, Mr Inacio...'

As he turned to go, he saw — out of the corner of his eye — Inacio withdraw a handkerchief from his jacket pocket, which he then used to dab at his sweaty brow. Bryn frowned: the weather was hot, so it would be reasonable to assume Inacio was simply feeling overheated. However, the sweating and lack of eye contact together was somewhat suspicious, not to mention the fact that Inacio, unlike his colleagues before him, didn't seem to be at all interested in the fate of Anne-Laure Chevalier. Was this the behaviour of someone who had something to hide?

'Excuse me,' said Bryn, pausing at the threshold, and then swivelling to face Inacio once more. 'I have a hunch you're not giving me the full picture here.'

The doorman's panicked expression in response to this told Bryn all he needed to know.

'I'm going to ask you a few more questions,' continued the police constable, 'and I'd like you to answer them honestly, please. If I think you're lying, I'll have to request you attend a formal interview at the station.'

This, of course, was an empty threat, as Bryn could hardly drag this man into the station and interrogate him about Anne-Laure Chevalier without Boyle finding out about it. Yet it had the desired effect, for Inacio's gnarled hands flew to his mouth and his eyes began to shine with unshed tears.

'Please, do not take me to the station!' he cried. 'Please! I will tell you all I know of Anna Laura! But first, you must promise I will not be in trouble for my crime!'

'In trouble?' said Bryn. 'What crime? Is it something to do with her?'

'No, but — please! Promise me! Then I will tell you!'

Bryn considered this. On the one hand, if this man had done something criminal, he should not escape justice. On the other, this was the first real lead Bryn had had on this whole Anne-Laure business, and he was reluctant to let it pass him by. He supposed he could just force Inacio into telling him what he knew with more threats of being taken to the police station, but something told him the doorman was not a bad guy. And if he was, Bryn supposed he could always listen to what he had to say and then take him to the station anyway — after all, he wasn't Boyle, and he couldn't be coerced into looking the other way, promise or no promise.

'All right,' said Bryn at last, 'I promise you won't be in trouble. Now, what do you know about Anne-Laure Chevalier?'

Inacio winced. 'Not here!' he hissed. 'I will tell you in my flat.'

Bryn looked at his watch: he had just over twenty minutes of his lunch hour left. 'I'm afraid I don't have time to go very far…'

But Inacio was opening a door at the back of the hallway that led to a narrow staircase. 'It is just down here,' he explained. 'Did you not know? All the doormen of Westminster Square live in the basements.'

Bryn had not known this. As he followed Inacio down the cold stone steps (his hand on his truncheon, just in case) he was struck by how gloomy this back staircase was, especially in comparison to the bright hallway in which they had just been standing. He supposed, many years ago, this route had been exclusively used by servants, as they ran up and down between the main floors and whatever had been down here. A coal storage room, perhaps? A wine cellar?

As they continued down the steps, Bryn became aware of a powerful aroma stemming from somewhere just below his feet. Somebody was evidently cooking, so it was not an entirely unpleasant smell — not like Boyle's office — but in this unventilated little space, it was overpowering, especially as the dish being prepared seemed to involve fish.

Moments later, Inacio was letting him into his flat at the bottom of the Westminster Square building. It was a dingy, airless space, no bigger than a bedsit and, apart from the bathroom, everything seemed to be squashed into this one room: the kitchenette, a small wooden table, a tatty old sofa, even the beds, one of which looked to be more suited to a camping trip than a permanent sleeping arrangement. The walls were grubby, although attempts had been made to cover them up with crucifixes, portraits of the Virgin Mary and faded postcards of what Bryn assumed must be Portugal. Damp clothes had been hung up to dry over every available surface. Indeed, the only bright spot in the whole room was a vase on the table that contained three red roses. They were just blooming, and looked intensely fragrant, although Bryn was still overwhelmed by cooking smells, the source of which was revealed to be a great saucepan of stew, simmering away on one of the two hobs.

'My kids,' said Inacio, gesturing carelessly at two little dark-haired figures in the corner, who were staring wide-eyed at the fuzzy picture of a small black and white television that looked as though it belonged in the 1960s. 'My wife is in the bathroom, I think, washing the baby.'

Indeed, as he said this, Bryn could hear the sounds of splashing and cooing coming from behind the bathroom door, which was slightly ajar.

'Please, have a seat at the table,' continued the doorman. 'Can I make you a tea?'

'Erm...'

The truth was, five minutes ago, Bryn had wanted a cup of tea, although now he felt slightly nauseous to be sitting in this hot and stuffy little flat. He could not quite believe people lived like this, especially in Westminster Square. He felt as though he had been transported to some slum in South America; it was impossible to reconcile the idea of this shabby accommodation being part of one of the finest properties in all of London. Did the people who lived above know that their doormen dwelt in such poor conditions under their feet? Why, it was like something out of the Victorian age! How could Central Square Properties possibly justify giving these men and their families such terrible flats?

Inacio seemed to have interpreted Bryn's 'erm' as a request for tea, for he put an old-fashioned kettle on the free hob and before long it was whistling away, adding to the noise of the bubbling stew, the crackling television, and the baby, who had begun to cry next door. Bryn sat down on a wobbly chair at the table, positioning himself right in front of the red roses, which he could not smell — although, as he was prone to hayfever, this was no bad thing. Then Inacio handed him a chipped but clean cup. The police constable thanked him, took a grateful sip, and then almost spat out his mouthful over the floor, it was so sweet.

'It is not good?' asked Inacio, looking concerned as Bryn forced himself to swallow the beverage. 'You can have more sugar if you like, I only put in four spoonfuls…'

'It's fine!' Bryn croaked, shielding the mug from the Portuguese man's attempt to sweeten it any further. 'And anyway, we should get on with this. I want you to tell me what you know of Anne-Laure Chevalier…'

He lowered his voice as he spoke, casting a look at the two children in the corner of the room, but their attention was entirely fixed on the old television set. In fact, they didn't even seem to have realised that a uniformed policeman had just strolled into their home.

'All right, I will tell you,' said Inacio, adding yet more sugar to his own tea. 'But we have a deal, right? I will not be in trouble.'

'Yes, we have a deal,' said Bryn, beginning to grow impatient with this man, and his attempts to get away with whatever he had done. 'Now please, tell me what happened on Saturday night.'

'Well,' said Inacio, 'my shift was quiet that evening, very quiet, in fact, because everybody was —'

'At the party at the Royal West, I know,' said Bryn, a little wearily, because he had heard this so many times now.

'Nobody had come into the building for some time, and because it was so empty, I — I decided to sneak out into one of the gardens.'

He hung his head in shame. Bryn shifted a little in his rickety seat, suddenly uncomfortable.

'Which garden was this?'

'The one on the south side, just opposite this building.'

Bryn pulled out his notepad and scribbled this down. 'And, erm —' He looked once more towards the oblivious children. 'Erm, what were you doing out in the garden at night?' he asked, unable to stop himself from imagining something suspect, even sordid.

'I was — I was — *stealing roses!*' wailed Inacio, burying his face in his hands and beginning to sob.

Bryn stared at him, wondering whether he had heard the man correctly. 'Excuse me? You were *what*?'

'Stealing roses,' murmured Inacio through his fingers.

'Yes, that's what I thought you said.' Bryn laughed as relief began to wash over him. 'Well, that's not so bad, is it?'

'Oh, but it is!' said Inacio, looking very serious. 'It *is*! I have a key to Westminster Square Gardens, in case any of the residents lose theirs, but I am not supposed to go in there, so if they found out I was stealing the roses... Sir, you cannot tell anyone, if CSP find out about this I will lose my job!'

'Your secret's safe with me,' said Bryn, feeling that firing a man for picking a few flowers was a little strong.

'I have been so worried about it all week!' moaned Inacio. 'I was so quiet, so careful, but since then I have been sure someone saw me and would report me.'

'Who on earth would do that?' Bryn asked, perplexed.

'Oh, plenty of people around here. Especially that old lady, Hilda Underpin, a few doors down. She spies on us doormen. I have been having nightmares about her telling CSP what I did.'

For want of any other way to react to this, Bryn wrote down the name *Hilda Underpin* in his notebook. Then, pointing with his pen at the vase on the table between them, he asked, 'And are these the flowers?'

Inacio shuddered. 'Yes, and what those flowers have cost me...'

Bryn shook his head, still feeling as though he was missing something here. 'If it was such a big risk, why did you do it?'

Inacio's lip wobbled. 'Because it was the birthday of my wife last Sunday, and she admires those roses every time she passes them. I do not make very much money, and even if I did, I do not have much time off to buy her anything. So I thought, I will pick her some roses. There are so many in the gardens, no one will notice if I take a few. But I have been eaten up with guilt ever since.'

'Did she like them?' Bryn asked.

'Huh?'

'Your wife, did she like the roses?'

'She loved them!'

'Well, there you go, then,' said Bryn, still feeling that this man was rather overreacting. 'It's probably best not to dwell on it anymore, I assume you've learned your lesson?'

Inacio nodded miserably. 'So — so you will not arrest me?'

Bryn tried to imagine the extent of Barry Boyle's fury if he turned up at the police station with a Portuguese doorman whose only crime had been picking flowers.

'No, I won't,' said Bryn, trying to sound kind, even though he was tempted to laugh. 'But perhaps, in return, you could tell me what happened in that garden, as I'm assuming this all relates to Anne-Laure Chevalier?'

'Oh yes,' said Inacio, wiping his forehead with his handkerchief once again and looking a little more cheerful. 'So that night, I crept out into the garden with some kitchen scissors, hid behind one of the rose beds and began to cut. It took me a long time, because rose stems are very tough — I did not know this — but I kept at it, cutting and cutting until they came away.'

'Right,' said Bryn, his lips twitching, because the image of this surly Portuguese man squatting in a rose bush was irresistibly funny. 'And what time was this, please?'

'I am not sure exactly. It was dark, so it must have been past ten o'clock. Yes, I would say not long after ten.'

Bryn wrote this down as well, then waited for Inacio to continue.

'A few minutes after I had arrived, I realised that there were two other people in the garden, at the opposite end to where I was, and they were having some kind of argument.'

'What kind of people?'

'A man and a woman.'

'And what did they look like?' Bryn asked eagerly.

'Him, I do not know. It was too dark, he was just a shadow in the distance. But her — I saw her as she walked past me a few moments later.'

'And?'

'And I think it was her, Anna Laura. She had blonde hair, she was very beautiful... I did not know her at the time, but when I saw all of the pictures in the newspapers... Well, I am sure it was her.'

Bryn tried to curb his excitement. Inacio could have seen any fair-haired, attractive woman in those gardens. Deciding it was Anne-Laure Chevalier might just be putting two and two together and making five. Then he was struck by an idea.

'Did you see what she was wearing?' he asked.

'Black,' said Inacio at once. 'Some kind of black cocktail dress, because I remember thinking she must be cold. She was carrying a gold handbag as well.'

Bryn felt a shiver run up and down his spine. There was very little chance Inacio could have known Anne-Laure Chevalier had died in a black dress with a gold handbag near her body, because — as far as he knew — the papers had not managed to get hold of this particular detail.

'You said they were having an argument?' Bryn prompted. 'Did you hear what it was about?'

'Not really,' said Inacio. He frowned. 'From where I was, it looked as though she was trying to leave, and he was trying to make her stay.'

'Make her how?'

'Well...' Inacio looked awkward. 'He was holding onto her by her arms — grabbing her, really — and she was trying to shake him off.'

Bryn fixed Inacio with a stern expression, as he wondered why the hidden man had not intervened to stop this violence.

'What about her neck?' he asked, a little coldly.

'Sorry?'

'Did he have her by the neck?'

As Bryn mimed a throttling motion, Inacio looked alarmed.

'I do not — No, I do not think so!' he stammered. 'Of course, I would have stepped in if he had tried to — well, tried to *strangle* her. But I thought it was just a quarrel between lovers, and it would be best not to interfere.'

Best for you, thought Bryn, *best for your job.* Perhaps Inacio could tell what he was thinking, for the doorman continued, 'He did not look as though he was going to...' he trailed off, unable to finish that thought. 'He seemed desperate. She was pulling away and he was pleading with her. Perhaps they were splitting up,' he mused.

'How can you know that, if you didn't hear anything he said?' asked Bryn, for this sounded flimsy to him.

'The tone of his voice, I suppose.'

'Could you tell if he was British? Or did he have an accent?'

'I am not sure. It is difficult for me to tell, as I am Portuguese, but I think maybe... not.'

'You don't think he had an accent?'

'I do not think so.'

'And you can't tell me anything about his appearance?' Bryn continued, trying not to sound too disappointed.

Inacio shook his head. 'I saw her when she came out of the garden, as I said — she walked right past me — but he stayed in there. I think he must have sat down on a bench or something. I waited for him to come out, but he did not, so after a while, I decided to sneak out. I do not think he saw me, or if he did, he did not care.' The Portuguese man looked at his fingers, which were clasped around his mug of sugary tea. 'Perhaps I would have behaved differently, if I had known she would turn up dead at the Royal West a few hours later. But I did not know, and I am afraid I was more concerned about the roses for my wife — and about keeping my job.'

He hung his head, ashamed, and Bryn saw little point in chastising him. Instead, he stared at what he had written on his pad:

Garden on south side
(Hilda Underpin)
Couple arguing
AL Chevalier = black dress, gold handbag
Grabbing wrists, man pleading? Break-up?
Man probably British

It wasn't much to go on, but it was something, and it did at least start to explain where the bruises on her wrists had come from. If only Inacio had got a better look at this man in the shadows…

'Well, thank you for your time,' said Bryn, closing his notepad and tucking it back into his utility belt along with his pen. 'This is very useful. I'll let myself out, shall I?'

Inacio looked confused. 'But wait!' he said. 'Do you not want to hear what she said?'

Bryn paused in the act of standing up. 'I thought you didn't hear anything of the argument?'

'Not the argument, no. But on the way out of the garden, she paused in front of where I was hidden, wiped the tears from her face, and turned back in his direction. Then she screamed at him, and I heard that — I heard that very clearly.'

'And what did she say?' Bryn asked, sitting down and withdrawing his notepad once again.

Inacio looked grim. 'She said, "*Don't follow me! I'm serious, this is it, you'll never see me again! I'm going to be free of you, and free of Westminster Square!*"'

★ ★ ★ ★

On his way home from work that evening, Bryn let himself into the garden on the south side of Westminster Square. He had not had time to investigate the scene of Anne-Laure's argument with the man in the shadows during his lunch hour, as after speaking to Inacio he'd had to hurry back to the police station. But the doorman had lent him the key to the gardens, and Bryn felt that there was no time like the present to have a look around.

Perched on the outside of the gardens, above the wrought iron gates, Bryn noticed a large black sign inscribed with gold lettering:

CENTRAL SQUARE PROPERTIES.
WELCOME TO WESTMINSTER SQUARE GARDENS

Please respect the following rules —
Only registered keyholders may access the gardens.
Always close the gates.
All children under the age of 12 must be accompanied by an adult.
No balls, bicycles or noisy games.
Plants must not be touched.
All dogs must be kept on leads.

Bryn stared up at this sign for a few minutes, before deciding that Westminster Square had the strictest regulations for a garden he had ever encountered. In fact, Central Square Properties might as well have added:

No having fun.

The sign also had the effect of making Bryn feel as though he was doing something wrong, despite the fact he was merely standing there in his police uniform, so nobody was likely to argue with him. But still, this sniffy set of rules did at least explain why Inacio had got himself into such a flap over the three roses, considering he had violated rule number five. And rule number one was interesting too, for it suggested that either Anne-Laure or her mysterious companion — or perhaps both of them — were registered keyholders of the gardens, otherwise they wouldn't have been able to get in there in the first place.

The garden was a surprisingly tranquil spot, despite it being wedged between two roads, one of which roared with the noise of rush-hour traffic. Its perfectly trimmed lawn and islands of tidy flowerbeds were surrounded on every side by trees and bushes that blocked out the sight of most of the quadrant beyond, thus giving the false impression of pastoral serenity.

After making sure to close the gate behind him, Bryn edged up the path of the enclosed garden, and no sooner had he set foot amongst the flowerbeds than his eyes began to water.

'Oh no!' he said, before loudly sneezing four times in quick succession. 'Oh bother!'

As he searched fruitlessly for a tissue in his utility belt, Bryn reflected this was another reason why he had chosen police work in Cardiff and then London: the countryside gave him the most terrible hayfever.

Forced simply to sniff and wipe at his streaming eyes and nose, Bryn hurried further into the garden, keen to get this over with as soon as possible. A little way in, just where Inacio had described, was a bush with exactly the same kind of vivid red roses the doorman had had in his flat. And sure enough, as Bryn edged closer, one hand over his mouth, he saw that three stems had been hacked away. The police constable thought he could even see where Inacio had been, for the dry earth behind the bush was compressed, as though a large man had recently stood on top of it. Bryn ducked under a thorny branch and positioned himself there, crouching where the rose thief would have crouched. If he looked to his right, he could just make out the end of the garden, where this argument had apparently taken place. But it was a little way away, and that part of the lawn was shielded from the sun by tree branches, leading Bryn to understand that Inacio was telling the truth; the couple arguing in the dark must have been completely cast in shadow.

He sneezed again, prompting an elderly couple who happened to be passing to give him a reproachful glance, presumably for disturbing the peace and quiet of the garden. What a nerve, thought Bryn, scrambling out of the rose bush, and sneezing some more. To give such a dirty look to an officer of the law!

Picking rose petals and leaves from his jacket, and brushing earth from the bottom of his trousers, Bryn made his way towards the end of the garden, to the spot where a mysterious man had grabbed Anne-Laure Chevalier by the wrists on the night she had died. But of course, there was nothing there — at least, there was nothing to help him with his investigation. Bryn stood on the perfectly-cut lawn, listening to the bees humming as they moved from flower to flower, and he began to feel foolish. What had he expected to find here? Some record of who that man had been? It would have been far too convenient if he had stumbled across some identifying object, like a driver's license. Besides, that argument was over a week ago now and anything found in this garden would have been thrown in the bin, or handed in to Central Square Properties.

Even so, Bryn cast his eye around for a few seconds, just in case. But it was only as he was turning to leave that he saw something glint in the corner of his eye. He moved his head from side to side, trying to see it again, assuming it had been a bit of litter, or perhaps the wing of an insect. But no, it was something silver, and it was half-buried between the roots of a tree. Like a magpie, Bryn dived for the gleaming object, dug around with his fingers to free it from the earth, and held it up to the light of the evening sun.

It was ring. A simple, silver band — one that only could have fitted a woman's finger — had been left or dropped or badly buried in this garden. It didn't look particularly elaborate or valuable, thought Bryn, although he was as much an expert on women's jewellery as he was on women's handbags. Something told him, from what he knew of Anne-Laure Chevalier, she wouldn't have worn something as plain as this. So it probably didn't belong to her at all, Bryn thought, his heart sinking. Most likely, some other woman had dropped it, and the silver band had nothing to do with the argument that had taken place here.

He began to walk away, still holding onto it, as presumably somebody was missing a ring, and he might be able to return it to them via the police station. It was still encrusted with earth, so to distract himself from all the pollen in the air, Bryn attempted to wipe it clean as he walked. There was a particularly stubborn speck of dirt on the inside of the band, which he rubbed at for almost a minute before he realised it wasn't earth at all — it was an engraving.

Stopping in his tracks, Bryn held up the ring to the sunlight once more, and saw that it had been inscribed with just two letters: *A.C.*

CHAPTER EIGHT

It was strange to be at home in the middle of a weekday, Magnus reflected. The flat was very quiet without Juliana and, in particular, Rosanna and Lee. Indeed, without his family there, it hardly felt like a home at all.

While he waited for Bryn to arrive, Magnus was slightly unsettled, and paced through the rooms, brushing specks of dust from surfaces and adjusting paintings that were hanging slightly askew. He could not stop thinking about the huge pile of paperwork waiting for him back at the office. He was anxious to get back to it, more because he didn't want to fall behind on his work than because it was particularly interesting. And yet, because of the unexpected phone call from Police Constable Bryn Summers yesterday evening, Magnus had to wait here for the young officer to come and say... Well, whatever it was he wanted to say, Magnus wasn't exactly sure.

The barrister was no fool, though; he suspected Bryn was coming to talk to him about Anne-Laure Chevalier, given that the only conversation they had ever shared was outside the Royal West Hotel on the morning after her death. It was because of this assumption that Magnus had thought it best to schedule this meeting when Juliana was at the flower shop. Somehow he doubted she would approve of him being mixed up in anything to do with Anne-Laure's death, especially as the news of their neighbour's demise seemed to have upset her. Magnus sighed: first the meeting about Central Square Properties' maintenance costs and now this... Since when had he made a habit of hiding things from his wife?

At ten minutes past one, a little after he was scheduled to arrive, the doorbell rang and Magnus found Bryn Summers on the threshold of his flat.

'Sorry I'm a bit late,' said the policeman, after they had shaken hands. 'I got talking to your doorman downstairs — Patrick, is it?'

'That's right. He's chatty, isn't he?'

'Very. Does he, erm, live in the building?'

'I believe he has a flat in the basement, yes,' said Magnus, surprised at the question.

Bryn looked a little uncomfortable. 'Have you seen it? Is it all right?'

'I think so, yes. I've not been down there myself, but I assume it's rather nice, considering this is Westminster Square.'

'Hm,' said Bryn, his tone and expression unconvinced.

Magnus, who was a little puzzled by all of this, assumed Bryn had not come round to talk about the living arrangements of his doorman, and so said, 'Do come in, won't you? I've just put the kettle on.'

The police constable thanked him, but no sooner had he stepped over the threshold than he began to sneeze.

'Oh dear,' said Magnus, reaching for a box of tissues on the telephone table. 'You don't have hayfever, do you?'

'Rather bad hayfever, I'm afraid,' sniffled Bryn. 'But I'm usually all right indoors.'

Magnus cast his gaze around the hallway, which Juliana had adorned with at least five plants. 'Unfortunately, this place sometimes feels more like a garden than a flat,' he said. 'Come on through to the sitting room; there are only a couple of pots in there and I'll take them out.'

Bryn, who was evidently trying to hold back another sneeze, merely nodded, and obediently followed Magnus through the flat.

'Have a seat,' said the barrister, gesturing at one of the leather sofas. Then, picking up a large vase of camellias, he added, 'I'll get these out of here and then make us some tea. How do you take it?'

'With a bit of — *atishoo!* — milk, please. No — *atishoo!* — sugar.'

'Right you are,' said Magnus.

His lips twitched as he moved the flowers into the hallway. There was something rather funny about a sneezing policeman; the spluttering and sniffing undermined the uniform's air of authority.

But then, Bryn was not exactly the most domineering figure in the first place, Magnus mused; not like that dreadful boss of his. The Welsh officer looked very young, although he was probably in his late twenties, considering he was a fully-qualified policeman. But he had an open, honest face, handsome but still quite boyish, and his big blue eyes and neatly-combed russet-coloured hair did not exactly give him an edge. Magnus doubted that Police Constable Bryn Summers would have been able to intimidate a kitten, let alone a hardened criminal, but then, perhaps there was steel underneath all that Welsh small-town innocence. And if there wasn't, there certainly would be after a few years on the beat.

When Magnus returned from both moving the flowers and making the tea, Bryn had finally stopped sneezing, and was looking at his surroundings with polite interest.

'This is a lovely room,' he said.

'Thank you,' said Magnus, looking around at it too and trying to see it from Bryn's perspective.

It was a large, rectangular space, the window and balcony of which were positioned at the rear of the house, so they looked down onto the back garden rather than Westminster Square itself. The furniture was comprised of two leather sofas, a couple of armchairs and a great mahogany table whose chairs were often used when Magnus and Juliana were hosting dinners in the conjoining dining room. The living area also featured a simple marble fireplace that was curiously modern in comparison to the building, so much so that Magnus suspected the previous tenant had probably almost come to blows with Central Square Properties over it. However, he himself thought the feature very complimentary to the rest of the décor in the room, which was generally unfussy. Westminster Square, he had discovered, did not feature much gilding or carvings. In fact, the fanciest feature in the room was probably the stucco patterns on the ceiling.

Juliana had, of course, further dressed up the space with her own decorations, and not just her plants and flowers. The floor was dominated by a large, floral-patterned Savonnerie carpet, although unusually it was English in origin, for it had been made in Axminster. Then, arranged about the cream-coloured walls were various pictures, either paintings of countryside scenes or line illustrations of birds. If Magnus remembered correctly, his wife had bought most of these from local artists in Kent, especially Tinterton, and — like her obsession with bringing flora into their home — this art gave the impression they lived in a country estate, not a central London flat.

'It is a tad eccentric,' Magnus decided, pouring Bryn some tea from the pot. 'But my wife has very strong ideas about interior design. I fully expect our retirement home to be a greenhouse.'

Bryn laughed. 'It's certainly more interesting than looking at the grey walls of a police station,' he said.

'Yes, how's it all going over there?' asked Magnus, settling himself onto the opposite sofa from Bryn. 'And are there any developments on the Anne-Laure Chevalier business? I assume that's what you came to talk to me about?'

Bryn nodded, but did not offer any further information.

After a moment, Magnus asked, 'Did you manage to talk to your superior about your doubts? That big man — I've forgotten his name.'

'Chief Superintendent Barry Boyle,' said Bryn, wincing. 'I tried, but it didn't go very well. In fact, I'm forbidden from talking about it anymore. I can't even mention her name.'

'That's a bit strong, isn't it?' said Magnus.

'Boyle's got a bee in his bonnet about —' Bryn lowered his voice, '— about *Anne-Laure Chevalier*. I think he knows something's not quite right about her death, but he doesn't want the bother of having to deal with it.'

'So you do still think there are loose ends?'

'Oh yes,' said Bryn, earnestly, 'now more so than ever. That's why I'm digging around, you see, although I have to do it in my lunchbreaks so Boyle doesn't find out.'

'This is your lunchbreak?' said Magnus, momentarily distracted. 'Oh, you must have one of Juliana's flapjacks to keep you going…'

He had brought the tin through with the tea, but had forgotten to open it. As soon as he did, however, Bryn reached forward eagerly and piled a couple of the sweet and buttery oat treats onto the edge of his saucer, popping a third into his mouth.

'Thank you,' he said, through a mouthful.

Magnus, chewing thoughtfully on a flapjack of his own, reflected on what he had read of the death recently, which wasn't much; media interest in Anne-Laure Chevalier finally seemed to be waning.

'So the official line is still that she died of natural causes, is that right?'

'Yes, but that's total nonsense,' said Bryn, looking cross, which was difficult to do with a mouthful of flapjack. With some effort, he managed to swallow, and then said, 'Look, Mr Walterson —'

'Please, call me Magnus. You've seen me in my jogging clothes, Bryn, I think we can dispense with formalities.'

'Magnus, then. I really can trust you, can't I?'

The barrister looked into the young policeman's earnest face and smiled. 'Of course you can.'

'Good, because I feel as though I need to talk this over with somebody, and I can't speak to anyone at the station, in case Boyle hears about it. That's why I looked you up in the phonebook, you see, because you told me you were a barrister, and you would want to see justice done. I hope you don't mind?'

'Not at all,' said Magnus. 'In fact, I'm rather flattered you thought of me. This whole business is very intriguing.'

Bryn nodded. 'When I went to Boyle to express my doubts about Anne-Laure Chevalier dying of natural causes, as we discussed, he became so irate he called in the medical examiner. You saw her the other day, I think, taking the body away. And, well, what she had to say was very interesting…'

Magnus listened as Bryn proceeded to tell him about this meeting, in which the medical examiner confirmed that cocaine had been found in the dead woman's blood, suggesting a drug-related death, even though this couldn't be proved without a full autopsy.

'And Boyle wouldn't permit that?' said Magnus, frowning. 'That seems very lax of him, very unprofessional, not to give a proper autopsy the go-ahead.'

Bryn shrugged. 'As I said, he's lazy. And without it, we can't prove she didn't die of natural causes, however unlikely it now seems.'

Magnus took another sip of tea, thinking over everything Bryn had just told him.

'So this medical examiner thinks it was suicide, does she?' he said.

'Well, she wouldn't swear it in court, but I think that's what she's leaning towards, yes.'

'It seems hard to imagine, a girl like that wanting to kill herself,' said Magnus, picturing the radiant young woman whose image had now graced so many newspaper articles. 'But of course, we don't know what was going on her life — or in her head.'

'No,' Bryn agreed quietly, 'although I do now know a little more about her movements on the night of her death, thanks to one of Westminster Square's residents.'

'Oh?' said Magnus.

Bryn replaced his cup and saucer on the coffee table between them — although he held onto one of the flapjacks — and then related a conversation he'd had with Inacio, a Portuguese doorman who lived and worked a few doors' down. Magnus listened with rapt attention as the police constable revealed that, according to this doorman, Anne-Laure Chevalier had argued with a shadowy figure in one of Westminster Square's gardens on the night of her death.

'That's very interesting,' said Magnus, grimly. 'And it certainly explains the bruises.'

'Only the ones on her wrists,' said Bryn quickly. 'Inacio was fairly sure this man didn't have her by the neck. I also think he would have intervened if he'd seen that level of violence — Inacio, I mean. I don't think he's a bad guy, you should have seen how cut up he was about stealing a few flowers...'

'But it could have happened before he arrived,' said Magnus. 'You said they were already in the garden when he crept in.'

'Ye-es,' said Bryn slowly: apparently he hadn't thought of this. Then he shook his head. 'Anyway, does it really make a difference? This man, whoever he was, still grabbed her.'

'It *might* make a difference,' said Magnus. 'Look, I'm not being callous, or condoning violence of any kind, but seizing someone by the wrists is not quite the same as seizing them by the neck. It's the difference between trying to make someone stay, as your doorman thinks was happening in that garden, and attempting to do them serious harm. Of course, both are threatening — both are deplorable — but there *is* a difference.'

'So do you think he did try and strangle her or not?' Bryn asked, confused.

'I don't know,' admitted Magnus. 'It's all a bit odd, isn't it? It seems unlikely she would turn around and scream at someone who had just tried to throttle her — if I were her, I'd have been out of that garden as quickly as possible. Plus, that's when Inacio got a good look at her, right? And he didn't mention anything about her neck…'

'No, although I didn't really ask,' said Bryn.

'But then, is it really likely that Anne-Laure Chevalier was attacked by two different people on the night of her death? Surely she didn't have *two* enemies…'

'But then, it could have been the same person; he could have followed her,' Bryn pointed out. 'Anyway, I don't think he saw himself as her enemy — quite the opposite, in fact.'

Magnus was about to ask Bryn to explain this statement, but the policeman was reaching into his utility belt and withdrawing what looked like a clear plastic freezer bag.

'I found this yesterday evening, at the spot where Inacio said they were arguing,' the police constable said, handing the pouch across the table.

Magnus took it, and discovered a simple silver ring sitting in a corner of the plastic.

'But this could belong to any…' He trailed off as he squinted at it more closely. '*A.C.*,' he read.

'See, it was hers!' said Bryn excitedly.

'Was it? Did your doorman see her with it at any point?'

'No, but — of course it has to be hers! Those are her initials.'

Magnus frowned. 'These are *some* of her initials,' he said, still examining the ring. 'I don't know, if I'd had a piece of jewellery engraved for her, I'd have put *A.L.C.*'

'But she was right there, where I found it — Inacio saw her! And maybe she went by "Anne" rather than "Anne-Laure." We don't know, because we haven't actually spoken to anyone who knew her.'

'My wife has,' mused Magnus. Then, at Bryn's confused expression, he clarified, 'Juliana — that is, my wife — spoke to Dame Winifred Rye the day after the body was found. She's this rather eccentric aristocrat who lives around here, and all she seems to do with her time is host events for charity. In fact, she was responsible for the party at the Royal West that night. Anyway, I only mention her because apparently she was fond of Anne-Laure — Juliana said she was very upset about the news. So I suppose she would be someone to ask, if you want to know what name Anne-Laure Chevalier chose to go by.'

Bryn drew out his notebook. 'You said she was called Dame Winifred — ?'

'Rye,' Magnus supplied. 'R-Y-E.'

'She's not like that mean old woman we met outside the Royal West, is she?' asked Bryn, shuddering at the memory

'Hilda Underpin? No, not all. Dame Winifred is actually very nice, if a little silly.' He returned his attention to the ring in the bag, which he was still holding between his fingers. 'So, assuming this does refer to Anne-Laure Chevalier, do we think he was trying to give her this ring, or was she was trying to give it back?' he wondered aloud. 'And what was it for? It's not exactly an engagement ring, but then you don't go around giving jewellery like that to your friends, do you?'

'I think there's a distinct possibility they were lovers,' said Bryn. 'Or at least, they had been. Inacio thought he might have witnessed a break-up.'

'And that would tally with the bruises, because of course most violence against women is committed by their partners, or at least someone they know,' said Magnus. He handed the ring back to Bryn. 'Can you take fingerprints from this?'

'I don't think so,' said Bryn. 'It was buried in the earth, and I'm afraid I will have smudged any prints when I wiped it clean. Besides, even if any could be found, it'd be difficult to sneak that past Boyle.'

'Shame,' murmured Magnus, although he hadn't just been playing devil's advocate earlier — he really wasn't sure what use this ring was in helping to understand Anne-Laure Chevalier's death.

'There's more,' said Bryn, who was now sat on the very edge of the sofa, so much so that Magnus was afraid that, in his eagerness to talk about the case, the policeman would slide right onto the floor. 'Just as Anne-Laure was leaving the garden, right when she passed Inacio's rose bush and he got a good look at her, she turned back to face her companion and screamed at him — it was the only bit of their conversation Inacio actually caught.'

'What did she scream?' Magnus asked, curious in spite of himself.

Bryn flicked back through his notebook, evidently determined to get the wording exactly right. 'She said: "*Don't follow me! I'm serious, this is it, you'll never see me again! I'm going to be free of you, and free of Westminster Square!*"'

Magnus let out a long, low whistle, feeling oddly deflated by how desperate this parting had sounded. Bryn, on the other hand, looked excited.

'Do you know what I think?' he said. 'I think it sounds as though she was planning on moving away, presumably to extract herself from this toxic relationship. And I think that man in the shadows snapped when he heard what she was planning. He must have followed her, tried to strangle her, and then —'

'Forced her to overdose on cocaine?' said Magnus, doubtfully. 'It seems unlikely, given that, according to your medical examiner, the state of her nose suggests she was a regular user, and therefore neither she nor anybody else would expect the drug to kill her. I'm not suggesting a cocaine habit is healthy, of course, but as far as I know it's fairly unusual for a heart or brain to just give out like that after inhalation, especially in one so young. If that is indeed what happened, Anne-Laure Chevalier was extremely unlucky.'

Bryn frowned he backed up on the sofa cushions, and Magnus could tell he was disappointed.

'What if there's another interpretation to what she screamed in the garden?' asked the barrister. 'One more in keeping with the theories of your medical examiner? What if by — what was it she said? — "... *you'll never see me again! I'm going to be free of you, and free of Westminster Square!*" she didn't mean she was moving away, she meant that she intended to end her life.'

Bryn's blue eyes widened: apparently, this had not occurred to him. Then he shook his head.

'But you just said —'

'— That as a regular user she wouldn't have expected the cocaine to kill her,' said Magnus. 'Yes, I realise I'm rather contradicting my own point here. But maybe if it was deliberate, and she took enough of it... Or maybe she wasn't even planning on doing it that evening, in that way. I don't know. I agree with you on one thing at last: this whole business is decidedly murky.'

'Well that's just it!' said Bryn, springing to the edge of the sofa once more. 'Boyle says I've been watching too many detective programmes on TV, and you probably agree with him, but it's not like that. I mean, I was speculating before, but it's not as though I truly suspect anything — or anyone. It's just... I have a hunch about this. All these loose ends, they're bothering me: the cocaine, the bruises, her peaceful pose on the sofa, our oversight in failing to properly investigate the scene of her death, the fact that none of her family or friends have come forward... And now this whole scene in the garden. It's all so *odd*. I'm sure we're missing something here, several things in fact. Don't you think?'

Magnus considered this. On the one hand, he could not help but think that Bryn was young, and keen, and he obviously wanted to prove himself, so was perhaps looking for a crime where there was none. And yes, his actions did seem as though they might be fuelled by one too many detective stories. Yet something told the barrister not to rule out the young police constable entirely. It seemed unwise to ignore Bryn's so-called 'hunch'. From both personal and professional experience, Magnus had come to realise that it was important to trust one's instincts; indeed, sometimes instinct was the only thing one had to go on.

'Look,' said Bryn, perhaps sensing that Magnus was weakening, 'it might have been suicide, or it might have been some sort of foul play. Or maybe it really was natural causes, or just a terrible accident… But at the end of the day, does it really matter? A woman is dead, and we still don't understand why. Isn't that reason enough to investigate? Don't we owe it to Anne-Laure Chevalier, whoever she was?'

'Yes,' agreed Magnus, seeing the earnest young policeman was right. 'Yes, I think we do.'

'So you'll help me?' said Bryn eagerly.

'I'll try,' replied the barrister. 'Although I'm not exactly sure *how*.'

'Well, as I told you before, I'm forbidden from talking about this at work, so it would be good to have you as a sounding board at the very least. You're a man of the law and — no offence — a little older than I am, so I expect you'll have plenty of wisdom and experience to bring to the investigation.'

'Flattery will get you everywhere,' murmured Magnus, choosing to ignore the comment about his age.

'Furthermore,' continued Bryn, 'it's pretty obvious I'm not from around these parts, and I don't know the area, or how things are done around here. But you do. You know Westminster Square, you know its residents, and given that Anne-Laure Chevalier lived, worked and died in this part of London, I'd say that knowledge might prove very useful.'

'Yes, I see what you mean,' said Magnus. 'All right then, Bryn. I'm not saying I agree that anything particularly untoward happened to this woman, but I'll help you with your unofficial investigation if I can. As you say, for her sake more than anything else.'

'So you're in?' said Bryn, extending a hand across the coffee table.

Magnus reached out and clasped the policeman's fingers with his own. 'I'm in,' he said. 'And I think this calls for another cup of tea, don't you?'

Bryn nodded, looking as though he could hardly contain his excitement, and once more he began to teeter dangerously close to the edge of the sofa. Magnus too leaned forward, although his motivation was to pick up the teapot and pour them both another brew.

'Out of interest,' he said, passing Bryn the milk, 'just so I know what I'm dealing with here, you understand — what *do* you think went on?' Then before Bryn could start reeling off all of the suspicious circumstances again, Magnus added, 'I mean, for a moment, let's forget about the facts, let's forget about evidence, and let's return to that hunch of yours. If you had to declare, right here right now, what happened to her, what would you say?'

Bryn did not even need a moment to consider this. 'I'd say I thought Anne-Laure Chevalier was murdered,' he said at once, 'and I'd say the person who killed her lives in Westminster Square.'

CHAPTER NINE

Two days after Magnus had agreed to help him solve the mystery of Anne-Laure Chevalier's death, Bryn made the short walk from Victoria Police Station to the south-east corner of Westminster Square, where the barrister was waiting for him. They had agreed that Magnus would take Bryn on a short tour of the quadrant, in order that the policeman could become more familiar with the famous London neighbourhood in which Anne-Laure had lived, worked and died.

Once again, to keep their unofficial investigation secret, and in particular to avoid the attentions of Police Chief Superintendent Barry Boyle, Magnus and Bryn met in the evening, after they had both finished work and the barrister had returned from Grey's Inn.

'I thought we could go for a stroll around the perimeter,' said Magnus, after they had greeted one another. 'Then we can talk while we walk. I'm not exactly sure what it is you want to know about Westminster Square, but it seems sensible to have the subject of our discussion in front of our noses. And after all, you're not going to get a feel for the place shut up in my flat.'

Bryn nodded, secretly relieved he didn't have to return to the barrister's jungle-like home and suffer another severe bout of hayfever. He was also pleased to have a genuine excuse to fully inspect Westminster Square; like so much of London, it was a location that fascinated him, perhaps because it was so different to the modest, rural and fairly isolated town in which he had grown up.

'The truth is, I want to know everything,' he told Magnus, as they began their walk along the square, which was in fact a rectangle, now Bryn came to think about it. 'I mean, it might not all be completely relevant for the case, but it can't hurt to have some background on the area, especially as I imagine I'll have to talk to some of Westminster Square's residents.'

'That makes sense,' said Magnus, 'and I'll try my best. But I've only lived here for ten years myself, which might sound like a long time, but I'm practically new in comparison to some of my neighbours.'

They continued along the street, passing a primary school, and then turned right onto the long northern side of Westminster Square. Not for the first time, Bryn was struck by the glamour of the large old buildings, with their stucco facades, grand pillars and their balconies set behind smart black railings.

'Westminster Square was originally built as a series of large terrace houses,' Magnus explained, evidently deciding to start his tour. 'And most of those houses are three bays wide, four or five storeys high, and have attics, basements and a mews house behind.'

'Which was for the carriages, right?' asked Bryn. 'Back in the day?'

'Right,' confirmed Magnus, 'but we'll get to that later, seeing as Anne-Laure lived in the Mews on the opposite, southern side.'

'How old is Westminster Square?' enquired the police constable.

'It dates back to the early nineteenth century,' replied Magnus. 'I believe its architect was commissioned to develop the square after Carlton House was dismantled and King George IV decided to make Buckingham Palace his home.'

'So he could take advantage of the address's proximity to the new palace?'

'Exactly. It's a strategic location, historically speaking as, being so close, it was an excellent base for the square's residents to court the king — especially as Carlton House had been dismantled not long beforehand. Also, it's near King's Road, which used to be the private route used by royalty to travel to Kew or Hampton Court.'

'Well, no wonder it's so grand, if it was specifically built for royalty,' said Bryn. His eyes roved over the parked cars lining the street before him, which included an Aston Martin, a Lamborghini, a Bugatti and several Rolls Royces. 'Blimey, where I'm from in Wales, the grandest car you're likely to see is a Volkswagen Golf!'

Magnus chuckled. 'You won't believe this then, but before the Second World War, although Westminster Square was certainly an upper class address, it wasn't regarded with the same esteem as similar areas in Mayfair and Belgravia, for example Grosvenor Square, St James's Square and Park Lane. But after the war had ended, most of the buildings in those addresses were converted for commercial and institutional use.'

'But not Westminster Square?'

'No. Westminster Square remained — and still does to this day — almost wholly residential, and as such it became an incredibly fashionable address in the second half of this century. The interiors of the buildings might have changed — most of the houses have been converted into flats and maisonettes by Central Square Properties — but the exteriors, with their Grade II-listed facades, remain the same. In fact, without the intrusion of any modern architecture, I expect the square looks almost exactly the same as it did when it was first built, save for all these flashy cars.'

They had walked almost exactly half the length of the northern side of Westminster Square, and Bryn slowed his pace to peer at an English Heritage blue plaque on the wall.

'I've seen a lot of these around,' said the young police constable.

'Yes, I think there is something like three hundred in the City of Westminster, and a number of them can be found in Westminster Square itself. And I expect we'll get another one in time, for our resident Hollywood star.'

'Who's that?'

'Didn't you know? Jem McMorran lives in Westminster Square.'

Bryn gave a little gasp of excitement. 'I didn't know that! *The* Jem McMorran? The star of *Pioneer of the Past?*'

'The very same.'

'Wow!' said the policeman again, completely bowled over by this fact; Jem McMorran was one of his favourite film stars. 'But he's one of our biggest actors! Have you seen him?'

'Of course.'

'Have you *met* him?'

'Many times. In fact, his fitness regime put my own to shame only the other day, when I encountered him dashing around the square having already completed a lap of Hyde Park. It was just before I met you outside the Royal West Hotel, in fact.'

'What's he like?'

'Charming,' said Magnus, a little grimly. Bryn was puzzled by his tone, until the barrister added, 'Oh, he's a nice enough young man. I just have the hump with him because he always leaves his sports cars in my parking space...'

But Bryn was hardly listening: he was craning his neck to gaze around at Westminster Square, hoping Jem McMorran might magically appear right there and then. Magnus smiled.

'If you're hoping to see him, I'm afraid you'll probably be out of luck. Jem McMorran is hardly ever here. If he's not away on a film shoot, he's at one of his other houses, wherever they are — America, I suppose. I think he only keeps a property in central London for convenience. But then, he's not unique in that. Plenty of Westminster Square residents treat their places here as a kind of town house, while spending most of their lives on their country estates.'

Coming to terms with the fact that he was not going to catch a glimpse of a Hollywood star, Bryn continued to follow Magnus around Westminster Square while the barrister regaled him with anecdotes about the area. After they rounded the north-east corner of the quadrant, they started down the southern side, where Bryn now knew Magnus lived. As they approached the barrister's house, the policeman was just feeling a little regretful that this pleasant and informative walk was passing so quickly, when they were waylaid by shouts coming from the nearest of the gardens.

'It's people like you who drag the good name of Westminster Square through the mud — or should I say, through the *poop!*'

Bryn sniggered at the shrill and croaky voice. It sounded as though, beyond the wrought iron gate of the garden, a local granny was having a rant. Magnus, however, shook his head.

'Come on,' he muttered, nudging Bryn forward. 'I know who that is, and if she sees us —'

'Magnus, is that you?' demanded a voice from beyond the foliage.

The barrister sighed, shot Bryn a resentful look, and then called, 'Good evening, Hilda! And how are you?'

The small, bony figure of Hilda Underpin hobbled into view around the rosebushes, peering out at them from over her large nose.

'What are you doing with that policeman? Are you being arrested?'

'Certainly not!' cried Magnus.

'Shame,' said Hilda. 'What a delicious scandal that would have been. Barrister and upstanding member of the local community hauled off to prison for... I don't know, fraud? Embezzlement?' She licked her dry lips at the thought.

'Hilda!' blustered Magnus. 'You shouldn't say such things!'

But the old lady wasn't listening. Her attention was now fixed on Bryn, who found himself cowering a little under her beady-eyed glare.

'You!' she called. 'Come in here! I have something that requires urgent police attention!'

'Really?' said Bryn, wondering for a moment whether this was somehow connected to Anne-Laure Chevalier's death.

'It won't be anything important,' muttered Magnus.

'I heard that!'

'Erm,' began Bryn, 'I'm not exactly on duty at the moment...'

'Well, you shouldn't be wearing your uniform then, should you? Come on, spit spot!'

Bryn looked to Magnus, who merely shrugged.

'Might as well get it out of the way,' he murmured. 'It'll be easier than arguing with her.'

'I heard that too!' called Hilda, as she shuffled towards the gate to let them in.

When they entered the private garden, which was the neighbour of the one in which Inacio had overheard the argument between Anne-Laure Chevalier and her shadowy companion, Bryn reflected that — even for Westminster standards — this was the least likely location for 'urgent police business' he had ever seen. In addition to Hilda Underpin, there was a second elderly lady standing in front of one of the benches, clutching at the lead of a little black terrier, but other than them, the garden was quite empty.

'Well, what exactly is the problem here, Mrs Underpin?' said Bryn, after it became apparent that nobody was willingly offering up any information.

'Isn't it obvious?' hissed Hilda.

'Erm, no.'

'*She* brought her dog into the garden and it — it *defecated* in one of the flower beds!'

'Oh,' said Bryn, trying not to laugh. 'Oh dear.'

'*Oh dear*?' Hilda looked furious. 'There are only two gardens in Westminster Square that permit dogs, and *this is not one of them*!'

'I'm sorry!' gasped the other pensioner, who was trembling under the combined gazes of Hilda, Bryn and Magnus. 'I'm new around here, I didn't know.'

'Can you not *read*?' Hilda sneered. 'Did you not see the sign? Did you not go through all of the paperwork given to you by CSP?'

Magnus took a step forward. 'Steady on, Hilda, it's not the end of the world.'

'You should be on my side, Magnus,' snapped the old woman. 'She's destroying the reputation of this area. Officer, arrest her!'

Bryn blinked at her. 'Excuse me?'

'Don't give me that gormless look, arrest her immediately!'

'I'm not —' Bryn began to say, but broke off as the other woman burst into tears.

'I'm sorry, I didn't know!' she wailed. 'I just came out here to give Whisper a bit of exercise, that's all.'

'Well, you should have read the sign. Officer!'

'I'm not arresting her,' said Bryn, now beginning to feel distinctly annoyed with the bullying old crone. 'She hasn't broken the law.'

'She's broken the *rules*,' said Hilda. 'She's disregarded the regulations of Central Square Properties and for that she should be soundly punished.'

Still crying, the other woman bent down with some difficulty and scooped her little dog into her arms. 'I didn't know...' she whispered again.

'Very well,' said Hilda, 'give her a caution, then. Fine her for wasting police time.'

'Excuse me, but it's *you* who's wasting police time, Mrs Underpin,' Bryn pointed out.

'She should be punished,' Hilda repeated, quivering with self-righteous anger.

Bryn looked to Magnus, who quickly turned his laughter into a cough, and then sighed: he was on his own with this one.

'Right then,' he said, turning to the sobbing woman. 'Mrs —?'

'Margret Witherwit.'

'Mrs Witherwit, I think it would be best if you leave now. And in the future, perhaps don't bring Whisper back into this particular garden, eh?'

'Of course.'

After shooting him a look of pure gratitude, the old woman fled from sight with surprising speed, her little dog still in her arms.

'Is that *it*?' roared Hilda, rounding on Bryn. 'What are you going to do about that?'

'About what?'

'*That!*' Hilda pointed a gnarled finger in the direction of the flowerbed. Bryn winced.

'I'm not going to do anything about that. Presumably either a gardener or the rain will clear it away.'

Hilda stared at him, and then at Magnus. 'Can you believe this?' she cried. 'The police are worse than useless these days. No wonder this country's in such a state...'

'Come on, Hilda,' said Magnus, who was still struggling to hide his mirth. 'I think you're overreacting a little. She made a mistake, and as a dog-lover yourself you must understand —'

This was evidently the wrong thing to say, for Hilda gave a little shriek of indignation. 'I would never bring Tam Tam to this garden, *never!*' she said. 'How dare you suggest such a thing! How —'

But her tirade was interrupted by a shout from behind them.

'Magnus! *Magnus!*'

Bryn turned to see, a little further down the street, an attractive woman with lots of auburn hair leaning out of one of the third floor bay windows.

'Erm, yes, Juliana dear?' called Magnus, looking faintly embarrassed.

'Your dinner is almost ready!' she shouted. 'If you don't come in soon, it'll go cold.'

And with that, she slammed the window shut. Hilda made a strangled noise of indignation.

'What is Juliana thinking?' she demanded, the issue with the dog instantly forgotten. 'Shouting out of the window like an Italian! I've never seen anything like it in all my days! Why, I thought I'd been momentarily transported to a fish market!'

'Oh, put a sock in it, Hilda,' said Magnus, whose mood seemed to have plummeted. 'Shall we continue, Bryn?'

The police constable made to follow him out of the garden.

'You can walk away from me now, Magnus, but I still need to have words with you!' called Hilda. When he didn't reply and kept on walking, she continued, 'I heard about your secret meeting in the Cosmopolitan Club last week!'

'I have no idea what you're talking about,' said Magnus calmly, closing the gate after Bryn with a definitive clunk.

As Magnus scowled, Bryn, who felt the atmosphere of their sunny evening walk had been rather spoilt, attempted to cheer the barrister by saying, 'Your wife seems like a character.'

'She is,' said Magnus, although he didn't look especially pleased about it.

'You should go in for dinner soon though,' said Bryn. 'That's the sort of thing my mum did back in Aberystwyth, when I was playing outside, and if I didn't go in there would be hell to pay.'

'Yes, exactly,' said Magnus, 'that's what your mother did in Aberystwyth. But it isn't really *done* in Westminster Square, not that you can explain that to Juliana...'

'But that's a good thing, isn't it?' asked Bryn. 'It would be worse if she was a colossal snob.'

'True,' agreed Magnus, 'but it might help us to fit in a bit more, if she wasn't always winding up Hilda Underpin. That's why she did it, by the way — she doesn't usually call me in for dinner like that, especially not when those windows are so difficult to open. I expect she saw us in the garden and decided to shout to me in an attempt to give the old lady a heart attack.'

This time, it was Bryn's turn to try and hide his laughter.

'But surely you do fit in around here?' he said, when he had regained control of himself.

'Mostly, yes,' said Magnus. 'Although the fact that my family is from Sweden originally means I'll never be fully accepted by some around here. They don't like foreigners, even someone like me who's lived in this country all my life, speaks perfect English, and has a wife who can trace her Kentish family back to medieval times, even if she is prone to hollering at me down the street. Although my "foreign-ness" is nothing in comparison to a couple of other figures who have moved into Westminster Square over the years.'

'Like who?'

'Oh, there's one chap called Vasyl Kosnitschev, this Ukrainian oligarch who arrived some time ago. He's not very popular, because he's surly and looks like one of Stalin's henchmen, and he has these big parties for his business associates, to which he rarely invites his neighbours. Not that I'd want to go, you understand...' Magnus trailed off. 'Goodness, now I come to think about it, you should talk to Vasyl about Anne-Laure.'

'I should?'

'Yes, he was her main employer, as far as I know. It was she who organised all those parties I just mentioned.'

Bryn whipped out his notebook from his utility belt.

'Vasyl probably doesn't know anything about her death,' the barrister continued, when he had finished spelling out the name for the police constable. 'When I spoke to him at this neighbourhood meeting last week, he seemed to view her demise as more of an inconvenience than anything else...'

'But it might be interesting to talk to him, seeing as he was her employer,' said Bryn. 'Frankly, it would be interesting to talk to anyone who knew her, considering it's not just her death but Anne-Laure herself who's a bit of a mystery at the moment.' He looked down at the scribbled name. 'Who was the other?'

'Sorry?'

'You said there were a couple of foreign figures who stood out around here.'

'Oh, yes. The other is a man named Sheikh Hazim bin Lahab, a gluttonous royal from the Arabian Gulf who swans around in robes and headdresses. I mean, I myself have no problem with what anyone wears, but people like Hilda Underpin... Well, you've just seen her reaction to a rogue dog and my wife leaning out a window, so you can imagine how Hazim's traditional Eastern costume goes down. And I think he, like Juliana, does it to be deliberately provocative. But I digress. Sheikh Hazim has nothing to do with Anne-Laure Chevalier.'

'No?'

'No. He was at the meeting too, and as excited as he was by the scandal of her death, he didn't seem to know her. Which is surprising, because if you watch who goes in and out of his house on a daily basis, it appears he knows half the girls in London.'

As Bryn raised his eyebrows, Magnus chuckled.

'Listen to me, I sound like an old gossip,' he went on. 'Perhaps, if I stay in Westminster Square too long, I'll turn into Hilda Underpin.'

Bryn shuddered at the memory of the vindictive pensioner, and then asked, 'How long do you think you will stay?'

'I don't know. I love Westminster Square. I love its location, its proximity to my work. I love its gardens, its security, its doormen. I love the beauty and provenance of the buildings. And I love the feeling of this place. There's something about the way Westminster Square is built, looking in on the gardens, that feels private, almost like an exclusive club. So there's a sense of camaraderie between those of us who live here, from the super-rich who invite each other to parties, to the drivers who tip each other off if they see a traffic warden coming. If I could, I'd stay here forever.'

'But you can't?'

'I doubt it. My wife hates it. She thinks Westminster Square is too elitist, too expensive, too urban. She doesn't want our children to grow up here. Rosanna, my eldest, has almost finished primary school and Juliana doesn't want her to stay in London. She wants her to go to a good school in Kent, but I'm not sure either of us can bear to send our daughter away to be a boarder. Plus, there are these silly issues concerning the management of the properties by Central Square Properties… Although I won't bore you with the details of all that, not when we're heading towards the most significant part of Westminster Square relating to Anne-Laure Chevalier: the Mews.'

They were approaching the south-east corner of Westminster Square now, and were almost back at the point where they had started the tour. Then, despite Bryn eagerly anticipating dipping into the next little street, the one in which the dead woman had lived, he became momentarily distracted by something to his right.

'Hold on,' he said, stopping in his tracks. 'Is that a tennis court over there?'

'Oh yes,' chuckled Magnus, as they crossed the road to peer through the foliage at the end of the central garden on the south side. 'That's another draw of the square: the fact it comes with its own private tennis court. Not that it gets much use, of course.'

'No?'

'Not really. Young Jem McMorran and his friends can be found there every so often, although — as I said before — he's not around much, as he's always off on film shoots and so on. Juliana and I will have a game every so often, and so will the children, but, believe it or not, my wife and I are some of the youngest people living in Westminster Square, so tennis is a little beyond the capabilities of many of the other residents. Then CSP don't exactly make it easy to hire the court…'

'What do you mean?'

'Oh, I'm sure you've seen all their rules about using the gardens, and it's ten times worse with the tennis court. You have to wear very specific shoes and clothes, at least one paid-up member must be on the court at all times — which is a bother when you have guests and want to send them off for a few hours. Not that it's even a few hours, because playing time is limited to one hour, and if you're even a little late, your slot will be given to someone else...'

'Hm,' said Bryn, who was only half-listening to Magnus' rant. Instead, he was thinking back to the day of Anne-Laure's death, before the party at the Royal West.

'So, am I right in thinking this charity tennis tournament that Dame Winifred organised took place right here?' he nodded towards the court, which was on the other side of the garden in which he had found the ring.

'Calling it a "*tournament*" is making it sound rather more competitive than it was,' said Magnus. 'In reality, Dame Winifred sold tickets for people to eat strawberries and drink champagne while watching a Hollywood film star beat a series of opponents without even breaking a sweat. Still, I suppose it was for a good cause.'

'Did you go?'

'No,' smiled Magnus. 'I can watch Jem McMorran beat people at tennis from my window.'

'So you don't know whether Anne-Laure was there?'

'Oh,' said Magnus, 'I hadn't thought of that. No, I don't know, but there's plenty who would. Maybe we could add it to the list of things to ask Dame Winifred?'

Bryn nodded and made a note of this. He wasn't sure it was important, whether Anne-Laure Chevalier had been at the tournament or not, but it didn't hurt to be thorough and confirm her movements on the last day of her life.

'Magnus!'

They turned and looked up. Once more, Juliana was leaning out of the window.

'Erm, yes, dear?' called Magnus, wincing.

'Your food is now on the table! Your children and your wife are sitting down to eat! Will you be gracing us with your presence?'

'Yes, of course!' cried Magnus. 'Right away!'

Without another word, Juliana retreated from the window, although this time she left it open, which struck Bryn as somewhat ominous — perhaps she would throw something at them next.

'Come on,' said the barrister. 'Let's have a quick look at the Mews.'

'You're not going in for dinner?'

'In a minute, in a minute.' Magnus looked harassed. 'But first we have to complete the tour.'

They proceeded to the corner of square and turned left. The architecture here was much the same, and if anything it was a little quieter without the noise of the main road that ran down the centre of the quadrant. However, at the end of the street, Bryn could just make out the side of a modern brick building — presumably an office block. Magnus was right: aside from the cars, Westminster Square and the surrounding area looked like something belonging to the distant past, and this artless intrusion instantly broke the spell.

Magnus, meanwhile, was waving at someone; a lanky, dark-haired young man who raised his arm above his head in awkward greeting and then ducked out of sight down the street just ahead of them.

'I don't suppose you've heard of Morris Springfield?' the barrister asked in a hushed voice.

Bryn shook his head.

'He could be considered another of our resident celebrities, at least in certain circles. He's a writer, and quite a successful one at that. His first novel, *Vacant Shadows,* caused a big stir a few years ago — the critics adored it — although I must admit I couldn't make head nor tails of it myself. Now, he mostly writes for the papers, although he did publish another novel not too long ago, and apparently he's working on a third...'

Bryn thought he might have seen *Vacant Shadows* in a bookshop, and was fairly sure from the dark, angry-looking cover it was not his kind of reading material. So instead of asking more about the author's career, he enquired, 'Does this Morris Springfield live on Westminster Square as well?'

'Not quite. He's on Westminster Row, the street he just walked down,' said Magnus, pointing. 'In fact, he's just behind the Mews.'

'Really? And do you think he might have known Anne-Laure?'

'I very much doubt it.'

'Really? They look to be around the same age, they didn't live very far from one another…'

'Yes, but from the limited amount I know about Anne-Laure, it sounds like she was a sociable creature, whereas Morris is a complete recluse. He's one of these writers who shuts himself away for days upon end, suffering for his art. No, I can't even imagine a situation where they would come face to face, let alone become properly acquainted.'

'I'm sure you're right,' said Bryn, privately thinking that beautiful women like Anne-Laure Chevalier rarely had time for eccentrics like Morris Springfield. 'I think I'm just clutching at straws because we have so little to go on…'

'Actually, I know I'm right,' said Magnus, 'because I've just remembered — Juliana ran into Morris a little while ago, and he said he didn't know Anne-Laure. Come on, let's have a look at the Mews.'

He turned and beckoned Bryn towards an archway that the policeman would have walked straight past, had it not been pointed out to him. On the right side of the entrance was another blue plaque, although this time it was an official notice:

Central Square Properties
PRIVATE MEWS
Residents parking only
Wheel clamps in use
No exercising of dogs

'People are rather preoccupied with dogs around here, aren't they?' noted Bryn.

Magnus led him through the archway and into the little street beyond, which featured an old-fashioned cobbled road flanked by square and rather squat-looking buildings, which were obviously contemporary conversions.

'So this used to be where the horses were housed and the carriages were parked?' said Bryn.

'And where the stable boys lived and worked. It's difficult to imagine now, isn't it? Especially as, I recently read, one of these places is going for over a million pounds. A million pounds — for a poky little place with only two bedrooms!'

'So Anne-Laure must have had quite a lot of money to afford one of these places, even to rent,' mused Bryn.

'Actually, I think she had a generous benefactor,' said Magnus.

'What do you mean?'

'Well, her flat — whichever one it is — actually belonged to Dame Winifred Rye, this woman who hosts all these fundraising events around here. In fact, as far as I'm aware, Dame Winifred owns quite a few of these properties. But that's by the by. The point is, according to Juliana, who spoke to her last week, Dame Winifred rented out one of her properties to Anne-Laure at a very reduced rate, at least when the girl first arrived in London. I think Dame Winifred was trying to help her find her feet — she's fond of helping young people, especially girls — although apparently Anne-Laure later tried to reimburse her.'

'Juliana found all of that out in one conversation?' said Bryn, as he rushed to make notes. 'Wow, considering that and her chat with the writer, I'm wondering whether I've teamed up with the wrong Walterson.'

'What do you mean?'

'I mean, your wife is doing better detective work than we are!'

Magnus laughed, and then his face suddenly fell.

'Oh dear! My wife! Dinner — I forgot!'

Once more, Bryn had to work hard to hide his amusement as Magnus spun around in panic.

'Bryn, we'll talk again soon,' he said, beginning to walk back towards the archway that led back towards Westminster Square. 'We'll decide how best to proceed with all of this. But for now I'd better run — otherwise the next murder you investigate might well be my own...'

CHAPTER TEN

Following their tour of Westminster Square, the next step Magnus and Bryn decided to take in their unofficial investigation was to revisit the scene of Anne-Laure's death. Whether or not it was the setting of a crime remained to be seen, but Bryn thought it might be useful to go back to the Royal West Hotel now that everything and everyone had calmed down, and examine the business conference room without Boyle breathing down his neck. Furthermore, the police constable thought it might be useful for Magnus to see the site first-hand. On the Sunday morning the body had been found, the barrister had not been allowed inside, so he was not familiar with the location in which Anne-Laure had been discovered — and possibly killed.

Once again, the pair had arranged to meet after work, and this time Bryn changed at the station, exchanging his police uniform for a shirt and chinos. Following his experience with Hilda Underpin, he was glad to be back in civilian clothing, as he didn't want to be drawn into another pensioners' dispute. In addition to this, he was hoping his everyday outfit would disguise his identity, because of course he had been there at the Royal West that fateful Sunday morning and didn't want anyone at the hotel — particularly its slimy General Manager — to recognise him as a policeman. If they did, there was a real possibility it might get back to Boyle, and then Bryn knew he would be in serious trouble.

However, as he approached the pillared façade of the hotel, Bryn was confident his civilian clothes would be enough to disguise him. In his short time on the beat, he had already learned that people tended to treat him very differently depending on whether or not he was wearing his uniform, and he was both far less conspicuous and far less respected without it. In fact, as he stepped into the grand entrance hall of the Royal West, he wondered whether he might have disguised himself a little too well; a fragrant and immaculately-coiffed blonde woman was looking at him from behind the reception desk with undisguised suspicion, even a little disdain.

'Good evening, sir, and welcome to the Royal West Hotel,' she said, in a clipped English accent. 'How may I help you?'

'Erm,' said Bryn, faltering a little, as he always did when faced with the well-to-do or the beautiful. 'Yes, good evening, I'm here to enquire about hiring a conference room at your hotel.'

This was the cover story he and Magnus had decided on, as they were sure it was the easiest way to get them access to the space in which Anne-Laure Chevalier had died. But Bryn was a little uncomfortable with the idea of putting their plan into action before his ally had arrived.

'Erm, my colleague will be arriving in just a minute,' he told the receptionist, 'so perhaps I should wait until then?'

As he gestured towards the waiting area, she gave him a broad smile that did not meet her eyes. 'I don't think that would be appropriate, would it, sir? Why don't you turn around, walk out of the door, and we'll say no more about this little incident?'

'Excuse me?'

She lowered her voice. 'Sir, you're obviously in the wrong place.'

'I am not!' he cried. 'Unless you're denying that this is the Royal West Hotel?'

She paused for a moment, evidently sizing him up, and then said, 'May I ask where you're from?'

'You may, although I'm not sure why it's relevant: I am from just outside Aberystwyth in Wales.'

'Are you from a very old Welsh family?'

'I'm afraid I don't know that.'

'What is your surname?'

'Summers.'

'Probably not, then,' she sniffed. 'Does your family own a castle?'

He stared at her. 'Of course they don't own a castle!'

'I've heard there are a lot of castles in Wales.'

'You've heard correctly, but none of them belong to my family.'

'That's a shame,' she said. 'Well, Mr Summers, as I said, I don't think it's appropriate for you to stay here any longer.'

'Excuse me?' cried Bryn again. 'You're telling me I can't hire a room at the Royal West because my family doesn't own a castle?'

'You're being a little unreasonable,' she said, the irony of which caused Bryn to splutter in indignation. 'I am simply doing my job and trying to maintain the illustrious reputation of the Royal West, which includes vetting guests. And I'm afraid you, Mr Summers, do not fulfil the criteria of this hotel's usual clientele.'

'Because I'm Welsh and not heir to a castle?'

'Because you've turned up here in cheap, un-ironed clothes, no tie, and an accent from goodness knows where!'

'It's from Aberystwyth, I just told you that!' he said, his temper rising. 'Would it help if I went away and put on a tie? Could we then continue this conversation when I returned?'

'No,' she said bluntly.

Bryn sighed. His fingers were itching to whip out his police badge, which was in the inside pocket of his jacket. He was desperate to see her reaction to it, especially if he were able to think of some sort of official warning to give her — inciting racial hatred, perhaps? It wouldn't stick, of course, but it would be highly satisfying to watch her snooty veneer crumble as she grovelled.

Yet somehow, he managed to restrain himself. After all, it was not worth risking his job by outing himself as a policeman just to get one over on this silly, snooty woman. But he wished Magnus would arrive. This was exactly the reason Bryn had wanted the barrister to help him in the first place; he had no experience in dealing with these types of people.

'Look,' he told the receptionist, trying to keep his cool, 'I'm not wanting to actually stay here, all I want to do is hire your business conference room...'

'I'm afraid nobody really comes to the Royal West for business,' she cut in. 'It's more of a *leisure* hotel, so I'm not sure it would suit your needs in this instance.'

'If it's a leisure hotel, why do you have a business conference room in your brochure?' asked Bryn, assuming this was so, even though he had never seen such a publication.

As the receptionist tried to think of an answer to this, a familiar figure emerged from the little room behind the front desk.

'What's this about the business conference room?'

Edwin Brackenwell, the General Manager of the Royal West, seemed much the same as he had done on the morning after Anne-Laure's death: smart, well-dressed and fussy-looking. But although he appeared slightly less hysterical this evening, his expression was undeniably anxious.

'I was hoping to hire the space,' said Bryn, 'for a business meeting.'

'Are you a journalist?' Edwin demanded.

Bryn had not expected this. 'Sorry?'

'Are you from *The Dawn Reporter*?'

'No, of course not.'

Edwin eyed him suspiciously, and then seemed to relax. 'We've had several journalists making enquiries recently, because of… Well, never mind.'

Evidently, he was hoping Bryn was one of the few people in this part of London who had not heard about Anne-Laure Chevalier's body turning up in his hotel. The policeman, who was simply relieved Edwin hadn't recognised him from that morning, decided to play dumb.

'Because of what?'

'I said never mind!' snapped Edwin. Then he turned to his receptionist. 'What seems to be the issue here, Penelope?'

'I didn't think Mr Summers here was an appropriate guest for the Royal West,' she said, without a trace of self-consciousness.

Edwin's gaze roved critically over Bryn, resting somewhere around his ankles, where his blue socks were showing above rather scuffed shoes.

'Yes, Penelope, I think I agree with you.'

'Excuse me,' said Bryn, beginning to feel incredibly frustrated by this whole situation, 'I'm not wanting to stay as a guest. As I've said several times, I simply want to hire the business conference room for a meeting…'

'How many credit cards do you have?'

Bryn was taken aback by the way Edwin had suddenly fired this query at him. 'What?'

'How many credit cards do you have?'

'Um, none.'

Edwin shook his head. 'Dear, dear, dear...'

'I don't really see what having a credit card has to do with anything,' said Bryn. 'Can't you just give me and my colleague, when he arrives, a quick tour of the business conference room?'

'A *tour*?' sneered Edwin, while Penelope giggled beside him. 'Where do you think you are, young man, Madame Tussaud's? The London Dungeon?'

'I'm certainly being treated like I'm in the London Dungeon...' muttered Bryn, who objected to being referred to as 'young man' by a person who was only a few years older than him.

'We do not do *tours*,' said Edwin coldly, 'and the Royal West Hotel only opens its doors to the most distinguished, the most celebrated, the most — Oh! Oh, hello!'

A change had suddenly come over Edwin Brackenwell. Whereas before he had been hunching over to scoff at Bryn, now he had drawn himself up to his full height to greet the person currently entering the hotel. Penelope too was sitting straighter in her seat, twisting herself around so as to best display her figure.

'A very good evening to you, sir!' cried Edwin, who seemed to have completely forgotten about the existence of Bryn. 'It's a *delight* to see you back at the Royal West, an absolute delight! I'm afraid this is appallingly lax of me, but I'm searching for your name, it's on the tip of my tongue...'

'It's Magnus Walterson,' said the barrister patiently, approaching the desk.

Having come straight from work, he was dressed in a grey suit, and although it was not particularly flashy, it was perfectly tailored and pressed, leaving Bryn in no doubt that it had been expensive. In that moment, he could see Edwin and Penelope looking at Magnus and mentally ticking boxes: smart, check; successful, check; wealthy, check; English, check.

Well, they were not entirely correct on that last one, as Bryn now knew, but it was obvious why they were being more welcoming to his companion than they had been to him, a skinny, baby-faced nobody from the middle of nowhere.

'Mr Walterson, of course, of course!' beamed Edwin. 'And will you be dining again with us tonight? We've been eagerly anticipating the return of you and your beautiful wife, and the chef has put together an especially impressive menu this week, if we do say so ourselves!'

He gave a smug little chuckle, and then glared at Penelope to do the same. Magnus did not smile.

'Hasn't my colleague here already asked you? I've come to enquire about hiring the business conference room?'

As Magnus said this, Bryn wished he had a camera to capture the shocked expressions of Edwin Brackenwell and his receptionist. Then they both began to twitter at once.

'Oh, he's *your* colleague!'

'We didn't realise —'

'It makes *so* much sense now.'

'— you must forgive us, but I'm afraid there's been a *teensy* misunderstanding.'

'What sort of misunderstanding?' asked Magnus, directing this question to Bryn.

'They wouldn't let me see the business conference room.'

'Why not?'

'A great many reasons,' said Bryn, keeping his voice light. 'Apparently I'm too badly-dressed, too Welsh, my family don't own enough castles, and I don't own enough credit cards. Oh, and this hotel's only for leisure anyway.'

'What a load of poppycock,' said Magnus, turning back to Edwin and Penelope, who were both stuttering uselessly. 'What's the matter with you? Don't you know who this man is?'

Bryn shot him a panicked look: was Magnus about to reveal his identity as a member of the Victoria constabulary?

'He is one of the most important up-and-coming lawyers in the country!' said Magnus. 'They are already predicting this man will take silk and be awarded the Queen's Counsel, and I expect he'll be one of the youngest ever to achieve this great honour. And you tried to turn him away from the Royal West!'

'It's her fault!' Edwin cried, pointing an accusing finger at Penelope. 'I could tell he was important immediately, but she filled my head with all her silly ideas and prejudices.'

'What?' said Penelope, looking incensed.

'It's true!' exclaimed Edwin, shooting her a warning glance. 'I'll give her an official warning! I'll have her pay docked!'

Penelope gasped.

'Please, just forgive us this terrible breach in etiquette!'

'There's no need for any of that,' said Bryn, even though he highly doubted Edwin would carry through on these threats; the hotel manager simply wanted to use his receptionist as a scapegoat. 'The only thing I want — the only thing I've wanted for this entire conversation — is to have a tour of your business conference room.'

'Of course!' said Edwin shrilly, almost tripping over his feet in his eagerness to emerge from behind the desk. 'Of course, of course! I'll show you both myself. It'll be my pleasure — an *honour!*'

He beckoned them to follow him through a door to their right. Bryn caught Magnus' eye as they walked behind him, and the barrister gave him a wink. He, at least, seemed to be thoroughly enjoying this whole charade.

'Thank goodness you arrived,' Bryn muttered under his breath. 'I thought they'd be asking me about the colour of my underpants next...'

'I wouldn't put it past them,' chortled Magnus.

'Sorry, what was that?' asked Edwin, turning around.

'I said this is a lovely room,' lied Magnus.

'Oh yes, yes, isn't it just?' said Edwin, looking around appreciatively. 'This is the Duke Room — named after the Duke of Westminster, of course. It's our main function space here at the Royal West, and we can certainly do you a deal to include it in the hire of the business conference room, should you need an extra area for coffee or break-out sessions, whatever you like! We can put the tables and chairs into a number of different arrangements to suit all your needs...'

While Edwin prattled on, Bryn looked around the Duke Room. He had not paid it much attention a few weeks ago: on his way in, he had been too eager to get a look at the body in the adjourning room, and on his way out he had been distracted by the fact that he was being manhandled by Boyle. But he did have a vague recollection of mess. The cleaner had evidently not been in here at the time, and he remembered this Duke Room, which was now spotless, being littered with crockery, glassware, party decorations, and flowers that had begun to pong. If he had stopped to take it all in, he thought the remnants of the previous night's event would have looked rather sad in the bright morning light.

Magnus, who was evidently thinking along similar lines, said, 'I've just remembered — isn't this where Dame Winifred's fundraising party took place the other week?'

Edwin spun around, his eyes wide. But he could not deny it. 'Um, yes,' he stammered. 'Yes, it was.'

'I was invited, of course, but I had a more pressing engagement,' said Magnus, before lowering his voice and adding, *'at the palace.'*

Bryn wasn't sure, but he suspected this wasn't true, and that Magnus was simply toying with Edwin Brackenwell. It seemed to be working, however, because the hotel manager looked so impressed by what Magnus had just said, he became noticeably less defensive about the subject of the party.

'Yes, well, Dame Winifred likes to host these events, doesn't she? And we're happy to oblige her, of course — after all, it's for charity! But it was just a little celebration, really, a local affair,' he concluded, with a dismissive wave of his hand.

Bryn gave a snort of surprise, which he quickly turned into a cough: it had been quite obvious, if only from the rubbish left behind, that Dame Winifred's charity bash had been far from a 'little celebration'.

'Gosh, wasn't that the party at which some girl was found dead?' asked Magnus, affecting innocence.

Edwin swallowed nervously, his Adam's apple bobbing up and down. 'Ah, well — we don't, *aha*, like to really talk about that.'

'Come on, old chap, it's only me,' said Magnus, giving him a gentle punch to the shoulder. 'I'm not going to gossip, am I? I'm a local — I wouldn't do anything to jeopardise the reputation of Westminster Square.'

These seemed to be the magic words, because Edwin visibly relaxed. 'No, of course you wouldn't, especially not a man of your standing... Well, between us, then, yes, that girl did die at the Royal West that night. Very unfortunate business. As you might have read in the papers, she died of natural causes — a brain haemorrhage or something, I suppose — but I wish she'd done it somewhere else. As you say, Westminster Square has a reputation to maintain!'

He gave a high-pitched little laugh, and then quickly stopped when he realised neither Magnus nor Bryn were joining in.

'Where did she die?' asked Bryn.

'In her room upstairs,' lied Edwin. 'Shall we continue with the tour?'

'But I thought she was local?' Bryn persisted. 'I read in the papers she lived in the Mews, so why would she have a room here?'

'It must have been somebody else's room, then,' said Edwin, whose face now looked a little shiny, as though he had begun to sweat. 'As I said, terrible business, we shouldn't dwell on it. Let's instead proceed to the business conference room...'

As he marched towards the door, clearly hoping to get them out of the Duke Room — and away from the topic of Anne-Laure's death — as quickly as possible, Magnus and Bryn exchanged another look behind his back, although this time it was one of defeat. Bryn assumed that Magnus, like he, knew they were going to get nothing more out of Edwin Brackenwell on the subject of the dead woman; he was too protective of his hotel. And even if they forced the issue, anything Edwin did reluctantly disclose might be, like this statement she had been found in one of the upstairs rooms, a complete falsehood. No, Edwin Brackenwell's usefulness had expired, and now they needed to get rid of him in order to have a proper inspection of the real location in which Anne-Laure's body had been found.

'The business conference room!' announced Edwin, throwing open the double doors with a flourish.

This space Bryn did remember, and he shivered a little as he crossed back over the threshold. She had been right here, the woman who had taken up so many of his thoughts since that morning. Or rather, her body had been right here, because Anne-Laure herself, that enigmatic person about whom they still knew so little, had long since departed.

'As you can see, we have plenty of space for large meetings right here,' said Edwin, gesturing at the long, shiny table that dominated the room. 'There are conference-calling capabilities — we have all the mod-cons here! — and we can certainly discuss menu options for morning coffee breaks, lunches, afternoon teas, that sort of thing. Now, if I could draw your attention to the spectacular view this room offers of Westminster, I think you'll find your guests highly stimulated by their surroundings. At the Royal West, we pride ourselves on not keeping our business clients cooped up like chickens — *aha!*'

Once more, Bryn let Edwin's blathering wash over him. Magnus' gaze, he saw, had strayed to the trio of sofas at the opposite end of the room, as Bryn had already told him exactly where Anne-Laure had been found. Edwin Brackenwell, however, seemed highly reluctant to venture further than halfway down the length of the table. Bryn would not have noticed this under normal circumstances, but knowing what he did, he suspected the hotel manager was still afraid to go anywhere near the spot in which the body had been discovered.

How were they going to get rid of him, Bryn wondered, as Edwin began an exhaustive description of the kinds of business events that the hotel had hosted over the years. They really needed him to leave, but Edwin seemed to be in full flow, clearly determined to secure their imaginary conference before the day was done.

Fortunately, their predicament was soon solved by a phone call. After one of the telephones on the conference table began to ring, Edwin snatched it up with an impatient, 'Yes, what is it?' He listened for a few seconds, gave a heavy sigh, and then concluded the call with, 'I'll be there right away.'

'I'm very sorry, gentlemen, but I'm going to have to leave you for a few minutes — that's CSP on the phone, wanting to discuss various maintenance issues…'

'Oh, say no more!' said Magnus, cringing. 'And you have my sympathies.'

Edwin cast him a grateful look before departing from the room. Magnus then turned to Bryn, his expression gleeful.

'What a piece of luck! Turns out CSP are good for something after all — he'll be away for hours!'

Together, they walked towards the three sofas at the end of the room, which were situated around a small coffee table.

'So she was here, was she?' said Magnus.

'On that one,' said Bryn, pointing at the sofa on the right and feeling oddly cold as he did so.

The sofa looked so shiny and innocuous it was difficult to believe that, mere weeks ago, a dead body had lain upon it. Surely Edwin should have thrown it away? But then, Anne-Laure had not suffered a messy death — at least, not outwardly; it wasn't as though there had been any blood to mop up.

'You said she looked as though she were sleeping?' said Magnus, his tone now business-like.

'Yes, she was curled up and facing into the cushions, so you could only see the back of her at first; her hair, her evening dress… The cleaner thought she was asleep for several minutes. In fact, she tidied up around her, which is a huge pain, because who knows what evidence she accidentally destroyed. Gosh, it'd be useful to talk to that cleaner, come to think of it, although I don't know how we'd do it without Edwin finding out…'

Magnus, meanwhile, still seemed focused on trying to picture the body. 'So she looked peaceful?'

'Yes.'

'Where was this bag? The one in which you found the cocaine?'

'She was lying on it, apparently. The medical examiner found it. I don't know how I missed it, because it was bright gold.'

'And had she taken off her shoes?'

'Yes. No wait, she hadn't. One of them had fallen onto the floor — right there — and one was still on her foot. They had those spiky, stiletto heels, you know?'

'Hm,' said Magnus. 'So they were the kind of shoes one would probably remove, if one were settling down to have a nap? Just as one probably wouldn't choose to lie on one's own handbag…'

Bryn felt a ripple of excitement in his chest. 'So do you think someone moved her?' he asked. 'To make her look peaceful? And they forgot to take off her shoes?'

'Maybe. Or she was so drunk or high she didn't think to remove them herself, and didn't even feel herself squashing her own handbag when she slumped down. We can't really tell, can we?'

'No,' Bryn agreed, although he felt disappointed; he had hoped Magnus was coming round to his way of thinking.

The barrister looked towards the double doors, through which Edwin had departed.

'Was this room used for the party?' he asked.

'I don't think so,' said Bryn, slowly. 'There were no decorations or anything in here, but as I said, the cleaner had already been in, so she could have tidied them away. I think there were a few glasses and so on scattered around, but I'm fairly sure the party was supposed to be in that Duke Room we just passed through.'

'Which begs the question, what was Anne-Laure Chevalier doing in here?' pondered Magnus. 'Could she have been coerced by someone into leaving the crowd next door?'

'I'm not sure, because the medical examiner said her death probably occurred at two o'clock in the morning, give or take a few hours,' said Bryn. 'Surely the party must have been over by then? At least, there wouldn't have been a big crowd left.'

'Hm,' said Magnus again. 'You know, when Juliana spoke to Dame Winifred in the flower shop, Winifred said she hadn't been able to find Anne-Laure after the party. She had wanted to thank her for organising it all, but in the end she went home without seeing her. She was very upset about it, apparently, because she thinks Anne-Laure was tidying up and checking people hadn't left anything behind...' He gave a wry smile. 'I fear that lady had a higher opinion of Anne-Laure than she deserved.'

'What do you mean?'

'Well, considering what we know, I'd say it was more likely Anne-Laure was snorting lines of cocaine than tidying up, don't you think?'

Bryn said nothing. He thought Magnus probably had a point, but it didn't seem fair to criticise Anne-Laure's behaviour, especially as she was no longer here to defend herself.

'But was she doing it alone?' he asked instead. 'Was she doing it here? Or was she elsewhere, and someone moved her here? And what time did Dame Winifred leave the party? Did she look in here when she was searching for Anne-Laure? And who else was even at this event anyway? Perhaps our man in the shadows made a late appearance?'

'Whoah!' said Magnus, holding up his hands to stop Bryn from saying anymore. 'Slow down! Unfortunately, the only person who can answer most of your questions is dead, so we're going to have to think outside the box a little. Who might be able to help us here? I still think it would be a good idea to talk to Anne-Laure's employer, Vasyl Kosnitschev. And although Juliana's already managed to get quite a bit out of her, it's probably worth speaking with Dame Winifred as well, because she was both Anne-Laure's landlady and the host of this party. Once she calms down a bit, she might find she knows more than she realises...'

He trailed off as a door just behind them opened and a young, olive-skinned woman pushing a cleaning trolley walked in.

'Oh!' she gasped, dropping a cloth in surprise. 'I'm sorry, I didn't know anyone was in here.'

'Not to worry, we're just looking at the conference facilities,' said Magnus kindly.

She lowered her eyes and muttered, 'I'll come back later.'

But as she and her trolley began to back out of the door, Bryn was struck by a sudden idea.

'Hold on a second!' he called. 'I don't suppose you know what happened here the other week?'

Her gaze flicked towards the sofa, and she looked worried, even a little scared. 'We're not supposed to talk about it...'

'I understand,' said Bryn. 'But I was wondering if you could tell me who it was that found the body. I think it was a cleaner, wasn't it?'

The girl nodded.

'What was her name?'

She looked between them for a few moments, clearly trying to work out what they were up to. 'Rafaela Ricci,' she said finally.

'And is Ms Ricci working today?'

'Yes.'

Bryn looked to Magnus, who gave a nod of encouragement.

'Look, Ms —?'

'Paola.'

'We were wondering whether you could help us with something, Paola,' continued Bryn. Then, deciding to stick with their cover story, he explained, 'We're lawyers from Grey's Inn, and we need to ask Ms Ricci a few questions about what she saw that morning. Perhaps you could go and fetch her for us?'

Paola's eyes had gone very wide, and it looked as though she were bursting to ask questions, but something held her back — perhaps a fear of lawyers.

'I'll go and get her now,' she said.

As she turned to go, Magnus called after her. 'And Paola? Maybe let's keep this from Mr Brackenwell for now?'

She looked surprised, but as she nodded an amused expression crossed her face. Bryn suspected she, like he, was not a fan of the General Manager of the Royal West Hotel.

A few minutes later, Paola returned with the older, stout cleaner Bryn had seen here on the morning after Anne-Laure's death. She scowled at both him and Magnus, leaving Bryn with the impression it would be more difficult to intimidate her into giving up information.

'Hello, Ms Ricci,' he began.

But before he could go on, Rafaela turned around and hissed at Paola, who was still hovering by the open door, 'They didn't ask for *you*, get out of here!'

The younger woman, looking severely disappointed to be missing out, slid silently away.

'You're not a lawyer,' Rafaela told Bryn accusingly, as soon as Paola was out of earshot, 'you're a policeman.'

'Well remembered,' he said, 'and seeing as you know who I am, you've probably worked out why we're here.'

'Mr Brackenwell says that if any of us breathe a word about that woman's death to anybody, we'll be fired on the spot and not given a reference.'

'Ah,' said Bryn, his heart sinking.

Rafaela folded her arms over her large chest. 'Luckily for you, I do not listen to what Mr Brackenwell says,' she said. 'And I do not think you listen to your boss either.'

Her lip twitched and Bryn smiled back at her, recognising a kindred spirit.

'Well, then,' said Magnus, 'now we've established we're all ignoring our superiors, let's think back on that morning. Rafaela, are we right in thinking you discovered the body?'

'Yes,' she said, her tone suddenly business-like. 'Mr Brackenwell asked me to arrive early that morning, at six o'clock, to ensure everything was tidied up after the party. I started in the Duke Room, but he made me move through here, because there was an early meeting booked in, for eight o'clock, I think.'

Bryn, who was now making frenzied notes, asked, 'Had the party taken place in here as well?'

'I don't think it was supposed to,' said Rafaela. 'There wasn't much mess when I came in, not compared to next door.'

'There were no decorations or flowers?'

She shook her head.

'But there was a little bit of mess?' prompted Magnus.

Rafaela screwed up her face as she tried to remember. 'I think there was an empty bottle of champagne and a plate of canapés on the table, as well as some rubbish. Oh, and there was a decanter full of whiskey. Then there was a glass down there...'

She nodded towards the significant sofa.

'What kind of glass?'

'A crystal tumbler. It smelled of whiskey, so I assume she'd helped herself to some from that decanter before she died. No, wait —'

Rafaela suddenly trailed off, walked towards the sofa, and mimed picking up something from the floor.

'No, there were two crystal tumblers. I picked them both up, when I thought she was sleeping. I had forgotten that.'

'Two?' said Bryn, straightening up: this sounded very much like Anne-Laure had not come into the business conference room alone. As far as he was concerned, Magnus and Marlene's theory of suicide was sounding less and less likely.

The barrister, meanwhile, was following his own train of thought. 'What happened to all the glasses and bottles and rubbish you cleaned up?'

Rafaela gave a huff of frustration. 'Nothing,' she said. 'As I've told you, I thought she was asleep, so I set the tumblers aside to be taken back to the kitchen, the whiskey to the bar, and everything else I threw away. But the glassware could have been dusted for fingerprints, if that's what you're thinking, only —'

'Only the police didn't do their job properly,' Bryn concluded.

'Well, yes,' she said. 'But Mr Brackenwell is to blame for that as well.'

Magnus looked between them, and then said, 'Ms Ricci, you seem to be in agreement with my friend here, given that you've mentioned fingerprints and so on, that there was something suspicious about this young woman's death, is that right?'

'Yes,' she said.

'And why do you think that?'

Rafaela laughed, as though the answer to this question was perfectly obvious. 'Because young and healthy rich white women don't just drop down dead like that!' she cried.

'It could have been a freak heart attack or brain haemorrhage?' Magnus suggested.

But Rafaela shook her head. 'What are the chances of that?' she said, dismissively. 'And if she was suffering from headaches or chest pains, why would she stay at this party until the early hours?'

Again, Bryn found himself in agreement with the cleaner, even though she probably wasn't aware that Anne-Laure had helped to organise the fundraising event.

Then, when neither he nor Magnus had spoken for a few moments, Rafaela said, 'That morning, I heard you talking about cocaine...'

The police constable hesitated, and then decided he might as well give her the full story; she would be in as much trouble with Brackenwell as he with Boyle if this conversation was discovered. 'Yes, we found the drug in her handbag, and blood tests reveal she snorted cocaine that night. So it's very likely she had a bad reaction to it, and that's how she died.'

'Then someone must have made her take it,' said Rafaela at once.

Bryn stared at her, surprised but not displeased she had jumped to this conclusion.

'What if she had taken it herself, on purpose?' asked Magnus.

Once more, Rafaela scoffed. 'Like I said, she was young, rich and white, not to mention beautiful. Why would she try and kill herself?'

Neither Bryn nor Magnus responded. There seemed no point in trying to explain to a poor, middle-aged, slightly overweight and very embittered immigrant that Anne-Laure Chevalier might have had problems.

'Before you found her that morning,' said Magnus, steering the conversation on, 'had you ever seen this woman before?'

Rafaela shook her head.

'You'd never seen her coming in and out of the hotel, or around Westminster Square, or with any men...?'

'No,' said the cleaner. 'Why do you ask about men?'

'We think she might have had a bad boyfriend,' said Bryn.

'So that's how she got the bruises...' murmured Rafaela.

'Well, the ones on her wrists, certainly.'

'It'll be him, then,' said the cleaner, with complete confidence. 'He'll be the one who killed her, you mark my words.'

'And what makes you say that?' asked Magnus.

For the third time, Rafaela gave a dismissive chuckle, but her expression was grim. 'It's *always* the bad boyfriends,' she said simply.

This statement seemed to echo around the business conference room, and neither Magnus nor Bryn disputed it. In the police constable's experience, and no doubt the barrister's too, Rafaela was correct: the angry, jilted lover usually was responsible when a woman was found beaten — or worse.

Magnus, however, was frowning, and this time it was he who moved towards the sofa, staring at it so intently Bryn could tell he was trying to picture the dead woman who had lain there.

'You both seem so convinced there was foul play involved in Anne-Laure Chevalier's death,' he said, 'and I can't help but think that perhaps this is because you were both on the scene that morning. I want to think that perhaps you noticed something subconsciously, and you haven't quite realised its significance yet, but I'm afraid I think it's more likely that, because you saw her, you're both more emotionally attached to this woman than I am, and so you're looking to make sense of her death. Because at this stage, although I admit it's all very strange, I'm just not convinced she was killed deliberately.'

Simultaneously, Bryn and Rafaela opened their mouths to object, but Magnus held up a hand.

'No, listen,' he said, 'I don't want to think about bruising or lost evidence or bad boyfriends anymore, I want to think about this: if Anne-Laure

Chevalier was murdered, why was it done at such a public event in such a public place? Surely it would be far easier to do it in private, where the body could be quietly disposed of? Why leave her lying around? And what you're both suggesting — the theory that she was coerced into overdosing — is not a crime of passion, but a cold and calculated move, and therefore not likely to have been carried out by an emotionally-unstable and violent ex-lover. And if she wasn't killed by a bad boyfriend, well then, what possible motive could somebody have for doing away with an apparently harmless party girl from Westminster? I'm afraid, as far as I'm concerned, the idea that she was murdered just doesn't make sense.'

Bryn could see where Magnus was coming from, and perhaps the barrister was right; he and Rafaela probably had been more affected by the sight of Anne-Laure lying on the sofa like a sleeping beauty who would never wake up. But still, they knew next to nothing about the dead woman, so he didn't exactly agree with Magnus' point that, aside from a spurned lover, nobody had had any reason to kill her. Who knew what Anne-Laure had been mixed up in before her death?

Bryn was about to point this out to the barrister when the double doors at the other end of the long table opened and Edwin Brackenwell came trotting back into business conference room.

'So sorry, gentlemen, so sorry!' he panted; evidently, he had dashed back to them straight after his phone call. 'Central Square Properties are, as you know, a demanding…'

He trailed off, his simpering expression morphing into one of anger.

'Rafaela!' he exclaimed. 'What are you doing in here?'

Bryn expected the cleaner to shrink under her boss' glare, but instead she straightened up and regarded him coolly.

'I was *trying* to clean,' she said. 'I was *told* this room would be empty…'

'Our fault entirely,' said Magnus easily, 'because, of course, we showed up without an appointment. Anyway, I think my colleague and I now have a feel for the place, so we'll let your cleaner get on.'

Edwin's eyes flickered between Magnus and Bryn, Rafaela and the sofa a few times, and the police constable could see that a small part of him was truly worried about what had occurred in his absence. But then he shook his head.

'Of course, Mr Walterson, Mr Summers. I'll accompany you back to reception, shall I? And Rafaela, just — just get on with it, will you?'

As Edwin led Magnus away, Bryn shot a grateful look over his shoulder at Rafaela, who was scowling at the departing form of the hotel manager. Bryn was pleased they'd had the chance to speak to her because, despite what Magnus said, Rafaela's certainty than Anne-Laure's death had been suspicious made his own opinions on the matter sound less outlandish.

Back at reception, Penelope greeted him with a much sunnier smile than he had been afforded upon entering the hotel, before fluttering her eyelashes at Magnus.

'How did you find our facilities, gentlemen?' she asked.

'Oh, very nice,' said Magnus.

Edwin gave a little squeak of pleasure. 'Wonderful, wonderful!' he cried. 'I'll go and get the paperwork then, shall I? So we can *seal the deal*, as it were! *Aha*!'

'Sorry, paperwork for what?' asked Magnus, looking politely puzzled.

'For hiring the business conference room, of course!'

'You are funny, Mr Walterson!' added Penelope, with a throaty, seductive laugh.

Magnus looked at Bryn, who had to bite the insides of his cheek to stop himself from laughing, and then went, 'Excuse me, I don't remember saying I was definitely going to hire the business conference room?'

Mirth froze on Edwin's face, making him look oddly grotesque.

'But — but you just said — you said it was very nice,' he stammered.

'Ah, yes. I see how this misunderstanding has come about,' smiled Magnus. 'Yes, you're quite right, the business conference room of the Royal West Hotel is exactly what I'm looking for.'

'So what's the problem?' wailed Edwin.

'I'm afraid it's the staff of the Royal West Hotel who I've found lacking,' replied Magnus, keeping his tone light and pleasant.

'Are you talking about that Rafaela woman?' Edwin growled.

'I'm talking about *you*, Mr Brackenwell. You and Penelope here, who were extremely rude to my colleague upon his arrival. As such, I can't give you our business, because I can't be sure you won't treat our esteemed clients in the same way. So I thank you for your time, and wish you both a goodnight.'

He nodded, turned on his heel, and walked back towards the entranceway. Bryn then took a couple of seconds to enjoy the shocked expressions on the faces of the hotel's General Manager and receptionist, before following Magnus out of the Royal West.

CHAPTER ELEVEN

Following Magnus' declaration at the Royal West Hotel that he still didn't believe Anne-Laure had been murdered, Bryn was surprised that the barrister agreed to continue helping him with his inquiry.

'I said I would assist you and I will,' said Magnus, when Bryn brought this up with him. 'At least, for a little while longer. Because we have a clear plan, don't we? To probe Vasyl Kosnitschev and Dame Winifred Rye about Anne-Laure's relationships, and about her movements on the day of her death. I also think it would be useful to try and find out a little more about her as a person. If we're still coming up against dead ends after that, well, I might take a step back. But let's see what we can find out this evening, eh?'

The police constable nodded gratefully. As the episode in the hotel had demonstrated, Magnus was a useful ally to have in Westminster Square, especially when he himself was out of uniform.

'Do you think Vasyl Kosnitschev will mind us dropping in on him like this?' he asked, for they were currently walking towards the Ukrainian's house, which was situated on the south side of Westminster Square, not far from Magnus' own flat. 'I mean, we haven't given him any notice…'

'I expect he will mind,' replied the barrister. 'He's not the most cheerful or friendly of men. But at least we now have an excuse for the call.'

He was referring to a discovery Bryn had made shortly after their trip to the Royal West: in an idle moment at work, when looking through recent police records for Westminster Square, Bryn had discovered there had been two attempted burglaries in the quadrant in the week preceding Anne-Laure's death: one at the main residence of Dame Winifred Rye, and the other, a few days later, at Hilda Underpin's flat.

Upon discovering these crimes, Bryn's imagination had gone into overdrive, because he thought they might be somehow linked to

Anne-Laure's death. But on closer inspection, it seemed as though the burglaries had been unsuccessful, for neither Dame Winifred nor Hilda had reported anything as being missing (although Hilda had obviously been apoplectic about the incident, for her ranting had been noted in painstaking detail by the officer on duty). Furthermore, after Bryn had told Magnus about the crimes, the barrister had been surprisingly blasé.

'I'm afraid burglaries are not uncommon around here,' he had said, 'given the obvious wealth of the area and its residents. I expect some opportunist targeted Winifred and Hilda because he thought they were defenceless old ladies with lots of jewels, which is probably true, but he must have been scared off by their high-tech alarms. If there's one thing CSP are good for, it's security.'

Bryn had been disappointed to hear the burglaries being explained away so rationally, although his discovery had given Magnus an idea as to how to proceed with their investigation. Seeing as Bryn was still forbidden from asking questions about Anne-Laure Chevalier by Boyle, they would need a cover story with which to approach Vasyl and Dame Winifred, and it made no sense for two lawyers to suddenly descend upon these Westminster Square residents for no apparent reason. Magnus' suggestion, therefore, was to pretend he was concerned about this recent spate of burglaries, and so — as a worried member of the community — had appointed himself as kind of unofficial neighbourhood watch figure, who was trying to improve the security of the area with the help of a junior policeman.

With this pretext, Magnus and Bryn approached the house belonging to Vasyl Kosnitschev. The oligarch was, according to Magnus, one of the few people on Westminster Square who owned an entire house, rather than a converted flat.

'And that should give you some indication of how rich he is,' said Magnus now, as he walked beneath the pillared entranceway and rang the doorbell.

As they waited for an answer, Bryn found he was looking forward to seeing the interior of this property. After all, he had visited a number of Westminster Square addresses during the period he had interviewed the various doormen, but they had all been divided into flats, just like Magnus' home. But because Vasyl Kosnitschev's building had remained a house, Bryn thought it likely it was one of London's most authentic examples of a nineteenth-century interior.

He realised how wrong he was as soon as a cowering butler beckoned them into the building. Far from the clean and elegant space of Bryn's imaginings, Vasyl Kosnitschev's hallway was in a state of complete disarray. The floor was covered with dust sheets; one of the walls was streaked with various shades of paint, as though someone had been trying to choose a colour; half of the banister seemed to be missing from the grand staircase; and — worst of all — most of a wall had been knocked down between the hallway and the neighbouring room.

In the midst of this chaos stood a middle-aged man in a pale suit, whom Bryn assumed was Vasyl himself. He had a beaky nose, bad skin and a stony expression, all of which made him seem thoroughly unapproachable, even intimidating. It was odd, therefore, that at the moment the policeman clapped eyes on the Ukrainian oligarch, he seemed to be receiving a thorough dressing-down by a petite young woman with shiny, chestnut-coloured hair.

'You didn't go through the proper processes!' she was shouting, in a shrill, plummy voice. 'You didn't seek any kind of permission to do this! Are you not aware that this is a Grade II-listed building? Do you not understand it has *significant* historical importance?'

'My goodness,' said Magnus, looking around at the mess.

He spoke quietly, but at his words Vasyl half-turned, noticing them for the first time.

'Magnus,' he said, before adding, in what Bryn thought was a colossal understatement, 'now is not a good time.'

'It's all right, I'll wait,' replied the barrister, smiling.

This was evidently not what Vasyl had intended, but Bryn was beginning to think that Magnus liked to deliberately misunderstand people to achieve his ends. He was reminded of the way Magnus had talked to Edwin Brackenwell and his snooty receptionist Penelope at the Royal West, using an agreeable kind of firmness to put them in their place. Perhaps this was what made Magnus such a formidable barrister, Bryn thought: he never allowed a confrontation to become unpleasant. Could he, as a policeman, cultivate a similar sort of manner?

If Vasyl still objected to their continued presence in his house, he did not have a chance to say so, for the young woman was soon berating him once again.

'You're destroyed all of the friezes, all of the carvings! I've never seen anything like this in all my years with CSP!' she cried, as though she were closer to the age of fifty than twenty-five. 'What made you *think* you could do this?'

'It is my house, Lavender, I can knock down a few walls if I want to.'

'It is *not* your house!' she shouted. 'You live in this building as a result of a generous twenty-year lease from CSP, on the understanding that you respect and retain its historical character! Doing all of *this* —' She gestured around at the hallway with a grimace, as though she could hardly bear to look at it. 'Doing all of *this* is in complete contradiction to the terms of your lease!'

Bryn thought she seemed close to tears, although ones of frustration and rage as opposed to distress. Vasyl, however, looked stubborn.

'I do not think it is,' he said. 'I think I am entitled to redecorate.'

'You most certainly are *not*,' spat Lavender of Central Square Properties, 'and if you'd read the paperwork of your lease agreement properly, you would know this. Perhaps, Mr Kosnitschev, you will pay more attention to the correspondence you will now be sent by our lawyers!'

And with that, she spun around and headed for the door, the dramatic effect of which was somewhat dampened by the fact that the heels of her shoes kept catching in the dust sheet.

'Oh dear,' said Magnus mildly, as he, Bryn, Vasyl and the butler watched Lavender totter down the front steps of the house and out of sight. 'I'm afraid you might be in a bit of hot water there, Vasyl.'

The oligarch scowled. 'What do you want, Magnus?'

'Just a quick word about neighbourhood security.'

'Oh, for God's sake...' growled Vasyl.

Undeterred, Magnus continued, 'This is Bryn Summers, one of our local policemen, with whom I'm working on a small project to decrease crime in Westminster Square and protect the wellbeing of its residents. You see, there have been a couple of break-ins over the past few weeks, and we're hoping to —'

'All right, all right!' interrupted Vasyl, obviously realising it was easier to agree than be subjected to the whole of the barrister's spiel. 'I will give you ten minutes. But with this and your battle against those maintenance charges, I am starting to think you need a hobby, Magnus... Come on, this way.'

He led them through the large hole in the wall and into the next room, which Bryn thought was probably some kind of salon, although it was difficult to tell what everything was under the dust sheets.

'Sit,' instructed Vasyl.

Hesitantly, Bryn lowered himself onto what he hoped was a sofa. Magnus settled beside him.

'Tea?' demanded the oligarch. 'Coffee? Horilka?'

'Horilka?'

'It is a Ukrainian spirit, a little like vodka.'

'Tea would be perfect,' said Magnus.

'Yes, for me too, please,' said Bryn quickly, anxious to avoid the Horilka.

Vasyl nodded towards the butler, who had crept into the room after them, and then he too sat on an armchair-shaped dust sheet. Clasping his bony fingers together, he said, 'I do not know how I can help you. I have not heard about any break-ins around Westminster Square. Who was targeted?'

'Dame Winifred Rye was hit a little while ago, and then Hilda Underpin a few days after that,' said Magnus.

'Well, she deserves it,' said Vasyl, before clarifying, 'Hilda, I mean. What did they take?'

'Apparently nothing.'

'That is a shame. It would be good to see that old witch lose a few jewels or whatever she has stashed away up there. Probably Nazi gold.'

Vasyl seemed to have no problem speaking so pugnaciously in front of a policeman and a barrister, just as he saw no problem in tinkering with a historically-significant building. Bryn supposed this arrogance had its roots in his immense wealth.

'So you haven't noticed anyone suspicious loitering around the Square?' asked Magnus. 'And as far as you're aware, nobody's attempted to break into this house?'

'No,' said Vasyl, his expression darkening. 'Although I would like to see them try. I have a very interesting collection of Soviet firearms upstairs, some of which may still work.'

While Magnus raised his eyebrows, Bryn muttered, 'I'll pretend I didn't hear that…'

But Vasyl shrugged, once again completely unconcerned by the policeman's presence.

'Of course, we always have to remain vigilant,' said Magnus, 'but because there's been so much media attention on the Square recently, it might be an idea to be extra cautious of our houses and valuables.'

Bryn thought this was a rather clever way of steering the conversation towards Anne-Laure, but Vasyl didn't seem to understand what Magnus was getting at. 'Media attention?' he asked.

'Yes,' said Magnus, 'following the death of that poor young woman, Anne-Laure Chevalier.'

'Ah,' said Vasyl, and although Bryn watched him closely for a reaction, it was difficult to identify any change in his naturally surly expression. 'I see what you mean.'

Unfortunately, the butler chose that moment to return bearing a tray with two cups of tea and a glass of amber-coloured liquid, which was presumably Horilka. Going by the smell of the steam emanating from his cup, Bryn thought he had been served a herbal, possibly lemon-flavoured tea, although when he took a sip he almost gagged: it was very bitter and earthy-tasting, a little like how he imagined tree bark must taste. Quietly, he replaced the cup on whatever the sheet at his feet was covering.

Vasyl, meanwhile, took a large glug of his Horilka and said, 'I am away a lot, so I do not always follow the British news. I did not know everyone was so concerned about Anna's death.'

'Anna?'

'It is what I called her. It is a nicer name than Anne, I think — someone like her did not deserve to be known by something so plain.'

Although this was probably the nicest thing Vasyl had said since they arrived, Bryn could not help but be a little bothered by it.

'Her name was actually Anne-Laure,' he pointed out.

'I do not see why someone needs two first names,' said Vasyl, before adding decisively, 'No, Anna was better.'

'She worked for you, if I remember rightly?' said Magnus, before Bryn could object.

'Yes.'

'Organising your events?'

'Yes.'

He was not giving much away, but Magnus persisted regardless. 'Is that all she did for you?'

'No,' said the Ukrainian, with a heavy sigh. 'Anna did a lot for me. She was in charge of my PR. At least, my PR in this country.'

'And what did that entail, exactly?'

'Various duties. My phone calls were diverted to her flat, she handled my letters and faxes, sometimes she drove me to meetings or ran errands on my behalf. For a few hours a day, she was a presence I could rely upon in London. As I said, I am away a lot. I often travel to South East Asia and South America for business, so I needed someone to — how do you put it? — *mind the fort* while I was gone.'

'Excuse me,' broke in Bryn, 'but may I ask what it is you do, Mr Kosnitschev?'

Vasyl gave him a swift, searching look, and Bryn had the impression he had just remembered that one of his guests was a policeman.

'Back in the Ukraine, I made a lot of money from real estate, and then from speculations on mining — bauxite, steel, palladium, that sort of thing. I also went into oil and shipping, the usual. After I moved to London, I began to trade these goods worldwide. That is why I travel, you see. I do not trust anyone to do this work for me, I would rather trust someone to stay here and mind my affairs, and that is what Anna did.'

'And how long had she been doing that?' asked Magnus.

'A number of years. Maybe six or seven? She came searching for me here, rang the bell and introduced herself. I would not normally give jobs to random women who turn up on my doorstep uninvited, but I was in need of someone to handle my PR, and I could tell there was something about Anna.'

'What do you mean?' asked Bryn, his curiosity getting the better of him. 'What was she like?'

'Smart,' said Vasyl at once. 'Organised. Capable. Quick. She was good at her job, very good. Her death has been a blow to me.'

From the way he talked, it was clear Vasyl meant in the professional sense, rather than the personal one.

'You make her sound a little like a robot,' Magnus observed.

'Do I?' Vasyl looked almost amused. 'Well, she was not like that. She could be charming when she wanted to be — very charming — and of course she was beautiful. Although I hired her for her professionalism, her looks and personality certainly helped win over many of my clients and business associates. You know, behind every big businessman there is always a woman like Anna, taking care of the details. And she was one of the best.'

'You said you trusted her?'

'Yes. She was sensible, practical. You know, she told me not to do all of this...' He gestured around at the rubble and the dust sheets. 'She practically begged me to rethink my decoration plans, or at least hire decorators who knew the law. She warned me it would anger CSP, and I would end up shelling out millions to fix it...' He sighed. 'She was probably right, but I went ahead and did it anyway. I was rather annoyed with her, you see — for suddenly dying like that.'

Bryn did not know whether or not to laugh: he wasn't sure whether Vasyl was in earnest. However the Ukrainian, upon seeing his uncertain expression, clicked his tongue in disapproval.

'I am joking,' he said, without so much as a smile. 'Anna's death... It is a loss. The more time passes, the more I realise what she meant to me.'

Magnus pounced upon this ambiguous statement. 'Your relationship with Anne-Laure, was it... purely professional?'

'What do you mean?'

Bryn shifted uncomfortably upon his dust sheet: Magnus was trying to ask the question he himself had been wondering, but would not have actually dared to ask the Ukrainian oligarch.

'I mean, did you have a friendship outside of work?'

'Not really, no.'

'Did you ever have a sexual relationship?'

For the first time that evening, the surly Vasyl Kosnitschev looked genuinely angry.

'Do you really think I would jeopardise my *professional* relationship with Anna by sleeping with her?' he snapped.

'She was very beautiful.'

'But she was not the only beautiful girl in London. Do you know how much money I have? I know I am no — what is the name of that stupid actor who lives around here?'

'Jem McMorran,' Bryn supplied helpfully.

'I know I am no Jem McMorran when it comes to looks, but plenty of women are attracted to fat wallets, in my experience. So why would I mess around with Anna?' Vasyl seemed to find the direction this conversation had taken extremely distasteful. 'Why are you even asking me this? I thought you came around to talk about the burglaries!'

Bryn's heart gave a lurch of fear, for he thought Vasyl had seen through their ploy, but Magnus remained calm.

'To be perfectly honest with you, Vasyl, Anne-Laure's death needs to be taken into consideration when we're talking about the security of Westminster Square. As we've discussed, it's brought a lot of media attention upon us, and we still don't have any answers as to how she actually died...'

'It was natural causes, was it not?'

'Yes, but what does that mean?' mused Magnus.

Vasyl shrugged. 'Why do you not ask your policeman friend here?'

'Oh, I haven't dealt with the case,' said Bryn quickly, 'and my superior officers aren't giving anything away.'

'Don't you think, considering how young she was, Anne-Laure's death was a bit... unusual?' asked Magnus.

'I suppose so,' said Vasyl.

He appeared supremely indifferent to finding out exactly what had happened to his employee. Bryn supposed this was because he was a pragmatic man: Anne-Laure could not be brought back to life, so what was the point in dwelling on her death?

'When you first heard she was dead, what did you think had happened to her?' asked Magnus.

Vasyl scratched at his chin. 'I suppose I thought she had been in some kind of accident,' he said thoughtfully. 'She did not seem ill to me.'

'Did you consider her death might have been suicide?' continued the barrister, and Bryn had to work hard not to give any indication of his frustration.

'Suicide?' Vasyl's brow furrowed, as though he hardly knew what the word meant. 'No, that cannot be it.'

'So she didn't seem unhappy to you?'

'Oh, I did not say that. There was always an air of unhappiness about Anna. No, not unhappiness, exactly — what is the right word? *Melancholy*. I do not think she was fond of her life in Westminster Square.'

'So perhaps she decided to end it?'

'No, I do not think so,' said Vasyl, 'because there was a change in her, over the last couple of years. She seemed... brighter. I thought she might be planning to move away, or maybe she was in love — I do not know, I cannot pretend to understand the emotions of women. But she did not seem suicidal, quite the opposite, in fact.'

Upon hearing this, Bryn was tempted to throw a triumphant glance in Magnus' direction, although he managed to restrain himself. In any case, the barrister looked rather flummoxed by what Vasyl had said, which was unsurprising given it contradicted his own theories.

Taking over the questioning himself, and keen to find out more about Anne-Laure as a person, Bryn asked, 'What did you know about her life outside of her work?'

'Nothing.'

'Nothing at all?'

'Well, I know she lived nearby, in one of Dame Winifred's flats in the Mews. I know she was English, in spite of her name. And I know that she was good at her job. Other than that... nothing.'

'Do you know if she had a boyfriend?'

'Why would I know that?'

'You must have spent quite a lot of time with her. Didn't you learn anything about her personal life?'

'I already told you, we were not friends,' said Vasyl impatiently. 'Anna kept herself to herself. I liked that about her. She did not babble on all day like most women...'

As though struck by sudden inspiration, Magnus leaned forward on the dust sheet.

'You said earlier she only worked for you for a few hours a day —'

'For which she was generously compensated,' said Vasyl, suddenly defensive.

'I don't doubt that,' said Magnus smoothly. 'But if she only worked for you part-time, what did she do with the rest of her day?'

'She had other jobs,' said Vasyl, as though this were obvious.

'Did she? You know that for sure?'

'Not exactly, no. But she was always making phone calls, rushing off to places... Anna was always busy.'

'Doing what?'

'Again, why would I know that? I assume it was more events work. You know she planned that party for Dame Winifred, the one she died at?'

This time, it was Bryn's turn to spot an opportunity. 'Were you there?' he asked.

'Yes,' said Vasyl, looking ever sourer than usual. 'It was not an enjoyable evening. I do not like these... *social* parties. I cannot stand small talk, I would rather discuss business.'

'Did you see her at the party?' continued Bryn.

'A little.'

'And did you notice anything different about her that night? Or did you maybe see who she spent the most time with?'

'No. I have to admit, I was slightly annoyed with her that night. The party had taken up too much of her time and attention when I needed her, so I am afraid I ignored Anna for most of the evening. I regret that now, of course, but I did not know I would never see her again.'

For a moment, Bryn thought he did look genuinely rueful.

'What time did you leave this party?' asked Magnus.

'Early, maybe around ten, ten-thirty. I remember because I had to make a business call to Argentina...' Vasyl trailed off, his eyes suddenly narrowing with suspicion. 'Why? Why are you asking me all of these questions? You are talking as though Anna's death was suspicious!'

Again, Bryn felt a flutter of anxiety, but Magnus merely laughed.

'I do apologise, Vasyl. I am obviously getting a little carried away with this new role of mine. Perhaps you're right — perhaps I do need a proper hobby!'

As the barrister chuckled, Vasyl managed a smile. 'As I said, Magnus, I cannot help you with these burglaries. I have seen nobody loitering around my house or in the Square, although I admit I am away a lot. But I wish you luck with this project.'

'Thank you,' said Magnus. Then, perhaps recognising this was his cue to leave, he rose from the dust sheet-covered sofa.

Bryn, hurrying to do the same, said, 'Thank you for your time, Mr Kosnitschev. I'll be making a note of what you've told us.'

The Ukrainian shrugged; apparently he did not care whether he was a responsible member of the local community or not. 'I will show you out,' he said.

They walked back through the hole in the wall and Bryn once more found himself standing amongst the mess of the hallway.

'Out of interest,' said Magnus, looking around, 'how exactly are you planning to redecorate this space, Vasyl? Assuming CSP don't stop you?'

The oligarch looked almost pleased to have been asked this question. 'I would like to make it less — what is the word? — *fussy*. I want to knock all of this through so there is just one big room downstairs, and I want to get rid of all these silly frills and details.' He gestured up at the floral-patterned stucco on the ceiling with an expression of disgust.

'Sounds nice and... contemporary,' said Magnus, after a small hesitation, while Bryn wondered why Vasyl hadn't simply bought a modern house or even penthouse instead. But then, he supposed the provenance of Westminster Square was probably too much to resist for wealthy individuals like Vasyl Kosnitschev, who could afford to buy property here.

'Yes, I am thinking of introducing some more contemporary touches,' continued their host, warming to his subject now. 'I have a friend back in the Ukraine who makes furniture out of old shipping materials, so I am thinking of commissioning him to do a few steel chairs and so on for me. Then another contact is a painter of murals, so I would like him to create a few urban scenes of Kiev and Odessa for my walls, so I have some of my country with me here. I would also like him to paint scenes of shipping and maybe mining too. I am very interested in industry, as I told you before.'

'Wow,' said Magnus, in a choked sort of voice. He looked as though he wanted to say more, but all he could manage was, 'Gosh!'

'Yes,' said Vasyl, looking happier than he had done all evening as he showed them towards the door, 'I think it will be a very rewarding project, as long as I can make CSP see sense.'

'Well, good luck!' said Magnus, and Bryn was fairly sure he could detect sarcasm in the barrister's voice.

'And thank you for your help this evening!' added the police constable, as the butler closed the door behind them.

Magnus and Bryn then walked a few paces along the south side of Westminster Square in silence until, when they had reached a safe distance from Vasyl Kosnitschev's house, Magnus burst out laughing.

'My God, what an absolute loon!' spluttered the barrister, tears of laughter springing to his eyes. 'Does he really think CSP would ever approve of his mad plans? I think they'd rather have that house burned to the ground than allow murals of mining and shipping scenes to besmirch its sacred walls!'

Bryn tried to smile, but not being familiar with CSP and its rules, he did not find the situation quite as funny as Magnus. Besides, he was feeling a little deflated following the meeting with the Ukrainian oligarch.

Magnus, noticing this air of dejection, managed to control his mirth to ask, 'What's the matter?'

'Oh, nothing. I just can't help but think that was a rather a waste of time...'

'Do you really think so?' asked Magnus, dabbing at his streaming eyes with a handkerchief.

'Don't you?'

Magnus looked up at the line of buildings ahead of them. When Bryn followed his gaze, he saw a curtain on one of the upper floors flutter against the window, as though someone had just ducked out of sight. The barrister frowned, and then took Bryn by the elbow.

'Let's do a lap of the Square while we talk,' he said, steering the policeman quickly past the house from which, if Bryn's suspicions were correct, someone had been watching them.

Again, they proceeded without talking until, once again, they reached the south-west corner of Westminster Square. Then Bryn, who was unable to rein back his curiosity any longer, asked, 'So what do you think we learned from Vasyl Kosnitschev?'

'A great deal,' said Magnus, pensively. 'For one thing, we finally managed to find out a bit about what Anne-Laure Chevalier was like as a person. Until now, all we've known about her is that she was beautiful and liked parties, which is not much to go on.'

'True,' said Bryn. 'I have to admit, I had slightly assumed she was just a fun-loving girl, but she sounds more businesslike than I expected. How did Vasyl describe her? Organised, responsible, smart —'

'And sad,' said Magnus thoughtfully. 'Or rather, *melancholy.*'

The young police constable bristled a little. 'You're not going to start on about suicide again, are you?'

'No, I'm not,' said Magnus. 'Because, from Vasyl's perspective at least, it seems unlikely she killed herself. It was interesting, what he said about her being happier before her death. I wonder if that's connected to what she said in the garden? *I'm going to be free of you, and free of Westminster Square!* Maybe you're right, Bryn — maybe she was planning on moving away.'

For a moment, Bryn felt himself puff up with pride, before Magnus immediately caused him to deflate again by continuing, 'Having said all that, I'm not sure we should entirely trust Vasyl's analysis of human emotions. This is, after all, a man who thinks it's entirely appropriate to destroy listed buildings with murals of mining. He didn't seem as though he was particularly interested in anything she said or did, only how efficiently she worked for him. So who knows what she was really feeling?'

'All right,' Bryn allowed, as they turned another corner onto the north side of the square. 'So we know a little more about Anne-Laure's personality...'

'We also know she had another job,' said Magnus, 'or perhaps a few other jobs. I think it's safe to assume Vasyl was right on that count, as she was obviously fairly well-off, and he can't have been paying her *that* much for the few hours she worked for him each day.'

'But is that relevant?' asked Bryn. 'Does it matter that she had other work?'

'Maybe,' said Magnus. 'We know she wasn't employed by Dame Winifred at least, because Winifred told Juliana the charity party was the first thing they had collaborated on for a long time. So who else was Anne-Laure doing PR or events for, and are they somehow connected to her death?'

'You are starting to think it's suspicious, aren't you?' asked Bryn.

'I'm trying not to form any opinions until we have more evidence,' replied Magnus. 'But even if, as Boyle and the medical examiner are assuming, it was a drug-related death, it would be interesting to know where she picked up that habit, and who she got her cocaine from, because I very much doubt it was Vasyl.'

'Hm,' said Bryn, in agreement.

'He became very irate when I asked whether he had been sleeping with her, didn't he?' mused Magnus.

'Do you think he was lying?' asked Bryn, doubtfully.

'I'm not sure. My instinct says no, and that he regarded Anne-Laure as one might regard a computer or a filing cabinet — she was intrinsic to his working life, but he didn't think of her outside of the office, as a person with her own life. Then again, his relentless insistence that he knew absolutely nothing about her private life is a little odd, considering he seemed to have a strange sort of respect for her, and they worked together for so long. Then of course, there's her name…'

'What, the "Anna" business?'

'Yes, that was very interesting.'

'But surely that's just a Ukrainian thing?' said Bryn. 'Maybe Anne-Laure was a bit of a mouthful for him, or he wanted to exert some power over his employee by designating her a nickname, something like that?'

'Oh yes, quite possibly,' said Magnus. 'But can't you see what I'm driving at here? Vasyl knew her as "*Anna Chevalier*". Consider the initials.'

Bryn stopped in his tracks and, without really realising what he was doing, he stared over to the other side of Westminster Square, where he could just about see the garden on the south side in which he had found a simple silver ring half-buried in the earth.

'A.C.,' he said.

CHAPTER TWELVE

Feeling they were on a roll, Magnus and Bryn decided to try and talk to Dame Winifred Rye as soon as possible. So after the barrister had rung ahead to check she was at home and willing to receive visitors (he was fairly sure turning up at an aristocrat's house out of the blue was a bad idea, especially when that house had recently been subject to a burglary), they made their way to her flat in the north-west corner of Westminster Square the very next evening.

Once more, they had decided to pretend that Magnus, as a result of the break-ins, had set himself up as an unofficial neighbourhood watch figure, in the hope that a conversation about crime would lead to one on Anne-Laure's Chevalier's death. As a further excuse for calling round, Magnus also had some paperwork for Dame Winifred to sign, which Bryn thought might regard his crusade against Central Square Properties — the police constable was a little hazy on the details. Yet in spite of these excuses to call round, Bryn still found himself being prepped by Magnus as they made their way up the north side of Westminster Square.

'As you know, Juliana spoke to Dame Winifred the Monday after it happened and... Well, Winifred was pretty upset, by the sound of it. I imagine she's calmed down a bit by now — it's been a few weeks, so the news must have sunk in, at least — but still. We might have to be sensitive with her.'

'Understood,' said Bryn, who had received plenty of police training about how to deliver bad news and cope with grieving friends and relatives.

'Furthermore,' continued Magnus, 'it might be a good idea not to mention the drugs.'

'Really?'

The barrister nodded. 'Like I told you the other day, Dame Winifred seems to have had a very high opinion of Anne-Laure. Of course, we still don't know that much about the girl, but Winifred seems to think butter wouldn't have melted in her mouth. Apparently, she completely refused to believe Anne-Laure had anything to do with drugs.'

'How do you know that?'

'Juliana tested the waters at the flower shop.'

'Again, am I working with the wrong Walterson here? Your wife has already got there before us...'

But as Magnus chuckled, Bryn reflected that the barrister had already been a huge asset to his investigation. Without him, Bryn wouldn't have been let into the Royal West, he probably would have been turned out of Vasyl Kosnitschev's house, and he wouldn't know half as much about Westminster Square and its inhabitants. No, he hoped it was clear that when he teased Magnus about the investigative prowess of his wife, he was very much joking.

After Magnus and Bryn were shown inside the building by its doorman — who was another Irishman, Bryn noted — they took the stairs up to the second floor, where they were shown inside one of the converted flats by a large, heavily-made up woman wearing a garish multi-coloured blouse and tight beige trousers that were rather unflattering on her sizeable posterior.

'Dame Winifred Rye,' she proclaimed, squashing Bryn's hand within her own.

'Bryn Summers,' he replied, 'police constable.'

'How *very* nice to meet you, dear. It's always lovely to know members of our local constabulary personally... And Magnus, a pleasure, as always. Come in, both of you, come in.'

As Magnus passed her in the doorway, Dame Winifred swooped towards him and planted a wet-looking kiss on his cheek. As she drew away, Bryn noticed a pink and orange smear on the barrister's face from her lipstick and foundation. As discreetly as possible, the police constable looked significantly at his associate and tapped at his own cheek. Fortunately,

Magnus seemed to get the message, for he took out a handkerchief and, under the guise of blowing his nose, wiped his face clean.

'Welcome to my humble abode!' trilled Dame Winifred, leading them through the flat. 'Do make yourselves comfortable, dears, and I'll fetch the tea...'

As she bustled away, Bryn looked around at the living room into which they had been shown. It featured a hodgepodge of styles: the wallpaper was dark and floral, the furniture old-fashioned and intricately carved, and the throws and cushions were made of rich red or purple-coloured velvet. It was, Bryn thought, the exact opposite of Vasyl Kosnitschev's building site of an interior.

'Goodness,' he said, quietly. 'This is all very lavish.'

'It's all very tasteless,' whispered Magnus. 'Winifred likes a designer brand, you can tell by her clothes, but I don't think she's blessed with good taste. I mean, pairing all this Victorian furniture with Art Nouveau fixtures and this William Morris wallpaper... It just doesn't *go*, and that's before you get onto all these clashing colours. You should have seen Juliana's face when she first came here, I thought she was going to explode with trying not to laugh. But having said that, Juliana has turned our flat into a veritable jungle, so I suppose we can't judge...'

'What's this about Juliana?' asked Dame Winifred, shuffling back into the room with a tea tray and causing Magnus to give a guilty start.

'Oh, erm, she sends her love,' said the barrister quickly.

'*Dear* Juliana,' smiled Dame Winifred, 'how is she? And the children?'

'Oh, they're all very well, thank you.'

'And how's that pretty little girl who works with her in the Station Garden? Daisy, is it?'

'Erm, yes,' said Magnus. 'I think she's fine too.'

'She's very sweet, that child — like a little flower herself. Although daisies are very common, you know, she'd be better off being called Jasmine or Dahlia...'

Magnus clearly didn't know how to respond to this, so he said nothing. Bryn recalled what the barrister had told him about Dame Winifred being fond of young people, and wondered whether she had children of her own. Somehow, he suspected not.

'Tea?' asked Dame Winifred, hovering over them with a Blue Arden teapot.

'Yes please,' said Magnus, holding up his cup and saucer while Bryn hesitated, the bitter taste of Vasyl's tea still on his tongue. Then, as though he had read his mind, Magnus said, 'Winifred always has the best beverages.'

'It's because I buy it all from Fortnum and Mason,' said the aristocrat, carelessly slopping the tea over the sides of the cups and onto the saucers as she poured. 'And I can never resist their biscuits either — do help yourself, by the way.'

Bryn did not need telling twice, and eagerly he reached for what turned out to be a spicy ginger snap. He crunched on it contentedly for a few minutes while Magnus took out a document from his briefcase and began to explain to Dame Winifred that he was organising a petition protesting against the high maintenance costs Central Square Properties were charging Westminster Square's residents.

'Of course, you're under no obligation to sign this,' the barrister said, 'but as you weren't able to make the meeting the other week, I thought I might as well fill you in and give you the opportunity to make your voice heard...'

'Oh no, I'd like to sign it,' said Dame Winifred, tweaking the document from Magnus' hand with crummy fingers and putting on a pair of purple reading glasses in order to study it more closely. 'Let's see, who else is here? The Wilkinsons and the Haylanders. Oh, and Lord Ellington, that's a bit of a surprise!'

'Yes, I thought so too,' agreed Magnus.

'He doesn't like to rock the boat when it comes to CSP,' Dame Winifred explained to Bryn, although he hadn't the faintest clue who they were talking about. 'Bevis Ellington always wants to be on the right side of those with a bit of power because he's a dreadful snob. But you managed to convince him, Magnus, well done!'

'I think it was more that he succumbed to peer pressure, to be perfectly honest.'

'Oh, well, at least his name's down,' she said, reaching for a glittery pen and scrawling her signature at the bottom of the page, 'and now so is mine.'

'Thank you, Winifred, that's very much appreciated.'

'Not at all, not at all. Don't forget, dear, I own a number of properties in the Mews as well, so I'm charged a ridiculous amount each month…'

She sighed and reached out towards the plate on the coffee table, before cramming a whole biscuit into her mouth. At the mention of the Mews, Bryn sat up a little straighter, wondering whether this was the point to start talking about Dame Winifred's former tenant, but Magnus gave an almost imperceptible shake of the head.

'Winifred, as I told you on the phone, Bryn and I are also working towards improving the security of Westminster Square. I understand you were subject to a break-in a few weeks ago…?'

'Oh yes,' said Winifred, with a dismissive wave of her chubby hand, 'but as I told the police, nothing was taken.'

This seemed to Bryn a very blasé attitude to have towards an attempted burglary, especially from someone who lived alone.

Perhaps Dame Winifred sensed this from their expressions, because she went on, 'Look, I have valuables, I don't deny that, but you should see the safe where I keep most of them. You need two keys and a combination code to get in, and I doubt even an explosive device would be able to make much of a dent in it. I expect this person, whoever he was, took one look at that safe and realised it wasn't worth the effort. And as I slept through the whole thing, I'm not particularly traumatised by the experience.'

'You say *most* of your valuables are in that safe?' said Magnus.

'Oh, I don't mean the rest are lying around. No, they're locked away in a safe deposit box elsewhere in London, and nobody but me is getting into *that*.'

'How did you know there had been a break-in if you slept through it and nothing had been taken?' asked Bryn, who had a sneaking suspicion that the ageing aristocrat might have simply dreamed up this story to entertain herself.

'The lock on the front door had been forced, and some of my things had been moved, as though the would-be thief had been searching through them. But there were no fingerprints, as it surely says in the police report. Anyway, these things happen. I sincerely doubt he'll come back…'

'Were you aware that the same thing happened to Hilda Underpin a few days later?' asked Magnus.

Upon hearing this, Dame Winifred looked so shocked it was almost comical: her eyes widened, her hand clutched at her chest and her pink mouth dropped open.

'Hilda was burgled? Just after me?'

Bryn nodded. 'Again though, nothing was taken.'

'How *odd*!' breathed the aristocrat. 'Does she have a safe too, perhaps?'

'I'm not sure about that,' continued Bryn. 'She, unlike you, made a big fuss about it, although with nothing taken and no clues as to who the perpetrator of both of these incidents is, there's not an awful lot we can do…'.

'Of course,' said Dame Winifred, helping herself to a third biscuit. 'But you don't think… No, I'm being silly.'

'What is it?' asked Magnus, leaning forward on the sofa.

Dame Winifred munched on her biscuit for a few moments before saying, 'I'm sure you'll think I'm being ridiculous, but you don't think these burglaries have anything to do with my poor Anne-Laure's death, do you?'

Bryn exchanged a look with Magnus, and he could tell from the barrister's expression that he too was surprised how easy it had been to steer the conversation towards Anne-Laure.

'What do you mean, exactly?' Magnus asked.

'Well,' she said, 'I've been going over and over it in my head, ever since it happened, and I just can't believe that lovely, healthy girl was ill. No, I think it's much more likely that she had some sort of accident, or…' The aristocrat hesitated, looking embarrassed. 'Or perhaps her death is somehow connected to these attempted burglaries.'

'Go on,' said Bryn, encouragingly.

'Well, if someone was sniffing around Westminster Square, they were bound to stumble upon the Royal West sooner or later. I would imagine there is a lot of money in those tills, and of course the hotel is full of antiques, paintings, expensive silverware and so on. So my theory is, this thief targeted the Royal West that Saturday night, slipping in unnoticed during my party and hiding somewhere until we all went home. Then he crept out to steal the candlesticks or whatever it was he wanted when he thought everyone was asleep. Only, Anne-Laure didn't go home until much later, so perhaps she disturbed him in the act, and he was forced to silence her? Perhaps there was a tussle that got out of hand? Perhaps...' But Winifred trailed off, shuddering. 'I know it all sounds very far-fetched — you probably think I'm being ridiculous.'

'No,' said Bryn quickly, thinking that this theory of Winifred's was no less outlandish than some of his own.

'But it does seem unlikely,' said Magnus gently. 'Nothing was reported stolen from the Royal West.'

'Yes, but after the altercation with Anne-Laure, this burglar might have become spooked and run off,' said Winifred.

'Did you see anyone suspicious creeping about your party?' asked Magnus.

'Well... no,' she admitted. 'But I was very busy, and there were a lot of people, so I certainly could have missed him.'

Magnus nodded, but his sympathetic expression suggested he was not convinced. 'If what my friend in the police here has told me is correct,' he said, indicating Bryn, 'Anne-Laure can't have suffered a violent death. She had no head trauma, no wounds on her body...'

Apart from all the bruising, thought Bryn, although he didn't think it would be helpful to bring this up in front of Dame Winifred.

'Well, of course I'm glad to hear that,' she said. 'I would sleep much easier knowing she had simply slipped away, or it had been quick and she hadn't known a thing about what was happening. I hope it *was* natural causes, is what I'm trying to say. But I'm afraid I can't help dwelling on it all... She was so *young*.'

She blinked back the tears that had sprung up, causing her clumpy mascara to smudge the skin around her eyes.

'You knew her when she first came to London, didn't you?' asked Magnus. 'Juliana told me you offered her one of your flats in the Mews for a very reduced rate?'

'Yes,' said Dame Winifred, a melancholic expression coming over her teary features. 'Although actually, it was me who convinced her to move to London in the first place.'

'Really?'

'Yes, about ten years ago now. I used to go to Brighton every couple of weekends to walk along the beach. On the day I met her, I had rather misjudged the weather, because as the train pulled into Brighton station, the clouds were turning black and it started to rain. Still, I was younger back then, of course, and hardier too, so I decided to walk along the beach anyway — I suppose I hoped the wind and rain would blow away the cobwebs of London! But I quickly realised I'd made a mistake. I was freezing half to death out there, so after I discovered one of those brightly-coloured beach huts had been left open, I took shelter there.

'I had been huddled there not five minutes before this girl knocked at the door and asked whether she could shelter inside as well. Naturally, I would have said yes to anybody — the weather was filthy, after all — but I admit I was rather taken with her. She was seventeen at the time, and very pretty, despite being soaked to the skin. She was a natural blonde, you know, which is rare. But it wasn't just her looks that caught my attention, it was more this aura of innocence she had. I almost thought a rather bedraggled angel had appeared in the hut that day...' She trailed off, a bittersweet smile on her overly made-up mouth. 'Anyway, she introduced herself as Annie Chambers and —'

'Wait, what?' interrupted Bryn.

'Sorry?' said Dame Winifred.

'We were under the impression you were telling us the story of how you met Anne-Laure Chevalier,' said Magnus.

'I am,' said Winifred, looking surprised. 'Annie Chambers was her real name, didn't you know?'

'No,' said Bryn, reflecting — not for the first time — how little they knew about the dead woman.

'She changed it not long after moving to London,' said Winifred. 'I'm not sure why she went for something quite so French — perhaps she thought it sounded sophisticated — but I wasn't surprised when she cast off Annie Chambers.'

'Why not?' asked Magnus.

'I'm afraid you're getting ahead of the story,' said the aristocrat, with mock severity. 'Do you want to know how and why she moved to London or not?'

'Yes,' said Magnus and Bryn together.

Dame Winifred took another sip of tea. In spite of her obvious grief, she seemed to be rather enjoying herself, and Bryn wondered how often she received visitors. Perhaps her habit of throwing fundraising parties was born from loneliness.

'Back in that beach hut, I got talking to Anne-Laure,' continued Dame Winifred, before adding as an aside, 'I always called her Anne-Laure, it's very hard for me to think she was ever Annie Chambers... Anyway, we fell into conversation, and she started telling me about her life, and it was just the saddest story. As I said, she was about seventeen, and it turned out a number of years beforehand both of her parents had been killed in a car accident. I still shudder to think of it: can you imagine anything quite so dreadful? So this poor girl had been shunted between foster homes for a few years, until finally she'd been taken in by her aunt, who sounded like a bitter old spinster to me, although Anne-Laure was far too polite to say so. That was what was so extraordinary about her, you see; she'd had this terrible start in life, and yet she seemed unsullied by it. She didn't have a bad word to say about anyone, or anything; she was just sweet and pure, if a little sad — although that was understandable, under the circumstances.'

Bryn found himself nodding, and recalled what Vasyl had told them a few days ago: "*There was always an air of unhappiness about Anna…*" The Ukrainian oligarch had attributed this melancholy to her dissatisfaction with life in Westminster Square, but perhaps it ran deeper than that, and was connected to this grief she had experienced as a child.

'Yes, she was still full of hope, and still fully aware her whole life was in front of her,' continued Dame Winifred, before chuckling, 'She told me she wanted to be an actress, isn't that funny? Although I suppose that's what most young girls want to do these days… Anyway, that was her big dream: she wanted to move to London and become the star of the stage, or perhaps the screen, I don't remember now. Only she was stuck, wasn't she? She had no money, she knew no one in London, and I must say she was a very young seventeen-year-old, very naïve. So of course I decided to help her,' said the aristocrat. 'I told her she could move into one of my flats in the Mews behind Westminster Square, and I'd give her a little money to start herself off— Oh, that reminds me, she hadn't even heard of Westminster Square! That was how little she knew about life back then!'

While Dame Winifred smiled, Magnus asked, 'And she agreed to leave Brighton, just like that?'

'Well, she took a little convincing. She hadn't seen much of the world, so it was a daunting decision for her. I think she also felt a little obligated to stay with this aunt who had taken her in… Oh, and she had some boyfriend who she was reluctant to shake off.'

'A boyfriend?' said Bryn, thinking of the man in the shadows of Westminster Square Gardens.

'Oh, I don't think it was *serious*,' said Dame Winifred. 'He was just a local boy, so it was only a childish romance, one in which I think she was quickly losing interest. In the end, she recognised I was offering her a once-in-a-lifetime opportunity, and if she didn't seize it with both hands, she might never be able to emerge from her unhappy childhood and pursue her dreams in London.'

With that, Dame Winifred sat back on the sofa, a rather self-satisfied expression on her face. At the sight of her, Bryn found himself re-evaluating his thought from earlier: perhaps she wasn't charitable because she was lonely, but because being munificent made her feel good. Although it was difficult to begrudge her this slight smugness when she obviously meant well. And after all, wasn't that why everyone gave to charity?

'Did she pursue her dreams, though?' asked Magnus. 'Did she become an actress?'

'Oh, well, I think that particular ambition fell by the wayside fairly quickly when she got to London and realised she was a small fish in a big pond,' said Dame Winifred. 'I don't think she was particularly upset about it, though, she was just happy to be in London. And for what it's worth, I always thought she was too smart to be an actress.'

'So what did she do, when she first arrived here?' enquired Bryn. 'Because she didn't start working for Vasyl Kosnitschev until around six or seven years ago, and I'm assuming she didn't sit back and live off your hand-outs before then.'

'Oh no, certainly not!' said Dame Winifred, her eyes wide. 'In fact, Anne-Laure was always very uncomfortable with being in my debt — which tells you a lot about her innate goodness, because a lot of girls would have simply sat back and let the money roll in. As for jobs, I think she had a couple of positions as a sales assistant, and did a bit of secretarial work, that sort of thing. It's difficult to remember now, and I didn't like to pry too much at the time. It was her own business, as long as she made the rent, which she always did.'

'The rent that you charged at a very reduced rate?' said Magnus.

'Well, yes, but she wasn't there so I could make money off her, was she? I was trying to do a good thing.'

She sighed and slumped where she was sitting, and Bryn could practically see the moment when she remembered, once again, that Anne-Laure was dead.

'Listen to me, harping on about the past,' she said, in a tight voice. 'I could do with another cup of tea. Shall I refill the pot or do you have to be getting on?'

'We can stay,' said Magnus, and Bryn nodded; Dame Winifred was proving a mine of information.

While the aristocrat disappeared into the kitchen, neither man spoke, each lost in his own thoughts. Bryn felt almost uncomfortable: Dame Winifred had painted a vivid picture of the young Anne-Laure and the image of the sweet, rain-soaked girl asking for shelter on stormy beach served as an unpleasant reminder that they weren't just playing detectives for fun; they were dealing with the death of a real person.

Furthermore, the police constable was beginning to suspect that the more they found out about Anne-Laure Chevalier, the less sense her death would make. It hardly seemed possible that the naïve youngster from Brighton Dame Winifred had described had ended up the fashionable, glamorous woman Bryn had seen dead in the Royal West, with cocaine in her bag and in her blood system. And yet the gulf between these two Anne-Laures — in fact, between Annie Chambers and Anne-Laure Chevalier — was perhaps key to understanding her death. What had happened to her, in the decade she had spent in London? How had she changed? What crowd had she fallen in with? There was still so much to find out.

When Dame Winifred returned with the teapot, Bryn noticed her eyes were red and watery, and with a jolt of sympathy he realised the tea had merely been an excuse, and she had left the room to cry in private. He wanted to offer his condolences, but Magnus was already reaching forward and taking the teapot from her trembling hands.

'Here, let me,' he said kindly, pouring tea into their three cups. 'I'm sorry we upset you, Winifred. We shouldn't have asked you so many questions about her.'

'Oh, it's all right, dear,' said Dame Winifred, dabbing at her eyes with a lacy handkerchief, her tears causing her thick make-up to come off in patches. 'In a way I *like* talking about her, it feels appropriate somehow. But then I remember that she's gone, really gone…'

'Perhaps we could talk about this party,' said Bryn quickly, before the aristocrat yielded to grief once more. 'As you know, we came round here to talk about preventing crime in Westminster Square, and so perhaps we can return to this idea that there was somebody at your charity event who shouldn't have been there.'

Magnus shot him a surprised, almost disapproving look, and Bryn supposed the barrister didn't want him to encourage Dame Winifred's wild theories about Anne-Laure's death having been caused by a burglar. But the police constable thought he knew what he was doing: he wanted to find out more about the party in order to understand what Anne-Laure had been up to that night and — perhaps more importantly — who she had been with.

'Well, as I said before, I'm afraid I didn't really notice anything or anyone suspicious. But hosting these kinds of parties is intense — you're constantly talking, checking everything's running smoothly, making sure everyone's happy — so I might well have missed somebody creeping in who wasn't on the guest list.'

'Do you still have the guest list?' asked Bryn.

'Of course.'

'Perhaps you could give us a copy of it at some point? It might help to know who was there — or rather, who was *supposed* to be there.'

'Yes, good idea,' agreed Dame Winifred, 'although I've filed it away somewhere, so I might have to dig it out later. Shall I drop it off at the station?'

'Just drop it round to me,' said Magnus easily, while Bryn swallowed down his panic that Dame Winifred would accidentally give him away to Boyle. 'No need to go all of that way,' continued Magnus. 'But while we're on the party, did you see much of Anne-Laure that night?'

She shook her head. 'Like I said, it was so busy... We spent a lot of time together in the run-up to it, during the planning stages, which was lovely — just like old times — but on the night itself I hardly saw her. She was very professional, Anne-Laure, so I expect she was doing something important behind the scenes. Then, as I told Juliana, I tried to look for her at the end, but couldn't find her, so I assumed she'd gone home. God, how I wish I had stayed, how I wish I'd looked harder...'

She broke off, shaking her head, clearly unable to say any more.

'So you can't remember seeing her with anyone?' pressed Bryn.

Dame Winifred gasped. 'Do you think she *knew* the burglar?' Then, reddening, she checked herself, 'I mean, assuming she was attacked and it wasn't natural causes… Oh dear, I'm getting carried away, aren't I? I just want an explanation, that's all. I want to *understand*.'

'Of course,' said Magnus gently, 'that's what we want too. That's why we're wondering whether you saw Anne-Laure with anyone unusual, or perhaps she told you about some boyfriend…?'

'I'm afraid I just don't know,' said Dame Winifred helplessly. 'Men were always very interested in her — well, it's easy to see why, isn't it, she was gorgeous! So it's very possible there was someone on the scene, but again, as I told your wife, Magnus, Anne-Laure always kept her personal life very private. Even from me, who had known her so long — who probably knew more about her than anyone else in London. She was very guarded like that.'

'I thought you said she was naïve?' said Magnus.

'She was, when I met her. But she changed, over the years.'

'Why do you think that was?'

'Oh, I don't know. She grew up, I suppose. She adapted to this big, brutal city we all live in.'

'Now you're starting to sound like Juliana,' smiled Magnus.

'What about Vasyl Kosnitschev?' asked Bryn.

'What about him?'

'What was their relationship like?'

'Oh!' She seemed surprised by the question. 'Fine, I think. He was very dependent on her. Anne-Laure was always taking phone calls from him when she was working with me on the party. Come to think of it, I don't know how he's going to survive without her.'

'You don't think they were… more than just colleagues?'

For the first time that evening, Dame Winifred burst out laughing. 'You mean, were they sleeping together? Anne-Laure and *Vasyl*? Have you seen that man? Have you met him? No, my Anne-Laure would never have gone for someone like that. Wait, are you suggesting he killed her?'

'No!' cried Bryn, horrified.

'Not at all,' said Magnus.

'There's just no way,' went on Dame Winifred with supreme confidence, ignoring their hurried objections. 'He was too reliant on her. Besides, do you know how much money that man has? He'd never try and rob the Royal West — all those antiques would seem like small change to him.'

She was, Bryn thought, completely obsessed with this idea of the hotel being subject to a burglary, but he could understand why: Dame Winifred was trying to wrap her head around Anne-Laure's death, and seeing as she refused to acknowledge the young woman's drug problem, she probably thought the idea of a tussle that had got out of hand — however unpleasant — was more likely than a natural demise. And ordinarily Bryn would have agreed with her, especially considering the hostile confrontation that had taken place in the garden earlier that evening. Only, while the bruising on her wrists and neck had been nasty, there had been no fatal wound on Anne-Laure's body to suggest a violent death. At least, no obvious fatal wound... For the hundredth time, Bryn cursed Barry Boyle for not granting the medical examiner permission to do a full autopsy.

'I think we should let you get on, Winifred,' said Magnus, draining the last of his tea. 'You've been very helpful, but we've kept you long enough, and Juliana will skin me alive if I'm late for dinner again. But thank you for the tea and talk.'

'Oh, it was my pleasure, dears,' she said, unable to entirely mask her disappointment that they were leaving. 'Any time, any time.'

As they rose to go, Bryn said, 'If you could look out for that guest list from the party...'

'Of course!' she said. 'I'll search for it right away. As I said, I doubt there will be another break-in here, but naturally I'd like to help you in your mission to prevent crime in the area. You know, as a neighbour.'

'That's very kind,' said Magnus, as he and Bryn followed her back through the hall and to the front door of flat. 'Well, look after yourself, Winifred.'

'And you, dear. Do give my love to Juliana and the children, will you? And pass on my regards to young Daisy too.'

'Of course.'

'I'll be popping into The Station Garden later in the week,' continued Dame Winifred, in what Bryn thought was a fairly transparent attempt to delay their leaving, 'so I'll see Juliana then, of course. But I was going to ask Daisy to come round for tea sometime, do you think she'd like that? Of course, the girl probably has far better things to do than socialise with an old biddy like me…'

'I'm sure she'd love to come to tea,' interrupted Magnus firmly, before adding with a wink, 'especially if you have more of those Fortnum and Mason biscuits.'

'Oh yes!' Upon hearing this, Dame Winifred visibly brightened. 'I could certainly get more in! They do some lovely rose-flavoured ones, you know, and I'm also particularly fond of their pistachio and clotted cream biscuits…'

She was still twittering away after she had reached out for Bryn, given him a forceful kiss on the cheek, and waved them both out of the door. And although the police constable quickly wiped the lipstick from his face, and even though he was rather pleased to be free of the eccentric and emotional aristocrat, he did find he felt sorry for her. He suspected that, aside from her parties, she had very little going on in her life, which was causing her to wallow in her grief and start theorising about this imaginary burglary. And while he hoped this Daisy girl — whoever she was — would prove a welcome distraction, somehow he doubted that anybody would be able to replace Anne-Laure Chevalier in Dame Winifred's heart anytime soon.

CHAPTER THIRTEEN

'Mum, is it true a lady who lived on our street was murdered?'

Juliana Walterson, who was walking her two children out of Westminster Square and towards their private primary school a few streets away, stopped in her tracks. She stared at her eldest, Rosanna, who had asked the question.

'Where on earth did you hear that?'

'School. Amelia says this lady lived in Westminster Square. Amelia says she was found in a hotel, dead. Amelia says she was *murdered*.'

Rosanna spoke with great relish. Juliana clapped her hands over the ears of her younger child, Lee, who smiled up at her benignly.

'For goodness' sake, Rosanna, what's the matter with you? Don't talk about such things in front of your little brother!'

'But is it true?' persisted her daughter, who, since turning ten, had not stopped asking questions.

'No it is not true,' snapped Juliana. 'For one thing, she didn't live in our street, she lived *behind* it. And for another, she wasn't murdered, she died of natural causes, okay?'

'Okay.'

Rosanna looked and sounded disappointed. Juliana, deciding it was safe to release Lee's ears, grabbed each of her children by the hand and pulled them along the pavement.

'Come on,' she said, 'we're going to be late for school — *again!*'

A few paces later, Rosanna had another question: 'Mum, why would Amelia say the woman was murdered if she wasn't?'

'Rosanna!' huffed Juliana, eyeing Lee once more. 'Please!'

'But *why*, Mum?'

'Because your friend has a very overactive imagination! Or she's very bored. Just like everyone else around here, in fact...'

'What do you mean?'

'Never mind.'

Juliana shook her head: she didn't entirely approve of Amelia and some of Rosanna's other friends. So many of them seemed to be spoiled and also, conversely, rather jaded. Juliana supposed they were all raised by nannies and bodyguards, and it was her and Magnus' fault for sending Rosanna and Lee to a fancy private school where they would obviously have to mix with these odd, half-abandoned children. But still, she didn't think Anne-Laure Chevalier's death was an appropriate topic of conversation in the playground, no matter how neglected these kids felt by their rich and busy parents.

Lee, his thumb in his mouth, asked, 'Mum, are *we* going to be murdered?'

'Now look what you've done!' Juliana told her daughter, absently removing Lee's hand from his face. Then, to her son, she cooed, 'No, darling, of course we aren't.'

'We might be,' said Rosanna cheerfully.

'Stop being so ridiculous!' Juliana snapped. 'This is one of the safest places to live in all of London. It's one of the only good things about being here.'

'What do you mean?'

Juliana raised her eyes skyward. 'Never mind,' she sighed again. 'Forget I said that.' Then, struck by a sudden idea, she asked, 'Hey, do you know who lives just a few streets away?'

'The dead lady?' said Rosanna eagerly.

'I mean, aside from her. Do you know which famous person lives in a place called Chester Square?'

'Spiderman?' suggested Lee.

Juliana ignored this: she was growing tired of superheroes entering into every conversation she had with her son. Instead, she asked, 'Have you heard of Margaret Thatcher?'

'Of course,' said Rosanna blithely. 'She was Prime Minister: the Iron Lady.'

Lee gasped. 'Is she *really* made of iron?'

'No, darling, now *you're* being ridiculous,' Juliana told him. 'But yes, you're quite right, Rosanna, Margaret Thatcher was Prime Minister, and now she lives in Chester Square. And I bet you can't guess how many policemen she has, standing outside her house, guarding her?'

'Seven!' cried Rosanna.

'Thousand!' added Lee.

Juliana briefly wondered whether she could convince Magnus to do this school run every so often, and then said, 'No, Margaret Thatcher has *one* policeman on guard outside her house.'

'Only one?' Lee sounded disappointed.

'Yes, so you see, that shows how safe this area is, doesn't it? If the Iron Lady — who I imagine plenty of people want to murder — only has one policeman standing outside her house, and we don't have any at all... Well, I think that means we're in no danger whatsoever, don't you?'

Rosanna and Lee were silent for a few steps, evidently both taking this in. Then, 'Mum, why do people want to murder Margaret Thatcher?'

'Oh, they probably don't, Rosanna, I was just being silly. I just meant she's rather unpopular.'

'Why's she unpopular?'

'I'll tell you if you can point to the Falklands on a map.'

'What's the Falklands?'

'Exactly, darling.'

But later, after Juliana had deposited both of her children at the school and was making her way back to Westminster Square alone, she reflected on this strange little conversation. It concerned her to hear that Rosanna and her school friends had been talking about Anne-Laure Chevalier, and especially that they had been speculating over the nature of her death. Juliana was fairly sure it was just childish chatter — that the dead woman had become a kind of bogeyman figure in the playground — but still, she didn't like this shadow that Anne-Laure's demise had cast over Westminster Square, especially if it was affecting her children.

Besides, Juliana thought, *what if she was murdered?* Magnus appeared to think this very unlikely, but his new policeman friend — Bryn, was it? — seemed to have all sorts of ideas about how the young woman had ended up dead in the Royal West Hotel.

Juliana had been aware that Magnus was involved in this unofficial detective work for the past week or so — her husband always told her everything — and at first she had found the idea of him and this policeman creeping around and asking questions rather funny. But the more she heard about it all, the more Juliana felt unsettled about an already unsettling event. It wasn't so much that Anne-Laure had taken drugs — that was unsurprising, considering the social circles she had moved in — no, it was more this shadowy figure in the garden that was bothering Juliana, especially as he had purportedly been rough with the poor woman. In fact, it made Juliana feel queasy to think a mysterious violent man was lurking around Westminster Square, especially when one took the recent burglaries of Dame Winifred Rye and Hilda Underpin into consideration. So although she hadn't exactly lied to her children, she hadn't been entirely truthful either: no matter what Magnus said, Juliana couldn't fully rule out her suspicions that poor Anne-Laure Chevalier had been bumped off by this crazed ex-boyfriend, and the fact that he might still be on the loose did not make her feel completely safe in her own neighbourhood.

Oh, but this was all Westminster Square's fault, thought Juliana, as she approached her home once more. If only they didn't live in such a wealthy, snobby part of London. Crime happened everywhere, of course, but the inhabitants of Westminster seemed to advertise how much money they had, so it was really no wonder some opportunist had decided to start robbing old ladies while they slept, and maybe even worse than that... If only Magnus wasn't quite so taken with this stupid quadrant, Juliana lamented, as she made her way up the grand staircase of her building, waving at Patrick the doorman as she went (and wondering, as she always did, why it always smelled so strongly of stew in the hallway).

It wasn't even as though Westminster Square was that nice, reflected Juliana. True, it gave an impression of magnificence, but if one looked more closely, it wasn't half as ostentatious as Central Square Properties would have people believe. The embellished ceiling above her head as she let herself into her flat was a prime example of this: at first glance, it looked as though its edges had been intricately carved from wood, but in reality it was just cheap stucco. And it was the same outside. Juliana had always assumed the exteriors of the quadrant's buildings were constructed of stone, but recently she had noticed some of the facades peeling slightly, and realised they were actually covered in plaster. In fact, Juliana was beginning to suspect much of the grandeur of Westminster Square was simply an illusion.

Listlessly, she glided through the flat, tugging open the windows, throwing open the balcony doors, and beginning the laborious process of watering all of her plants and flowers. As she gathered up some dead leaves that had fallen into the pot of one of her palm plants, she found herself wishing Anne-Laure Chevalier *had* been murdered, as having a killer on the loose might convince Magnus they'd all be better off living in the countryside. Of course, Juliana checked herself, she wished the poor woman hadn't died at all, but a murder on the Square would certainly be a good excuse to start renegotiating the terms of their lease...

After she had drifted into the living room, still armed with the watering can, Juliana laid eyes on an object that was currently causing her much offence: a small sketch of London by none other than J.M.W. Turner. Magnus' mother had gifted this piece of artwork to him and Juliana for their twelfth wedding anniversary the other month, and although Juliana was sure her mother-in-law had meant well, and while she was surer still this little sketch had been incredibly expensive, she couldn't for the life of her work out what she was supposed to do with this scratchy London scene. As though it weren't bad enough she had to stare at the real thing, day in, day out — why on earth would she want to display a representation of this toxic, soul-destroying city?

Juliana scowled as she looked down at the picture, which was currently lying on one of the coffee tables. Her hand twitched and, given her already bad mood, she was tempted to pour the contents of the watering can on top of it. She imagined how good it would feel, to watch the ink smudge and dribble off the page, as though London itself were being washed clean away. Or perhaps she should simply throw it out of the window and be done with it: if she was lucky, Hilda Underpin would spot her lobbing expensive pieces of artwork into the square, and have a fit.

But then Juliana's artistic sensitivity kicked in, and she laid the watering can down at a safe distance from the Turner sketch: she might think this picture was a piece of rubbish, but there were probably plenty of people who wouldn't, and it would selfish to deny them the chance to own it, especially when she could make a quick buck off her mother-in-law in the process.

So, deciding there was no time like the present — and in want of anything better to do — Juliana picked up the phone and the address book, looked up Sotheby's, and dialled the number.

'Good morning, Sotheby's auction house, how may I help you?' asked an exceedingly posh receptionist on the other end of the line.

'Oh yes, hello. My name is Juliana Walterson and I want to speak to someone about valuing a piece of artwork, a Turner sketch.'

'Where are you calling from please, Mrs Walterson?'

'Um, London. Westminster Square.'

'Westminster Square?' The receptionist suddenly sounded much more interested. 'Hold on a moment, Mrs Walterson, I'll just transfer you to Jerome. He's in our real estate department and he also deals with large private placements. He works very closely with Central Square Properties.'

'But I don't want to talk about real estate, and this is just a single item...' said Juliana, but she had already been put on hold.

After half a minute or so of listening to the Vivaldi that was being blasted into her ear, a man picked up on the other end of the line and addressed her in a slow, pinched voice.

'Hello, Mrs Walterson, my name is Jerome Nightingale, and it's an absolute *pleasure* to speak to you this morning. Now, what do I have the honour of being able to help you with today?'

'Um,' said Juliana, completely thrown by his ingratiating tone, which sounded entirely insincere. 'I was hoping I could talk to you about a picture.'

'Just one painting?' Jerome sounded disappointed.

'Actually, it's just a sketch, but it is by Turner.'

'Hm,' said Jerome. 'The problem is, Mrs Walterson, that's not exactly my remit. I deal with large private placements, like collections of books or statues, which I sell on to museums or high net worth individuals…'

'Well, I did try and explain this to the receptionist, but she transferred me to you,' said Juliana impatiently, 'and you did then say you'd be honoured to help me.'

There was a short pause before Jerome said, in a somewhat strangled voice, 'Yes, I did, didn't I?'

Pushing her advantage, Juliana then described the small sketch that Magnus' mother had acquired, and made an appointment to bring it into Sotheby's and have it valued. Jerome, who still sounded a little put-out to be dealing with a single piece of artwork, was nevertheless fairly helpful, and reassured her that, after Sotheby's had inspected the picture, it could probably be put up for auction in the next month or so.

'And is there anything else I can have the gratification of helping you with, Mrs Walterson?' he asked, as soon as they had finalised her appointment, for he was clearly keen to get her off the phone.

'Actually, there might be,' said Juliana, partly because she'd just had an idea and partly just to spite him for his rudeness. 'Did you say you were involved in real estate for Westminster Square?'

'I did, Mrs Walterson.'

Juliana frowned: why did he keep calling her 'Mrs Walterson'? Was there somebody else on the line she didn't know about? However, keeping her temper, she went on, 'Mr Nightingale, would I be able to ask you a question about my lease in Westminster Square?'

'Of course, Mrs Walterson.'

'I just want some advice,' she said, 'so this is purely theoretical, and I'd appreciate it if you kept this matter just between us, all right?'

'All right...' he said slowly, sounding intrigued.

'Let's say that my husband and I are halfway through a twenty-year, long-term lease of our flat from CSP,' said Juliana. 'We bought it — or rather, we signed the contract — in 1984, so we still have ten years left, according to the terms of our lease. Do you follow me?'

'I do, Mrs Walterson.'

Juliana grimaced, but continued, 'Now, let's say that my husband and I don't want to stay on in Westminster Square for another decade. Let's say — and I'm just speaking theoretically here, remember —let's say we want to move to the countryside instead. What would our options be, regarding that long-term lease?'

'Well, as far as I'm aware, you don't have multiple options, not really,' said Jerome. 'The only thing you can do is negotiate an early exit from your lease with CSP.'

'That's possible, is it?' said Juliana.

'It is.'

'And presumably we'd be reimbursed for the ten years left, given that we wouldn't be living there.'

'Ye-es,' said Jerome, sounding uncertain.

'What's the issue?' demanded Juliana.

'Look, I don't know how much you paid for your property,' said Jerome. 'Let's see, if it's a flat in Westminster Square, and you acquired it in 1984 for a twenty year lease, I'd say it must have been around... four hundred thousand pounds?'

Juliana's eyebrows shot up: this was exactly correct. 'Yeah, around that,' she said.

'All right,' continued Jerome, 'so the most you're going to get off CSP if you sell it back to them now is two hundred thousand pounds.'

'*What?*'

'And that's if you're lucky and they don't add a load of extra charges and penalties for leaving early, that sort of thing,' continued Jerome.

'But —' Juliana hesitated: she was by no means an expert on money matters, but this seemed very low — 'what about inflation? What about the fact that house prices around here are going through the roof? CSP should be *encouraging* us to sell, they could probably make far more on that property if we moved out — millions, in fact.'

'Be that as it may,' said Jerome, 'they'll hold you to the lease you signed. And that lease says you'll stay there for twenty years.'

'But that's preposterous!' cried Juliana. 'There's very little one can commit to for that long — one's children, I suppose, and one's marriage too — but a poxy house in the middle of London? No, thank you!'

'CSP would argue you had been given an extraordinary opportunity, Mrs Walterson: the chance to live in a historic, beautiful area before, as you say, the house prices sky-rocketed.'

'Well I don't agree,' snapped Juliana, dropping all pretence that this was a hypothetical situation. 'Westminster Square is a dreadful place to live, and I want to leave. Is there nothing else we can do? What if I find someone else to take over the lease? Could we renegotiate with CSP then?'

'I doubt it,' said Jerome. 'Because it won't make any difference to the money they're making, will it? Besides, I don't think they'd let you choose your replacements. As you may know, CSP are incredibly fussy about who it allows to live in the area…'

'Unless they have shedloads of money,' Juliana grumbled, thinking of ridiculous characters like Lord Ellington and Sheikh Hazim, who made far more of a spectacle of themselves than she ever did, in spite of what Hilda might think. 'So there's really nothing I can do?' she continued. 'If I want to get out of this place, we're going to end up losing a significant amount of money, when you consider house prices and inflation and so on?'

'I'm afraid so, Mrs Walterson.'

Juliana leaned against the wall next to the telephone table, her whole body heavy with disappointment. Then, unbidden to her mind, came the words that, according to Magnus, Anne-Laure Chevalier had screamed at her attacker in one of the gardens: *I'm going to be free of you, and free of Westminster Square.* That pitiable girl, Juliana thought for the hundredth time; by the sound of it, Anne-Laure had felt just as trapped in this place as she did — probably more so — and the tragic thing was, the young woman had never managed to escape.

As tears began to prick at the corners of Juliana's eyes, she heard a low chuckle from the other end of the line.

'What is it?' she demanded of Jerome, blinking hard, although there was no way he could have known she was about to cry.

'Oh, it's just that I've finally worked out why your name is so familiar, Mrs Walterson!'

'Is it because you've said it three hundred times during the course of this conversation?' she asked coldly.

'No, it's because of your husband. He's the lawyer, isn't he? The one who's been kicking up a fuss about CSP's maintenance costs?'

'What on earth are you talking about?' asked Juliana, feeling less upset and more angry now. 'What maintenance costs?'

'You know, the charges for doormen and gardening and so on? The ones that go up and up practically every month? I mean, for what it's worth, I agree with him — it's criminal the amount CSP are now charging on top of the leases. So we were all rather impressed by the petition your husband put together...'

'Right, well, very good,' interrupted Juliana tersely. 'But actually, I have to go now. Thank you for your help, Mr Nightingale, and I'll make sure to call round at Sotheby's next week. Goodbye.'

'Goodbye, Mrs Walterson, and might I say how *delightful* it was to —'

But Juliana slammed down the phone, unable to listen to him for another second. She felt suddenly cold, despite the heat of the day, and a horrible sense of dread was creeping over her. But then, she had to be mistaken: Magnus didn't keep secrets from her, did he?

Without really thinking about what she was doing, she marched into Magnus' study. She rarely ventured into her husband's workspace at home, with its shelves and shelves of old books and its antique mahogany desk. It wasn't as though he didn't want her in here, more that she herself found paperwork of any sort very boring, and so kept her distance from both this room and the administration involved in running their house and lifestyle. Now, however, Juliana was starting to suspect her disinterest in financial matters might have been a mistake...

She began to search through the documents on the moulded top of the desk, which was inset with tooled green leather. Most of them concerned legal matters, and she found a couple of personal letters from Magnus' friends, which she carefully replaced, but after ten minutes or so of looking, she found what she was looking for: a bill from Central Square Properties labelled *Maintenance Costs* and dated 1st May, 1994.

'*Three thousand pounds a month!*' Juliana shrieked, so loudly she could probably be heard from the other side of the square.

She stared at the bill, unable to believe what she was seeing, shocked by both the amount and the fact that, apparently, Magnus didn't tell her everything after all.

CHAPTER FOURTEEN

Following their meeting with Dame Winifred Rye, Magnus had decided to take a step back from his and Bryn's investigation. After all, while the aristocrat had offered them plenty of background information on Anne-Laure Chevalier's life — most notably that she was once an orphan from Brighton named Annie Chambers — they had learned very little about her more recent existence, and nothing at all that might explain the strange circumstances of her death. If both Dame Winifred and Vasyl Kosnitschev were to be believed, Anne-Laure had been incredibly protective of her private life, and Magnus was starting to think it probably wasn't worth the effort of finding out more about any friends she might have had, or what might have happened in the days preceding her demise. Because, at the end of the day, unlike Bryn, the barrister still thought the only person responsible for Anne-Laure's death was probably Anne-Laure herself, and the only real mystery was whether she had overdosed accidentally or on purpose.

But how was he going to tell Bryn that he thought he had contributed enough to this unofficial detective work? Not only did the police constable seem to be entirely convinced of his theory that Anne-Laure was murdered, he also appeared to be very keen on carrying out this investigation. Most likely he was bored, the barrister thought, and although he didn't necessarily agree with Bryn's speculations, Magnus found he liked the eager young Welshman, not least for the way he was surreptitiously standing up to his big bully of a boss.

But on the other hand, Magnus was worried that his involvement in this whole business was upsetting Juliana. He had kept her up to date with his and Bryn's findings over the past couple of weeks, but he was beginning to think this might have been a mistake. For one thing, Juliana had a very overactive imagination, so Magnus suspected she too would jump to the conclusion of murder. For another, Juliana would seize upon anything she could to increase her hatred of Westminster Square, so much so that Magnus was sorely regretting telling her about the break-ins and the shadowy man in the garden, because now she was convinced Westminster was full of violent criminals, which was obviously not true. Indeed, Magnus thought his wife had been unusually and exceptionally cold toward him over the past few days, and he had no doubt she had been obsessing over Anne-Laure's death and drawing her own terrible conclusions. It was ironic, really, because Magnus had just discovered Juliana was going to put a very charming Turner sketch gifted to them by his mother up for auction, so he rather thought it should be *him* being cold with *her*, and not vice versa.

Anyway, although it was a shame to break up his and Bryn's partnership, it was probably for the best, Magnus thought, as he left the flat for work one morning (without a kiss from his wife). Yes, it was time to stop creeping around Westminster Square whispering about murder, and instead trust that the police had known what they were doing, and let the woman rest in peace. The question was, how was he going to tell Bryn?

Magnus was so consumed by this question as he turned right out of his building and started walking towards Victoria Station, he didn't notice another person walking the other way along the pavement until he had almost crashed into her.

'Magnus, you great oaf! You almost bowled me right over!'

Magnus looked down at the small, angry figure of Hilda Underpin, who was glaring at him and cradling her bag, inside of which her chihuahua was trembling.

'Look, you've scared Tam Tam!' she continued. 'Look at him, he's terrified!'

'Sorry, Tam Tam,' said Magnus automatically. 'But don't those kind of dogs always shake like that...?'

'No they do not,' snapped Hilda. 'Anyway, I'm glad I've bumped into you, Magnus — or rather, you've bumped into me — because I wanted to talk to you about something.'

'Can't we talk about it later, Hilda? I'm actually on my way to work right now —'

Hilda, ignoring this protestation, went on, 'What are you and that policeman up to?'

Magnus blinked at her. 'What policeman?'

'Don't play dumb with me, Magnus, I've seen you walking around the square with that gormless-looking officer multiple times now.'

'Oh, so it was *you* spying from the window the other day,' said the barrister. 'I suppose I should have guessed…'

'I'm entirely within my rights to look out of my own window,' she sniffed. 'Why are you always skulking about together? What's going on?'

Magnus sighed. 'If you must know, Hilda, we're trying to improve the security of Westminster Square and the surrounding area.'

'Well then, why aren't you talking to me?' she asked. 'I had a break-in the other week.'

Magnus paused: he hadn't really thought this through. Of course, Hilda's flat had been the location of the second burglary — one of the very burglaries he and Bryn had used as an excuse to talk to Vasyl and Dame Winifred — but given he doubted Hilda would be any use in their Anne-Laure investigation, Magnus was not about to subject himself to more time in the mean old lady's company than was strictly necessary.

'Yes, but Constable Summers has seen the police report of your break-in,' he said at last, 'and you were very thorough in what you told them, so I don't think it'll be necessary to talk to you again.'

Hilda narrowed her eyes: evidently, this answer displeased her.

'Nevertheless, I think you and — what's his name, that stupid-looking policeman?'

'I assume you're talking about Constable Summers?'

'Yes, him. I think you and Constable Summers should come round for tea at my flat this week, and I can tell you about my burglary in full.'

'I'm not sure that's entirely —'

'And while we're at it,' said Hilda loudly, drowning him out, 'you can tell me what else you're up to, Magnus.'

'What do you mean?'

'Well, I know you held a meeting for Westminster Square residents and didn't invite me — that was very rude. I also think you and that Summers boy are up to more than just neighbourhood watch business, otherwise why would you go and see that awful Ukrainian? So you can either come round for tea and tell me all about it, or I'll go to the police station myself and ask that lard-like Chief Superintendent what's going on.'

'No,' said Magnus quickly, thinking of Bryn's fragile position with Barry Boyle. 'No, don't do that. We'll come round.'

Hilda's gave him a twisted, triumphant smile.

'Lovely,' she croaked. 'Shall we say four o'clock on Thursday?'

'Myself and Constable Summers will still be at work…'

'Then you'll have to excuse yourselves, won't you?' she said, beginning to hobble away. 'And don't be late, please. I abhor lateness.'

* * * *

'You know, between you and me, I'm a little afraid of Hilda Underpin,' said Bryn, as he and Magnus met once more at the south-east corner of Westminster Square that Thursday afternoon.

'That's nothing to be ashamed of,' Magnus assured him. 'I think most people in Westminster Square are scared of her. Well, apart from my wife.'

Dragging their feet, the two of them began to walk up the south side of the square, towards Hilda Underpin's building, which was not far from Magnus' own and which overlooked the tennis court.

'Well, I'm sorry to drag you into this,' said Magnus. 'It's just, when she started talking about Barry Boyle —'

'Oh, I quite understand,' said Bryn quickly. 'And as frightening as I find Hilda Underpin, she doesn't have the same power over my job as Boyle does. Anyway, it might be useful to talk to her, mightn't it?'

'Do you think?' Magnus looked doubtful.

'Of course,' Bryn laughed, for he thought this was fairly obvious. 'Hilda's the neighbourhood busybody, isn't she? She's always nosing into everyone's business. So if anything odd or suspicious has happened around here, she's bound to know about it.'

'I see what you mean,' said Magnus, although he still sounded unconvinced.

'Then there's that thing she said about Anne — I mean, *you know who* — on the day we found the body,' continued Bryn, looking over his shoulder for Boyle, even though he knew the Police Chief was back at the station with a large portion of chips.

'What did Hilda say?' asked Magnus, frowning. 'I don't remember.'

Bryn withdrew his notebook from his utility belt, in which he had been jotting down anything even vaguely connected to Anne-Laure Chevalier. He then flipped back to one of the first pages, and said, 'It was the day we met, remember? Outside the Royal West. We were talking about the death and Hilda crept up on us, eavesdropping on our conversation. She started speculating — rather eagerly, if I recall — about how... erm, *the woman* had died, and said, "*If she was murdered, I'm not surprised*".'

'Blimey, I'd forgotten that,' said Magnus.

'There's more,' said Bryn, his eyes still on the page. 'When I asked whether *you-know-who* had been in some kind of trouble, Hilda replied, "*she was trouble*" and then went on to state, "*If she was murdered, that girl got exactly what was coming to her*".'

Magnus let out a low whistle as Bryn closed his notebook. 'Goodness, you're right, that *is* interesting. I think I'm so used to Hilda's nastiness I didn't take it in at the time. And perhaps she was just being poisonous, but it might be worth speaking to her about how, in her opinion, Anne — I mean, *you-know-who* — deserved to be murdered.'

'Especially,' said Bryn, 'as Hilda's opinion on her completely contradicts what we've been told by Vasyl and Dame Winifred.'

By now, they had reached Hilda's building and, after being let in by a chubby Portuguese doorman who was clutching a copy of *The Dawn Reporter,* they made their way up to Hilda's flat, which was on the top floor.

'I suppose — she takes — the lift,' gasped Bryn, for he and Magnus had opted for the stairs. 'But isn't it a little — inconvenient for an old lady to — live all the way up here?'

'I think it probably suits her — very well,' said Magnus, who was also out of breath. 'After all — the top of the building gives her — a better view from which to — spy on everybody.'

Feeling rather hot, they finally arrived on the top floor of the building and rang on Hilda Underpin's front door, which was immediately tugged open.

'Three minutes past four,' the old woman announced, staring at an ugly old pocket watch rather than them. 'You're late.'

'Good afternoon, Hilda, and it's very nice to see you too,' said Magnus, evidently deciding a charm offensive was the best way to cope with her. 'You remember my friend, Police Constable Bryn Summers?'

Hilda eyed him scathingly. '*What* Summers?' she demanded.

'Bryn.'

'Brian?'

'No, *Bryn*. It's Welsh.'

'Oh, for goodness' sake!' Hilda snapped, slamming the door shut behind them. 'I can't be doing with all this foreign nonsense, I'm going to call you Brian.'

'But that's not my name,' Bryn pointed out patiently, marvelling that this woman could be so rude to someone she knew was a policeman, even if he wasn't in uniform.

But Hilda wasn't listening. Instead, without another word, she had started hobbling further into her flat, leaving Magnus and Bryn no choice but to follow her.

When the barrister had told him they had been summoned to tea at Hilda Underpin's home, Bryn had imagined walking into a flat full of flowery curtains, lacy furnishings, a plethora of doilies and perhaps a few pictures of kittens. In his mind, this was the kind of environment inhabited by sweet old ladies, like his dear grandmother — or, *mamgu*, as he called her. But, of course, Hilda Underpin was no sweet old lady, and therefore her living room came as a complete surprise to the young police constable. Instead of finding the expected abundance of floral cushions and chintzy china ornaments, Hilda's approach to decor appeared to be almost Spartan. The sofa, armchairs, carpet and curtains were all beige in colour, which, alongside the bright white walls, made the room feel distinctly chilly. The only decoration to be found was either religious in nature, such as the lines of different crucifixes Hilda had had nailed on either side of the door, or — even more bizarrely — military-themed. After just a cursory glance around the room, Bryn spotted a green beret hanging from a hook, several medals and what he hoped were some purely ceremonial knives in a display case, and, over on the bookshelf, what looked like an old army ration tin, though it was battered and dirty. All in all, the policeman wasn't sure whether Hilda's living room reminded him more of a church or a war museum.

'Sit down,' instructed Hilda, who had already seated herself at a little table by the window, where she had already laid out the teapot and cups.

They obediently slid into uncomfortable wooden seats and Bryn glanced out of the window. Magnus had been right about the view: Hilda's flat offered a magnificent panorama of Westminster Square, and the garden where he had found the ring in particular. Bryn also could not help but notice there was a pair of binoculars, a notebook and even an old camera on the chair nearest the window.

'Tea?' the old woman asked, starting to pour it before they had a chance to answer. 'I'm afraid it's probably a little cold and over-brewed, given you were so late, but you'll have to put up with it.'

Magnus looked as though he wanted to object to this, but he contented himself by rolling his eyes at Bryn.

'And I suppose you'll want biscuits, won't you?' she said.

Bryn didn't reply. He did, indeed, want a biscuit, but he was too afraid to ask for one. Hilda, however, was opening another old tin — which was mercifully cleaner than the one of the shelf — and waving it under his nose.

'Go on, help yourself, Brian. Take two, you need fattening up, you look like a beanpole. It's absurd for a grown man to be so skinny... Go on, take two!'

Hesitantly, Bryn helped himself to two of the sticky biscuits.

'I didn't make them,' said Hilda, now offering the tin to Magnus. 'I buy them from a convent in Cheshire, and my butter too. I approve of putting good girls to work like that, you see — nuh-uh, Magnus, only one for you! Your jogging's not having much of an effect, is it?'

Sadly, Magnus withdrew just one biscuit from the tin. Without having one herself, Hilda shut the lid with a clatter.

'So,' she said, with the air of someone preparing to pounce, 'what exactly are you two up to?'

'As I told you the other day, we're starting up a little campaign to improve security around Westminster Square,' said Magnus, while Bryn took a sip of tea, which was indeed tepid and over-brewed.

'Yes, yes,' said Hilda impatiently, 'you're worried after my break-in. But what are you visiting that dreadful Ukrainian and Winifred for?'

Bryn raised his eyebrows: Hilda certainly had been keeping an eye on them.

'Well, for starters, Dame Winifred's flat was broken into a few days before yours...' began Magnus.

He was clearly playing for time, but Hilda let out a shout of laughter and slapped her claw-like hand against the table.

'Ha!' she cried. 'What did the thief want to rob *Winifred* for? She doesn't have any money! I doubt anybody would be able to find as much as a penny in her place!'

'Well, they certainly didn't take anything,' said Magnus, 'but Winifred claims that's because her valuables were locked away, either in a safe or elsewhere in London.'

'Lies!' hissed Hilda gleefully. 'That woman is as poor as a church mouse. Her husband was a gambler, you see, so he left her with next to nothing.'

'She didn't strike me as poor,' mused Bryn, thinking wistfully of Dame Winifred's cosy furnishings and Fortnum and Mason tea and biscuits.

'Then you're a fool,' said Hilda bluntly. 'It's all just pretence. She probably buys designer clothes cheap, to make everyone think she has money. Or perhaps you think she syphons some of the takings from her charity parties? A few hundred here, a couple of thousand there...'

'Hilda!' gasped Magnus. 'That's a terrible thing to say!'

But the old woman shrugged. 'Her husband ate up all of their savings in the casinos, everybody knows that,' she said, determinedly.

'What about her flats in the Mews?' asked Magnus.

'Pocket money,' said Hilda, dismissively. 'Her income from those flats is probably the only reason she can afford to stay living in Westminster Square. It's lucky old Lord Rye had a heart attack when he did, really, otherwise he'd have sold off those properties to fund his degenerate habit and she'd probably be living in some godawful hovel in, I don't know, *Battersea* by now.' Hilda cackled from behind her teacup. 'Oh, I'd *love* to see what Winifred made of Battersea...'

Bryn stared at her. She was, without a doubt, one of the most horrible people he had ever met, and he had dealt with several hardened criminals in his short time on the beat.

'Anyway, as usual, it's all because of a *man*,' continued Hilda. 'Winifred should never have married him. She did it for the title, of course, and the money — she's a social climber, that one — but look what it got her: an utterly useless husband who messed everything up and then keeled over to avoid having to pick up the pieces.' She tutted. 'Of course, it's because men aren't really *men* anymore. Not like they were in the good old days. Not like Tarquin.'

'Who's Tarquin?' asked Bryn, who was finding Hilda's bile strangely mesmerising.

At his question, Magnus made a throat-slitting gesture, but it was too late.

'Tarquin was my dear, late husband,' said Hilda, an almost dreamy expression stealing over her face. 'And such a man has never walked this earth before or since. Perhaps that's why God took him from me so early, perhaps he was too good for this wicked world.'

'Hilda —' began Magnus, trying to cut into the conversation, but there was no stopping her now.

'Tarquin was a war hero, you know,' she told Bryn, perhaps realising he was less likely to interrupt her than Magnus. 'He was a "Green Beret". I expect you don't know what that means — young people are so ignorant these days. Well, I'll tell you. Green berets were the official headwear of the British Commandos in the Second World War, and so it became their nickname too, you see?'

'Erm, yes,' said Bryn.

'And you probably also don't know that the British Commandos were formed during the Second World War, in June 1940, at the orders of the Prime Minister himself, sir Winston Churchill. How do you like that, eh? And because Tarquin was such a high-ranking member of the British Army, he was cherry-picked to join the Commandos, which was the greatest honour of his life. Do you know what the purpose of the British Commandos was back then, Brian?'

'Erm...'

Hilda gave a hiss of disapproval. 'Britain needed a force that could go into German-occupied Europe and carry out raids. Tarquin went all over the place with the Commandos: France, Austria, Eastern Europe... It was dangerous work, of course, because he was up against the greatest evil this continent — perhaps this world — has ever seen: the Nazis. But Tarquin wasn't afraid, oh no! As I said, men were true men back then. They ran into the line of fire, willing to give up their lives for their countries. Do you know, he and his comrades kept pills in tiny pockets in their sleeves, so that if they were caught by the enemy, they could make the ultimate sacrifice to avoid questioning? Do you really think the youth of today possess even a fraction of that kind of bravery? Of course they don't! They're all a bunch of drug-abusers, layabouts and *artists*.'

She spat the last word out, as though, in her opinion, it was the gravest crime of all.

'He certainly does sound very brave,' said Bryn, uselessly.

'I can show you some of his memorabilia,' said Hilda, turning in her seat. 'I have all of his medals over there, his uniform's in the wardrobe, and there are all sorts of knickknacks in his wartime ration tin up there.'

She pointed at the bashed-up object on the bookshelf. 'I never could bear to throw any of it away, you see...'

'Perhaps we could have a proper look at all of that another time?' suggested Magnus, clearly desperate to try and take back control of the conversation. 'Because at the moment, we're really just wondering whether you know anything that will shine a light on who this person responsible for these two burglaries might be?'

'I see,' said Hilda, looking both sour and disappointed.

'Assuming it *was* the same person,' Bryn said, almost to himself than them.

This thought had not occurred to him before, and he could tell by both Magnus and Hilda's faces they were intrigued.

'In police training, we're taught not to dismiss coincidences,' explained Bryn. 'Two crimes might seem similar, but unless there's concrete evidence to link them, we were always told we should treat them as separate incidents.'

'Ha!' Hilda looked almost impressed. 'He's not as stupid as he looks, is he, Magnus?'

Magnus, however, was frowning. 'But don't you think there *is* enough evidence to link them?' he asked. 'They both happened in Westminster Square within a week of one another, and in both cases the target was a property belonging to a single, elder— I mean, woman of *mature years*. And nothing was taken from either flat.'

'Nothing that's been noticed,' said Bryn, unsure why he was playing Devil's advocate against a barrister from Grey's Inn.

'Excuse me,' said Hilda, butting in, 'I *know* nothing was taken. I've checked.'

'Everything?'

'Everything.'

'All right,' said Bryn, 'I'm not disagreeing with you, Magnus — you're probably right — I just think it's wise not to make assumptions.'

'Understood,' said Magnus, with a respectful bow of his head.

A diversion then occurred as the living room door swung open. At first, Bryn thought the wind had pushed it — or perhaps the spirit of

Tarquin Underpin — but then he saw Hilda's ratty little dog come trotting into the room.

'Ah, here's Tam Tam!' said the old woman, looking genuinely delighted for the first time that afternoon. 'Come here, Tam Tam! Come on!'

The white chihuahua, which Bryn thought resembled a bleached rat, sniffed pathetically as it approached the table.

'That's right, Tam Tam! Come to Hildy!'

'Why's he called Tam Tam?' asked Bryn.

'Because he has Chinese eyes, of course,' said Hilda, which caused Magnus to gasp and Bryn to almost choke on his tea in horror. The old woman then handed Bryn the tin of biscuits. 'Give him a biscuit, Brian — go on.'

Still coughing, Bryn reached down and offered Tam Tam a biscuit. The ugly little creature sniffed at it for a few moments, and then sunk its teeth into Bryn's fingers.

'*Ow!*' cried the policeman, snatching back his hand. 'Did you see that? It bit me!'

But Hilda was shaking with silent laughter.

'It drew blood!' Bryn continued, showing Magnus the bite marks, which were indeed beginning to bleed.

'Oh, don't be such a crybaby, Brian!' wheezed Hilda. 'Tam Tam was just playing!'

Bryn scowled and surreptitiously wiped his fingers on her tablecloth, tempted to kick the wretched animal across the other side of the room like a football.

'*Anyway*,' said Magnus loudly, looking highly frustrated that the conversation had been diverted yet again, 'could we get back to the point? Considering the... *interest* you take in this neighbourhood, Hilda,' he went on, his gaze flicking towards the binoculars on the chair, 'Bryn and I were wondering whether you had noticed any suspicious characters loitering around Westminster Square lately?'

'Well, of course I have.'

'You have?' Bryn said, forgetting his throbbing hand for a moment and sitting up a little straighter in his chair.

'Westminster Square is *full* of suspicious characters,' said Hilda with relish.

'For example?' Magnus prompted.

'Where do I even start? Let's see... There's that disgusting Arab, the fat one, who looks like he eats a whole camel for breakfast, lunch and dinner. I wish he'd go back to whatever desert he came from. There's that so-called writer, who pens all that lefty liberal nonsense in the newspapers. I don't like the look of him one bit, and he always seems to be mooching around. And there's that *dreadful* butler of Lord Ellington's, who looks as though he comes from Transylvania. I wouldn't be surprised if he's some relative of Frankenstein's creature, and —'

'All right,' said Magnus, cutting in, before Hilda could list every single person who lived on or around Westminster Square. 'I see where you're going here.'

'And don't even get me started on all the *foreign* doorman and chauffeurs — none of them are to be trusted an inch, you mark my words. Do you know, the predecessor to the doorman downstairs was *asleep* when my flat was broken into? He won't get another job anytime soon... And, I'll tell you this for free: there's something dodgy going on with the tennis court. I've seen the same woman there every afternoon for the last three Saturdays. What's she done to deserve that prime spot, eh? Has she struck some secret deal with CSP? I think you should investigate that, Magnus.'

'I'll bear it in mind, Hilda.'

Bryn looked up from his notes. He had diligently written "fat Arab", "mooching writer", "Transylvanian butler", "sleeping doorman" and "tennis woman". But even without knowing Westminster Square, he could tell this was all completely useless information: Hilda was simply casting aspersions on people she didn't like the look of.

'Why are you doing all of this, anyway?' the old woman demanded of Magnus. 'What's in it for you?'

'Again, I'm just concerned for the security of my neighbourhood and the safety of my neighbours,' said the barrister, sounding tired.

'After all,' Bryn piped up, seeing a way forward, 'there's been a lot of media attention on the square, what with the death of that poor young woman —'

Hilda took the bait: 'Urgh, don't even talk to me about *her*!' she cried, in the manner of someone who very much wanted to talk about Anne-Laure Chevalier.

'Why?' asked Bryn, trying not to sound too eager. 'Did you know her?'

'I should think *not*!' Hilda looked outraged by this suggestion. Then she sneered, '*Anne-Laure Chevalier*. Never trust the French, that's what Tarquin always used to say. Never forget how quickly they surrendered in the Second World War — never forget it, Brian!'

'Erm, I don't think she was actually French,' began Bryn.

'Well even worse, then!' snapped the old woman. 'Why would you have a French name if you weren't French? She probably thought it sounded *exotic* — how typical of that little tramp!'

Magnus and Bryn exchanged a look: even coming from Hilda, this sounded especially vicious, not least when taking into consideration the fact that Anne-Laure Chevalier was dead.

'Sorry, Hilda, I feel like I'm missing something here,' said Magnus. 'Did Anne-Laure wrong you in some way?'

'She wronged the whole of this square!' snarled the old woman. 'You must have seen her around, you must have seen the things she wore: shiny great high-heels, short skirts that came to above her knee — *above her knee*, Magnus!'

'I'm sure she didn't mean to offend you personally,' the barrister sighed.

'Oh, but she did,' said Hilda. 'She knew what she was doing, that one. She was all smiles and charm when you spoke to her: "*Good morning, Hilda. How are you, Hilda?*"' The old woman's voice became high-pitched and exaggeratedly common as she impersonated the dead girl. '"*I'm entitled to wear what I want, Hilda. You're starting to upset me, Hilda...*" But I could see right through her. I knew she was laughing on the inside, and that she enjoyed all of the attention she received from dressing that way. She relished in flaunting her body like some — some *fallen woman!*'

'Hilda!' said Magnus, sternly. 'I think you're being a little unfair.'

But Hilda gave a snort of derision. 'Of course you'd think that, you're a man! You probably enjoyed gawking at her yourself.'

'Don't be ridiculous,' Magnus snapped, his temper clearly rising. 'I don't spend all of my time spying out of the window like you. I didn't even know she existed until the other week.'

'A likely story,' sniffed Hilda, although she did seem a little quelled. 'Anyway, I'm not sorry to see her gone. Like I said to you before, she got what was coming to her.'

'So, just to be clear,' said Bryn, who was feeling slightly angry himself now, 'you're saying you think Anne-Laure Chevalier deserved to die for — what — wearing high heels and a short skirt?'

'Oh, it wasn't just that,' said Hilda, completely unembarrassed by Bryn's accusation. 'It was also the way she acted, wasn't it? You could tell she thought a lot of herself, that one — she was a vain, conceited creature and —'

'Again, is that really reason to wish her dead?'

'*Let me finish!*' Hilda's nostrils flared as she banged her hand against the table once more. 'Anne-Laure Chevalier was a narcissistic little hussy who enjoyed making a spectacle of herself in this noble neighbourhood. She wasn't a good girl. She didn't dress correctly, she didn't behave correctly, and she was certainly no Christian, otherwise she would have exercised some restraint over her disgusting carnal urges...'

'What are you saying, Hilda?' asked Magnus, who sounded more interested than angry now.

'Oh, you should have *seen* the way she carried on with that *man*!' Hilda cried, now practically spitting with rage and indignation. 'They were obviously trying to be discreet, but I saw them — I see *everyone!* And they were completely shameless, holding hands in the street, kissing, groping at one another, and doing goodness knows what in the gardens... Disgusting!'

'Wait, so you're saying Anne-Laure Chevalier had a lover?' said Bryn.

'Of course I am — keep up, Brian! In fact, she probably had hundreds of them! But recently, before she died, she was always with *him*. Oh, it turned my stomach...'

'Do you know who this man was?' the police constable asked, repressing a shiver of anticipation as he considered how close they might be to a real lead here.

'I know *everybody*,' said Hilda, smugly. She bent down, scooped up Tam Tam, and began stroking him so forcefully that the little dog began to whine and even Bryn felt a stab of sympathy. Then, over the noise, the old woman asked, 'If I tell you, is he going to be in *trouble*?'

Her eyes glittered with malice.

'Maybe,' said Magnus, seizing upon the opportunity to appeal to her malevolence. 'As you've no doubt worked out, the circumstances around Anne-Laure Chevalier's death were unusual, to say the least ...'

'I'd rather like it if he was in trouble,' said Hilda, who didn't seem to be listening to the barrister. 'I can't bear him either, especially the way he swaggers around as though he owns the whole of Westminster. He's just like her, in fact: a vain, immoral reprobate who probably —'

'Sorry, who are you talking about here?' Magnus interrupted.

The old lady licked her lips, as though she were about to eat an especially delicious meal — or perhaps the trembling dog on her lap. Bryn had the impression she had kept this particular morsel of gossip back deliberately, until she was quite sure he and Magnus were hanging off her every word.

'Oh, he's that dopey-looking actor who lives on the square,' she said. 'You know, the one who's made all those dreadful pictures in Hollywood.'

Magnus looked at Bryn, then back at the old woman, and said, 'Hilda, are you suggesting Anne-Laure's lover was *Jem McMorran*?'

CHAPTER FIFTEEN

'You know, I bumped into Jem McMorran the morning I met you,' said Magnus, after he and Bryn had finally escaped the miserable haunt of Hilda Underpin and were standing, once more, upon the pavement of Westminster Square. 'Which was, of course, the same morning Anne-Laure's body was found.'

'Oh?' said Bryn, who was still trying to get his head around the old woman's revelation about the Hollywood actor.

'Yes,' said Magnus thoughtfully. 'We were both on our morning jog — well, Jem was on more of a run, really, he'd been all around Hyde Park — and he was in remarkably good spirits.'

'Really?'

'I mean, that in itself wasn't unusual,' continued the barrister. 'I don't know him well, but on the few occasions we've talked Jem's struck me as a fairly chirpy individual. Of course he is: he's young, he's handsome, he's rich and he has a wonderful career.'

'That's what everyone says about Anne-Laure, though,' said Bryn. 'It doesn't mean she wasn't unhappy.'

'True,' Magnus allowed. 'All I'm saying is, if Jem McMorran was in a secret relationship with her, why was he in such a good mood on the morning after her death?'

'I imagine because he didn't yet know she was dead,' said Bryn. 'It was really early, remember? Why...?' He trailed off, realising what his companion was getting at. 'Magnus, you don't think —?'

'No,' said the barrister, quickly. 'I don't.'

'We can't even be sure Hilda's telling the truth about him and Anne-Laure,' said Bryn, with an anxious look up at the top of the building they were still standing outside, from which he was sure the old woman was watching them through her binoculars. 'I mean, I know she's always spying on everyone, but she seemed to really, really hate Anne-Laure, and she's obviously not keen on young people in general, so perhaps she just made it up? Maybe she wanted to prove her point about Anne-Laure's alleged lax morals, or she wanted to taint Jem McMorran's reputation, or maybe she was just amusing herself, because it must be very boring up there.'

'I certainly wouldn't put it past the old witch,' agreed Magnus. 'But really, there's only one way to find out... ' His gaze drifted to their right, to the north-east corner of Westminster Square. Then he nodded, saying, 'Jem lives over there. I've never been to his flat, and I know he's not often about — he's always on film shoots and so on — but it might be worth a try.'

'You mean, call on him *now*?' asked Bryn.

'Why not?' said Magnus.

As they set off up the south side of the quadrant, Bryn felt a thrill of exhilaration. He suspected this was partly due to their finally being free of mean old Hilda Underpin, not to mention that Magnus was now demonstrating a renewed enthusiasm for the investigation; lately, Bryn had had the impression the barrister was trying to extricate himself from the case. But the policeman had to admit, at least to himself, that much of his excitement concerned the fact that they were not only about to meet a Hollywood star, but in his own — undoubtedly luxurious — flat.

Bryn was not especially aware of or up-to-date with celebrity gossip, however even he had a fairly good knowledge of Jem McMorran's career, simply because the actor was so famous, and easily one of the biggest British names currently working in Hollywood. As his name suggested, he had grown up in Scotland, but had been working from London since his late teens, and had long ago lost any Scottish accent he might have had. He'd first found fame in a lead part in a BBC costume drama, for which he had received a lot of attention, both from critics praising his performance and women praising his looks. This had led to a string of increasingly serious parts until, around a decade ago now, Jem

McMorran had had his big break by being cast in the action-adventure film, *Pioneer of the Past*.

Bryn smiled as he recalled travelling into Aberystwyth as a teenager to see the film with his school friends. He had already been captivated by the posters of Jem McMorran striking a pose against a jungle backdrop, a compass in one hand, an ancient map in the other, but the film itself had surpassed even his highest expectations. The story of the solving of an ancient Aztec mystery had been captivating, and the special effects had been extraordinary for their time. But really, it was Jem McMorran's performance that had made the film. It was as though he had been born to play the charming and witty young explorer, who seemed to think nothing of all the dangers thrown at him by the Mexican jungle.

The flipside of this, however, was that Bryn wasn't sure Jem McMorran had ever found a film that suited him as much as *Pioneer of the Past,* although he had since tried his hand at serious dramas, romantic comedies, and even a horror film, although that had been a major flop. Perhaps this was why the actor had made *Pioneer of the Past II: The Pharaoh's Tomb,* and the other two sequels, which had been set in Turkey and Greece respectively. They had all been enjoyable enough, but even a fan like Bryn had to admit that there had been a steady decrease in quality as the films had continued.

Was the actor in a rut? Bryn considered this, as he and Magnus continued to walk towards his flat, and concluded probably not: Jem had worked consistently for the last ten years or so, and he was still a very recognisable face, due to both his good looks and the iconic nature of the *Pioneer* films. But what of his personal life, Bryn wondered. On this subject, the policeman's knowledge was hazier. He thought Jem might have had a few high-profile relationships in Hollywood with a couple of actresses — or maybe they'd just been flings — but he hardly had a playboy reputation. Although equally, Bryn was fairly sure the actor wasn't married, so there was nothing to suggest he hadn't been in a relationship with Anne-Laure. In fact, the more he thought about it, the more it seemed to make sense. They had been neighbours, they had probably moved in the same glamorous circles and, from the little he knew about each of them — and as he had pointed out to Magnus just now — there were certain, undeniable similarities between Anne-Laure Chevalier and Jem McMorran. Furthermore, from a purely aesthetic perspective, they would have made a striking, almost perfect-looking couple; Barbie and Ken dolls come to life.

'Bryn? Hello?'

Magnus waved a hand in front of his face. The policeman blinked, realising that he had not been paying attention for a good few minutes. To his surprise, they were now at the north end of the square, being beckoned into a building by a doorman who was — remarkably — neither Portuguese nor Irish, but Italian, going by his accent.

'Good afternoon,' said Magnus, pleasantly. 'We were wondering whether we could have a word with young Jem McMorran upstairs? Is he around?'

'He is…' But as Bryn felt another surge of anticipation, the doorman eyed them suspiciously. 'You are not from the press, are you?' he asked. 'I always have to turn away journalists for Mr McMorran. You are probably from *The Dawn Reporter* or something, are you not?'

'*The Dawn Reporter?*' Magnus looked disgusted. 'How dare you? No, I'm actually a barrister at Grey's Inn: my name is Magnus Walterson and I also live on Westminster Square.' With a flourish, he produced a business card from his jacket pocket. 'I'd like to talk to Mr McMorran about a few issues concerning local maintenance costs and security. He missed our neighbourhood meeting, you see, as I believe he was on a film shoot at the time. I've come round to fill him in on what was discussed.'

The doorman took Magnus' business card and his gaze roved over it several times, as though he was looking for a secret message hidden in the scant text it contained.

'I don't know, Mr Walterson…' he began. 'I am under strict instructions from Mr McMorran's bodyguard not to let strangers into the building.'

'I am not a stranger, I am a neighbour and casual acquaintance,' said Magnus, patiently. 'If you call up to Mr McMorran, he will confirm this.'

But still, the doorman hesitated. 'The bodyguard's a big guy, Mr Walterson... Perhaps you can call the agent of Mr McMorran and make an appointment?'

To Bryn's great surprise, it seemed as though Magnus' powers of persuasion were finally failing him. Then he remembered: in his own pocket, he had the means to enter almost any building without question.

'I didn't want to have to do this,' he said, affecting a deep, commanding voice and flashing his police badge at the doorman, 'but you've left me no choice. So, we'll ask you again: may we go up to Mr McMorran's flat?'

The doorman, who at the sight of the police badge had jumped back as though he had been scalded, squeaked, 'You didn't tell me you were *police*... Yes, yes, go on, then! He's on the second floor!'

'Good improvisation,' noted Magnus a few moments later, as he and Bryn were walking up the stairs. 'You scared the life out of him.'

'It's usually a fairly good way of getting people to cooperate, although that was quite extreme, I must admit. I wonder what he's been up to?'

'Perhaps he's another flower-picker, like Inacio?' suggested Magnus.

'Maybe,' Bryn laughed. 'Anyway, hopefully it won't get back to Boyle that I'm abusing my power...'

They reached the second floor, where they found the door of Jem McMorran's flat slightly ajar and loud rock music coming from within. Evidently unwilling just to barge in, Magnus rang the doorbell a few times, although it seemed unlikely it could be heard over the din inside the flat.

'Jem?' called Magnus, pushing the door open a little more. 'Jem?'

When there was no reply, Magnus looked at Bryn, shrugged, and stepped over the threshold.

'Jem, it's me, Magnus Walterson, from across the road! Sorry to intrude, but I don't think you can hear the bell. *Jem? Are you here?*'

As with Hilda Underpin's flat, Bryn had had several preconceptions of what a famous actor's London accommodation might look like. He had imagined a modern, open space of stylish but minimalist design, perhaps featuring a few decadent details like a giant fish tank, or maybe even one of those new PlayStations Bryn wanted so badly, but could not afford.

Yet once more, the reality was quite different to his conjectures. While he followed Magnus through Jem's flat, he noted that there were indeed a few swanky details: great canvases of modern art on the wall, a PC computer even more modern than the one they used in the station, and the most sophisticated coffee machine Bryn had ever seen. However, these trendy fixtures were almost completely undermined by the fact that every room was in a state of total chaos. Every surface and much of the floor space was littered with clothes, magazines, scripts, crumbs, not to mention empty cans of beer, bottles of spirits and cartons of half-eaten takeaway... It might even have been more disgusting than Barry Boyle's office, Bryn thought, for at least the Chief Police Superintendent confined his mess to his desk. No, the nearest thing Bryn could compare Jem McMorran's flat to was a drug den in Cardiff that he had once broken down the door of during a police raid.

And where was Jem McMorran? While Bryn stood in the doorway of the living room, where the music continued to blare from state-of-the-art speakers, Magnus did a quick search of the flat and came back shaking his head. Then, just as Bryn was wondering whether the actor had gone out, his gaze fell on the back of the grubby sofa, from which white, spongey stuffing was escaping in several places. There appeared to be a thin line of smoke issuing from the other side, and for a moment the policeman thought the sofa might be on fire — then he spotted the feet dangling over one of the ends, clad in mismatching and rather holey socks.

He pointed this out to Magnus, who nodded, and then pointed over at the speakers. Understanding, Bryn crossed the room and twisted a dial until the music was almost inaudible. The figure on the sofa stirred.

'What —?'

'Good evening, Jem,' said Magnus, smiling down at the young man lying spread-eagled on the tatty sofa with a cigarette wedged between his lips. 'I hope you don't mind my friend and I letting ourselves into your flat, I don't believe you could hear the doorbell over all that — aha — *interesting* music.'

'Magnus?'

Jem frowned, rubbed at his eyes, and managed to push himself up into a sitting position, the cigarette still dangling from his lips. Bryn, walking over from the speakers, took in the sight of the dazed and sleepy-looking actor and felt an overwhelming surge of disappointment. While Jem was usually remarkably handsome, today he looked in a terrible state. His skin was sallow, as though he were physically ill, and there were dark circles under his red-rimmed eyes. His thick chestnut-coloured hair, which was usually neatly combed, fell into his face in greasy tendrils, or else stuck up at the back where he had been lying on it. As well as the mismatching socks, he was clad in a stained t-shirt and what looked like old pyjama bottoms. The effect of all of this, plus the patchy stubble he was sporting on his chin and jaw, not to mention his general aroma of tobacco and alcohol, was that Jem McMorran more resembled a hobo than a Hollywood actor. In fact, Bryn found himself hoping the star was doing a little method research for the part of a down-on-his-luck character — otherwise what on earth had happened to him?

'Do you mind if we sit down, Jem?' asked Magnus, who seemed unperturbed by the state of both the flat and the actor — or at least, he was pretending to be.

'Yeah, sure,' said Jem, taking a drag on his cigarette, which had almost burnt down to his fingers. 'Pull up a pew.'

This was easier said than done, Bryn thought, because the only other seat in sight was an armchair that, for some reason, was lying on its side. Magnus, however, fetched two dining chairs from the adjoining room and placed them both in front of Jem's sofa, on the other side of a dirty coffee table.

'This is about the parking, yeah?' said Jem, peering at them blearily. 'I've used your spot again, haven't I?'

'Actually, you haven't, at least not to my knowledge,' said Magnus. 'Jem, may I ask — are you all right?'

'Oh yeah, fine, fine,' said the actor, stubbing his cigarette out directly onto the wooden surface of the expensive-looking coffee table. 'Never better.'

'Forgive me, but you look a little… below par,' said Magnus.

'I've had a few big nights, that's all,' said Jem, rubbing at his red eyes. 'One night turned into two turned into three… I'm afraid I've drunk far too much over the last few days, and probably taken a few things I shouldn't've.' He grinned at Bryn. 'You know how it gets…'

'Ah, I should probably introduce my companion here,' said Magnus, jumping in before Jem could incriminate himself any further. 'This is Police Constable Bryn Summers of the Victoria Police Station.'

'Police?' Jem seemed more confused than afraid. 'Magnus, you've not grassed me up about the parking, have you?'

'As I already said, Jem, this isn't about parking.'

'Oh yeah,' said the actor, reaching for a packet of rolling papers and a pouch of tobacco, half of which was scattered over the table, 'yeah, I forgot…'

As he began to construct another cigarette with shaking fingers, Bryn wondered whether he was still drunk or high. Jem seemed far too dazed to be suffering from simple tiredness, and his words were slurring a little, as though he was having difficulty getting them out.

'Do you want a drink or something?' he asked, when neither Magnus nor Bryn had spoken for almost a minute. 'What time is it? Is it time for a beer?'

'I'll get us all some water,' Magnus decided, standing up and departing the room.

Jem watched him go, and then looked at Bryn. 'I always park in his spot,' he whispered, with a slight giggle. 'I don't mean to be a pain, but I have too many cars. I've a Ferrari, a Lamborghini…' He trailed off, clearly not able to remember any more. 'Anyway, I wish Magnus wouldn't get in such a flap about it…'

'I don't think he is in a flap about it,' said Bryn, feeling the need to defend his friend. 'We just want to talk to you about some neighbourhood business, that's all.'

'Neighbour business,' repeated Jem, imitating Bryn's accent, although not in an unkind way. 'You're Welsh, aren't you? I'm quite good at accents — I've always been able to mimic people — but I've never played a Welshman. Perhaps I'll tell my agent that...'

'All right,' said Bryn, not knowing how else to respond; it seemed Jem McMorran was easily distracted.

Fortunately, Magnus returned not long afterwards with three glasses of water. The largest, which was a pint glass, he handed to Jem. The actor took it eagerly, gulped down half its contents, and then said, 'I didn't realise how thirsty I was.'

'I'd drink the rest if I were you,' Magnus advised, 'and while you're doing that, I'll explain why Bryn and I are here... You see, there have been a number of break-ins around the neighbourhood over the past few weeks, so we're just knocking on doors and finding out whether anyone's seen anything suspicious.'

'Break-ins?' said Jem.

'Yes, one at Dame Winifred Rye's flat and one at Hilda Underpin's. Do you know them?'

'I know *of* them,' said Jem. His expression had turned a little sour.

'It seems nothing was taken,' continued Magnus, 'but it's worrying that they were targeted, given that they're both fairly elderly ladies who live alone. We're trying to prevent the same thing happening again, so if you've noticed anybody strange hanging around...'

'Nah, I haven't,' said Jem.

This was unsurprising, Bryn thought, given the actor had not even noticed their presence in his own flat until they had turned off his music. He watched Jem drain the last of the water and look around for more. Magnus, who had not yet taken a sip from his own glass, handed it to Jem and said, 'You haven't seen anything odd? Because, given you're so well-known, your flat might well be a target too.'

'Ha, unlikely, given the state it's in at the moment,' said Jem, with the first flicker of self-awareness he had displayed since they'd been there; evidently, the water was having a positive effect.

Magnus shot Bryn a look that suggested he was going in for the kill, and then continued, 'We have to be careful, you see, because of all the extra media attention Westminster Square has received recently…'

'*Extra?*' Jem repeated, in a tone of voice that suggested he was used to constant media attention.

'Yes, because of the death of that poor woman at the Royal West — Anne-Laure Chevalier.'

Magnus had timed this statement exactly right: Jem had been lifting his glass of water to his mouth and, upon hearing her name, had given a start and slopped half of its contents down his front.

'Oh, damn!' he said, wiping at his t-shirt — somewhat in vain, Bryn thought, because it was already dirty.

Magnus, however, was watching Jem closely. The actor seemed to be taking a long time about checking on the state of his clothes.

'Sorry, what were you saying?' he asked at last.

'I was talking about Anne-Laure Chevalier,' Magnus said again.

Even now, when he was prepared for it, Jem seemed to flinch at the name. However, when he spoke, his voice was more level than it had been all evening.

'I don't know who that is,' he said.

'Yes you do,' Magnus pressed, 'she's the young woman they found dead at the Royal West Hotel a few weeks ago. You must have heard about her — it was all over the news.'

'Oh, yes — of course.' Jem seemed to realise he'd made a mistake. 'Yeah, I did hear about that. Only, I wasn't sure that's who you meant. I'm always travelling, you see, so sometimes I get mixed up between the news in America and the news here.'

'Understandable,' said Magnus. 'Although I would have thought you'd remember Anne-Laure's death, given she died just a few streets away from your flat.'

'Yeah, yeah, I do,' said Jem, with a touch of impatience. 'I told you, I remember now. Anyway, I have a lot of houses...'

'Of course.' Magnus smiled, although Bryn detected a chilliness about his face and hoped he never had cause to go up against the barrister in court. 'Did you know Anne-Laure, Jem?'

'No,' said the actor at once.

'Not at all? You'd never even met?'

Now, Jem took a little more time answering. 'Not that I recall — although I tend to meet a lot of people in my job, so who knows? Maybe we bumped into each other at a party and I don't remember...'

'That seems unlikely, don't you think?' said Magnus. 'She was a very beautiful woman, Anne-Laure. Don't you think you'd remember her?'

'I work in Hollywood,' said Jem, his confidence appearing to grow. 'I'm surrounded by beautiful women.'

Magnus inclined his head in acknowledgement of this statement. Bryn looked between them a few times, feeling a little as though he were a spectator at a tennis match. This gave him an idea.

'You won a tennis tournament a few weeks' ago, didn't you?' he asked.

Jem visibly relaxed. 'Yeah, I did,' he grinned. 'Well, it wasn't difficult — hardly anyone around here knows one end of the racket from the other. Present company excluded, of course.' He nodded at Magnus.

'Did you go to the party afterwards?' asked Bryn.

Jem, seeming to sense they were heading back to the topic of Anne-Laure, hesitated.

'For a bit,' he said. 'But I can't bear those charity events — not because they're for charity,' he added quickly. 'I just can't stand all those old bores standing around, patting each other on the back for being so generous, when really they've hardly donated anything at all...' He trailed off, perhaps realising he had gone off-topic. 'So yeah, I left early. It was dull. It wasn't my kind of party.'

Going by the appearance of his flat, this was fairly obvious.

'So you didn't see Anne-Laure at the party?' Magnus asked.

'I don't know, maybe… Like, I said, I'm not aware I met her.'

'Anne-Laure planned that party, you know.'

Magnus, Bryn noticed, kept using her name, and he wondered whether the barrister was trying to elicit some kind of emotional reaction from Jem. But the actor merely shrugged. 'Again, it wasn't my kind of party.'

'It's such a tragedy, don't you think?' said Magnus, leaning forward on his dining chair and peering down at Jem on the sofa. 'Anne-Laure was so young — she had most of her time still ahead of her. It's so very sad, the life of such a promising person being suddenly snuffed out like that.'

Jem swallowed, but said nothing.

'According to my friend here,' said Magnus, gesturing at Bryn, 'there are rumours going around the police station that Anne-Laure's passing wasn't a result of natural causes, as was reported in the press, but that it might have been a drug-related death, and perhaps even a suspicious one…'

Jem leapt from the sofa, unable to withstand the barrister scrutiny's any longer.

'What is this?' he cried, running his hands through his greasy hair. 'What are you playing at, Magnus? Why are you barging into my flat and talking about — about all this? It's nothing to do with me. I didn't even know her!'

Magnus watched Jem pace through the debris of his living room for a few moments, like a big cat surveying his prey.

'Jem, we have reason to believe you *did* know Anne-Laure,' he said calmly. 'In fact, we've been told you might have been in some kind of relationship with her.'

Jem spun around. His face had turned very white. 'Who told you that?' he demanded.

'Is it true?'

'Who told you?'

Magnus sighed. 'Hilda Underpin. She says she used to see you with Anne-Laure from her window…'

Jem laughed, although it was a rather unnatural high-pitched sound. 'And you believed her? *Hilda Underpin*? That old hag will say anything to stir up trouble — she hates me!'

'So you're saying she was mistaken?'

'Yes,' said Jem resolutely. 'She must have seen me with another blonde.'

'So you're romantically involved with a blonde woman at the moment?'

'I don't have to answer any these questions,' snapped Jem. 'How do I know you're not from the press?'

'It's me, Jem,' said Magnus, sounding weary. 'Why would I set you up?'

But the actor seemed jittery and upset now. He clasped his shaking hands together as he paced, his lips moving silently, almost as though he were in prayer.

'I think you should go now,' said the actor. 'I'm leaving for a shoot tomorrow. It's only Pinewood, but they're putting me up nearby for a few days, so I have to pack.'

'All right,' said Magnus. 'But Jem, are you sure there isn't more you can tell us about Anne-Laure Chevalier?'

'*I said I didn't know her, all right?*' the actor cried, thoroughly agitated now. 'And I don't see what these questions have to do with neighbourhood security. Now please, Magnus, I need to pack. I need to get all this stuff together...'

He began to pick up items from the floor seemingly at random, items it was unlikely he was going to be taking with him to a film studio: a tie, a dirty old mug, a handful of cassettes. He didn't seem to know what he was doing as he bundled these objects into his arms, and while Magnus watched him with a sympathetic expression on his face, Bryn was struck by an idea.

'Mr McMorran — Jem. May I use your bathroom before we go?'

'Oh, yeah, yeah,' said the actor, almost tripping over a paperback book lying on the floor. 'It's the last door on the right.'

As Bryn left the room, he reflected that while he was in no way an expert on women, he did know — mostly from his sisters — they often left a trail of accessories behind them. If Jem and Anne-Laure had been in some kind of relationship, there might still be evidence of her presence in his flat. And again, growing up with sisters had taught Bryn the most likely place for this would be in the bathroom.

His first impression of the messy, damp and mildew-stained room was not promising, because he could not see anything that immediately struck him as feminine. Jem's towels, many of which were lying on the floor, were all a manly shade of slate grey, and the shaving foam and shower gels around the bathtub all proudly declared themselves to be '*For Men.*' But then there were two toothbrushes in the holder by the sink... Bryn moved closer, carefully and quietly opening the mirrored cabinet above the taps.

'Jackpot,' he murmured.

For he doubted very much that Jem would have use for the various items of make-up, the perfume, and the dainty little hairbrush he discovered inside. Of course, he checked himself, they hadn't necessarily belonged to Anne-Laure — in fact, given he was a Hollywood star, Jem probably had no trouble at all convincing women to stay the night and leave all their cosmetics in his bathroom. But still, Bryn thought, as he picked up the small brush and held it up to the light, the person who had left this particular item behind had definitely had long, blonde hair...

'Bryn?'

Beyond the bathroom door, the policeman heard Magnus and Jem move into the hallway: evidently, the actor was still keen on chivvying them out of his flat.

Bryn made to shut the bathroom cabinet, but then, on a whim, he reached past a lipstick to pull out a small bottle of amber-coloured perfume. He sprayed a little into the air and sniffed. It was fresher than he had expected, although pleasantly so — it put Bryn in mind of summer. It also smelled vaguely familiar. As he replaced it carefully in the cabinet, Bryn mused that although he couldn't have sworn to it in court, he was fairly sure the last time he had smelled this perfume had been early one morning a couple of weeks ago, in the business conference room of the Royal West Hotel.

CHAPTER SIXTEEN

Following the meetings with Hilda and Jem, Anne-Laure Chevalier began to visit Bryn in his dreams.

At the beginning, for the first night or two, she was simply there, shimmering somewhere in the background of his unconscious mind. He would dream of his parents' home in Aberystwyth, and there would be a blonde figure sat at the kitchen table, visible only out of the corner of his eye. Or else, a nightmare version of Barry Boyle — bigger and more ferocious than even his real-life counterpart — would be berating Bryn for some small error in his police work, and during his tirade Anne-Laure would drift past the window of the office, vanishing as suddenly as she had appeared.

When he was awake, and he remembered these dreams, Bryn told himself not to worry about them. A combination of boredom at work and curiosity about the case meant his conscious thoughts often turned to Anne-Laure and her mysterious death, so it was probably to be expected that she was also straying into his dreams.

However, as the week wore on, and Bryn tried to concentrate more on the dull details of his job during the day, the spectre of Anne-Laure remained a presence in his night-time imaginings. In fact, the less he tried to think of her when he was awake, the more she infiltrated his unconscious contemplations, until he no longer dreamed of home or work or anything other than her. And what strange dreams they were, for they always started in a vaguely recognisable way, but descended into violence or trauma.

Bryn dreamed of Anne-Laure and Dame Winifred Rye, sitting in a little beach hut in Brighton, both wearing evening gowns and drinking champagne. Dame Winifred told Anne-Laure she wanted to host her next charity party right there, in the beach hut, and when the girl told her it was far too small, Winifred became upset. She stormed out towards the sea and shut the hut door behind her, locking the girl inside...

Bryn dreamed of Anne-Laure and Hilda Underpin, having afternoon tea in Westminster Square gardens, not far from where he had found the ring. As Hilda filled Anne-Laure's cup from the pot, she began to talk of her late husband, the war hero, only when she showed Anne-Laure an old black and white photograph it was only of her dog, Tam Tam. Anne-Laure then took a sip from her cup, and immediately spat her mouthful onto the grass, discovering it was not tea, but blood. 'It's a test,' Hilda explained. 'Only good girls get tea…'

And Bryn dreamed of Anne-Laure and Jem McMorran, sitting in the rubble of Vasyl Kosnitschev's house, lining up empty bottles of Horilka, as though they were playing a giant game of dominos. 'We don't have enough,' she told him, and Jem nodded towards the ceiling, from which hundreds more bottles were suspended on wires. Only, when Anne-Laure reached up to pluck at one, all of them crashed down, the glass smashing around her feet while she screamed…

Bryn woke from this last dream with a gasp, sitting bolt upright in bed and staring around at his dark room. And there, in the corner by the door, lay the body of Anne-Laure Chevalier, positioned just as he had found her in the Royal West Hotel, only now her eyes were wide open, and staring straight at him.

With a whimper of fright, Bryn groped for the bedside lamp and switched it on. As light plunged into the room, he saw that the corner by the door was quite empty. *It wasn't real,* he told himself firmly, *you were still dreaming. She wasn't there.*

Still, Bryn felt shaken, and as he pushed back the covers he discovered he was drenched in cold sweat. He reached for the glass of water on his nightstand, drank deeply, and then climbed out of bed, trying to clear his mind.

'Pull yourself together, Summers,' he told himself. 'You're a policeman, for goodness' sake.'

Reluctant to return to his nightmares, Bryn walked to his only window, pulled aside the curtain, and looked out. He lived in a little bedsit on the top floor of a building right next to Clapham Junction

Station, and from here he could look down onto the tracks. It must have been late, Bryn reflected, because now even the trains had stopped, and they usually rattled by from very early in the morning until very late at night, shaking the floor and the walls of his accommodation every time they passed.

He supposed he was lucky, living just five minutes from Central London; in order to get to work, all he needed to do was catch a train to Victoria, so it was practically door-to-door. But it was difficult to feel grateful as he stared down at the almost monochrome world beyond his window, and as he imagined how much pollution he was being subjected to by living here. He wasn't far from Clapham Common, but he wished he could see a little green from his window. At this, Bryn chuckled to himself, realising he was beginning to think like Magnus' wife, and then his mirth turned to a cringe, as he imagined what the barrister, who lived in such a grand building in Westminster Square, would make of this meagre abode.

The thought of Westminster Square brought him back to Anne-Laure Chevalier and his nightmares. What was the matter with him? Why was both his conscious and unconscious mind obsessed with this? He was fairly sure a psychiatrist would have a few theories about why this highly desirable woman kept appearing in his dreams, despite the fact that she was dead, but Bryn was sure there was more to it than that. Was he suffering some sort of post-traumatic stress from seeing her body? He didn't think he had been particularly affected that morning in the Royal West — in fact, to his shame, he remembered being thrilled, thinking that this corpse would liven up his life at the Victoria Police Station (which, in fairness, it had). But then, the mind worked in funny ways... Who knew what his brain was trying to tell him? He might have been bothered by any number of things concerning the case. And perhaps it was natural that he, as a relatively young person, would be bothered by this unexpected and early death; after all, Bryn reflected, he and Anne-Laure Chevalier were almost exactly the same age.

The police constable stepped away from the window and, rather tentatively, looked around his bedsit, which he was relieved to find was still free of dead bodies. The space was poky and unglamorous, and although there was a separate bathroom, everything else was crammed into this one room: his bed, a lone chair and table, and a kitchenette that was rather sticky from years of use by other tenants. It wasn't quite as bad as Inacio the doorman's flat under Westminster Square, but having been around so many grand homes recently, Bryn couldn't help but feel his own was rather lacking. So maybe his nightmares had nothing to do with Anne-Laure, he thought — maybe it was more this room, and it was time to think about moving out.

Bryn climbed back into the bed, which squeaked under his weight, and found he felt a little calmer now — although he thought he might spend the remainder of the night with the light on. His mind was too busy, that was all. These dreams were just a continuation of his thoughts during the day, when he tried to think of the case from every possible angle. They would surely wear off in time, especially if he and Magnus got to the bottom of the whole business.

He turned over onto his side to avoid a protruding bed spring, and found himself looking at the spot by the door where, for a moment, he thought he had seen her. Now Bryn was more composed, he was able to think back on that image with a more logical brain. It had been her open eyes that had frightened him, he realised, but the more he considered it, the more it seemed to him that the expression he had had seen — no, the expression he had *imagined* — on her face had been beseeching, almost as though Anne-Laure Chevalier were asking for his help.

★ ★ ★ ★

Magnus found himself whistling as he walked along the street that evening, although he was unsurprised by his own good mood: it was Friday, the sun was still out, and he was heading towards one of his favourite pubs in London, The Lion of Westminster.

He had suggested to Bryn that they discuss the latest developments in the Anne-Laure mystery in that particular pub for several reasons. Firstly, the policeman was too allergic to pollen for them to meet in Magnus' own flat. Secondly, although close, the pub was a few roads behind Westminster Square to the south-east, meaning they would have a little more anonymity there, and would be able to talk without fear of being spied on by people like Hilda Underpin. And thirdly — and perhaps most importantly — Magnus had had a busy week at work, and thought he deserved a drink.

The Lion of Westminster — or 'the Lion', as it was more commonly known — was a very traditional-looking English tavern: its façade was almost entirely black, with the exception of the gold lettering of its name and its many-paned windows, some of which were made of bullseye glass. Its exterior also featured a couple of window boxes, some Victorian-style streetlamps and a hanging wooden sign depicting a roaring red and gold lion, all of which seemed to complement the pub's grand surroundings.

As it was Friday, the Lion was busy, although because the weather was fine, most people were sitting at the little tables outside, or else standing and chatting with a pint in their hands. Magnus, however, headed straight inside, which was dark and cool in comparison, and just as he was making his way to the bar, he was tapped on the shoulder by Bryn.

'Hello there, Magnus. Goodness, this is fun, isn't it? A proper old English pub!'

'I thought you'd like it,' smiled the barrister, as they shook hands. He found Bryn's wide-eyed appreciation of all that London had to offer rather endearing, especially as it seemed so at odds with a policeman's persona.

'Although — goodness,' said Bryn again, still looking around, 'they're not short on animals in here, are they?'

Magnus chuckled, for this was something of an understatement: the Lion of Westminster played host to around two dozen pieces of taxidermy, which were either mounted on the walls or propped up on cabinets and mantelpieces. Most of these animals were — or had once been — examples of British wildlife, such as stags, foxes, badgers and stoats, although there was what looked to be a leopard skin by the fireplace, and the stuffed head of a male lion had been hung in pride of place above the bar. Magnus had grown used to this unusual design scheme over the years, but he had to admit, when considering it from Bryn's perspective, walking into this pub was not dissimilar to entering a museum of natural history.

The barman, a stocky, middle-aged man with a kindly smile saw Bryn's slightly alarmed expression and said, 'Don't worry, none of them are recent kills.'

'It's an, erm, *interesting* choice of décor,' said the policeman, now eyeing the ferocious lion warily.

'Isn't it?' grinned the barman. 'A new pub couldn't get away with it these days, and I'm not saying I approve of our more exotic exhibits. But it does give the Lion a traditional feel, and you know most of it has come our way for free.'

'Really?' said Magnus. 'I didn't know that.'

'Yeah, almost all of them are family heirlooms, I believe. Well, taxidermy's not really in fashion any more, is it? You know, it's always women who bring them in. I have a theory that these modern girls get sick of having these dusty old creatures in their houses, particularly in their bedrooms, so they come here to get rid of them. And I can understand that. It must be a bit distracting, having a great stag's head glaring down at your bed when you're trying to, well, *you know...*'

He winked at Bryn, who reddened.

'Bryn, might I take this opportunity to introduce Gerry, one of the finest barmen in Westminster,' said Magnus, jumping in. 'No, scratch that, one of the finest barmen in all of London! Gerry, this is Police Constable Bryn Summers, an upstanding member of our local constabulary.'

'Always good to meet a local bobby,' said Gerry, extending his hand across the bar.

'Always good to drink at a local pub,' replied Bryn.

'Looks like we'll get on just fine, then,' smiled the barman. 'Now, what can I get you two gentlemen?'

Bryn ordered a pint of Harvey's beer and Magnus, who wasn't much of a drinker, a dry sherry. Then they headed to a little table right at the back of the bar, where it was quiet and there was no one nearby who might eavesdrop on their conversation. After they had taken a couple of sips of their drinks and exchanged a few pleasantries, they quickly fell to discussing their usual subject: Anne-Laure Chevalier.

'We haven't really had a chance to talk about everything since that day we saw Hilda and Jem,' said Bryn.

'No,' agreed Magnus, recalling how he had been called to dinner by Juliana shortly after they had been booted out of the actor's flat. 'You were telling me about finding some cosmetics in Jem's bathroom that you think might have belonged to Anne-Laure...?'

'Yes. Cosmetics, perfume, a hairbrush...'

'It's a shame you didn't keep that hairbrush,' said Magnus. 'Can't you use hair follicles to do DNA tests? We could have proved it was hers — that she'd been there.'

'I did consider it,' said Bryn, 'but then, how would we get a DNA test past Boyle?'

Magnus sighed heavily. 'I forgot. Goodness, Boyle's always in our way, isn't he?'

'I am fairly sure that perfume was hers, though,' said Bryn. 'The scent reminded me of that morning in the Royal West.'

'Which is rather creepy, when you come to think about it,' said Magnus. 'And unfortunately not a lot of use, as we only have your word to go on with that.'

'But at least it makes *me* more confident that Jem might have been lying to us.'

'Oh, I think we can be quite sure he was lying. Or at least avoiding the truth.'

'Yes, for a professional actor he's not very good at hiding his emotions, is he?' said Bryn, who seemed to have found the whole appointment with Jem McMorran rather disappointing.

'No,' Magnus agreed. 'But I have to say, I feel a bit sorry for him.'

'Really?'

'Yes, he was in a right old state, wasn't he? Goodness knows how much he'd drunk — and what he'd taken. I can't quite believe the change in him since we last bumped into each other, that morning after her death.'

'So it must be connected to her, mustn't it?' Bryn pressed. 'He must be feeling, I don't know — heartbroken? Grief-stricken? Guilty?'

'Hm,' said Magnus. 'It certainly looks that way, doesn't it? But still, as you said the other day at Hilda's, we mustn't rule out coincidences. We have to accept there's a possibility the old bat was mistaken, and she did see Jem with another blonde woman...'

'But surely you don't think that!' burst out Bryn. 'This is *Hilda* we're talking about — she said it herself: *I know everybody*. Is she really likely to make that kind of mistake?'

'Probably not. But then, perhaps she even misled us on purpose. As we know, she seems to have a lot of antagonism towards young people.'

But Bryn was shaking his head. 'Then why was Jem so jittery when you started talking about her?'

'Because he was suffering from some sort of hangover or come-down?'

'And why did he throw us out shortly after you specifically asked him whether he'd been in a relationship with Anne-Laure?'

'Because he'd had enough of us, I don't know,' said Magnus. 'Look, Bryn, I'm not disagreeing with you. In fact, I'm ninety percent sure Hilda was telling the truth and Jem was lying, but if you want to investigate this properly, you can't just jump to conclusions.'

Looking a little stung, Bryn took a sip of his beer. Magnus felt a twinge of guilt: perhaps he was being unfair. After all, it *had* been Bryn who had advised caution when he himself had taken it for granted that the two Westminster Square break-ins had been carried out by the same perpetrator. And with regard to this Anne-Laure case, while he was trying to be as open-minded as possible, it did seem likely she and Jem had been in some kind of relationship.

'I suppose what I'm getting it is that even if Hilda's right — even if Anne-Laure Chevalier and Jem McMorran were an item — have we really learned anything new about her death?' he asked.

Bryn immediately opened his mouth to reply, and then shut it. 'No,' he said, after a while. 'I suppose we haven't. Unless…'

'Unless we think Jem was the man in the garden that night?' finished Magnus.

'He could have been,' said Bryn. 'Didn't Hilda say she had seen them in the garden together before?'

Magnus nodded, but he was unconvinced. 'I don't know. I'm having a difficult time imagining Jem grabbing a woman like that. He's never struck me as an aggressive person. But obviously, it takes all sorts, and we shouldn't rule him out.'

'Perhaps we should have shown him the ring?' mused Bryn.

'Again, it doesn't seem likely that was from him, does it?'

'Why not?'

'Because that ring was a plain, cheap-looking thing, and Jem McMorran is a multimillionaire — or I assume he is, given the success of those *Pioneer* films.'

'Perhaps that's why she threw it away,' said Bryn, with a slight smile.

'Maybe,' said Magnus. 'But don't forget about those engraved initials. Now I come to think about it, I wonder what Jem called her: Anne-Laure or Annie or Anna… It might be useful to know.'

The barrister took another sip of his sherry, turning everything over in his mind for a few moments. 'The trouble with this whole business,' he said, 'is that every concrete fact is somewhat undermined by some unknown quality — by a question mark.'

'What do you mean?'

'Well, we know for fact that Anne-Laure Chevalier died from an overdose of cocaine…' He held up a hand, before Bryn could dispute this and start talking about the lack of autopsy again. '… But was her death accidental or on purpose? Another example: we know for a fact that, on the night of her death, Anne-Laure had a violent argument with a man in one of the gardens. But who was he? Again, we know for a fact that Anne-Laure was planning on leaving Westminster Square. But did she mean she wanted to physically move away, or was she planning on ending her life? And we know for a fact that there were two attempted burglaries in Westminster Square in the weeks preceding Anne-Laure's death. But are they of any relevance to this case? I would assume not, but — to return to our motto — we shouldn't rule anything out.'

'I see what you mean,' said Bryn. 'And something I've noticed with all of this is that there are a number of things we *almost* know, but — in the interest of not jumping to conclusions — we can't be one hundred percent sure about.'

'Such as?' asked Magnus.

Bryn pulled out his police notebook, which, as he was in plain clothes, was in his pocket rather than his utility belt.

'I'd say it was more than likely that the ring in the garden belonged to Anne-Laure,' he began. 'Just as it seems more than likely that whoever grabbed her wrists in the garden also grabbed her neck, either then or later, and that he was the one who gave her that ring. I'd also say it was more than likely that Hilda's right, and Anne-Laure and Jem were lovers, especially as Dame Winifred seemed to think she was popular with men — who's to say she wouldn't fall in with a movie star?' Bryn flipped back through the notebook, still reading his scribbles. 'And I'd also say it was more than likely that Anne-Laure had some sort of other work on the side, which was separate from Vasyl's PR stuff — probably still party-planning, though. But again, there's no real proof for any of this,' said the policeman, shutting his notebook. 'It's just speculation by us, and by others.'

'Hm,' said Magnus, 'and I'm assuming you still think it's more than likely that Anne-Laure Chevalier was murdered as well?'

Bryn's gaze did not waver, and the barrister had to admire the young man for sticking to his guns. 'I do,' he said. 'And I'm starting to think you're becoming more and more intrigued by this case, Magnus.'

The barrister chuckled as he took another sip of his sherry. 'I suppose you're right,' he said. 'I must admit, before we went to see Hilda, I was thinking of taking a step back from all of this. It didn't really seem as though we were getting anywhere and, well, to be perfectly honest I'm not sure how much Juliana likes all this amateur sleuthing — she's in a very odd mood at the moment.'

'But you've changed your mind?' said Bryn, looking hopeful.

'A little,' Magnus confessed. 'I'm still not sure we're looking at a murder case here — that just seems too far-fetched to me — but equally I can't deny that there's nothing odd about this woman's death. Not to mention the fact that, as I said before, the more we find out about it, the more questions we seem to have.'

'So you'll carry on investigating with me?' said Bryn, who seemed to want to elicit some sort of confirmation from him.

'I will,' said Magnus, hoping he wasn't going to regret agreeing to this. Then, before Bryn could grow too enthused, he added, 'But the issue is, *how* are we going to carry on investigating? We've talked to everyone we know of who had some sort of connection with Anne-Laure: her employer, her landlady, her possible lover and Hilda, if you can call having a nemesis a connection. I don't know who or what to try next. And it's not as though, even if we do find out anything significant, we can take to Scotland Yard. I imagine your friend Barry Boyle would block us even if we had the killer's confession signed in Anne-Laure Chevalier's blood.'

'Probably,' said Bryn gloomily. 'Anything to protect the reputation of the Royal West and the rest of Westminster... But there must be something we can do, surely? We can't just try and forget our doubts — it's not right.'

'Not right for whom? Us? Anne-Laure?' asked Magnus, curiously. 'Or her killer, if he even exists?'

'For all of us,' said Bryn, and the barrister noticed the policeman was beginning to look rather pale and clammy. He took a steadying gulp of beer and then continued, 'You're going to think I'm weak, or perhaps I'm cracking up or something, but... I dream about her,' he whispered. 'Well, they're not dreams, really... I have these nightmares about Anne-Laure. That's crazy, isn't it?'

'No,' said Magnus firmly. 'It can't have been pleasant, being one of the first to see her body and —'

'But I'm not sure it's just that,' said Bryn quickly. 'I don't feel traumatised at seeing her corpse — she wasn't the first. It's more...' He trailed off, looking embarrassed. 'Look, I don't believe in ghosts or anything like that, but I feel as though she's haunting my dreams because I'm not finished with this case. I still have more to discover before I can put it all from my mind and have a decent night's sleep. And then she can rest in peace too.'

Magnus considered this as he drained the last of his sherry. His first thought was that it did indeed sound as though Bryn were losing the plot a little, given all this talk of dreams and hauntings. And there was no shame in that: after all, the policeman was new on the job, bored, bullied, and very green to be dealing with seeing the body of a woman his own age. Magnus doubted whether anybody had checked in with the young policeman to see how he was coping after that potentially upsetting morning at the Royal West.

But then, once more, the barrister reminded himself to trust his companion, and especially to trust in Bryn's instincts. While it didn't seem as though they were any closer to understanding the mystery of Anne-Laure's death, there was no indication that Bryn was leading him on a wild goose chase either. And wasn't the younger man right? Didn't they owe it to both themselves and the dead woman to at least try and find out the truth?

'Tell you what,' said Magnus, at last, 'why don't we take a few days' break and have a think about everything? And during that time,' he pressed on, before Bryn could argue, 'perhaps you could put together a proper document on what we've learned, instead of flipping back and forth through that little notebook of yours? I'd appreciate a copy of what you wrote down during our various meetings, and it might make it clearer how we should proceed.'

'That's a good idea!' said Bryn, and in his eagerness to reach for his notebook he elbowed over his pint glass, which was fortunately now empty. 'Yes, I'll get started on that straight away!'

'Do,' said Magnus, righting the toppled glass. 'Describe it all, don't leave anything out. In my experience, it's often the smallest details that have the biggest impact on these cases. Who knows, perhaps we already have the exact piece of information we need to crack this mystery, we just haven't realised it yet...'

CHAPTER SEVENTEEN

The following few days at the Victoria Police Station were as dull as ever for Bryn, who was still mostly confined to his desk. However, his seemingly-endless administration duties did give him the opportunity to work on the document he had agreed to put together for Magnus, compiling everything they knew and suspected about the Anne-Laure Chevalier case.

Bryn kept his notes on his desk at all times, sometimes pausing in the act of sorting through a pile of letters or stapling leaflets about vehicle crime to jot down a quick memory from one of his and Magnus' recent meetings with Vasyl Kosnitschev, Dame Winifred Rye, Hilda Underpin and Jem McMorran. He supposed it was a little risky, putting together these notes at work, right under Barry Boyle's bulbous nose, but experience had taught Bryn that the Chief Police Superintendent was supremely uninterested in anything he did. In fact, Boyle didn't ever give him a second glance on the few trips he made past Bryn's desk each day, which were usually to top up the supply of junk food in his disgusting office.

But one Tuesday afternoon, just as Bryn was thinking about detailing Hilda's late husband's army experience on the off chance it might be relevant, he was distracted by a conversation taking place between two of his colleagues at a neighbouring desk.

'It's not many people who can stand up to Boyle, but she's giving it a good go,' said Shona Walsh, a female constable with a few years' experience on Bryn.

'Rather her than me,' shuddered her companion, John Brockhurst, who was a middle-aged, mild-mannered sergeant. 'Who is she, anyway?'

'I think she's something to do with that woman who died at the Royal West a few weeks' back. You know, the one we're not supposed to talk about?'

'You mean Anne-Laure Chevalier?' piped up Bryn, before remembering he was not supposed to mention her name in the police station.

'That's right, her,' said the other constable, appearing a little bemused by Bryn's sudden interruption. 'I think she might be some sort of relation...'

'Wait,' said Bryn, scattering envelopes over his desk to cover his notes and edging closer to his colleagues. 'Are you saying that a relation of Anne — I mean, of that dead woman — is in the police station *now*? Talking to Boyle?'

'I think so,' said Walsh. 'She's in reception, and Boyle's at the front desk, trying to make her go away. I was instructed to take them coffee — you know how Boyle likes to treat me like a secretary rather than a police constable, just because I'm the only woman around here,' she added, with a very sour expression. 'Anyway, when I went in, this lady was having a right old go at him.'

'Blimey,' said Brockhurst.

'A go at him about what?' asked Bryn eagerly.

'I'm not really sure. She seemed to think we'd messed up somehow, but I didn't hear much, because when I brought in the coffee Boyle started shouting at me for interrupting — even though he specifically phoned through to ask for it! He's such a pig,' she concluded, bitterly.

'Is this woman still here?' asked Bryn. 'Are they still in reception?'

'I assume so, I only just came back, so — Hey, Summers, where are you going? *Summers?*'

But Bryn ignored his colleague, for he was already hurrying towards the gloomy corridor that led to the reception of the Victoria Police Station, which was the only place where members of the public were able to venture, unless they had a pre-arranged meeting or were under suspicion.

Bryn heard them before he saw them. As he crept further along the corridor running adjacent to the front desk, Barry Boyle's voice, which still betrayed traces of his working class origins, was as loud and strident as ever, but now it was competing with a shrill female voice as well.

'I told you, I'm not leaving here until I have some answers!' the woman was crying.

'And I've told you, Mrs Chambers, you can't speak to me like this in my own police station!'

'You dare to tell me what I can and cannot do after the mistakes you've made with this whole business! I should go to your superiors! I should go to the *press*!'

'Are you threatening me, Mrs Chambers, because I could have you arrested for —'

'Oh, what a load of rot!' interrupted the woman's voice. 'As though you're going to arrest me for simply asking questions about my dead niece! You're a very foolish man, Mr Boyle, a very foolish man indeed!'

Still hidden, Bryn stuffed his knuckles into his mouth to stop from bursting into laughter: he had never heard anyone talk to Barry Boyle like this.

'I'm getting fed up with you!' the Police Chief Superintendent roared. 'You've got what you came for, now get out of my sight — and clear up that flat while you're at it!'

'I'm still waiting for an explanation, Mr Boyle! I want to know how this whole mix-up occurred!'

'Well you're going to be waiting a long time,' retorted the Police Chief Superintendent. 'Now, if you'll excuse me, I have important police work to be getting on with…'

'Don't you walk away from me, Mr Boyle! *Mr Boyle*?!'

Almost too late, Bryn realised from the sound of heavy footsteps that Barry Boyle was leaving the reception area and heading straight into the corridor. Quickly, the police constable threw himself behind the nearest door, which led to a dark and damp-smelling cleaning cupboard, and waited until Boyle — who was swearing loudly to himself — strode past on his way back to his office. Then, when he was quite sure the coast was clear, he headed back towards the reception, which was now empty.

'Miss Chambers?' he called, walking out through the main entrance of the Victoria Police Station. 'Hello? Miss Chambers?'

She turned, having only made it a few steps along the pavement, and Bryn took in the sight of her. The woman appeared to be in her late fifties, and it was difficult to believe she was any close relation of Anne-Laure's, for while she was not exactly ugly, she had a very plain, almost forgettable face. Her skin was sallow, her hair lank and mousy-coloured, and she was wearing a long, shapeless brown dress that did absolutely nothing for her tall, bony figure. However, despite her dowdy appearance, Bryn detected an aura of sharpness about this person, especially in her beady dark eyes.

'Yes?' she snapped. 'Who are you?'

'Police Constable Bryn Summers. I was one of the first officers on the scene when your niece was discovered.'

He held out a hand. She shook it, giving a little huff of impatience.

'Miss Agnes Chambers. And they won't tell me a thing in there — it's absurd!'

'It's a busy time,' Bryn lied, for things were rarely busy in the Victoria Police Station. 'But still, that's no excuse. I'm very sorry for your loss, Miss Chambers.'

'Well, thank you,' she said, and as she waved aside his condolences Bryn noticed what was clutched in her hand: a large transparent bag the police usually used for evidence and, within it, a gold handbag he had seen once before.

'You came to pick up her belongings,' he realised.

'Yes.' Her gaze also went to her hand. 'I told them they could give that dress and those shoes to charity — ghastly-looking things, I don't know what she was thinking. But I suppose I should have a look through this. And they want me to clear out her flat, if you can believe it. As though I have time for all of that when I have to catch a train back to Brighton! I'll have to come back another day…'

Bryn was getting the impression she felt more annoyed and inconvenienced than particularly bereft, but he was aware this aunt could be a valuable source of information about Anne-Laure.

'Is it Victoria you're heading to, then?' he asked.

She checked her watch. 'In a moment, yes. If I can remember the way...'

'Perhaps you'd allow me to accompany you?' asked Bryn, seizing his chance. 'I can show you where to go and carry your bags while I'm at it. To make up for the shoddy treatment you received back at the station there.'

'All right,' she said, handing him both the transparent sack of evidence and her own ugly carpetbag, which was so heavy Bryn thought it had stones inside. 'I'm glad to know at least *some* of London's policemen still have manners...'

They set off along the road that led towards Victoria. It wasn't far to the station, especially as Agnes Chambers was setting such a brisk pace, so Bryn quickly racked his brains as to how best to tackle her on Anne-Laure. Fortunately, however, her aunt seemed to be in the mood to talk — or rather, rant.

'I just can't believe that disgusting man back there — who does he think he is, talking to me like that? I don't know how you can bear working with him.'

'Neither do I,' Bryn admitted.

'The audacity of him,' she continued, 'speaking to me like that, after the mistakes you lot have made, it's simply unacceptable!'

'Sorry, what mistakes have we made?' asked Bryn, curiously.

'Why, the cremation, of course!'

'The cremation?'

'Yes, didn't you know? That tubby fool back there sent my niece off to be cremated at the government's expense — as though she were a tramp who'd drunk herself to death behind some bins! And all because I, her next of kin, didn't come forward early enough to claim the body! Well, how could I, when nobody bothered to inform me she was dead?'

Bryn stopped in his tracks.

'Sorry — Boyle had Anne-Laure cremated without telling you?'

'He had *Annie* cremated, yes,' corrected Agnes. 'That was the problem, you see: I heard about this Anne-Laure person being dead on the radio, but how I was I supposed to know it was my brother's child? Silly girl. What did she have to change her name for? And couldn't the police have checked up on something like that?'

'Yes, we should've, I'm very sorry,' said Bryn, apologising even though he'd had nothing to do with the official Anne-Laure Chevalier case since that morning at the Royal West.

Agnes let out another impatient exhalation. 'I appreciate that, Mr Summers, I do. It's a damn sight more than I got from your colleague.'

'Well, it's dreadful,' said Bryn, now growing annoyed on her behalf. 'You didn't get to say goodbye, you didn't get to give her a proper send-off...'

'Oh, I don't care about any of that,' Agnes sniffed. 'It's the principle of the thing, you know? It should have been handled better — I should have been informed. I had no great love for the girl, I don't mind admitting that, but it should have been done properly. If only for the sake of her father, my poor late brother...' She checked her watch. 'You know, I'm not sure why we're dilly-dallying here, Mr Summers, I do have a train to catch.'

'Oh right, sorry,' said Bryn, jumping to attention.

As they continued along the street, he found himself wondering at Agnes' rather callous attitude to Anne-Laure's death: as he had suspected a few moments ago, she didn't seem in the least bit upset about the fate of her niece; instead, it was the lack of correct protocol that seemed to be bothering her.

'You weren't particularly close, then?' he asked, tentatively. 'You and Anne — I mean, you and Annie?'

'No,' she said bluntly.

'But you took her in, didn't you? After the death of her parents?'

'I didn't have much of a choice,' grumbled Agnes. 'I thought she was going to stay in foster care until she became an adult, but both she and social services made such a *fuss*. I was practically forced to take her.'

'How old was she?'

'Eleven when they died. Almost thirteen when she came to stay with me.'

Bryn forced himself not to make a retort: did this woman have no heart? Why had she been so reluctant to give a home to her brother's orphaned child? But in spite of his silence, however, Agnes seemed to know what he was thinking.

'Look, I know how it sounds. And I had sympathy for the girl, I did. It was a dreadful thing, that car crash. To be perfectly honest with you, it completely devastated me, losing my dear brother like that…'

She trailed off, and for the first time Bryn detected a hint of softness about her, a little like when Hilda Underpin had spoken of her late husband.

'But what you have to understand is that I have never been a sociable person,' continued Agnes, her curt manner returning at once. 'I don't particularly like company — I'm far happier on my own — and for that reason I chose not to marry and not to start a family. So of course I didn't want to be suddenly saddled with this moping teenager, no matter who she was. I knew it would turn my life upside-down, and it did.'

'So she was a difficult child?' asked Bryn, struggling to understand Agnes' perspective on this.

'Oh, she was all right. She wasn't a bad girl. She was just — how would you put it? — a dreamer. She always had her head in the clouds. Do you know, she wanted to be an actress?' Agnes gave a snort of laughter. 'I mean, how completely ridiculous!'

'You and Anne — *Annie* were very different, then,' was all Bryn allowed himself to say.

'Exactly,' said Agnes. Then, with a martyrish sigh, she continued, 'But I took her in, I gave her a roof over her head. I fed her and gave her money for clothes. And we were fine — I suppose I got used to her. I can't deny I was looking forward to her finishing her college course and moving out, but we were getting along okay, before that *dreadful* woman came along…'

'Sorry,' Bryn said again, wrong-footed by this sudden change of direction. 'What woman?'

'That awful aristocrat from London who filled Annie's head with all sorts of *ideas*…'

'Are you talking about Dame Winifred Rye?'

'Oh, probably. Yes, that sounds about right; an absurd name for an absurd woman. In my opinion, it's nothing short of kidnap, whisking a young girl away like that, spoiling her rotten.'

'You didn't approve of Annie's move to London, then?'

'No I did not,' Agnes snapped. 'She had a life in Brighton, and she just upped and left it without a second thought: her home, her remaining family, her college course, even her boyfriend — well, that was no loss, he was a complete no-hoper. But the rest of it...' Agnes broke off, shaking her head. 'She was a silly girl.'

By this point, they had reached Victoria Station. As they stood under the great glass roof, and after Agnes had checked her train back to Brighton on the big information boards overhead, Bryn was expecting her to try and dash off at the first possible moment. But, once more, it seemed Anne-Laure's aunt was keen to continue with her story, and it occurred to the policeman that, as much as she claimed to like her own company, perhaps she was a little lonely after all.

'And Annie wasn't happy in London, you know,' Agnes went on, after she had double-checked her train tickets, 'at least, not at first. I expect it was a big shock for her, this busy, polluted city — I can't bear London, myself,' she added as an aside, looking around at Victoria in disgust. 'Annie even phoned me once, telling me she wanted to come home, that she'd made a mistake. She was crying, if I remember rightly.'

'And what happened?'

'What do you think happened? I told her she'd made her bed and she had to lie in it. Oh, don't look at me like that, young man, she was just a little homesick, that was all. And I'd already rented out her room — I run a B&B by the seafront, you see, so there was no way she could come back. Plus, I wasn't about to mollycoddle her, not when she'd thrown all my years of care back in my face.'

Once more, Bryn refrained from saying anything, even though this all seemed rather cold-hearted to him.

'Did you speak to Annie regularly?'

'We didn't speak at all. That was the last time I ever heard from her, that phone call. I expect she viewed me as some kind of villain after that, but, as I said, it was all her doing. Anyway, judging by those expensive clothes, she did all right for herself. I mean, look at this ridiculous handbag…'

She reached out and took the transparent container for evidence that Bryn had forgotten he was holding, and pulled it open to get at the gold handbag inside. The policeman gave a little shudder: the last time he had seen this object was when Marlene the medical examiner had extracted it from under Anne-Laure's body. Agnes, however, seemed to have no qualms about inspecting her dead niece's belongings, not even in the middle of Victoria Station.

'It's a horrible-looking thing, isn't it?' she muttered, turning the sparkly bag over so it caught the light. 'Designer, I expect. Let's see what she kept inside…'

She fumbled at the clasp and Bryn, despite the fact he had already seen the contents of this bag, stepped forward and peered in eagerly.

'Lipstick, hair-grips, lots of loose change — well, she was always bad with money,' said Agnes, narrating the contents of the bag as she found them. 'A purse full of bank cards — goodness, I suppose I'll have to deal with all of that, won't I? Her finances, if she has any. What's this? Addresses?' She flicked through a little purple book, a sour expression on her face. 'I dread to think what's in there. Who on earth did she fall in with in London? Here, hold it for a minute, there's loads in here…'

She thrust the address book at Bryn and produced a set of keys from the handbag.

'Did I tell you I have to go and sort out the contents of her flat? Apparently I'm a glorified cleaner now! I told Boyle I couldn't very well do it this afternoon, not when I have a train to catch, I'll have to do it another day. So that awful Rye woman will have to wait a few weeks.'

A slow, satisfied smile spread across Agnes' face at the thought of inconveniencing Dame Winifred like this.

'If you want, I could help you clear it out,' offered Bryn, hardly daring to imagine how much of an insight into Anne-Laure's life her flat would give him and Magnus. 'You know, whenever it's convenient for you. To make up for all that cremation business.'

'Yes, that'd be good,' said Agnes vaguely, still peeking into the handbag. 'Now, what's this?'

She drew out the large compact. Bryn found he was holding his breath as she opened it but, unsurprisingly, the packet of cocaine had been removed. Instead, it was a simple mirror, in which Agnes Chambers surveyed her own reflection critically.

'Well, it's unsurprising she was carrying around one of these, she always was a vain girl. She was beautiful, of course — there's no denying that — but she knew it, which is a very unattractive quality in a woman. My brother's wife was the same, both in looks and in temperament. That must have been where Annie got it from. Well,' Agnes sighed, 'I did try and stamp it out of her, but clearly it didn't work. That's London for you, isn't it? I imagine it corrupts most people in the end.'

She shut the compact with a snap and dropped it back into the handbag.

'Heaven knows what I'm going to do with all of this rubbish. I should have left it at the police station. I suppose it can go to charity as well. You get all sorts in Brighton, so I don't doubt even this ghastly handbag will find a home somewhere…'

She dropped the offending object back into its plastic evidence bag and looked at her watch again.

'Well, it's almost time for my train,' she announced. 'I'm much obliged to you for walking me here, Mr Summers. As I said, it's rather restored my faith in the London police.'

'You're very welcome,' said Bryn. 'And, as I said, if you need help with Annie's flat…'

'Yes, yes,' said Agnes Chambers, sounding a little impatient to be going over this again. 'Now, what am I missing? I feel like I'm forgetting something?'

'Your own bag?' Bryn suggested, sliding the heavy, ugly thing off his shoulder and handing it over.

'Ah yes,' said Agnes, snatching it from him. 'Yes, I'll be needing that. Well then, goodbye, Mr Summers.'

'Goodbye, Miss Chambers.'

Bryn watched her for a few moments, marching across Victoria Station and towards her platform, checking her ticket against the information board for a third time. What a curious woman, he thought; it was difficult to tell whether she had always been indifferent to her niece, or whether she had become embittered by Anne-Laure's abandonment of her. Either way, and not for the first time, the police constable could not help but feel rather sorry for Anne-Laure Chevalier: it can't have been easy, spending her teenage years in the company of her pitiless aunt, especially after being shunted from foster home to foster home, and after suffering the trauma of losing both of her parents in an accident. Really, it was little wonder the girl bolted to London with Dame Winifred at the first chance she got, even if the big city did initially prove to be rather a shock to her system. To her, a miserable, unloved orphan, it must have felt as though her fairy godmother had finally shown up in the form an eccentric aristocrat.

Returning to the present, Bryn glanced around the station to see that the tall, rigid figure of Agnes Chambers had now disappeared, presumably onto the train bound for Brighton. Then he gave his arm a little shake, so that the small, purple address book he had managed to stow up the sleeve of his uniform dropped out into his other hand.

CHAPTER EIGHTEEN

After Magnus had finished reading Rosanna and Lee their bedtime stories, he returned to the living room to find Juliana curled up in an armchair, ensconced in a book of her own.

'I like that new story of Lee's,' he said, settling himself down onto the sofa, 'the one with the pirates and so on. I must admit, I prefer it to that boarding school stuff Rosanna's into at the moment…'

'Mm-hm,' said Juliana, without looking up from her novel.

'I've told them they can both have twenty minutes more reading time,' continued Magnus, 'and then I'll go and turn out their lights.'

This time, Juliana didn't bother to reply; she simply turned a page and continued to read. Magnus frowned.

'Juliana? *Juliana?* How long are you going to keep this up for?'

She lowered the book, glaring at him over the top of the pages. 'I don't know what you're talking about, Magnus,' she said.

'Yes you do,' he snapped. 'You've been cold with me for almost a week now! What have I done?'

'Really,' Juliana sighed, returning to her reading. 'I don't see why *I* should be the one to tell you…'

'Well who else can I ask?' he cried. 'Patrick downstairs? Your mother? *John Major?*'

'Don't be ridiculous, Magnus.'

Highly frustrated now, he rose from the sofa, moved towards her, and plucked the book from her hands. She scowled as she followed its progress towards the coffee table — and out of her reach.

'Come on, Juliana,' he said, 'let's talk about this, shall we? Why are you so upset? Is it because I'm staying too late at work? Have you had another run-in with Hilda Underpin? Or perhaps you don't like the fact that I'm doing this investigation with this policeman?'

'Hm, yes, all of the above,' said Juliana. 'But to be perfectly frank with you, Magnus, I'm used to being upset about your work and that spying old hag.'

'So it's the investigation that's bothering you?'

'Not really, no — although I've no idea what you're both up to.'

'Well what is it, then?' cried Magnus, throwing his hands into the air and wondering whether any of his friends' wives were this difficult. 'I don't understand! And seeing as we're being frank, Juliana, I'm actually a little annoyed at *you* for not consulting me before you talked to Sotheby's about that Turner sketch my mother gave us.'

'Oh, don't talk to me about Sotheby's, Magnus Walterson!' retorted Juliana, her chilliness suddenly giving way to a flash of anger.

Magnus hesitated: what was going on? Evidently, Sotheby's had something to do with her bad mood, but he still couldn't work out what he was supposed to have done. He hadn't dealt with the auction house in years.

'Juliana, please,' he said, trying to curb his impatience with her, 'just tell me what the matter is, will you? I'm sure it's all a big misunderstanding...'

'Oh, it's *not* a misunderstanding!' she cried. 'You've deliberately lied to me, Magnus, and I'm furious about it!'

He stared at her. 'I — I haven't,' he said, thoroughly bewildered. 'I always tell you everything, darling, you know that.'

'You haven't told me about all your secret meetings.'

'I have! I told you, Bryn and I went to see Vasyl Kosnitschev, Dame Winifred Rye, Hilda —'

'Not those meetings!' she cried. 'The secret meetings about CSP — about the maintenance costs!'

'Ah,' said Magnus slowly, '*those* meetings.'

As guilt and dread began to trickle through him like cold water, Magnus realised his crusade against Central Square Properties had been put on the back-burner over the past few days and weeks. In fact, he had been so distracted by the Anne-Laure Chevalier investigation he had almost entirely forgotten about the issue of maintenance costs.

'How did you, erm, find out, darling?'

'So you're not denying it?' she demanded.

'Erm, no. No I'm not...'

'I found out from Sotheby's of all places — *Sotheby's!*' she shouted, leaping from her armchair.

'Shh, you'll disturb the children...'

But Juliana wasn't listening. She was pacing up and down the living room now, growing more and more irate.

'I called them about that *awful* Turner sketch your mother gave us — and don't start on at me about that, it's a horrible little piece. Why would Turner of all people want to draw *London*? I can't even bear to look at it.'

Obediently, Magnus shut his mouth; he had indeed been about to object.

'Anyway, while I was on the phone, I asked the man from Sotheby's whether it was possible to get out of our lease here in Westminster Square...'

'Oh, *Juliana!*'

'Don't "*oh, Juliana*" me!' she snapped. 'You know I'm not happy here, Magnus, and I have the right to ask whether we can get out of that dratted lease you signed a decade ago, the one that confines us to this wretched place for twenty years.'

'You speak as though you're in prison...'

'I feel like I'm in prison! A dirty, noisy, concrete prison called *London!*'

'Juliana, this is one of the most enviable addresses in the country! In the world!'

'Not for me,' she said, stubbornly.

Magnus rubbed at his eyes. Their conversation had been diverted into this now-familiar discussion about his wife's hatred of where they lived.

'Can we return to Sotheby's?' he asked. 'What did they tell you about the lease?'

'They told me the only way we could get out of it was for CSP to pay us back for the time we wouldn't be living here. So, if we moved out in the next few months, they'd pay us two hundred thousand pounds — half of the four hundred thousand we paid in 1984.'

Magnus' brow furrowed. 'What, without any interest? What about inflation?'

'Exactly, Magnus: *what about inflation*? Don't you see what you've consigned us to by signing that lease? A huge loss!'

Magnus couldn't argue with this: if they had been able to buy the property outright, they could have made an enormous profit selling it now, after ten years, house prices being what they were.

'CSP really are a bunch of crooks,' he muttered, temporarily forgetting about Juliana's rage.

'There's no need to tell me that! Especially not now I know how much they're charging us for maintenance issues each month!'

'Ah,' said Magnus, 'you — erm — found out about that, did you?'

'Yes I did! Because the man at Sotheby's had heard of you, Magnus! Apparently you're causing a bit of a stir over at the CSP office, because you've organised this, I don't know, *protest* against the maintenance charges. Apparently you've put together a petition! And everyone knew about this apart from *me*! Do you have any idea how humiliating it was for me to find out from a stranger what my own husband had been up to behind my back?'

'I'm sorry, Juliana,' said Magnus. 'Although, to be fair, Hilda Underpin also didn't know…'

'*I don't care about that wretched woman!*' shouted Juliana. 'I care about *us* — about our marriage, our family! What were you thinking, keeping this from me?'

'I don't know,' he admitted. 'I suppose I thought if you found out how much CSP were charging us each month, you'd be even more unhappy living here.'

'Well you were right,' said Juliana bluntly. 'Now I've discovered we're three thousand pounds down every month, I hate Westminster Square even more, and I didn't think that was even possible. I mean, for God's sake — three thousand pounds, just for the privilege of having a tennis court we can hardly use and living in an ugly old building made of plaster pretending to be stone!'

'Hang on, how do you know it's three thousand pounds?'

'Because I went into your office and found the latest bill.'

'Juliana!' Now it was Magnus' temper rising. 'Juliana, that office contains a lot of sensitive, highly confidential material —'

'Oh, I'm not interested in your work, I'd fall asleep with boredom as soon as I laid eyes on any of *that*...'

'You shouldn't have gone through my papers!'

But Juliana was unrepentant. 'Don't you dare paint me as the bad guy in this situation, Magnus! Not when you've been the one holding secret meetings and putting together petitions behind my back. And as for that three thousand pounds each month...' She broke off, shaking her head, evidently too incensed to continue.

Magnus fell back onto the sofa, suddenly feeling exhausted by this whole discussion.

'Look, I'm sorry,' he said. 'I was wrong not to tell you about all of it. But I don't know what you want me to do, Juliana. You're acting as though it's my fault we live here, but you agreed to sign that lease back in '84 — you agreed to living here for twenty years.'

'So I'm not allowed to change my mind?'

'Of course you are. But I don't know what you think we should do. As you now know, if we try and get out the lease, we make a huge loss.'

'But if we stay here, we're making a huge loss from these maintenance costs anyway. Three thousand pounds every month for another ten years is, what —?'

'A lot,' said Magnus quickly, not wanting to give her a chance to do the mental arithmetic. 'And that's assuming CSP don't put it up again, which they undoubtedly will attempt to do. Which is why I'm trying to fight this, Juliana. I am trying to do the right thing here, even though — I know, I know — I shouldn't have kept it from you.'

His swift apology and admission of guilt seemed to be having a calming effect on Juliana, for she finally stopped her pacing and came to sit next to him on the sofa.

'I don't know what we should do,' she said, her voice now soft and sad. 'I don't like it here, Magnus. I never have.'

'Darling, we get out to the country almost every second weekend…'

'It's not just the fact we're in a city,' said Juliana. 'I don't like the atmosphere here. At best it's snobby and prejudiced and a little bit mean, and at worst…' She broke off. 'I can't stop thinking about that woman, Anne-Laure Chevalier. What if she *was* murdered?'

'I think it's very unlikely,' said Magnus, not entirely truthfully.

'I wouldn't put it past a few people around here,' Juliana muttered.

Magnus dared to reach out for her hand and squeeze it. 'Don't dwell on all of that, it's not good for you — for anyone. You should hear Bryn talking about it, apparently he's having all sorts of nightmares.'

'Maybe you're right,' Juliana said, looking at their entwined hands. 'I think I'm just trying to find any excuse to get out of here. Because a part of me does think we should just accept the financial loss and move on. We could get a place in Kent, near enough to London that you can commute, of course, but away from all these ugly buildings and busy roads. The children could go to nice local schools, and they could play outside without me constantly worrying they're going to be knocked down by traffic. I could start gardening again, and maybe get a horse… I miss riding. I miss everything about the countryside.'

Her eyes were glittering with unshed tears. Magnus didn't know what to say. The trouble was, he *liked* London — loved it, even — and had been truly happy here over the past decade. There was so much to enjoy in this dazzling great city; so many sights and shows and exhibitions and events to be experienced. They were fortunate to have the means and opportunity to live in Westminster Square, but for some reason his wife just couldn't appreciate this. In truth, he didn't think she had ever given London a chance — she had been determined to hate it from the start — and while he couldn't very well force her to live somewhere that made her unhappy, it pained him to think of moving away from a place where he was so content.

As he considered how in the world he was going to try and articulate all of this to Juliana, the flat's buzzer sounded.

'Who on earth is that?' he asked, checking his watch. 'It's almost nine o'clock.'

'Ignore it,' said Juliana at once. 'They've probably got the wrong flat. Or it's Jehovah's Witnesses.'

Magnus hesitated, and then just as he was about to relax there was another buzz. Was it his imagination, or did it sound more urgent this time?

'Don't answer it, Magnus,' Juliana said sternly. 'We're having an important talk here.'

But when the buzzer sounded for the third time, Magnus stood up.

'They're going to disturb the children,' he said, walking towards the hallway.

Although, in truth, he was keen to put a stop to his and Juliana's 'important talk'.

'Magnus, come back! *Magnus!*'

Knowing he would be in trouble later for ignoring his wife like this, the barrister pulled open the front door of his flat. He then leapt back as a long-limbed figure came barrelling over the threshold, gibbering excitedly.

'Bryn?' said Magnus, closing the door behind the policeman. 'What are you doing here?'

'I've — I've made a discovery!' cried Bryn, who was still in his police uniform, and whose face was flushed with exhilaration. 'I've — I've something to — *atishoo!* — show you, Magnus. *Atishoo!*'

'Oh goodness, the pollen,' said Magnus, leading the policeman by the elbow down the hallway. 'Come into the living room again, I'll move the flowers out.'

'Right you are — *atishoo* — Magnus.'

'And try and keep it down, will you? My children are in bed.'

Juliana was back in her armchair when Magnus returned to the living room. She had evidently been intending to ignore him in favour of her book again, but when he walked in with a sneezing policeman she stared at them, open-mouthed.

'Juliana, this is Bryn, the police constable I've been telling you about. Bryn, this is my wife, Juliana.'

'Pleased to — *atishoo* — meet you.'

He stretched out his hand, which Juliana merely eyed suspiciously.

'What's the matter with him?' she hissed at Magnus.

'Hayfever.'

'*Hayfever?*' Juliana regarded Bryn with an expression that was half-pitying, half-contemptuous.

'Yes, he's allergic to all the pollen you have in here. So perhaps we can move some of these plants out?'

Juliana looked from Magnus to Bryn and back again, her lips very thin, and Magnus thought she might be taking Bryn's allergies as a personal slight. Then, after the policeman sneezed four more times in succession, Magnus barked, 'Come on, Juliana, help me with this,' and reached for the nearest vase.

A few minutes later, the room was free of flowers and foliage, Bryn was sniffling into a tissue, and Juliana was in the kitchen making tea.

'Why did you come round?' Magnus asked, ignoring the fact he had answered the door. 'You know this place is like a jungle. And it is rather late...'

'Sorry,' Bryn murmured, through a faceful of tissue. 'As I said, I've something to show you, and I wanted to discuss it straight away.'

'Couldn't you have phoned?'

'Oh yes, I didn't think of that...'

'Well, never mind,' said Magnus, feeling he would rather talk to Bryn about, well, anything, than Juliana about their future in Westminster Square. 'What's the latest, then?'

But before the policeman could answer, Juliana had returned with a tray of tea.

'Are you recovered?' she asked bluntly, as she handed Bryn a cup.

'Almost,' he said. 'Sorry about all of that sneezing.'

'It's you I feel sorry for,' she told him. 'How do you manage long walks in the countryside?'

'Well, I suppose I'm not really a countryside kind of person,' he said.

Juliana stared at him, as though he had just said he didn't breathe oxygen.

'Milk? Sugar?' she asked coldly.

'A bit of milk, please, and no sugar,' said Bryn, watching Juliana with a slightly fearful expression.

'And how long have you been in London for, Mr Summers?'

'Oh, just a few months.'

'And do you like it?'

'Very much.'

'Is this your first job?'

'No, I was in Cardiff before. I did my training there.'

'How long did you have to train for?'

'Juliana, leave the poor man alone,' said Magnus, who had spent the exchange looking around hopefully for the biscuit tin and, to his great disappointment, found it missing. 'Honestly, darling, only you would have the nerve to interrogate a policeman.'

'I'm not interrogating him, I'm simply exchanging pleasantries,' Juliana retorted, in a tone that was bordering on unpleasant. 'I want to know more about this person you've been playing detectives with, Magnus.'

'Well, that's all there is to know, really,' said Bryn, modestly.

Juliana regarded him through narrowed eyes, an expression that Magnus knew meant *I'll be the judge of that*.

'Anyway, darling, Bryn's come round because he has something to show me regarding this Anne-Laure Chevalier case…' began Magnus.

He spoke pointedly, hoping she would go away and leave them to it. But instead, Juliana sat back in her armchair and regarded them both on the sofa with a rather cynical smile.

'That's what you're calling it now? The Anne-Laure Chevalier *case*? Goodness, you really are taking this sleuthing seriously, aren't you? And I thought you told me there was no way she was murdered, Magnus?'

As Bryn turned to him looking slightly betrayed, Magnus explained, 'I said I thought it was *unlikely*, Juliana. But my friend here has a more suspicious mind than me, which is why we're continuing with our inquiries.'

'*Inquiries*, eh?' Juliana was definitely mocking them now. Then she turned her sharp gaze on Bryn. 'Why do you think she was murdered?'

'Don't let's go into all of that now,' said Magnus, before Bryn could answer, anxious not to start talking about bruising and the lack of an autopsy again. 'You said you had something to show me, Bryn? Oh wait — I've just remembered. It's the notes I asked you to write up, isn't it?'

He couldn't help but feel a little annoyed that the policeman had called round unannounced and this late simply to pass on information he already knew. But Bryn was shaking his head.

'Actually I haven't finished those notes, they're still on my desk at work. No, it's something else. You see, earlier today, Anne-Laure's aunt appeared in the police station…'

He paused, looking over at Juliana, clearly wondering whether he should continue while she was still here. Magnus, who was also keen to get rid of his wife, mostly because she was being so difficult, said, 'Erm, darling, don't you have to check on the children…?'

'I thought you said you would do that, Magnus?' she replied, smiling sweetly. 'Anyway, I want to hear about Anne-Laure's aunt.'

Magnus shrugged at Bryn, and the policeman, understanding that Juliana was here to stay, proceeded with his story. It emerged that, just after lunch, a woman named Agnes Chambers had got into an argument with Barry Boyle at the police station, because the police had had the body of her niece, Annie Chambers, cremated without her knowledge.

'Wait, who's Annie Chambers?' cut in Juliana.

'That's Anne-Laure's real name, I told you that,' said Magnus, impatiently. 'She changed it when she moved to London.'

'Why?'

'We don't know,' admitted Bryn. 'But that's an interesting question…'

'And she was cremated without her aunt knowing about it?' Juliana gasped. 'That's outrageous!'

'I think it was due to some mix-up over her new name. Her aunt was her next of kin, but didn't know she went by Anne-Laure Chevalier, or had forgotten, so didn't come forward.'

'How *awful*!' cried Juliana, whose scepticism had now completely disappeared. 'That poor woman must have been simply devastated, not to have a chance to say goodbye!'

'Actually, I don't think she really cared about that,' said Bryn, before going on to explain that Agnes Chambers had seemed rather unfeeling towards her niece — in fact, the policeman seemed to think she had always been cold towards the girl, even when Anne-Laure had been an orphan of eleven.

'That's terrible!' said Juliana, shaking her head. 'What a tragic life that girl had...'

'Juliana, would you stop interrupting?' said Magnus, who was far more interested in hearing the facts than being emotional about everything like his wife. 'Let Bryn finish the story, will you?'

The policeman, after looking nervously between the bickering couple, filled them in on how bitterly Agnes had reacted to Dame Winifred Rye convincing Anne-Laure to move to London, and how the relationship between aunt and niece had completely broken down soon afterwards. Then he explained that, when she had finally come forward, all the police could offer Agnes Chambers in place of a body was a bag of Anne-Laure's belongings and the opportunity to clear out her flat.

'Imagine what we could learn from her flat!' said Juliana, who looked excited in spite of herself.

'Well, we're going to have to wait to find out,' said Bryn. 'I did offer to help, but Agnes refused to sort out the flat until her next visit to London. To be perfectly honest, I think she just wants to hold off on it to inconvenience Dame Winifred, whom she seems to view as some terrible, corrupting influence on Anne-Laure.'

'I doubt Winifred will mind,' said Juliana. 'Considering how she felt about the girl, she probably won't be in a rush to have the flat cleared out. It'll probably feel a bit final.'

'What about these belongings, though?' Magnus asked, keen to get to the purpose of Bryn's visit. 'You said she was given a bag of Anne-Laure's stuff?'

'Just her handbag, actually — the one she was found with. I've seen it before, on the morning after her death, but it was interesting to get another look. The drugs had been removed, of course — Agnes didn't seem to have any idea about that, although she did seem to think that Anne-Laure had been tainted somehow by London. But the lipstick and keys and everything else was still there, as was this.'

And from his own bag, Bryn withdrew a small, purple book with the word *Addresses* emblazoned across the front in silver letters.

'Is that *hers*?' Juliana asked, leaning forward.

Bryn nodded. 'I've been going through it all afternoon, to see who all her friends and acquaintances were. Vasyl Kosnitschev is in there, of course, as is Dame Winifred Rye. And guess who's under M?'

'Jem McMorran,' said Magnus, before adding to Juliana, 'Hilda thinks they were lovers.'

She gaped at him. 'Lovers? Anne-Laure and Jem McMorran — *the* Jem McMorran?'

'The one and only.' Magnus looked back at the policeman. 'Well, good work, Bryn — that proves they knew each other at least, doesn't it?'

'Oh, that's not all I found,' said Bryn eagerly.

'It's not?'

'No, when I went through all of the addresses, I paid particular attention to the people who lived in or around Westminster Square, given what Anne-Laure shouted in the garden.'

'"*I'm going to be free of you, and free of Westminster Square!*"' Magnus said, for Juliana's benefit. 'So did you find anyone?'

'There are three people who live locally that, according to this book at least, Anne-Laure Chevalier knew: Lord Bevis Ellington, Sheikh Hazim bin Lahab and Morris Springfield.'

Juliana laughed. 'Well, Morris won't have killed her,' she said, with confidence. 'He wouldn't hurt a fly. Do you know him?' she asked Bryn, and when the policeman shook his head, Juliana continued, 'He's this rather weedy writer who comes into my flower shop almost every week to buy a bouquet for his ailing mother. It's very sweet.'

Bryn checked back through his police notebook. 'When we asked whether she had seen anyone behaving suspiciously lately, Hilda Underpin said Morris Springfield had been "mooching" around the Square...'

'Urgh, *Hilda*!' scoffed Juliana. 'I doubt he was *mooching*, he was probably just crossing the street. Don't forget that this is a woman who berates me for wearing jeans!'

'And she did start listing everyone she could think of, when we asked her about any unsavoury characters she might have seen around,' added Magnus. 'So I'm not sure we should set too much store by her misgivings. But hang on, Juliana, didn't you speak to Morris shortly after Anne-Laure's death? And he told you he didn't know her?'

Juliana looked a little unnerved. 'You're right,' she said. 'How odd.' Then she shook her head. 'But do you know what? He was very upset at the time, because his mother had just been taken ill, so he was all over the place. In fact, I think my talking about death unnerved him even more, so I wouldn't be surprised if he hadn't really known what he was saying when I asked him whether he knew Anne-Laure.'

'You're probably right,' agreed Magnus. 'But I wonder how they knew one another?'

'Yes, Morris doesn't exactly strike me as the sociable sort,' said Juliana. 'In fact, I had him down as a complete recluse. I actually think it's far more surprising his name was in her address book than Jem McMorran's — how would they have even met?'

'Maybe she was a fan of his novels?' Bryn suggested.

Juliana laughed. 'I don't think anyone's a fan of his novels, not really,' she said. 'Critics just pretend to like them because they're *highbrow*.' This last word she accompanied with air quotes. 'I can't see a girl like Anne-Laure getting much enjoyment from those weighty tomes...'

'I don't know, I wouldn't rule it out,' said Bryn, repeating his and Magnus' new mantra.

When Juliana stared at him in surprise, Magnus explained, 'Lately, we're feeling like the more we find out about Anne-Laure Chevalier, the less we know her. Depending on who you speak to, she's composed or she's melancholy, she's chaste or she's loose, she's glamorous or she's humble, she's an angel or she's the devil. Was,' Magnus corrected himself, after a pause. 'She *was* all of those things. So you see, learning she was a fan of Morris' incomprehensible literature wouldn't particularly shock me at this stage.'

'Even so,' said Juliana, 'it's much more likely one of those other two bumped her off.'

'Juliana, I thought we talked about this — we're not assuming she was murdered at this stage...'

'Oh, shush, Magnus,' said his wife. 'Don't tell me you don't think there's anything deeply suspect about both Lord Bevis Ellington and Sheikh Hazim La... whatever his name is.'

'Sheikh Hazim Lahab,' supplied Bryn.

'Yes, him.'

'I wouldn't exactly call them *deeply suspect*,' said Magnus, reasonably. 'They're both rather eccentric, it's true, but I've never felt there's anything particularly sinister about them.'

'Hang on,' said Bryn, suddenly sitting up very straight. 'Isn't Sheikh Hazim bin Lahab the man you were talking about the other week, when we took the tour of Westminster Square? He's the rather large royal who walks around in traditional costume all the time?'

'That's him,' said Juliana, pulling a face.

'What of it?' asked Magnus.

'Well, I might be wrong,' said Bryn, reaching for his trusty notebook once more, 'but I thought you said that you had spoken to him about Anne-Laure at some meeting recently, and though he was excited by the scandal of her death...' He trailed off, until he located the exact page. 'Yes, here it is. Magnus, you said, "*he didn't seem to know her. Which is surprising, because if you watch who goes in and out of his house on a daily basis, it appears he knows half the girls in London."'*

'Urgh, that's true,' said Juliana.

'That *is* true!' said Magnus, thinking more of the sheikh's denial than his female callers. 'And — goodness me — do you know who also denied knowing her, at that very same meeting? *Lord Bevis Ellington*!'

'You're kidding!' said Bryn.

'Excuse me, but what meeting are you talking about?' asked Juliana.

Magnus, thinking it best to ignore this question, lest they get back onto the subject of CSP's maintenance costs and his wife's hatred of Westminster Square, said quickly, 'Yes, I remember now: Hazim was gossiping away about Anne-Laure's death, making a few lewd remarks about her, if I remember rightly —'

'Urgh,' said Juliana again.

'— And Ellington suddenly burst out in her defence. Hazim then teased him about it, and Ellington quickly backtracked, saying he hadn't known Anne-Laure, he'd just read about her in the papers. But it was a bit odd.'

They lapsed into silence, while Magnus was lost in his reminisces and Bryn scribbled furiously in his notebook. Then, a few minutes later, Juliana cleared her throat.

'Well,' she said, 'I think it's obvious what you have to do next, isn't it?'

'What?' asked Magnus.

'Go and talk to Lord Ellington and Sheikh Hazim. And Morris, if you like. Ask them why their names were in Anne-Laure Chevalier's address book, when they all claimed not to know her — because I think that's very fishy.'

'So do I,' agreed Bryn.

'Yes, it is a little strange,' said Magnus, 'and so probably worth looking into. But — wait a minute,' he turned to his wife, 'are you actually encouraging us to carry on with our investigation now? I was under the impression you thought it was a little silly? And I thought this Anne-Laure business had unnerved you?'

'It has, and I do think it's silly,' said Juliana, although he thought he detected a glint of excitement in her eye as she began replacing the empty tea cups on the tray. 'But if you're going to force me to stay on in Westminster Square, Magnus, at least I'll have something to entertain me.'

CHAPTER NINETEEN

As he and Magnus made their way towards the house of Sheikh Hazim bin Lahab the very next evening, Bryn felt as though he were walking with a spring in his step.

It had, of course, been extremely enlightening talking to both Hilda Underpin and Jem McMorran, and in particular learning that Anne-Laure had almost certainly been in some kind of relationship with the Hollywood film star. But even that juicy revelation had failed to shed much light on the circumstances surrounding her death, especially given Jem's reticence to talk about her, and so despite their conversation in the Lion of Westminster, Bryn had been starting to feel as though the investigation was grinding to a halt.

But no longer, he thought, as they approached the south-east corner of Westminster Square. Because, ever since the appearance of Agnes Chambers, and ever since he had nabbed that address book from under her nose, the Anne-Laure case felt as though it were moving forward once again.

Sheikh Hazim bin Lahab. Lord Bevis Ellington. Morris Springfield. Bryn had committed them to memory now, the names of Anne-Laure's three neighbours who had denied knowing her, and whose names had then showed up in her address book. Had she somehow got on the wrong side of one of these men? Could one of them have orchestrated her death? And might one of these individuals have been the shadowy man who had grabbed her in the garden on the night of her demise? Bryn hardly dared to hope he and Magnus were about to uncover a sinister plot, but at the very least Hazim, Ellington and Morris might be able to tell them a little more about Anne-Laure Chevalier and her life — and Bryn was very interested to know why all three of them had categorically denied being acquainted with her.

'That's it,' said Magnus, nodding at the building in front of them, which looked to Bryn like all the other grand Georgian properties on Westminster Square, 'that's where Hazim lives.'

'Which floor?' asked Bryn.

Magnus chuckled. 'All of them,' he replied. 'Sheikh Hazim owns the entire house.'

'Wow... So he's like Vasyl, then?'

Again, Magnus laughed. 'Sort of. Although I expect Hazim's bank balance would make the Ukrainian oligarch look like a peasant in comparison. And they don't exactly have a similar temperament.'

'No?'

'Not really. You'll recall from our meeting that Vasyl's a very serious and rather humourless sort of man, while Hazim... Well, you'll find out. Let's see if my theory about Eastern hospitality turns out to be correct.

As Magnus rang the doorbell, Bryn recalled the barrister had advised that Hazim be the first of the three men they visit, simply because a conversation with him was unlikely to require an appointment. Lord Ellington, Magnus explained, was obsessed with protocol, and therefore would be offended if they didn't go through the proper process of pre-arranging a meeting. Equally, Magnus thought that Morris Springfield would be very unsettled if they suddenly showed up on his doorstep without warning, as he had the sensitive disposition of an artist. But Magnus had explained that, as far as he was aware, it was customary for men of the East such as Hazim to happily welcome guests at any time of the day, with or without prior warning.

A few moments later, the door of the sheikh's house was opened by a person Bryn assumed was a butler, although he couldn't be sure. The man before them was clearly Western, with pale skin and a ginger moustache, yet other than that, he looked as though he had just stepped out of an Arabian palace. He was dressed in a double-breasted kaftan embellished with gold and silver thread, and a small but beautifully embroidered waistcoat made of silk. His hair — which was presumably as red as his moustache — was covered by a large white headdress, and his feet with *babouche* slippers that curled up at the toes. All in all, he cut a striking but slightly comical figure, as though he had been caught playing dress-up. In fact, had Bryn not known he was about to enter the house of an Eastern prince, he would have assumed this man before him was an extra in a pantomime of *Aladdin*.

'May I help you?' asked the butler-figure, in a cut-glass English accent.

'Yes, hello,' said Magnus, stepping forward. 'My name is Magnus Walterson. I'm a barrister and also an acquaintance of the sheikh's. My associate here is Constable Bryn Summers of the Victoria Police Station. We were hoping to have a word with your employer about neighbourhood security — I trust he doesn't mind us dropping in like this?'

Once more, Bryn felt Magnus' tone and manner left little room for contradiction. Indeed, after looking them up and down a few times, the curious-looking butler beckoned them inside.

'Do come in, gentlemen. If you wait in the gallery, I will see if His Majesty is willing to receive you.'

Bryn hopped over the threshold, eager to see what the interior of this Westminster Square property looked like, especially considering Vasyl's, Winifred's, Hilda's, Jem's and even Magnus' were all so very different. But as the butler led them through the hallway and into a room on the right, the police constable found himself rather disappointed: he was now standing in a long gallery lined with paintings, and although they portrayed various Eastern scenes, these images were the only remotely exotic feature of the space, which was otherwise rather dull.

Magnus, however, gave a low whistle of appreciation and headed straight towards the nearest picture, which was of some ruins Bryn thought might be ancient Egyptian.

'Very nice,' he commented. 'David Roberts, is it?'

The butler, who was halfway out of the room, paused. 'Yes, I believe so, sir.'

'I'm guessing they're copies of the lithographs in the Mathaf Gallery?' Magnus continued, gesturing at the thirty or so framed scenes around the room.

'You're quite correct, sir,' said the butler, before giving a little bow and departing the room.

'The Mathaf Gallery — which isn't far from here, actually — specialises in Orientalist paintings,' explained Magnus, for Bryn's benefit.

'And what's a lithograph?' asked Bryn.

'Oh, it's a printing process that uses ink and a greasy substance to reproduce an image. David Roberts was particularly famous for it. He was a nineteenth-century Scottish painter who travelled extensively around Egypt and the Near East, and created lithographs from the sketches he had made during his travels.' Magnus paced up and down the gallery, peering at each image in turn. 'They are rather impressive, I must say; like snapshots into another world, because of course Roberts was working before photography really got going. And Hazim clearly agrees, going by how many prints there are here…'

'Are you interested in art, then?' asked Bryn, who could barely tell a Monet from a Picasso.

'A little,' replied Magnus. 'If I had the time, I'd probably go hunting through London's auction houses and antique shops for bargains. But then, if I did purchase anything, it'd probably get thrown out by Juliana…'

'Surely not!'

'Oh, I'm afraid so,' said Magnus.

The barrister continued his progress around the gallery, although now he seemed to have an air of dejection about him. Bryn reflected on his own meeting with Magnus' wife the previous evening: as he had suspected from his first glimpse of her the other week, hanging out of the window and hollering about dinner, Juliana Walterson was as fiery as the colour of her hair.

'Hey, what do you notice about this place?' asked Magnus suddenly.

Bryn looked around, nonplussed by this question.

'Erm, it's… big?' he suggested, for the first thing that came to mind was that it was the size — as well as the paintings — that made this space resemble an art gallery.

'Exactly,' said Magnus, with a knowing smile.

'Sorry, I don't understand,' said the policeman.

'Think back to when we were in Vasyl's place,' said the barrister. 'His house has almost exactly the same layout as this, doesn't it?'

'Erm, I suppose so. But this space was his living room, and it was smaller, even when you consider he was in the process of knocking through that wall in the hallway.'

'Exactly,' said Magnus again, 'it was *smaller*.'

'I'm not really sure what you're getting at here, Magnus...'

'That girl back at Vasyl's — Lavender, was it? — you know, the one from Central Square Properties? Do you remember, she was making a huge fuss about how Vasyl had torn that place apart without CSP's permission? She was incensed, because he wasn't allowed to pull walls down and redecorate a Grade II-listed building?'

'Yes,' said Bryn, still unsure why Magnus had suddenly brought this up again. 'It sounded like he was going to be in serious trouble with their lawyers...'

'And yet, Sheikh Hazim has done exactly the same thing. In fact, I think he must have knocked down a wall over there —' Magnus gestured at the opposite end of the large gallery. 'But somehow, I doubt CSP will have made the same amount of fuss.'

'Why do you think that?'

'I heard Hazim managed to get this place freehold,' said Magnus, lowering his voice now. Then, in answer to Bryn's puzzled expression, he added, 'That means there's no lease arrangement, and he's the undisputed owner of all of this: the house, the basement, the garden, even the land beneath us. I wasn't sure it was possible to even do that in Westminster Square, until I saw this gallery. But the fact that CSP has obviously turned a blind eye to his renovations means he *must* own it — or else he's paid them a sizeable chunk of money to keep them happy. I suspect it's the former, given that out of all of my neighbours, I reckon Hazim is the only one wealthy enough to afford actually buying a property like this outright. But either way, it shows you how hypocritical and corrupt CSP are...'

He trailed off as, behind him, a door opened and the extravagantly-dressed butler returned. Bryn wasn't sure how much of their conversation Hazim's man had overheard, but Magnus seemed totally unabashed.

'Well? Have we been granted an audience?'

'You have,' said the butler. 'Gentlemen, if you would like to follow me into the *majlis*...'

'The *majlis?*' muttered Bryn, as he followed Magnus to the end of the gallery. But the barrister merely smiled and shook his head, shooting Bryn an expression that clearly read *you'll see.*

As the butler opened the door of the adjoining room, Bryn could hear the unmistakable sound of at least one sports programme being played on either a TV or a radio beyond, for commentators were shouting above the roar of a crowd. With this in mind, and considering the rest of the house he had seen so far, the policeman imagined he was about to walk into a fancy games room, perhaps complete with a dartboard and billiards table.

But Bryn should have learned by now that it was almost impossible to predict what lay within the walls of Westminster Square, and — not for the first time — his mouth fell open as he entered a new interior. Just as when he had first laid eyes on the butler, it felt as though he had been transported into a story from one of the *1001 Arabian Nights*. If he had not been certain that the space beyond the gallery was a room, he would have assumed he had strayed into the lavish camp of a sultan journeying through the desert. The fine walls, windows and ceiling of the historic Georgian building were completely covered by pleated cream-coloured cloth, which was draped from a point above their heads to the edges of the room, as though they were in a large and luxurious tent. Small lanterns hung at intervals around the circumference of this fabric, and the floor was covered with overlapping silk Persian carpets, and over a hundred low *majlis* cushions that were arranged in a horseshoe shape around the edges of the makeshift den.

Yet not all of the features within Hazim's lounge area looked authentically Eastern. Bryn was fairly sure he wouldn't have been able to find a vast crystal chandelier like the one above their heads in a real

Arabian tent, and the two large televisions in the centre of the *majlis,* both of which were showing different football games, also looked very out of place in their modernity.

In the midst of these dichotomous surroundings sat an extremely overweight Arab man, who was dressed in a similar outfit to his butler, although the embroidery on his kaftan was far more extravagant. He leered up at them as they walked in, his wide mouth curving into a smile. Bryn thought that, cross-legged on his *majlis* cushion, he resembled a particularly fat toad perched on a lily pad.

'Magnus, my friend, good to see you!' he cried, stretching out a chubby hand and not bothering to heave himself up from the floor.

'Likewise, Hazim,' said Magnus, who had to lean down to greet the Eastern prince. 'Please allow me to introduce my associate here, Mr Bryn Summers of—'

'Of the local police, yes, so Steve told me.'

As Bryn too bent down to grip at the sheikh's podgy fingers, it took him a few moments to work out that 'Steve' must be the red-moustached butler. Close to, he also noticed that Hazim bore the scent of an extremely strong and musky perfume. It was like no aftershave Bryn had ever smelled in Britain, so he assumed the cloying aroma — which was so potent he could almost taste it in his mouth — must have been imported from the sheikh's homeland.

'Have a seat,' said Hazim, in a commanding voice, 'pull up a cushion. You're just in time — I was about to have some dinner.'

'That's very kind of you, but we don't want to trespass for too long,' said Magnus. 'In fact, we're only here to have a quick word about—'

'Nonsense!' interrupted Hazim. 'There's plenty to go around! Steve, bring in the food, will you? It's well past dinner time!'

While the butler departed, Bryn chanced a look at his watch: it had only just gone six o'clock.

'Do you like football?' asked Hazim, who didn't seem to be particularly curious as to why they were there; perhaps, Bryn thought, he had people coming in and going out of his *majlis* all the time.

'I'm more of a rugby fan myself,' confessed Magnus.

'What about you, Bryn?'

'I quite like football, yes,' he replied, looking up at both of the screens that had been set up in front of Hazim. 'Who's playing?'

'Manchester United versus Liverpool,' said the sheikh, pointing a stubby finger at the screen on the left, before moving his arm right and continuing, 'and that's Arsenal versus Aston Villa. They're just friendlies, given the season's officially finished now, but it doesn't hurt to keep an eye on things, does it? Man U are pretty smug, after winning the Premiere League last month, but Liverpool aren't a bad team at the moment. And I'm looking forward to seeing what Blackburn Rovers are going to do next, as I don't think they're going to take their runner-up status lying down, do you?'

'Erm, no,' said Bryn, who had not really been keeping up with English football — or indeed football of any kind — during his time in London.

'Are you able to concentrate on both games at once?' wondered Magnus, as Sheikh Hazim's eyes flicked between the two screens. 'Isn't it a bit distracting, moving from one to the other, hearing both commentaries?'

'Oh no,' said Hazim, scratching his large belly. 'In fact, this is nothing. Ever since Sky Sports started, I can put three or four games on at the same time. I'll get Steve to fetch us another TV if you'd like to see…?'

'No, that's all right,' said Magnus quickly, 'I believe you.'

At that moment, Steve the butler did return, but rather than a television, the trolley he wheeled into the *majlis* bore several silver trays piled with food. Spicy cooking smells suddenly wafted through the room, replacing the smell of the sheikh's perfume, and Bryn, who only had a rather sad leftover pasta dish waiting for him back in Clapham, clutched at his suddenly growling stomach.

'Stuffed lamb!' announced Hazim, as Steve began to unload tray after tray onto the carpet in front of them.

'What's it stuffed with?' asked Magnus, leaning forward to inspect the biggest dish, the meat of which was glistening with grease.

'Chicken, of course!' roared Hazim, as though this were obvious. 'Then there are stuffed pigeons over there, some vegetables, and — what's that? — oh, another stuffed lamb… Where's the cheese, Steve?'

Bryn gazed around at the vast feast that had been laid out before them; it looked as though it would feed at least ten people. Magnus was apparently thinking along the same lines, for he said, 'Erm, are you expecting any other guests, Hazim?'

'Huh?' asked the sheikh, who was already tearing strips of meat off one of the lamb dishes with his fingers.

'It's just, there's quite a lot of food here,' said Magnus.

'Is there?' Hazim stuffed the greasy chunk of lamb between his lips and continued speaking with his mouth full. 'There's enough for you and Bryn, don't worry. And if there isn't, Steve can get the kitchen to make more. Go on, help yourself.'

'Oh, that's not what I meant,' said the barrister quickly. 'Anyway, I'm not sure I should eat here, Juliana's making dinner…'

'Never mind Juliana!' cried the sheikh, spraying the carpet with half-chewed food as he spoke. 'Go on, Magnus, eat! And you, Bryn!'

Unwilling to disobey this direct order, the policeman helped himself to a few of the vegetables rather gingerly, for the grotesque sight of Hazim stuffing his face and spitting all over the *majlis* had caused him to lose his appetite. It also didn't help that the smell of the greasy meat lingering with the sickly aroma of the sheikh's perfume was making him feel rather nauseous.

When Magnus followed suit, and piled a couple of vegetables into a napkin, their host seemed satisfied that they were enjoying his hospitality, for he then turned his attention back to the football, chewing noisily as he watched.

'That Tony Adams knows what he's doing, doesn't he?' Hazim commented, to nobody in particular. 'I think he is one of the best players Arsenal's ever — *Ooh, so close!*' he cried, dropping his food onto the floor as one of the red-shirted players on the right-hand screen hit the crossbar of the goal.

While Steve swooped down to remove the sticky piece of lamb from the silk carpet, Bryn looked to Magnus: how on earth were they going to hold Hazim's attention from the food and football long enough to discuss Anne-Laure?

'And Steve!' cried the sheikh, leaning over to help himself to a whole stuffed pigeon. 'Where's my cheese?'

The butler blinked at him. 'You would like the cheese course now, sir?'

'Of course I want it now! Bring me the cheese, Steve!'

The amount of food the gluttonous sheikh had crammed into his mouth in just a few minutes seemed to have given him a burst of energy, so much so that Bryn wondered whether he was on the verge of a toddler-style temper tantrum.

Magnus, however, seemed to think they had nothing to lose by finally cutting to the chase.

'Hazim, the reason we're here is that we wanted to have a quick word with you about neighbourhood security,' he said, beginning their now well-worn opening gambit.

'About what?'

'Neighbourhood security.'

Hazim turned an astonished expression upon Magnus. 'Is work at Grey's Inn drying up or something?'

'Pardon me?'

'Are you a burglar alarm salesman now?' he laughed.

'Of course not,' said Magnus impatiently. 'It's just, over the past few weeks, there have been a couple of break-ins around Westminster Square and...'

'Have there?'

'Yes. Someone attempted to burgle the flats of Dame Winifred Rye and Hilda Underpin.'

Hazim shrugged. 'Who?'

'Come on,' scoffed Magnus. 'You must know who Hilda Underpin is. She's the elderly lady who lives a few doors' down, the one who's always —'

'— Sticking her nose into other people's business,' finished Hazim, nodding. 'Yes, I remember now. She shouts at me every time I leave the house, calling me all sorts of names... I think she might be a racist, you know.'

'I'm afraid you're probably right,' agreed Magnus.

For some reason, Sheikh Hazim seemed to find this rather funny, for he threw back his head and laughed so hard Bryn could see all the chewed up food in his mouth.

'I quite like her,' Hazim said, when he'd recovered himself.

'You — you *like* her?' Magnus looked confused. 'You're saying you're fond of the mean old lady who shouts racist abuse at you every time you leave your house?'

'Well, she has a little spirit. She speaks her mind, unlike most of the Brits I have encountered around here. Anyway, I just yell back. She pretends to be furious about it, but I can tell she enjoys the sparring...'

Bryn conjured the mental image of this obese eccentric Arab prince and nasty little Hilda Underpin shouting at one another across Westminster Square and had the sudden urge to laugh. Repressing this, he asked, 'And are you familiar with Dame Winifred Rye?'

'Should I be?'

'She lives on the other side of the square,' said Magnus. 'She's famous around here for her charity parties.'

'Oh yes, yes,' said Hazim. 'She is that woman with the awful clothes and five layers of make-up?'

'Erm, yes, that's right,' said Magnus, looking awkward at having to confirm such an unflattering description of Dame Winifred. Then he continued, 'The burglar didn't actually manage to steal anything from either Hilda or Winifred, but it is a concern, especially as they're both on their own.'

'Hm,' said Hazim, his eyes straying back towards the TV; evidently, he was growing bored with this conversation.

'So we're just trying to keep an eye on things around here,' said Magnus, raising his voice a little to compete with the commentators on the TVs, 'especially given that we've been subjected to a lot of media attention recently, because of Anne-Laure Chevalier.'

'Who?' asked Hazim, still watching the football.

'The young woman who was found dead at the Royal West the other week.'

'Oh yeah... *Come on Cantona, wake up!*'

Magnus shot a frustrated look at Bryn, before continuing, 'I don't suppose you knew the girl, did you, Hazim?'

To the policeman's surprise, the sheikh looked faintly annoyed. 'I already told you this, back at that meeting in the Cosmopolitan Club — I've never met her. Which is a shame, because when I saw those pictures of her in the paper... *Wow*. I will just say I wouldn't have minded becoming — aha — *intimately* acquainted with her, if you catch my drift.'

Apparently, his lascivious thoughts concerning Anne-Laure Chevalier were more appealing than even football and food, for he spent the next few moments staring off into the distance, temporarily distracted from both TVs. Magnus cleared his throat.

'I'm afraid I have no idea what you're talking about,' he said firmly. Then, nodding at Bryn, he went on, 'And I'm not sure you're telling us the whole truth here, Hazim, because we happen to have something in our possession that contradicts what you're saying.'

On cue, Bryn withdrew the small purple address book from his pocket.

'This belonged to Anne-Laure,' he explained. 'We found it in her handbag after she died.'

Hazim stared at it, and then laughed wheezily. 'What is it, a list of her conquests?'

'Excuse me?' said Magus.

'In my experience, Western girls — particularly ones that look like that — tend to be pretty fast, so I wouldn't be surprised if that book detailed all the men she'd gone to bed with.'

Bryn frowned: he wouldn't have felt it was appropriate for the sheikh to have spoken about anyone in this way, but the fact he was referring to a dead woman made the conversation especially distasteful. Magnus too looked unimpressed.

'Well, apparently it's just addresses of acquaintances, considering you're in here and — what did you say just now? — you hadn't been *intimately* acquainted with her?'

Hazim looked sour. 'I'm in there?'

'Unless there's another Sheikh Hazim bin Lahab living at this address, then yes, you are. Which is rather interesting, considering you just said you'd never even met her.'

Hazim picked up another piece of lamb in a rather transparent attempt to play for time. Bryn could not help but notice that he seemed to have forgotten about the football.

'Look, I might have met her,' he admitted. 'I like women, all right? They're my vice. Speaking of, *Steve, where's my cheese?*'

'Coming, sir, coming!' cried the butler's distant voice from beyond the room.

Hazim turned back to Magnus and Bryn. 'What was I saying? Oh yes, I can avoid whiskey, I can turn down a bacon sandwich, but women... Women I cannot resist.'

'Do me a favour,' said Magnus, 'if you ever meet my wife, don't compare women to alcohol or pork or cheese in front of her. For your own sake.'

Bryn, however, was reflecting on what Hazim had just said, and feeling more sickened by the minute.

'Are you saying you and Anne-Laure Chevalier...' he swallowed. 'Are you saying you had a *sexual* relationship?'

'What? No!' Hazim looked surprised. 'Although, as I said, I would have paid a lot of gold for a few nights with a woman like that. Did you see those pictures of her in the papers? I should have kept them...'

'You should have kept pictures of a dead woman?' Bryn asked, unable to keep the judgement from his voice.

Hazim gave a sigh of frustration; evidently, they were failing him as an audience. Fortunately, however, before the conversation could turn too awkward, Steve returned with a huge platter of cheese. As far as Bryn knew, cheese was not a staple of Middle Eastern cuisine; indeed, from the look of the large plate — on which the policeman recognised cheddar, edam, stilton, manchego and gruyere — Hazim's taste for cheese was another of his distinctly Western habits, like watching football.

'Clear all this away, Steve,' commanded Hazim, gesturing at the other plates. 'Assuming you've both finished?'

Magnus and Bryn nodded, both unwilling to be subjected to any more greasy meat. But Bryn was shocked by how much food had been left untouched, even by the greedy Hazim.

'That's quite a lot of leftovers,' he said, with a small laugh.

'What are leftovers?' demanded Hazim.

'You know, food you reheat the next day.'

The sheikh pulled a face that suggested this was the oddest thing he had ever heard. 'We don't keep food overnight,' he said. 'Anything left goes in the bin, presuming my staff don't want it.'

'And you enjoy meals of this size every day?' said Magnus, his tone disbelieving.

'Every day, three times a day,' said Hazim, patting his enormous belly. 'Sometimes four or five, if I'm particularly peckish. *Now, bring us some tea, Steve!*' he bellowed, as the butler departed the *majlis*, laden with largely untouched trays of meat.

Waggling his fingers with anticipation, Hazim then reached towards the cheese platter before him, cut off a large chunk of the edam, squashed it up between his fingers and crammed it into his mouth. As he chewed contentedly, he turned back to the TV.

'What's happening here, then?' he wondered aloud. 'Were Man U and Liverpool drawing before? Did we miss a goal? Oh, I can't hear what's going on...'

He reached for the remote control, presumably to turn up the volume. Magnus, looking slightly panicked, said quickly, 'Hazim, I'm not sure we got to the bottom of this Anne-Laure business. We're still wondering why your name's in her address book when you claim not to have known her?'

'Well, as I was saying, I like women,' said the sheikh, reaching for the stilton now, which — in Bryn's opinion — smelled almost as bad as he did. 'I like to surround myself with them. You should see my accountant — she looks like a top model.' He licked his lips at the thought of her. 'I like the presence of women, you see: in my office, in my *majlis*, in my bed. Yes, sometimes I pay for them to keep me company between the sheets too, if you know what I mean…'

'Yes we do,' said Magnus at once, before the sheikh could elaborate.

Bryn frowned: he felt thoroughly bemused by this whole speech. 'I still don't see what this has to do with Anne-Laure Chevalier,' he said.

'What I'm saying is, how am I supposed to remember this one woman, out of all the rest?' Hazim demanded, as though this were obvious, and they were being exceptionally slow and unreasonable.

'She had quite a memorable face, you said so yourself,' pointed out Bryn.

'I wasn't talking about her face,' said the sheikh, his lecherous expression returning. 'Anyway, however memorable it was, I don't recall it, so how am I supposed to know why I am in that address book? We probably met years ago. What did she do?'

'She was in events,' said Bryn. 'She did PR, planned parties, that sort of thing, mostly for Vasyl Kosnitschev.'

'Oh, that old bore!' scoffed Hazim. 'Well, there you go, then. She probably organised a few of my parties over the years — I throw great parties, by the way. They're not like Vasyl's dull evenings, when you can hardly stay awake, so I bet you this girl was grateful to have the opportunity to plan something a bit more exciting, a bit more *exotic*, especially as I have far more money than that Ukrainian…'

'But you don't remember for sure?' said Magnus, interrupting him mid-boast.

Hazim shrugged. 'As I said, I cannot keep tabs on everyone who comes in and out of here, can I?'

Bryn could well believe this, considering Hazim had invited them in without a second thought, and had spent most of their visit with an eye on the two televisions. The sheikh probably would have forgotten all about them by the end of the week.

'You should ask Steve, if you're so desperate to know,' Hazim said, cutting yet another slice of cheese. 'Steve! *Steve!*'

Once more, the butler reappeared in the doorway of the tent-like room carrying yet another tray, although this time it bore three cups and a long-spouted silver teapot.

'Ah, tea!' said Hazim, his eyes lighting up with pleasure. 'Pour some for our guests, Steve. And do it in the proper Arabian way.'

Steve handed Bryn a cup and stood over him with the teapot.

'Hold it steady, sir,' he instructed.

Bryn tensed: as he was still sat on his *majlis* cushion, the distance between the cup and pot was one of several feet, so he half-expected to be scalded by the boiling beverage at any moment. Yet, with a deft upward sweep of his wrist, the butler poured a thin strand of tea straight into the cup.

'Very good!' cried Hazim, clapping his hands as though his butler were a dog or a young child.

'Thank you,' Bryn said to Steve.

He blew on the tea to cool it, took a sip, and almost gagged: it was one of the sweetest things he had ever tasted. Why, the butler must have heaped several tablespoons of honey into the pot to make it so syrupy. As Westminster Square cups of tea went, it wasn't the worst — that dubious honour still belonged to Vasyl Kosnitschev's bitter infusion — but it certainly wasn't the best, which had been Dame Winifred's Fortnum and Mason blend. No, Bryn would have put this sugary concoction on a par with the similarly sweet tea he had drunk at Inacio the doorman's basement flat, and perhaps slightly below Hilda Underpin's cold, overly-stewed beverage of the other day.

Meanwhile Magnus, who was holding out his cup for the butler to repeat his party trick, asked, 'Steve, do you remember a woman coming here by the name of Anne-Laure Chevalier?'

Evidently put off by the question, the butler's hand twitched and the line of tea he was pouring missed Magnus' cup by a few centimetres.

Fortunately, it splashed on the other side to the one the barrister was holding, but Bryn was forcibly reminded of Jem McMorran slopping water down his front at the mention of the woman's name.

'Oh, Steve!' cried Hazim, disappointed. 'Look what you did!'

'A thousand apologies, sir,' gasped the butler, reddening with mortification. 'I'll fetch you a new cup.'

'There's no need,' said Magnus, 'this will do just fine. Fill me up.'

The barrister watched Steve carefully as he poured and, this time, the butler's aim was true.

'So, Anne-Laure Chevalier?' prompted Magnus.

'Was she not the young lady who was found at the Royal West?' Steve asked.

'She was.'

Steve looked at Hazim, evidently unsure what to say.

'These two think I knew the girl, because my name was in some address book she had,' supplied the sheikh. 'But I do not remember her, so I am wondering whether she planned one of our parties a few years ago? She was in events, you see.'

'Right,' said Steve, staring at his employer as though trying to read his mind: evidently, he did not see.

'I said you would remember her if she was here,' went on Hazim, and Bryn noticed that Magnus looked annoyed the sheikh was leading this line of questioning.

'I, um —' Steve faltered.

'Do you know? If you are really that interested, I could ask my accountant — you know, the one I said looked like top model — to go through the invoices. Because if she planned a party or two, there must be some kind of financial record...'

'Oh, *Anne-Laure Chevalier!*' cried Steve, in a rather unconvincing tone of abrupt recollection. 'Yes, you're quite right, sir, she planned a couple of your parties a few years back. Goodness, it must have been around 1990, if I remember rightly.'

'There you go, then,' said Hazim, looking smug. 'Mystery solved.'

'Even so,' said Magnus, looking between the sheikh and his butler with a wry expression, 'We wouldn't mind having a look at those invoices, if your accountant can dig them out... My colleague here is tying up a few loose ends concerning her death.'

'Oh, fine, fine,' said Hazim. 'Steve, go and phone Bethany, will you? And before you do that, send in the entertainment. Actually, before you do *that,* take away all this cheese.'

'Very good, sir.'

The barrister was still staring at Hazim, his eyes slightly narrowed.

'Well,' he said eventually, 'thank you for your time, Hazim...'

'You are not going?' the sheikh said, his gaze back on the TVs.

'You've been very hospitable, but we only came to inform you about those break-ins, really, and I must be getting back home to Juliana and the children...'

Bryn checked his watch again: it wasn't even seven o'clock, but it felt far later. He supposed this was due to there being no windows in the cloth walls of Hazim's tent-like *majlis,* and so they couldn't see the late midsummer light outside.

'You cannot go *now!*' Hazim cried, waving his cup so tea slopped over his expensive carpets. 'We have hardly even begun!'

Considering he hadn't been expecting them, he seemed very keen to make them stay.

'How can you leave when the entertainment is about to start?' Hazim continued.

Bryn looked to the football, which had been on for some time now, decided this was not what their host was referring to, and asked, 'What entertainment?'

But before Hazim could answer, there was a jingling sound from just beyond the *majlis,* as though many small bells were ringing at the same time. The first thing that sprang to Bryn's mind was Christmas, specifically Santa's sleigh, but then he checked himself: it seemed very unlikely an Arab sheikh would be receiving a mythical Western figure, especially in the middle of June. Indeed, as six beautiful woman, scantily-clad in veils and bells, filed into the tent-like room, Bryn began to realise that the entertainment on offer was rather more adult than a visit from Father Christmas.

'Oh God,' said Magnus.

'Ah, my girls!' cried Hazim, spreading his fat arms wide. 'Come in, come in!'

They jangled towards him, their skipping steps, brightly-coloured outfits, and glittering accessories reminding Bryn of a flock of exotic birds showing off their feathers. Two of the girls looked like traditional belly dancers, for they were olive-skinned and voluptuous, but the others were paler, skinnier and — with the exception of one redhead — blonde. It was these Western girls Hazim seemed to prefer, for he stretched out his hands to two of them, beckoning them closer.

'Now I have two very special guests over there,' he told the group of belly dancers, 'so once Steve sets up the music — *Steve, are you setting up the music?* — I want you to —'

'Actually, I think we'll be on our way,' said Magnus loudly.

Hazim looked amazed. 'But the girls…' he began.

'Yes, we've got to be getting on,' said Bryn, staring determinedly at a lantern on the opposite wall and trying not to feel so hot and bothered.

At that moment, Steve came dashing into the room clutching a huge stereo, which he proceeded to plug into one of the sockets that, until that point, had been occupied by one of the TVs.

'Oh, Steve!' cried Hazim. 'Not the Man U game!'

'Sorry, sir, sorry…'

A few of the girls looked down at the scrambling butler disdainfully, their bells still tinkling as they folded their arms and tapped their feet with impatience.

'Well, thank you very much for a lovely evening,' said Magnus, and as he stood up Bryn hurried to his feet as well.

'You can't go!' cried the sheikh, who was still holding onto one of the blonde girls. 'The party's just getting started!'

'Hazim, I'm a married man, and Bryn here is an officer of the law, this isn't at all appropriate —'

'Relax, relax! It's just dancing. They're not, you know —' he lowered his voice to a stage whisper, '— *women of the night*. It's far too early for that. Although, if you're interested, I can definitely make arrangements for later…'

'Let's go, Bryn,' said Magnus.

At that moment, a blast of music erupted from the stereo so loudly that everybody jumped in fright and clapped their hands over their ears.

'*Steve!*'

'I'm sorry, sir, I'm so sorry…'

'Are we dancin' or what?' demanded the redheaded girl, who had a thick East End accent.

'Of course you are, fix it, Steve — fix it!'

Bryn then felt himself being nudged in the ribs by Magnus and, while everyone was distracted with the music, they were able to slip out of the *majlis* and head through the house the way they had come, until, blinking into the sunshine, they emerged back outside on the south-east corner of Westminster Square.

CHAPTER TWENTY

After Magnus had rung him to arrange a meeting, Lord Bevis Ellington had invited the barrister and Bryn over to his flat the very next evening. The Labour lord lived in the north-east of Westminster Square, a location which Magnus seemed to find rather amusing.

'I'm sure it's just a coincidence, but it seems very fitting Ellington lives up here, right at the top of the Square,' he said, as they walked towards the building in question.

'What do you mean?' asked Bryn.

'Well, as you'll soon see, Ellington is completely obsessed with royalty and aristocracy —'

'But I thought you said he was from the Labour Party?'

'Yes, he is — funny, isn't it? Unusual. Anyway, I'm sure his flat was the only one available at the time he moved to this part of London — whenever that was — but it just strikes me as rather appropriate he's up here.'

'I'm still not sure I understand,' said the policeman.

'Think about it: this is as close as one can get to the Queen in Westminster Square. Why, you can almost see over the wall into Buckingham Palace Gardens from up here. I expect Lord Ellington enjoys his proximity to Her Majesty very much, not to mention this end of the square is the nearest to Downing Street and the Palace of Westminster.'

'Oh, I see,' said Bryn, with a smile. Then, thinking back on the tour Magnus had conducted a few weeks' ago, he asked, 'Didn't you say that was the original purpose of Westminster Square? To serve as accommodation for nobles and dignitaries, given it's in such a strategic location to the palace and parliament?'

'Yes, well remembered,' said Magnus. 'I suppose, over the years, living in close proximity to one's workplace has become less important, given the rise of the car. You and I are both very fortunate with our commutes, but some people travel for miles and miles to get into London each day. Yet Lord Ellington, as you're about to discover, is an old-fashioned sort, so I imagine he prizes being this close to the great and the good of Britain pretty highly.'

By now, they had reached Ellington's property, which was a flat, but one that took up the entire ground floor, so it almost looked as though the Labour Lord owned the entire building (in fact, considering what Magnus had just told him, Bryn wondered whether Ellington might encourage this false impression). At the door, they were greeted by an enormous individual in an ill-fitting suit, who looked more like a rugby player than a butler: he was well over six feet tall, with square shoulders, a blonde crewcut, and an extremely red face.

'Good evening, Gregor,' said Magnus, pleasantly. 'My friend and I have an appointment with Lord Ellington.'

'Yeth,' grunted the butler, 'He'th ecthpecting you.'

As he spoke, Bryn saw that Gregor was missing both of his front teeth, and this was perhaps the reason for his pronounced lisp. He had a strong accent that might have been Scottish, considering his name, but his rumbling voice and speech impediment made it difficult to tell for sure.

'Thith way, pleath,' continued Gregor, standing aside to let them in.

Bryn tried to give the butler a wide berth as he passed him; the policeman was not exactly short, but he was skinny, and next to this man he felt like spindly twig in comparison to the thick trunk of a vast baobab tree.

As he and Magnus then followed Gregor through the hallway, Bryn reflected that, out of all of the Westminster Square interiors he had seen so far, Lord Ellington's seemed to be the most authentic. He hadn't altered any of the architecture, like Vasyl Kosnitschev and Sheikh Hazim bin Lahab; he hadn't filled the spaces with garish furnishings or wartime memorabilia, like Dame Winifred Rye and Hilda Underpin; and he hadn't made a huge mess of his accommodation, like Jem McMorran.

Indeed, even Magnus' flat — which Bryn thought would have been nice and traditional, if it hadn't been for all those wretched plants and flowers of Juliana's — looked positively bohemian in comparison to the clean and rather austere look of Lord Ellington's home.

Furthermore, the few adornments Bryn could identify, from the coat stand to the doorstoppers, looked decidedly British, at least to his untrained eye. There were also a number of oil paintings lining the walls, which, without exception, depicted English countryside scenes, horses, or sombre men in white wigs, whom Bryn assumed were important aristocrats and politicians of the past.

Gregor led them directly into what appeared to be an office, for the focal point of the room was a vast antique table with two pull-out wings on either side, which the policeman thought might have been called a 'partner desk'. Framed by the bookshelves behind, an elderly man was writing at this fine bureau, although he looked up when they entered.

'Ah, Magnus, welcome,' he said with a smile, replacing the cap of his fountain pen and rising to meet them. 'And this must be Police Constable Bryn Summers. Lord Bevis Ellington, at your service.'

As Bryn shook Ellington's bony hand, he reflected that the Labour Lord was not quite as old as he had first thought: the impression of frailness might have been down to the fact that he was rather tall and thin, and although his hair was very white, he could have been naturally fair. Now that the policeman was getting a better look at him, he thought Lord Ellington might only be in his early sixties. Close to, he also bore the thick, woody aroma of tobacco.

'We'll go through to the living room, I think,' said Ellington, in a crisp, nasal voice. 'Gregor, would you bring us through some drinks? Perhaps a little of the twelve year-old Glendronach, or you could open up that Balblair?'

'Actually, I won't have any whiskey,' cut in Magnus.

'You won't?'

'No, perhaps I could have a soft drink instead?'

'A soft drink?' Ellington looked genuinely perplexed, as though he had never heard of the term before.

'You know, a Coca Cola or an orange juice,' said Magnus.

Ellington looked to Gregor.

'Thir, we don't have Coca Cola or orange juith,' said the butler, with a shrug.

'Well, any soft drink will do,' said Magnus. 'Whatever you have.'

Gregor looked as though he were trying to do a particularly difficult sum in his head, and then said, 'Water?'

'Water sounds fine,' said Magnus, with a faint note of incredulity in his voice.

'For me too, thanks,' said Bryn, trying not to laugh as Ellington and Gregor exchanged a bemused glance.

'Two waters and a drop of Balblair then, Gregor,' the Labour Lord said, with a dismissive wave of his hand. 'Magnus, Bryn, follow me.'

He led them into a living room, in which two sofas and an armchair were positioned around a marble fireplace, and the walls were lined with paintings depicting yet more pastoral scenes. Settling into the armchair with a practiced air, Ellington motioned that Magnus and Bryn should take the sofa opposite, and when they too had sat down, he surveyed them with his pale blue eyes, which were rather bulging.

'Well then,' he said, with a thin smile, 'what was it you wanted to talk to me about? You said something about security, Magnus?'

But no sooner had the barrister launched into their usual spiel than Ellington held up a hand to stop him.

'Of course, it's for exactly this reason I have Gregor,' he said, smugly. 'He's a butler first and foremost, but he serves as a bodyguard too, so he accompanies me everywhere. Do you know, the House of Lords don't provide any kind of protection — isn't that just absurd? I think it's absolutely outrageous that a man of my status has to make his own arrangements, don't you?'

'Erm, yes,' said Magnus. 'But I'm not sure it's your personal safety that's at risk here. We're fairly sure the person who targeted Dame

Winifred Rye and Hilda Underpin was trying to rob them rather than do them any harm — thank goodness — because on both occasions the burglar scarpered after finding nothing of any value in their flats.'

'Hm,' said Ellington, in the manner of someone only half-listening. 'Gregor's been in the Marines, did you know that? Well, it was the best place for him, as a young man, because I'm afraid he hasn't even half a brain cell. He dropped out of school up in God-knows-where he's from in Scotland — some slum in Aberdeen, I expect — so the Marines were probably the only ones who would take him. Anyway, he's retired from all that now, and he's been with me for about ten years. He's a gentle giant, really, although if anyone crosses me —' Ellington clicked his long fingers together, and the sudden snapping sound made Bryn jump. 'So although I'm grateful for your concern, Magnus, I'm fairly confident no one is going to mess with me or Gregor. Ah, speak of the Devil!'

He looked around keenly, for at that moment the butler-bodyguard had entered the living room carrying three delicate crystal tumblers on a silver tray. As he offered Bryn one of the waters, the policeman wondered how many glasses Gregor had broken in his time: his calloused hands were about twice the size of the policeman's own, and looked as though they could do some serious damage, even accidentally.

'Over here, Gregor, over here!' said Ellington impatiently, as soon as Magnus had taken his water.

When the butler had lumbered over to the armchair, Bryn could not help but notice the drink he placed on the little round table next to Ellington was not just a 'drop' of whiskey, as his employer had requested; instead, well over half of the crystal tumbler was full of amber-coloured liquid. Still, Ellington did not seem to object to this liberal serving, for he presently picked up the glass, took an enormous gulp, and smacked his lips together with pleasure.

'It's a lovely little number, that Balblair,' he said. 'Spicy, but with some sweet notes of honey and vanilla. Balblair is one of the oldest distilleries in Scotland, you know.'

'Goodness,' said Magnus, politely.

'Did you know that, Gregor?' demanded Ellington.

'No, thir.'

'And he calls himself a Scot!' Their host laughed and took another huge gulp of his drink. 'Gregor doesn't even like whiskey very much — he certainly can't keep up with me!'

At the rate Ellington was going, Bryn wondered whether anybody would be able to keep up with him.

'To return to the point,' said Magnus, before Ellington could become too diverted by the subject of whiskey, 'as I said before, Bryn and I are more concerned about what these attempted burglaries mean for your property and belongings than you yourself, Bevis — although naturally your personal safety is our utmost concern.'

'And as I said, I wouldn't worry, Magnus!' cried Ellington. 'What thief is going to even attempt to rob this place, when Gregor's around? He'd have to be an absolute halfwit. Isn't that right, Gregor?'

'Yeth, thir. An abtholute halfwit.'

'There you go,' said Ellington, as though this had straightened everything out.

'With all due respect,' said Magnus, through gritted teeth, 'not everybody has a Gregor figure at their disposal.'

'Obviously!' laughed Ellington, draining the rest of his drink.

'So with that in mind,' said Bryn quickly, for it looked as though the barrister was already losing his patience, 'Magnus and I were wondering whether you'd seen any suspicious characters loitering around the area lately?'

'Suspicious characters?' repeated Ellington, looking amused. 'Goodness, where do I even begin? This place is full of suspect individuals!'

'Funny, that's what Hilda Underpin told us,' noted Bryn.

'Well, she would know — dreadful woman.'

'What we mean is have you noticed any strangers loitering around the Square over the past few weeks?' clarified Magnus. 'Or perhaps you've noticed something unusual or out of place in the area recently?'

'I'd love to help you, Magnus, I would, but I'm afraid I'm far too busy to spend my days spying out of my window like that old bag, Underpin. You might not know this,' he added to Bryn, 'but I'm a Member of the House of Lords.'

'Actually, I did know that,' said Bryn.

Ellington looked pleased. 'It's an incredibly important role, of course, so I'm always going back and forth between here and Westminster, and the palace too, of course. Do you know, there are a few very high-up members of the royal family — I won't say who, it wouldn't be proper — but they say having me in Westminster Square is absolutely essential.'

'That's... great,' said Bryn, for Ellington seemed to be searching his face for some sort of response, and the policeman thought it best to act impressed.

'Yes, isn't it? I believe I was born for this role, even though — between us — I actually come from rather a modest background.'

'Do you?'

This, Bryn thought, was far more interesting, not to mention surprising, for Lord Bevis Ellington gave the impression he had been born with a silver spoon in his mouth.

'Yes, I grew up in Yorkshire, you see, where I worked with the mining unions as a young politician. I became a bit of a hero up there, because of my contributions to that industry, the way I stood up for better wages and so on.' He gave a self-indulgent little chuckle. 'I never forget about the good men who do the true work in this country, and I'll continue to speak up for them until my last breath...'

Bryn wasn't sure he believed this, for it struck him that Lord Bevis Ellington was trying to have his cake and eat it: on the one hand, he seemed to revel in the grandeur of his position and the lifestyle it afforded, but on the other he still wanted to be thought of as a man of the people who fought for the rights of the working classes. It was a jarring juxtaposition, and as a consequence one that made Ellington seem rather false.

'If we could perhaps return to the subject of Westminster Square?' suggested Magnus.

'Oh yes, yes. Actually, hold on: Gregor, fetch me another drink, will you? And this time make it a double.'

Bryn raised his eyebrows: if the amount of whiskey Ellington had just knocked back wasn't a double (and really, it had looked more like a triple to him), what on earth was?

As the butler departed once more, Magnus continued, 'Obviously, these attempted burglaries are a concern in themselves, but what Bryn and I are particularly aware of is that Westminster Square has been in the spotlight over the past couple of weeks.'

'Westminster Square's *always* in the spotlight!' cried Ellington. 'It's the most enviable address in London! Why, my friend in the royal family was saying only the other day that —'

'I'm talking about the less than positive attention this area has received in the media lately,' Magnus interrupted, before Ellington could launch into a boastful anecdote.

'Less than positive?' The Labour Lord looked perplexed. 'I'm sorry, you've lost me, Magnus.'

'Well, you may have been too busy running back and forth from the palace to remember,' said Magnus, with a hint of derision, 'but a few weeks ago a young woman was found dead at the Royal West Hotel under… let's say under *unusual* circumstances.'

Lord Ellington's bulbous-eyed gaze did not move from Magnus' for several seconds, before he snapped, 'Of course I remember that, it was a complete embarrassment to Westminster! I don't know what that dreadful manager at the Royal West was thinking, allowing the press to get hold of all that…'

'I don't think he had a choice,' said Magnus. 'It wasn't as though she was a little old lady who died in her sleep. She was a young, beautiful and apparently healthy woman who suddenly dropped down dead. No wonder the press were excited.'

'Well, it's all very unpleasant, if you ask me,' sniffed Ellington. 'The way those vultures at *The Dawn Reporter* and so on will pick at any corpse for a story. Anne-Laure's dead, leave her be.'

'You remember her name, then?'

'Of course I remember her name, it was all over the news. Wasn't that exactly what we were just talking about?'

He seemed suddenly flustered and angry, which Bryn thought was an overreaction to Magnus' question.

'Yet you'd never met her?' the barrister pressed.

'Why do you say that?'

'Because you told me so at that meeting about CSP's maintenance costs, remember?'

'Oh yes, of course,' said Ellington quickly. 'Well then, why are you asking me again?'

'Because my colleague and I have reason to believe that might not be the case.'

Ellington looked between them sharply, and there was something hawk-like in his expression, as though he were deciding which of them to swoop down on, talons outstretched.

'Where on earth did you get that idea? I bet it was that old witch, Underpin, wasn't it? You can't believe anything she says, she's a malicious, slanderous old hag.'

'Steady on,' said Magnus.

'Well, it's true,' snapped Ellington. 'How dare she spread lies about me like that? As though I would associate myself with a common little girl like Anne-Laure Chevalier? Doesn't Underpin know who I am? I am a Member of the House of Lords!'

'Yes, I think everybody knows that,' said Magnus, patiently.

For a politician, Bryn didn't think Lord Ellington was a particularly convincing liar. He was too easily rattled, too quick to temper.

'Actually, Hilda Underpin didn't say anything about any association you might have had with Anne-Laure Chevalier,' said Magnus. 'As it happens, we received the information from Anne-Laure herself.'

'You're being preposterous!' declared Ellington, but he looked worried.

Bryn, realising now was the moment, withdrew the purple address book. 'This was found in the handbag she died with,' he explained. 'If you look under "E", you'll find yourself.'

Lord Ellington looked as though he were afraid to look at it. 'Preposterous,' he said again.

Bryn flicked through the pages until he reached Lord Ellington's name, scrawled in Anne-Laure's small, neat handwriting, and showed it to their host.

'How am I supposed to know how that got there?' Ellington demanded. 'And how does that even prove that I knew her? She probably made a note of my name and address because she knew I was a man of standing around here. The fact I'm in that book doesn't prove anything! She could have found that information from the Yellow Pages!'

'True,' Magnus agreed. 'But there aren't a huge number of addresses in that book, which has led us to speculate she only made a note of people with whom she was in regular contact.'

'Well, your speculations are incorrect,' said Ellington. 'Your — Oh, Gregor, thank goodness!'

For at that moment, the butler returned, this time with just one tumbler on his silver tray, although it was so full of whiskey it looked as though it were about to overflow. Ellington practically snatched the glass when it was presented to him, and while he drank deeply, Magnus seized his opportunity.

'Gregor, when was the last time Anne-Laure Chevalier came to this flat?'

The redness began to drain from Gregor's features. 'A few weekth —' he began, but he was interrupted by a splutter from Ellington.

'You don't have to answer that, Gregor!' he cried.

The butler bit his lips, looking fearful. Bryn smiled: Magnus had used exactly the same tactic on Lord Ellington as he had on Sheikh Hazim the night before: target the help.

'I'd like to hear what Gregor has to say,' said the barrister pleasantly.

'I don't have anything to thay.'

'Yes you do, you said Anne-Laure Chevalier was here a few weeks — what? Ago? Before she died? What were you going to say, Gregor?'

Bryn felt rather sorry for the butler as he looked between Magnus and Lord Ellington; indeed, it was odd to see such a big man look so scared.

'All right!' burst out Ellington. 'All right, I'll tell you what you want to know. But this has absolutely nothing to do with my butler, so leave him out of this, will you?'

'Very well,' said Magnus.

Ellington nodded over at Gregor, who retreated back from the sofas, his expression one of undiluted relief. His fingers, Bryn noticed, were flexing in and out of his palms, and the policeman wondered whether this was a nervous twitch he had developed in the Marines.

'I trust, if I tell you about my connection to Anne-Laure, it will remain between us?' Ellington said. 'I trust what I say will stay in this room?'

'Of course,' Magnus said.

Bryn, however, did not answer; as a policeman, he could not swear to keeping secrets that might impact on a case. But Ellington didn't seem to notice his silence: perhaps he had forgotten he was sitting opposite a policeman. For the first time, Bryn wondered whether his unobtrusiveness might actually be an asset if he wanted to be a detective.

'All right,' said Ellington again, in the manner of someone steeling himself for something. 'Well, not many people know this, but being a Member of the House of Lords is not a particularly lucrative vocation.'

'Really?' Bryn could not quite disguise the doubt in his voice.

'No,' said their host firmly. 'And let me assure you, I am not an extravagant man. I live a very modest lifestyle, as you can see —' He gestured around at the opulent surroundings of his Westminster Square accommodation without a trace of irony. 'But one needs a bit of pocket money every so often, if only to order a drink or two at the pub now and again...'

Bryn said nothing, but from what he'd seen this evening, he sincerely doubted Ellington only had *a drink or two* anywhere.

'Now this is all very hush-hush, as I have a reputation to maintain, but for some time now I've been dabbling in a little work on the side.'

'What sort of work?' Magnus asked.

'Just a bit of trading, a deal every few months, that sort of thing.'

'Trading what?'

'Oh, nothing fancy. Mostly rice and other food staples, sometimes a bit of jewellery — as I said, it's just dabbling, really.'

'And what does this have to do with Anne-Laure?' asked Bryn.

'Why, she was my *rabbateur*, of course.'

Bryn stared at him. 'Your *what*?'

'A "*rabbateur*" is a colloquial business term,' Magnus explained. 'It's French, but translated into English it means "beater."'

Bryn shook his head: this wasn't becoming any clearer.

'Traditionally, a beater is the person who, in estates up in Scotland and so on, goes out with the hunt and beats the ground to disturb the game birds, which then fly up into the range of the guns,' said Ellington. 'In business, it refers to someone who has a similar sort of role, in that they network, identify clients and steer them towards... Well, someone like me.'

'Presumably not to be shot,' said Bryn.

Magnus snorted with laughter, but Ellington didn't crack a smile. Unfazed, Bryn continued, 'So Anne-Laure drummed up business for you?'

'She did.'

'And she did it well?'

'Oh yes. In many ways, she was a natural fit for the role, because she was young and fairly smart, not to mention attractive — or so people seemed to think, I couldn't really see it myself.'

Bryn almost laughed: was Lord Ellington really suggesting he had failed to notice Anne-Laure's beauty?

'Clients fell over themselves for her,' their host continued. 'Well, the male ones did and, let's face it, most of them are men. She only had to flutter her eyelashes and they would promise her anything. More importantly, they would sign anything.'

'She sounds like a huge asset,' noted Magnus.

Their host looked a little sour. 'I suppose she was,' he said, unconvincingly. 'Anyway, there you go: that's why my name's in her address book. She did a little a work for me, that's all, and — as I said — I'd appreciate it if you kept quiet about my trading ventures. I wouldn't want it to get back to the palace or to Downing Street.'

'Naturally,' said Magnus.

There was a slight pause, and Bryn had the impression that Ellington was gearing up to making some excuse to get rid of them — after all, he had answered all of their questions. But then Magnus picked up his empty tumbler.

'Do you know what, Bevis? You've spoken so highly of that Balblair I'm tempted to give it a try.'

Instantly, Ellington lit up, all resentment of a few moments' ago forgotten.

'Oh, you must!' he said, clicking his fingers for his butler. 'We all must! Gregor, fetch our guests some Balblair, will you? And just a splash more for me.'

Bryn goggled at their host's empty glass: how on earth had he drunk all that whiskey so quickly? Gregor too seemed thrown, although perhaps not by the rate his employer consumed alcohol.

'Now, thir?'

'Yes, now!' snapped Ellington.

Bryn frowned as the butler shuffled miserably from the room: why had he been so reluctant to leave?

While they waited for the drinks to arrive, Magnus kept Ellington occupied with small talk, allowing the Labour Lord to brag about his latest trip to the palace and name-drop several aristocrats and high-profile politicians into the conversation. Then, when Gregor reappeared, and Magnus and Bryn had made several enthusiastic comments about the whiskey (of which, thankfully, they had received conventional-sized servings), the barrister allowed Ellington to take a significant swig of his drink before he returned to his line of questioning.

'Forgive me for harping on about this, Bevis, but I am still a little curious about this Anne-Laure business...'

Ellington, whose gaze was a little unfocused now, said, 'What do you mean?'

'Well, how did it work exactly, her being your *rabbateur*?'

Ellington shrugged. 'I would send her off to parties and networking events, and sometimes overseas to meet clients, and she would come back with the goods. As I said, she was very competent.'

Again, Magnus waited until the Labour Lord had taken another glug of his drink before asking, 'So you liked her, then?'

'I wouldn't say that.'

'No?'

'No.'

Behind Ellington, Gregor shifted from foot to foot, the floorboards creaking under his weight. When it became clear Ellington wasn't going to say any more, Magnus ventured, 'Vasyl Kosnitschev spoke highly of Anne-Laure.'

'Well, that old Commie probably lusted after her, didn't he?' said Ellington, with a flash of malice. 'He was probably as smitten with her as the rest of them. Fortunately, I'm immune to the charms of women — I mean, women like *that*,' he corrected himself quickly.

'Like what?' pressed Magnus, ignoring Ellington's embarrassment. 'I'm still not quite sure why you didn't like her, Bevis.'

'Because she was a grasping opportunist!' burst out their host, with surprising passion. 'Because she didn't know her place! I mean, who even was she? I don't know where she came from, who her parents were, what she was even doing in London, before she started working for that Ukrainian!'

'Didn't you ask her?' Bryn enquired, thinking this was a very strange complaint to make, considering Ellington could easily have questioned Anne-Laure when hiring her.

'I should have. But she was steering so much business towards me, I didn't like to pry. Why look a gift horse in the mouth? Why question your *rabbateur*, when she has almost superhuman powers of charm and persuasion?'

'To which you were completely immune?' said Magnus.

'Oh, I didn't like the way she put on airs and graces, as though she were a member of the aristocracy. I can't be sure, but I sensed a very *aspirational* streak in Anne-Laure. Her whole demeanour was very *nouveau riche*.'

Bryn thought this was very hypocritical, considering Ellington himself had boasted about his working class origins not fifteen minutes ago. Perhaps the Labour Lord realised he sounded foolish, for he quickly added, 'She was greedy. Grasping. Completely obsessed with money, as far as I could tell — always making sure I paid her exactly the right amount, making a huge fuss if even a few pennies were off. It's very uncouth in a person, especially a woman, to be that preoccupied with material gain.'

Bryn frowned: as someone who was only just scraping by in London, he could not appreciate this attitude one bit. In his experience, the only people who didn't worry about money were the ones who had far too much of it.

'Towards the end, she became so greedy she asked me for an advance — can you believe it! The cheek of the girl! As though I didn't pay her enough for simply quaffing champagne and flirting with old men, she wanted *more*! Of course, I refused point blank, but it did make me rethink her position. To be perfectly honest, I was rather relieved when I heard she had died. I mean —' He looked horrified, as though he hadn't realised his words would sound so blunt out loud. 'I mean, I was relieved from a business perspective, because I no longer had to face the unpleasantness of firing her. Otherwise, of course it was a terrible tragedy. It's a dreadful thing, to lose someone so young like that...'

Bryn took a sip of his own whiskey to stop himself from saying anything he would regret, and felt a little pacified as the fiery liquid burned down the back of his throat. Magnus, however, did not seem distinctly ruffled by Ellington's lack of sympathy for the dead woman.

'You were going to fire her for asking for an advance?' he said, somehow managing to make the question sound non-accusatory.

'Yes. Well, I mean, I was thinking about it. It was her attitude as much as anything... We weren't a good fit.'

His words, Bryn noticed, were becoming a little slurred.

'And did Anne-Laure tell you why she wanted this advance?'

Ellington laughed. 'Why would she do that?'

'Presumably there was a reason she wanted extra money. I just wondered whether she'd mentioned it to you, when she asked?'

Their host shook his head. 'She was probably starting some scheme on the side, knowing her. No doubt she was investing in something behind my back.'

'That's not a crime, is it?' Magnus asked Bryn.

As the policeman shook his head, Ellington said, 'I don't know why she wanted the money. I wasn't particularly interested in her private life.'

Apart from being desperate to know where she was from and who her parents were, thought Bryn, who couldn't help but think that Vasyl had been far more convincing than Ellington on this score.

'You never saw her with Jem McMorran, did you?' asked Magnus.

'Jem McMorran? *The* Jem McMorran!' Again, much as he had when Magnus had said he wanted a drink, Ellington seemed to brighten. Then he scoffed, 'Why on earth would someone like *him* have any time for someone like *her*? He's a star — an icon — an *Adonis*!'

Gregor cleared his throat loudly. Again, Ellington ducked behind his whiskey glass.

'... So they say,' he mumbled.

Magnus' lips twitched. 'And you don't know whether she had a boyfriend or anything like that?'

Ellington smirked. 'You sound like a journalist for *The Dawn Reporter,* Magnus. I'm afraid, if you were thinking of making her your mistress, you're a little late.'

'Don't be absurd,' said Magnus calmly. 'Anyway, I never knowingly met her. Unlike you, my name's not in that address book.'

Their host, recognising the slight, looked immediately chastened.

'Anyway,' said Magnus, pushing his advantage, 'we rather got off the subject there, didn't we? I do hope you'll heed our warnings about Westminster Square security, Bevis, despite Gregor's reassuring presence.'

'Yes, yes,' said Ellington, who had begun to hiccup. 'But will you — *hic* — have another drink, Magnus?'

'Actually, I think we should be off. We've taken up far too much of your time already, and I have to be back for dinner.'

'Dinner!' cried Ellington, as though he had forgotten all about it. 'Why, you can — *hic* — eat here! Stay! Gregor — *hic* — what are we having for dinner?'

'Roatht beef and potatoeth, thir.'

'There you - *hic* - go!'

But fortunately — for Bryn was dreading a repeat of yesterday's dubious *majlis* experience — Magnus managed to make their excuses and they bade goodbye to Lord Ellington, who now seemed too sozzled to rise from his chair. Then, after they had followed the butler back through the flat to the front door, Magnus asked one last question before they left: 'What did you think of Anne-Laure, Gregor?'

The butler looked thrown at the prospect of having to give an opinion. He cast his gaze around for Ellington, but his employer was back in the living room, probably looking around for more whiskey.

'Pretty,' Gregor said at last.

'Just pretty?'

The butler appeared to be doing some serious thinking. 'Pretty and... fragile. Thee wath like thome kind of little bird...'

He trailed off and, apparently unable to look at them anymore, looked down at his hands instead. Bryn thought, unlike Ellington, this big man must have harboured some affection for Anne-Laure Chevalier, for his blotchy face was suddenly overcome with sadness. Magnus gave him a reassuring pat on his huge arm.

'We'll be off, then,' he said. 'Thanks for the drink.'

The butler gave a shrug of his huge shoulders and closed the door behind them. Then, when they were safely out of earshot of the building, Magnus looked at Bryn.

'Hm,' he said.

'Hm,' Bryn agreed.

They did not have to say any more: it wasn't as though they had any answers but both Hazim and Ellington had provided a very interesting perspective on the Anne-Laure Chevalier mystery.

'Why don't you go and write this all up?' suggested Magnus. 'And while you're at it, I'm going to make a phone call.'

'A phone call?'

'Yes, to Morris Springfield — Juliana has his number from the flower shop. Considering all we've learned from his two compatriots in Anne-Laure's address book, I think it's a good idea to talk to that writer as soon as possible…'

CHAPTER TWENTY-ONE

The writer Morris Springfield lived in Westminster Row, a street running parallel to the south side of Westminster Square, with only Anne-Laure Chevalier's former address, the Mews, in between. To Bryn's inexpert eye, Westminster Row looked like a slightly more modest version of the four streets that made up Westminster Square, for although its terraces still boasted similarly pristine white facades, smart black doors, and wrought iron balconies and railings, the individual properties seemed smaller here, slightly more modern, and there was not a pillared entranceway in sight.

Nevertheless, it was still an undoubtedly grandiose part of London to live, which was somewhat surprising, given Morris Springfield was a writer. As far as Bryn was aware, most modern authors were not half as well-off as their eighteenth-, nineteenth- and early-twentieth-century predecessors, many of whom featured on the blue plaques he had seen around the City of Westminster and Greater London. Indeed, as Morris only had two rather elitist novels to his name, Bryn couldn't quite understand how the writer could afford to live in Westminster, unless he did other work on the side, like Lord Ellington and his trading — and like Anne-Laure Chevalier's *rabbateur* role, now Bryn came to think about it.

As it happened, the police constable's curiosity about how Morris Springfield was able to afford his flat was somewhat satisfied as he and Magnus were buzzed into the writer's building the evening after they had talked to Lord Ellington. As Bryn had suspected from the outside, the accommodation in Westminster Row was far more cramped than that of Westminster Square, and as they made their way up the narrow staircase towards Morris' top floor flat, the floor creaked so loudly under their feet that Bryn thought it might give way at any moment. In fact, by the look of the staircase, the carpet of which was scuffed, the banister scratched and the surrounding wallpaper peeling, the police constable wouldn't have been surprised if the whole building was in serious danger of falling apart.

Morris Springfield only opened the door halfway after Magnus had knocked, peering at them through the gap, yet this still gave Bryn an opportunity to take in the writer close-to: he guessed Morris was of a similar age to himself, although there was something oddly adolescent about his rather greasy hair, which came to just below his ears, and which seemed to emphasise — rather than disguise — his receding hairline. Other than that, Morris Springfield gave the impression of someone who spent a great deal of time indoors, for his skin was pale, his posture bad, and he was eyeing his guests with great deal of suspicion, despite the fact Magnus had made an appointment.

'Ah, Morris,' said the barrister, with his usual easy manner, 'how nice to see you. This is my associate, Police Constable Bryn Summers of the Victoria Police Station.'

'Pleased to meet you,' said Bryn, extending a hand.

Hesitantly, Morris took it, although he barely brushed Bryn's fingers with his own before letting go.

'Would we be able to come in for a quick word?' Magnus asked. 'As I told you on the phone, we're making the rounds of people in the area because we have a few security concerns...'

Morris didn't look especially happy to be receiving them, but he nodded, and then stood aside to let them pass through the door.

Bryn's first impression of Morris Springfield's flat was that it wasn't much bigger than his own bedsit back in Clapham. The writer did at least have a separate bedroom, but the living area was very small indeed, and there was only just room for a threadbare sofa, which had been crammed under the window. It didn't help that half of the room was taken up by a kitchenette, and the sloped ceiling also made what once must have been an attic look especially poky.

But Bryn could not help but think that Morris could have created an illusion of space if he hadn't filled the flat with quite so many books.

Indeed, in this respect — and unlike most of Bryn's other experiences with Westminster Square's properties — Morris' flat was almost exactly as the police constable would have imagined a writer's accommodation to look: piles of newspapers, bits of manuscripts, not to mention countless tall towers of tomes seemed to occupy every surface and half of the floor space, so much so that it looked far more like a second hand bookshop than somebody's living quarters. There were also a number of cardboard boxes scattered about the place, and although it looked as though Morris were in the process of moving in or out, Bryn suspected these simply held more books.

In a way, the whole scene reminded the police constable of the chaos of Jem McMorran's flat, but while that clutter had been completely random — and probably a result of slovenly housekeeping on the actor's part — these mountains of books almost served as decoration, and the only real mess he could identify was a couple of used coffee cups buried amongst the various papers.

'I've been writing all day, so I haven't had time to tidy,' said Morris, speaking for the first time and revealing a rather reedy voice.

'That's quite all right,' said Magnus, picking his way towards the sofa and nodding at a pile of books occupying one of the cushions. 'I'll just move these aside, shall I?'

'Yes,' said Morris, and as he gave no indication as to where Magnus was supposed to put them, the barrister simply dropped the books onto the floor.

Bryn moved to sit next to Magnus on the sofa, but only when he had taken his seat did he realise this left no room for Morris. There followed a few awkward seconds while the writer dithered over where to sit, until he eventually decided to pull over one of his cardboard boxes and use it is a makeshift stool.

'This is quite a place you have here,' said Magnus, and Bryn wasn't sure whether he meant this as a compliment or a criticism.

Morris, evidently taking it as the former, said, 'Thank you.'

'Have CSP sorted out that sinking business yet?' the barrister continued.

Bryn stared at him. '*Sinking?*'

'Yes, apparently, some of these houses are sinking, because of their proximity to the Thames. It's something to do with disturbed foundations.'

'They're only sinking a few millimetres a year!' piped up Morris defensively.

'Are they? Well, that's not too bad, I suppose,' said Magnus. 'Still, you should be badgering Central Square Properties to sort it out, Morris — they should be thinking about how to fortify those foundations. It's their responsibility after all, and you pay enough to live here, so it's the least they can do.'

Bryn frowned. He was rather puzzled by the fact that Morris Springfield had chosen to live in this tiny and apparently sinking flat in Westminster, when for the same price he probably could have rented or even bought a property of around one hundred and fifty square metres in somewhere like Camden. For Bryn, who could barely afford the rent of his tiny bedsit in Clapham, it made no sense: Morris might be richer than him, but he wasn't anywhere near as wealthy as people like Sheikh Hazim, or even Magnus, so what on earth was he doing around the corner from them?

'Why did you decide to live here?' Bryn asked, before he could stop himself.

Morris looked at him with a rather scathing expression. 'Because of Westminster's rich literary history, of course.'

'Oh,' said Bryn, a little put-out by Morris' manner. 'Is it particularly famous for writers, then? I mean, I've seen a few plaques, but —'

'Ian Fleming lived not far away from here on Ebury Street — the author of *James Bond*, for goodness' sake! Then Somerset Maugham lived in Eaton Square, as did Diana Mitford, who wrote a little — though I suppose it was her sister Nancy who was more of an author...'

'Oh, right,' said Bryn politely, thinking Morris had stopped, but it seemed as though he were just getting started.

'Then also in Belgravia you have Mary Shelley, the author of *Frankenstein*; and Joseph Conrad, who wrote *Heart of Darkness*, lived on the other side of Victoria. Mark Twain and TS Eliot were just two of the many writers who lived in neighbouring Chelsea. But perhaps my personal favourite is Alfred, Lord Tennyson — his blue plaque is on Upper Belgrave Street.'

'And what did he write?' asked Bryn.

'*What did he* —?' Morris broke off, shaking his head. 'Only some of the finest poetry this country has ever known! Tennyson was Poet Laureate for most of Queen Victoria's reign, you *must* have heard of him. He wrote the famous lines: *I hold it true, whate'er befall; I feel it, when I sorrow most; 'Tis better to have loved and lost Than never to have loved at all.*'

'Ah, yes, that does ring a bell,' said Bryn, a little annoyed that Morris seemed to be judging him for his lack of literary knowledge. 'Although, being Welsh, I'm more of a Dylan Thomas man, myself.'

But Morris didn't seem to be listening. He was gazing out of the window above their heads, apparently overcome by the power of the poetry he had just recited by heart.

'So you're hoping for a blue plaque yourself someday, eh, Morris?' said Magnus, his voice laced with amusement. 'That's why you're staying in Westminster?'

'Pardon? Oh, no!' Morris reddened, as he caught up with what Magnus had said. 'Of course not! I couldn't begin to compete with men like Tennyson. I simply want to soak up the literary atmosphere of Westminster, and feel inspired by the greats who lived here before me.'

'I see,' said Magnus, and Bryn thought the barrister, like he himself, was not entirely taken in by the writer's show of modesty. 'Well, speaking of Westminster, and Westminster Square in particular, we should probably talk about this security issue, Morris…'

As Magnus proceeded to tell him about the break-ins at Dame Winifred Rye and Hilda Underpin's properties, Morris looked politely concerned, but professed not to know either woman.

'I'm not familiar with many people in Westminster Square,' he said, with an air of superiority.

'Hilda Underpin is that elderly lady who shouts at everyone,' Magnus explained.

At this, comprehension seemed to dawn on the writer's pasty features. 'Oh, *her*,' he said, with a shudder. 'She's an awful person. I don't know about the other woman, but I'd say that Hilda person had something like a burglary coming to her, wouldn't you?'

Neither Magnus nor Bryn answered, and the police constable was rather surprised at this flicker of spite, even with regard to someone like Hilda Underpin. But Morris did not appear to notice their unspoken disapproval.

'She accused me of skulking around the Square the other week,' he continued. 'Apparently it's a crime to stroll down a street these days, because that old bat came hobbling over and started accusing me of all sorts.'

'Really?' Magnus laughed. 'What did she say?'

'Oh, that I should iron my shirt, that I should comb my hair, that I looked scruffy carrying around my notebook... Never mind that it contained the precious first draft of my next novel! No, it looked *scruffy*! She even accused me of loitering and spying — the irony!'

'I'd just ignore her, if I were you,' advised Magnus. 'If you make a fuss, she only goes after you harder. My wife can attest to that. And so, I believe, could Anne-Laure Chevalier.'

Bryn gave a little start: this was not the way they usually dropped the dead woman's name into a conversation. Evidently, Magnus was trying something new, and perhaps this was a wise move, because Morris — who had been enjoying castigating Hilda — suddenly looked very sombre.

'W-who?' he managed to stammer.

'Anne-Laure Chevalier. You know, that poor girl they found dead at the Royal West? By all accounts, she and Hilda were at loggerheads when she was alive. The old lady accused her of all sorts of things.'

'Like what?' Morris asked.

'Oh, Hilda seemed to be very offended by Anne-Laure's way of dressing and behaving. She thought she was a flirt, to put it politely. And she had some madcap theory that Anne-Laure was having an affair with Jem McMorran. You know, that actor?'

'I know *of* him.'

Although he couldn't be sure, Bryn thought Magnus was trying to elicit some sort of reaction from Morris. But the writer looked more confused than jealous or upset.

'Did you know her, Morris?' asked the barrister.

'Who?' The writer immediately seemed to sense this was a silly question, because he quickly added, 'You mean, Anne-Laure Chevalier? No, I didn't.'

'Not at all?'

'No.'

Magnus nodded at Bryn, who, for the third time in three days, withdrew the little purple address book to contradict what their host had just said.

'This was hers,' he explained, flicking through to the letter 'S' and showing Morris his own name.

As soon as he saw this, Morris jumped back as though he had received an electric shock.

'What is this?' he demanded. 'What are you playing at, Magnus? Why have you brought the police here? I haven't done anything!'

It was by far the most defensive reaction they had had to the address book so far, which Bryn thought was interesting. Magnus, meanwhile, retained his usual composure.

'No one's accusing you of anything, Morris,' he said. 'My associate here is simply tying up a few loose ends regarding Anne-Laure Chevalier's death, and — as I said — I want to improve the security of Westminster Square and the surrounding area.'

'What sort of loose ends?' Morris asked at once.

Bryn hesitated: Morris Springfield was clearly no fool. In all their other meetings, nobody had questioned the way he and Magnus had steered the conversation towards Anne-Laure Chevalier; in fact, nobody else had had any reservations about giving their opinion on her. The writer, on the other hand, seemed suspicious, and Bryn didn't know how to react, for he and Magnus had not planned for this eventuality. Fortunately, however, the barrister seemed unruffled.

'I'm afraid we're not at liberty to divulge any information on the Anne-Laure Chevalier case,' he said smoothly. 'At the moment, it's between the police and lawyers.'

Morris seemed to accept this, but he didn't look any less nervous.

'Well, what do you want to know?' he asked, avoiding Magnus' gaze and directing this question straight to Bryn.

'We want to know what your relationship was to Anne-Laure Chevalier.'

'*Relationship!*' Morris spluttered. 'We didn't have any kind of relationship!'

'All right, put it this way,' the policeman corrected himself. 'We want to know why you're in her address book.'

Morris shook his head and began to mutter to himself. Bryn caught the odd word such as '*ridiculous*' and '*completely unnecessary*' before the writer sprang to his feet and began to pace around the room — a difficult feat, considering all the books, manuscripts and boxes.

'Fine, I'll tell you,' he said, 'but I do think this is a bit over the top, Magnus. And to be perfectly honest, I'd rather this didn't go any further than you two, because I'm a bit embarrassed by it all.'

'Embarrassed?' said Magnus. 'Why?'

Morris took a deep breath, in the manner of a man steeling himself for a great divulgence.

'The reason I'm in that address book is that Anne-Laure Chevalier and I… once went for coffee.'

'*Coffee?*' said Bryn, both amused and disappointed: he had been expecting something far more scandalous.

'Yes, coffee!' cried Morris. 'I presume the reason she wrote down my address and phone number is because we met outside my flat here, and we walked to a cafe in Sloane Square together, but we never saw each other again, so she needn't have bothered putting me in there, really.'

He gestured at the little address book as though it were a person who had greatly offended him. Bryn, still feeling a little let down by this non-revelation, thought this would be the end of the matter, but it seemed Magnus had more questions.

'When was this trip to Sloane Square?'

'Oh, a few years ago — maybe three or four. Not long after I moved here. And as I said, it was a one-off.'

'And was it going for a coffee, as in... a date?'

'Oh, no!' Morris looked surprised. 'No, nothing like that. Just as friends, or *prospective* friends would be a better term. We're both from Brighton, you see — we grew up there — and I think she wanted to talk about that. She was probably a little homesick, now I think back on it.'

'Did you know her back in Brighton?' asked Bryn, for if this man was around the same age as him, he had to be around the same age as Anne-Laure too.

'No!' Again, Morris looked almost shocked by the question. 'No, not at all. I went to an all-boys' school back in Brighton. I didn't — *aha* — meet many girls when I was growing up.'

This, Bryn thought, was unsurprising. In fact, he very much doubted Morris met many girls now. Although, given he was hardly a lothario himself, the police constable wasn't really one to judge. Magnus, meanwhile, was frowning.

'How did she know you were from Brighton, then?' he asked.

'Pardon me?'

'If you didn't know one another when you lived in Brighton, how did you both know you were from the same place?'

Morris shrugged. 'Well, I didn't know. It was all her. We bumped into each other on the street one day, and she must have recognised me from the newspaper or something, because she started chattering on about *Vacant Shadows* and what a big fan of my work she was.' He looked rather pleased with himself as he said this. 'She told me she was from Brighton as well — so I presume she must have read that in one of my profiles — and asked me for coffee, just like that.'

Bryn raised an eyebrow: if he had been relating a story of how he had been asked out for coffee by someone who looked like Anne-Laure Chevalier, he would not have sounded half as blasé about it as Morris Springfield — and he flattered himself that he had a little more going for him, personality-wise, than the awkward, arrogant writer.

'I don't quite understand why you're embarrassed about this, Morris,' said Magnus. 'You went for a coffee with a woman. Why keep it secret? Why lie to Juliana about knowing Anne-Laure?'

'I didn't lie,' said Morris sharply. 'I just — your wife caught me on a bad day, that's all. My mother had just been taken very ill, and I hardly knew what Juliana was on about, because I'd barely registered the news that day. I think that's understandable, don't you? That I didn't remember the girl who'd just died at that hotel was the same one I'd had coffee with a few years' ago, because I was far more concerned about my dear mother being so sick?'

'Of course,' said Magnus, 'but might I remind you, Morris, you denied knowing Anne-Laure Chevalier a few minutes ago, and then professed to find going for coffee with her embarrassing. I don't really understand why.'

'Isn't it obvious?' said Morris, pausing in his pacing to look down at them both on the sofa.

'No.'

'Anne-Laure was — Well, she — I mean, Anne-Laure wasn't really what I look for in a girl.'

'You don't like beautiful women?' said Magnus, his tone mocking.

'I like *intelligent* women,' said Morris. 'My ideal partner would be well-read, well-spoken, clever and opinionated, and I'm afraid Anne-Laure was none of those things. In fact, to be perfectly blunt, I think she was a bit of a bimbo.'

'Was she?' said Bryn, before he could stop himself; this was not the impression they had gleaned from Vasyl or Lord Ellington, both of whom had entrusted her with their business interests.

'Yes, she was,' said Morris, sitting down on his cardboard box once more. 'It was a complete waste of time, that coffee.'

'What did you talk about?' asked Magnus.

'Oh, Brighton mostly,' said Morris, sounding irritated. 'Brighton, Brighton, Brighton. She was obsessed with it. I think she wanted to go back there, or go back in time and relive her childhood there, I don't know.'

Again, this struck Bryn as odd: it wasn't as though Anne-Laure had had a particularly happy childhood in Brighton — quite the opposite, in fact.

'We talked about my work as well,' continued Morris, softening a little. 'She told me she'd read both *Vacant Shadows* and *Splinters of Innocence* and had been very impressed with them.'

'She can't have been that dim, then,' noted Magnus.

'Sorry?'

'Well, with all due respect, Morris, your books are a little hard-going at times. Juliana gave up on *Vacant Shadows,* and I'm afraid I found it a bit of a struggle to get to the end.'

Curiously, Morris did not look at all put-out to hear this. On the contrary, he looked rather pleased.

'All I'm saying is, if Anne-Laure Chevalier had read and enjoyed both of them, she was probably a little smarter than you're giving her credit for.'

'Oh, but I don't think she really *got* them, you know? I don't think she truly appreciated the themes, the use of symbolism, the subtlety of prose... In fact, looking back on it, she probably hadn't read them at all. I bet she only said that to impress me.'

'You think she was trying to impress you?' Bryn asked, hoping his voice didn't betray too much doubt.

Morris shrugged again. 'Maybe.'

'So you didn't see her again?' asked Magnus.

Morris shook his head, his lank hair flopping about at his temples.

'And you weren't... tempted to set up another meeting?'

'Why would I do that?'

'Well, without putting too fine a point on it, Anne-Laure was a very attractive woman.'

'But how does the saying go? *Never judge a book by its cover.* As I said, she wasn't my intellectual equal.'

'Even so...'

'No, I'm sorry, but no.' Morris seemed irritated now. 'I can't abide talk of designer bags and — and, and, who's who on the London party scene.'

'Is that what she wanted to talk about?' asked Bryn.

'That sort of talk rots the brain,' said Morris, ignoring the question. 'Look, I think of my brain as I do my body. If one eats junk food and quaffs fizzy drinks and alcohol all day, one becomes fat and lethargic, even ill. It's the same with the mind. If one reads trashy novels, and talks to people with inferior intellects... Well, the effects are almost as adverse. Do you see what I'm saying?'

'Yes,' said Bryn, although at that moment he thought he would rather talk to almost anybody than Morris Springfield.

Perhaps the writer sensed his disapproval, for he continued, 'Look, I'm not trying to be harsh. Maybe Anne-Laure wasn't exactly a bimbo — maybe that was the wrong word — but neither was she particularly bright or interesting, and therefore I'm afraid I couldn't waste any more time on her. I look for much more in a woman.'

'Well, I wish you luck on your romantic quest,' said Magnus, 'especially as your standards are so high. I just hope your prospective partners aren't quite so picky.'

'Thank you — Wait, what?'

'Shall we go, Bryn?' asked Magnus loudly, before Morris could dwell too much on his last comment.

'Erm, yes,' said the policeman, scrambling to his feet.

'Thank you very much for your time, Morris,' said Magnus. 'We'll keep you updated on the security situation around here, although you probably don't have too much to worry about, given you don't actually live *on* Westminster Square.'

Morris winced a little as he heard this, as though it were a sore point. Then, as he shook Magnus' hand, he said, 'I don't imagine a burglar would be very interested by the contents of my flat. My belongings have far more intellectual worth than monetary value.'

He gestured proudly round at the piles of books and papers.

'I don't know, you could have a few jewels stashed in here,' said Magnus, bending down to peek under the lid of one of the nearest cardboard boxes.

He was obviously joking, but Morris gave a cry of alarm, leapt forward and slammed the top of the box shut. Magnus stared at him.

'Don't!' he cried. 'Those are my story notes! They're incredibly private!'

Magnus held up his hands, as though surrendering. 'Sorry, old chap. I was just messing around. I didn't mean to pry.'

Morris seemed to relax. 'Right,' he mumbled. 'I just — I don't like people seeing my unfinished work, that's all. My rough drafts are just that — rough. What would people think, if they were able to glimpse into the unglamorous early stages of the writing process? They would be disappointed. Why, they might even question my talent!'

'Heaven forbid,' said Magnus, who looked as though he were trying not to laugh. Then he clapped Morris on the shoulder. 'Well, it won't happen again. In fact, we'll leave you to your writing now. Come on, Bryn.'

They proceeded out of Morris' flat and down the creaking staircase once more, and only when they were back on Westminster Row did Magnus seem to feel it safe to roll his eyes and say, 'Writers, eh?'

Bryn didn't smile. 'That was all very odd,' he said.

'What, Morris, his flat, or the Anne-Laure Chevalier stuff?'

'All of it.'

'Yes, it was a bit, wasn't it?' Magnus checked his watch. 'Look, Bryn, I've got to be getting back for dinner, Juliana —'

'— Will be expecting you, I know,' said the policeman, who was now used to Magnus having to run off each evening to appease his wife.

'But we need to discuss this further, not just Morris, but Ellington and Hazim too. Why don't we have dinner this weekend? Not at my flat — the pollen in the dining room will kill you — but we could go to Lei Sing's instead?'

'Who's Lei Sing?'

Magnus laughed. 'It's not a person, it's a restaurant: Lei Sing's Taste of China. It's just a couple of roads away from here, and it does amazing Chinese food.'

'Sounds good to me,' said Bryn, who rarely allowed himself to eat out, given London was so expensive. In fact, the thought of delicious Chinese food at this time of day was making his mouth water.

'Great, I'll book us a table for around seven-thirty on Saturday, then,' said Magnus, already backing away in the direction of Westminster Square, as though he could hear Juliana calling to him here, in Westminster Row. 'Oh, and Bryn?'

'Yes?'

'Bring your notes.'

CHAPTER TWENTY-TWO

As they entered Lei Sing's Taste of China the following Saturday, and Bryn gazed around the restaurant in appreciation, Magnus, who had been there many times before, tried to see the scene through the policeman's eyes.

Lei Sing's, no doubt because of its Westminster location, was rather grander than most of the Chinese restaurants that had been popping up around London over the past few decades. It was a relatively large and beautifully decorated space, with carved wooden panels and a warm red and gold colour scheme, which reflected the traditional colours of China. Chinese culture was then further emphasised by the dragon statuettes, the paintings of warriors adorning the walls and cabinets, and the arrangements of Oriental-style flowers, such as orchids and lotuses, on the tables.

This commitment to China was one of the things Magnus liked best about Lei Sing's. As well as the decoration, the food was entirely authentic — no chips or other British cuisine had snuck onto the menu — and all of the staff seemed to be genuinely Chinese, or at least the children of Chinese immigrants. Their waiter introduced himself as 'Johnny', but Magnus was sure this was a Western name he'd adopted, because to look at his high cheekbones and jet-black hair, the man was obviously from somewhere in the Far East. Furthermore, when he spoke, he had a slight but noticeable accent, leading to Magnus to suspect English was not his native language and he hadn't been born in the UK.

Once Johnny had led them to a small, white-clothed table by the window, and they had sat in comfortable high-backed red seats, they ordered a bottle of wine and some crispy Peking sesame prawn toasts for a starter. Then, after they had exchanged a couple of pleasantries and perused their menus for a few minutes, Magnus decided to get straight to the point and asked, 'So what did you think of our three hosts this week?'

He chuckled as the young policeman's expression changed to one of wide-eyed mystification.

'Yes, I know what you mean,' he agreed, 'they're interesting characters, aren't they?'

'And so *different*,' said Bryn. 'In fact, it's difficult to believe they all live in Westminster Square — or near it, in Morris' case. But I feel as though, in the last few days, I was transported to the Arabian Desert, some kind of country estate, and — I don't know — a Victorian-era writer's garret. Actually, it reminds me of what Morris said about Anne-Laure: *never judge a book by its cover*. It seems the same can be applied to the buildings of Westminster; you never know what you're going to find beyond those grand facades.'

Magnus laughed again. 'Do you know, I think you're getting the hang of Westminster Square,' he said. Then, remembering the issue in hand, he continued, 'But let's talk about these three men, seeing as we haven't had a chance to discuss any of those meetings yet. First, Sheikh Hazim.'

'Well, that was the weirdest evening, definitely,' said Bryn at once. 'I mean, I appreciate that eating dinner in a *majlis* setting is an Eastern custom, but it was quite surprising to find a whole tent set up in there, and then there were those Western touches: the football, the cheese…'

'What about the fact that, once again, Hazim denied knowing Anne-Laure?' said Magnus, in an attempt to steer Bryn back on track. 'Before we showed him the address book?'

The policeman hesitated. 'I'm not sure,' he said. 'Actually, a part of me thinks he could have been telling the truth.'

'Really?' Magnus was rather surprised to hear this: in his experience, Bryn always leaned towards the more outlandish theory. He was a born conspiracy theorist.

'Yes,' said Bryn, looking thoughtful. 'Because it didn't sound as though he had a particularly high opinion of women, did it? He barely seems to see them as people — just objects for his amusement, like those belly-dancers.' He reddened at the memory. 'So really, why would he remember Anne-Laure? To him, she's probably just one of many who came through that flat, who worked on a party…'

'You believe that too, then?' asked Magnus. 'That she organised a few of his events?'

'It makes sense, doesn't it? That's what she did for Vasyl, so it was obviously what she specialised in...' Bryn trailed off, seeming to realise that Magnus was not wholly convinced. 'I don't know, what you do think?'

'I'm not sure,' said Magnus, pausing for a few moments while Johnny returned with the wine. Then, when the waiter had filled their glasses and departed, he withdrew a sheet of paper from his bag, which he handed to Bryn. 'What you say makes sense, especially when you consider this...'

'What is it?' asked the policeman, frowning down at the document.

'An invoice Anne-Laure apparently sent in 1990, detailing the costs for organising a couple of parties,' said Magnus, who had been sent this by Hazim's secretary the previous day.

Bryn looked up. 'So doesn't this prove it? That he hired her to plan his events?'

'Maybe,' said Magnus, with a shrug. 'Only, it's typed, isn't it? And there's no signature. Hazim's secretary could have written that up yesterday.'

'But why would he bother organising that?'

'Why indeed?'

Bryn regarded him quizzically as Magnus took a sip of wine.

'Come on, then,' said the policeman, 'what are you thinking? What's your alternative theory?'

'I'm not certain I really have one,' said Magnus. 'But that scene with Steve the butler, when he was pouring our tea, was very strange indeed.'

'Oh yes, I'd forgotten about that. It looked as though they were trying to communicate without words, didn't it? As though Hazim was trying to get Steve to cover for him?'

'Exactly,' said the barrister. 'But why? If Anne-Laure was just planning a few parties, why the secrecy? I suppose I'm wondering whether she was involved in something a little more... *illicit*.'

Bryn gasped. 'You don't think she was one of his... *belly-dancers*?' he said, whispering the last word and blushing again.

'Oh, no, not that,' said Magnus, shaking his head. 'I'm fairly sure the work she was doing for Vasyl made her enough money to resist joining Hazim's harem.' He shuddered. 'And don't forget she was also doing work on the side for Ellington, as his *rabbateur*. But remember what Ellington said about her: she was greedy. Now, I'm not saying that's necessarily true,' Magnus added quickly, before Bryn could jump to the dead woman's defence, 'but I don't think I'm incorrect in saying she was a hard-working, ambitious woman who liked to make money — and there's nothing wrong with that. So what if Ellington wasn't the only client she had on the side? What if she was also doing *rabbateur* work, or a similar role, for Hazim?'

Bryn looked thoroughly impressed. 'Goodness, I hadn't thought of that,' he said. Then his brow furrowed once more. 'But that still doesn't explain why Hazim lied about it. I mean, allegedly Ellington didn't want it getting out and tarnishing his reputation...'

'Which I doubt is the case for Hazim,' cut in Magnus, 'given he doesn't seem to give two hoots about what other people think of him. No, I think it more than likely that his work with Anne-Laure was on the border of the law, which is why he wants to keep it quiet, especially when policemen such as your good self are sniffing around.'

Bryn returned the invoice to him across the table and said, 'You make a convincing case, Magnus.'

'One would almost think it was my job or something...'

'What about Ellington, then?' asked Bryn. 'What are your thoughts on him?'

'Hm, rather difficult to say, as Ellington's a duplicitous character as it is.'

'Yes, I noticed that,' said Bryn. 'All that carrying on about being a man of the people while living the high life and boasting about visiting the palace.'

'Precisely,' said Magnus. 'He's a slippery sort of person, Lord Bevis Ellington. But still, we learned a lot about Anne-Laure from him. We suspected, didn't we — from what Vasyl told us — she had some other work on the side, but now we know for sure she was making money elsewhere, as a *rabbateur* for Ellington.'

'And do you believe he lied about knowing her to protect his reputation?'

'It seems more likely he would react in that way than Hazim,' mused the barrister. 'But who knows? "Trading" is a vague term, and he was vaguer still when describing the kinds of deals Anne-Laure was helping him with. Perhaps he's the one involved in dodgy business, not Hazim.'

'Or perhaps they both are?'

'Yes, that's a possibility too,' sighed Magnus, hoping against hope Juliana didn't get wind of any of this, for it would not improve her opinion of Westminster Square and its residents. 'Anyway, there's no point dwelling on that at the moment, given we have no proof. It might be more useful to talk about what we learned about Anne-Laure as a person from Lord Ellington.'

'What, that she was *grasping*?'

Magnus smiled at Bryn's defensiveness. The policeman seemed to have become rather attached to Anne-Laure — or at least, the idea of Anne-Laure — over the past few weeks. It was a shame, really: from what they knew of her, she could have done with a knight in shining armour when she was alive.

'I might be wrong, but I imagine Lord Ellington disliked Anne-Laure's can-do attitude to making money because it reminded him of himself, in his younger days. After all, they're both from modest backgrounds and they both climbed their way up the social ladder. How did he describe her? *Aspirational? Nouveau riche?* I bet he's been called the same — and worse — in his time.'

'You'd think he'd be a bit more sympathetic, then,' said Bryn.

'Ah, but it probably wasn't nice for him, having her as a constant reminder of his own beginnings. I expect that explains his rather spiteful attitude, unless of course we're wrong and she was ruthlessly avaricious. And on that note, it's probably worth paying attention to Lord Ellington's attitude towards her, given he was so immune to her charms.'

'What do you mean?'

'Well, Ellington likes to think of himself as a lifelong bachelor by choice, but I think it's safe to say he's not particularly interested in women. You heard how he started speaking about Jem McMorran, he sounded like a giddy schoolboy. And by the sounds of it, Anne-Laure Chevalier — especially in this *rabbateur* role — tended to rely on her feminine allure. How did Ellington put it? "*She only had to flutter her eyelashes and they would promise her anything — more importantly, they would sign anything.*"'

'So you're saying Ellington may be giving us a more truthful picture of her, because his judgement isn't clouded by desire?'

'Perhaps,' said Magnus. 'Or maybe he's just vindictive, it's difficult to say. The other thing worth mentioning is the attitude of the *lithping* Gregor.'

'I can't believe you tried to use two men's butlers against them in two days,' grinned Bryn.

'You noticed that, did you? Actually, I was referring to what Gregor said at the door, when he described Anne-Laure as —'

'A pretty, fragile little bird,' finished Bryn, who had withdrawn his notebook by this point. 'Yes, that was a bit weird, wasn't it?'

'Was it? I mean, yes, it was an odd way of putting it,' Magnus allowed, 'but I'd say that description of Anne-Laure bears more relation to what we've been told by Vasyl and Winifred than anything else: that underneath all her beauty and apparent business prowess, Anne-Laure was a rather melancholy, delicate creature...'

'You're about to mention suicide again, aren't you?' said Bryn, his eyes narrowed. 'You're about to tell me you still think she deliberately overdosed?'

'I was going to say no such thing,' Magnus told him, not entirely truthfully.

Bryn looked as though he didn't believe him, but the barrister was spared having to justify himself any further, for at that moment a diversion occurred in the form of their starter. The crispy Peking sesame prawn toasts were quite as aromatic as Magnus remembered, which was a relief, for he had been the one to recommend them from the menu. Then, while Johnny was back and topping up their wine glasses, they took the opportunity to order their main courses before resuming their conversation.

'What about Morris, then?' asked Bryn, dipping the corner of his prawn toast into the accompanying dish of chilli sauce. 'Because he was the most upset about his name being in the address book, wasn't he? He didn't like being caught in a lie like that.'

'No, he certainly didn't,' Magnus agreed. 'And to be perfectly honest, if it weren't for that overreaction, I might have been inclined to believe his excuse about his mother; that he was so worried about her he wasn't really taking on board what Juliana was saying about Anne-Laure that day, and therefore he denied knowing her accidentally. But then, instead of laughing it off when we presented him with the address book, he almost jumped out of his skin.'

'I'm not sure Morris is the sort of person who would laugh anything off,' said Bryn.

'True. Nevertheless, it was a very odd reaction. In fact, a lot of what he told us was rather strange. That business about Anne-Laure being a bimbo, for example — do you believe that?'

'No,' said Bryn immediately. 'That sounds like complete rubbish to me. How could she have been doing all that work for Vasyl and Lord Ellington and possibly Hazim if she was a complete airhead? In fact —' He looked through his notebook for a few seconds. 'Yes, I thought so: both Vasyl and Ellington went out of their way to call her smart, and, as we just discussed, Ellington wasn't exactly her number one fan, so he didn't need to say that.'

'I think even Morris knew he was talking nonsense when he divulged that she'd read his terrible books,' said Magnus. 'Because, speaking as someone who could barely finish *Vacant Shadows*, there's no way she could have made it through both of them if she was even half as dim as he was implying. No, I'm with you, Bryn: we might not know much about Anne-Laure, but I think it's safe to say she wasn't lacking in the brain department.'

'Why would Morris say that, then?' wondered Bryn. 'Do you think it was just intellectual snobbery? Perhaps she had a practical rather than creative mind? Or maybe it was just old-fashioned misogyny? He was blind to her intelligence because she was a woman?'

'Possibly,' said Magnus. 'But I've been thinking over that little story he told us.'

'Story?'

'Yes, about her accosting him on the street and asking him for coffee and his not being terribly impressed with her, which is why they never met up again. And I wonder... Well, I wonder whether it wasn't the other way around.'

'What do you mean?'

'Think about it: Morris was embarrassed to reveal he'd been for coffee with Anne-Laure, which strikes me as very strange. First of all, because it was only coffee, not a full-blown dinner date, and secondly because — well, at the risk of sounding very superficial, what single man wouldn't want to be seen with a woman who looked like that? So I'm wondering whether his embarrassment was due to the fact that *he* asked *her* out. She might have accepted because she was dazzled he was a semi-famous writer, or perhaps he was the one to bring up Brighton and that convinced her, but either way she would have discovered pretty quickly, as we did the other day, that Morris Springfield is not exactly blessed with charm or social skills. So perhaps she told him she didn't want to see him again, and to soothe his bruised ego, Morris convinced himself she was a bimbo, she was intellectually inferior to him, she wasn't what he looked for in a woman and all that other drivel he told us.'

'Do you really think so?'

'It's a theory,' shrugged Magnus. 'Again, perhaps I'm being very shallow, but I find it rather difficult to believe someone like Morris Springfield would reject someone like Anne-Laure Chevalier, brains or no brains. But who knows?'

'The level of his embarrassment was strange, though, you're right,' said Bryn, looking sadly at the now-empty plate between them; their starter had been so delicious, they had devoured it in mere moments.

'Unfortunately, despite learning quite a bit from these three men, I'm not sure we're any clearer on how Anne-Laure died,' said Magnus.

'No,' agreed the policeman. Then, perking up a little, he added, 'But I did finally compile all those notes for us, so here's a copy for you.'

Magnus took the proffered sheets of paper, which were neatly typed and stapled together. On the first page was a list of people titled, *Westminster Square residents with a connection to Anne-Laure Chevalier*:

Vasyl Kosnitschev (employer)
Dame Winifred Rye (landlady/benefactor)
Hilda Underpin (acquaintance)
Jem McMorran (lover?)
Lord Bevis Ellington (employer)
Sheikh Hazim bin Lahab (?)
Morris Springfield (acquaintance)

'There they all are,' said Magnus, refraining from adding that he found it deeply unlikely any of these seven people were capable of murder, no matter how eccentric some of them might be. 'And actually, I have something for you in return.'

Once again, he reached into his bag and withdrew a different piece of paper.

'Dame Winifred finally sent it round — I had to remind her, as she's deeply entrenched in planning her next event. It's a list of people who were at that party on the night of Anne-Laure's death.'

He watched Bryn's eyes rove over the list. 'Ellington's on here, along with Gregor, and so are Hazim and Steve. No Morris, though.'

'He's not rich enough,' said Magnus. 'And Hilda wouldn't have been invited for the same reason — well, and the fact nobody likes her.'

'Jem's on here, though,' noted Bryn. 'Well, we knew that, didn't we? And of course Dame Winifred was obviously present that night…' He sighed, and placed the list on top of his notes. 'I'm beginning to feel a bit overwhelmed by all of this.'

'Don't be,' Magnus advised him. 'We're making good progress.'

'But nothing we just talked about was in any way conclusive. We don't know anything for sure.'

'Well I know one thing,' said Magnus, holding up the list of names in Bryn's notes, 'and that's that these people are a pack of liars.'

Bryn stared at him. 'Do you really think so?'

'Oh yes, definitely. As a barrister, you learn to spot a lie a mile off, and none of these characters exactly have expert poker faces. Of course, we've already caught three of them telling fibs via the address book, but I'd say most of them — if not all — are still not telling us the whole truth.'

'All of them?' Bryn repeated quietly.

'Morris and Jem are definitely both lying, that's obvious,' said Magnus, 'and Hazim and Ellington are almost certainly keeping information back as well. Dame Winifred seems to be lying to herself more than anyone, talking about Anne-Laure as though she were sugar and spice and all things nice — I wonder if Winifred truly believes that? And then with Vasyl it's hard to tell, but he wasn't exactly forthcoming, was he? In fact, now I come to think about it, the only person who I feel was truly honest with us about her opinions on Anne-Laure — honest to a fault, in fact — was Hilda Underpin.'

Shortly afterwards, Johnny the waiter returned, this time with their main courses. Once again, Magnus and Bryn were temporarily distracted from the conversation, as they fell upon their dishes. Magnus, who was something of a regular at Lei Sing's Taste of China, had ordered his favourite, the stir-fried fresh lobster with ginger and spring onion noodles, which was quite as flavoursome and succulent as ever. Bryn, meanwhile, had gone for the slightly more modest choice of Cantonese sweet and sour chicken, which he reported to be 'one of the best things I've ever tasted'.

Then, once they had finished praising the food, Magnus said, 'The other thing I'm interested in, with regard to Anne-Laure, is all these different perspectives we're getting on her.'

'What do you mean?'

'Well, everybody's opinions of her vary considerably, don't they? For some, she was an innocent angel —'

'You mean, for Dame Winifred.'

'— And to others, she was a disgraceful harlot.'

'Hilda,' said Bryn, with a nod.

'Then Vasyl tells us she was an efficient, organised employee —'

'— But Ellington tells us she was a grasping opportunist,' continued the policeman. 'While his own butler calls her a fragile little bird.'

'Hazim considered her entirely forgettable —'

'What about her aunt?' added Bryn. 'She thought Anne-Laure was some kind of heartless deserter.'

'And Morris decided she was a dumb blonde,' concluded Magnus. 'Do you see what I mean? It sounds as though we're referring to about five different people here, not one. She can't have been all of those things, surely? So are we ever going to get an accurate idea of what she was really like?'

They lapsed into silence for a few moments, mulling this over as they chewed, before Bryn said, 'You know who we forgot about? Jem McMorran. I wonder what *he* thought of her?'

'I think we have a pretty good idea,' said Magnus, before scowling. 'I wish we hadn't hurried to his flat after speaking to Hilda. We should have waited, thought out a strategy for questioning him. Or at least, I should have interrogated him more. He was just in such a state, I didn't want to push him over the edge…'

'We could try him again?'

'If he ever comes back from this film shoot,' replied Magnus gloomily. 'And I'm fairly sure, if or when he does, he's going to be steering well clear of us. I think —'

But Magnus broke off, for at that moment a shrill and horribly familiar voice rang out across the restaurant.

'*Don't you speak to me like that, you dim-witted immigrant!*'

'What on earth —?' began Bryn, turning around.

But Magnus, who was facing the door, had already seen the source of the noise: Hilda Underpin. The old lady was standing just inside the entranceway of Lei Sing's Taste of China, a walking stick clutched in one hand, a handbag containing Tam Tam in the other.

'Oh God, it's *her*,' said Bryn, ducking down in his seat.

But Magnus didn't think there was any danger of Hilda seeing them just yet. She was far too busy berating Johnny and one of his fellow waiters, a Chinese girl who was even shorter than the old woman. Every so often Magnus caught phrases like, '*you people are completely unacceptable*' and '*who do you think you are, coming to my country and telling me that?*'

'What's she upset about?' hissed Bryn, now so low in his chair he was in danger of sliding onto the floor.

'I'm not sure, but I think — yes, I think I should intervene,' said Magnus, untucking his napkin and rising to his feet.

'What? But then she might come over *here*!'

'Well I can't just stand by while she's awful to the staff here, she'll eat them alive! Excuse me, Hilda!' he called, beginning to walk towards the door and trying to ignore the fact that most of the people in the restaurant were now staring at him. 'Hilda!'

The old woman paused in the act of jabbing a finger at the poor Chinese waitress and turned to face him.

'Oh,' she said, looking at him as though he were something unpleasant on her shoe, 'it's *you*.'

'Is there some sort of problem here, Hilda?'

'That's none of your business.'

Ignoring the irony of this, considering here was a woman who spent almost her entire existence spying on other people, Magnus proceeded, 'Well, you're causing rather a disturbance in this restaurant, Hilda, and as I'm sure everyone here wants to carry on with their meal in peace, why don't we try and sort this out as quickly as possible? What is it you're doing here?'

'What do you think I'm doing here?' she sneered. 'I've come to collect food, haven't I? But these foreigners are refusing to serve me.'

'We're not refusing to serve you,' began Johnny, 'we're just —'

But Hilda interrupted him, holding up a hand to her ear and crying, 'What? *What?* Can you understand what he's saying, Magnus, because I can't! *Speak — English — please!*'

'He is speaking English, stop being difficult,' said Magnus. Then, turning to the waiter, he asked, 'Can you explain what's going on here?'

'We're not refusing to serve her,' said Johnny again. 'She is very welcome to sit down at a table and order food — she can even keep that dog with her if she wants. But she's not asking to do that. She wants to order a takeaway meal, a service we do not provide at Lei Sing's Taste of China.' He drew himself up to his full height, which was not particularly tall, and continued with a slightly superior air, 'We are a reputable fine dining experience in Westminster, not some backstreet eatery in Chinatown.'

'All right,' said Magnus, turning back to the old woman. 'Hilda, why don't you sit down and —?'

'I don't want to sit down! I just want them to give me some fish or some chicken and I'll be on my way!'

'Why would I give you anything, when you're refusing to pay for it?' demanded Johnny, folding his arms.

'Wait — what?' said Magnus. 'Hilda, if you want to eat from here, you have to pay for it.'

'*I* don't want to eat from here!' Hilda said. 'How dare you suggest such a thing? I wouldn't touch this foreign muck with a barge pole! No, I just want them to give a little something to Tam Tam.'

'What?' said Magnus, now so bemused he looked down at the white chihuahua in her arms as though the little animal could offer some sort of explanation. 'You've come to a top London restaurant to ask for scraps for your dog?'

'Not scraps — I would never feed Tam Tam scraps. But yes, I've run out of dog food, and the supermarket is too far away, so I thought I'd ask here. And look at the reaction I get!'

She glared at Johnny. The waitress, Magnus noticed, had managed to slip away.

'You know, it's probably because they serve dog meat here,' Hilda continued. 'I bet it's not chicken or fish or whatever they say it is on the menu, but *dog*. They don't want to serve Tam Tam, because he'll be able to tell.' She gasped. 'Oh my goodness, he'll be a cannibal!'

'Of course we don't serve dog meat!' cried Johnny. 'And would you keep your voice down!'

'All of their lot eat dog,' went on Hilda. 'I shouldn't have brought Tam Tam in here. Don't take your eye off him, Magnus, or he'll end up in a stew!'

As she cradled the chihuahua close, Magnus reflected that even if Hilda were right, the tiny dog would make a very meagre meal.

'You're being ridiculous,' he told her. 'The way I see it, you have two options. Either you can politely ask Johnny here for some scraps and bones from the kitchen for Tam Tam, and reimburse Lei Sing's for their trouble. Or you can go away, walk to the supermarket — you'd be there by now if you hadn't caused this fuss — and stop spoiling everybody's evening. What'll it be?'

She pursed her thin lips in disapproval. 'You think you're such a big man, don't you, Magnus?' she grumbled. 'Such a big, important lawyer?'

'*What'll it be, Hilda?*'

She murmured something almost inaudible.

'Sorry, we didn't quite catch that,' said Magnus. 'Maybe you're not speaking English?'

'I said, scraps and bones from the kitchen!' she snapped.

'Scraps and bones from the kitchen, *what*?' asked Magnus.

She looked at him with undisguised hatred.

'Scraps and bones from the kitchen, *please*.'

Magnus nodded at Johnny, who shot him a look of pure gratitude, said, 'Give me a few minutes, I'll ask the chef,' and then departed.

'Right, then,' said Magnus, wishing to escape Hilda's company as quickly as possible. 'Good evening to you, Hilda.'

But to his horror, as he began to make his way back to his table, he found that the old lady — rather than settling herself down on a chair by the entrance — was following him.

'You're not with that brainless-looking policeman again, are you?' she said, as she spotted Bryn, who was staring up at the ceiling as though willing her to disappear. 'What are you two up to, Magnus? Why are you always skulking about together? If I didn't know you were happily married to that *woman*, I'd say you'd caught old Bevis Ellington's disease...' She wheezed with laughter.

'It's not a disease, Hilda,' said Magnus, patiently.

But she wasn't listening. 'What are you doing here, Brian?' she demanded, sitting down in Magnus' seat, so he was forced to pull up a chair from a neighbouring table. 'This all seems a bit fine for the likes of you, even if it is *Chinese*.'

She plonked Tam Tam on the table, and the little dog immediately trotted towards Magnus' half-eaten meal. The barrister, anxious to protect his stir-fried lobster, whipped the plate out of the way.

'Hello? *Brian*? Are you deaf now, as well as stupid?' asked Hilda, helping herself to a prawn cracker. 'I asked you a question!'

Bryn, looking as though he wanted the ground to swallow him up, said, 'Magnus and I are just discussing neighbourhood security.'

Hilda took a bite of the prawn cracker, made a horrified face, and promptly spat it out onto Magnus' side plate. 'Disgusting!' she croaked. 'What's the matter with these people?' Then, wiping at her wrinkly mouth, she continued, 'And what's the matter with both of *you*? Do you really expect me to believe you're *still* discussing my burglary? I wasn't born yesterday, you know.'

Her gaze shifted to the papers on the table. Just in time, Magnus managed to snatch them away. Hilda raised her eyebrows.

'So you are up to something,' she said. 'Tell me what it is.'

'It's none of your business, is what it is,' said Magnus.

'Is it some kind of police work? Perhaps I should ask one of your superiors, Brian. Maybe that fat man with the red face...'

'No, don't!' cried Bryn, before he could stop himself.

Hilda grinned, revealing crooked yellow teeth. 'Doing something you shouldn't be, are you?' she said. 'Tsk, tsk, Constable Summers...'

'Oh for goodness' sake, Hilda!' cried Magnus, before she could bully Bryn any further. 'We're not doing anything remotely wrong. If you must know, during our rounds of Westminster Square, a lot of people mentioned Anne-Laure Chevalier's death, and many of them had quite strong opinions about her — yourself included. So I thought we should compile this information for the police, should they need it, but Bryn here is advising me against it, because his superior — Police Chief Superintendent Barry Boyle, who you just referred to — has closed the case. Satisfied?'

Magnus had chosen his words carefully here, so that even if Hilda did go running off to Boyle, Bryn wouldn't be in any sort of trouble. But the barrister didn't think it worth keeping from the old lady that they were interested in Anne-Laure Chevalier: knowing Hilda, if she felt anything was being kept from her, she was likely to do some digging of her own. No, it was much better to tell her this half-truth and, indeed, Hilda seemed rather disappointed that they weren't up to anything more scandalous.

'Oh, *her*,' she said, looking even more repulsed than when she had eaten the prawn cracker. 'I don't know why you want to be bothering with *her*. It's as I told you: that little tramp is better off dead.'

'Hilda, she was a human being,' said Magnus.

'Not much of one,' the old woman sniffed. 'Look at all the fuss she's caused. Even in death she's still drawing attention to herself. I'm glad she's dead, but to be perfectly honest with you I wish she'd never come to Westminster Square in the first place. Or at least, I wish she'd left when she said she was going to, rather than dropping down dead or getting herself murdered or whatever happened to her. Then we wouldn't have had this whole to-do.'

She pulled Tam Tam back towards her and began to stroke him so forcefully the tiny dog's dark eyes bulged in discomfort.

'Hilda, how can you say all that?' said Magnus, shaking his head. 'How can you speak so unkindly about —'

'Hold on,' broke in Bryn. 'What did you just say? You wish she'd left when she said she was going to?'

'Yes, and then she could have died on somebody else's doorstep, couldn't she? Or carried on with her immoral behaviour elsewhere. I could have lived with that, as long as I didn't have to watch her draping herself over that dreadful actor every day, or whoever else she was falling into bed with.'

'Anne-Laure Chevalier told you she was going to move away from Westminster Square?' Bryn asked.

'That's what I just said, wasn't it?'

'When? When did she tell you this?'

Tam Tam began to wriggle, apparently trying to escape his mistress' clutches, but she held him fast.

'I don't know, maybe a week or so before she died? We were having another of our arguments, because she was wearing the most inappropriate outfit I had ever seen in Westminster: a tiny skirt, a practically see-through blouse that was unbuttoned far too low... I went out to order her to put on something appropriate, and she told me this was appropriate for the summer, so then I began to give her a piece of my mind.'

Tam Tam let out a yelp of pain and finally Hilda released him. He clambered back onto the table and began to lick at the bowl of leftover chilli sauce that had come with their starter. Magnus sincerely hoped that it would make him sick later, preferably on Hilda's bed.

'That girl always turned on the tears when I criticised her,' Hilda continued. 'I'll say this for your wife, Magnus, she knows how to stand up for herself. But Anne-Laure was a weak, silly thing — and probably far too used to men protecting her. So that day, when I was merely suggesting she dress like a respectable Christian woman, she began to cry — crocodile tears, of course — and then started on about how I wouldn't have to put up with her for much longer.'

'What exactly did she say?' asked Bryn, eagerly.

'Oh, she was snivelling on about what a difficult time she was having, and that she couldn't cope with me that day. Then, when I pointed out I couldn't cope with her any day, she said something like, *"Well, you'll be pleased to hear you won't have to cope with me at all after next week, because I'm moving away from London on Monday.'''*

'And?'

'And what? I was very pleased to hear it. But then, in true Anne-Laure style, she had to go and die instead, making a great spectacle of herself and the Royal West in the process.'

'You're sure she said she was moving away?' said Magnus.

'Of course I'm sure. In fact, I was eagerly anticipating the sight of a removal van...' She gave a huff of disappointment.

'Why didn't you tell us this before?' asked Bryn.

'You didn't ask. All you wanted to know was who I'd seen her with.'

This, Magnus thought, was perfectly true, although it was frustrating: this latest testimony from Hilda felt significant. Then, just as Tam Tam was eyeing what was left of Bryn's dinner, Johnny edged towards their table once more, carrying a plastic bag.

'Scraps and bones for your dog,' he said, handing it to Hilda.

She looked down her nose at the contents of the bag. 'Hm,' she said, 'is that it?'

Tam Tam, his attention now claimed by the meaty smells coming from the plastic bag, nosed at it hopefully.

'How much does she owe you, Johnny?' asked Magnus.

'Nothing,' said the Chinese waiter. 'It's on the house.'

'Well, that's nice, isn't it, Hilda?' said Magnus brightly.

'But on the condition you never come back to Lei Sing's Taste of China again.'

'Ha!' croaked Hilda, as though he'd made a great joke. 'You couldn't pay me to come back to this dump. Come on, Tam Tam, we're going.'

She looked at the waiter expectantly, who stared back at her.

'Oh, I have to carry it to the door myself, do I?' she said, picking up the bag. 'What is the world coming to?'

And without another word, she scooped up her dog from the table and hobbled out of the restaurant, the plastic bag of free food clutched under one arm.

'Such a charming woman...' Magnus murmured.

Johnny shook his hand and thanked him for his help, and then Magnus pulled his plate of stir-fried lobster back towards him — though cold, it had fortunately not been touched by Tam Tam — and said, 'Well, Bryn, it seems you were right.'

The policeman, who had been staring at the door, as though to check Hilda was truly gone, said, 'Huh?'

'When Anne-Laure yelled — what was it? — *I'm going to be free of you, and free of Westminster Square*, it seems she wasn't intending to take her own life. If Hilda is to be believed, and I think she can be on this, it appears Anne-Laure was genuinely intending to move away from London. And if that's the case, and if we consider all these loose ends that need tying up, well... Her death being an unfortunate accident is looking less and less likely, isn't it?'

Suddenly, he had Bryn's full attention. 'So are you saying you finally think it was murder?' the younger man asked.

Keen for his companion not to get too excited, Magnus continued, 'The only trouble with it being murder is that we're missing one key ingredient as far as the crime is concerned.'

'And what's that?'

'A motive. Nobody — at least, nobody we've talked to — had any reason to want Anne-Laure Chevalier dead.'

'At least, not one we're aware of,' pointed out Bryn.

'True,' agreed Magnus, looking back at the list of names. 'But let's see... Vasyl heavily relied upon her as an employee and Dame Winifred thought of her as a beloved protégée, so neither of them seem likely suspects. Hazim doesn't seem to have cared about her enough to plot her demise. And while Morris and Ellington were a bit disdainful of her personality, that's not really reason enough to bump her off, is it? Again, we don't know much about Jem...'

'Oh, I wish we could talk to him!' burst out Bryn once more.

'... Although if he was in a relationship with her, why would he want her dead? No, when you look at it in terms of motive, the only person who seemed to bear a grudge against Anne-Laure Chevalier was Hilda Underpin.'

The policeman laughed. 'Now there's a thought!'

Magnus, however, didn't smile. Now he was the one watching the door of Lei Sing's Taste of China through which Hilda had so recently departed.

'Magnus?' said Bryn. '*Magnus*? You're not seriously suggesting *Hilda Underpin* is capable of *murder*?'

The barrister frowned. Unfortunately, through his work at Grey's Inn, he'd had some experience in dealing with murderers, and so he knew as well as anybody that all sorts were capable of taking a life; in fact, he was often surprised by how normal and unassuming some killers appeared, at least during their trials. Furthermore, it wasn't even as though Hilda Underpin was normal and unassuming, was it? She was probably the nastiest person Magnus had ever met. What if her vendetta against Anne-Laure Chevalier had become an obsession, had got completely out of hand…?

'She's about eighty-five years old!' cried Bryn. 'She can't even walk to the shops! How on earth would she even go about it?'

'You're right,' said Magnus, snapping out of his reverie. 'Of course, you're right. It's a mad idea…'

'Besides,' said Bryn, 'she's not doing a very good job of covering it up if she did do it, is she? Considering she's been saying from the start how glad she is Anne-Laure is dead, and being quite vocal about how much she disliked her when she was alive. I mean, if I'd just murdered someone, I'd probably be keeping quiet about them in public.'

'Yes, good point,' said Magnus, looking down at Bryn's typed-up notes. 'Yes, I was being silly… The wine must be going to my head!'

But still, he thought, it might be wise to keep Hilda's name on this list for now, just in case.

Bryn, reaching for the menu, presumably to study the dessert options, said, 'I'm just glad you finally believe it was murder.'

'I'm more willing to believe it *might* have been murder,' Magnus corrected him.

The policeman, however, seemed happy enough with this.

'And not to burst your bubble, Bryn, but if you're right with this theory — and, as I said, I'm beginning to think you are — well, that means we have a lot of work to do. We need to prove Anne-Laure Chevalier was killed deliberately, and that's not going to be easy.'

'Why, because the body's gone? Because Boyle wouldn't let us collect evidence?'

'Yes, on both counts,' said Magnus. Then he held up the list of names so that Bryn could see. 'But also because, like I told you earlier, this lot are a pack of liars. We've spoken to them all about Anne-Laure Chevalier and I'm pretty sure every one of them has at least withheld a bit of the truth, and most of them have told us barefaced whoppers. So the question is, what *is* the truth? Who was Anne-Laure Chevalier, and what happened to her, in the weeks and days and hours before her death? And, for whatever reason, might one of these people have killed her?'

CHAPTER TWENTY-THREE

Around six weeks after her fateful party at the Royal West Hotel, Dame Winifred Rye, ever the philanthropist, hosted another fundraising event. This time, the party was a smaller, afternoon affair, and therefore she was hosting it in her own flat, on the north-west side of Westminster Square.

Magnus was not particularly enthused by the idea of spending half of his Saturday at this event. He disliked the notion of schmoozing with people who were more concerned with appearing to be generous than actually coughing up money, which was why they went to functions like this, rather than donating quietly to charities on a regular basis, like he and Juliana did. But Dame Winifred had personally invited him, and Magnus had felt he couldn't refuse her, seeing as he had missed the event at the Royal West (a fact that grated on him now, because perhaps if he had been there he would have noticed something that might have shed a little more light on Anne-Laure Chevalier's death). Besides, with the dead woman in mind, Magnus had decided that attending the party might be an interesting way of continuing his and Bryn's quest for further evidence and motives: according to Dame Winifred, the guest list of the party included Vasyl Kosnitschev, Sheikh Hazim bin Lahab and Lord Bevis Ellington.

The event was already in full and merry swing when Magnus arrived that afternoon. The furniture in Dame Winifred's living room had been pushed against the walls in order to make more room for the mingling guests, and the doors leading out onto the terrace at the back of the building had been thrown wide open. Adorning the various surfaces were beautiful flower arrangements Magnus knew came from The Station Garden, for he would have recognised his wife's handiwork, particularly the signature purple ribbons, anywhere. As a result of all of this, the effect of the mismatching decoration was lessened, and the aristocrat's accommodation looked slightly less eccentric than usual.

Magnus, never one to make a grand entrance, slipped into the room unnoticed and immediately cast his eye around for a drink and something to eat. As it was an afternoon party, Dame Winifred was only serving canapés with the champagne, but in Magnus's experience his neighbour never shirked on quality when it came to consumables. Just as her tea was from Fortnum and Mason's, he imagined her *hors d'oeuvres* were from some fancy caterer — or perhaps the Harrods food hall. There were a number of servers dotted about the room (all of them young and female, which was a pleasant contrast to the guests, who were mostly old men) and when Magnus tapped the nearest waitress on the shoulder, he found that he recognised her: it was Daisy, the pretty dark-haired girl who worked with Juliana at the flower shop. She was dressed in a smart blouse and skirt and carrying a silver tray of champagne flutes.

'Mr Walterson!'

'Hello, there,' said Magnus, helping himself to a drink. 'Is Juliana not paying you enough at the Station Garden?'

'Sorry?'

Magnus chuckled. 'I was just wondering why you're being a waitress today?'

'Oh, Dame Winifred was one girl short and she asked me to help out.'

'That's nice,' said Magnus. 'You've been spending a bit of time with her, so I hear from Juliana?'

'Yes,' said Daisy, 'she's been very good to me over the past few weeks, so doing a bit of waitressing was the least I could do…'

She spoke a little tonelessly, as though there was no real feeling behind her words. Magnus knew, from what his wife had told him, that Daisy had a very good head for numbers, so perhaps — in spite of what she said — she considered serving drinks a little beneath her.

Before Magnus could probe, however, Dame Winifred herself appeared. Today, she was wearing as much make-up as usual, and her bright orange face clashed considerably with the shapeless pale pink dress she was wearing for the occasion, which made her look like a gigantic blancmange.

'Magnus!' she trilled, hurrying over to kiss him on the cheek. 'How lovely to see you! Welcome, welcome! I see you're being entertained by my little flower!'

'Sorry?'

'Daisy here!' laughed Dame Winifred, throwing her pink-sleeved arm over the girl's slender shoulders, which almost caused the tray of champagne to go crashing to the floor. 'I call her my Little Flower, because — well, look at her! She's a *darling*!'

Daisy reddened, although whether it was from the compliment or the effort of supporting both Winifred's arm and the drinks, Magnus didn't know.

'Are you all right, dear?' Winifred asked her. Then, before Daisy could answer, she turned back to Magnus and said, 'She's *such* a treasure, agreeing to help out this afternoon. She's completely saved the party, because I was one girl short.'

'Really, it's no trouble, Dame Winifred,' said Daisy, attempting to free herself from the aristocrat's grip.

The older woman gave an animated gasp and said, 'How many times, you naughty thing! It's *Winnie*! We must dispense with formalities, now that we're such good friends!'

'Sorry, I forgot,' mumbled Daisy.

Dame Winifred chortled and gave the girl's small freckled nose a gentle tweak. 'You dear creature... Now, I'm about to make a speech, so off you trot and hand around those drinks, so everyone's nice and quiet while I talk. Thank you, Little Flower!'

She waved Daisy away, one hand on her heart. Then she turned to Magnus and said, 'I can't tell you how envious I am of Juliana, having that girl to herself all day. I'm quite tempted to steal her away, but I don't suppose your wife will thank me for it...'

'No,' said Magnus, privately thinking that Daisy probably wouldn't thank her either.

Had Dame Winifred been like this with Anne-Laure, he wondered? If so, it was easy to see why she had drifted away from her fairy godmother figure; there was only so much of this cloying behaviour one could take. But equally, if Dame Winifred had been as affectionate with her as she had been just now with Daisy, it made complete sense that Anne-Laure had initially warmed to the aristocrat, and chosen her and the life she was offering in London over her cold Aunt Agnes and staying in Brighton, a place that had held nothing but misery for her.

Presently, Dame Winifred moved to the other side of the room, tapped a spoon against a glass, and waited for the room to fall silent.

'My dear friends,' she said, beaming around at them all. 'Welcome to my humble abode! Thank you *so* much for taking the time out of your busy schedules to pop round today, I can't tell you how much I appreciate it!

'Now, do forgive me, but I'm going to get the vulgar money talk out of the way first. As you know, the point of this event is to raise money for the GGEF — the Global Girls' Education Fund. For this, I have a punch bowl waiting on that table over there for your cheques —' Here, Dame Winifred pointed at the object on one of the coffee tables on the opposite side of the room, before continuing, 'and the suggested amount is a thousand pounds — although, of course, you may be as generous as you like!'

Her eyes twinkled, as though she fully expected all of her guests to cough up far more than that.

'As some of you may know, I have a soft spot for young people — especially girls,' she continued, 'so it simply breaks my heart to know that, in many parts of the world, young women cannot reach their full potential because they have not received proper — or indeed any — education. So this is where the GGEF comes in. The Global Girls' Education Fund works tirelessly to promote the importance of schooling in countries such as Mali, Pakistan, Somalia, Yemen...'

While Dame Winifred continued to talk, Magnus took a sip of his champagne and looked around the room. There were around thirty-five people present, and because so many of them were besuited men, it took Magnus a little while to pick out Vasyl and Ellington in the crowd, both of whom were looking very bored by their hostess's speech. Hazim did not appear to have arrived yet, for Magnus couldn't see him, and the sheikh was usually the most conspicuous person in the room.

But how did Dame Winifred collect all of these businessmen, Magnus wondered, looking at the other guests. He almost suspected she, like Ellington, and possibly like Hazim, was doing some sort of secret business on the side, otherwise how would she have come into contact with all of these high-flyers? But then, the idea of Dame Winifred negotiating deals was laughable: she had no subtlety whatsoever, and she'd never struck Magnus as a particularly intelligent woman; well-meaning, maybe, but not the sharpest knife in the drawer. No, she must have simply amassed these people through her charity work and, once more, Magnus supposed that they all kept turning up at her parties in order to look like great philanthropists.

A few minutes later, a smattering of applause alerted him to the fact that Dame Winfred had finally stopped talking. While most of the crowd looked around for more drinks, Magnus made his way towards the large crystal bowl Winifred had indicated in her speech. Deciding he might as well get it out of the way, he scribbled out a cheque for a thousand pounds and prepared to drop it in with the others already there, reminding himself this was for a good cause, and he wasn't simply paying through the nose for a couple of drinks, canapés, and an afternoon in dull company. But just as he was leaning over the bowl, someone came up behind him and threw in something that made a great clattering noise against the glass.

Magnus jumped back: for one wild moment, he thought a snake had been inexplicably thrown amongst the cheques, for the foreign object was long and undulating. But then, on closer inspection, he saw that it was actually a string of prayer beads, and even to Magnus's untrained eye it looked as though it were made of...

'Pure gold!' shouted a recognisable voice, and Magnus turned to find Sheikh Hazim standing behind him. 'Ninety-nine beads of it!' He picked up the extravagant rosary and dropped it into the bowl a few times, clearly enjoying the long clink that sounded from the crystal.

Dame Winifred, perhaps roused by the noise, came tottering over.

'What's this?' she asked, looking pleasantly interested.

'The prayer beads, they're pure, twenty-four carat gold,' Hazim announced loudly. 'I don't know how to do bank transfers — I do not have time for all that — but these beads should cover the cost of my entrance. They're worth at least ten thousand.'

'Oh, *darling!*' said Winifred, reaching out to embrace him. 'How generous you are!'

Hazim submitted to a hug, but he didn't look happy about it. 'You know, I don't normally touch women over the age of twenty-five,' he said, patting her awkwardly on the back.

Dame Winifred pulled away giggling and pinched him on the flabby cheek. 'You are a tease, Hazzy!'

Magnus watched this display with both revulsion and interest: he couldn't recall ever seeing Dame Winifred and Sheikh Hazim interacting before. He would have assumed they wouldn't get on, but obviously they were rather friendly, which struck him as a little strange.

'Whatever they're worth, I guarantee the amount you get for those beads will be ten times what Ellington gives you,' said Hazim loudly, spotting the Labour Lord nearby.

Bevis Ellington scowled, but did not dispute this. Magnus, depositing his own rather paltry cheque on top of Hazim's golden beads, couldn't exactly blame him.

The party plodded on. Magnus, fuelled by champagne and delicious canapés, fell into conversation with a couple of aristocrats, the Duke of Wexford and an elderly Earl who might have been from one of the southern counties of Ireland. They weren't particularly interesting, and when Magnus tried to liven things up by steering the conversation towards Anne-Laure, neither man seemed especially keen on discussing the Westminster scandal that was, by now, old news. Indeed, the ancient Irish aristocrat was too intent on trying to flirt with one of the waitresses to pay Magnus too much attention. The barrister found this deeply embarrassing, and was very impressed when the object of the Earl's affection — a striking Eastern European girl with white-blonde hair who was at least a third of the Irishman's age — fixed a polite smile on her face and pretended she couldn't see his wandering glances or hear his suggestive comments.

About an hour and a half into the party, just as Magnus was beginning to think it wouldn't be too impolite to leave — after all, he had showed his face and paid the money — he heard a name that made him stop in his tracks: *Jem McMorran*.

'I thought he would be here,' someone was saying. 'Dame Winifred said he was due to appear, so I'd almost call that false advertising.'

To Magnus's amusement, the speaker was none other than Lord Bevis Ellington. He was talking to Vasyl Kosnitschev, who was looking surly, although whether this was because he didn't care about the whereabouts of Jem McMorran or because he simply always looked like that, the barrister didn't know. But seeing that here were two of his quarries talking to one another about a third, Magnus realised he had to be part of this conversation, and so excused himself from his discussion with a minor royal from Sweden and sidled towards Lord Ellington and Vasyl.

'Sorry, I couldn't help but overhear — did you say Jem McMorran was coming later?' he asked, deliberately misunderstanding Ellington's earlier statement.

'No, he's not!' cried the Labour Lord. 'He was *supposed* to be here, Winifred told me so, but it seems he's still away.'

Magnus, half wondering whether Dame Winifred might have made this up to get Ellington to come to her party, said, 'Jem's been away a while now, hasn't he? Almost a month?'

'Well, these film shoots take time,' said Ellington. 'And I think it's an action film he's working on, and those are especially arduous. Plus it's shooting in the States, so maybe he's staying on there for a bit...'

'You seem to know a lot about his movements,' observed Vasyl.

The Ukrainian oligarch had spoken tonelessly, without apparent reproach or mockery, but nevertheless Ellington reddened.

'Well, he is our local celebrity, so one likes to keep abreast of what he's doing! In fact, I'm practically obliged to; my friends at the palace and in parliament always want to hear what Jem McMorran is up to, they can't get enough of him. Especially the women,' he added sourly.

'I wouldn't mind knowing what Jem McMorran had been up to myself,' said Magnus.

He was speaking more to himself than to Ellington and Vasyl, because, out of all the people he and Bryn had talked to, the Hollywood actor had been the most transparent liar: it was obvious Jem McMorran had had some connection to Anne-Laure Chevalier, and very likely he had been in a romantic relationship with her. So now, with so many people under suspicion and so little evidence, Magnus was particularly keen to question the actor again, and more thoroughly, and he could not help but think that the timing of Jem's absence was rather convenient, perhaps even fishy.

'Magnus?' said Ellington.

The barrister, returning from his musings, blinked and said, 'Sorry, what?'

'I asked, what do you want to keep tabs on Jem for?' Ellington's tone was accusatory.

'Oh, you know, these security issues,' said Magnus, with a careless wave. Then, hoping his two companions hadn't heard otherwise, he continued, 'Jem's one of the few people in Westminster Square I haven't spoken to about these break-ins, so if you see him back in the area, perhaps you could let me know?'

Vasyl nodded, but Ellington merely sniffed. 'Never mind this alleged burglar, I think the biggest thief in Westminster Square is Dame Winifred Rye: a suggested donation of *a thousand pounds?* That's daylight robbery! I know she thinks of herself as a great hostess, but she's not *that* good.'

'It *is* a little steep,' Magnus agreed, while Vasyl nodded. 'But I suppose it's for a good cause…'

'Puh,' said Ellington, 'what do I care about girls in Mali and — where else did she say — *Yemen?* Why is their lack of education my problem? I'm more concerned about social issues in this country, thank you very much. Before looking elsewhere, I'd like to elevate the working classes in the UK.'

You'd like to elevate yourself, more like, thought Magnus, but managed to hold his tongue. At that moment, however, Hazim lumbered over, clutching his fat belly with mirth.

'What are you going on about now, Ellington?' he chuckled, physically elbowing his way into the conversation.

The politician drew himself up to his full height, which was considerable, and said, 'I'm merely questioning why Dame Winifred wants us to send all this money overseas, when there are so many worthier causes closer to home — *at* home, in fact.'

'No you are not, you just have tight hands as usual,' declared Hazim.

'Tight hands?' repeated Ellington. 'I suppose that's some Arab saying, is it?'

But Hazim ignored him, and instead withdrew from the pocket of his robes a fat roll of banknotes. The appearance of this much money — Magnus thought the sheikh must be holding thousands of pounds — seemed to silence Ellington, who eyed the notes as though hypnotised by them. Magnus recalled what the Labour Lord had said about Anne-Laure being greedy, and wondered whether the same description might be applied to Ellington himself.

'I might throw this into the bowl as well as my beads,' said Hazim, fingering the roll of banknotes as though it were a particularly fat cigar. 'You know, for the *girls*… What do you think?'

When it became apparent neither Ellington nor Vasyl was going to reply, Magnus said, 'I think that sounds very generous, Hazim.'

'What about you two?' the sheikh demanded, giving Ellington and Vasyl a toad-like grin. 'Why don't you match my donation?'

He was toying with them, Magnus knew, but Vasyl at least refused to play along.

'Most of my available finances are tied up with my house at the moment,' said the Ukrainian coolly. 'Bevis here might call our hostess the biggest thief in Westminster Square, but I think that title belongs to Central Square Properties, who are trying to bleed us all dry.'

'Hear, hear,' murmured Magnus.

'And you, Ellington?' prompted Hazim.

'No, I'm afraid I can't!' the politician cried, his voice a little shrill. 'Normally, I would, but I'm afraid, like Vasyl here, I don't have the funds to spare. In fact, I'm actually waiting to receive some money I'm owed, it's rather inconvenient to tell you the truth…'

As he trailed off, Magnus wondered whether Ellington was referring to the deals he did on the sly. Hazim, however, seemed to think his neighbour was merely making excuses, for he clapped him on the back and said, 'Well, get back to me when you can play with the big boys, Bevis. Meanwhile, this will have to do for all of us.'

He held up the roll of cash and then, with another wide grin, waddled off into the crowd towards the bowl. While Ellington then sighed and blustered to himself, Magnus turned to Vasyl. 'So you haven't managed to sort out your issues with CSP, then?' he asked.

'No,' said the Ukrainian, looking even grimmer than usual. 'I have invested over ten million in that house, and they have the audacity to tell me I can't paint the banisters or knock down a couple of walls? It is crazy! I have never known anything like it in all my years of buying property. And I am trying to improve it! When I moved in, it was so very old-fashioned, with its little rooms and stucco ceilings. They should be paying me to modernise it!'

Modernising was one way of putting it, Magnus thought, remembering the building site that had been Vasyl's house a few weeks' ago, and the steel furniture and industrial murals he was planning on introducing to the historic Georgian interiors.

'To be frank with you, Magnus, I am not sure I can be bothered with it anymore,' continued the Ukrainian.

'Bothered with what?'

'All of it. The house, CSP, Westminster Square. London is not the only place where I have business interests, and at the moment living here seems an unnecessary complication, especially without Anna.'

It took Magnus a few seconds to remember that 'Anna' was Vasyl's name for Anne-Laure Chevalier.

'Speaking of,' he said, spotting an opportunity, especially as Ellington had just slunk off to find another drink, 'Can I ask you a question about Anne-Laure Chevalier?'

'I thought you already asked me several questions about her?'

'I just have one more: do you know if she was in a relationship with Jem McMorran?'

If Vasyl was surprised by this question, he didn't show it. 'I already told you, Magnus, I did not pry into her personal life. I do not know if she had any boyfriend or not.'

'But Jem McMorran is hardly *any* boyfriend — he's a Hollywood star, for goodness' sake!'

But apparently this didn't make a difference to Vasyl Kosnitschev. 'I do not know,' he said again. 'I cannot tell you anything about Anna's private life. It was of no interest to me.'

Not long after this, Magnus managed to extricate himself from the conversation and, after thanking Dame Winifred — who seemed a little giggly from drink — he headed towards the door, intending to slip out of the party quietly. On his way out, however, he was diverted by the sight of Daisy, who seemed to be hiding behind a coat stand.

'Hello?' said Magnus. Then, because she looked a little flustered, he added, 'Are you all right?'

'No!' she cried. 'That man — the fat one in the headdress — he just tried to, to —' She lowered her voice. 'He just tried to *grope* me.'

Magnus frowned. 'Hazim did?'

She nodded, trying to flatten her hair. 'He came up to me and started paying me all these compliments. But he was standing so close — I thought I was going to choke on his horrible perfume — so I tried to get away and... Well, he tried to stop me, and he was very handsy about it.'

Magnus frowned. 'Right, that's not on at all. I'm going to have a word...'

'No, don't,' she said, catching his arm. 'It's fine, really. I gave his hands a slap as I escaped.'

'Even so!'

But Daisy shook her head. 'Please, Magnus, I'm okay. He just surprised me, that's all. But I don't want to make a scene at Winnie's party...'

She fixed him with a beseeching look and, somewhat reluctantly, Magnus nodded. He was surprised at Hazim. Although he knew the Arabian sheikh to be thoroughly lecherous, somehow he hadn't expected him to start being inappropriate with every young waitress that passed his way. What on earth was the matter with him?

'You tell me if that happens again, Daisy,' he said sternly. 'Then I'll definitely be having a word — possibly with my friend at the police station.'

'Please,' said Daisy, 'let's just forget about it. I don't want it to spoil Winnie's evening.'

'You're very loyal.'

Daisy shrugged. 'Dame Winifred has been good to me over the past few weeks. We've talked a lot, she's taken me for tea at Fortnum and Mason's, she's even bought me presents, like a new dress...'

'That's nice,' said Magnus.

But Daisy looked a little uncomfortable. 'Between you and me, it's almost too much,' she said. 'She's being too generous. And I'm not stupid: I know she's doing it because she's so sad about Anne-Laure Chevalier, so I can't help but feel I'm taking advantage of her grief.'

'Oh, Daisy, of course you aren't. You're just offering a lonely woman some comfort, that's all.'

'But I'm not Anne-Laure.'

No, you're not, thought Magnus. At least, this shy girl before him bore little relation to the glamorous woman in the designer dress who had been found in a top London hotel with cocaine in her system.

'I'm sure Dame Winifred knows perfectly well you're Daisy Fenway,' Magnus reassured her. 'I think she just wants a little company, that's all. I wouldn't feel bad about being on the receiving end of her generosity. In fact, I'd enjoy it if I were you.'

'You're probably right,' said Daisy, although she still looked unconvinced.

Magnus located his jacket on the coat stand. 'Look, Daisy, I'm going to slip away while I have the chance. But you will look after yourself, won't you? Let me or Dame Winifred know if Hazim or anyone else does anything like that again?'

She nodded. 'Thanks, Mr Walterson,' she said. Then, indicating the room at large, she continued, 'This isn't really my scene either. I can't wait to get back to The Station Garden on Monday.'

'Juliana will be pleased to hear it.'

A few minutes later, during the short walk back across Westminster Square to his own flat, Magnus reflected on Dame Winifred's newfound attachment to Daisy. It was obvious that, in the girl, the soppy old aristocrat was looking for a replacement for her recently deceased young friend. But now Magnus came to think on it — and especially on the differences between Daisy and Anne-Laure — perhaps in the girl from the flower shop Dame Winifred saw something of the girl Anne-Laure had once been; the angelic creature she had met on a stormy Brighton beach and whisked off to London. Yes, perhaps it wasn't the death of Anne-Laure Chevalier that had upset Dame Winifred so profoundly, but the demise of the person who had once been Annie Chambers.

CHAPTER TWENTY-FOUR

It was Saturday afternoon, the sun was shining, the air was still, and Juliana Walterson was furious.

When she had first become unhappy with living in central London, Magnus had assured her — no, *promised* her — they would get out of the city at least every second weekend. In the time that had elapsed since, and in addition to her favourite spots in Juliana's native Kent, they had discovered many beautiful pockets of countryside in the south-east of England, from Virginia Water in Surrey to the South Downs National Park in Sussex to the New Forest in Hampshire. But recently, despite their increasingly-frequent disagreements about living in Westminster Square, these weekends away seemed to have fallen by the wayside.

This Saturday was the last straw, as far as Juliana was concerned: they had been planning on taking the children to the Tankerton beach at Whitstable, in order to take full advantage of the fine weather, but Magnus had cancelled at the last minute, as apparently he had to work on an important case over the weekend. Juliana was livid: if Magnus didn't go, none of them could, for she was not confident behind the wheel, and refused to drive through London, especially on her own. Magnus had suggested taking the train — pointing out Victoria Station was exceptionally close — but Juliana couldn't be bothered with that, especially when it meant packing two children and their belongings onto public transport all by herself. No, not for the first time, Magnus had thoroughly sabotaged the weekend, and Juliana was finding it difficult to forgive him for it.

What sort of case required weekend work anyway? Juliana was aware Magnus was very high up in Grey's Inn, but she also thought family should always come first. Besides, how come Magnus had time to go creeping around playing detectives with that policeman, but he didn't have even a day to spare for a trip with his children? It was ridiculous.

Still, there was no point taking Magnus's shortcomings out on their children, Juliana had decided, so she was trying to salvage the day with a picnic. She and Rosanna had spent some of the morning mixing up homemade lemonade, and Lee had attempted to make a few sandwiches, although Juliana had taken over when most of the butter had ended up in his hair. Then, just after half past twelve, the three of them had headed out of the house — Juliana not bothering to call goodbye to Magnus in his study — crossed the road, and headed towards one of the gardens of Westminster Square.

As they lay a rug across the grass and began to unpack the food, Juliana's mood began to improve a little. They had brought their lunch over in a Hermés picnic hamper, which had been a wedding present from her parents, and Juliana never failed to enjoy lifting up its lid and seeing how neatly the china plates, crystal glasses and bronze flasks and containers fitted together. Really, it was too good for children, she thought, but Rosanna and Lee were very well-behaved, and knew the crockery and glassware had to be removed from the hamper with great care.

In any case, they were far more interested in the food, the appearance of which also caused Juliana to brighten. She had felt guilty about the cancellation of Whitstable, and so had gone a little overboard in her spending at the bakery earlier that morning, so the hamper was now filled with good bread and pastries, as well as cheese, cold meats, yoghurt, fruit and litres of the lemonade she and Rosanna had concocted.

Indeed, Juliana had to admit, at least to herself, that it was a very pleasant way to pass a Saturday lunchtime. It was warm, the food was good, and her children were as dear as ever, chattering happily about their friends and all the things they wanted to do now the summer holidays were here. Really, if she ignored the sound of the traffic on the main road, which ran down the other side of the garden, Juliana could almost imagine herself in the countryside. She would say this for Central Square Properties: they employed good gardeners, who knew how build up the flowerbeds around the railings, offering these green spaces as much seclusion as possible.

A little while later, when they had finished eating and packed away the leftover food in the Hermés hamper, Juliana was pleased to discover the children wanted to remain in the garden. Rosanna stretched out on her stomach, propped herself up with her elbows, and found where she had left off in her latest book. Lee, on the other hand, seemed to have been energised by his meal, for he took up a mini football he had brought with him from the house, and attempted to keep it up in the air with only his feet and knees, counting under his breath as he did so.

Juliana, delighted they were both occupying themselves, lay back on the picnic rug beside her daughter and closed her eyes. The sun was hot on her skin, and the heady scent of the flowerbeds completely intoxicating. If she ignored the sound of the nearby cars, and concentrated instead on the humming of the bees and the gentle *thwack thwack* of Lee keeping his football in the air, she really could be in Kent — she could be home. Moving her hands to the back of her head to form a pillow, she sighed deeply, feeling content and sleepy from the sunshine and all of the food — which was a stark contrast to her mood earlier that day. Then, before she knew it, she was running through the garden of her Kentish childhood home, and her parents were preparing for a Midsummer party that very evening, and she was creeping up to one of the outdoor tables, preparing to steal an iced bun from one of the tins...

'Stop that! You there — how dare you? Stop that at once!'

Juliana jerked awake, startled and confused. No one had ever spoken to her so sharply when she had been a child, even when she had pilfered food from the adults' table, and it took Juliana a few moments to work out that she was the adult now, and she wasn't in Kent, but in the middle of central London.

She sat up, attempting to smooth down her wild, copper-coloured hair, and looked around to see what had woken her. Rosanna was looking up from her book, and Lee was now clutching his mini football to his chest, looking fearful. With competing feelings of dread and annoyance, Juliana followed her son's gaze towards the edge of Westminster Square gardens, where a familiar and thoroughly unwelcome face was peering through the railings.

'I should have known it was you, Juliana!' cried Hilda Underpin.

Juliana shielded her eyes from the bright light and, without moving from the rug, called back, 'What do you want?'

'I want the residents of Westminster Square to obey the rules,' said Hilda, pressing her ugly little face between the metal bars of the railings like a prisoner. 'And that includes you, Juliana!'

'For goodness' sake, we're not breaking any rules!'

'Yes, you are!'

'No, we're not! We're perfectly entitled to sit in here and have a picnic. And if it's your own stupid rules you're talking about, I'm not even wearing jeans today, as you can see.'

She held up the long skirt of her summer dress to demonstrate this. Hilda scowled.

'I am referring to the rules outlined by CSP,' she shouted, through the bars. 'The rules of Westminster Square Gardens. And you are breaking rules three and four.'

Juliana sighed, tempted to throw a half-eaten sausage roll in the direction of the idiotic old woman. 'I suppose you're going to remind me what rules three and four are?' she said.

'Rule three,' said Hilda, clearing her throat and apparently reciting from memory, *All children under the age of 12 must be accompanied by an adult.*'

Juliana goggled at her. 'Are you blind? They *are* accompanied by an adult — they're with me!'

'You were asleep,' snapped the old woman, 'so I wouldn't call that sufficient supervision. Who knows what your feral offspring could get up to while you're out for the count?'

While Rosanna and Lee, still respectively clutching book and ball, exchanged a hurt expression, Juliana jabbed a finger in the old woman's direction.

'Don't you talk about my children like that!' she hissed. 'Insult me all you like, but leave them out of this.'

Ignoring her, Hilda continued, 'Rule four: *No balls, bicycles or noisy games.* Your son is thoroughly disregarding that stipulation, given that he is playing a game that features both a ball *and* a lot of noise.'

'Oh, for pity's sake!' cried Juliana, throwing her hands into the air. 'First of all, he's not being in the least bit noisy, and secondly, that ball is tiny! I'm sure that rule is referring to full-on games of cricket and football, not a small boy practicing kick-ups on his own!'

'You're *sure*, are you?' said Hilda, nastily. 'Tell me, Juliana — where does it specify that on the sign?'

'Mum, it's fine,' mumbled Lee. 'I'll read my book...'

'You'll do no such thing,' said Juliana, trying not to lose her temper with him too: why on earth was he choosing this moment to demonstrate the fact that he had inherited Magnus's diplomacy? 'Lee, you will continue to do your kick-ups. In fact —' Juliana leapt to her feet. 'In fact, I shall join you.'

'Juliana!' cried Hilda, warningly.

'Come on, darling, pass me the ball.'

'*Juliana!*'

'How many can you do, Lee? I bet I can double it!'

'Juliana, I'll report you to CSP! I'll report you to the police!'

'The *police!*' Juliana threw back her head with laughter. 'Please, go ahead! And when you do, ask for Constable Bryn Summers — it ought to give him a laugh!' Then, marching forward and snatching the ball from her son, she said, 'Watch this, Lee — I was good at kick-ups as a girl...'

'How dare you?' shouted Hilda, dropping her handbag in her rage. 'Have you no respect for your elders? Have you no respect for Westminster Square? You're a bad woman, Juliana Walterson, a —'

But she wasn't allowed to finish, for at that moment, a small diversion occurred in the form of Tam Tam, who came tumbling out of Hilda's handbag, squeezed through the railings of the garden, and bolted straight towards the flower bed.

'Oh ho!' cried Juliana, as the chihuahua began to scrabble at the flowers. 'What's this, then?'

'Tam Tam!' shouted Hilda. 'Come here, Tam Tam!'

Juliana watched the ratty animal kick up soil, her hands on her hips.

'Tell me, Hilda — what rule is it that says all dogs in the gardens should be kept on leads?'

The old woman ignored this. 'Tam Tam, come to Hildy!'

'And I'm sure it's not showing very much respect for Westminster Square, letting your dog dig up all of the flower beds. What will CSP think of *that*?'

'Juliana, he's making a mess. Pass him through the railings, will you?'

But Juliana was now kicking the miniature football towards Lee. 'I'm sorry, Hilda, I can't hear you over all this noise I'm making playing ball with my son!'

'*Juliana!*'

With a bellow of rage, Hilda disappeared from view. For a few hopeful seconds, Juliana hoped they had got rid of her for good, but then she reappeared in the garden, marching across the lawn with surprising speed with one so old.

'Tam Tam!' she screamed, heading straight towards the flowerbed.

She seized the dog by the scruff of his neck. Tam Tam, suddenly finding himself soaring through the air, gave a yelp of fright, and then, after Hilda had aimed a few sharp slaps at his fluffy white bottom, began to whine pitifully.

Juliana, feeling instantly sorry for the poor creature, threw the ball back to Lee and said, 'Oh, there's no need for that, Hilda. He was just digging, just doing what dogs do.'

'You stay out of this!' snapped Hilda, stuffing the writhing dog back into her large handbag and zipping it shut. 'I've still a good mind to report you.'

'*You* report *me*?' Juliana cried, her temper flaring once more. 'Go on, then — go and tell CSP I was playing ball and making noise. But if you do, I'll show them the mess your dog just made. Look at the state of that flowerbed!'

Juliana was not exaggerating: in just a few short minutes, Tam Tam had managed to kick up a lot of soil, not to mention several carefully-planted pansies, and now the flowerbed boasted a hole at least a foot deep. Juliana wondered what on earth had possessed the little creature to launch into such frenzied digging; perhaps he had been trying to make an escape tunnel.

'So?' she demanded of Hilda, for the old woman was unusually quiet. 'Are you going to report me?'

Hilda looked from the destroyed flowerbed to Juliana and back a few times. 'On this occasion, I've decided to be... lenient.'

'Oh, how big of you!' cried Juliana. 'How *generous!*'

'But if I see that ball here again...'

'Oh, go away, Hilda,' sighed Juliana, turning her back on the old woman. 'Leave us alone, otherwise I really will go to Central Square Properties...'

To her immense relief, Hilda did finally depart the garden after that, although she cast dark looks over her shoulder as she did so. When Juliana heard the gate slam shut, she felt her whole body sag with exhaustion: how long would it go on for, this animosity between her and Hilda? She didn't think she had the energy for it anymore, and yet, she wasn't going to let herself or her children be bullied by that elderly tyrant.

Lee tugged at her hand. 'Mum?' he whispered. 'Mum?'

'Hm?'

'What's wrong with that old lady?'

She smoothed down his hair, which was dark, like Magnus's. 'That's a very good question, darling. I'm afraid I've no idea.'

Rosanna, meanwhile, had abandoned her book and was inspecting the ruined flowerbed.

'That dog's made *such* a mess!' she announced gleefully.

Juliana moved to stand beside her. 'Oh dear,' she said: the pile of earth around the hole looked like the beginnings of a compost heap.

'What shall we do?' asked Rosanna.

Juliana hesitated. She was quite tempted to leave it as it was, as a testament to Hilda and her badly-behaved dog, especially as she would no doubt need something to use against the old woman in the near future.

But then, there was no way she was going to go through the bother of contacting CSP about it, especially as she disliked that organisation almost as much as she did Hilda. Besides, Juliana was a gardener through and through, and there was no way a gardener could stand aside and leave a mess like this around a flowerbed.

'Let's tidy it up,' said Juliana, kneeling down to inspect the damage more closely. 'But carefully, we might be able to salvage some of these pansies…'

She and Rosanna set to work. What had taken Tam Tam seconds to destroy took them far longer to put right, for they had to sift through the earth to find the poor, battered flowers before replacing it in the hole. Juliana wished Daisy were here: her assistant's father was one of the best gardeners she knew, and she was sure Daisy would have a better idea of what do with the bedraggled flowers than she did.

'What's that?' asked Rosanna, pointing at something white and flimsy in the soil.

'Oh, for goodness' sake!' said Juliana, realising it was the corner of a plastic bag. 'What is the matter with people? Dropping litter in this beautiful garden?'

She gave the corner of the bag an experimental tug, fully expecting it to come loose. But it didn't. It seemed heavy — or perhaps it was just lodged under a weighty pile of earth.

'Help me dig it out, will you?' she asked her daughter, and the two of them scrabbled in the earth until the plastic bag finally came loose.

'There's something inside it!' cried Rosanna excitedly, wiping her dirty hands on her dress.

'Maybe it's treasure!' cried Lee, who had ambled over.

Juliana rubbed her hands on the grass so they were a little cleaner, and then turned over the plastic package. There was, indeed, something inside this bag, which had been taped shut before being buried. But what? It was thin and rectangular in shape, suggesting some kind of book…

'Open it, Mum, open it!' cried Rosanna.

Juliana hesitated, torn between excitement and apprehension. A naive part of her was thinking along the same lines as her children, and imagining that this really was a long-lost treasure of some sort. But then, she could not help but wonder whether this thing — whatever it was — had been buried for a reason, and perhaps it wasn't suitable for young eyes...

'Please, Mum, please!'

'All right,' said Juliana, making a snap decision, 'all right.'

She wiped her hands once again, and then started to unpick the sellotape from the side of the bag. Rosanna and Lee leaned forward so eagerly, their heads obstructed her view of her hands, and she had to wave them away.

'Just a moment,' she said, as the tape finally came loose. 'Hold on...'

Juliana unravelled the bag, which turned out to be the regular supermarket kind, and put her hand inside.

'Is that it?' said Lee, sounding highly disappointed as she pulled out the object inside. 'It's just an old notebook.'

'Maybe it's valuable,' said Rosanna.

'Or maybe it's a book of treasure maps!' said Lee, perking up.

'Lee, why don't you open it, as you've got clean hands,' suggested Juliana, relieved they had dug up nothing more offensive than a jotter. 'I expect it's someone's old school notes, although why you'd bury them, I've no idea...'

Her son carefully took the book and opened it at a random page.

'It's just a load of writing,' he said, sounding dissatisfied again. 'Just a list of times and stuff — *bo-ring*. I can't even read this!'

From what Juliana could see over his shoulder, her son was right: it did appear to be some sort of list, and the handwriting was almost illegible.

'Oh well,' she said, attempting to dust her hands clean. 'It was a bit of excitement, at least. I might run across the road and get some gardening gloves, and then we can continue with the flower —'

'Mum, there are pictures!' said Lee suddenly, turning a few more pages. 'They're all of a lady.'

'A lady?'

Rosanna giggled. 'She's not got many clothes on there...'

Juliana wheeled round, snatched the book from Lee's hands, and held it above her children's heads, so they could no longer see it.

'Hey!'

Juliana ignored her son, and instead stared at the page at which he had been looking: it featured a rough sketch of a woman sat in front of a dressing table mirror, her silky robe hanging open and revealing lacy underwear. The artist had apparently drawn this picture through a window, and he had captioned it: *23:06 — Gets ready for bed*.

'Oh God,' said Juliana, turning back through the book and discovering it contained pages and pages of times and images, all concerning Anne-Laure Chevalier. There were even a few photographs. 'Oh my God...'

'Mum, what is it?'

Rosanna was reaching up to take back the book, but Juliana shut it with a snap. She felt sick, and as she looked down at her two puzzled children, she couldn't think what to say.

'Who's that lady, Mum?' asked Lee.

'No one. She's just a made-up woman, like in a story. Come on, let's go...'

'Go?' chorused the children.

'But what about the flowerbed?' asked Rosanna.

'I want to see the book!' cried Lee.

'That's enough!' Juliana snapped. 'The gardener can deal with the flowerbed, we've saved the worst of it. Now, Rosanna, can you please pack up the hamper? Lee, I'm trusting you to fold up the rug *neatly*, and not forget your ball. Then we're going home.'

'*Home?*'

'Yes, home,' said Juliana, gripping the book tightly between her earthy fingers, as though it were trying to escape her. 'There's something I want to show your father.'

CHAPTER TWENTY-FIVE

Bryn wasn't working that Saturday, and so had spent much of his lunchtime sitting outside a pub near Clapham Common with a couple of friends from his building. It had been an exceptionally pleasant way to pass the time, and he felt sleepy and content when he returned to his bedsit later that afternoon, not to mention a little hot in the face. He peered into the mirror on his wall and discovered, as he had thought, he had caught the sun. Then, as he prodded at his red nose, deploring his pale complexion, he noticed something in the reflection of the room behind him. A light was flashing on the old phone he had inherited from the person who had lived here before him: he had an answerphone message.

'*Hi Bryn, it's Magnus. Sorry to call you on a Saturday, but there's been a bit of a... development with this Anne-Laure business. Something pretty significant, I think. Are you able to pop round the next time you're in the area?*'

Bryn played and replayed this message three times with mounting excitement. What could Magnus be referring to? What did 'a development' mean? And how was it 'pretty significant'? He picked up the phone's receiver with his right hand, the fingers of his left hovering over the keypad, but then he hesitated: no, he wasn't working today, but he could be in Westminster Square within half an hour, considering the train from Clapham Junction to Victoria was so quick. And if Magnus had found out something momentous about the Anne-Laure Chevalier case... Well, Bryn wanted to hear about it in person.

As it turned out, it only took a little over fifteen minutes from his own door to Magnus's, due to there being a train ready and waiting for him at Clapham Junction. After he was buzzed in by the Irish doorman, he hurried up the steps two at a time, and was rather surprised to find that it was Juliana, and not her husband, who opened the door.

'Oh good, you got Magnus's message,' she said, by way of greeting. 'I'll clear out the flowers.'

'Thanks,' said Bryn, before sneezing three times in a row.

He could not help but notice that Juliana did not seem quite as in control as usual. She too was a little red-faced, although he didn't think it was sunburn.

'Hello, Bryn,' said Magnus, offering his hand as the policeman entered the living room. 'Were you working today?' Then, before Bryn could answer, he added, 'No, of course you weren't, or you wouldn't have received my message. Well, thank you for coming over. I hardly know what to make of it myself...'

'What to make of what?' asked Bryn, trying to keep the eagerness from his voice.

'Oh, it's just *awful*!' said Juliana, coming in, picking up two vases, and heading out of the room again. 'I've never seen anything like it in all my life!'

Magnus indicated that Bryn should sit down on the sofa. 'Juliana's had a bit of a shock,' he explained in an undertone. 'She's a bit upset.'

But before he could elaborate, his wife was back for more flowers. 'I don't think we should keep this from the rest of the police any longer,' she said, gathering up the last of her living room plants. 'It's too terrible, Magnus...'

'Sorry,' said Bryn, anxious not to be rude but desperate to know what they were talking about. 'Could you enlighten *this* policeman? What's the development you mentioned on the phone?'

Magnus began to relate how Juliana and the children had been having a picnic in one of Westminster Square's gardens earlier in the day, and had been interrupted by Hilda Underpin. Tam Tam, it emerged, had started digging in one of the flowerbeds and when Juliana had gone to tidy up the mess, she had made a startling discovery.

'What did she find?' asked Bryn keenly.

Magnus gestured at the coffee table between them. Bryn wasn't sure what he was supposed to be looking at: all he could see were a few magazines, a novel of Juliana's, and a slightly grubby notebook, which presumably belonged to one of the children.

'That,' said Magnus, and to Bryn's surprise he pointed at the notebook. 'Take a look.'

Curiously, the policeman picked it up, wondering what could possibly be contained within to have made Juliana borderline hysterical. He had his answer soon enough: almost every page was covered with scribbly handwriting about one woman, and one woman only:

14.03: Returns from the shops, carries two bags
09.32: In green dress today, third time she's worn it
22:15: Heading out — to where? Followed her as far as Victoria

'My God,' said Bryn, a chill sweeping through his whole body. 'This looks like she had a —'

'*A stalker!*' cried Juliana, returning to the room and waving around a tea tray so carelessly she looked in danger of spilling the contents all over the carpet. 'Anne-Laure Chevalier had a stalker!'

'Juliana, calm down,' said Magnus, as she dropped the tray onto the coffee table with a clatter. 'Come and have a seat, I'll do the tea...'

'I will *not* calm down!' she said, although she did lower herself onto the sofa next to him. 'It's sick! What's the matter with people? What's going on?'

'I think only one person is responsible for this book,' said Magnus, 'or I assume so from the handwriting...'

'That doesn't make it any better! She had a stalker, Magnus — a stalker!'

'All right, all right,' he said, 'nobody's denying that. But let's not lose our heads. Let's discuss this.'

Bryn, who was still holding the offending object, tried to take in what he was seeing. But the scrawled words seemed to blur in front of his vision, and it was all he could do not to tear the whole notebook apart with his bare hands.

'What — what *is* this?' he asked.

'It's an account of all her movements,' said Juliana, her voice still high and shrill. 'It goes back months, even years — he was watching her for ages! And have you seen the pictures?'

Bryn shook his head.

'There are sketches of her — some of them pretty sordid, so they were probably out of his disgusting fantasies — and bits of poetry dedicated to her, and a couple of photographs too. Whoever that belongs to was completely obsessed with Anne-Laure Chevalier!'

Bryn swallowed, trying to quell the nausea bubbling inside him. Magnus, who seemed calmer than his companions, ventured, 'You keep saying *he*, Juliana…'

'Oh, of course it was a man, Magnus! No woman would do that, for goodness' sake!'

Bryn, still trying to catch up with what was going on, asked, 'And you found it buried in one of the gardens?'

'Yes, in a plastic bag,' said Juliana.

'I wonder why?' said Magnus. 'It's obviously an inflammatory object, especially given Anne-Laure's demise, so why would you bury it? Why not burn it, or shred it, to get rid of it once and for all?'

'You can't pretend a man who puts together a book like that thinks *logically*, Magnus!' cried Juliana.

While they squabbled amongst themselves, Bryn turned back to the book. Holding the pages at their very corners, as though the paper were in danger of contaminating him, he flicked through it. Juliana was right: there were pictures. Some of them were rather fuzzy photographs, which had evidently been taken at a great distance, and they showed the beautiful blonde woman going about her business in Westminster, apparently oblivious to the voyeur. Others were sketches, crude both in quality and subject matter. After seeing one particularly vulgar — and hopefully imagined — drawing of Anne-Laure, Bryn shut the book and replaced it on the table, feeling sicker than ever. He wished he hadn't seen any of it: somehow, looking at the contents of the stalker's notebook — all of which had presumably been made without Anne-Laure's consent — made Bryn feel complicit in a crime.

'Have some tea,' ordered Magnus, perhaps noticing that Bryn looked rather green.

The policeman took the proffered cup and saucer, even though he didn't feel like drinking anything at all. Yet when he took a tentative sip out of politeness, he was surprised by the soothing effect of the hot, familiar drink. He noticed that Juliana too had quietened down a little since Magnus had poured her a cup of tea.

'Right,' said the barrister, appearing to take charge of their little meeting, 'obviously this is a pretty shocking and unpleasant discovery, but it's also an extremely important piece of evidence. As such, I've taken the liberty of spending a couple of hours with that notebook this afternoon, and I've made a couple of observations that might be useful for our investigation.'

'Such as?' asked Bryn, reassured by Magnus' logical response to the situation.

'Well, as Juliana said, these notes go back a couple of years, so we're talking about a long-term obsession here.'

Juliana shuddered.

'And is it just Anne-Laure?' asked Bryn. 'He wasn't watching anyone else?'

'Not according to this notebook, no,' said Magnus. 'And he doesn't follow her every day. There are gaps of time — perhaps when she got wind of what was happening, or perhaps when she was away for Ellington, I don't know — when it goes quiet.'

'Oh well, that's all right, then!' cried Juliana sarcastically.

Magnus ignored her. 'I think the most interesting thing about it — if you can call any of this interesting — is that it seems to confirm some of what we've learned. According to this... *individual*, Anne-Laure visited Vasyl's house pretty regularly — almost every day, in fact — but she was also seen at Ellington's place once or twice a week.'

'Doing her *rabbateur* work, presumably,' said Bryn.

'She also visited Winifred every so often,' Magnus continued, 'especially towards the end of her life — which makes sense, given she was planning her party.'

'What about Hazim?'

'Urgh, what about him?' said Juliana, making a face.

'We have a theory that Anne-Laure was doing some work on the side for Hazim as well,' explained Bryn.

'A theory that's yet to be proved, unfortunately,' said Magnus. 'If this book is to be believed, Anne-Laure only visited Hazim once over the past couple of years — although, interestingly, it was only two weeks before her death.'

'And Jem McMorran?'

'More interesting still: he doesn't appear at all in this book.'

'What?' said Bryn, taken aback by this. 'Not at all?'

'Not at all,' said Magnus, shaking his head.

'But Hilda was convinced they were having some sort of affair — and Jem all but confirmed it for us!'

'You know what that means, then?' Juliana cut in, nodding at the book. 'He wrote it.'

Bryn almost laughed, but then thought better of it. After all, she had a point: if Jem and Anne-Laure had been seen together on multiple occasions, and yet none of their meetings had been recorded, perhaps he was the book's author.

'Hilda didn't make it sound especially one-sided, Anne-Laure and Jem's behaviour,' mused Magnus. 'From what she said, it sounded as though Anne-Laure had returned his affections.'

'But she would think that,' said Bryn, 'because Hilda was under the impression that Anne-Laure was some sort of... loose woman.'

'Urgh, I *hate* Hilda!' burst out Juliana.

'But no, this is crazy,' continued Bryn, shaking his head. 'I can't believe *Jem McMorran* would stalk someone.'

'It does seem a little unlikely,' agreed Magnus.

'Why?' said Juliana, with derision. 'Because he's handsome? Because he's a Hollywood star? That doesn't mean anything! Men like him are probably the worst of the lot!'

'But Jem McMorran must have women throwing themselves at him all the time,' said Magnus. 'Why obsess over this one in particular?'

'You talk as though we're all the same,' sniffed Juliana. 'Maybe because Anne-Laure had something the others didn't? Or maybe she rejected him, and he wasn't used to it — couldn't accept it — and so it prompted this... *fixation.*'

Bryn looked between husband and wife, wondering which side he fell on. Again, he thought Juliana was talking a lot of sense: Jem McMorran might present a glossy image to the world, but who knew what he was really like, underneath the Hollywood glamour? He was an actor, after all, and hadn't they already seen him in a pitiful state the other week? But then, as much as he tried to convince himself that Juliana was right, he couldn't shake his gut instinct that Jem McMorran didn't have it in him to compile something like this. The notebook might have been depraved, but diligence and patience had gone into creating it, which Bryn doubted the actor possessed.

'I'm just not sure he fits the profile of a stalker,' said the policeman eventually. 'I mean, Juliana's right — who knows what people are really like underneath it all — but someone like Morris Springfield seems more of the type, don't you think?'

'Oh, poor Morris!' cried Juliana. 'You're just saying that because he's socially awkward!'

'I'm not,' said Bryn, which wasn't entirely true. 'But think about it: he's a writer, and there are bits of poetry in there, and because of his job he's always present in Westminster Square, unlike Jem, who goes off on film shoots.'

'Maybe Jem going off for film shoots accounts for the gaps in the notebook!' said Juliana, who now seemed determined to blame the actor.

Magnus, however, was still thinking about the writer. 'Morris, like Jem, also isn't mentioned in the notebook,' he said.

'But why would he be?' asked Juliana, turning to her husband. 'You told me that Anne-Laure and Morris Springfield had been out for an unsuccessful coffee date a few years ago, and that had been the extent of their relationship. So why would he have had any more contact with her? Why would he appear in those awful notes?'

'That's true,' said Magnus. 'Plus Morris wasn't exactly impressed with Anne-Laure, was he? So why would he have gone to all of this trouble?'

He gestured at the notebook. Bryn, however, sat up a little straighter.

'But Magnus, remember what you theorised in Lei Sing's the other day? You said that maybe it was the other way around: that Anne-Laure had been unimpressed with Morris, and he had changed the narrative to save face. So perhaps it wasn't Jem who she rejected and he couldn't let it go — perhaps it was Morris!'

But Juliana shook her head. 'I just don't believe that,' she said. 'I know Morris is a bit odd, but he's sweet and sensitive…'

'You're just saying that because he's good to his mother,' said Magnus.

'Well, maybe I am, but that's what I think,' she said, stubbornly.

They lapsed into silence, and Bryn had the impression Juliana was silently fuming at her husband. Magnus, however, seemed unperturbed by her temper. Instead, he took a long sip of tea, and then said, 'You know, if we take emotion out of this, and look at it entirely logically, there's one very obvious person who might have written this book.'

'Is there?' said Bryn, nonplussed.

'Think about it. Who spends their whole time spying on Westminster Square? Who had an almighty grudge against Anne-Laure Chevalier? And Bryn, when we went to her house, who had *a notebook, a pair of binoculars, and a camera* by the window?'

'My God,' said Bryn, realising Magnus was right, 'Hilda Underpin.'

Juliana burst out laughing. 'Don't be so ridiculous — there's no way she would have written that!'

'Why's there no way?' Magnus asked her. 'She's always keeping tabs on people in Westminster Square, you know that more than most.'

'Well, it doesn't look like an old lady's handwriting for starters.'

'That's not a very scientific method of deduction, Juliana…'

'Oh, come on! What about all those dirty drawings? You're seriously suggesting a little old lady is responsible for them? Magnus, the person who put this book together was sexually obsessed with Anne-Laure Chevalier!'

'So was Hilda Underpin, in a way,' said Bryn, thoughtfully.

'*What?*'

'I mean, Hilda Underpin was obsessed with her sexuality,' Bryn clarified. 'Every time we've mentioned Anne-Laure to her, Hilda's been fixated on how loose she apparently was. She's called Anne-Laure a "hussy", a "fallen woman", she deplored the clothes she wore, not to mention was horrified by her alleged public displays of affection with Jem McMorran. So maybe this notebook is just a bizarre manifestation of Hilda's unshakeable belief that Anne-Laure was — how did she put it — a "bad girl"?'

But Juliana was shaking her head. 'You're both being absurd.'

'Out of everybody we've spoken to, Hilda's certainly the most likely person to have put together a record of someone else's movements,' said Magnus. 'And didn't you say Tam Tam dug it up?' he asked Juliana. 'I mean, why did he start digging there?'

'He's a dog!' Juliana cried. 'That's what they do! He'd been shut up in her handbag for who knows how long, so when she dropped it to shout it me, he bolted towards the first bit of earth he could find.'

'And what was her reaction to his digging?'

'She was mortified, of course. But that was because she'd just told me off for breaking all these stupid Central Square Properties rules, and then her dog goes and destroys half the flowerbed, not because she was worried her sordid notebook was going to be uncovered.'

'No?'

'No! She left me in the garden with that mess,' Juliana continued. 'Surely she would have offered to clear it up herself, if she had buried something questionable nearby?'

'It *is* Hilda, though,' said Magnus. 'Who knows how she thinks?'

Yet Bryn thought the barrister now sounded a little more convinced by Juliana.

'What about the other people we've spoken to?' he asked, feeling that they had exhausted the subject of Jem, Morris and Hilda. 'What about our other suspects?'

'Well, if we're going to rule out Hilda on the grounds of a lack of attraction to Anne-Laure, I think we can say the same for Lord Bevis Ellington,' said Magnus. 'I'd venture it was very unlikely he put this together, when, like Morris, he didn't seem to think much of her — or women in general, really.'

'Unlike his bodyguard, Gregor,' pointed out Bryn.

'True,' said Magnus. 'Yes, that's a possibility, but he was rather an oaf, wasn't he? Could he have put in all of this work?'

'It's not *work*!' Juliana scoffed. 'It's — Well, I don't know what it is, apart from *completely depraved*.'

'Then there's Sheikh Hazim,' interrupted the policeman, before Juliana could launch into another rant.

'Who certainly makes no secret of his sexual appetite,' said Magnus, 'and who sees women more as playthings than people. Yes, he fits the bill there, but I can't really imagine him peering out into Westminster Square and making notes on one particular girl, especially as his *majlis* doesn't even have a window...'

'Also, you're forgetting that both Ellington and Hazim are in the book,' said Juliana. 'Are you suggesting they're writing about themselves in the third person?'

'I'm not suggesting anything,' said Magnus, sounding wearied by her constant interruptions. 'We're just brainstorming here, Juliana.'

'What about Vasyl Kosnitschev?' asked Bryn.

'Well, he probably *would* be the sort to make meticulous notes,' allowed Magnus, 'but so far he's demonstrated complete indifference to Anne-Laure's personal life, so it would be quite a surprise if he'd been stalking her. Plus, once again, his name appears frequently in that book — in fact, he's probably mentioned the most, given that she saw him almost every week day.'

'Well that's everyone, isn't it?' said Bryn, feeling disappointed that they'd failed to draw any concrete conclusions.

'Apart from Dame Winifred Rye, yes.'

Juliana happened to be taking a sip from her cup as Magnus said this, and accidentally inhaled a mouthful of tea.

'*Dame — Winifred — Rye?*' she spluttered, while Magnus clapped her on the back. 'You're not — *serious?*'

'Not really, no,' Magnus admitted. 'I mean, I was a little intrigued by her behaviour towards young Daisy at that party the other day…'

'Who's Daisy?' asked Bryn.

'What behaviour?' asked Juliana.

Magnus explained that Daisy was Juliana's assistant at The Station Garden, a girl who Dame Winifred had recently taken under her wing, and Bryn vaguely recalled mention of this during their meeting with the aristocrat a few weeks' ago.

'I'm not sure I like it,' sniffed Juliana. 'Daisy's *my* friend, not Dame Winifred's.'

'I'm not sure Daisy likes it either,' said Magnus. 'She hasn't said anything about Dame Winifred to you, has she?'

'No. She tells me she prefers working for me, but I assumed she was just being polite, especially as Dame Winifred keeps taking her for tea and buying her little trinkets. Daisy's very well-mannered,' Juliana said, for Bryn's benefit.

'Actually, I don't think she was just being polite,' said Magnus. 'When I saw them together at the party, Dame Winifred was being very clingy with her. I think Daisy finds her a bit much, to be honest.'

Juliana, who looked pleased to hear this, said, 'I'm not surprised, Dame Winifred *is* a bit much at times.'

'What if she was like that with Anne-Laure too, then?' asked Magnus. 'What if she wanted to mollycoddle her to such an extent that she went too far, became slightly obsessed, started keeping track of her movements?'

'But this isn't mollycoddling, Magnus, it's *stalking!*' said Juliana, jabbing a finger towards the notebook. 'And, once again, there's clearly a sexual element to those pictures. Surely you're not suggesting Dame Winifred —?'

'No,' said Magnus quickly, 'I'm not. My theory is that Dame Winifred Rye views young people like Daisy and Anne-Laure as surrogate children, so I suppose that doesn't really add up.'

'No it doesn't,' said Juliana, folding her arms. Then, looking between them, she said, 'You have to admit, both of you, the obvious author of that book is Jem McMorran.'

'I think Morris Springfield wrote it,' said Bryn.

'And I believe, if we're looking at it logically, Hilda Underpin is the most likely candidate,' said Magnus, with a hint of a smile. 'So I suppose, for now, we'll all have to agree to disagree.'

Juliana gave a huff of frustration. 'Never mind agreeing or disagreeing, what are we going to do about it?' She rose to her feet, suddenly restless, and began to pace around the room. 'I thought we might have had something here,' she continued, nodding at the book, 'something that might have helped us with the case. But now we discover that horrible book is completely useless in telling us any more about how the poor girl died.'

'I wouldn't say that,' said Magnus quietly.

'What do you mean?' asked Bryn.

'Well, assuming she was murdered, and by the person who wrote this, we're able to build up more of a profile of our potential killer, aren't we?' mused Magnus. 'At Lei Sing's, I said that one of the biggest problems we have with this case is a lack of motive: nobody we've spoken to had any reason to want Anne-Laure Chevalier dead — at least, no reason that they've revealed to us. But if we take away all of the people we've questioned — and, let's face it, there's no guarantee our little group *does* include the guilty party — and just focus on this notebook, well, the motive is quite clear, isn't it? He or she — and, all right, let's say for the sake of argument it *is* a he — was obsessed with her. Most likely, sexually obsessed. Maybe he was a spurned ex-boyfriend, maybe he was a current boyfriend who she tried to get rid of — don't forget we still don't know the identity of the shadowy man in the garden: he and the author of this book are likely one and the same person. Or maybe he didn't know her at all. But whichever way you look at it, and whoever was responsible, Anne-Laure Chevalier's death now looks like it was the work of someone who was infatuated, unhinged and probably seeking some kind of vengeance.'

'Like a crime of passion?' said Juliana.

'Crimes of passion are violent, usually caused by a sudden burst of rage,' explained Magnus grimly. 'They're prompted by arguments getting out of hand, or the shock of finding a partner in bed with someone else, that sort of thing. But this wasn't like that, was it? If Anne-Laure's overdose wasn't accidental, her murder was planned — premeditated.'

Bryn found himself nodding. He didn't know how to express it aloud without seeming insensitive, but there was a flutter of hope in his chest: they might not have solved the case, but the truth — and the justice he would ensure came with it — felt closer than before.

'All right,' said Juliana, who had stopped her pacing and was now perched on the arm of the sofa, apparently a little soothed by Magnus's summation. 'Well, I don't want that book in my house any longer, and as I assume you're going to show it to your superiors, Bryn, I think you should take it for today...' She trailed off seeing the expression on his face. 'You *are* going to show it to your superiors, aren't you?'

'Um, no, I don't think I will, at least not at this juncture.'

Juliana's mouth fell open. 'But it's evidence! That proves she was followed, probably harassed, and who knows what else!'

'But unfortunately it doesn't prove she was murdered,' said Magnus, 'and therefore I doubt Chief Superintendent Barry Boyle is going to be particularly interested in it.'

'Is stalking not a crime?' demanded Juliana.

'It is, but given the victim is dead, I think you're going to have a job getting Boyle to investigate this any further.'

'But she's probably dead because of the stalking!' Juliana cried, leaping to her feet once again. 'Magnus, I can't believe what you're saying here!'

'Juliana, calm down! I agree with you, it's dreadful, but there's no point going to the police when Boyle is so determined to bury this case. Let's sit tight for a little longer, try and compile more evidence, and attempt to weed out an actual suspect from amongst Anne-Laure's former acquaintances. And then we'll go to Boyle — when there's no way he can ignore what we're telling him.'

'And when there's no way I'll get fired for my trouble,' muttered Bryn, feeling highly resentful of the Chief Superintendent, for he, like Juliana, thought this notebook deserved to go straight to the Victoria Police Station.

Juliana looked between them a few times and then gave another sharp exhalation of disapproval.

'Fine,' she said. '*Fine*. But we'd better get to the bottom of this. I can't bear the thought of there being no justice for that woman.'

Bryn, who wasn't sure how he felt about Juliana inserting herself into their investigation, said, 'Neither can I.'

'And you'd better take that notebook away with you anyway, Bryn,' Juliana continued. 'I want it out of my sight.'

Bryn eyed it warily: in truth, he wanted it out of his sight too.

Perhaps sensing his unease, Magnus suggested, 'I could keep it in the study…'

'No you cannot,' his wife snapped. 'What if the children find it? They're already asking questions about what we dug up in the garden, and I don't want them going anywhere near it, either accidentally or on purpose.'

Realising he had little choice in the matter, Bryn picked up the notebook, although very gingerly, as though it were likely to explode.

'I wish I'd never found it,' Juliana announced. 'I mean, if it can be used as evidence later, great, but otherwise I wish it had stayed buried. Or I wish the author — whoever that sick individual is — had just destroyed it.'

'Yes, I'm still wondering why he didn't,' said Magnus. 'As I said before, why not shred or burn it, or at least throw it away with the rubbish — and preferably somewhere far away from Westminster Square?'

'Maybe he didn't want to get rid of it permanently?' said Bryn, staring down at the cover of the old jotter as though mesmerised. 'Maybe, rather than destroying it completely, he only wanted to hide it, so he could go back for it later?'

Magnus nodded. 'That makes sense, especially considering this level of… Well, this level of obsession. But why in the garden? Why not stash it somewhere in his house?'

But Bryn found he knew the answer to this straight away, and it sent a cold chill running down his spine: 'Maybe because you and I had already been to his house, asking questions. And maybe he was worried that, next time, it would be the police knocking on his door with a search warrant.'

The three of them stared at one another, and Juliana made a little noise of distress at the back of her throat.

'What on earth have you two got yourselves into?' she asked.

CHAPTER TWENTY-SIX

Apparently it was a good week for developments in the Anne-Laure Chevalier case, because when Bryn returned from work the following Tuesday, he discovered another message waiting for him on his answerphone:

'*Good afternoon, Constable Summers, this is Agnes Chambers here. As I mentioned to you the other week, I have been tasked with the duty of clearing out Annie's flat, so I am coming up from Brighton tomorrow afternoon. If you're still able to assist me, I'd very much appreciate the help, especially as your colleagues have made such a pig's ear of this whole situation. I should be in the Mews at around two o'clock, so I hope to see you there.*'

Bryn, who had until that point completely forgotten about the existence of Agnes Chambers and his offer to help her, hurried to write down the time. What a bit of luck this was: just as he and Magnus were looking for more evidence to prove Anne-Laure had been murdered, he was going to have access to the place she had lived, which was surely going to be full of clues, if he could only manage to identify them.

The next day, Bryn took a late lunch and arrived at the Mews a little before two o'clock. When he and Magnus had come here on their tour of the area a few weeks' ago, he hadn't known which property had belonged to Anne-Laure — or rather, which property had belonged to Dame Winifred, and been rented by Anne-Laure. But now, he was not only going to get a chance to peer through the windows, but actually go inside and see whether Anne-Laure's accommodation gave any indication as to how or why she had died.

'Ah, you're here. Good.'

Bryn turned to find Agnes Chambers marching down the cobbled street towards him. She was dressed, once more, in long and dowdy clothes, and going by her expression it didn't seem to have occurred to her that he might not have turned up. Apparently, Anne-Laure's aunt was a person who expected her demands to be met.

'Good afternoon, Miss Chambers.'

'Yes, yes,' she said impatiently, before withdrawing a set of keys from her ugly carpetbag. 'Let's get this over with, shall we? It's this one here, I believe...'

She was heading towards one of the boxy terraced houses, which was even smaller than Morris Springfield's building on Westminster Row, although it still featured the white walls, black door and large windows that were characteristic of the area.

'Apparently, Dame Winifred told the police she rented out the whole property to Annie,' said Agnes, as she tried various keys in the lock of the front door, 'both upstairs and down. What can the girl have wanted with all that space?'

Bryn didn't know how to respond to this: even with both floors, the property didn't look especially large. It might have been a little big for just one person, but it was hardly extravagant in comparison to some of the other examples of accommodation around here.

'Aha, here we are,' said Agnes, as she found the correct key at last. 'Well, let's see what kind of state she left it in, shall we...?'

As Bryn followed her inside, he braced himself for the effect of seeing all of Anne-Laure Chevalier's belongings scattered around the space, as though she were soon to return to them. The scene of her flat would capture the moment she had left it that fateful evening, as though her life had only been put on pause, and not stopped entirely.

However, contrary to this, when Bryn did get his first look at Anne-Laure's flat, he found — to his great surprise — it looked exactly like the home of someone who had recently died: the open-plan kitchen, dining and living room area was completely tidy, other than a dozen or so cardboard boxes piled neatly in the centre of the space, all of which bore descriptions in marker pen such as: *clothes, shoes, crockery, linen.*

'I don't understand,' said Agnes, staring at the boxes. 'Has someone been in before us? The police didn't say so.'

But Bryn was looking behind them, at the wall next to the door, against which three large suitcases were lined up. He recalled what Hilda Underpin had told them in Lei Sing's, about what Anne-Laure had said to her the last time they had spoken: '*Well, you'll be pleased to hear you won't have to cope with me at all after next week, because I'm moving away from London on Monday.*' Here, it seemed, was the proof Anne-Laure had been intending to go through with that plan.

'It looks like she was moving away, doesn't it?' the policeman said to Agnes.

'Moving *where*?' Anne-Laure's aunt demanded, as though Bryn could answer her question. 'I didn't know about this.'

He refrained from pointing out that, considering she hadn't spoken to her niece in many years, it wasn't exactly surprising she hadn't been kept in the loop about Anne-Laure's plans.

At that moment, there was a knock on the door, and Bryn turned to let in Magnus, who he had informed about the clear-out of the flat the previous evening.

'Who are you?' asked Agnes. 'You don't look like a policeman.'

'My name is Magnus Walterson, and I'm a lawyer. I just came round to check that everything's going all right in here?'

'Oh!'

Agnes's eyes widened and she looked both surprised and a little impressed; she was perhaps under the impression that Magnus had been sent by the police to make up for the cremation debacle, and Bryn knew that the barrister had kept his introduction deliberately vague for this reason.

'Well, as it happens, Mr Walterson, we've only just come in, and we've just found all of these boxes lying around. It seems my niece was about to move out.'

'Oh?' For a second, Magnus's gaze flicked towards Bryn, although he also appeared to think it wise to feign ignorance. 'Well, at least that'll make your life easier, Miss Chambers.'

'What do you mean?'

'Well, it must have been such an inconvenience for you, coming all the way here from Brighton, so thank goodness much of the work has already been done for you.'

Agnes sniffed, seemingly pleased he had acknowledged her long journey. 'Yes, I suppose you're right. I wouldn't mind having a peek in a couple of boxes just to check that what she says is inside is actually there.

'Of course...'

'But then it might be an idea just to take everything to a charity shop or two. I don't want any of this stuff — I expect it's a load of old rubbish.'

'Well, then,' said Magnus, striding forward and beginning to unfasten the tape on one of the top boxes. 'Shall we start with crockery here?'

As Agnes moved to follow him, Bryn said, 'I'll check upstairs. See if that's packed away as well.'

'Hm,' said Agnes, peering into a box of what was presumably plates and mugs wrapped in old newspaper.

Bryn took the stairs two at a time, wondering whether there might be more to discover on the first floor. But he quickly came to the conclusion that Anne-Laure hadn't occupied the upstairs of her little home for some time. There were two bedrooms up here, which she had presumably used for guests, and a bathroom, but all three spaces were almost completely empty. The two double beds had been stripped of all linen, the wardrobes didn't have so much as a blanket inside, and there was a thin coat of dust on the mantelpieces. Not for the first time, Bryn found himself wondering whether Anne-Laure had actually had any friends: she seemed to have had plenty of business acquaintances, and at least one lover, but had she had anybody in whom she could confide?

The thought of this made him feel a little depressed as he returned back downstairs, accidentally dirtying his hand on the dusty banister as he did so. To the right of the room in which his companions were inspecting the boxes was another bedroom. This was smaller than those upstairs, but apparently Anne-Laure had preferred to sleep here, because there were still sheets on the bed, as well as a book and a glass of water on the nightstand. Neatly folded on a nearby chair were a pair of jeans, some comfortable-looking black trousers and a couple of tops, one blue and one light pink in colour; while a pair of casual loafers was tucked underneath. Somewhat incongruously, two silky black evening gloves were also hanging over the arm of the chair. Bryn knew very little about women's fashion, but he could only assume that Anne-Laure had intended to wear these to Dame Winifred's fundraising party, and had either changed her mind at the last minute or forgotten about them. In any case, other than these few items, the rest of the bedroom — including the contents of the cupboards — had been cleared out: Anne-Laure had clearly not intended to spend much more time here.

Bryn made a few notes, although this all looked perfectly normal to him, and then drifted through to the ensuite bathroom. This space had been tiled in blue, and featured a large mirror above the bath, which Bryn would not have enjoyed himself. As with the bedroom, a few personal items were still cluttered around the sink and shower, and Bryn headed straight towards a bottle of perfume, which looked remarkably similar to the one he had found in Jem McMorran's flat.

'What do you know?' he said to himself, as he spritzed a little of the fresh, summery scent into the air. 'It's exactly the same.'

When he returned to the dining-living room area, the others were still peering into boxes. Anne-Laure's aunt seemed to have taken more of a liking to Magnus than she had to him, presumably because the barrister was older, looked wealthier, and had a nice English accent. Leaving them to it, Bryn wandered into the kitchenette area of the open-plan room, in case there was anything of any significance to be found there.

Once more, as much as Anne-Laure had packed away, there was still signs of the fact that she had intended to spend a little more time in this accommodation, if only a night or two. Although the cupboards were now mostly bare, inside the fridge he found some very old milk, butter and juice, all of which he threw straight into the bin. As he then pulled the bin bag out, holding his breath so he didn't gag at the smell, he noticed that there were a surprising number of dead flowers beneath the items he had just thrown in, and he wondered whether Anne-Laure had bought them from Juliana's shop. Then, unable to hold his breath any longer, he tied up the handles of the bin bag, and took it outside onto the Mews, so the smell couldn't contaminate the little house any longer.

'I don't know why she had to have quite so many clothes,' Agnes was saying, as Bryn came back in. 'Young women these days! When I was a girl, I rotated a few outfits, and that was that.'

'Hm,' said Magnus, non-committal. 'At least they might fetch a good price at Oxfam or somewhere similar…'

Bryn edged past them towards the desk in the corner of the room, and at last he found something significant. The wooden surface of the table had evidently been cleared, but once again it featured a few items to which Anne-Laure had presumably intended to return.

The first thing Bryn saw was an invoice addressed to Vasyl Kosnitschev for PR work, which Anne-Laure had evidently meant to pass onto him at some stage. But Bryn was more interested in what was lying on top of this sheet of paper: a British passport. As he flicked through it, he saw her name was listed as *Anne-Laure Chevalier* — so she'd obviously changed it legally. The identification also featured the best headshot Bryn had ever seen; even in a passport photo — which, in the policeman's experience, made everyone appear washed-out and ugly — Anne-Laure looked like a model. Bryn flicked through the pages for a few seconds, noting there were a surprising number of stamps inside, and then his attention was caught by a thin rectangle of card, which had been lying beneath the passport: an aeroplane ticket.

Bryn picked this up, frowning. Once more, it bore the name *Anne-Laure Chevalier* and the flight listed was a direct journey from London Heathrow to Los Angeles International Airport, or LAX. The policeman swallowed as he saw the date: Anne-Laure's flight to America had been due to leave on Monday, just as she had promised Hilda, and just a day after her body had been discovered at the Royal West Hotel.

Bryn's first instinct was to call out to Magnus, for this felt like a truly significant find. But he was still over the other side of the room, inspecting yet another box of clothes with Agnes, and, once again, the policeman didn't think it a particularly wise idea to let Anne-Laure's aunt in on what he had just found, at least not at this stage. If or when they proved the murder, she would of course have every right to know about it, but at the moment she would almost certainly be more of a hindrance than a help.

So Bryn slipped both the passport and the airline ticket into a pocket on his utility belt, and was about to walk away from the desk when he noticed something had fluttered onto the floor. Stooping, he picked it up, and saw that it was a small square of notepaper, which read:

Darren Dodge — Sunday, 2pm. The Dawn Reporter Office, Fleet Street

Bryn stared at this note. He recognised Anne-Laure's handwriting from her address book, so it was obviously she who had written this. But why had she been intending to meet up with a journalist? Presumably, considering she was going to his office, he wasn't another secret boyfriend and instead she had wanted to see him in a professional capacity. But regarding what?

The timing, too, was interesting: why had she wanted to meet with this man just before she left the country?

As Bryn folded up the note and pushed it into his utility belt along with the ticket and the passport, he remembered a journalist from *The Dawn Reporter* had been outside the Royal West that morning, causing him a headache after Boyle had made him stand guard outside the hotel. What had been his name? Bryn couldn't recollect it now, but he thought he would have remembered somebody called Darren Dodge.

'I think we're done here,' Magnus announced, summoning Bryn from his reverie. 'The contents of these boxes seem to match their labels, so we might as well ship them off to a few charity shops as they are.'

Agnes nodded fervently. 'Well, I must say, this has been a far quicker task than I anticipated.' Her expression suddenly darkened. 'You would have thought someone might have told me she was moving out, so I knew what I would find when I arrived here. But what do you expect from people like that dreadful Dame Winifred woman?'

'Yes, I wonder if she knew?' Bryn pondered, because Dame Winifred certainly hadn't mentioned the fact that Anne-Laure had been intending to move out of her accommodation.

'What do you mean?' asked Agnes.

'Oh, nothing, nothing.'

'Miss Chambers, if there's nothing you wish to keep from your niece's belongings, I can make arrangements to have these boxes taken away,' said Magnus.

'Really?'

'Of course, it's no trouble.'

'Well, I'd very much appreciate that, thank you, Mr Walterson, Constable Summers.' Agnes looked at her watch. 'Goodness, I thought I'd be here for hours, but I can now catch a much earlier train back to Brighton!'

She looked delighted at the prospect of leaving London, and seemed to have no qualms about getting rid of Anne-Laure's possessions, which were, Bryn remembered, her last link to her dead brother's child. Still, Agnes Chambers had not even spoken to her niece for about ten years, so what were all these clothes and shoes to her? Just physical proof that a member of her own family had sought a better life than the one she had tried to provide.

Once Agnes had said goodbye, leaving the keys on the counter of the kitchenette, Bryn turned to Magnus.

'Why did you offer to take care of the boxes?' he asked. 'Do you think they contain anything significant?'

'Not unless you think loads of fancy designer clothes are significant, no,' replied the barrister. 'That woman was just grating on my nerves a bit, and I wanted to talk to you while we still had access to this place. I assume, from the glint in your eye, that *you've* found something significant?'

Bryn nodded, and pulled out the passport, aeroplane ticket, and notepaper.

'So she wasn't just moving away, she was leaving the country,' said Magnus, after studying the ticket.

'Yeah, I guess she wasn't exaggerating when she said she wanted to get away from Westminster Square,' replied Bryn.

'The destination is interesting too,' continued the barrister.

'LA? Why?'

'Think about it: who out of Anne-Laure's acquaintances is most likely to be found in LA? Or rather, a little northwest of LA?'

'Northwest...?'

'I'll give you a clue: its name is emblazoned in giant white letters on a hillside, and the streets are full of stars — quite literally, in fact.'

'Are you talking about Hollywood? Oh, you mean Jem McMorran!'

Magnus nodded.

'It does slightly disprove the theory she was being stalked by him,' said Bryn, 'if she was jetting out there to see him — or maybe jetting out there *with* him.'

'But then, you and I didn't really buy that, did we?' said Magnus. 'That was Juliana's theory.'

'Maybe she was flying out there to try and launch an acting career of her own?' said Bryn. 'Haven't we been told more than once that she wanted to be an actress when she was younger? Maybe she never truly gave up on that dream?'

'It's possible,' said Magnus. 'It's also worth noting a lot of business goes on in LA. She could have gone there on behalf of Vasyl or Ellington or even Hazim. Although I doubt she would have packed quite so much for her trip if she were only going for a few days or even weeks of business... It looks like she was planning to make a permanent move.'

They both looked towards the three large suitcases by the door. Then, realising they hadn't actually checked inside, they unzipped each one in turn, but there appeared to be nothing suspicious inside. Instead of the wads of cash and pouches of drugs Bryn's overactive imagination conjured up, the suitcases merely contained more clothes, shoes and toiletries.

'Speaking of Jem McMorran,' he said, standing up once more, 'that perfume I found in his bathroom did belong to her — there's an identical bottle next door. I mean, I guess there's a slim chance that Jem has a girlfriend with exactly the same perfume as Anne-Laure, but —'

'It seems unlikely,' Magnus concluded. He sighed. 'I do wonder when young Jem is going to return to Westminster Square. Out of everybody we've spoken to, he's the one I want to question further, because at the moment it's looking more than likely he and Anne-Laure were planning on moving to America together.'

'What about this journalist, though?' asked Bryn. 'Where does he fit in?'

Magnus looked down at the piece of paper bearing the reporter's details and shook his head. 'I've no idea. I wasn't expecting anything like this.'

'Do you remember the name of the journalist who caused all of that fuss outside the Royal West on the morning after her death?' Bryn asked. 'Because he was from *The Dawn Reporter*, wasn't he?'

Magnus made a face, presumably at the mention of the tabloid, although it could also have been because he had strongly disliked the pushy journalist. 'Nicholls,' he said. 'Nicky? No, Ricky, that was it: Ricky Nicholls.'

'So not Darren Dodge, then,' said Bryn, feeling a little disappointed. 'Not the man she had been intending to meet with later that day.'

'No,' said Magnus. 'But I think it might be an idea to give this Darren Dodge a call. I'd be very interested to know what Anne-Laure wanted to talk to him about.'

They lapsed into silence as they looked around the empty, packed-up flat and then, simultaneously seeming to decide there was nothing more they could do there, Magnus picked up the keys and Bryn followed him back out onto the Mews.

'I'd better do something about this,' said Magnus, picking up the bin bag Bryn had left out there earlier. 'Otherwise CSP will be out for someone's blood — Dame Winifred's, I expect, in the absence of Anne-Laure...'

But Bryn was hardly listening: he crossed over to the other side of the street, where he scrutinised the ground floor of the little house from which they had just emerged. Magnus followed him.

'It's strange to think it was once stables, isn't it?' the barrister said. 'Or at least, the downstairs part would have been for the horses and carriages.

Then the grooms — or *sais*, as they were sometimes called — would live upstairs, above the horses. Can you imagine the smell?'

'Hm,' said Bryn, now staring at the window on the left-hand side of the door.

'Are you all right?' Magnus asked, apparently realising that he had lost his companion's attention.

Bryn turned. 'Do you remember the sketches in that notebook?'

'Unfortunately, yes.'

'And how it appears that many of them are imagined?'

'I would hope so, yes.'

'There's one —' Bryn coloured to recall it, '— there's one that shows Anne-Laure at her dressing table, in her underwear and a robe, and the caption reads something like, *A before bed.*'

'Regrettably, the children saw that one, before Juliana realised what she'd dug up,' said Magnus. 'You're lucky you weren't around when my wife came in with that book; she was beside herself. Anyway, what of it?'

Bryn nodded towards the window. 'I think that one was from life. I reckon he sketched it right here. Look, when we stand at this spot, we can see straight into her bedroom — my view of the dressing table right now is identical to the one in that picture.'

He broke off, shuddering. Magnus sighed heavily.

'Well, we knew he was following her,' he said.

'But this isn't just making a note of how many bags of shopping she buys of an afternoon — which is still incredibly weird, don't get me wrong — this is lurking outside her bedroom at night, watching her undress, and drawing her. This is extremely sinister behaviour.'

All of a sudden, Bryn didn't want to stand there any longer. He took a few strides further along the pavement, almost to avoid being tainted by the association of remaining on that spot.

'I agree with you, I do,' said Magnus, 'but we know he's a creep, don't we? The fact he loitered around outside her house doesn't really tell us anything new.'

'It might, considering what we've learned today,' said Bryn.

'What do you mean?'

Once more, the policeman took out the aeroplane ticket from his utility belt. 'We've been speculating Anne-Laure wanted to go to LA to pursue love, or a career in acting, or business, or whatever it was. But what if *she* was the one being pursued? What if it wasn't so much a case of her going somewhere because she wanted to, but leaving somewhere because she had to? I mean, if I were Anne-Laure, and I knew someone was following me, spying on me, maybe even threatening me, I'd want to get out the area as quickly as possible — and to somewhere far away, where I couldn't be tracked down.'

'Yes, I see what you mean,' said Magnus. 'But assuming she got wind of what he was up to, why didn't she go to the police?'

Bryn shrugged helplessly. 'I don't know. I wish she had. Because, for all her plans, it didn't work, did it? Right now, as far as I can tell, it looks like this — this *madman* found out what she was intending to do and decided that, rather than letting her go and have a life on the other side of the world, he'd rather she didn't have a life at all.'

CHAPTER TWENTY-SEVEN

'Magnus?'

'Hm?'

'*Magnus!*'

'What?'

'I can't sleep!'

Magnus groaned into his pillow. Until this moment, he had been sleeping perfectly well, despite being vaguely aware of Juliana tossing and turning and huffing and puffing beside him.

'Count sheep or something,' he mumbled, attempting to turn his back on her, but she held onto his shoulder to stop him.

'That doesn't work. Nothing works. I haven't slept a wink.'

'Well, what do you want me to do about it?' he moaned, trying to pull the blanket over his head to block her out, but again she stopped him.

'I can't stop thinking about Anne-Laure Chevalier.'

'Oh, *Juliana*...'

'It's going round and round in my head. I think we should talk about it, and then I'll be able to sleep again.'

'Talk about it — what, *now*?' Blearily, he opened his eyes and peered at the clock on the bedside table. 'Juliana, it's half past three in the morning! I need to sleep!'

'So do I, Magnus, so do I! I'm going to get some tea, and then we'll talk. Do you want any?'

'What?'

'Do you want some tea?'

'I want some sleep!'

But Juliana merely sighed, kicked off the covers, and switched on one of the bedside lamps, causing Magnus to yelp as bright light suddenly flooded the room.

'*Juliana!*'

But she was already putting on her dressing gown and padding out of the room, calling, 'I'll be back in a minute...'

Magnus grunted, rolled over, and shut his eyes tightly against the dazzling light. Then, seemingly seconds later, he was being shaken awake once again.

'I know you said you didn't want any,' Juliana said, 'but I've brought you tea as well. It's Lemon Verbena, so there's no caffeine. Come on, Magnus, sit up.'

With a growl of frustration, Magnus heaved himself into a sitting position, his eyes sticky with tiredness. Why had he married this impossible woman? At that moment, her beauty, brains and feisty spirit seemed far less appealing than usual, especially in comparison to the prospect of a decent night's sleep.

'Put the light on, Magnus, there's no point sitting in the gloom.'

Obediently, he reached out for the lamp next to him. He knew, from bitter experience, he might as well do what she said: it was the best chance he had of her leaving him alone before dawn.

'Here's your tea,' said Juliana, waiting until Magnus had finished plumping up the pillows behind his back to hand him the steaming mug. 'I left the bag in, just as you like it.'

'Thanks,' Magnus grunted.

Juliana clambered back into the bed beside him, pulled the blankets over herself, and picked up her own mug. 'So,' she said.

'So?'

'Anne-Laure Chevalier.'

'What about her?'

'Oh, don't play dumb, Magnus!'

'I'm not playing *dumb*, I'm playing tired — I *am* tired!'

'I can't stop thinking about that notebook,' Juliana ploughed on. 'I keep picturing it when I close my eyes. I almost wish we still had it.'

'You almost wish —? *What*? You ordered poor Bryn to take it away from the house! You didn't want it near the children, remember?'

'Yes, I know, and I still stand by that, but I don't like the thought of it still being out there. I want to burn it or something.'

'Juliana, it could be important evidence…'

'I know, I know. It's just such a horrid, nasty object, you know? That poor woman. Do you think she knew she was being followed? Do you think she suspected anything? I'd have been terrified out of my wits, if it had been me.'

Magnus said nothing, but these were interesting questions: how much had Anne-Laure known? Bryn now seemed fairly convinced the author of the notebook was the reason she had wanted to move away, and Magnus supposed this did make the most sense. But he wasn't sure he should tell Juliana that. After she had reacted so badly to finding out about the secret meeting concerning Central Square Properties' maintenance charges, he knew he had to be very careful about keeping things from his wife. However, he didn't think it was especially wise to disclose that Bryn had all but confirmed Anne-Laure's stalker had been loitering outside her house at night, and that there was a chance he had been so distraught at the idea of her leaving that he had killed her. No, it wouldn't do Juliana any good at all to know about that.

'She *must* have known,' Juliana said eventually, answering her own question. 'Because he attacked her, didn't he? She had those bruises on her neck and her wrists — I bet that was his handiwork.'

Again, Magnus said nothing, but assuming the author of the notebook wasn't Hilda Underpin, he thought it unlikely his wife was wrong on this count.

'In fact, he was probably that man in the gardens, wasn't he?' Juliana continued. 'The one who tried to give her the ring?'

'I'd forgotten about the ring,' said Magnus, speaking for the first time. 'Although, as Bryn says, we shouldn't rule out a coincidence.'

'Honestly, Magnus, I don't know why you're always so cold and analytical about everything.'

'Well, it is my job, darling…'

'Don't "darling" me! You can't use your calm lawyer voice to convince me this is all okay, because it isn't! I'm worried, Magnus!'

She replaced her cup of tea on the bedside table and drew the blankets more tightly around her body, as though they could offer her some protection. Magnus, meanwhile, peered around at their bedroom, searching for some inspiration as to how to calm her down. It was a large, airy room, and because of Juliana's aversion to big, bright lamps, the light from each of their bedside tables didn't quite reach the far corners of the space, which were shrouded in shadow. Honestly, thought the barrister, taking a sip of his tea, Juliana really did know how to pick her moments: of course she was feeling unnerved, dwelling on the idea of stalkers and murderers in the middle of the night. If they had been sitting on the balcony in the sunshine while having this conversation she wouldn't have felt half so rattled.

'Look, Juliana,' he said, aware he had to tread carefully here: it was more than his life was worth to accuse her outright of being overdramatic. 'I hear what you're saying, I do: the fact that Anne-Laure Chevalier was being followed by this person is worrying enough, and the idea of him attacking and possibly even killing her is downright horrifying. But I'm not sure there's anything to be gained by going over and over it like this. You'll accuse me of being callous again, and perhaps I am, but it's done now — as tragic as it is, Anne-Laure's gone.'

Juliana was silent for a while, and after a few moments Magnus dared to hope that he might have convinced her to try going back to sleep. But then she shook her head.

'*He* hasn't gone, though.'

'Sorry?'

'The stalker — whoever he is — he hasn't gone, has he? He hasn't disappeared just because she's dead. In fact, if he killed her, and if he thinks he's got away with it, he's probably feeling more powerful than ever.'

'What do you mean?'

'I mean, what is it those crime dramas always tell us? That those who have killed once are more likely to do so again? He's totally deranged, Magnus — you only need to take one look at that notebook to see that — so I don't imagine he's just going to stop this behaviour, do you? He's probably picking out his next victim as we speak.'

'Juliana, you're being —'

'Paranoid? Am I? This man lives in our area, Magnus — he probably lives in or around Westminster Square! What if he targets me next? Or worse, what if he targets *Rosanna*?'

Magnus felt as though somebody had just tipped a bucket full of ice down the back of his pyjama shirt: he hadn't considered this. In his mind, the mysterious author of the notebook had been obsessed with Anne-Laure, and Anne-Laure only. But Juliana was right: presumably the man was still out there, somewhere. What if he had already decided on the newest object of his dubious affections? This idea was abhorrent enough, before Magnus even considered the safety of his wife and daughter.

'I hadn't thought of that,' he admitted, rather sheepishly.

'Well you should've.'

Again, she threw off the covers, wriggled out of the bed, and headed towards the window. Then, pulling aside the heavy curtain, she stood staring down into Westminster Square, her arms wrapped around her body in an attempt to keep herself warm.

'Juliana, come on,' said Magnus, wearily. 'What are you doing over there? Come back to bed, you'll get cold.'

But she ignored him, instead asking, 'Do you know what you always say, when I ask you why you want to stay in Westminster Square?'

Magnus rubbed at his eyes: he felt too tired to be quizzed like this. 'I don't know... It's a good area? It's convenient for my work? It's historically-significant and —?'

'You say it's safe,' Juliana interrupted. 'You always tell me, Westminster Square is *safe*.'

'Well it is. Half of that maintenance money I'm so upset about goes towards security.'

Juliana wheeled round. '*How can you say it's safe when someone's been murdered?*' she cried, so loudly that Magnus had to shush her for fear she would wake the children. 'Not to mention the fact that two other people have been burgled in the past few months.'

'First of all, those two burglaries were unsuccessful,' said Magnus. 'And secondly, Anne-Laure wasn't failed by CSP's security system — she died in the Royal West Hotel, not in her own home, so if anyone's to blame for security there it's Edwin Brackenwell.'

'Who?'

'The manager of the Royal West.'

'Oh, for goodness' sake, Magnus!' Juliana turned back to the window. 'Again, you're spectacularly missing the point: I'm not worried about faulty burglar alarms or sleeping doormen or however these things happened. I'm worried because there's a very dangerous man on the loose! He's probably out there right now!'

She gestured at the window, perhaps a little more violently than she had intended, for her knuckles rapped against the glass. Magnus sighed. Seeing her standing there, in her long white nightdress, silhouetted against the large window and framed by the long, dark curtains, he could almost imagine Juliana was part of some Gothic scene; that she was looking down onto a shadowy street on which, at any moment, a Jack the Ripper-like figure would materialise from the mist with a swish of his cloak and a gleam of his knife...

But when Magnus heaved himself from the bed and went to stand beside his wife, the view from the window was exactly the same as it always was at night: Westminster Square was well-lit by old-fashioned streetlights, and the roads, pavements and gardens were completely quiet and still, aside from a cat streaking out from beneath one parked car and disappearing under the next.

'Juliana, there's nothing out there,' said Magnus, wrapping his arms around his wife, both to keep her warm and in an attempt to make her feel safe. 'This is the City of Westminster, remember? Most people are in bed by ten — and if they're not, they're partying until dawn.'

'When do they think Anne-Laure was killed again?' she asked.

'Um, I don't remember, exactly,' lied Magnus, because now she mentioned it, hadn't the medical examiner theorised Anne-Laure had been killed at around two in the morning? 'But listen, it's just not dangerous around here at this time — at any time,' he quickly corrected himself.

'But all of this Anne-Laure business proves it is!' Juliana said, still staring out of the window.

Magnus, feeling this conversation was going round and round in circles, said, 'I don't know what you want me to say, darling. Bryn and I are trying our best to work out what on earth happened to the poor girl, and we've already explained why it's best not to involve the police at this stage, so I'm not sure what else you want me to do about it.'

Juliana, tilting her head a little, so her curly hair tickled his face, said, 'I want you to consider the idea that we wouldn't be having this conversation — that none of this would be anything to worry about — if we lived in the countryside.'

Magnus's arms slipped from her waist as annoyance began to prickle at his insides.

'So that's what this is about, is it?' he said, coldly. 'Of course it is. I don't know why I'm surprised — this is what it's always about, isn't it?'

Juliana, sensing his infuriation, spun around to face him. 'There's no need to be like that — it's perfectly true. The countryside is much safer than the city, that's just a fact.'

'This was a one-off, tragic death, Juliana,' said Magnus. 'It could have happened anywhere.'

'What *nonsense!*' she snapped. 'Anne-Laure Chevalier may have been born in Brighton, but she was a Londoner through and through, even in death. Or are you telling me the countryside is full of girls in designer dresses overdosing on cocaine in expensive hotels?'

'Of course not, don't be silly. I'm just saying, people die everywhere, you can't up and move house every time something unfortunate happens nearby.'

'A murder is more than *something unfortunate*!' cried Juliana. 'A murder is pretty bloody worrying!'

Magnus began to pace the room, suddenly flooded with exasperation. 'You know, you had me there for a moment, Juliana. I honestly believed you were spooked out by the thought of this weirdo creeping around Westminster. But I should've known your theatrics were part of your grander plan to get us out of London. After all, there's not much that scares you, is there?'

'*Theatrics?*' she repeated, her voice rising dangerously. '*Grander plan?*'

'I thought you cared about the case for its own sake, for Anne-Laure's sake.'

'I do!'

'But you're just using it as yet more leverage to try and get us to leave Westminster Square.'

'So what if I am?' she fired back. 'I can be simultaneously concerned about the case and worried for my family, can't I?'

'*Are* you worried?' asked Magnus. 'Or are you just pretending to be, to convince me it's too dangerous to live in the middle of London anymore?'

'How dare you!' she shouted. 'How can you think I would be so conniving? Of course I'm worried — we're probably living in the same neighbourhood as a cold-blooded killer! And I don't know about you, Magnus, but when I consider where we should live, I prioritise the safety of Rosanna and Lee above whether it's a *good area* or *convenient for your work* or —'

'You're twisting my words,' Magnus growled. 'That's not what I meant, and you know it. Of course the wellbeing of our children is my top priority.'

'Then allow them a proper childhood!' Juliana yelled. 'Let them grow up where it's green, and the air is fresh, and they can ride their bikes on the roads, and stay out all day without me worrying that something terrible is going to happen to them!' She drew a shuddering breath. 'You might think Anne-Laure Chevalier's death is merely *something unfortunate* that happened nearby, but I see it as a wake-up call, Magnus: it's time to get our children out of this corrupt, dangerous, *disgusting* city, before it destroys them like it destroyed that poor girl.'

'Juliana…'

'No,' she said, batting away his attempts to placate her. 'No. I've had enough, Magnus. I want to get Rosanna and Lee out of here, and if you won't come with us…' She swallowed. 'If you don't come with us, I'll just have to do it myself.'

For the second time that evening, Magnus felt as though something extremely cold was trickling down his spine. 'What did you say?'

'You heard me: I'll do it myself.'

Magnus stared at her, unable to quite believe what she was saying — what she was implying.

'I want to go to sleep now,' said Juliana. 'We can talk about this in the morning.'

'*What?*' demanded Magnus. 'You can't just drop that on me, and then decide to go to sleep!'

'Why not? I've said all I have to say — in fact, I've been saying it for years, if only you'd have listened.'

She began to head towards the door.

'Where are you going?' Magnus called.

'I'm going to check on the children. I want to make sure we didn't wake them up with our shouting. Then I'll sleep in the spare room.'

'There's no need for — Juliana? *Juliana!*'

But she had already gone, closing the door behind her with a little more force than was strictly necessary. Magnus gaped at it, wondering what on earth had just happened. Was he in fact still asleep, and this was some awful dream? He and Juliana had always squabbled; long ago, he had learned these disagreements were part and parcel of being married to such a fiery woman. But any ill-feeling between them always blew over quickly; their arguments were both swift to escalate and to dissolve. But this — this was different. In saying she was prepared to move the children to the countryside without him, it sounded as though she had been giving their marriage some serious thought, and had found it wanting. Magnus had no idea what to make of this. On the one hand, it was a complete shock, the idea that — from Juliana's perspective at least — things were that bad between them. And it was truly unnerving to even contemplate a life without her and the children. But then again, Magnus was angry, because however much Juliana insisted to the contrary, she'd had him convinced she was genuinely scared about Anne-Laure's stalker, when it was far more likely she was using the shadowy figure as just another point on her long list of reasons why they should move away from Westminster Square. And so Magnus couldn't be sure whether this latest development — this ultimatum she had presented to him — was genuine, and something he should truly be worried about, or whether it was just another of her ploys to get her own way.

Sighing, he shuffled back towards the bed and pulled the covers over himself once more. It was much colder beneath the blankets without Juliana next to him, and his mind was so busy going over the scene they'd just had, he couldn't get back to sleep, in spite of how tired he was, and the lateness of the hour. He tossed and turned for a long time, rehashing what she had said, and how he should have responded, and debating with himself whether he should go into the spare room, wake her up, and continue having this out with her out right now.

Eventually, Magnus's thoughts turned back to Anne-Laure Chevalier, and what he and Juliana had talked about before their discussion had turned so ugly. Now he dwelt on it, he had to admit that his wife, however irrational she could be about other matters, had a point about Anne-Laure's killer. Magnus supposed, until now, he had always felt a little removed from the Anne-Laure Chevalier case, as though it were a diverting television drama, rather than a real crime that had happened on his doorstep. Even though he lived in Westminster Square, even though the list of suspects he and Bryn had compiled was made up of neighbours, even friends, because Magnus had never knowingly met Anne-Laure, he had never really thought her fate would have much effect on his life — at least, not in any significant way. But now Juliana had reminded him that it was real, and it was here — right in the heart of London — that Anne-Laure had lived and died. Therefore, if Bryn was right, and she had been killed deliberately, Magnus had to conclude that somewhere around Westminster Square lurked an extremely dangerous person; someone who thought he had got away with murder.

CHAPTER TWENTY-EIGHT

After helping Agnes Chambers clear out the little house in the Mews, it took Bryn a full day to pluck up the courage to phone Darren Dodge, the journalist from *The Dawn Reporter* Anne-Laure had intended to meet the day after her death. The police constable had always been rather wary of the media; he knew, from TV dramas and crime novels more than real life experience, that policemen and journalists didn't always get along, as often their agendas were completely at odds. He was also still rather haunted by the memory of the pushy Ricky Nicholls from the same paper, who had almost caused a riot outside the Royal West Hotel, and prompted Bryn to feel so out of his depth that Magnus — then a complete stranger — had had to rescue him.

Still, in spite of his misgivings about the press, in the end Bryn could not allow a potentially significant lead like this to grow cold, and so when the station was quiet the following lunchtime, he dialled the number that he had found in Anne-Laure Chevalier's address book.

'Dodger here, what can I do you for?'

Bryn paused, stumped by both the familiar greeting and the gravelly, East London accent, which sounded rather more as though it belonged to a wheeler-dealer than a journalist. *Although perhaps they aren't dissimilar figures*, he thought to himself.

'Erm, hello,' he said. 'Is that Mr Darren Dodge of *The Dawn Reporter*?'

'Might be, might be,' said the other man. 'Depends who's asking, don't it?'

'My name is Constable Bryn Summers of the Victoria Police Station.'

This time it was Darren Dodge's turn to hesitate. 'A copper, eh?' he said at last. Then, in a slightly more obliging tone, he asked, 'How can I help you, Constable?'

'I wanted to talk to you about a meeting you were due to have with a woman a few months ago...' Bryn began, and then trailed off, wondering what name — if any — Anne-Laure had given this man.

'You're going to have to be a bit more specific than that, mate,' said Dodge. 'I have a lot of meetings with a lot of women, if you know what I mean...'

Bryn could practically hear the cheeky wink that accompanied this statement. Still not sure how to proceed with regard to Anne-Laure's name, the policeman told Dodge the date he had been due to meet her.

'Hold on, hold on, I'll have a look through my diary,' said the journalist, and there followed a great deal of rustling on the other end of the line. 'Two o'clock did you say? That was Annie, that was. Only she didn't turn up, did she?'

'No, I don't suppose so,' said Bryn, reflecting that it would have been most surprising if she had. 'Mr Dodge, I wonder if I could have a word with you in person about this meeting?'

'What meeting? Like I said, she stood me up, the silly cow. I wasn't happy about that, Constable — I'm a busy man, you know.'

'I'm sure you are,' said Bryn, 'but perhaps I could have a few minutes of your time this week to discuss any... *interaction* you might have had with Anne — I mean, with this Annie person?'

'Do I have a choice in the matter?' grumbled Dodge.

'No, not really,' said Bryn, reflecting that there was no need for the journalist to be made aware of the fact he wasn't on official police business. Then, feeling a little more confident, he continued, 'I'll drop round at *The Dawn Reporter* office tomorrow lunchtime, shall I?'

★ ★ ★ ★

Although he felt he had conducted himself fairly well during the phone call, Bryn nevertheless invited Magnus along to the meeting with Darren Dodge. It made Bryn feel better to know that someone as calm and firm as Magnus would have his back during the encounter, in case the journalist proved to be as slippery as Bryn suspected he would.

But Magnus seemed out of sorts when they met at Victoria Station the following day. He looked pale and strained, and his eyes were puffy, as though he hadn't slept well. Bryn, who had never seen Magnus looking anything less than cheerful and well-rested, cautiously asked after his health, and the barrister quickly assured him that everything was fine. Not wanting to pry any further — for although they were now friends, they weren't exactly close confidantes — Bryn said nothing more, but as they caught the District Line to Blackfriars Underground Station he did keep casting sidelong glances in Magnus' direction, hoping he was all right.

The offices of *The Dawn Reporter*, like those of many other major publications, were on Fleet Street, which was situated just at the boundary of the City of Westminster, at the site of the London Wall. As Magnus and Bryn walked between the tall, tightly-packed buildings, and the iconic dome of St. Paul's Cathedral loomed just ahead, the policeman asked, 'Has Fleet Street always been associated with journalism?'

'It's certainly always had a link to printing and publishing,' said Magnus. 'If I remember rightly, several printing companies set up here during the sixteenth century, mainly publishing court documents, but also books and plays — don't forget, that was Shakespeare's time.

'The newspapers started to set up here around two hundred years later, in the 1700s,' Magnus continued, 'and production really expanded with the abolishment of the "newspaper tax" in 1855, which led to papers becoming far cheaper — "the penny press" — and the consolidation of many smaller newspapers into a few nationally important ones. So by the beginning of this century, Fleet Street and the surrounding areas were completely dominated by the national press and related industries.'

'You say "were",' noted Bryn. 'What happened?'

Magnus shrugged. 'Around ten years ago or so, a few major publications moved their enterprises to cheaper parts of London — after all, we are right in the heart of the city here, and office space doesn't come cheap. But it's a shame, because Fleet Street is practically synonymous with the British Press. I'm no fan of *The Dawn Reporter,* but I'm pleased at least some of our major so-called newspapers are still based here. Ah, speaking of...'

They had reached a modern-looking building, the mirrored windows of which gave it an anonymous, almost unfriendly appearance. Beside the main entrance was a modest brass plaque reading: *The Dawn Reporter.*

'Here we go,' said Magnus, who seemed a little cheerier once Bryn had pressed the buzzer, introduced them, and the door had clicked open. 'Behind enemy lines we go...'

As with the architecture outside, the newspaper headquarters had a contemporary feel, which was at odds with its historic setting. A receptionist led them into a bright and largely open-plan space, in which scores of journalists were tapping away at computer keyboards, and then indicated they should head towards the offices at the edge of the room. Here, the inhabitants were divided from their colleagues by frosted glass partitions. After she had knocked at the central office, been greeted by a terse 'Yeah?' from within, and poked her head around the door, Magnus and Bryn followed the receptionist into what turned out to be a small, sparse room dominated by a metal desk and piles of paperwork.

Darren Dodge was making notes on a document when they entered, frowning down at it as he turned slowly from side to side in his swivel chair. He was a short and rather squat man who looked to be in his midforties, and had thinning dark hair and an unshaven chin. The buttons of his shirt, which was very crumpled, were straining against his large paunch, and his tie was loose and hanging askew. On first impression, he was a dishevelled, almost sad figure, although Bryn could not help but notice that, as Dodge looked up at them, his dark eyes were keen and alert.

'Constable Bryn Summers, I presume?' he said, tucking his pen behind his ear and offering his hand to Magnus.

'Actually, that would be me,' cut in Bryn, stepping forward to clasp the journalist's rather clammy hand.

Darren Dodge's eyes seemed to glitter as he took in Bryn's youthful appearance; evidently, he thought the policeman was an easy target, and Bryn wasn't sure he was mistaken in that regard.

'And I'm Magnus Walterson, a lawyer,' said Magnus, in his best barrister voice.

Dodge's expression suddenly soured: apparently, journalists thought as little of lawyers as they did of the police.

'Have a seat, gentlemen,' he said, giving a small and mocking bow as he indicated the plastic chairs in front of his messy desk. 'Would you like a coffee or something?'

After Bryn had accepted this offer and Magnus had declined, the receptionist was dispatched with the coffee order, and Dodge surveyed his visitors over his clasped, stubby fingers.

'Why the lawyer? What's going on here?'

'We'll ask the questions, Mr Dodge,' said Bryn, surprising himself with his own assertiveness.

Dodge grinned, revealing a large gap between his two front teeth. 'You're making me curious, that's all. I'd completely forgotten about that Annie woman until you called me yesterday, and now I can't stop thinking about her. You shouldn't make a journalist curious, you know,' he added, shaking his finger at them as though they were disobedient children.

Bryn resented being cautioned in this way, but Dodge's advice was more timely than even he knew. They were playing a risky game here: the journalist, whether he knew it or not, potentially had some very useful information about Anne-Laure Chevalier; however, if their questioning piqued his interest too much, Dodge might decide to start doing his own investigation, and the last thing Bryn needed was *The Dawn Reporter* sniffing around. No, he had to tread very carefully here.

'We'd like to talk to you about the contact you had with this woman, Annie,' began Bryn.

'I don't know what to tell you, other than I'm afraid you've wasted your time,' cut in Dodge. 'I never met her. Like I told you on the phone, she never showed up to that meeting. Pretty blooming rude of her if you ask me...'

Neither Bryn nor Magnus reacted to this outwardly, but in Bryn's mind's eye he pictured Anne-Laure's body sprawled over the sofa in the Royal West Hotel that very same day.

'Let's rewind a bit,' he decided, determined to break through Dodge's tough and slightly defensive demeanour. 'What was the purpose of this meeting? What were you due to discuss?'

Dodge shrugged. 'I dunno. She was the one who set it up, you'll have to ask her.'

It was strange, Bryn thought, hearing Anne-Laure Chevalier being referred to in the present tense. But of course, if they had never actually met, Dodge would have no way of knowing that the woman he had spoken to on the phone was the same person whose image had been splashed over the papers — including his own — a few days' later. This, the policeman thought, was something of a relief, and he made a mental note to only speak about Anne-Laure as though she were alive.

'So she called you, did she?'

'Yeah, she did.'

'And what did she say, exactly?'

Dodge's gaze roved over Bryn's uniform, and the policeman had the impression he was being sized up. Eventually, however, the journalist appeared to decide not to play games — at least, not for the moment.

'She told me she had a story for *The Dawn Reporter* — a big one. I pressed her for details, but she didn't want to say too much on the phone. So that's why we agreed to meet in person.'

'Did she give you a surname?'

'Nah, she just said I should call her Annie.'

'And you didn't ask for one?'

'Why would I? Most of our sources don't want to be named, especially those of them what've grassed up their neighbours and friends and whatnot. I assume this Annie girl was the same.'

Before Bryn could pursue this point, the receptionist re-entered carrying two small, polystyrene cups. After Bryn had taken a sip from the one she handed to him, he concluded that this was one of the worst coffees he had ever had, and scowled down at the lukewarm concoction, which he now saw was filled with undissolved instant coffee granules and clumps of powdered milk. Dodge, on the other hand, threw back his drink as though he were downing a shot in a bar, and smacked his lips together, apparently having greatly enjoyed the so-called coffee.

'So, Annie,' said Bryn, sliding his polystyrene cup onto a corner of the desk unoccupied by paperwork, 'what did she sound like on the phone?'

'What do you mean?'

'What sort of person do you think she was?'

'I dunno, do I? Young, kind of posh...'

'What sort of mood was she in?' asked Bryn.

'What?'

'I mean, did she sound distressed at all? Upset?'

Dodge considered this. 'Not really, no. She sounded... determined. Yeah, that's the word. Sure of herself. I thought she meant business, by the way she was speaking. That's why I was surprised when she didn't show up.'

'So, just to be clear, this Annie told you she had a story specifically for *The Dawn Reporter*?' said Bryn.

'For *me*,' interrupted Dodge, 'specifically for me.'

'Why was that, do you think?'

'I know why it was: I'm the best in the business, aren't I?'

'What do you mean? You're the best at what?'

Dodge's eyes gleamed once again. 'At stirring up a scandal. If you look at all the juiciest headlines of the last few years, I'm behind them. Do you remember the divorce of Carly and Emilio, that golden Hollywood couple? I was the one who tracked down the nanny, I was the one who got her to publicly admit to having an affair with him. And remember old Jonathan Crabb, the politician? It was me who had that room bugged, I was the one who recorded him buying all those drugs.'

Bryn remembered both of these scandals only too well, and wasn't sure he approved of Dodge revelling in the destruction of people's personal and professional lives for his own — and the public's — entertainment. Nevertheless, he pushed his unease aside, and instead asked, 'So, you think Annie picked you because she had an especially scandalous story she wanted to sell to *The Dawn Reporter?*'

'That's what she led me to believe, yeah.'

'But you have no idea what it was?' Bryn allowed just a hint of scepticism to creep into his tone.

'I wish I did. But I've been going over and over it since you called yesterday, and she didn't give much away. Although I guess if the police are involved it has to be something pretty exciting…'

His voice rose expectantly, as though he hoped Bryn would drop him a crumb or two, but the policeman ignored him.

'Can you remember exactly what she said during the call?' he asked.

Dodge scratched at his unshaven chin as he considered this. 'She opened by telling me she had a big story, and I of course asked what it was. But she didn't want to tell me over the phone, which isn't unusual, by the way. Either she would've been afraid I'd take her information and then not cough up any cash for it —' He said this in such a matter-of-fact way that Bryn wondered whether this had been known to happen before at *The Dawn Reporter*. 'Or else there's a chance she wasn't able to talk, because she was afraid of being overheard, or someone was listening in — you'd be surprised how many phones are tapped these days.

'Anyway, I pushed her a bit, she pushed back, and eventually she said something like, "*It's a huge story involving people in high places. The consequences of you publishing it will be huge. The fallout will keep your paper going for days, maybe months.*" So, you can see why I was pretty interested to meet her.'

Bryn sat back in his seat: what on earth had Anne-Laure discovered?

'What do you think she was talking about?' he asked. 'What were you expecting her to tell you that day?'

Again, Dodge thought about this for a few moments. 'My first thought was that she was someone's mistress. She sounded young, she had a husky, sexy voice... I assumed she'd seduced some politician or celebrity or member of the royal family and wanted to shout about it for a bit of money and attention. But then, as I said, her manner was firm, almost business-like, and a sex scandal like that wouldn't have *huge* consequences, unless it was someone really, really high-up. It wouldn't keep us going for *months*. So I wonder if she'd stumbled across something else; a big political cover-up, perhaps, or large-scale corporate fraud...'

He exhaled, and his expression turned hungry, as though he were desperate for some clue as to what Anne-Laure had discovered. For once, Bryn found himself sympathising with the journalist.

'You must have *some* idea yourself, seeing as you're here?' went on Dodge.

But Bryn, once more, refused to indulge him. 'So she told you about this big story she had, and that got your attention and then, what, you agreed to meet?'

'Yeah, but there was a bit of debate about money first, if I remember rightly. She was keen to know how much *The Dawn Reporter* would pay for her information — very keen, actually. That's another reason I wonder whether she was some kind of businesswoman: she was especially preoccupied with money, and she weren't no pushover, let me tell you.'

'And what did you tell her about the kind of reimbursement she could expect?'

'What could I tell her, without knowing what she was going to tell me? All I could say was that, as far as *The Dawn Reporter* is concerned, we pay big money for big stories and small money for small stories. It's as simple as that.'

'And did she seem satisfied with your response?'

'Yeah, I think she was. As I said, I believed her when she said she had this great scoop for us. We get a lot of jokers and chancers calling us, as you'd imagine, so you learn to tell pretty quickly who's having you on and who's the real deal. In fact, it wasn't until she stood me up I even considered she was a prankster.'

Bryn looked up from his notebook, on which he had been scribbling a few phrases, and wondered whether they had exhausted Darren Dodge as a source of information. He didn't trust the journalist one inch, but he also didn't think Dodge was deliberately withholding much. So was there anything more to press him on? As though to silently ask this question, the policeman glanced at Magnus, who he realised hadn't spoken for the entirety of this meeting, other than to refuse a coffee.

'When did this phone call take place, Mr Dodge?' the barrister asked quietly. 'Can you remember the date?'

'Blimey, I dunno. It was a couple of months ago now. I don't write down stuff like that.'

'Perhaps you can remember how much time elapsed between the day of the phone call and when you were due to meet.'

'Ah, that I can remember,' said Dodge. 'It was about a week or so, because —' His eyes suddenly widened. 'I've just remembered — she said she needed some time to gather "evidence" — that's what she told me. She said it was more than a theory, this thing she was presenting me with: she had physical proof.'

'What proof?' asked Bryn at once.

'I've no idea,' said Dodge. 'And it wasn't as though I even asked her for that. Mostly, my sources come to me with tip-offs and I do the rest of the digging myself. But no, Annie said she had something to show me, she just needed to get hold of it first. She probably thought she would get more money out of us that way, and she wouldn't have been wrong.'

'And you've no idea what it was?'

'None. Could've been anything, couldn't it? Some dodgy invoices, some saucy photographs, a bloody knife... Like I told you, she wasn't giving anything away until I guaranteed her the money. Sensible girl.'

He looked half-impressed, half-regretful. Bryn closed his notebook.

'Well, thank you for your time today, Mr Dodge,' he said. 'You've been very helpful. And perhaps, if you do remember anything else about this Annie woman and the conversation you had with her, perhaps you could get in touch? It's probably best to contact my colleague here,' he added, as Magnus handed the journalist a business card.

Dodge stared at the card, and then between Magnus and Bryn.

'Woah, woah, is that it?' he demanded. 'Is that all you're giving me?'

'Excuse me?' said Bryn.

'I was under the impression this would be a mutual exchange of information,' said Dodge. 'You know, I scratch your back, you scratch mine? I want to know what *you* know about this woman.'

Bryn hesitated, unsure how to counter this, but Magnus said smoothly, 'You forget we are not journalists, Mr Dodge. I'm sure it works that way with your fellow reporters, but this is police work, and as such we are not obliged to tell you anything at all.'

'Yeah, but even so,' began Dodge, looking sour. 'Give me a hint, won't you? Who is she? What's she done? I'm assuming young Annie must've caused a bit of a stink…'

'Why do you say that?' asked Bryn.

'Because I've got a copper and a lawyer knocking at my door and asking questions about her, that's why!' laughed Dodge. 'If I had to guess, I'd say you wanted to question Annie about her connection to something large and criminal, only someone offered her money to keep quiet — more money than even *The Dawn Reporter* would've given her. That's why she didn't bother turning up to our meeting. Unless she's left the country, of course. Yeah, maybe she's done a bunk!'

He scrutinised their faces for a reaction.

'Good afternoon, Mr Dodge,' said Magnus, standing up and offering his hand.

'I'll do a little digging, shall I?' Dodge called, after Bryn too had grasped his stubby, ink-stained fingers. 'I'll see what I can find out about it?'

He was trying to goad them into staying; evidently, he hoped that if they feared he was close to uncovering the truth, they would sit back down, try to reason with him, and in doing so reveal more than they intended. But Bryn was fairly sure Darren Dodge was bluffing. If he hadn't already linked Annie from the phone to Anne-Laure Chevalier, there was little chance he was going to now, especially as the glamorous party girl's death was old news. It was also highly convenient that Dodge was under misconception that the woman he had spoken to was still alive.

'You do that,' said Magnus, blithely. 'And good luck with your investigation, Mr Dodge. We'll be in touch if we need to ask you any more questions.'

CHAPTER TWENTY-NINE

In the days that followed the meeting with Darren Dodge of *The Dawn Reporter*, Bryn could not help but feel a little disheartened about the lack of progress he and Magnus were making with the Anne-Laure Chevalier case. Before they had gone to talk to the journalist, things had been clearer: in spite of being a highly disturbing object, the discovery of the notebook had felt like a positive step, especially after Magnus had pointed out that it gave them both motivation for Anne-Laure's murder and a better profile of her killer. But now the conversation with Darren Dodge had thrown Bryn, because it seemed to contradict the idea that Anne-Laure had died at the hands of an obsessive, unhinged stalker. If the journalist were to be believed, it sounded more like Anne-Laure had stumbled across some dangerous information, tried to make a bit of money from it by going to the papers, and had subsequently been found out and permanently silenced.

At the moment, Bryn wanted nothing more than to dissect these two options with Magnus, who had had to dash back to work immediately after their meeting with Darren Dodge. But the barrister had been rather elusive of late, and therefore Bryn had been forced to go over and over the matter in his own head, and was starting to feel a little loopy as a result. Indeed, a few lunchtimes after the one he had spent in Fleet Street, the young police constable found himself wandering aimlessly around Westminster Square in the hope that if he walked around the area in which Anne-Laure had lived enough times, he might finally understand how and why she had died. He was also half-hoping he might run into Magnus: Bryn was reluctant to bother his friend when the barrister clearly had a lot on his plate, but he didn't think there was anything wrong with hanging around the Square on the off-chance they might bump into one another.

This lunchtime, however, all was quiet, and after Bryn had done an entire lap of Westminster Square he came to a halt outside one of the gardens, feeling a little overheated from the effort of walking under the glare of the midday sun. He noticed the gate a few yards ahead of him had been left slightly ajar, presumably by the young woman he could see over the top of the flowerbed, who was sitting on a bench with a newspaper. Bryn was just about to pull the gate closed, so that Hilda Underpin couldn't hobble out from behind a bush and start berating everyone in sight, when he paused: this was the garden in which Juliana had found the offending notebook.

As far as Bryn had gathered, Magnus's wife had headed straight back to the house with the vile object, and the policeman now wondered whether there had been anything else buried in that flowerbed — or indeed, nearby. He had not forgotten about the ring initialled *A.C.* that he had found in this very same garden, nor that this had been the location of a violent argument between Anne-Laure and a shadowy man. So, checking his watch to confirm he still had half an hour left of his lunchbreak, he pushed open the gate and proceeded into the garden, immediately feeling sniffly and tingly-eyed as he stepped amongst the flowers.

It only took Bryn a few moments to work out where Juliana had discovered the notebook, for the flowerbed at the opposite end of the garden looked rather sad in comparison to its pristine neighbours. It was filled with purple, white and yellow blooms Bryn thought might have been pansies, only they looked very bedraggled, as though the earth around them had been recently disturbed. Wondering if there might be anything else there that hadn't been found, he made his way towards it, past the woman with the newspaper, and then crouched down by the edge of the flowerbed, his nose beginning to tickle as he sensed the pollen in the air.

Now he was here, he felt a little foolish, peering down at some dishevelled pansies as though they might be able to help him solve a crime. And it was worse still when he began to sneeze in quick succession, for it felt as though the garden wanted him out of its gates as quickly as possible.

But after casting a self-conscious look over his shoulder, and discovering his companion had still not looked up from her newspaper, Bryn pulled his truncheon from his utility belt and began to use it as a makeshift spade.

After about five minutes of digging in this manner, Bryn's eyes were streaming, he had sneezed at least two dozen times, and his legs were aching from crouching on the balls of his feet for so long. He had made a lot of mess, but found absolutely nothing buried in the flowerbed, save for a few stones and a particularly fat earthworm. Then, just as he was trying to keep his balance through yet another sneezing fit, somebody spoke.

'Um, excuse me?'

Bryn gave a start. The woman who had been sitting on the bench with her newspaper was now standing above him, looking understandably puzzled by what he was up to. Bryn, feeling rather embarrassed to have been caught scrabbling around in the dirt in his police uniform, leapt to his feet. Only this made him feel still more self-conscious, because he now saw that the young woman was extremely pretty: she had shiny dark hair, a peaches-and-cream complexion, and bright blue eyes that were looking at him in some concern.

'Erm, I was just —' Bryn began, before realising he had no idea how to explain what he had been doing. 'I was just — *atishoo!*'

'Do you have hay fever?' she asked, reaching into her handbag. 'Here, have these.'

She produced a packet of tissues. For a moment, pride stopped Bryn from accepting them, but she pressed them into his hand, and then he reasoned he would probably make a better impression on this attractive woman if he wasn't sneezing and spluttering all over the place.

'Thanks,' he murmured, wiping at his streaming nose.

'Hold on,' she said, returning to her handbag, 'I think I have — *aha!*'

This time, she pulled out a half-empty packet of pills.

'You probably shouldn't — *atishoo!* — offer drugs to a policeman,' Bryn jokingly advised her.

'They're antihistamine tablets!' she laughed. 'They're good, honestly. Take one, and you'll see.'

As they looked legitimate enough, Bryn did so. Then he asked, 'Why do you have — *atishoo!* — antihistamine tablets in your bag?'

'Oh, I get hay fever too,' she said. 'It's not as bad as yours seems to be, but I often have to take one of those in the morning, because I work with plants and flowers all day.'

'You're a gardener?'

'A florist. And I must say, I'm not entirely sure what you're doing with that flowerbed…'

'Oh,' said Bryn, 'I wasn't really — *atishoo!* — gardening, I was just — Hold on,' he said, interrupting himself. 'Do you work with Juliana Walterson? Are you Daisy?'

She looked startled and then — Bryn was pleased to see — rather impressed.

'How do you know that?'

'I'm a friend of Magnus',' he said. 'I've heard him and Juliana talk about you.'

'In a good way, I hope.'

'Oh yes,' Bryn assured her quickly, 'all good.' Although inwardly, he wished the Waltersons had prepared him for quite how pretty she would be; he currently felt even more awkward and tongue-tied than usual.

'I'm afraid I don't know who you are,' said Daisy, looking up at him, her head slightly tilted to one side.

'Oh!' he said. 'Police Constable Bryn Summers. I mean —' He realised this sounded formal and foolish. 'I mean, just Bryn.'

'Hello, Just Bryn,' she said, her cheeks dimpling as she smiled. 'Daisy Fenway, pleased to meet you.'

Automatically, he held out his hand, but just in time he remembered it was rather dirty from his digging, and snatched it back. She laughed, and then he laughed too, and for a moment they simply stood there, smiling at one another. Bryn knew he should probably say something, but he was afraid to open his mouth: the antihistamine tablet seemed to be taking effect already, but he was terrified of accidentally sneezing on her.

After a short time, Daisy turned back towards the bench, and for a few heart-sinking seconds Bryn thought their little interaction was over. But then, over her shoulder, she asked, 'So how do you know Magnus?' and Bryn almost tripped over his own feet in his eagerness to follow her.

'We're doing some work together on neighbourhood security,' Bryn said as he sat down next to her on the bench, having decided it would be best to tell her their official cover story. 'There have been a couple of break-ins around Westminster Square recently, and—'

'Oh, like at Winnie's!' she said. Then, colouring a little, she continued, 'I mean, at Dame Winifred's. She makes me call her "Winnie"...'

'I forgot you were friends,' Bryn admitted.

'Hm,' said Daisy, her smile faltering.

'Or you're *not* friends?'

'I suppose we are,' she said. 'But really, I think I'm just a replacement for that poor woman who died. You know, Anne-Laure Chevalier?'

'Oh, yes,' said Bryn, after pretending to search his memory for the name.

'Winn— I mean, Dame Winifred — was friends with her. Well, not friends, exactly, she was a kind of benefactor figure to Anne-Laure, I guess. She was completely distraught by her death, and I think she likes having me around to distract her from her grief.'

'Mm,' said Bryn, thinking Daisy would be a very pleasant distraction from anything. Then, realising he was staring at her, he cleared his throat and asked, 'It's not really fair you should have to play second fiddle to someone who's... Well, someone who's not around anymore.'

'I'm not really bothered by that,' said Daisy. 'It's more that Dame Winifred is a bit... *intrusive*.' She was looking uncomfortable now. 'She spends most of her time asking me questions.'

'What sort of questions?'

'Oh, all sorts. How long do I want to stay in London, do my parents miss me, what are my hopes for the future, that sort of thing. And she asks me some quite personal stuff too, like —' She was blushing now. 'Like, what type of men I find attractive, and how many boyfriends have I had, and do I have a boyfriend now...'

Do you? Bryn wondered at once, although fortunately he refrained from expressing this aloud.

'I think she just wants to get to know me,' said Daisy, 'and I feel a bit guilty for talking about her like this when she really has been so kind to me. But it's a bit much, you know? I talk to my friends about that stuff, not middle-aged women I hardly know.'

'Mm,' said Bryn again, wondering whether the type of men Daisy found attractive included gangly, red-headed policemen, and concluding it was probably unlikely.

'The trouble is, I feel a bit indebted to her,' continued Daisy. 'Lately, I've been wanting to keep my distance, but she has a way of reeling me in. Like, the other week, she asked me to fill in as a waitress at this party — Magnus was there, actually — which was fine, but then this sheikh that lives around here, he tried… Well, he became a bit handsy.'

'Sheikh Hazim bin Lahab?' said Bryn sharply, suddenly snapping out of his dreamy mood as he was flooded instead with the urge to go and throttle the man — not that he would be able to find Hazim's neck under all that flab.

'Yeah, that's him,' said Daisy, looking miserable. 'So anyway, after that, I didn't want to help out with any more parties —'

'Understandable.'

'But then the other day, Winnie — I mean, Dame Winifred — asked me to do some more waitressing, this time at a dinner she was hosting for her biggest donors. And because Sheikh what's-his-name was going to be there, I said I didn't want to do it. But she wasn't very happy about that. She actually got a little bit upset, saying she felt let down, and weren't we friends anymore, that sort of thing. Anyway, in the end, I felt so bad I agreed to do it, and it was fine, really. I think she must've told him off, because he didn't go near me all night. But I felt a bit, I don't know, a bit *pressured*, does that make sense?'

Bryn nodded, his brow furrowed. As much as he believed Daisy, he was surprised to hear Dame Winifred had tried to guilt-trip her in this way. Furthermore, the notion that the aristocrat was having secret dinners for her biggest donors was news to him, and he wondered whether Magnus knew anything about this.

'Does she hold these private dinner parties fairly regularly, do you think?' he asked Daisy.

'Every couple of months, I reckon.' Then, perhaps sensing his suspicion, she said quickly, 'Oh, I don't think there's anything dodgy going on! Dame Winifred just wants to schmooze those rich men into giving more money to her charities. I shouldn't have said anything, really, because you mustn't think badly of her. She means well. I just don't particularly enjoy waitressing, that's all. I didn't leave Kent just to pour wine for old bankers. I'm actually quite smart, especially with numbers. I know I only work in a flower shop, but I do all the accounting, and someday I hope to have a business of my own...'

She's perfect, thought Bryn, who had talked to very few women in London, and had certainly not encountered anyone even half as appealing as Daisy. His companion, however, seemed to mistake his enraptured silence for boredom, and said, 'I'm so sorry, I don't know why I'm telling you all of this, we've only just met! I should let you get back to your...' She wrinkled her nose. 'Your gardening?'

'Oh, don't worry about that,' said Bryn, who at that precise moment had absolutely no idea why he had been digging up the flowerbed. He dared to shift a little closer to her on the bench and then, desperate to prolong their conversation in any way he could, asked, 'So where did you grow up in Kent? Are you from the same place as Juliana?'

Prompted by his questions, she began to tell him a little more about herself. Over the next few minutes Bryn learned that Daisy's father was the gardener at Juliana's family estate, and that although she was from a fairly modest background, her parents had sent her to a top girls' school in Tunbridge Wells.

'Which I hated,' said Daisy. 'It was so competitive, so ruthless, and I'm afraid I failed almost everything apart from maths. But nevertheless, my parents wanted me to move to London and "make something of myself". I'm not sure working in a flower shop was exactly what they had in mind...'

'Well, it's like you said, isn't it?' Bryn remembered. 'It's all training for when you have your own business someday.'

She looked pleased he had been listening so carefully, and then asked, 'And what about you, Bryn? I'm assuming you're from Wales?'

He grinned. 'What gave me away?'

In turn, he told her how he had left his home village just outside of Aberystwyth after dropping out of his Electrical Engineering college course and deciding he wanted to be a policeman. He explained how he had moved to Cardiff for his training, and was newly qualified when he had been transferred to London for his probationary period just over six months ago.

'So it's been a big change, getting used to all of this,' said Bryn, gesturing around. Then, realising he was merely pointing to a few rose bushes, he added, 'I mean, to the city as a whole.'

'Oh, I know what you mean,' said Daisy. 'London's just so big and —'

'So dirty,' said Bryn.

'And everyone's so busy —'

'And everyone *thinks* they're so important —'

'So sometimes you feel — you feel —'

She couldn't think of the word, but Bryn could: '— and it makes you feel a bit *lost*.'

Daisy glanced up at him, her expression serious. 'Yes,' she said, 'that's exactly it.'

They held one another's gaze, and this time there was a little more to their shared look; Bryn now felt absolutely certain that — in addition to being a very good-looking girl — Daisy was a kindred spirit; another small-town soul trying to keep up with life in the big city.

They were sitting very close on the bench now; one of his knees was touching hers, and he could see every individual freckle on her nose. The sun was warm overhead, and the air was thick with the fragrance of roses (some dim part of Bryn's brain registered that he had finally stopped sneezing). It was, he knew, a moment he couldn't let pass.

'Daisy,' he said, without really knowing how he was going to proceed.

'Yes?'

'I wonder, would you —?'

But before he could continue, there came the sound of someone loudly clearing their throat. For a moment, Bryn imagined it was Hilda Underpin, and was sorely tempted to arrest her on the spot, and decide what to charge her with later — presumably "interruption of a potentially romantic moment" was not a crime, although it should've been. But, to his surprise and annoyance, when he turned around it was Magnus who was peering over the railings of the garden, and he looked amused.

'Sorry to interrupt,' called the barrister. 'It's just —'

But Daisy had leapt to her feet. 'Oh no!' she cried. 'I was supposed to be back at The Station Garden ten minutes ago, so Juliana could go to lunch!'

'Yes, she's due to meet me now. I rarely get any free time during the day to meet her,' continued Magnus, 'so I told her I'd see if I could find you whilst she held the fort at the shop.'

'I'm *so* sorry, Mr Walterson!' gasped Daisy, swinging her handbag over her arm and folding up her newspaper.

'Not to worry.'

'I completely lost track of time...'

'Clearly,' smirked Magnus.

Daisy looked rather pink as she glanced between Magnus and Bryn. Then, whistling, the barrister pretended to study something interesting in the sky.

'Come and see me in the flower shop some time,' Daisy said quietly, so only Bryn could hear. 'I mean... if you want to.'

'I do want to,' said Bryn, far too eagerly. 'I mean, that'd be good.'

She grinned, began to hurry towards the gate, and then spun round again. 'And take one of these first!' she called.

Bryn saw a glint of something silver in the air, and instinctively caught what she had thrown in his direction: the remainder of the antihistamine tablets. Then, with an odd ache in his chest, he watched her dash out of the garden, give Magnus a quick wave as she passed him, and then hurry off along Westminster Square in the direction of Victoria Station.

'I hope I didn't interrupt anything there,' called Magnus, who was still looking very entertained by what he had just witnessed.

Bryn, pocketing the pills, made his way over to the garden railing and said, 'I don't know what you're talking about.'

He had wanted to see his friend for the last few days, but now he felt very resentful of Magnus's sudden appearance. Although he obviously didn't want Daisy to get into trouble with Juliana, he wished they had been able to talk all afternoon.

'I assume you worked out that was my wife's assistant?' said Magnus.

'Yes,' replied Bryn, still a little sullen.

'Of course you did,' Magnus said. 'We'll make a detective of you yet.' Then, with a sideways glance, he asked, 'So what did you think of young Daisy?'

'I thought she was very nice,' said Bryn. Then, realising his friend knew exactly what was going on, he abandoned pretence and said, a little accusingly, 'You didn't tell me she was so pretty.'

Magnus's eyes sparkled with mirth. 'I'm a little too old and much too married to be making those sorts of statements about young ladies. You, on the other hand... Do you know, I've never thought about it before, but the pair of you are rather well-suited.'

'I think she's a little out of my league...'

'Don't underestimate yourself,' said Magnus, with fatherly severity. 'You should ask her out on a date, Bryn.'

'That's what I was trying to do,' grumbled the policeman. Then, feeling this conversation was too becoming too uncomfortable to continue with, he said, 'Don't you have to be getting to lunch?'

'I have a few minutes, while your girlfriend runs to The Station Garden.'

'She's not my girlfriend!'

'Not *yet*...' Seeing Bryn's expression, Magnus hastily continued, 'Actually, I was wondering whether you had time for a quick word about what we learned from Darren Dodge the other day?'

Bryn looked at his watch: he still had ten minutes left of his lunchbreak. Trying to remind himself that talking to Magnus about the case had been exactly why he had been wandering around Westminster Square, he forced himself to push thoughts of Daisy from his mind and said, 'I think that's a good idea. Dodge put rather a different spin on Anne-Laure's death, didn't he?'

'I'm afraid he did,' said Magnus. 'In fact, he's completely muddied the waters. The way I see it, we're now looking at three different motives for her murder.'

'Three?' said Bryn, who had only counted two. 'Are you sure?'

'I think so, yes. The first, as we've already discussed, is that Anne-Laure was killed because somebody pretty unhinged was obsessed with her. They followed her, kept track of her movements in that notebook, and it was likely this was the same person who accosted her in the garden, and who was responsible for the bruising on her wrists and neck. Presumably, this person found out Anne-Laure was leaving London for Los Angeles — which was fairly common knowledge, remember, because she'd told Hilda and shrieked it for half of Westminster Square to hear in the garden that night — so I'm assuming this person panicked, followed her into the Royal West and —'

'And what?' Bryn asked, for he had been wondering this himself. 'Forced her to overdose? It doesn't quite make sense. Why would she have taken drugs with someone she knew to be dangerous?'

'I don't know,' Magnus admitted, 'and I'm still afraid we're missing something regarding the body…'

'If only Boyle hadn't been so pig-headed about an autopsy!' Bryn burst out, not for the first time. 'And if only he hadn't gone and had the body cremated!'

'Let's not get distracted,' said Magnus. 'Let's try and focus on the motive for a moment. Because that's what is particularly perplexing me right now. Until the other day, it looked as though romantic and sexual obsession was the only reason we could find for someone to want to kill Anne-Laure, but Darren Dodge has opened up two new possibilities.'

'So I see that the first possibility is information,' cut in Bryn, for he had been going over this ever since that day in Fleet Street. 'Anne-Laure was involved in something shady — or she had stumbled upon something shady by accident — and she realised she could make a quick, easy buck by taking it to *The Dawn Reporter*.'

'We know Anne-Laure liked money,' continued Magnus. 'Darren Dodge said she was very focused on how much she'd get for the story — and there's all those designer clothes in her flat. I think it's worth considering that going to the papers with an explosive scoop is something she would do. Only, in this case, the person — or people — involved must have found out about it beforehand. Somehow, they learned what she was trying to do, and decided she had to be silenced. Permanently. The method of her death makes more sense in this case: it was deliberate, premeditated. And who's going to ask questions about a dead party girl with cocaine in her system?'

'Well, apart from us,' Bryn admitted, 'but I see your point. What's this third option, then?'

'That she was killed because of money,' mused Magnus. 'As I said, it's clear that wealth meant a lot to Anne-Laure. Not only did she have a somewhat extravagant lifestyle, she was actively looking to make more money. She worked multiple jobs, remember, and she asked Lord Ellington for an advance just before her death.'

'I wonder if that was because she was looking to start a new life in America?' said Bryn. 'Because she wanted to get away from her stalker?'

'Quite possibly,' said Magnus. 'But what if she went a little far with her pursuit of wealth? Presumably she had access to Vasyl and Ellington's account details, maybe Hazim's too, if we're correct in thinking she was working for him as well. What if she took a little of their money for herself, thinking they wouldn't notice, but one of those men found out and wasn't best pleased about it...?'

Bryn considered this for a few moments. Because she was the victim, and because people like Hilda were so rude about her, his instinct was to always stand up for Anne-Laure, and to try and think the best of her wherever possible. So he didn't like the idea that she was some sort of thief, but equally he couldn't deny that Magnus made a convincing argument: one of the only consistent facts they knew about Anne-Laure Chevalier was that she was drawn to wealth and the glamour that went with it.

'That wouldn't explain why she went to *The Dawn Reporter*, though,' said Bryn. 'I mean, she's hardly going to tell Darren Dodge she's stealing from some rich businessman or politician, is she? That would land her in far more trouble than anybody else.'

'But we don't know for sure Anne-Laure's death had anything to do with her going to the papers. We've been assuming so, because of the convenient timing of it, but what's to say it wasn't just another money-making scheme that never came to fruition?'

'But what about this huge story she was going to divulge?'

'Yes, I've been thinking about that. But do you remember what Darren Dodge said, about when he first started talking to her? From the sound of her voice, he thought she was a mistress wanting to sell a kiss-and-tell story to *The Dawn Reporter*, and changed his mind when she hit him with her assertive negotiating technique, which she'd obviously perfected working for Vasyl and Ellington. But what if Dodge's first instinct was actually correct? After all, we're almost certain that Anne-Laure *was* sleeping with an internationally-famous celebrity...'

'Jem McMorran,' said Bryn.

'It wouldn't be the biggest scandal Dodge had ever exposed, but perhaps she exaggerated to try and get more money out of *The Dawn Reporter*? And Jem is a huge star. Plus, who knows what kind of evidence she was trying to get hold of to prove it...'

Bryn didn't particularly want to dwell on that. And, again, although Magnus was presenting him with a series of very reasonable points, he couldn't quite shake the feeling that there was more to this *Dawn Reporter* business than a sleazy kiss-and-tell.

'Okay,' he said, 'I hear what you're saying, I do. But let's assume for the moment that it's the second option: let's say Anne-Laure was killed because she found out something scandalous, decided to go to the papers about it, and someone had her bumped off to keep her quiet. If we think about our list of Anne-Laure's acquaintances — which is not exhaustive, I know — is there any way we could work out what on earth was going on?'

Magnus looked thoughtful. 'Again, what was it Dodge said she had told him? It was a huge story involving a high-up person?'

'*People* in high places,' Bryn corrected him, for he remembered making a note of this exact phrase.

'*People*?' Magnus raised his eyebrows. 'Well, assuming for the moment it's just one of our Westminster Square friends, they're most of them people in high places. Lord Bevis Ellington and Dame Winifred Rye perhaps most obviously, given they're high up in British society, but Vasyl Kosnitschev and Sheikh Hazim Lahab are well-known international businessmen. Then Jem McMorran and Morris Springfield are of course famous in their respective fields. In fact, the only person I'd say wouldn't be of any interest to *The Dawn Reporter* is Hilda Underpin.

'As we just discussed, I would assume if she was going to Dodge with a story involving Jem it would be a straight-up kiss-and-tell,' continued Magnus. '"*My two-year secret affair with Jem McMorran*," that sort of thing. Morris, on the other hand, seems a bit of a stretch. What would she have found out about him? He doesn't seem to lead a very scandalous life, holed up in his flat, writing his obscure books and articles? Unless he's had us completely hoodwinked, I think we can tentatively rule him out.

'The others, however, seem likely candidates for a good old-fashioned scandal. Who knows how on earth Vasyl Kosnitschev really makes his money, and Anne-Laure was close to him, remember, so she could have discovered something incriminating. And Lord Ellington has always struck me as a thoroughly dodgy individual. I wouldn't be surprised if the reason he didn't want to tell us about her *rabbateur* work is because some of his dealings aren't strictly legal. And it's not as though Sheikh Hazim is exactly a paragon of morality, is it? I'm not sure about Dame Winifred, though…'

'Actually, Daisy said something about Dame Winifred earlier, which I thought was interesting,' said Bryn, trying not to go red as he mentioned his new friend's name. 'She said Dame Winifred has been holding dinners for her biggest donors. People like Sheikh Hazim bin Lahab…' He scowled at the thought of the gluttonous Arab getting "handsy" with Daisy.

'Really?' said Magnus.

'Yeah, and the way Daisy was talking, it sounded as though they were almost done in secret, these meet-ups.'

'That's very interesting,' said the barrister. 'Of course, the innocent and most likely explanation is that Dame Winifred is simply wining and dining a few businessmen in the hope they'll cough up even more money for the GGEF, or whatever she's fundraising for these days.'

'All right,' said Bryn, feeling a little guilty that he was distrusting a philanthropist like Dame Winifred. 'What's a less likely and less innocent explanation, then?'

Magnus appeared to give this some thought. 'I'm not sure… The only thing I can think of is that a lot of fraud goes on within the charity sector. At best, charities are used as tax avoidance schemes, at worst… Well, at worst not all of the money reaches those in need.'

'You're suggesting Dame Winifred is syphoning off the money she raises from all these parties?'

'I'm not suggesting anything of the sort,' said Magnus quickly. 'I'm just saying it's been known to happen, in similar circles.'

'It would certainly be a juicy scandal,' said Bryn, thinking back to the mysterious story Anne-Laure wanted to sell to the papers. 'Dame Winifred is a high-up person, definitely.'

'And so are the kind of businessmen who donate to her charities, people like Sheikh Hazim. But it all seems very unlikely, doesn't it? Firstly, that Dame Winifred would have the temperament to skim money from her fundraising in the first place, and secondly that Anne-Laure would betray her generous benefactor by selling her out to the papers, and thirdly that Dame Winifred would seek violent revenge… It's laughable!

I mean, they were friends, they worked together on that last party. No, I think Vasyl or Ellington are more likely candidates — they're both cold-hearted enough to seek retribution like that, and Hazim could be too.'

'So, in conclusion, we're no closer to knowing anything at all,' said Bryn, nudging the edge of the railing with his foot in frustration.

'I wouldn't put it like that,' said Magnus. 'I think we're getting closer and closer, but right now we have too many lines of enquiry open. It would be nice to confirm a few things, to draw a line under them. Personally, I wish Jem McMorran would show up again: I'd like to show him that airline ticket, and the notebook. I'd be interested to see how he reacted to them…'

'How who reacted to what?' came another voice.

Magnus spun around, but Bryn had already seen Juliana approaching from the direction of Victoria Station, her fiery hair glowing brightly in the sunshine.

'Oh, we're just discussing the usual,' said Magnus, kissing her on the cheek.

Juliana didn't push him away, but Bryn thought he detected a hint of chilliness in her manner towards her husband, and wondered whether this was the reason Magnus had been a little downcast of late.

'You look like a pair of old women gossiping over a garden fence,' said Juliana. 'Speaking of, I bet Hilda's lurking around here somewhere, listening in…'

She peered around, apparently spoiling for a fight, but Magnus took her arm.

'Come on, darling, let's go and have some lunch, shall we?'

'Yes, *let's*,' said Juliana, straightening up and turning towards the south side of Westminster Square. 'I'm absolutely starving. Do you know, Daisy was supposed to come back at half past, but she didn't appear until almost quarter to?'

'Oh dear,' said Magnus, mildly.

'It's not like her to be late,' said Juliana, pulling Magnus towards the edge of the pavement. 'Apparently she lost track of time talking to some *charming man* in the gardens. You know, I think she was rather taken with him... Well, bye, Bryn!' she said loudly, looking over her shoulder at him and winking.

In that moment, Bryn wanted nothing more than to call Juliana back and quiz her on exactly what Daisy had said. But he forced his expression to remain passive as he said, 'See you later,' in a relatively normal voice. Then, when he was quite sure neither Magnus nor Juliana were going to look back at him, he allowed his face to break into a broad grin.

CHAPTER THIRTY

In the days that followed their last conversation, Bryn found himself dwelling a lot on Magnus's theory that Anne-Laure Chevalier might have been killed over money. Had she, over the course of her business dealings with Vasyl Kosnitschev, Lord Bevis Ellington or even Sheikh Hazim bin Lahab, found a way to skim some cash for herself from one of their bank accounts? It wasn't beyond the realms of possibility, and Magnus was right; however feeble their grasp of Anne-Laure's true character might be, it seemed safe to say she had always been interested in the accumulation of wealth, and would certainly have been looking to make quick money to help her start afresh in Los Angeles.

But even so, Bryn remained sceptical. It wasn't as though he didn't think one of those three businessmen had it in him to dispose of a thieving employee; in fact, if one of them had done it, Bryn doubted he would have even got his hands dirty, and instead would have dispatched somebody else to finish her off. But then, it depended on how much she had taken. When at least two of them were multimillionaires, would they have even bothered to go to the trouble of killing her for, what, a few thousand pounds?

Furthermore, what was especially bothering the policeman was that Magnus's theory of a money-related death seemed almost completely unconnected to both their discovery of the stalker's notebook and the revelation that Anne-Laure had attempted to sell a scandalous story to *The Dawn Reporter*. Instinct told Bryn that these were two of the most significant leads they had regarding the probable murder of Anne-Laure Chevalier, and he wanted to concentrate on them, rather than speculate on a third and — in his opinion — less likely motive.

For this reason, not long after he and Magnus had had that conversation over the railing of one of Westminster Square's gardens, Bryn decided it was time he looked up an old friend: Lucas Jones, who worked for the Criminal Investigation Department, or CID, for the Metropolitan Police Service.

Bryn had met Lucas when he had been completing his police training in Wales. Looking back, those years hadn't been the easiest of Bryn's life: he had been even less sure of himself than he was now, and had suffered from acute homesickness, especially during the first few weeks. Perhaps sensing weakness, some of his fellow trainees and even a few of his superiors had picked on him, always purporting that they wanted to 'toughen him up' — although admittedly none of their treatment had been half as bad as the bullying to which Barry Boyle had since subjected him to.

Lucas, on the other hand, had been different. He was a few years older than Bryn, and at the time had been training to be a detective with the CID in Cardiff, something Bryn had found immensely impressive. He had never called Bryn names or tried to trip him in the corridors like everybody else, but had instead recognised that the young trainee was more brainy than brawny, and it had been Lucas' advice and guidance that had inspired Bryn to start thinking seriously about a career in detective work.

Lucas had been transferred to London around a year ago — about six months before Bryn had moved here — and the young police constable had not yet plucked up the courage to go and say hello to him. Would he even remember the unpromising trainee he had unofficially mentored back in Cardiff? But now, with the latest developments in the Anne-Laure Chevalier case, Bryn finally felt as though he had an excuse to see his old friend, and so they had arranged to meet for lunch that Friday.

The police station in which Lucas now worked as a plainclothes CID officer was near Hanover Square, which was a forty minute walk from Bryn's own branch, and therefore too long for him to complete twice in one lunch hour, especially if he actually wanted to have a few minutes with his friend when he arrived. So Bryn decided to catch the Victoria line from Victoria Station instead, dawdling as much as he could before he ducked into the Underground, on the off chance that — once again — he would bump into Daisy. It had only been a couple of days since he had met her in Westminster Square Gardens, and he had not quite steeled himself to visit her at the flower shop just yet, especially if Juliana was going to be there, smirking at them and no doubt committing everything they said to memory to report back to her husband. But still, Bryn thought, he would have to be brave and just go for it soon, or Daisy might think he wasn't interested. Or worse, someone might come along and sweep her off her feet before he had the chance.

These thoughts and worries kept him occupied throughout the journey on the Underground, and he was in rather a daze when he emerged from the Oxford Circus tube station, so was unprepared for the crowds of shoppers and tourists that immediately began to shove at him from all sides. Managing to extract himself from the tide, he headed down Regent Street, and then towards Hanover Square.

He found Lucas already waiting for him outside a modern-looking building not unlike the office of *The Dawn Reporter* in Fleet Street. He was a tall, good-looking man in his mid-thirties, with shiny dark hair, bright green eyes, and a fairly muscular physique. Bryn didn't know whether Lucas was seeing anyone, but he made a mental note not to bring him anywhere Daisy, just in case.

'Summers!' cried Lucas, transferring his takeaway coffee cup to his left hand so he could grip at Bryn's fingers with his right. 'What's occurin', boyo? How are you?'

'I'm tidy, thanks,' said Bryn, joining in with the Welsh slang. 'It's good to finally catch up with you, Lucas.' He looked around at the bustling streets of London's premier shopping district and said, 'It's quite something around here.'

'Oh yes, we're a long way from the valleys now,' said Lucas.

'I think I'm a long way from Westminster,' said Bryn, reflecting on how much quieter it was around Westminster Square. 'It took me much longer than I thought to get here. Speaking of…' He consulted his watch. 'I only have about half an hour left of my lunch.'

'Lucky I have something quick in mind then, isn't it?' said Lucas, giving Bryn a little prod on the shoulder to get him moving.

What Lucas had in mind, it turned out, was a little Japanese restaurant hidden away down a nearby side street. To Bryn's untrained eye, its interior looked fairly traditional, with bonsai plants, sliding screen doors and lots of bamboo detail to the decoration. In fact, the most modern feature was the conveyer belt transporting little wooden boats of sushi around the room.

'I'm not being funny,' said Bryn, who was now finding it difficult to slip out of Welsh slang, 'but I've never had Japanese food before.'

Lucas laughed. 'You mean, they don't do sushi in the wilds of West Wales? You're in for a treat, my friend.'

He turned out to be perfectly correct, for after he and Bryn had pulled themselves up onto stools at the bar-like table, they sampled some of the prawn teriyaki, California rolls, vegetable gyoza and pumpkin katsu that was trundling by. Bryn found he rather liked it, once he'd come to terms with the fact that most of it was cold and completely different to the traditional, stodgy fare he had grown up with.

As they ate, he and Lucas caught up on one another's lives. His companion, it turned out, was now a Detective Sergeant with the CID, which was a rewarding — if very demanding — position to have in the Met, the biggest and busiest police force in the country by a significant margin. In turn, Bryn told Lucas how his probationary period with the Victoria Police Station was going, which sounded a lot less exciting in comparison to the CID.

'But don't forget you're finding your feet,' said Lucas, as prudent as ever. 'You might be qualified now, but you've still a lot to learn, so better it's too quiet than too chaotic, I say.'

Bryn also couldn't help but have a small moan about Barry Boyle, considering Lucas had protected him from similar figures in the past.

'I've heard of him,' said the Detective Sergeant. 'He's a big fat bloke, right? He's a bit of a laughing stock in some of the other branches, because everyone knows he just wants a quiet life until he retires.'

'Well, he certainly goes out of his way to achieve one,' said Bryn.

Lucas paused in the act of helping himself to another salmon avocado maki. 'Why do you say that?'

Bryn, feeling this was as good a time as any to bring up what he had come here to discuss, lowered his voice and said, 'Do you remember that woman who died a couple of months ago?'

'God, which one?' said Lucas.

'Sorry, I forget you work with the big boys,' grinned Bryn. 'Her name was Anne-Laure Chevalier, she was a PR girl and socialite who died at the Royal West Hotel.'

'Oh yes, I remember,' said Lucas. 'The papers had a great time printing lots of photographs of her in skimpy dresses for a few weeks. Gosh, that must've been a bit of excitement for you over there. They said she died of natural causes, didn't they? Which obviously means it was a drug overdose...'

Bryn, surprised and impressed by this cynical and fairly accurate reaction, said, 'Actually, I was there on the morning the body was found, and I'm still not sure anybody's got to the truth of how or why she died.'

'Oh?' said Lucas, his voice cautious.

Bryn, realising he didn't have time to go into all of the ins and outs of the case, went on, 'Let's just say that there were a number of suspicious circumstances surrounding her death.'

'Such as?' said Lucas, more reluctantly still.

Bryn hardly knew where to start. 'Well, there was cocaine found in her system, you're bang on with that point, but she'd also been knocked about by someone, because her body was badly bruised in places.'

'But let me guess: Boyle didn't want to do a full autopsy?'

'Got it in one. Only, well, I've been doing a little unofficial investigating with a barrister friend, and the whole business just gets shadier and shadier. A witness saw her having a violent argument on the night of her death, she was working for a number of pretty dodgy characters around the City of Westminster. Then there's the fact she was intending to sell some kind of scandalous story to the papers — oh, and it looks like she was being stalked by someone.'

Lucas let out a long, low whistle. 'I shouldn't be listening to this,' he said. 'Do you know how much the CID hate hearing about potential murders? You're just trying to add to our workload.' He sighed. 'I don't suppose she could have done it herself, could she? That it could have been suicide?'

'It's unlikely, because she had a meeting booked for the next day and a plane ticket to America for the one after that.'

'Hm,' said Lucas, looking grim. 'That does seem unlikely.'

'The thing is,' continued Bryn, 'I voiced my concerns just after her body was found and, well, Boyle didn't take too kindly to his authority being questioned. In fact, he outright forbade me from even mentioning her name again. So everything I've done on this case so far has been on the quiet. Only now, it's getting to the stage where I might need a little more help...'

'And that's where I come in, is it?' asked Lucas. 'You can't ask any CID officers at Victoria, in case they go to Boyle, so you're asking me?'

'Erm, that's about the size of it, yes,' admitted Bryn.

'What do you need?' asked Lucas.

Bryn thought back to Magnus's theory about Anne-Laure siphoning money from businessmen's accounts and said, 'If possible, I'd like to get a look at her bank statements.'

'Oh, only her bank statements?' said Lucas, sarcastically. 'Bryn, do you know how difficult it is to get hold of stuff like that? Normally, you need a court order!'

'But you could sneak me one or two, couldn't you?' pressed Bryn. 'Just the latest few? I mean, she's dead, so it's not doing anyone any harm.'

'It might do my career some harm, if anyone finds out about it...' muttered Lucas. 'What else do you need?'

'Advice, I suppose. As I said, she appears to have had some kind of stalker, because we found this notebook of all of her movements and so on. So I was wondering, is there any way I can get the handwriting analysed? To try and find out who wrote the wretched thing?'

'You could,' said Lucas, before adding hastily, 'but don't get too excited. First of all, you would need handwriting samples of some suspects.'

'I could get that,' said Bryn, thinking he and Magnus could do their neighbourhood watch act again, this time with a questionnaire.

'But hold on, then you'd have to send it all away to be assessed, and that doesn't come cheap. It's a couple of thousand at least, and even if you could scrabble together those funds, I'm not sure they'd accept anything that didn't come directly from the CID.'

'And you couldn't...?'

Lucas shook his head. 'Look, I can try and get you the bank statements. I'm not promising anything, but, as you said, it's not really doing anyone any harm. But I'm afraid you might have to think outside the box, as far as this handwriting issue is concerned.'

Bryn nodded, trying not to feel too disappointed. 'Can I ask you something else?'

Lucas, who had finally taken the opportunity to pop the salmon avocado maki into his mouth, looked wary as he chewed. 'Mm?'

'How do you do it? After you've talked to the suspects, after you've compiled a load of evidence, how do you narrow it down to get at the truth?'

Lucas swallowed his mouthful. 'You know, there aren't really any hard and fast rules...'

'I know, but I'm not trained in this like you are. It'd be good to know I wasn't doing everything completely wrong.'

'I'm sure you're not,' said Lucas. 'But, let's see... I assume, knowing you, you've taken extensive notes.'

'Oh yes,' said Bryn eagerly, 'I've pages and pages of them.'

'Good,' said Lucas. 'Keep hold of them, keep reading them. Chances are, you've already come into contact with the key to the case, you just haven't realised it yet. It might be something someone said offhand, it might be something you saw out of the corner of your eye... In my experience, it's these little things that turn out to be important, the ones you don't think twice about at the time but for some reason you make a note of them anyway. It's almost as though your subconscious is a few steps ahead.'

'You know, Magnus said something similar a while back,' said Bryn, before quickly explaining, 'that's my barrister friend, the one who's helping me with the investigation. He said it was often the smallest details that have the biggest impact on his court cases.'

'He's right,' said Lucas. 'Of course, the trick is to identify them. And the way to do that is to try and cut away everything else, to eliminate all the excess information — the red herrings, if you will.'

'And how do you do that?'

'Good question. By doing everything you've already been doing, I suppose, and trying to work out what's the *least* likely motive, who are the *least* likely suspects. Everybody has secrets, after all, you just have to identify which of them are related to the case, and which aren't.' He shrugged. 'And if all else fails, I'd just go with your gut.'

'Yes, I must admit that's what I've been putting most of my faith in so far — my instincts. That's why it'd be good to get hold of those bank statements, because I'm almost certain they'll eliminate one of our motives, although I can't really explain why I think that.'

Lucas removed his napkin from his lap, scrunched it up, and dropped it onto his plate to signify he had finished eating. Once more, he looked a little uncomfortable.

'I shouldn't be giving you advice, really,' he said.

'Why not?'

Lucas cocked his head to one side. 'Look, Bryn, I know you're a smart guy, but what you're doing here, is it really... *wise*?'

'What do you mean?'

'Well, this "unofficial investigating", it's not exactly your job, is it?'

'No one else is doing it,' said Bryn, a little stung by the criticism. 'And I just know there's something off about the whole business. In fact, I'm ninety-nine percent sure she was killed on purpose. So I can't just sweep that knowledge under the carpet, can I? Where's the justice in that? I can't let someone get away with murder!'

Lucas rolled his eyes, but he looked amused. 'You always did have the moral compass for police work, even if you're not always the most practical bobby on the beat.' He gave Bryn another clap on the back. 'Well, just as long as you're careful. From what I've heard, Boyle is not a man to cross, and I certainly don't want to get mixed up in all of this.'

'Of course,' said Bryn quickly, 'I would never want to get you into trouble...'

Lucas held up a hand to stop his protestations. 'So, as long as my name stays out of it, I'll see what I can do to get hold of a couple of her bank statements. But let me tell you: if you're right, and this does turn into a big murder case, nobody at the CID is going to thank you.'

'No,' Bryn agreed, a little sadly. 'In fact, I think the only person who would have thanked me for doing any of this died two months ago at the Royal West Hotel.'

They finished their lunch shortly afterwards, and once they had agreed to go for a proper catch-up drink in the near future, Bryn dashed back towards Oxford Circus tube station, and impatiently endured the lengthy journey back to Westminster. Then, most unfortunately, as he dashed through the door of the Victoria Police Station, he barrelled straight into Barry Boyle, who was eating a Big Mac while shouting orders at Constable Shona Walsh.

'Where've you been, Summers?' demanded Boyle, spraying Bryn with half-chewed food as he spoke.

'I've been on my lunch, sir,' said Bryn, feeling unnecessarily nervous, as though Boyle had the ability to read his mind and discover he had been talking to someone from the CID about Anne-Laure Chevalier.

'Do you see this rota here, Summers?' said Boyle, snatching a piece of paper from the wall with his greasy fingers and waving it at Bryn. 'This rota here says you should have been back at two o'clock on the dot, and now it's twenty past!'

'I'm sorry, sir.'

'Tell me, Summers,' went on Boyle, after tearing off another mouthful of his burger, 'are you being accidentally stupid or deliberately disobedient?'

'I just lost track of time, sir—'

'*Accidentally stupid or deliberately disobedient?!*'

Bryn hung his head. 'Accidentally stupid, sir.'

'Good,' said Boyle, smiling nastily. 'It better not happen again, Summers.'

'It won't, sir.'

For a moment, Bryn thought this was the end of it, but as he sat down at his desk, he realised Boyle was following him. The Police Chief Superintendent lowered his fat posterior onto the edge of Bryn's workspace.

'Um, can I — can I help you, sir?' asked Bryn, wondering whether his desk was about to give way under Boyle's weight.

'What are you up to, Summers?'

'Excuse me?'

Boyle crammed the last of his hamburger into his mouth so carelessly that chunks of ketchup-smeared food fell onto Bryn's desk.

'I said, *what are you up to, Summers?*'

Bryn pushed his chair back a little to avoid the onslaught of half-chewed food.

'Just — just my job, sir. Just the paperwork you gave me.'

'Do I look stupid?' demanded Boyle, who had sesame seeds caught in his moustache.

'Um, no, sir.'

'You're up to something, Summers — I know it. You're always taking long lunches; you're always hanging around Westminster Square… You're not even complaining about all the paperwork I'm giving you. What's going on?'

Bryn swallowed. He hadn't realised he had been quite so obviously distracted of late, especially enough that Boyle would have noticed. But then, the Chief Superintendent had his spies, not to mention a sizeable vendetta against him.

'I—' Bryn faltered.

'Your mind's not on the job,' Boyle continued. 'So where is it, Summers?'

In that moment, all Bryn could think about was Anne-Laure Chevalier and, once more, he was terrified Boyle was able to somehow know this just by looking at him. In fact, by the way he was talking, he suspected Boyle had a pretty good idea already.

'What are you doing in Westminster Square? Why are you always late back from your lunches?'

'Because — because of a girl!' Bryn blurted out, and relief flooded through him as, in his mind's eye, Anne-Laure's corpse was replaced by the very much alive figure of Daisy. 'I've met a girl!'

Boyle stared at him. Clearly, whatever he had been expecting, it had not been that.

'A *girl*?' he repeated, as though he had never heard the word before.

'Yes,' said Bryn, wishing that they were having this conversation in Boyle's stinky office, because most of his colleagues were listening in and smirking. 'Yes, she's called Daisy, and she's really nice and extremely pretty. She works at a flower shop in Victoria Station, and I met her in Westminster Square a little while ago, and well…'

He trailed off, his face burning. He wasn't enjoying confessing this to the office at large, but it was a partial truth, and therefore probably the safest way to wriggle out of these accusations. Boyle's eyes were wide, as though he had never heard anything quite so extraordinary in his life. Then, just as Bryn thought he was going to recommence his yelling, the Police Chief Superintendent threw back his head and roared with laughter. He guffawed so heartily that one of the buttons on his jacket popped off, and then his mirth must have moved a morsel of food from his mouth to his windpipe, for he began to cough and splutter, flailing around so much that most of Bryn's paperwork went flapping to the floor. The young Police Constable wondered whether he dared to pat Boyle on the back — it might be more than his job was worth to raise a hand to his superior officer, even if he was trying to stop him from choking — but eventually Boyle grabbed a cup of water from Bryn's desk, drank deeply, and seemed to recover himself.

'A *girl*!' he gasped. 'Daisy from the — flower shop!' He wiped away tears, which had either been caused by laughter or coughing, Bryn wasn't sure. 'I didn't know you had it in you, Summers! In fact, I'm still not convinced. What are your moves, eh? Did you handcuff her to the railings? Did you flash her your *truncheon*?'

'I just talked to her, sir,' mumbled Bryn, over the increasing noise of laughter coming from around the office.

'You know she'll only be interested in the uniform,' Boyle sneered. 'If she ever sees you out of it — as though you'd be so lucky! — she'll realise exactly what you are: a pasty, weedy, ugly, dim-witted...' He paused, evidently searching for a word insulting enough, '*Welshman.*'

Bryn looked at the floor. Aside from the slight on his nationality, he feared Boyle was right: apart from being a policeman, what else did he have?

Nevertheless, he was determined not to reveal that the bullying Chief Superintendent had got to him, so he forced himself to look Boyle in the piggy eyes and said, 'Thank you for the advice, sir.'

'Any time,' Boyle grunted, clearly disappointed at Bryn's lack of reaction. 'And Summers?'

'Yes, sir?'

'You'd better start coming back from your lunches on time, and you'd better start concentrating on your work, all right?'

'All right, sir.'

Boyle reached out and poked him in the chest. Bryn tried not to show it, but the force of the fat fingers knocking against his skinny ribcage almost winded him.

'I'm watching you, Summers,' growled Boyle. 'I'm just waiting for an excuse...' Then, heaving himself from the desk, he gestured down at the debris of crumbs, fast food packaging and paperwork he had created on the floor and added, 'Now clean up this mess.'

* * * *

Bryn still felt rattled when he returned to his Clapham bedsit that evening. It had been a strange sort of day. On the one hand, he had caught up with an old friend and at least attempted to get hold of Anne-Laure Chevalier's bank statements, which could prove to be an important factor in cracking the case, so he should have felt more positive. But he couldn't help but dwell on Lucas's barely disguised disapproval of what he was doing, not to mention the CID officer's attempts to warn him off the investigation.

Then there had been the run-in with Barry Boyle. Bryn was used to being bullied by his Chief Superintendent, but Boyle had been especially forceful in his conviction that something was going on, which was worrying. Given that Boyle was right, Bryn would have to heed Lucas's advice and be very careful around him. Furthermore, Boyle was not usually so personal in his victimisation, and Bryn was still cringing at the memory of having to use his feelings for Daisy to shield himself against his superior's interrogation.

He wished he had used a fake name, but of course he'd been put on the spot, and his main priority had been steering Boyle's suspicions away from Anne-Laure Chevalier. Yet the memory of Boyle laughing about 'Daisy from the flower shop' made Bryn angry, and more than a little concerned. Was this the reason he hadn't yet summoned the courage to go and see her in The Station Garden? Did he, in his heart of hearts, agree with Boyle's claim that there was nothing to him but his uniform, and once Daisy found this out she wouldn't be interested anymore — if she was even interested in the first place.

'Oh, pull yourself together,' Bryn told his reflection in the bathroom mirror, after he had splashed cold water on his face in an attempt to both wake and cheer himself up.

The thing to do, he thought, drying his face on a towel, was to hurry up and solve the case. That would lay all of this to rest: Lucas's pessimism, Boyle's smugness, even his own feelings of inadequacy. Bryn wasn't exactly sure, if or when he discovered the identity of Anne-Laure's killer, how he was going to triumphantly reveal it without Boyle completely steamrollering over him, but he supposed he would have to cross that bridge when he came to it. The important thing to keep in mind was that Boyle would be wrong and he would be right. Bryn would be vindicated — a hero, even. And surely then he might have a chance with Daisy?

Feeling a little buoyed by these thoughts, Bryn began to lay out all of his notes across the floor of his bedsit, so he could examine and analyse them just as Lucas had advised. They were already fairly well organised, considering he had typed them up for Magnus just before their meeting in Lei Sing's Taste of China restaurant, and he was able to lay them out in the order they had spoken to each suspect: Vasyl Kosnitschev, Dame Winifred Rye, Hilda Underpin, Jem McMorran, Sheikh Hazim bin Lahab, Lord Bevis Ellington, Morris Springfield. Then, for good measure, he placed the pieces of evidence they had gathered so far directly in front of him on the floor: the engraved ring, the address book, the stalker's journal, and the aeroplane ticket to Los Angeles.

'Right,' said Bryn aloud, 'let's see if I can figure this out.'

But he had barely read — or rather, reread — a word before the phone suddenly began to ring. Bryn gave a cry of frustration: he was almost certain this would be his mother, wondering whether he was safe, whether he was eating properly, whether he had found a nice girl yet. And while there might have been a small amount of progress on the latter front, he was not about to tell her that; it was bad enough most of Victoria Police Station already knew.

He snatched up the receiver without taking his eyes from the collage of paperwork he had created on the floor of his bedsit.

'Hello?' he said, a little impatiently, bracing himself for the usual questions.

'Bryn, it's Magnus.'

'Oh, hi, Magnus.' Bryn was pleasantly surprised. 'How are you? Is everything all right?'

'Everything's fine,' said the barrister, who sounded more excited than worried. 'In fact, I think I know what our next step should be, regarding Anne-Laure's death.'

Bryn smiled. Whatever Magnus was going to say, it was good to be reminded that somebody else was involved in this case, and he wasn't just going it alone.

'Oh? What are you thinking?'

'Well, I was out jogging earlier, and guess who I saw returning to their flat at long last?'

'Who?'

'Jem McMorran,' said Magnus. 'Bryn, he's back — so I think it's time we had another word with him, don't you?'

CHAPTER THIRTY-ONE

'Jem!' cried Magnus. 'Jem, we know you're in there — open up!'

Bryn stood back while his companion hammered on the door. He was in his police uniform today, and as a result the doorman had had no issue with waving them upstairs. Jem McMorran, on the other hand, didn't seem very keen on talking to them.

'Come on, Jem!' continued Magnus, taking a short break from his knocking. 'Let us in!'

There came a creaking sound from the other side of the door, suggesting someone was standing just behind it, listening. Upon hearing this, Magnus leaned forward and lowered his voice.

'Jem, I think you should open the door,' he said, eyeing the peephole. 'I have Police Constable Summers with me, and we're willing to talk to you off the record. As the alternative is Constable Summers obtaining a search warrant for your flat, or hauling you down to the station — both of which will cause something of a scandal, especially if the press find out about it — I would advise that you let us in.'

This was, they both knew, an empty threat; there was no way Bryn could have gained permission to search the flat of a Hollywood film star or dragged him down to Victoria Police Station without Barry Boyle noticing. However, Jem seemed to think it sounded plausible enough, for after a moment's hesitation, he opened the door.

'I'm assuming this isn't about the parking space?' he said, attempting a wry smile.

To Bryn's slight surprise, Magnus's face remained stony: apparently, he was in barrister mode today. 'May we come in?' he asked.

Jem shrugged and stood aside. Evidently, being away on a film shoot had been good for him, for he looked rather better than he had done the last time Magnus and Bryn had seen him. True, he still had an air of dishevelment, and was a far cry from the glossy, handsome figure he presented on the big screen, but today he had managed to shave, comb his hair, and find some clean jeans and a t-shirt.

Furthermore, his flat was completely transformed. Bryn supposed a cleaner must have visited in Jem's absence, for he couldn't believe the actor would have tidied and scrubbed this space all by himself, especially not to this extent. The furniture had been righted, all the clothes had been cleared away, the scripts had been arranged into neat piles, and someone had clearly run a vacuum cleaner and a cloth around the place, because every surface was now free of dust and crumbs. In fact, as Bryn gazed around at Jem McMorran's living space, with its contemporary paintings and state-of-the-art technology, he thought it looked much more like the sort of flat in which he would have expected the actor to live: a swanky, modern bachelor pad.

'Can I get you a drink?' asked Jem, after he had directed them to the sofa in his living room.

'Just water, I think,' said Magnus, his manner still stern.

'And for me too, please,' added Bryn.

When Jem returned from the kitchen with the two glasses, he had a bottle of beer under his arm, which he uncapped by bashing it against the side of the coffee table. Now it was devoid of papers and food wrappings, Bryn was able to see several sizeable dents in this table, suggesting opening beer bottles against it was a regular occurrence.

'So,' said Jem, after slouching into his armchair and taking a large swig of beer, 'to what do I owe the pleasure?'

He looked expectantly towards Bryn — or rather, towards his uniform — but it was Magnus who leaned forward to speak.

'A couple of weeks ago, during our last visit, we asked you whether you knew a woman named Anne-Laure Chevalier,' he said, cutting right to the chase.

This time, Jem was more prepared to hear her name. 'And I told you I didn't know her,' he said smoothly. 'And I'm unlikely to have got to know her in the meantime, am I? Seeing as she's dead?'

He attempted a smile, although it didn't quite reach his eyes. Magnus did not return it.

'So you still stand by that statement, do you? You didn't know her at all?'

'I didn't say that,' said Jem quickly. 'It's like I told you last time, I might have *met* her. I meet a lot of beautiful women, so maybe—'

'I'm not interested in *might*s or *maybe*s,' interrupted Magnus. 'I'm interested in the truth. And the truth is, you were in a romantic relationship with her, weren't you, Jem?'

'I—' The actor faltered. 'No—'

'Yes, you were,' said Magnus firmly. 'We have substantial evidence to prove it.'

Bryn shifted uncomfortably on the sofa cushion. In fact, they had very little to prove it, other than Hilda's gossip, an airline ticket to LA, and a bottle of perfume and a few strands of blonde hair in Jem's bathroom, none of which were exactly incriminatory.

Nevertheless, Magnus's bluffing seemed to be having an effect, for Jem put down his beer with slightly shaking hands and said, 'If this is Hilda Underpin spreading lies again…'

'Never mind her,' said Magnus curtly. 'Answer the question, please: were you or were you not in a romantic relationship with Anne-Laure Chevalier?'

The actor didn't seem to be able to hold Magnus's gaze any longer, so he looked to Bryn instead, almost as though to appeal for his help. The policeman felt a little sorry for him; clearly, Jem was well out of his depth with Magnus's questioning.

'If I was,' he said, before quickly adding, 'and I'm not saying it's true, I'm just saying *if* I was in a relationship with her, what does it matter? Why are you asking me about this?'

'Why do you think she doesn't matter, Jem?' asked Magnus.

'That's not what I said!'

'Is it because she's gone? Do you think Anne-Laure Chevalier doesn't matter because she's dead?'

Jem, who had winced on the words 'gone' and 'dead', exclaimed, 'You're twisting my words! I would never —'

Magnus leaned forward still further on the sofa. 'Anne-Laure Chevalier died in the middle of the night in an empty business conference room, completely alone,' he began.

Jem's hands moved to the side of his face, as though he wanted to block out what Magnus was saying.

'Her body lay there, quite abandoned, until around six o'clock in the morning, when she was found by a cleaner — a cleaner!'

'Stop it,' murmured Jem, his fingers now creeping towards his ears.

But Magnus ploughed on: 'In death, Anne-Laure looked so peaceful that at first the cleaner thought she was asleep. But she wasn't asleep, Jem, and there had been nothing peaceful about her demise — in fact, there was severe bruising on her neck and wrists.'

The actor looked up, horrified. '*What?*'

'Bruising, Jem. Before she died, someone must have knocked her around, grabbed her by the wrists, the neck...'

'No!'

'She must've been so scared,' Magnus continued, with relish, 'she must have been terrified, that night in the business conference room, in those few hours or minutes before her death. If only someone had been there, someone she was close to, someone she trusted. If only she hadn't been so completely on her own and —'

'*I said, stop it!*'

Jem was hunched over now, his fingers still clasping at his face. Bryn didn't think he had seen anything quite so pitiful in some time: Jem McMorran, the world-renowned film star, now looked like a dog who had been beaten, and was cowering against the possibility of further blows.

'What's wrong, Jem?' asked Magnus, in a detached sort of way, as though he didn't really care about the answer.

'I loved her, okay?' burst out Jem. 'Are you happy now? I loved her!'

And, to Bryn's great surprise, the actor then broke down completely; he bent over still further in his chair, covered his eyes with his palms, and began to cry, his whole body trembling with grief. The policeman looked at Magnus, who was regarding Jem with more sympathy than he had shown that afternoon: apparently, the callous lawyer act had merely been a means to get to this point.

It was a little awkward, sitting opposite a sobbing Hollywood star and not knowing what to do with him. If he had been a friend, Bryn might have thrown an arm around his shoulders, and made a few jokes until he pulled himself together, but Jem wasn't a friend and his anguish didn't seem to be the kind that could be fixed by a few witty comments. So instead, Magnus and Bryn merely sat there, until Jem eventually recovered himself, and sat up a little straighter, his eyes red and watery.

'Are you all right?' asked Magnus, in a kinder tone.

'No,' admitted Jem. He seemed unapologetic about his thoroughly un-British breakdown. 'How can I be, when she's gone?'

Bryn, who could not quite shake the idea of the stalker's notebook from his mind, dared to ask, 'And, erm, did Anne-Laure return your affections?'

Jem wiped at his face with a sleeve. 'Of course,' he said, as though he had never before considered the possibility that someone wouldn't love him. 'We were together for a couple of years — in secret, naturally — but we were in love, and we were happy. And now —'

His voice wavered, and it seemed as though he were on the verge of tears again.

'You say *in secret...*' Bryn began, but Magnus held up a hand to stop him.

'I think you should tell us all about it from the beginning,' decided the barrister, before adding, 'When you feel up to it.'

Jem nodded, sniffed, and took another long drink from his bottle of beer.

'We met at a party a few years ago,' he said. 'I don't remember when or where, exactly. It wasn't like in the stories: lightning didn't strike as soon as I laid eyes on her, it wasn't love at first sight or anything like that. I mean, I noticed her, of course I did — it was difficult not to — but, at the risk of sounding sleazy, there are a lot of beautiful women in my industry, so I didn't pay her much attention at first.'

'What changed?' asked Magnus.

Jem's gaze flicked towards Bryn. 'Can I speak openly?'

Bryn, knowing he was wary of the uniform, nodded.

'This probably won't come as a surprise to you, but I've always been susceptible to… *chemical stimulants*, let's say. I mean, nothing *really* bad,' he added quickly, perhaps fearing their disapproval, 'mostly alcohol, a bit of weed, and coke, obviously…'

'Obviously,' murmured Magnus.

'Look, my job comes with a lot of pressure,' said Jem defensively. 'I keep strange hours — I often film early in the morning and late at night, so sometimes I need a pick-me up. Plus, everyone's watching me all of the time. Do you know what it feels like, to constantly have to be *on*?'

Bryn said nothing. He wanted to sympathise with the actor, who did seem to be genuine, but it was a little difficult to feel too sorry for him, sat in his City of Westminster flat surrounded by all of his mod-cons.

'So I have this habit,' continued Jem, perhaps realising he wasn't going to receive much compassion on this score, 'and sometimes I bring a bit of coke or whatever to a party, no big deal. I mean, I didn't used to charge for it or anything, mostly I just shared it out among friends…'

Bryn raised his eyebrows but, again, decided not to comment. Magnus, however, asked, 'What do you mean, you didn't *used* to charge for it?'

Jem looked at his feet. 'Well, I might as well tell you: I'm not that great with money. That probably sounds absurd, because I earn millions for every film I do, but it just seems to… go. I don't know what I spend it on.'

'Drugs?' Magnus suggested. 'Sports cars?'

'I guess, yeah…' said Jem, looking decidedly sheepish now. 'Anyway, I know I can always make more — I'm not washed up just yet — but sometimes I get a bit short of cash between projects, and that's why I started charging a bit for my… distribution services.'

'You mean, you became a drug dealer?' said Bryn.

'No, no, not at all. It was just — Look, it was Anne-Laure's idea, she had a great head for business, by the way. And that's all it was at first: a business relationship. We would move a bit of pot or coke around parties, and make some pocket money while we did so. It wasn't *that* bad...'

'Apart from the fact it's completely illegal,' pointed out Bryn.

'Yes, but no one was getting hurt,' protested Jem. 'It wasn't as though we were getting people hooked on heroin. We were just sharing out a few... *party favours.*'

'That's one way of putting it,' said Magnus, looking nervously between Jem and Bryn, as though he suspected the latter to start kicking up a fuss. 'But let's move on, shall we?'

'I'm just being honest,' said Jem. 'I'm just saying, that's how I got to know Anne-Laure. That's how I came to realise that she wasn't just beautiful, she was also clever, and fun, and sweet — well, sweet when she wanted to be. And she didn't fawn over me, like so many other people do. She genuinely seemed to see me as a friend and, conversely, that's when I started to see her as something more.'

'So you made the first move?' asked Magnus.

'I made a lot of moves,' said Jem. 'I practically pursued her.'

Considering the existence of the notebook, Bryn thought this was a poor choice of words, but Jem soon clarified what he meant.

'At first I thought she was playing hard to get, but after a while I realised she genuinely didn't want to be in a relationship — not with me, not with anyone. She was like that, very independent and very private. But eventually, I managed to win her round, although it was no easy task. We started dating, properly dating, and it was... It was...' He looked momentarily elated, and then suddenly forlorn. 'Sorry, it's all still sinking in. Plus, I've never really spoken about her before, because we had to keep it secret.'

'Why?' asked Bryn again.

'Well, my agent wasn't particularly happy about it. When you're a fairly young actor like me, being in a relationship is bad for business, so my agent wanted me to appear... attainable, let's say. Or at the very least she wanted me to date somebody equally as famous. She also knew about the fact we were moving these drugs around, and thought Anne-Laure was a bad influence on me, although really it was the other way around. My agent made me swear to keep my relationship with Anne-Laure secret, because she was convinced it would get me into trouble.'

'What do you mean?'

'Well, if the papers got hold of pictures of me even taking drugs, for example, it would all be over, so God knows what they would have done if they'd found out I was sharing them out at these parties...'

At the mention of the papers, Bryn looked at Magnus: was this what Anne-Laure had been trying to do? Take a picture of her internationally-famous boyfriend taking and dealing cocaine and sell it to *The Dawn Reporter*? It was certainly a more explosive story than a standard kiss-and-tell, but it seemed a pretty low thing to do, even for someone keen to make money.

'Did Anne-Laure mind the fact you wanted to keep your relationship secret?' asked Magnus.

'Oh, no.'

'Really? Because I would imagine most women would want to shout that they were dating a handsome Hollywood actor from the rooftops.'

'Ah, but she wasn't like that,' said Jem, glossing over the compliment with a practiced air. 'No, as I said, Anne-Laure was very, very reserved, even with me. She would have hated attention like that. So I think it suited her, really. If anything, it was me who wanted to tell everyone, and Anne-Laure who held me back.'

'All right,' said Magnus, 'let's fast forward a bit, to a few months ago. You were planning on leaving Westminster Square together, weren't you?'

Jem nodded. 'I've no idea how you know this stuff, but yes, we were. We were going to move to LA.'

'Why?'

'It was her idea. I suppose, if I'm being honest, it was because of me. Anne-Laure was always able to shut herself off from the parties, the drugs, the whole toxic lifestyle, but I never could. Never can. I'm a mess. I always drink too much, spend too much, stay too late. I think she was trying to save me.'

'I'm not sure LA is the best please to recover from those sorts of bad habits,' noted Magnus.

'But I would have been closer to Hollywood there,' said Jem, 'and I'm better when I'm working on a film, as you can see. And she wanted to save herself too. I don't think she'd ever been happy here. She hated people like Hilda Underpin, she hated living in that little flat — in fact, she hated the whole of Westminster.'

'Why?' asked Bryn.

'I don't know. She wouldn't really talk about it. She just wanted to get out.'

'So you bought your tickets,' prompted Magnus, 'packed up your flats —'

'*She* packed up *her* flat,' corrected Jem. 'I was going to hold onto this place, as it's so convenient. But yeah, we made plans to leave. We were going to go on the Monday after —' He swallowed. 'Well, the Monday after that tennis tournament.'

'What was Anne-Laure like, in the weeks before the tennis tournament?' asked Magnus.

'She was…' A frown crossed Jem's handsome features. 'Actually, she wasn't great. She was a bit worried, almost jumpy. She really wanted me to stop spending — I think she was worried we wouldn't have enough funds to start our new life together. I mean, I wasn't that bothered. I just assumed we'd both get work out in LA and we'd be fine.'

'Did she take on any extra work?' asked Magnus.

Jem shook his head. 'I don't know. Anne-Laure's jobs were always a bit of a mystery to me.'

Bryn raised his eyebrows: Jem did not seem to know very much about Anne-Laure Chevalier, considering they had been in a relationship for a couple of years. At this stage, the policeman almost thought he and Magnus had a better grasp of her character and lifestyle.

'Let's move on to the day of this tennis tournament, if you don't mind,' said Magnus. 'Can you talk us through it?'

'There's not much to say, really,' said Jem. 'Anne-Laure and I didn't spend much time together that day. She was working hard behind the scenes to make sure the tournament and the party at the Royal West afterwards ran smoothly, and I — Well, I was just supposed to show up and win at tennis.'

'So you didn't see her much?'

'We caught up briefly between the events. She congratulated me on my victory.'

'Did she seem all right then?' asked Bryn.

'She was a bit agitated, but I think that was due to the stress of managing it all.'

'And that was the last time you saw her?'

'No,' said Jem, 'I went to the beginning of that party at the Royal West. But you know what those sorts of things are like, Magnus, they're full of incredibly boring people. So I just went to show my face, really, and to support Anne-Laure — although nobody knew about us, of course. Then I decided to go and meet up with some friends in Ephemeral.'

'Ephemeral?' asked Bryn.

'Yeah, it's a nightclub in Mayfair,' explained Jem. 'I managed to grab Anne-Laure for a few minutes to tell her where I was going, and she agreed she'd meet me there when she had finished with the party. Obviously, she never showed up.' Jem's face crumpled once more. 'Oh God, I wish I'd stayed with her…'

'And what time was this?' asked Magnus. 'When did you last see her?'

'I don't know, early. About nine, nine-thirty?'

'And how did she seem then?' asked Bryn.

'The same, really.'

'How about physically?' persisted the policeman.

'What do you mean?'

'Well, as Magnus said, when her body was found, there was some severe bruising to her wrists and neck —'

'Yes,' said Jem sharply, suddenly sitting up. 'What are you talking about?'

'We're talking about the distinct possibility that Anne-Laure was subjected to violence before her death.'

Jem looked aghast. 'But who? *Why?*'

'Who and why indeed?' asked Magnus. 'As you've probably ascertained, there are a number of loose ends when it comes to Anne-Laure's death.'

'But —' Jem started to respond, but Magnus shook his head.

'Let us ask the questions first, Jem, then you'll get your turn. Did you notice any bruising on Anne-Laure when you said goodbye to her, at the party?'

'Of course not,' said the actor, looking affronted. 'Do you think I would have left her there, if she'd been hurt?'

'Is it possible you might have overlooked them?' continued Magnus.

Jem looked almost angry now. 'I think I would have noticed if my own girlfriend had been beaten up,' he snapped.

Bryn, remembering Inacio's guess that he had overheard the argument in the garden at around ten o'clock, thought Jem was probably right: it seemed whoever had grabbed Anne-Laure had done so after the actor had left the party. Unless that meant the shadowy figure in the garden had been Jem himself...

'Can anyone confirm you were at this club?' asked Magnus, apparently thinking along the same lines.

'Of course,' said the actor, now glowering at them both. 'I'm pretty recognisable, you know. Why do you ask?'

Magnus, who seemed to be back on the offensive, ignored this question and said, 'Did you not think it odd, that Anne-Laure didn't turn up at Ephemeral?'

'Not really, no,' said Jem. 'I knew she'd be working late, and she'd been known to pull all-nighters in the past, so I assumed that was what had happened — that or she'd just gone to bed. I thought we'd catch up with one another in the morning.'

'I saw you the next morning,' said Magnus. 'We bumped into one another during our respective jogs, remember? You'd just run around Hyde Park. You seemed happy.'

'Well, of course I was happy,' said Jem, bitterly. 'That was probably the last time I was truly content. Because I didn't know, did I? As far as I was concerned, I was in love with a wonderful woman, we were about to start a new life together, everything was rosy. Then just a few hours later, I heard what had happened on the news, and I just — I just fell apart.'

Bryn recalled the state of both the actor and his flat the last time they had visited, and could not contradict him.

'It's the guilt that gets me,' said Jem, putting his head in his hands once more. 'I should have been with her, of course, but it's my fault, really, what happened to her…'

'Your fault?' asked Bryn.

The actor looked up. 'I'm not stupid, you know. The papers might have said she died of "natural causes", but I've heard the rumours, I know it was an overdose. And who got her into that stuff, eh?' He pointed a finger at his own chest. 'She never liked it, not really. She liked making money from it, but she was never as keen on it as I was. In fact, she never took it on her own.'

'Had you taken any cocaine together that evening?' asked Bryn.

Jem looked shame-faced once more. 'Yeah, in the bathroom, before I said goodbye to her.'

'And she took it too?'

'Yeah… So I don't know why she had more later. Maybe she was tired. Maybe she thought she needed a pick-me up to come out to the club. Whatever the reason, it was my fault.' His eyes swam with unshed tears. 'It should have been my body they discovered at the Royal West the next morning, my name in the headlines, not hers. I wish it had been.'

He seemed to crumple as he dissolved into grief once more. This time, Magnus reached out a hand and held the actor by the shoulder, steadying rather than embracing him. Bryn, meanwhile, sank back into the sofa cushions, and considered everything Jem McMorran had just told them. He had to assume that, for the moment at least, Jem had told them the truth. He'd had nothing to gain and everything to lose by divulging his drug habits, and — although Bryn very much enjoyed his work on the big screen — he did not think Jem was a good enough actor to fake this kind of inconsolable heartache.

Another interesting aspect of their discussion, the policeman reflected, was that Jem seemed wholly convinced Anne-Laure had died of an accidental overdose. Even being told about the bruising had not altered his opinion, although Bryn supposed his conviction might be being swayed by his own sense of guilt. For a moment, the policeman wondered whether he and Magnus should correct Jem's misconception — if indeed it was a misconception. But he quickly decided against it. Telling a grief-stricken person their dead lover might have been murdered seemed unwise, especially when they were yet to find out the identity of the killer. And the fact that Jem McMorran had the money and means to make a huge amount of fuss about the case only set Bryn more against the idea.

But that was not to say that the conversation with Jem was now over. Bryn thought the actor could still tell them a thing or two about the case, whether he knew what he was doing or not.

'Mr McMorran,' he said, when Jem was sitting up and sipping at his beer again, 'I wonder whether I can make a slightly unusual request of you?'

'What is it?' asked Jem, looking wary.

Bryn tore out a page of his notebook and handed it to Jem, along with a pen. 'I wonder whether you could write something on this piece of paper?'

'Excuse me?'

'Just a sentence or two. Maybe, *The quick brown fox jumps over the lazy dog,* or something similar?'

Jem looked at him as though he had gone slightly mad, but nevertheless picked up the pen and began to write. A few moments later, he handed the paper back to Bryn, saying apologetically, 'Sorry, my hand's a little shaky.'

Bryn and Magnus looked at the words. As the policeman had suggested, Jem had written out, *The quick brown fox jumps over the lazy dog,* and in doing so revealed his handwriting to be large, rounded and a little shaky. In fact, if Bryn had been given this anonymously, he might have assumed it had been penned by a child only just learning to write. In any case, the handwriting sample revealed two things: first, Jem McMorran was not used to writing — which was unsurprising, given he was an actor; but more importantly, it seemed very unlikely that he had written the notebook detailing Anne-Laure's movements, for that contained pages and pages of small, scrawling handwriting. Perhaps, Bryn thought, it wasn't necessary to send the notebook off to the handwriting specialist after all.

'Look, what's this about?' said Jem. 'Why are you getting me to write out children's poems?'

'It's not a poem, it's a pangram,' said Magnus, mildly. 'A phrase that contains all the letters of the alphabet.'

'Never mind what it is, why did you make me write it out?' asked Jem, with a touch of impatience.

Bryn looked to Magnus, silently asking his permission before he withdrew the notebook.

'Because this rather disturbing object has come into our possession,' said the barrister, 'and we wanted to know whether you had anything to do with it.'

Jem, looking baffled, took the notebook. Then, as he began to leaf through it, his face grew very pale.

'What — what is this?'

Neither Magnus nor Bryn answered, and it seemed as though Jem didn't expect a response, because he continued to flick through the pages, his features a mask of horror. He seemed almost transfixed by the detailed account of his dead girlfriend's movements, until, quite suddenly, he seemed to come out of his trance, and closed the book with a snap.

'Who wrote this?' he demanded. 'Who's responsible for this — this *thing*?'

'That's a good question,' said Magnus.

Jem's gaze flicked from the book to the piece of paper on which he'd written the pangram.

'You can't think it was *me*?' he said, colour returning to his face in angry red blotches.

'We don't, not anymore,' said Magnus. 'But we had to rule you out: you see, you're not mentioned in there, not once.'

'I would never — This is absolutely — How could you *think* that I would be such a creep, that I would do something so perverted? I *loved* her!'

'We know, we know,' said Magnus, in a soothing voice. 'Your absence in those pages merely struck us as odd, that's all, especially considering the voyeur was so... meticulous. Surely he or she must have caught you and Anne-Laure together at some point, if you were together as much as you say you were.'

'We were,' said Jem at once, 'I'm not keeping anything back from you anymore.'

He sounded desperate, but Bryn was inclined to believe him.

'I wonder why he left you out?' mused Magnus.

'How am I supposed to explain the actions of perverts?' snapped Jem defensively, interpreting Magnus's question as non-rhetorical. 'I don't believe it. This looked like she was being stalked or something! And you say someone bruised her on the night of her death! What's going on, Magnus?'

'That's what we're trying to find out,' said the barrister, and Bryn noted his reply was fairly non-committal. Perhaps he wasn't keen for Jem to jump to the conclusion of murder either.

'I have something else to show you,' said Bryn, spotting an opportunity to deflect Jem's attention still further. He held up the little plastic wallet containing the engraved silver ring he had found in the garden and said, 'Do you recognise this?'

Jem's expression almost spoke for him: he looked rather offended by the small piece of jewellery.

'Where did you get that, Poundland?' he asked. 'No, of course I don't recognise it! First because I'm a man, and that's a woman's ring, and second because it looks cheap and tacky.'

Inwardly, Bryn had to admit he had a point there.

'So you never saw Anne-Laure wearing it?'

Jem burst out laughing. 'Wearing *that?* Are you being serious? Anne-Laure had expensive taste — believe me, I should know. She wouldn't have been caught dead wearing that.' He seemed to realise he had chosen his words badly. 'I mean, it's not hers, it can't be.'

Bryn handed him the plastic wallet. 'What do you make of the engraving?' he asked.

'*A.C.?*' Jem read, squinting down at the silver ring. 'Nah, it's not hers. She never went by just "Anne".'

'What about "Annie"? Or "Anna"?'

'No, it was always Anne-Laure...' Jem looked confused and, once again, Bryn realised how in the dark he was about certain aspects of Anne-Laure's background.

'That's what we thought,' said Magnus, his voice reassuring. 'We just wanted to double check, that's all. It's nothing to worry about.'

Jem visibly relaxed. Bryn, however, keen to continue making use of Jem as a source of information, said, 'I wonder if you can help us out with one more thing, Mr McMorran? We're going to name a few people who live around here, and perhaps you can tell us what you know of any connection they might have had to Anne-Laure?'

The actor looked perplexed, but shrugged. 'All right, I'll try.'

'Vasyl Kosnitschev,' began Bryn.

'He was her employer,' said Jem at once.

'Did they get on?' pressed the policeman.

'I think so. He was very reliant on her, I reckon she knew all of his secrets. But they seemed to get on, yeah.'

'All right,' said Bryn, after pausing to write this down. 'What about Dame Winifred Rye?'

'She was her landlady,' said Jem, answering as though he were being tested. 'Yeah, Anne-Laure didn't like her.'

Magnus and Bryn exchanged a look of surprise. 'Really? Are you sure?' asked the barrister.

'Yeah, I don't really know why,' went on Jem, 'but she wasn't a big fan. Maybe they had a falling-out about the flat, I don't know.'

'Are you aware that Dame Winifred helped Anne-Laure find her feet when she first moved to London?' asked Bryn.

'What?' Jem laughed. 'No, she didn't! Are you being serious?'

'That's what Dame Winifred told us. In fact, it was her idea for Anne-Laure to come here in the first place.'

Jem looked astonished. 'I didn't know that. Anne-Laure never said. Well, I don't know, maybe she did like her, underneath it all — to be honest, it was sometimes a bit difficult to tell with Anne-Laure, she was so closed off. Maybe she just found Dame Winifred irritating.'

'Dame Winifred has a reputation as being a little… overbearing,' said Bryn, thinking of Daisy.

'Yeah, yeah, that was probably it, then,' said Jem. 'She probably just found her overbearing.'

'She did also agree to plan the tennis tournament and the charity party at the Royal West for Dame Winifred,' Magnus pointed out.

'Yeah, but she did that for the money,' said Jem. 'Like I said, she was keen to raise as much cash as possible for our move to America.'

'What about Hilda Underpin?' asked Bryn.

'Oh, Anne-Laure definitely hated *her*,' said Jem. 'That old bag was completely awful to her. She was always having a go at her about what she was wearing and how she was acting. To be honest, it was a bit weird, how obsessed Hilda was with Anne-Laure. I sometimes thought she was a bit jealous of her, and that's why she was always so mean. She reminded me of an old witch in a fairy tale who wanted to steal Anne-Laure's youth and beauty…'

He trailed off with a slightly self-conscious laugh, but neither Magnus nor Bryn seemed to think what he had said was in any way ridiculous. In fact, Bryn could not help but think that Jem's comments about Hilda echoed those Magnus had made, when they and Juliana had been speculating as to the identity of the notebook's author. Perhaps, then, it was Hilda who had small, scrawling handwriting…

'What about Lord Ellington?' Bryn continued.

'Who?'

'Lord Bevis Ellington, the Labour lord who lives in Westminster Square. He's tall, white-haired —'

'Oh him, yeah,' said Jem. 'The one who's — Well, I think he might have a bit of a… soft spot for me.'

'I think you might be right,' said Magnus, trying to repress a grin.

'But I don't think Anne-Laure knew him, did she? She never mentioned him.'

Once again, Magnus and Bryn shared a glance of surprise: Anne-Laure and Jem might have been lovers, they might have been planning on running away together, but apparently there was plenty she hadn't told him.

'All right,' said Bryn, 'what about Sheikh Hazim bin Lahab?'

'That Arab guy? I don't think she knew him either. Why?' Jem peered at Bryn' notes. 'You don't think any of these people have anything to do with that book, do you? Or the bruises?'

'We're just exploring every possible avenue,' said Magnus, in vague lawyer speak.

'What about Morris Springfield?' asked Bryn.

'I don't know him either.'

'Morris Springfield? He's an author who lives on Westminster Row…'

'He has dark hair and he looks a bit like a vampire, as though he could use some sun,' supplied Magnus.

But Jem shook his head. 'I've never even heard of him. What's he written?'

'Oh, a couple of pompous novels, I wouldn't bore yourself with them,' the barrister advised.

'I don't think Anne-Laure knew any authors,' said Jem, apparently trying to be helpful. 'But who knows, she did like to read. She was much smarter than I am.'

He seemed to have no qualms about admitting this, which Bryn thought was unusual, and not unappealing. He had the impression that, if you ignored the drinking, drug-abuse and general hedonism, Jem McMorran was a fairly decent guy.

'Okay, one last one,' he said. 'Darren Dodge.'

'Who?' Jem laughed. Then, when Bryn repeated the name, he said, 'Sounds like a character from *EastEnders*.'

'He's actually a journalist from *The Dawn Reporter*.'

'Urgh.' Jem's reaction to hearing the name of the tabloid was one of instant disgust. Presumably, as one of the UK's most well-known celebrities, he'd had more than a few encounters with the paper. 'No, why would Anne-Laure know anyone from that rag?'

Why indeed, thought Bryn. He found himself hoping Anne-Laure hadn't been planning to expose Jem to *The Dawn Reporter*, as it would surely break the actor's heart all over again to learn this.

'Well, I think that's everyone,' said Bryn, tucking away his notes. 'And probably everything, too.'

He looked at Magnus for confirmation, and the barrister gave an almost imperceptible nod.

'You are going to try and find the person who wrote that horrible book?' said Jem, as the three of them stood up. 'The one I presume gave her those bruises? I know it might not seem important, given that she's — she's — Well, given that she's gone, but —'

'It *is* important,' Magnus assured him, laying his hand on Jem's shoulder once more. 'Both the book and the bruises are evidence of criminal activity, and we don't take that lightly. Rest assured we're trying to get to the bottom of it.'

Jem, who had winced at the words 'criminal activity' said, 'And what I told you earlier? About the drugs?'

Magnus looked at Bryn, and the policeman realised this was up to him.

'As you've been so helpful, I'll pretend I didn't hear that, just this once,' said the policeman.

'But you should try and sort yourself out, Jem,' said Magnus, in the manner of a stern father. 'You should see poor Anne-Laure's passing as a warning: it might be too late for her, but it's not too late for you. Get help, clean up your act, you're worth more than this.'

'You know, you sound a bit like her,' said Jem, showing them towards the door with a sad smile. 'That's the sort of thing she used to say to me.'

'Well, she was right,' said Magnus, firmly.

Bryn remembered, when he had met Jem McMorran the last time, he had been surprised by how small the actor had been, in comparison to the strapping figure he presented on the big screen. But now, as he stood in his vast, largely-empty hallway, practically hunched over with wretchedness, Jem looked smaller still. It was as though he had shrunk during the course of their conversation; as though talking about Anne-Laure had literally drained him.

'You take care of yourself, Jem,' said Magnus, shaking his hand.

'That's the trouble, isn't it?' said the actor. 'I can't. Now she's gone, I don't know what to do with myself. My fame, my films — they don't mean anything anymore.' He took a shuddering breath, evidently trying to hold himself together until after they had gone, and said, 'Without Anne-Laure, I'm nothing.'

CHAPTER THIRTY-TWO

In spite of Barry Boyle's threats and warnings, Bryn now found it exceptionally difficult to concentrate on the boring paperwork of Victoria Police Station when his mind was full of theories about the death of Anne-Laure Chevalier.

For the last few days, he had been careful to avoid Westminster Square at lunchtime, and had always come back from his break at least five minutes early, in order to demonstrate that — outwardly, at least — he was being careful to toe the line. But that didn't mean that, in his head, Bryn wasn't constantly replaying the interviews he and Magnus had conducted with their various suspects, and trying to make connections between their often wildly different accounts of Anne-Laure's movements, relationships, and even her personality.

In the evening it was easier, for Bryn was free to pore over the notes he had made over the past few weeks, which were still scattered across the floor of his bedsit. Now, they were laid out in a completely different order to before, and were covered in more markings, scribbles and even luminous bands of highlighter pen, where Bryn had wanted to draw his own attention to something he thought especially significant. Often, he would stay up late into the night, reading and rereading just one of their suspects' accounts, for he always felt as though the answers were almost within reach... It was not a particularly healthy way to live, especially as the beautiful and terrible dream-figure of Anne-Laure had begun to haunt his nightmares again. Yet when he felt as though all of the information he needed was right here it was difficult to turn off the light and try and put the matter from his mind in favour of sleep.

When it came to his day job, he wished for the hundredth time Boyle would give him something different to do, although now it wasn't because he was bored, but because he wanted to think about something other than Anne-Laure, before it sent him completely mad. If only Boyle would let him patrol, or put him on security duty somewhere nearby, or perhaps he could even go into a school to talk about police work — if only Boyle would let him do anything at all, other than this endless administration.

The hours in the office had, however, given Bryn ample opportunity to reflect on his and Magnus' meeting with Jem McMorran. It had been an illuminating encounter, during which the actor had told them so much Bryn knew it would be a long time before he finished sifting through the notes he had made. But it felt good to have at least a few of his and Magnus' theories confirmed: as they had suspected, Jem and Anne-Laure had been in a romantic relationship, and they had also been planning on running away together two days after the party at the Royal West. These admissions, along with the small matter of the drugs, seemed to be the major revelations of the meeting, but Bryn wondered whether there was anything important to be discovered from Jem's other, more throwaway comments. The policeman would have to give it some thought.

Meanwhile, however, he felt fairly confident in moving Jem down the list of people most likely to have killed Anne-Laure Chevalier. Bryn knew from his police training that boyfriends were usually *more* likely to be suspects — and Magnus would probably have reminded him of this — but from what they had seen and heard, Bryn highly doubted Jem had it in him to take someone's life, let alone the life of someone he loved. True, the actor had had access to the cocaine that had probably killed her, but what would he have had to gain from her death? As far as Jem had been concerned, everything had been wonderful between him and Anne-Laure. The only possible motive Bryn could see was one of vengeance, as there was a slim chance Jem had found out Anne-Laure was trying to sell him out to *The Dawn Reporter* and had seen red. But if that were the case, he had done an exceptional job of pretending not to know about Anne-Laure's link to Darren Dodge and the paper, let alone playing the grieving boyfriend. And besides, although Bryn couldn't pretend to know that much about her, he could not quite believe that the reserved, business-like and slightly melancholic Anne-Laure Chevalier would have betrayed her lover like that, no matter how desperate she had been to make money.

So, as usual, Bryn felt as though he were swimming in information about the case, and there were very few facts to hold onto. But even so — and hopefully this wasn't just his imagination — things did seem a little clearer. He was beginning to entertain a couple of theories that were so outlandish he hardly knew where they had come from, which surely meant he was either going completely round the bend, or that somewhere in back of his brain connections were being made without his even realising it. In fact, it reminded Bryn of what Lucas had said at the Japanese restaurant the other day: '… *it's almost as though your subconscious is a few steps ahead.*'

With this in mind, during a particularly quiet period in the Victoria Police Station one afternoon, Bryn pulled a blank sheet of paper towards him and began to make a 'To Do' list:

Chase up Lucas for A-L's bank statements
Try and get invited round to tea at Hilda's again

(This, Bryn thought, would be an exceptionally unpleasant task, but unfortunately a very necessary one, if what he suspected had happened turned out to be true.)

Buy a copy of Vacant Shadows by Morris Springfield
Compare invoices
Look at The Station Garden catalogue

Then finally, and perhaps most importantly, Bryn wrote:

Go and visit Daisy

'Bryn?'

He quickly threw an elbow over his 'To Do' list so the person who was approaching — his colleague, Shona — couldn't see what he was up to. Although, as he smiled at her in greeting, he reflected that his list probably wouldn't seem particularly incriminating to a casual observer. In fact, the most damning item on there was probably the last point; Bryn had been teased mercilessly by almost everyone in the office ever since he had made the mistake of revealing the name of his crush. Even now, almost a week later, his colleagues were still sporadically bursting into renditions of 'Bicycle Built for Two', especially the chorus:

Daisy, Daisy,
Give me your answer, do.
I'm half crazy
All for the love of you…

'The internal post is here,' said Shona, just as Bryn was bracing himself for yet more mockery.

'Oh?' he said, wondering why she was telling him this; he was so junior, he hardly received any mail.

'Yes, there's something for you,' she said, 'from the CID.'

It took all of Bryn's restraint not to grab it from her hands. But Shona was looking curious, almost suspicious, so he shrugged and said, 'That must be a mistake, surely? But I'll take a look — thanks, Shona.'

Apparently satisfied, she handed him the envelope and departed. Bryn saw from the ink stamp that it had, indeed, come from the Criminal Investigation Department near Hanover Square.

Good old Lucas, he thought, as he tore open the envelope.

Inside were a few sheets of A4 paper folded neatly together. There was no accompanying letter or even a compliments slip enclosed; evidently, Lucas had wanted to send this information as anonymously as possible. With slightly trembling hands, Bryn smoothed out the papers, his feverish gaze trying to take in everything written there all at once.

They were indeed a few months' worth of bank statements, and they did indeed belong to Anne-Laure Chevalier. Tracing a hand down each page, Bryn scanned through the itemised list as quickly as possible, his finger running past relatively large amounts made to upmarket clothes boutiques and smaller payments made to more mundane shops such as Sainsbury's and Boots. None of it looked particularly unusual for a London-dwelling woman in her late twenties who had apparently had plenty of disposal income. In truth, Bryn was beginning to worry that it all looked far too innocuous. But then, on the third page, he saw it.

'Ah ha!' he said under his breath, jabbing a finger against the paper so forcefully he nearly dropped it. 'There it is!'

Bryn stood up, intending to show Magnus immediately. But then he remembered where he was, and what he was supposed to be doing, and realised Boyle wouldn't take kindly to him simply marching out of the police station in the middle of the afternoon. Besides, Magnus wouldn't even be in Westminster Square at this time of day, and he was a hard man to get hold of lately, for he seemed to be knee-deep in some new case at work.

Trying not to feel too deflated, Bryn decided he would make copies of the bank statements and send them to Magnus instead. That way, the barrister could read them at his leisure, and Bryn wouldn't feel as though he was bothering him too much. So, with a whistle, he walked over to the photocopier, made a few duplicates of the documents, and returned to his desk, being careful to tuck the copies under his To Do list, which was in turn obscured by a large ring binder.

For the rest of the afternoon, he tried to focus on his work, feeling as though he had made some significant progress on the Anne-Laure case. It was a bit difficult to sit still when all he wanted to do was study what Lucas had sent him properly, but the delivery had put Bryn in a good mood, and he wasn't even fazed when Barry Boyle came lumbering through the shared office, heralded by the smell of fast food and body odour.

'Walsh!' he bellowed. 'Walsh, I need you!'

Constable Shona Walsh rolled her eyes: it was a well-known fact that, because she was one of the only women working in Victoria Police Station, Barry Boyle treated her like a secretary, despite the fact she had more experience than several of her male colleagues, including Bryn.

'Yes, sir?' she said, through gritted teeth.

'Walsh, make this bigger for me,' demanded Boyle, thrusting a handwritten letter into her hands. 'I can't read a word of it.'

'You know, there is a receptionist who can do this for you, sir,' said Shona.

'I'm not walking all the way to reception!' bellowed Boyle. 'Just do as you're told, Walsh!'

Shona scowled, but did not object. Bryn felt sorry for her, although somewhat relieved that, for once, he was not the one being picked on.

'Someone's left this!' Shona announced, having lifted up the lid of the photocopier and discovered a document still resting on the glass. 'Who does this belong to?'

As she waved the piece of paper through the air for the office to see, Bryn's heart seemed to freeze in his chest: apparently, he had forgotten to remove the last page of the original bank statement from the photocopier. He opened his mouth to try and salvage the situation, but before he could think what to say, Shona was examining the paper.

'Looks like a bank statement,' she continued, evidently trying to help find its owner. 'Account holder is — blimey! Account holder is *Anne-Laure Chevalier*.'

The name had an instantaneous effect. The office, which had been abuzz with noise moments beforehand, was now completely silent. It might have been a couple of months since she had died, but everyone remembered who Anne-Laure Chevalier was.

'Um...' said Shona, before biting her lip, as though she guessed she had accidentally landed someone in trouble, 'I can just leave it here, and —'

'*What did you say?*' came a booming voice.

Bryn closed his eyes. For a second, he had hoped that Barry Boyle had returned to his office, or that perhaps, by some miracle, the Police Chief Superintendent hadn't heard or been listening to what Shona had said. But he strode up to the female constable, snatched the document from her hands, and stared at it with his small piggy eyes.

'*What is this?*' he shouted, almost incoherent with rage.

MYSTERY IN WESTMINSTER SQUARE

The other employees of the Victoria Police Station seemed to shrink with fear as Boyle brandished the paper with such force he almost hit Shona in the face.

'*Who does this belong to?*' Boyle roared. '*Who brought this here?*'

Bryn raised a tremulous hand. 'I did,' he said. 'It's mine.'

There seemed little point in denying it. Once Boyle recovered from his temper tantrum, it wouldn't be too difficult to for him to work out who the paper belonged to, and Bryn didn't want to risk getting any of his colleagues into trouble in the meantime. The game, it seemed, was up.

'*Summers!*' Boyle roared, crossing the room with surprising speed for a man of his size, slamming his palm down on Bryn's desk, and leaning almost his whole weight on his arms, so the tabletop creaked in protest. '*Explain yourself, Summers!*'

Boyle's bright red face was very close to Bryn's, and his breath was so foul-smelling it was all the young police constable could do not to retch.

'I'm sorry, sir,' he mumbled, leaning as far back from Boyle as he dared.

'Did I ask you to apologise?' Boyle roared.

'No, sir.'

'What did I ask you to do?'

'Explain myself, sir.'

'*So explain yourself, Summers!*'

Bryn's skin was prickling with panic. 'I was —' he began, hoping in vain that a plausible explanation was on the tip of his tongue. 'I mean, I thought —'

'Let me tell you what *I* think, Summers,' said Boyle, lowering his voice to a sneer. '*I* think you ignored me when I told you *repeatedly* not to stick your nose into this little tart's death. *I* think you completely ignored me, when I informed you that our top priority was protecting the reputation of Westminster and the Royal West. *I* think you thought you could do better than people with far more experience and expertise than you, so you decided you'd have a go at playing detective. How am I doing so far?'

Bryn said nothing: again, there seemed little point in contradicting him, not when Boyle was largely speaking the truth.

'Where did you get this?' Boyle demanded.

'Nowhere,' said Bryn at once, determined to protect Lucas.

But Boyle had already spotted the torn-open envelope on Bryn's desk, and snatched it up, squinting at the ink post stamp.

'Who do you know in the CID?'

'No one,' said Bryn. 'I — I wrote to them anonymously.'

Boyle scrunched up the envelope in his fist and said, 'I don't believe you. We'll see if that's still your story after I've had a word with our friends near Hanover Square…'

Bryn swallowed. He had always been aware that he had been risking his own neck, investigating Anne-Laure's death on the quiet. But the thought that he might now have landed Lucas in hot water as well made him feel truly awful, especially when he recalled Lucas had warned him to keep his name out of it.

Boyle straightened up to address the office at large.

'Let me make this clear once and for all,' he told his staff, who had all been watching the confrontation between him and Bryn unfold. 'Anne-Laure Chevalier was a silly bimbo who accidentally overdosed after too much partying at the Royal West. She caused great inconvenience to a great deal of people, but fortunately we managed to contain the situation by putting out the official story that she died of natural causes. It was a little white lie to appease the press and protect the reputation of the Royal West, of Westminster, and of the stupid girl in question.'

Bryn almost snorted at this: as though Barry Boyle cared one jot about Anne-Laure's reputation! His hands were balled into fists, and his fingernails dug into his palms so painfully that he was afraid he would draw blood. Almost everything Boyle had just said was untrue: Anne-Laure *hadn't* been a silly bimbo, she *hadn't* accidentally overdosed or died of natural causes, and she'd been working, rather than partying, at the Royal West.

'As Police Chief Superintendent of this station,' Boyle continued, 'I should not have to explain myself or my actions to anybody at all. But apparently, some of you are having difficulty understanding the decisions I made regarding this idiot girl's death, so I hope you now feel sufficiently informed. And in case you don't, here's a summary: dumb blonde dies, end of story. Now, if I hear so much as a whisper about this business — and if even a whiff of this conversation leaves this station, let alone reaches the press — I will come down on each of you so hard that you'll regret the day you were born. Understand?'

He glared around at his inferiors, all of whom seemed to be too afraid to respond.

'*Understand?*' he bellowed.

'Yes, sir,' everybody murmured.

'Good,' said Boyle grimly. 'And as for *you*...'

He jabbed a fat finger at Bryn, his face turning purple with rage once more.

'As for you, I want you out of this station in ten minutes.'

Bryn stared at him, his chest suddenly feeling painfully tight. 'Wh — what?' he stammered.

'You heard me, Summers, get the hell out. You're fired.'

'Fired?' Bryn repeated, hardly able to choke out the word. 'You can't do that, you've no —?'

'Oh, do you want an official reason?' Boyle jeered. 'Let's see. There's breach of police confidentiality, for starters. Then there's poor conduct at work, sloppy time-keeping, and of course gross insubordination... That's what I'll put on the forms, anyway. But really, between us, I just don't like you, Summers. You've been a thorn in my side since you arrived, with your constant whining and interfering, and this disobedience is the last straw. But honestly, you should think of this as a favour, this dismissal. You're no great shakes at police work, Summers. How can you be, when you're such a poor excuse for a man?'

It cost Bryn every bit of strength he had to keep his face blank, to hide from Boyle how hurt and frustrated he was by this whole situation. Because he knew he would regret it forever if he lost any more face; if he begged to keep his job or, worse, if his emotions got the better of him and he became teary. That, he knew, would only prove Boyle's theory that he was somehow lacking.

The Police Chief Superintendent, perhaps a little disappointed Bryn hadn't crumbled, said, 'Pack up your stuff, Summers. I never want to see your ugly face in this station again. You have ten minutes.' He checked his watch. 'Actually, you have eight.'

Under the gaze of the whole office, Bryn began to collect his scant belongings from his desk, his face burning with humiliation. This was a hundred times worse than when everyone had been teasing him about Daisy, or anything Boyle had subjected him to before. His fingers were shaking as he picked up all of his pens and the little cactus he had bought to brighten up his desk, and it was only when he had an armful of belongings that he realised he had nowhere to put them.

'Here,' said Shona, emptying a box of printer paper and bringing it to Bryn's desk. 'Take this.'

'Walsh, did I ask you to help him?' asked Boyle, who was watching Bryn pack up with his arms folded.

But Shona ignored him. Boyle rarely had the attention span to be angry with more than one person at once, so perhaps she thought she was momentarily safe from his wrath. In any case, Bryn thanked her. He suspected she felt bad for accidentally landing him in it with the bank statement, and he wanted her to know he didn't bear her any ill will: this was all his fault.

After what felt like an eternity, but in reality must have only been a few minutes, Bryn finished putting his belongings in the pathetic cardboard box. He then went into the station's bathroom to take off his uniform, stealing a moment to look at himself in the mirror before he did so.

This is it, he thought, realising, perhaps for the first time, how much broader and stronger his skinny frame looked in his official get-up. How much it suited him. *I'll never wear this again.*

Afterwards, when he was back in his civilian clothes, he handed his uniform to the receptionist — who seemed to have been made aware of the situation — and then walked slowly and wordlessly out of the Victoria Police Station.

Outside, and completely incongruously, it was a beautiful day. The sun was blazing, and there were no clouds in the sky or even a hint of a breeze.

Bryn, clutching at his box of belongings, wandered towards Westminster Square without really knowing why. Perhaps he hoped he would run into Magnus again. Or Daisy. Or Juliana. He craved any friendly face who might offer him even a word of comfort. In fact, right now, he would have even appreciated an encounter with Hilda Underpin, because at least she would have distracted him from the horrible, unavoidable truth.

'I've been fired,' he said aloud, as though by stating this to the largely empty Square it would sink in quicker.

At the sound of his own words, Bryn sat down on the front steps of one of the houses in the south-east corner of the quadrant, not even caring he looked like a vagrant, and would surely be chased away by a doorman before long. He felt utterly hopeless. Everything he had worked towards for the past few years had come to nothing. All of his dreams of becoming a detective were now shattered.

'I've lost my job,' he said, trying these words instead.

But no, he thought, a flicker of defiance flaring up inside him. *No. My job has been taken from me.* Because hadn't Barry Boyle just admitted he had always had a grudge against him? Was it even legal, to fire someone without proper warning? Because while Boyle had made all sorts of threats against him, there hadn't been anything *official*...

Feeling marginally more optimistic, Bryn moved the cardboard box onto his lap. Rifling through the contents, he pulled out Anne-Laure's bank statements, which — aside from the one he had left in the photocopier — he had managed to smuggle out directly under Boyle's nose. He stared at her name, and in that moment felt nothing but resentment. Bryn had sacrificed his time, his efforts, and now his job to try and get to the bottom of her death, and for what? She would never know and she would never thank him. It had all been completely pointless.

He moved his fingers to the top of the bank statements, intending to tear the paper into little pieces there and then. But he couldn't do it. Something stopped him. Because it wasn't pointless, was it? Trying to uncover the truth, pursuing justice? That was what police work was supposed to be about, no matter what Boyle said.

Weeks ago, Bryn had known, by instinct if nothing else, that Anne-Laure Chevalier's death was an injustice that needed to be investigated, and nothing had changed on that score. Indeed, he and Magnus had merely found more evidence to support his theory of murder. So he couldn't give up now, could he? It didn't matter that he had returned his uniform, that he had been cast out of Victoria Police Station. All of his detective work up until now had been unofficial anyway.

Bryn forced himself to momentarily cast aside worries for his long-term future. (What was he going to do about his career? How was he going to afford to live in London? How was he going to afford to *eat*?) Because something else had occurred to him now: if he could solve the murder of Anne-Laure Chevalier and take his findings to someone above Boyle, maybe he would be given a reprieve. Maybe he could make the case that he had only behaved recklessly and rebelliously in order to uphold the law — in order to catch a killer. Surely then, somebody more benevolent than Boyle would realise he was worthy of his job.

Of course, solving the murder was no easy task. But it was also not impossible, Bryn thought, as he finally found the strength to stand again, and picked up his box of belongings from the pavement. Ideas were already falling into place in the back of his mind, and vague niggling feelings were now growing into lucid suspicions. He had the evidence, the motivations, and now he was no longer in the employ of Barry Boyle, there was nothing and no one stopping him from his investigation. He would uncover the truth, both for Anne-Laure's sake and his own. All he needed was a little more time to piece it all together, to prove it — and it just so happened that time was the one thing Bryn now had in abundance.

CHAPTER THIRTY-THREE

As September rapidly approached, Magnus felt as though there was a distinctly 'back to school' feel to the last days of the summer holiday, and not just for his children. He had enjoyed a few relatively quiet months at work, which was not unusual in July and August, given everyone was on holiday. But now, in the week or so before Rosanna and Lee returned to their studies, he had been plunged into a huge case at work, which was keeping him busier than he had been in some time.

The case involved the arbitration of a conflict over a pipeline installation in the Gulf. Apparently, a Korean subcontractor was owed six months' worth of pay for the infrastructure work they had completed, and the whole affair had blown up into a three-way battle between the Korean subcontractor, the American contractor, and the Gulf company in question. Not only were the details of this case keeping Magnus working late into the night, he was also having to attend the arbitration tribunal at the ICC Chamber of Commerce in Luxembourg. This was unusual, as for the sake of his family the barrister usually tried to avoid travel, and sent his solicitors to do the depositions and witness statements on his behalf. But in this matter, it was unavoidable, and Magnus' relaxed and peaceful summer soon became a very distant memory.

In addition to the stresses of work, he was under the usual pressure from Juliana. On the most part she was supportive of his job, but she couldn't quite get her head around the fact that Magnus was having to work so hard while the children were still on holiday, no matter how many times he tried to explain to her that the legal profession didn't keep to the same schedule as the schools. However, in order to appease her, he forced himself to put down his paperwork for a few hours every day and spend time with Rosanna and Lee, who were not at their most pleasant, both being restless and slightly bored after too long a break from their lessons. This meant Magnus then had to work until past midnight to make up the time, but it was probably worth it, in order to stop Juliana from complaining.

His marriage, he knew — despite having had no time to properly reflect on it — was still a little shaky. He and Juliana hadn't had a major argument since the episode in which she had woken him up in the middle of the night, worried about stalkers and murderers loitering around Westminster Square, and then stormed off to sleep in the spare room. But then, neither had they had many minor disagreements either, and Magnus found this a little worrying. Juliana was a tempestuous character who enjoyed purging her emotions on a regular basis, so the new, politer version of his wife was unsettling. It was almost as though she, like the children, was restless and bored — although it was a far more serious prospect to be jaded by a marriage than a school holiday.

They were both cowards, Magnus thought; both unable to face up to the fact that significant cracks were appearing in their partnership. He knew he had to talk to her — he knew together they had to figure out a way to plaster over those cracks before everything began to fall apart in earnest — but he was so exhausted and overworked he couldn't quite bear the thought of even beginning the conversation.

One evening, however, when he was reading Rosanna and Lee their bedtime story, it occurred to him to ask their opinion on the matter.

'Do you like living where we live?' he asked, looking up from *The Lion, the Witch and the Wardrobe*.

'Dad,' said Lee, prodding him on the shoulder, 'I want to know what happens to Lucy…'

Magnus shut the book, eliciting groans from both of his children.

'But seriously, do you like living in London?' he asked.

'Yes,' they both said automatically, obviously anxious to get back to the book.

Magnus, feeling this wasn't going quite as he had intended said, 'What about Kent? Do you like visiting Granny and Grandad there?'

'Oh, yes!' they both said, with a little more enthusiasm.

This, Magnus thought, was unsurprising: Juliana's parents spoiled Rosanna and Lee rotten every time they went to stay.

'All right, apart from Granny and Grandad, and all the sweets and presents they give you, what else do you like about Kent?' Magnus asked.

'All the trees I can climb!' said Lee at once.

'The rope swing by the river!' said Rosanna.

'Blackberry picking!'

'Rolling down the hill and getting all grassy!'

'Swimming in the lake!'

'The woods!'

'The sea!'

They went on like this for some time. In the end, Magnus had to hold up his hand to stop them. They truly were Juliana's children.

'Great,' he said, a little weakly. 'And what do you like about living here, in Westminster Square?'

They gave this some thought.

'The house,' said Rosanna, gesturing around at her room.

'My friends,' said Lee. 'Not school, though.'

'Yeah, my friends too,' agreed Rosanna.

'What about *London* though?' Magnus pressed. 'What about the museums and the galleries and all the famous buildings?'

'I guess…' said Rosanna, wrinkling her nose.

They lapsed into silence for a few moments. Then Magnus, a little desperately, said, 'What would you miss the most, if you didn't live in London?'

They looked a little worried now, and Lee, in a matter-of-fact voice rather beyond his years, said, 'That's obvious, isn't it? You and Mum.'

Magnus's heart gave a little twinge, and he pulled both his son and daughter into an embrace. They submitted to this for a few seconds, and then tried to wriggle out of his grasp.

'Dad, read the book!' demanded Rosanna.

★ ★ ★ ★

The other side-effect of having far too much work and far too little time was that Magnus had not had much of an opportunity to see Bryn over the past few weeks, which he felt bad about. When Bryn had phoned him with the news that Barry Boyle had discovered his secret investigation into Anne-Laure Chevalier's death and promptly sacked him, Magnus had been surprised, but not shocked. He had always known, as had Bryn, that they had been taking a big risk with their detective work. In a way, Magnus was glad that — if Barry Boyle had had to find out — at least it was Bryn's own fault, and that it wasn't he or someone else who had landed the young Police Constable in trouble by accident. But still, Magnus was not without sympathy: after all, Bryn had been trying to do the right thing, and look where it had landed him.

They had met just once since Bryn's dismissal, snatching an hour in the taxidermy-stuffed interior of the Lion of Westminster before Magnus had had to return to work. He had expected to find Bryn defeated and morose, perhaps plunged into a depression over this blow to his career, but instead the former police constable was oddly buoyant.

'I think I can solve it now, Magnus,' he had said.

Magnus had been both stunned and a little worried to hear this. He had thought, considering the circumstances, Bryn might have given up on the whole Anne-Laure Chevalier case, seeing as it had cost him his job. But on the contrary, his young friend now seemed more enthused than ever.

'Are you sure that's wise?' he had ventured, back in the pub. 'Perhaps you should concentrate on deciding what to do next instead? I mean, are you going to try and stay in the police force? Is that possible? Is there anything we could do to dispute Boyle's decision? It sounds like there must be, he didn't give you any warning at all... Or are you going to change careers entirely? And what about London? Would you want to stay here or go back to Wales?'

But Bryn had waved aside these big questions, as though they were of no importance whatsoever. 'Never mind all that, it's the case that matters. We're so close to the truth now, Magnus, I refuse to be distracted. Solving Anne-Laure's murder is the only thing I care about.'

The trouble was, Magnus now felt exactly the opposite. While his young friend was presumably scrutinising every piece of evidence they had found, every statement they had collected, and going over and over the various theories they had formulated, the barrister felt rather relieved he had the excuses of work and family to keep him removed from it all. It wasn't as though he had suddenly changed his mind and decided Anne-Laure's death was entirely unsuspicious after all — far from it. He supposed he just had a more cynical mind than Bryn, who was idealistic to a fault. Every day, Magnus heard about or came into contact with unsolved cases, so why should that of Anne-Laure Chevalier be any different? He wanted to know what had happened to her, of course he did, but realistically, it was likely they would never find out the truth.

Still, in spite of his best efforts to push both Bryn and Anne-Laure from his mind, at least temporarily, something troubled Magnus's conscience. Was he letting Bryn down, neglecting the case as he was? Magnus knew he was under no obligation to help him — in fact, when it came to the case, the barrister felt he had already gone far beyond the call of duty. So why did he feel oddly guilty, when he reflected on how much time and effort Bryn was still setting aside for the investigation, while he, Magnus, was no longer contributing at all? It wasn't as though it would be particularly helpful, encouraging the now ex-Police Constable to continue with what would likely be a fruitless undertaking. Perhaps, then, it was merely the idea that he had left Bryn on his own; that, through no fault of his own, Magnus had practically abandoned a good person in unfortunate circumstances who was still trying to do the right thing. And perhaps, mixed in with all of that, it wasn't just Bryn he felt he was letting down, but Anne-Laure Chevalier as well.

The only thing Magnus promised Bryn that evening in The Lion of Westminster was that he would let him know if any of their suspects did or said anything unusual over the next few days and weeks. And, given Magnus was soon to be holding a follow-up meeting about Central Square Properties' maintenance charges, he thought he might at least have an opportunity to keep an eye on a few of the more dubious characters in Anne-Laure's life.

Magnus highly regretted scheduling this meeting for the end of August, but at the time he had made the arrangements he hadn't been so swamped at work, and he supposed it was his responsibility to continue leading the attempted rebellion against CSP. Once more, for the sake of numbers, he had hired out the back room of the Cosmopolitan Club on Westminster Square, and on the evening in question he waited for his guests at the head of the table, nursing a cup of coffee; he was not in the habit of drinking caffeine much after midday, but it had become an unfortunate but necessary habit of late.

Out of the people they had questioned about Anne-Laure's life and death, Morris Springfield, Jem McMorran and Vasyl Kosnitschev were not expected to attend the meeting. Morris, of course, did not live in Westminster Square, and Magnus had limited the meeting to residents of the quadrant, for fear of most of the area turning up. Jem had sent his apologies and explained he was on a publicity tour for his latest film, the one he had shot at the end of last year. Magnus was both unsurprised and unbothered to hear this; he, like Bryn, was fairly sure that Jem had been truthful during their last meeting — on the whole, anyway — and at the moment it seemed sensible to prioritise other people in the investigation.

Vasyl, however, seemed a noteworthy absence. The Ukrainian oligarch had a lot at stake with CSP, being one of the few people in Westminster Square in possession of an entire house, and when Magnus thought back on their previous meeting, Vasyl had been one of the people most willing to take action against their common enemy. He'd had the surprisingly good grace to send Magnus a letter full of vague explanations about how he was out of the country, but it still struck the barrister as a little odd he hadn't made an effort to be here, considering how much the oligarch had to lose, quite literally, from CSP and their inflated charges.

As for the other persons of interest, they were all soon present and correct, filing in with the rest of the guests. Hilda Underpin, whom Magnus had reluctantly invited this time, arrived first, presumably so she could spy on everyone else coming in after her. She was carrying Tam Tam under her arm and when she came across a group of guests lingering in her path by the door she jabbed at them violently with her walking stick. Dame Winifred Rye made her entrance a few minutes later, her yellow floral dress looking particularly bright and garish against the grey, blue and black suits of almost everybody else. She made a great show of kissing and waving at many of the other people present, and although they all seemed to humour her, Magnus could not help but wonder whether she was as popular as she thought she was. Next came Lord Bevis Ellington, who had mercifully decided to forgo his riding gear this time. He, with slightly less aggression than Hilda, pushed his way through the guests to take up the seat right next to Magnus, evidently keen to position himself as far up the table as possible. And last of all was Sheikh Hazim bin Lahab, who lumbered in at least ten minutes late, when everyone else was seated and Magnus was about to start the meeting. He did not bother to apologise for his tardiness, or perhaps he was simply unable to, for he was stuffing great fistfuls of sticky dates into his mouth as he sat down, and Magnus could not help but notice that a food-stained napkin was still tucked into his collar, presumably from his dinner.

'Well, good evening, everyone,' Magnus began, a little thrown by suddenly having these four suspects in one place. *Not that I'm investigating anymore,* he reminded himself. 'And welcome back to the Cosmopolitan Club, who have kindly allowed us to use this room once again.'

Hilda gave a huff of disapproval. 'Welcome *back*?' she cried. 'Some of us are here for the first time! Some of us weren't invited to the *other* meeting!'

'As you may recall,' Magnus continued, ignoring her, 'the last time we met we discussed the fact that we were all similarly unhappy with the rising rates CSP charge us for the so-called maintenance of our properties.'

Next to him, Lord Ellington leaned forward. 'I wouldn't say I was *unhappy*, exactly...' he began. 'I wouldn't want it going on any kind of record that I had *criticised* Central Square Properties. Really, I'm just here as an interested party.'

'You did put your name to the petition, Bevis,' pointed out Magnus.

'Yes, I know. But I'd rather that didn't get bandied about, to be perfectly honest with you,' said Ellington. 'I have a reputation to maintain, after all.'

'Reputation for *what*?' snorted Hazim from the other end of the table, although his words were barely audible through his mouthful of dates.

Ellington did not dignify this with an answer.

'Well, as we're on the subject of that petition,' Magnus continued, 'I should cut to the chase and say that it seems to have had absolutely no effect whatsoever. I'd be lying if I said I had thought it was going to solve all of our problems, but I least expected a bit of correspondence from CSP on the matter. Whereas in fact, I've heard nothing at all.'

Groans and sighs of disappointment rippled around the table. Magnus, knowing very well what the answer to his next question would be, asked it anyway, 'I don't suppose anyone else has heard anything?'

Everybody shook their heads.

'How *do* they get away with it?' said Dame Winifred, looking outraged. 'It didn't used to be like this, did it? I don't really remember, because my husband dealt with all of that, way back when. But I'll tell you this: if he were still alive, he'd be right here, leading the charge with you, Magnus.'

'He'd be right here under the table, you mean,' sneered Hilda. 'If I remember rightly, Lord Rye had quite a weakness for drink.'

Dame Winifred gasped in outrage, as did a few of the other guests; the aristocrat might have been a rather silly figure, but she was certainly more beloved and sympathetic than Hilda Underpin, who was generally viewed to be the wicked witch of Westminster Square.

'Thank you for that vote of confidence, Winifred,' said Magnus loudly, before an argument could break out. Then, trying to regain control of the discussion, he said, 'So what we really need to decide today is what we're going to do next. I, for one, am still supremely unhappy with these maintenance charges. I know it's a privilege to live in Westminster Square, and I'm also aware that historic buildings like ours cost a certain amount to maintain. But I feel we are yet to receive a proper explanation as to why the charges have gone up so drastically over the past few years, even taking inflation into account. Which forces me to conclude there is no reason at all, and CSP are simply trying to take us for a ride. I don't know about the rest of you, but I'm not happy with that.'

A smattering of applause followed this little impromptu speech, and a few cries of 'Hear, hear!' Only Lord Ellington looked uncomfortable, probably because he didn't want to be drawn into anything that might make him look bad to his contacts in parliament or the palace. Magnus held up a hand to quieten the noise.

'The only action I think we can take at this stage is to write a follow-up letter to CSP,' he said. 'And this time, I'll word it more strongly — far more strongly. As you know, I'm a barrister, so I'll pepper this correspondence with some frightening-sounding legal jargon and see if that gets us a reply. After all, they still owe us a response to our petition.'

Dame Winifred raised a bejewelled hand. 'But Magnus, don't CSP have their own lawyers?' she asked.

'Doubtless they do,' he replied, before cracking his knuckles, 'but you don't get to where I am in the legal profession without learning to write some pretty intimidating letters. Maybe I'll view it as a challenge: try and pen CSP something so threatening even their lawyers will shake in their boots.'

Most of the room chuckled. Then Sheikh Hazim raised his hand.

'Magnus, when you write this letter, could you add in something from me?' he said. 'Could you tell them I still have a problem with the pipes in my house? I think there are mice or rats running around inside them, because they make a terrible sound at night. It sounds like I have a ghoul. I cannot sleep, with all that noise.'

Magnus, who did not intend to write anything of the sort in his letter, asked, 'Have you not told them yourself, Hazim?'

'I did, and they just told me it was probably air bubbles, and it would stop after a while, but it has not. So put that in your letter, will you, Magnus?'

'I'm not sure that would entirely relevant to —' the barrister began, but he was interrupted by an elderly lady whose name he couldn't remember.

'I have something for your letter as well, Mr Walterson,' she said. 'At the end of the last year, CSP rewired a part of my flat, only they didn't exactly tidy up after themselves. There are still exposed wires hanging down from one of my light fixtures, and very often when I switch on one of the living room lamps I get a small electric shock!'

'That doesn't sound great,' Magnus admitted, 'but I think, when it comes to individual issues like that, it might be better to contact CSP separately, otherwise —'

'Does anyone else have a problem with their plaster?' interrupted an elderly neighbour called Mr Wilkinson, who was sitting next to Hilda Underpin. 'Some parts of my walls are peeling off so much it looks as though I'm in the process of redecorating. And as for that stuff on the ceiling, whatever it's called —'

'Mr Wilkinson, if we could please focus on the matter at hand,' said Magnus, desperately trying to return everyone's attention to the legal letter.

'Stucco!' burst out Wilkinson. 'That's what it is. And a ruddy mess they've made of it too. Why, in my dining room — hey!' he suddenly shouted. 'Hey! Mrs Underpin, control your dog!'

Magnus looked up from his notes to the cause of this minor commotion. At that moment, Tam Tam was stood on the table, brazenly licking the froth off Mr Wilkinson's pint of beer.

'He's just thirsty,' said Hilda.

'It's *my* drink!' cried Wilkinson, outraged. 'Also, it's *beer!*'

'He seems to like it,' observed the old woman, making no move to stop her pet.

Wilkinson, looking outraged, tried to shoo Tam Tam away. The little dog, wearing a moustache of foam, growled at him with surprising ferocity, and then returned to licking at his drink, in which he was now down to the dark-coloured beer.

'Mrs Underpin!' exploded the elderly gentleman.

'Hilda,' said Magnus wearily, feeling as though Rosanna and Lee showed more maturity on a daily basis than some of the people sat around this table, 'please would you control your dog?'

Grumbling to herself, Hilda pulled the scrawny little creature towards her. Tam Tam took a few unsteady steps along the table top, leaving Magnus in no doubt that the alcohol had gone straight to the creature's head. Perhaps to save herself the embarrassment of everyone looking at her drunk dog, Hilda stuffed him into her handbag, zipped it closed above his head, and then said, 'Can we get on, please? I can't dilly dally here all night.'

Magnus sighed. 'Yes, let's move on, shall we?' he said, hating to agree with Hilda. 'Do we all approve of this idea of the letter? I don't think I can include your individual concerns, as it might rather undermine the stern legal tone I want to take, but I do of course encourage you to air your grievances to CSP directly.'

Apparently, however, the people at the meeting in the Cosmopolitan Club wanted to air their grievances to Magnus directly, and for the next quarter of an hour or so he was besieged by complaints about their properties and Westminster Square at large. They moaned about a creaking staircase, the roadworks at the weekend, the scruffiness of one of the doormen. They condemned an overgrown tree in one of the gardens, the smell of damp in an entrance hall, a wobbly paving slab in the north of the quadrant. And they lambasted a leaky tap in a third floor flat, the overzealous traffic wardens, and the fact that all of the pansies in one of the flowerbeds had been dug up and crudely replanted (Magnus looked at Hilda upon hearing this, wondering whether she would have the good grace to look embarrassed by what Tam Tam had done the other week — she did not).

After a while, the barrister stopped listening to them. He sorely regretted calling this meeting, and in doing so accidentally electing himself as the unofficial spokesman of the residents of Westminster Square. As though he had the time to be dealing with grievances about leaky taps and wobbly paving slabs! Most of these people were retired, and yet they were coming to him, a busy professional with a family, to sort out their petty problems.

That is, assuming they did want these issues fixed. As far as Magnus could tell, they were all rather enjoying themselves, comparing notes on how they'd each been wronged by CSP. *Why do you live here, if you have so many complaints?* Magnus wanted to ask them. And, more to the point, *Why do I live here?*

Something had changed in him. Perhaps it was the conversation with his children the other night, or maybe it was Juliana's threat of a few weeks' ago, or more likely his wife had simply ground him down after all these years. It could even have been that the murder of Anne-Laure Chevalier had had more of an effect on him than he had previously thought. Whatever the reason, Magnus didn't think he had it in him anymore, to put up with all of these people, with Central Square Properties, and by extension with living in Westminster Square. Was he really coming round to Juliana's way of thinking at last? Did he truly feel as though a better life awaited him and his family in the countryside? It seemed so. Because no matter how much he loved the provenance of Westminster, and living so close to work, and having all of the attractions of one of the greatest cities in the world right on his doorstep, none of that seemed very important in comparison to the happiness of his family. And compared to Juliana and Rosanna and Lee, all these complaints about overgrown trees and peeling plasterwork, let alone the whole headache of the maintenance charges, seemed utterly insignificant.

'All right,' said Magnus at last, holding up his hands in surrender, 'I hear you. You're unhappy. But as I said before, we can't include these individual issues in my letter, although I will certainly mention you are all very dissatisfied with how CSP are managing your properties, and Westminster Square as a whole. So what I suggest you do is each put pen to paper and write your own letters. I don't think a barrage of complaints arriving on CSP's doorstep over the next week or so is going to do our case any harm. If anything, it'll convince them we are united, and we mean business. Does that sound like an agreeable plan?' he asked, and then without waiting for an answer, he continued, 'Well, thank you all very much for coming this evening, and we'll return to this matter in a few months' time. Goodnight, everyone.'

His guests looked visibly shocked to be dismissed so abruptly, but then they stood up and began to file out of the meeting room, grumbling amiably to one another as they went. Magnus watched them go for a few moments and then, when nobody was paying any attention to him anymore, put his head in his hands and closed his eyes. All of a sudden, he felt exhausted. He didn't think he had the strength to get up and make the short walk home, let alone face the chatter of his family and the mountain of paperwork waiting for him in his study. Perhaps nobody would notice or mind if he simply stayed right here, in this hard wooden chair at the back of the Cosmopolitan Club, until he felt more like himself again.

'Magnus, dear, are you all right?'

Someone laid a heavy hand on his shoulder, and he looked up to see Dame Winifred Rye peering down at him, her lipstick-smudged mouth pursed in concern.

'Oh, yes,' he said, rubbing at his eyes. 'Just a bit tired, that's all.'

'You should trot off home,' she said. 'Tell dearest Juliana you need looking after. Tell her that from me — from all of us, in fact. You did a good job here tonight, Magnus, thank you.'

'You're welcome,' he said, not entirely sincerely.

'Come on, then,' she chided, 'chop chop!'

He still didn't want to move, and he resented her for trying to make him. But then, Dame Winifred meant well, didn't she? She was a kind soul, in spite of her interfering nature and clownish appearance. But then Magnus checked himself, remembering his and Bryn's conversation of the other week: was it really possible this eccentric woman was involved in some kind of dodgy scheme connected to her fundraising? Stealing from those who needed it most was truly despicable, and Magnus didn't want to believe it, but he knew from professional experience that charity fraud was an unfortunately common occurrence, and it was usually well-connected people like Dame Winifred who had the nerve to attempt it.

'It was a good turn-out tonight, wasn't it?' said Dame Winifred, apparently completely unaware of what was going through Magnus's mind as she looked around at the emptying room. 'I'm surprised Vasyl didn't come, though, seeing as he has that big house.'

'Oh, he sent me a message saying he was abroad,' said Magnus, standing up at last. 'I expect I'll have to fill him in when he gets back.'

'Ha, I think that's unlikely!' croaked a voice.

Magnus and Dame Winifred turned to see Hilda Underpin still lingering at the table. Just as she had been one of the first to arrive, the barrister was unsurprised that the old lady was one of the last to leave. He intended to ignore her comment — he was too jaded to deal with her anymore — but Dame Winifred seemed curious.

'What do you mean, Hilda?' she asked, rather coldly — evidently, she had not yet forgiven the old lady for the insulting remark she had made about the drinking habits of the late Lord Rye.

'I mean, that Russian isn't coming back!' said Hilda, jabbing at Tam Tam's nose, which was poking through a gap in the zip of her handbag. 'He's gone for good!'

'How do you know that?' asked Magnus, ignoring her possibly deliberate mistake concerning Vasyl's nationality.

'I saw him leaving with a load of suitcases last week,' said Hilda. 'And since then, men have been in and out of that house, packing boxes into removal vans. Haven't you seen? I went to look at it the other day, and when I peered through the living room window, I saw it was completely empty inside.'

'So you're saying he's moved out?' said Magnus.

'How strange!' said Dame Winifred. 'He didn't mention anything at my party…'

Hilda gave an impatient click of her tongue. 'Are you two stupid?' she demanded. 'He hasn't moved out — well, he has, but not by choice — he's *bolted*!'

'Bolted?' repeated Magnus and Dame Winifred together.

'Yes, bolted, hightailed, run away,' said the old woman. 'Why else would he leave so suddenly, and have his packing done afterwards? You mark my words, something's amiss there. He's probably been up to no good, and it'll have caught up with him, forcing him to leave the country. Well, I can't say I'm surprised. They're all a bunch of criminals, aren't they, these *foreigners*...'

Apparently feeling as though she had made her point, Hilda swung the handbag containing Tam Tam over her shoulder and began to shuffle out of the meeting room. Then Dame Winifred, who looked rather bemused by the whole conversation, shrugged, waved at Magnus, and also departed.

The barrister, however, stayed where he was. He was unwilling to admit it, but Hilda was right: Vasyl Kosnitschev's abrupt departure *was* surprising. And if the nosy old bag was also correct in assuming he had bolted because he had done something criminal, the timing of it started to look downright suspicious. Because surely it wasn't merely coincidence that the Ukrainian oligarch had done a runner so recently after the death of his apparently devoted and reliable employee, Anne-Laure Chevalier?

CHAPTER THIRTY-FOUR

In spite of his busy schedule, not to mention his reluctance to get pulled back into the investigation, Magnus did not feel as though he could keep from Bryn what he had learned about Vasyl Kosnitschev. The police constable — or rather, former police constable — had a right to know one of Anne-Laure's acquaintances had suddenly disappeared, especially as the man in question was the person who had spent more time with her than anyone else, aside from perhaps Jem McMorran.

However, when Magnus informed Bryn of this latest development over the phone, his friend seemed surprisingly unexcited by the news.

'Oh?' he said. 'That's a bit strange, isn't it? Do people normally leave Westminster Square so abruptly?'

'No,' said Magnus, a little impatiently. 'That's why I thought perhaps it was connected to Anne-Laure's death somehow.'

'Do you think so?' said Bryn, and Magnus had the impression he was being politely humoured.

'Maybe,' the barrister replied, beginning to doubt himself. 'Anyway, I know you're still investigating, so I thought you'd want to know.'

'Yes, thank you,' said Bryn. 'I'll bear it in mind.'

Magnus was about to bid him goodbye, but he hesitated. 'Sorry, you'll bear it in mind? Don't you want to do a little more than that? I would have thought you'd want to come and see the house at least. He departed in a rush, so he might have been careless and left something significant behind. I suppose it's a long shot you'd be able to see it through the windows, but isn't it worth a try?'

'Yes, perhaps it is,' said Bryn, still not sounding very enthusiastic about the idea.

'Come and see the house,' Magnus said, making the decision for him. 'I'll go with you, so it looks less odd, now you won't be in your uniform.'

They made arrangements to meet the next day after Magnus had finished work, and then the barrister hung up the phone, frowning. He was a little confused by what had just happened: why on earth had he just agreed to go sniffing around Vasyl's house? No, he hadn't agreed to it, he'd suggested it. Was he not determined to keep his distance from this whole business, at least until the arbitration case was over and his marriage was back on track? He would have almost suspected his young associate had somehow manipulated him into making this proposal, only he knew by now Bryn didn't have a sly bone in his body. No, it had been Bryn's reluctance to see the severity of Vasyl's abrupt absence that had frustrated Magnus, and caused him to make the suggestion. As he reflected on this, his confusion and frustration turned to worry: he hoped, in the wake of his dismissal, his young friend was all right.

But when they met outside Magnus's house the following day, the barrister was surprised how cheerful Bryn seemed. He didn't look great — he was rather thin and hollow-eyed — but he had a spring in his step that was rather unusual, even alarming, considering he had just lost his job.

'You seem very chipper,' observed Magnus, after they had shaken hands.

'Do I? Well, it's a very nice day,' said Bryn, brightly.

'You're not too cut up about the job, then?'

'Oh, well, a bit, yes,' Bryn admitted, which came as something of a relief to Magnus. 'But I'm trying to get on with things, you know?'

'Of course. And, I hate to sound like a bore, Bryn, but are you eating properly?' asked Magnus, once more taking in the slightly sunken look to his friend's features.

'Oh, yes. You get used to beans on toast for dinner after a while.'

Magnus didn't know whether to laugh or not: he wasn't sure Bryn was joking.

'Don't look so worried,' the younger man urged him. 'I'm fine, honestly. In fact, it's good I have this case, as it's taking my mind off everything. You know, giving me something to focus my energies on...'

'Hm,' said Magnus, not entirely sure it was helpful for Bryn to be prioritising Anne-Laure above himself right now; after all, as much as they both wanted justice for her, Bryn's lack of job and money was perhaps the more pressing issue at the moment.

'Speaking of,' said Bryn, either not noticing or pretending not to notice Magnus's disapproval, 'shall we have a look at Vasyl's house?'

The barrister nodded, and together they made their way to the Ukrainian oligarch's former residence. From the outside, it looked like every other façade in Westminster Square, but as they approached the steps and peered through the large windows, they could see the interiors of the front rooms were completely empty.

'He really has gone, then,' murmured Magnus, who until this point had only half believed Hilda Underpin.

He leaned awkwardly around the doorway to get a closer look through one of the windows, but there wasn't much to look at in the room beyond, which was dark and bare.

'I'm sorry, Bryn,' he said, as he squinted through the gloom. 'I thought there might be a little more to see…'

'We could always go inside?' suggested his companion.

'What?'

Magnus turned to find his companion poking the front door with his index finger, revealing it to be slightly ajar. He hesitated: on the one hand, he knew he shouldn't go snooping around in other people's houses, especially in broad daylight, and right under the nose of Hilda Underpin and her binoculars. But on the other, the house was unlocked, Vasyl was gone, and Magnus's curiosity was getting the better of him. Wordlessly, he nodded at Bryn, and the two of them proceeded into the oligarch's former home.

The last time they had been there, the hallway had been a complete mess: the floor had been covered with dust sheets, paint samples had been smeared across the walls, half of the bannister had been missing, and there had been a great hole in the wall of this space and the neighbouring room.

Magnus wouldn't have thought it possible to have created more chaos than that, but now, looking around, he saw that somehow Vasyl had managed it. The bannister was now completely gone, as was half of the staircase carpet, and by the looks of it the Ukrainian had been planning to install a metal handrail, for there were various bits of steel lying around. The paint samples were still present, but now somebody had begun work on several murals, most of which were industrial in style and subject, although the one on the ceiling was an abstract and rather risqué depiction of several nudes. The wall between the entrance hall and the salon had disappeared, as had all of the furniture in both rooms, giving the space an imposing, cavernous appearance, rather like a warehouse. And generally, wherever they looked, they saw half-empty paint pots, rolled-up dust sheets, workmen's tools, trailing wires, sheets of glass, scraps of metal — all the rubble of a renovation project suddenly abandoned.

'It's not *exactly* in keeping with the tone of Westminster, is it?' said Bryn, wryly.

'No...'

For some reason, Magnus was failing to see the funny side of the situation. He had no love for Central Square Properties, but this was ridiculous: Vasyl had deliberately destroyed a piece of English heritage, and for what? He was no longer even here to enjoy it.

'Let's take a look around,' he said. 'Although if the rest of the house is like this, there's not going to be much to see...'

Indeed, Magnus felt a little foolish as he began to pick his way through to the salon. What was the point of this? Vasyl Kosnitschev was hardly going to have left a note behind, confessing to killing his employee, so what were they really looking for? As he watched Bryn crouch down to inspect some scraps of old paper — presumably workmen's instructions — Magnus cursed himself for getting involved in this all over again. He couldn't even blame Bryn, because it had been his own silly idea to investigate Vasyl's abrupt departure.

They were just about to leave the salon and explore a different space when there came the sound of approaching footsteps behind them —

female ones, going by the clipping noise of the heels. Magnus turned to see a small, smartly-dressed and vaguely familiar brunette woman coming towards them from a room on the other side of the hallway. She would have been very attractive, had it not been for her sour expression.

'Who are you?' she demanded, in a high, plummy voice. 'Well?' she continued, when neither of them immediately answered her question. 'I'm waiting. What are you doing here? If you've been sent to pick anything up, you're too late — it's all gone. But you can tell your boss from me that we're on to him. You can tell him that CSP are —'

'It's Lavender, isn't it?' Magnus interrupted, remembering he had indeed seen this woman before, in this very house, berating Vasyl for his decorative efforts. 'You work for Central Square Properties?'

She folded her arms. 'Who are you?' she asked again.

'Magnus Walterson. I live just a few doors' down and —'

'Oh, I know who *you* are,' said Lavender, for she had raised her eyebrows upon hearing his name. 'You're the one leading that little rebellion against us, aren't you? You're the one writing petitions about the maintenance charges?'

'Oh, so you've received my correspondence?' said Magnus, feigning surprise. 'I am glad. I was beginning to think it had been lost in the post, considering I'm still waiting for a response.'

Lavender narrowed her eyes, but offered no apology or explanation. Then she looked at Bryn, her gaze requesting he identify himself.

'Bryn Summers,' he supplied.

'Police Constable at the Victoria Police Station,' Magnus added.

He felt this encounter might go better if Lavender were unaware Bryn had recently lost his job and, indeed, she looked a little taken aback to learn she had been so standoffish to an officer of the law.

'And might I ask what you're both doing here?' she said, her icy tone thawing only a little.

'We came to see Vasyl, of course,' said Magnus, as though this were very obvious. 'But I'm beginning to think we've rather mistimed our visit.'

Lavender snorted. 'Do you think?' she sneered.

The three of them looked around the debris, as though just making sure the Ukrainian oligarch wasn't about to pop out from behind a pile of bricks and shout, *Surprise!* Then Lavender gave a huff of annoyance and said, 'Didn't you know? He's gone! Vanished, just like that.' She clicked her fingers together, the sharp sound echoing around the empty rooms.

'And, erm, you don't know where he's gone?' asked Bryn, tentatively.

'No, we don't,' snapped Lavender. 'Because if we did...' She took a deep breath to try and quell her rage. 'If we did, we would be hitting him with some serious legal action. I assume you know the kind of thing I'm talking about, Mr Walterson?'

'I can imagine, yes,' said Magnus, wincing a little.

'Because of what he did to this place?' Bryn asked, apparently recalling what had been said the last time they had been here. 'Because he didn't have permission to renovate or redecorate or —'

'He didn't have permission to do *anything*!' Lavender cried, her nostrils flared like an angry bull. 'This is a Grade II-listed building! It is of the *utmost* historic importance! And as such, there are *rules*. Lease-holders in Westminster Square have to ask the permission of CSP if they want to make significant alterations to their properties...'

'And insignificant,' muttered Magnus, who was fairly sure CSP would object to him putting a nail in the wall to hang a painting.

Lavender chose to ignore this comment. 'It says in the lease of every single Westminster Square property that the tenant must ask permission from CSP before he or she makes any changes,' she continued.

'In fairness, those leases are nearly two hundred pages long,' said Magnus, who recalled going through his with a fine tooth comb a decade ago. As a lawyer, he would never have neglected to read an important contract, yet even he had been sorely tempted to skip a few paragraphs of the seemingly endless document.

Once more, Lavender pretended she hadn't heard him. 'And generally, CSP refuse such requests, because they are not in keeping with the character and provenance of Westminster Square,' she went on, and Magnus had the impression she was ranting more to herself than to them now. 'In the past, we've had to turn down requests for balcony extensions, open-plan kitchens, conservatories... But never, *never* have we had to deal with something like this before. I mean, just look at it! Look what he's done!'

She was apoplectic with rage and, although she was from the enemy's camp, Magnus couldn't help but sympathise: Vasyl had well and truly destroyed any character the interior of this house had ever had.

'Did he ask permission for any of it?' wondered Bryn aloud.

'Once,' said Lavender, begrudgingly. 'About a year ago we received a couple of letters saying he wanted to knock down this wall and re-carpet that room.' She gestured at the place where a wall had once been, between the entrance hall and the salon, and then waved vaguely towards the upper floors of the house. 'We refused, of course. I mean, what an idea! What was he trying to do? Attempting to make it into some kind of open-plan American home?'

'I don't think he was going for an *American* look, exactly,' murmured Magnus.

'Anyway, the next thing I heard, he was doing it anyway,' continued Lavender, looking utterly furious. 'I came here a couple of months ago, and he had torn a great hole in the wall, not to mention messing up the stairs and playing about with paint. Of course, the damage was already done by that point, but I made it quite clear that it wasn't acceptable, this renovation, and we sent him a couple of cease and desist notices. But did he listen? No! He just made it even worse. My God,' she said, looking around as though catching sight of it all again for the first time. 'I've never seen anything like it my life!'

Magnus, realising she didn't seem to remember that they had been witness to that earlier scene, said, 'I wonder what was going through his head? Do you think he thought you were bluffing, or did he know CSP would be angry but did it anyway?'

'I've no idea how that absurd man thought,' said Lavender. 'But if you ask me, it's all because of that girl's death.'

Magnus blinked at her: he had not expected this. He exchanged an optimistic glance with Bryn, and then said, 'Sorry, what do you mean?'

'That girl, the one who died in the Royal West, what was her name? Anne-Lauren something.'

'Anne-Laure Chevalier,' supplied Bryn.

'Yes, that's the one. Kosnitschev called her his PA or his PR girl or his events manager or something like that, but really, she was his right-hand woman. Before she died, everything went through her, including his correspondence with CSP. I remember I used to get frustrated with her, because she'd make these ridiculous requests, but once she was out the picture, I realised how much she must have been holding him back, because his demands became completely outrageous. And then of course he just went ahead and did all of this —' She gestured around at the house in disgust, '— without asking any kind of permission at all.'

'So what are you saying about Anne-Laure?'

'I'm saying she was far more sensible than I gave her credit for at the time. I believe she tried to stop his renovation plans, because she understood he would land himself in all sorts of trouble if he did exactly what he wanted with this house. I don't think it's coincidence that only a few weeks after she died he started tearing this place apart. You mark my words, she was the one who held him back.'

Magnus frowned: he vaguely recalled, the last time they were here, Vasyl saying something similar about Anne-Laure's influence over him. In fact, hadn't the Ukrainian even made an uncharacteristic joke that he had started the renovations because he had been annoyed with Anne-Laure for suddenly dying like that?

'I wish she was still around,' said Lavender, 'if it meant this place might still be in one piece.'

Bryn pulled a face. 'And if it meant she was still *alive*,' he said pointedly.

Lavender did not appear to be insulted by his tone. 'You know, with that kind of mind, and — I'll admit — those looks, Anne-Laure Chevalier could have had a job with us, at CSP. She would have fitted right in.' Lavender sighed. 'What a waste.'

Magnus, reflecting that Anne-Laure had already been Vasyl's right-hand woman, a *rabbateur*, had dabbled in social drug-dealing, and possibly still harboured ambitions to be an actress, didn't really think she had needed any more jobs.

'So what are you going to do now?' he asked Lavender. 'What's going to happen to this house?'

'Well, we've a court order to take it back from him, and it doesn't look as though he's going to object, does it? But officially, its ours, because he's violated so many terms of his lease. And I don't just mean decorating without our permission — although that's by far his most serious offence — he's also flouted parking rules, been late in paying his maintenance charges…'

'So he'll lose his money, will he?' asked Magnus, not wanting to go anywhere near the subject of maintenance charges. 'He'll lose whatever he paid to lease this property?'

'As he should!' said Lavender, suddenly flaring up once more. 'That's his penance for completely ruining the house! For destroying one of the icons of the City of Westminster! Do you know how much the district council are up in arms about this? And rightly so!' She took a deep breath, apparently trying to calm herself down. 'The real kick in the teeth is the fact that we went out on a limb for him, allowing him to live here. This is one of the most expensive properties in Westminster Square, considering it's still a house, and there was quite the scandal when he bought it.'

'Why?' asked Bryn.

'Because he was a foreigner, of course,' said Lavender, impatiently. 'Because, by rights, this house should have gone to a member of the royal family, or somebody high-up in parliament, or at least an icon of British entertainment. Not some jumped-up Ukrainian who made his money God knows how.'

The sheer snobbery of this irritated Magnus, who commented, 'Say what you like, but I imagine that jumped-up Ukrainian was one of the few who could actually afford a place like this.'

'Well, it didn't go down well, let me tell you,' said Lavender. 'People around here didn't like it. But we gave him a chance, and look how he's repaid us. He's destroyed it.'

'Can you not have it repaired?' asked Bryn.

'We can try. We can hire some of the finest builders, decorators and restorers in the business, but it will never be the same. He's demolished a piece of the past, and although we can attempt to imitate, say, the Georgian banister, it's not going to be an actual Georgian banister, is it? It's going to be a late twentieth-century Georgian-*style* banister.' She sighed. 'But, as I said, we'll attempt it. I wish we knew where he was, at least, so he could foot some of the bill.'

'Really?' asked Magnus, surprised.

'Oh yes,' said Lavender, a ruthless glint in her eye. 'You're a lawyer, Mr Walterson, I would have thought you'd know what happened when clients violate the terms of their leases…'

'Naturally,' said Magnus, who disliked being patronised by this angry young woman, 'but I would have thought the fact that CSP were keeping the whole amount Vasyl paid for the house — which would be, what, several million? — that would more than cover the cost of the repairs. Once you fix it up and put it back on the market, you'll probably make quite a tidy profit, especially considering the rising house prices around here.'

Lavender gave him a chilly smile, but did not confirm or deny his suspicions.

'So you have no idea where Vasyl is now?' asked Bryn, perhaps in an attempt to break the sudden tension between Magnus and Lavender.

'As I already told you, no. And believe me, we've tried to find him. Our investigators have uncovered links to some crazy traders in the Ukraine, the Czech mafia, and a couple of particularly threatening Russian businessmen, so it looks like Kosnitschev has had to disappear on purpose. A newspaper in Prague reported he was last seen in Rio de Janeiro, and another in Kiev was speculating he was in Argentina, but who knows? I think it's safe to say, however, that sorting out this mess is not at the top of his list of priorities at the moment. He probably won't even notice we've taken the house back.'

She looked bitter as she said this, as though she wanted Vasyl to be aware of what CSP were doing; she wanted him to know he was being punished. Magnus, who was disliking her more and more as time went on, suddenly found he had had enough of her and of the house.

'Well, I suppose we'd better be off, Bryn,' he said. 'After all, it doesn't look as though our friend is coming back any time soon.' Then, to Lavender, he said, 'We'll leave you to your…'

'Damage assessment survey,' she said shortly, before turning her back on them and walking away without another word.

Outside, Magnus took in a deep breath of fresh air — he had only just realised how dusty it had been inside the house — and said, 'Well, I'm sorry, Bryn. That was a complete waste of time.'

'I wouldn't say that, exactly,' said his companion, reaching into his jacket pocket and pulling out a scrap of paper, which he handed to Magnus.

The barrister looked at what seemed to be a handwritten and fairly innocuous note to some decorators:

Remove all traces of decorative stucco from the ceiling — to be replaced with smooth surface. VK.

'So what, Vasyl didn't like stucco? None of us do,' said Magnus.

'No,' laughed Bryn, 'look at the handwriting.'

'Oh!'

Magnus glanced back down at the note. Vasyl Kosnitschev's handwriting was medium-sized, neat and rather square, a little like computer print. Magnus thought he would have been able to tell, just by a glance, that the person who had written this was not a native English speaker — more to the point, not a native user of the Latin alphabet.

'So we can be fairly sure Vasyl didn't write that notebook,' he concluded.

'No, and I didn't think he did,' said Bryn. 'I mean, first of all, it would be very odd to keep tabs on someone he had an excuse to see almost every day through his work. And second, it would be even stranger to make all of those notes in English.'

'I also happened to believe him, when he said he had no romantic interest in Anne-Laure,' said Magnus. 'He was a very serious businessman, I don't think he would have wanted to jeopardise that, especially as he was so reliant on her. Of course, there is the "A.C." ring, and he did call her Anna…'

'But is it likely a man such as him would have given her such a cheap piece of jewellery?' said Bryn. 'You saw Jem McMorran's reaction to it, and he's not nearly as rich as Vasyl.'

'Hm,' said Magnus. 'So you think we can rule him out as the stalker?'

'Actually, I think we can rule him out as the murderer,' said Bryn. 'Think about it: he had no motive. In fact, he had a lot to lose from Anne-Laure's death. From what Lavender was saying, and from what he himself told us the other month, Vasyl Kosnitschev relied heavily on Anne-Laure. She was, as Lavender just said, his right-hand woman. So why would he kill her? In the wake of her death, things have completely fallen apart for him, first with this renovation business — which she warned him against — and second with this running away from the Czech mafia or whatever Lavender was talking about. That second point might be unrelated to Anne-Laure's demise, but at least it proves he had bigger fish to fry than go to all the trouble of killing his own employee — especially an employee who, by the looks of things, he couldn't do without.'

'You make a convincing case,' said Magnus, approvingly. 'And I see your point: Vasyl Kosnitschev would have been well and truly shooting himself in the foot if he had murdered Anne-Laure — more so than he's shot himself in the foot with this house.'

At the mention of the property, they both seemed to realise they were lingering outside it, and began to walk slowly back towards Magnus's house instead.

'I sense you didn't think it was Vasyl in the first place, though,' the barrister said to his young companion, recalling their earlier phone call. 'Even before we went into the house and talked to Lavender, I think you had mentally crossed him off your list.'

'I suppose I had,' said Bryn. 'You see, I'm working on a theory at the moment…'

He trailed off. Magnus, who could not help but be intrigued, tried to cajole him into revealing more by saying, 'Oh? What sort of theory?'

'It's a bit wild,' admitted the Welshman, 'and I'm not sure I've managed to fit all the pieces together just yet. I just have this feeling we've been missing something huge — something that's been under our noses the whole time — and I think I might finally know what it is.'

'I must say, you're being very cryptic here, Bryn.'

'Sorry. As I said, this theory is still a work in progress.'

Magnus considered this for a few moments. On the one hand, he was burning with curiosity, and wanted to shake Bryn by the shoulders and force him to reveal everything he was thinking. But on the other, he knew he was supposed to be taking a step back from this Anne-Laure Chevalier business, and if Bryn was content to work on this theory alone there seemed little point in Magnus involving himself for the sake it.

Still, a sense of loyalty and propriety prompted the barrister to remark, 'Well, if there's anything I can do to help…'

'Actually, I do have a couple of favours to ask you,' said the former policeman at once. 'Tiny things, I promise.'

The barrister sighed. 'All right. What do you need?'

Bryn pulled out a further few sheets of paper from his jacket pocket. 'First of all, perhaps you could take a look at these?'

The barrister unfolded the documents and looked at the details at the top of the first page. 'How on earth did you get hold of Anne-Laure Chevalier's bank statements?' he asked.

'That's a long story,' said Bryn, 'and not unconnected with why I no longer have a job. But never mind that for now. I'd like you to have a glance over them, if you have a moment.'

'What am I looking for?' asked Magnus, bemused.

'You'll be able to spot something fairly incriminating straight away,' said Bryn, with confidence, 'but I'd like to know the whys and wherefores, if you're able to explain them to me. I think you, as a lawyer, will have a much clearer idea of what's been going on with Anne-Laure's money.'

This all sounded very obscure to Magnus, but looking at a few pages of bank statements was hardly a gruelling task, so he folded the documents back up and tucked them away in his own pocket.

'And what was the other favour?' he asked. 'You said there were a couple?'

'Oh yes. Well, I was wondering whether you would be able to wangle me another invitation for tea at Hilda Underpin's flat.'

Magnus stared at him: this was getting stranger and stranger.

'Hilda Underpin's flat?' he repeated.

'Yes.'

'*The* Hilda Underpin?'

'The one and only.'

'What on earth do you want go there for?'

'There's something I want to check. Last time we were there, she said something that I didn't think anything of at the time, but I've looked over and over my notes, and I think it might be the key to everything, Magnus.'

'You're not saying Hilda Underpin did do it, are you?' asked Magnus, almost afraid to hear the answer.

'I'm saying she played her part.'

Magnus couldn't help but chuckle. 'I'm not sure this enigmatic persona quite suits you, Bryn...'

'Huh?' The Welshman blinked. 'Oh, sorry. It's just, it's been so blurred, this Anne-Laure business, and I think it's finally coming into focus. I can almost see it with perfect clarity. But I don't want to say too much, in case I'm wrong.'

'Fair enough,' said Magnus, reminding himself once again that he was supposed to be leaving Bryn to it. 'What do you want me to say to her? What's your excuse for going round?'

Bryn shrugged. 'Anything you like. We could pretend we're doing another round of visits to raise awareness about neighbourhood security, I suppose...'

'We?' said Magnus. 'I'm coming along too, am I?'

'If you like,' said Bryn, in the manner of someone offering a great treat. 'I mean, you don't have to, but we might learn something interesting.'

'I'll see how I feel,' said Magnus, non-committal, although privately he thought they would have to learn something very interesting indeed to make up for tolerating tea with Hilda Underpin.

CHAPTER THIRTY-FIVE

'You're very early,' snapped Hilda Underpin, as she opened the door to her flat and glared up at her visitors.

Magnus and Bryn exchanged a weary expression. Considering the last time they were here she had told them off for being a few minutes late, they had made a conscious effort to be exactly on time. Perhaps unsurprisingly, it seemed there was no pleasing the old lady.

With a grunt of disapproval, Hilda led them into her beige-coloured living room, which was still populated by an abundance of crucifixes and military memorabilia, and Tam Tam jumped out from under the sofa. The little dog appeared to be in a very excitable mood today, because he ran around and around Magnus and Bryn's feet barking shrilly, until the barrister was sorely tempted to aim a sharp kick in the ratty creature's direction.

'Sit down, sit down,' ordered Hilda, directing them to the table by the window.

Her binoculars, notebook and old camera were still sitting on a nearby chair, and Magnus was reminded of his theory that she had been the one keeping diligent notes on Anne-Laure Chevalier's movements.

'Seeing as you arrived so early, this tea is going to be very weak,' said Hilda, picking up the teapot. 'It hasn't had time to brew.'

'We could always wait five minutes,' Magnus pointed out.

But Hilda ignored him, and started pouring into three cups liquid that looked so pale Magnus doubted it had ever seen a teabag.

'And no biscuits today,' she informed them. 'I only give out biscuits on the first visit.'

'Fair enough,' said Magnus, trying not to feel disappointed: the biscuits from the convent she had given them last time had been rather good.

'Maybe if you returned my hospitality and invited *me* round to tea at *your* flat...' said Hilda pointedly.

This time it was Magnus's turn to pretend he hadn't heard her. The idea of Juliana's reaction to his telling her he had invited Hilda Underpin round for tea was too terrible to contemplate.

Then Hilda said, 'I don't mean you, Brian. I don't want to see where you live. It's probably some shack in Brixton, is it not?'

'Close enough,' said Bryn, affably.

Perhaps disappointed she hadn't managed to get a rise out of either of them yet, Hilda went on, 'So what do you two want, anyway? I presume this isn't a purely social call... Is this about that silly little tart again?'

Magnus, recalling they had been forced to reveal something of their investigation to Hilda in Lei Sing's Taste of China restaurant, said, 'Actually, this isn't about Anne-Laure Chevalier, who I presume you're referring to there. I've taken my associate's advice on that one, and decided to let the matter drop — after all, if the police think the case is closed, the case is closed.'

The irony of what he was saying was not lost on Magnus, especially as Bryn nodded authoritatively, as though he were pleased the barrister was finally seeing sense.

'Glad to hear it,' croaked Hilda. 'As I said before, that vile girl is better off dead.'

Upon hearing this, Bryn's expression darkened. Magnus had noticed that his young friend had become strangely attached to Anne-Laure over the past few months, and always seemed to take slights against her to heart. So before Bryn could say anything to jeopardise their agreed cover story, the barrister continued, 'We're just following up on our last visit regarding neighbourhood security, Hilda.'

'Oh,' she said, looking thoroughly unimpressed, 'is that all?'

'I'm afraid so,' said Magnus. 'As you were subject to a burglary a few months ago, it would be lax of us not to check up on you.'

'I told you, they didn't take anything,' Hilda huffed.

'Are you absolutely sure about that?' said Bryn, and Magnus was surprised to see him leaning forward and looking especially alert.

'Yes, Brian, I'm quite sure,' Hilda snapped.

'You checked all of your belongings, every little thing?'

Hilda looked to Magnus. 'Who does this boy think he is, interrogating me like this?'

'He is a policeman,' the barrister reminded her; as with Lavender from Central Square Properties, he felt it wise not to reveal Bryn's unemployed status to Hilda.

'Hmph,' said Hilda. 'For the last time, no, nothing was taken.'

'And you haven't noticed anything or anyone suspicious in Westminster Square since our last visit?' asked Magnus.

'Apart from the pair of you loitering about, no,' said Hilda shortly.

Magnus dared to take a sip of his tea, which was so weak it simply tasted like dirty hot water. He wasn't quite sure how to advance: it was Bryn who had wanted to come here and talk to Hilda regarding one of his theories, and seeing as the old woman didn't seem to want to discuss Westminster Square security any more than they did, the barrister hoped his young friend would soon take control of the conversation.

As if on cue, Bryn pushed back his chair, rose to his feet, and walked over to a glass display case, which contained several ceremonial knives.

'What are you doing, Brian?' Hilda demanded, her eyes narrowed.

'Did these belong to your husband?' he asked, leaning so close to the cabinet his nose was almost touching the glass.

The old lady hesitated, and Magnus could almost see her inner struggle, as she tried to decide whether to be insulted or flattered by Bryn's question.

'Yes, they did,' she said eventually.

'They're remarkable,' said Bryn, his gaze roving over the knives, which were arranged as carefully as if they had been in a museum. 'You said his name was Tarquin, is that right?'

'Yes,' said Hilda, and Magnus didn't think he was imagining that her voice was a little softer now. 'Tarquin Underpin, Officer of the British Commandos, also known as...'

'The "Green Berets", I remember you telling us,' said Bryn, nodding up at an example of the headwear in question, which was hanging on a hook on the wall. 'Actually, I've been thinking about your husband ever since,' he continued, now examining the beret more closely. 'It really is an extraordinary thing, what he did for this country, back, as you said, when men were true men. I don't suppose —' he appeared to check himself. 'No, I'm being impudent, never mind...'

'No, what?' asked Hilda, sitting up a little straighter. 'What is it?'

Magnus had no idea what Bryn was playing at, but whatever it was, the old lady seemed to be falling for it hook, line, and sinker.

'Well, I was just wondering whether I could have a look at some of this memorabilia you have,' said Bryn, looking bashful. 'I used to love looking at my grandfather's mementoes, and he wasn't in the *commandos*, like your husband. But no, I'm sure it's too personal...'

'It's not!' cried Hilda, jumping up with surprising agility for one her age. 'It's not too personal. I'll show you right now.'

'Oh, I'm sure you don't have time for that...'

'I do, Brian, I do! Sit back down, I'll get it all out.'

Bryn slid back into his seat and smirked at Magnus behind Hilda's back. The barrister shook his head in amused disbelief; perhaps he had been wrong in thinking there was no slyness in his young companion.

'Here we are,' said Hilda, who was depositing knives, medals, documents yellowed with age, and even an old ration tin onto the table. 'I kept everything from Tarquin's time in the commandos, every single thing...'

Magnus studied Bryn's expression, wondering whether he was regretting his request to see Hilda's late husband's memorabilia, but the Welshman was looking politely interested.

'Well, then,' said Hilda, pushing away Tam Tam, who was evidently wondering what was going on. 'Shall we start with the medals?'

To his credit, Bryn continued to look absorbed for almost a whole hour, as Hilda showed them Tarquin's wartime belongings, explaining every one of them in painstaking detail. Some of them, like the ration cards and the photographs, came with a diverting story, but Magnus inwardly groaned as she drew out the seventh or eighth European train ticket and made them study it at great length.

As she talked, a change seemed to have come over Hilda Underpin, who looked happier than Magnus had ever seen her. Any joy he had ever known her to display before today had been the savage kind, and usually in the face of someone else's misfortune, but when she spoke about her late husband's adventures and heroics, she seemed to glow with pride and love. In fact, it made Magnus feel a little guilty: had he ever asked her about her Tarquin? He doubted it.

'And here are our letters,' she said, when she had finally exhausted all of the objects on the table. She drew a flowery box from a shelf and opened it, revealing sheets and sheets of handwritten notes. 'While Tarquin was away, we wrote to one another all the time, and then when he returned we compiled all the letters in order. I was going to have it bound, so we had a little book of our love story, but somehow after he died I never got round to it...' She sighed.

'It's not too late,' said Bryn brightly, subtly sliding the box towards Magnus.

Magnus, who thought he had an idea of what Bryn was up to now, peered at the first letter, which dated all the way back to 1940:

> *Dearest, darling Tarquin!*
> *You've only been gone a day, and my heart's so heavy I can hardly breathe. How are we to get through this war? How can I even survive this day without you? I know you must do your duty, I know Mr Churchill needs the best of men (and you are, my love, the very best) so I will endeavour to go on, even though it feels as though half of my soul — half of myself — has been taken away from me...*

Magnus pushed the box back towards Bryn, feeling a little embarrassed to be reading such a private love letter. He was also hardly able to believe it had been written by the mean old lady currently sitting before him. But he did not fail to notice that her old-fashioned handwriting was very beautiful, almost like calligraphy, so unless it had significantly changed over the next fifty years, it seemed very unlikely she had been the author of the notebook recording Anne-Laure's movements after all. And while Magnus was grateful to have yet another person crossed off their list of possible stalkers, he wondered whether this was the reason Bryn had requested to see all of these wartime souvenirs. It had got results, certainly, but surely there were quicker ways of extracting an example of handwriting from Hilda Underpin?

Meanwhile, the old lady herself was reaching into the box.

'Ooh, guess who this is?' she asked, holding up a black and white photograph of a small and rather plain-looking young woman.

'That's never you!' gasped Bryn.

Hilda Underpin actually giggled, a sound which made Magnus feel a little sick. 'Wasn't I pretty? You can't see it in the black and white, Brian, but I had all this bright red hair back then, almost like his wife over there.'

She waved vaguely at Magnus without actually looking at him, and the barrister realised he had become something of a third wheel: apparently, Hilda only wanted to speak to Bryn now.

'I sent it to Tarquin with one of my first letters, to keep him company,' continued the old woman, still smiling at the photograph in Bryn's hand. 'Apparently he carried it in the pocket of his uniform the whole time he was away, next to his heart.'

'That's amazing,' said Bryn.

She sighed again, and then gave his hand a little slap.

'Naughty, naughty, Brian, you can't keep it!' she chided. 'You'll have to put me back, the photograph belongs with the letters.'

'Of course,' said Bryn, dropping the picture back into the box.

Magnus cleared his throat, shuffled rather obviously in his chair, and tried to catch Bryn's eye to silently request that they leave — they had, after all, been stuck in this flat for some time now. But, to his surprise and slight annoyance, Bryn's whole attention was fixed on Hilda.

'I bet he looked really smart in his uniform,' said the Welshman, with a smile.

'Yes, Tarquin was so handsome,' said Hilda. 'Didn't I show you a photograph of him?'

'Oh, you did,' said Bryn, 'it's just sometimes difficult to get the full effect, in black and white. I wish I could see it in real life, but I don't suppose you have it...'

'But I do!' cried Hilda. 'Didn't I just tell you? I kept absolutely everything from Tarquin's time in the commandos. Come with me, I'll show you.'

She began to bustle out of the room, and as Bryn made to follow her, Magnus caught his friend by the arm.

'What's going on?' he hissed. 'What is all this?'

'Trust me,' said Bryn.

Magnus let him go, but wondered whether the young man had gone slightly mad. Perhaps his mind had been warped by losing his job. After all, who voluntarily spent more than a few minutes in the company of Hilda Underpin?

'Brian? *Brian*! Are you coming?'

Upon hearing Hilda's voice, Bryn leapt to attention. Magnus, curious in spite of himself, joined them in the hallway. There, Hilda had opened up a closet and was pulling out a khaki-coloured jacket.

'There you are,' she said, holding it up for Bryn. 'Straight from the war. It hasn't even been washed, so it's still a little grubby.'

'Wow,' he said. 'That's incredible.'

Privately, Magnus had to agree: there was something very impressive about this little piece of the Second World War being right here, in Hilda's hallway.

'Can I take a closer look?' asked Bryn, reaching out for the uniform.

Magnus expected Hilda to snatch it away, but in fact she pushed the jacket towards the Welshman, saying, 'Of course, try it on if you like.'

Bryn hesitated. 'Are you sure?'

'Yes, yes,' said Hilda, helping Bryn detach the jacket from its hanger. 'You're nice and tall like Tarquin, although he was a little broader than you — more muscular.'

'Most people are,' admitted Bryn.

'Oh, *you*,' laughed Hilda, helping Bryn slide his arms into the jacket, while Magnus began to feel a little nauseous again.

The jacket did indeed fit Bryn fairly well, although it was a little wide at the shoulders. Still, Hilda frowned as she helped to button him up.

'It's not quite right,' she said. 'Oh, I know… Hold on a minute.'

She hobbled off back into the living room. Magnus took the opportunity to whisper, once again, '*What's going on?*'

But his friend did not appear to be listening. He was fiddling with both sleeves of the jacket, turning them inside and out, as though he were worried they were too long for his arms.

'Bryn!' hissed Magnus.

'Hold on a second,' said his companion, now peering at the cuffs, like he was checking for loose threads.

'Bryn, this dressing-up lark is getting a bit strange…' began Magnus, but he couldn't say any more, because Hilda was returning to the hallway clutching an armful of medals and the green beret from the wall.

'Here you are, Brian,' she said. 'Stay right there.'

Bryn kept his torso obediently still as she reached up and started pinning the medals to his chest, although his hands were still patting at the jacket rather nervously.

'Magnus, put the beret on him, will you?' said Hilda, talking to the barrister for the first time in about half an hour.

Muttering under his breath, Magnus fixed the hat on Bryn's russet-coloured hair.

'There,' said Hilda, taking a step back a few moments later. 'Don't you look handsome? Not as handsome as Tarquin, obviously, but not too shabby. Come and look at yourself.'

She slid her bony arm through Bryn's and pulled him towards a full-length mirror that was hanging opposite the front door of Hilda's flat. Magnus once again followed them, feeling slightly as though he were Bryn's bodyguard.

'Wow,' said Bryn again, taking in the sight of his own reflection — or rather, the top half of his reflection. 'I look like a real commando. Thanks so much for letting me try it on, Mrs Underpin.'

'Oh please, call me Hilda,' said the old woman, with another giggle. 'Or Hildy, if you like. That's what Tarquin always called me…'

She had not let go of Bryn's arm, and was standing next to him before the mirror. From where Magnus was stood just behind them, if he ignored Bryn's jeans, his friend looked like a soldier posing for a photo with his grandmother before going off for war.

'So *handsome*…' sighed Hilda again, reaching up and beginning to stroke Bryn's chest rather absently, as though she were petting a cat.

This, Magnus thought, was a distinctly un-grandmotherly action, and it did at last seem to bring the young man to his senses. Bryn gave a little start, and then quickly disentangled himself from the old woman's clutches.

'Well, we'd better be going,' he said, beginning to unpin the medals from the jacket.

'Already?' Hilda looked highly disappointed.

'We've got to be getting on,' said Bryn, handing her the medals while Magnus stepped forward to remove the beret from his head. 'We've taken up more than enough of your time…'

Hilda looked down sadly at the memorabilia being returned to her, and then said, 'Well, perhaps you could come back another day? You could try on the whole uniform — the trousers too. I could take a photograph!'

'Erm, yes, maybe,' said Bryn, and Magnus was relieved to hear the reluctance in his tone. 'Well, thank you very much, Mrs Underpin —'

'Hildy!'

'Erm, Hildy, yes.'

Bryn shook the jacket from his shoulders, and Magnus hurried to put it back on the hanger.

'Are you sure you won't stay?' asked the old woman. 'You can have a biscuit if you like.'

'Oh, that's fine, thank you…'

'Goodbye, Hilda,' said Magnus firmly, delighted to be finally leaving.

She looked at him in surprise, as though she had only just remembered he was there, and said, rather coldly, 'Yes, goodbye, Magnus.' Then, in a softer voice, she cooed, 'And bye bye, Brian. Take care of yourself. Do come again soon, you can drop in at *any* time…'

Eventually, they managed to escape. In silence, they hurried down the stairs and out of Hilda's building, and it was only when they were a safe distance away, on the other side of Westminster Square, that Magnus rounded on his young friend.

'What on earth was all that about?' he demanded.

Bryn blinked at him innocently. 'What was what about?'

'All that…' Magnus could think of no other word for it. 'All that *flirting*!'

'I wasn't flirting,' Bryn laughed.

'Well, she certainly was. And you didn't exactly discourage her. You know, Bryn, I heard from Juliana that you finally plucked up the courage to ask young Daisy out on a date. But perhaps I should tell Daisy that you've suddenly developed a taste for older women — *much* older women.'

'Magnus, don't you dare!' gasped Bryn, looking suddenly serious. 'You know I'm mad about Daisy. And I need all the help I can get with winning her over, especially now I don't have a job.'

'Well, if your charm today is anything to go by, I don't think you have anything to worry about on that score…'

'Oh, stop it,' said Bryn, 'I was investigating.'

'Investigating what?' asked Magnus. 'How to tame mean old ladies? Because, I must say, I've never seen Hilda so benevolent.'

'Yes, that was an unexpected side-effect,' Bryn admitted. 'But never mind all that. Magnus, do you realise what's just happened? We've finally found out how Anne-Laure Chevalier died!'

'*What*?'

Bryn had definitely lost his marbles, Magnus thought. Flirting with old ladies was one thing, but maintaining there was any kind of connection between a lengthy discussion about a long-dead Second World War commando and the recent death of a glamorous London socialite was pure insanity.

'Bryn,' he said, a little worried now. 'Are you all right? Do you need a cup of tea — a proper one? You're not making any sense.'

'I'm fine,' said the former policeman brightly. 'In fact, I'm more than fine. Look, let's walk for a bit, and I'll explain.'

Telling himself this was the very last time he was going to give Bryn the benefit of the doubt, Magnus nodded, and they began to stroll around the perimeter of Westminster Square.

'If we're right in saying Anne-Laure was murdered,' began Bryn, 'how did the killer do it?'

Magnus frowned: hadn't they covered this a hundred times already? 'I thought we had decided a murderer must have coerced her into overdosing on cocaine?' he said.

'That seems unlikely, doesn't it?' said Bryn. 'Considering what we were told by Jem McMorran?'

'Jem? And what was that?'

Magnus's head contained far too much information on his arbitration case to remember every little thing the Hollywood actor had told them the other week.

'Jem McMorran, who would certainly have known Anne-Laure best, not to mention her drug-taking habits, told us — and I quote: "*She never liked it, not really. She liked making money from it, but she was never as keen on it as I was. In fact, she never took it on her own.*" Jem admitted that they'd done a few lines together in the bathroom before he left the charity party and went to the nightclub, and then he expressed surprise that she'd had more later on.'

'So what's your point?' asked Magnus.

'My point is, she didn't take any cocaine later on,' said Bryn, matter-of-factly. 'The traces of the drug the medical examiner found in her nose and in her blood system were from earlier that evening, from when she and Jem had taken it in the bathroom at around half past nine.'

'All right,' said Magnus. 'But if it wasn't a fatal overdose, how did she die?'

'Well that's the question, isn't it?' said Bryn. 'That's what's been bothering me, ever since Jem McMorran said that. There were no wounds on her body, other than the bruising, which wouldn't have killed her, and although I considered suffocation, it seems unlikely she would have looked so peaceful in death, and that the medical examiner wouldn't have picked up on it. And then I remembered the glasses.'

'Glasses?' said Magnus, trying to keep up.

'Yes, the two crystal tumblers that Rafaela the cleaner tidied up in the business conference room of the Royal West Hotel that morning. She said they had been on the floor, right next to the body, leading me to conclude that Anne-Laure had been drinking with someone after the party. And that's when I realised: she was poisoned.'

'*Poisoned*?' Magnus almost laughed, it seemed so far-fetched. 'Are you sure?'

'Almost positive,' said Bryn. 'Think about it. Somebody wanted Anne-Laure dead, but they wanted her to go quietly, without a struggle or a scandal, so they decided to slip her something that would make it look like she had simply overdosed on cocaine — either accidentally or on purpose. Which tells us two more things about our killer: one, that they knew Anne-Laure well enough to know about her drug habit, and two, that they were close enough to Anne-Laure to convince her to have a drink with them at the end of the night.'

'But hold on a minute,' said Magnus, before Bryn could get too carried away. 'Poison? Surely the medical examiner would have picked up on that?'

'Not necessarily,' said Bryn. 'I've been doing a little research, and although most poisons tend to leave some kind of trace, they're still difficult to detect, especially if a coroner is not specifically looking for poison — which, of course, Marlene Hardwitt wasn't, because we'd already found the cocaine, and Barry Boyle forbade her from doing a full examination of the body.'

'But that would have to be a pretty sophisticated poison,' said Magnus. 'I'm no expert, but I imagine most readily-available fatal toxins *would* leave a trace, even if your medical examiner wasn't doing a full autopsy.'

'But it *was* a sophisticated poison,' said Bryn, 'and it wasn't readily-available.'

'But — *what*?' said Magnus, now thoroughly confused. 'Who around here has access to something like that?'

'We just saw her,' said Bryn. 'Hilda Underpin does.'

Magnus's mouth fell open and he stopped in his tracks. 'You're not being serious!' he said.

'I am.'

'But she's a little old lady! Are you saying she's been buying premium poison on the black market or something?'

'No, I'm saying she's had premium poison in her flat for — let's see — around fifty years now.'

'*What?*' Magnus was tempted to walk away right then: the Welshman was definitely mad. 'Bryn, you're not making any sense!'

'Listen,' said Bryn, 'the first time we went to Hilda Underpin's flat she told us about Tarquin, right?'

'She told us quite a bit about him today...' muttered Magnus.

'But do you remember exactly what she said about him the first time, about how valiant he was?'

'I expect you're going to remind me,' said Magnus, feeling very out of his depth.

'She said about Tarquin and his men — and again, I quote: "*They ran into the line of fire, willing to give up their lives for their countries. Do you know, he and his comrades kept pills in tiny pockets in their sleeves, so that if they were caught by the enemy, they could make the ultimate sacrifice to avoid questioning?*"

'*That's* the poison you're talking about?' said Magnus, disbelievingly. 'Bryn, that was fifty years ago! And Tarquin's long dead!'

'But you heard what she said today,' said Bryn, his tone impatient now. 'She said she'd kept every single thing Tarquin had owned during his time in the commandos — *every single thing*, Magnus. And this afternoon, I went through those things, and I tried on that jacket, and there was no trace of a poisonous pill, even in the little pockets I found sewn into the sleeves.'

Magnus gaped at him: so that was the reason Bryn had wanted to look through all of Tarquin Underpin's memorabilia, and try on the dead man's jacket.

'Considering Tarquin made it through the war and didn't have to sacrifice himself to avoid questioning, I can only assume the pill made it back to Westminster Square and remained in that sleeve until a few months ago, when it was dropped into the drink of Anne-Laure Chevalier.'

'But — but —' Magnus was shaking his head: Hilda Underpin was one of the worst people he knew, and although he wouldn't have put much past her, sneaking undetected into the Royal West Hotel in the middle of the night to poison Anne-Laure seemed very unlikely. 'But she had no motive,' he said, 'I mean, aside from the fact she didn't like Anne-Laure's clothes. And she wasn't even at that party — or at least, she wasn't on Dame Winifred's guest list.'

This time it was Bryn's turn to stare at Magnus for a few moments before, quite suddenly, he burst out laughing. 'Oh, you think I'm saying *Hilda Underpin* murdered Anne-Laure Chevalier?'

'Aren't you?' said Magnus, thoroughly perplexed.

'No!' Bryn chuckled. 'Of course not. As you say, she had no motive!'

'But you just said — the pill — it was in her flat!'

'It was in her flat since Tarquin's return from the war, yes,' said Bryn. 'But don't forget, Hilda's flat was broken into shortly before Anne-Laure's death.'

A cold shiver suddenly ran up and down Magnus's spine. 'So you're saying...'

'The killer broke in for the pill, yes,' continued Bryn. 'Hilda told us nothing was taken — but I bet she didn't think to look in the sleeve of Tarquin's army jacket. Perhaps she didn't even remember the pill was there. As she told us just now, she hardly touched it since his return from the war.'

'But if she didn't know it was there, how did the killer?'

'The same way I did. I expect they came around for tea, heard Hilda's boasts about her brave husband, and put two and two together. Then, when they decided they wanted to bump off Anne-Laure, they broke in to get it.'

At some point during this discussion, they had resumed their stroll around the Square, and they continued in silence for a good few minutes. Then Magnus let out a long breath he didn't even realise he had been holding.

'Blimey, Bryn,' he said. 'That actually all makes sense. I mean, it's completely barmy, but it *does* make sense.'

Bryn shrugged a little bashfully. 'Let's not get carried away. It's going to be almost impossible to prove, considering Boyle had the body cremated, and it's not exactly like I've cornered the killer. Not yet, anyway.'

'No,' Magnus agreed, 'but you've done something almost as impressive. Bryn, after all this time, you may have finally found the murder weapon.'

CHAPTER THIRTY-SIX

Following Bryn's performance at Hilda Underpin's house, and the subsequent revelation that they may have discovered how Anne-Laure had been killed, Magnus was finding it harder than ever to keep his distance from the investigation, in spite of his workload. Then, a few evenings after they had spoken to Hilda, the barrister finally found the time to glance over the documents Bryn had given him, and his lukewarm interest in the case suddenly turned to burning curiosity.

'We need to speak to Lord Ellington,' he informed Bryn over the telephone, skipping past the *hello*s and *how are you*s.

Bryn, who did not seem bothered by the omission of pleasantries, said, 'Ah. Am I right in thinking you've just had a look at Anne-Laure Chevalier's bank statements?'

'Yes, and you were correct — they make for interesting reading.'

'Don't they just?' Bryn agreed. 'Do you think you can explain it, in business terms? I mean, I can see something dubious is going on, but I wouldn't be able say exactly what.'

'Oh, I think I know what's happened,' said Magnus, studying the documents before him with a frown. 'But Bryn, does this mean—?'

'I'm not sure,' said Bryn, before Magnus could finish his sentence. 'I have a theory, nothing more. I think it would be best to speak to Lord Ellington, as you say, and for you to tackle him over those bank statements. Then, depending on what he says, I might have a few questions of my own...'

Once again, this seemed very cryptic to Magnus, almost irritatingly so, but Bryn had known what he was doing with Hilda Underpin, hadn't he? There had been a reason for all those theatrics with Tarquin and the jacket. So perhaps Magnus simply had to trust that his young friend knew what he was doing, and that he preferred to keep his cards close to his chest until it was time to play his winning hand. In any case, there seemed little point discussing the ins and outs of the investigation over the phone, so in the end Magnus said he would arrange a time for them to call on Lord Ellington, and they left it at that.

Still, in the period leading up to their meeting with the Labour Lord, Magnus found himself dwelling on the question Bryn had not allowed him to ask: *Does this mean Ellington killed Anne-Laure Chevalier?* It wasn't beyond the realm of possibility. In fact, when he considered the poison pill angle, it was more than probable. Lord Ellington had been at the party at the Royal West that evening, at least according to Dame Winifred's guest list, and as he had been one of Anne-Laure's employers it was unlikely she would have thought twice about accepting a drink from him at the end of the night. And now, with these bank statements, Magnus was even beginning to see a motive emerge…

All of this was still whirling around the barrister's head as he and Bryn were let into Lord Ellington's flat by Gregor, the politician's hulking butler and bodyguard. Once more, they were led through the fairly traditional-looking hallway, and into the grand living room, where Ellington himself was sitting in an armchair by the fireplace, nursing a large glass of whiskey.

'Good evening, gentlemen,' he said smoothly, offering his hand from where he sat, so both Magnus and Bryn had to bend down to greet him, like courtiers paying their respects to a king. 'What can I offer you to drink?'

Magnus, remembering the effectiveness of plying Ellington with whiskey at their previous meeting, said, 'I wouldn't mind a spot of something strong, if you have it?'

Bryn looked a little surprised, and then hastened to agree, 'Yes, and for me too, please.'

Ellington looked pleased as he turned to his butler. 'Why don't you open the Jura this evening, Gregor?' Then, swallowing his own drink in one gulp, he added, 'You might as well refill me while you're at it — it'll save you a trip.'

With an ungainly bow, Gregor said, 'Yeth, thir. Thank you, thir.' Then he took Ellington's crystal tumbler in one of his massive hands and departed the room.

'Well, take a seat, won't you?' said the politician, regarding Magnus and Bryn coolly from his armchair. 'I'm keen to discover what you want to discuss with me this time. I'm hoping we're not going to spend the evening dissecting these maintenance charges again?'

'No,' said Magnus, as he and Bryn lowered themselves onto the sofa opposite the politician. He had slightly abandoned that particular campaign since the last meeting in the Cosmopolitan Club. 'I sent off that letter to CSP, so there's nothing to do at the moment but wait for a reply.'

Ellington received this news with a blank expression, and Magnus remembered he — more so than anyone else — had been sceptical about making too much of a fuss about the issue.

'On the last occasion you were both here, you told me you wanted to talk about Westminster Square security,' continued Ellington, 'although when I reflect on our conversation all I seem to remember is gossiping about the death of that silly girl, Anne-Laure Chevalier.'

Ellington may be a drunk, but he's no fool, Magnus thought. Then, deciding he didn't have the time or the patience to play games, he said, 'Well, I'm afraid you're going to be disappointed, Bevis, because discussing Anne-Laure Chevalier is exactly what we want to do this evening.'

Next to him on the sofa, Magnus could sense Bryn looking at him curiously, but the barrister did not return his gaze. Instead, his attention was fixed on Lord Ellington, whose bulging pale eyes now looked particularly icy.

'You seem to have a preoccupation with the girl, Magnus,' observed their host, after a few beats of silence. 'One might even call it a little unhealthy, fixating on the dead like this.'

'Well, I'm grateful for your concern, but you don't need to worry about my health,' said Magnus, deliberately missing the point. 'In fact,

I'd rather you used your energy explaining to us exactly what your relationship with Anne-Laure was.'

'What gives you the right to come into this flat and ask these sorts of questions?' demanded Ellington, leaning forward in his chair.

Magnus pointed at Bryn. 'He does. Police Constable Bryn Summers gives me the right.'

Ellington appeared to be a little taken aback, and Magnus wondered whether he had forgotten Bryn's profession. It was remarkable, really, the effect a policeman's presence had on a room, and the barrister thought they might as well use this to their advantage before news of Bryn's firing became public knowledge.

'So is this some sort of interrogation, then?' chuckled Ellington, slumping back in his chair but not quite managing to look relaxed. 'Am I about to be dragged down to the police station?'

'That depends on what you tell us, doesn't it?' said Magnus, pleasantly. 'But if you want to stay in your armchair there, I'd advise you not to keep anything back this time.'

'What do you mean?'

'I mean, you weren't entirely honest with us before, were you, Bevis? You didn't disclose all of the details of your dealings with Anne-Laure Chevalier.'

At that moment, there was a great crashing sound from behind them, which caused Magnus, Bryn and Lord Ellington to give a start of fright. Looking over the politician's head, Magnus saw Gregor had re-entered the room, and perhaps he had tripped on the edge of a rug, because the tumblers of whiskey he had been carrying were now in pieces on the floor, along with the silver tray.

'That's baccarat crystal, you brainless oaf!' snarled Ellington, with a sudden flash of temper as he took in the sight of the shattered glass on the floor. 'Clean it up — no! On second thoughts, get me a drink first — I'm parched! Then tidy up that mess, you clumsy fool!'

Gregor hurried from the room muttering, 'Yeth, thir. I'm tho thorry, thir. Right away, thir.'

With a very ugly expression, Ellington turned back to Magnus and Bryn. 'You were saying?' he demanded, as though no interruption had taken place.

'I was saying we would like to talk to you about this *rabbateur* role Anne-Laure had with you.'

'What about it?'

'Well, what did this job entail exactly?'

Ellington gave a huff of irritation. 'You're a man of the world, Magnus, you know what a *rabbateur* is. It's like I told your young friend here last time: I sent Anne-Laure out to network on my behalf. She talked me up to potential clients in her own charming style, and then steered them my way.'

'Potential clients for your trading deals?' clarified Magnus.

'That's right, yes.'

'And how did you reimburse her for this service?'

Ellington hesitated, clearly unhappy with having to answer so many questions. 'I paid her as and when I needed her — I suppose you could say I employed her on a freelance basis. As I told you before, I just dabble in trade, so I only needed her a few times a year.'

'And how much did you pay her?' asked Magnus.

'I don't see how that's any of your business, but as you seem to think there's something untoward going on, and as the girl herself isn't here to object, I'll tell you: I paid Anne-Laure a few thousand pounds every time she sent a client my way. And, on the occasions that I dispatched her to do negotiations on my behalf — which became increasingly frequent, considering my mostly male and middle-aged clients responded to her so well — I paid her about the same.'

'A few thousand pounds?' Magnus said. 'That was all?'

Ellington looked angry. 'What do you mean, *that was all*? It's a ridiculous amount to pay someone to go to a few parties, bat her eyelashes and laugh at a few jokes. What that girl was doing was hardly rocket science, Magnus, it was professional flirting!'

'Professional flirting on your behalf,' Magnus could not resist reminding him. 'Professional flirting you did rather well out of, Bevis.

In any case,' he continued, thoroughly enjoying being back in barrister mode, especially after all the paperwork he'd had to do recently, 'I'm not really interested in what she did, I'm interested in what you paid her, and I'm especially interested in why, when you say you only gave her a few thousand for her *rabbateur* services, why you were in the habit of depositing up to half a million pounds into her bank account.'

Ellington gaped at him: clearly, he had not been expecting this.

'What?' he said at last, before forcing his features into a smile. 'What rubbish is this? Where are you getting this nonsense from?'

'From Anne-Laure Chevalier's bank statements,' said Magnus, drawing them from his jacket pocket and offering them to the politician. 'I've taken the liberty of highlighting the relevant deposits so you can see, quite clearly, when Anne-Laure Chevalier received vast sums of money from Lord Bevis Ellington.'

The Labour Lord regarded the proffered documents as though Magnus were offering him a ticking time bomb. Then, when he finally snatched at them and began to read, his paper-thin skin grew even paler than usual. He stared at the bank statements for so long Gregor had time to return to the room and hand out fresh glasses of whisky, his hands trembling the whole time.

Eventually, when it became clear that Ellington was going to remain tight-lipped, Magnus said, 'I have two questions: why did you transfer all of that money into Anne-Laure's account, and why did you do it on multiple occasions? I must admit, at first I thought you were paying *her* for some service — some absurdly expensive service, mind you — but then I noticed that within a few days the money always left her account again, going to all sorts of interesting-sounding companies and individuals, especially in the Far East.' He looked Ellington straight in the eye. 'So I can only conclude, Bevis, that you were using Anne-Laure to do a few under-the-table commissions.'

Ellington's upper lip curled into a sneer. Then, without turning in his seat, he addressed his butler-bodyguard, who was attempting to creep out of the room.

'Gregor, stay here, will you?' he said. 'I might be in need of your… services.'

As Gregor turned at the door, Magnus looked between both men. Surely Ellington couldn't be threatening them? But on the other hand, he and Bryn were here because they had not ruled out their host as being a killer. Magnus swallowed, suddenly feeling a little nervous.

Bryn, meanwhile, who had hardly spoken since they had arrived, said, 'Perhaps, Magnus, you could explain what you mean by under-the-table commissions? I'm afraid I'm not well-versed in trading, or business generally, for that matter.'

'Of course.'

Magnus took a large sip of whiskey and then rose from the sofa. Although he was painfully aware of how much smaller he was than Gregor, he knew from his work that being on his feet was a much more effective and intimidating position from which to cross-examine a defendant.

'First, I think it's important we're all clear on exactly what Bevis's deals involve here,' Magnus began, pacing behind the sofa as he spoke. Then, knowing his young friend would remember from his exhaustive note-taking, he said, 'Bryn, the last time we were here, what did Lord Ellington tell us he was trading in?'

'Mostly rice and other food staples, and sometimes a bit of jewellery,' said Bryn at once.

'Well, that's not true for a start,' said Magnus bluntly. 'If I had to guess, I'd say Lord Ellington's deals involve arms and heavy military and transport equipment — items, in short, that are subject to embargo.'

'Preposterous!' burst out Ellington. 'You're talking utter claptrap, Magnus. You're basing that on nothing at all.'

'Not quite,' said Magnus. 'You see, I thought there was something fishy going on the last time we were here, considering how you denied knowing Anne-Laure Chevalier, when in fact she had been your employee. This suggested there was something dodgy about her working for you, or something dodgy about the work itself, and seeing as there's nothing illegal about being a *rabbateur*, I had to conclude it was the latter. Furthermore, when you consider the amount of money we're looking at in those bank statements alone, it strikes me that a little more than rice and a bit of jewellery is at stake here.'

Ellington looked down at the incriminating documents, which were still in his hands. 'Where did you get these, anyway?' he demanded.

'Never you mind,' said Magnus, batting away the attempt to change the subject. Then, turning to Bryn, he continued, 'Let's say Government X in South-East Asia wants to buy some heavy equipment. Lord Ellington gets wind of this — he gets wind of everything through his royal and political connections — and he sets up a deal wherein Government X buys the equipment for, say, twenty million dollars from Company Y, and he takes, I don't know, one million from the arrangement. Is that about right, Bevis? You take a five percent commission?'

Magnus half expected Ellington to start spluttering with rage and indignation, but he seemed to have momentarily cowed the man into silence.

'I'll take that as a yes,' continued the barrister. 'So far so good. Depending on what he's trading in, it's fairly clean business, and Bevis probably repeats that deal three or four times a year to make a bit of pocket money. Who knows, he might even pay tax on it. The point is, it's a pretty easy way for him to supplement his income, and all he needs to do is capitalise on his contacts. But complications arise when you consider Bevis here has been selling potentially problematic equipment, and so he sometimes has to work on the border of the law — or laws, as we're talking about international deals here. That means he sometimes had to grease a few palms along the way, and I believe that's where Anne-Laure Chevalier must have come in.

'To go back to our example of before,' the barrister went on, 'let's say Government X, who wants this military and possibly embargoed equipment, have a minister of defence. And this individual — Minister Z, we'll call him — informs Bevis that in order for the deal to go through smoothly, he wants a little extra for himself, maybe half a million dollars.

And Bevis agrees. But, of course, our friend is a man of repute, and he doesn't want to be seen to be giving money to corrupt politicians in the Far East, let alone be accused of bribery — perish the thought! So he sends the commission through his *rabbateur*, Anne-Laure: half a million is paid into her account by Lord Ellington and then, a few days later, that money is transferred out again to Minister Z. The deal goes through and everyone's happy: Government X gets its embargoed equipment, Company Y gets its twenty million, Minister Z gets his bribe, Lord Ellington gets his commission, and Anne-Laure gets paid for the use of her bank account, her *rabbateur* work and her discretion. Does that sound about right, Bevis?'

As Magnus took a large swig of whiskey to reward himself for making sense of it all, Ellington began to clap very slowly.

'What a *fascinating* theory, Magnus,' he said, his voice thick with sarcasm. 'Unfortunately, it's going to be very difficult for you to prove it, especially as I'm not sure you've acquired these bank statements by innocent means. And even if you could find evidence of my trading in embargoed equipment or paying the odd minister or president a little extra, what are you going to do about it? As you've kindly pointed out, I have friends in powerful places.'

'Oh, but we're not here to take you to task for your trade deals,' said Magnus. 'Franky, Bevis, I couldn't care less about what you get up to in your spare time. That's not to say I hope it doesn't catch up with you some day — I hope it does, and causes a huge scandal — but I don't have the time or the energy to be the one to expose you. No, what we're interested in today is what you did to Anne-Laure Chevalier.'

Ellington's expression of smugness faltered a little. 'What do you mean, what I *did* to her? I didn't do anything to her.'

Magnus looked to his left: it was Bryn's turn. He had played his part, he had acted the accusing barrister, and in doing so had uncovered some of Ellington's guilt. But now it was the turn of the former policeman to take the stage and, fortunately, Bryn was rising to his feet on cue.

'Lord Ellington, the last time we were here, you didn't give us the impression you had been particularly fond of Anne-Laure,' the Welshman began. 'You called her "greedy", "grasping" and "completely obsessed with money". You resented the fact she checked and double-checked you had paid her correctly, and you were furious when she dared to ask you for an advance a few weeks before her death.'

'Which is perfectly justified!' Lord Ellington cried. 'What right did she have, as a freelance *flirt*, to ask *me* for extra money? It was ridiculous, it was insulting, it was —'

Bryn held up a hand to stop him. 'My point is, you didn't like her,' he said. 'You were unmoved by her beauty, you were blind to her business prowess — in part, I think, because she was female — and you disliked that a woman with no family, status and little education was playing with you and the big boys, and playing well. I would even go as far to say that the combination of Anne-Laure's modest background and big ambitions reminded you a little of yourself, which you found unpleasant.'

'I don't have to sit here and listen to this,' Ellington growled. 'You're insulting me in my own house. Who do you think you are, young man?'

Bryn, apparently taking a leaf out of Magnus's book, ignored the politician entirely, and continued, 'But as well as not liking Anne-Laure, you didn't trust her. Even though, as we've seen, you had to assign her vast sums of money. You were paranoid about what you perceived to be her grasping nature — again, perhaps you saw yourself in her there — and you only put up with her because you needed to; she and her bank account were necessary parts of these schemes Magnus has just outlined.

'But then, I think something changed a few weeks before her death,' Bryn went on, 'and your feelings of resentment and mistrust intensified when she had the gall to ask you for this advance. Perhaps you even found out she was intending to leave Westminster Square with Jem McMorran — after all, Hilda Underpin knew, so that piece of information must have been on its way to becoming public knowledge.'

'With *Jem McMorran?*' gasped Ellington, and Magnus recalled he had a soft spot for the Hollywood actor. 'Are you saying that dratted girl was — she was with *Jem McMorran?*'

Bryn waved this question away, perhaps feeling it wasn't relevant to the discussion. Instead, he said, 'Around this time, something else happened, didn't it, Lord Ellington? A man named Zafran, who was a minister or government official you were trying to bribe, got in touch to say he hadn't received his money. The half a million you had promised him hadn't made it into his account, and if it didn't make an appearance in the next few days, he would call the whole deal off, and you would lose your commission.

'I bet that sent you into a spin, didn't it?' said Bryn. 'And I bet you knew who to blame. You were aware she was after money, you had heard through the grapevine she was planning to leave the country, so all your worst fears about her suddenly seemed to be confirmed: Anne-Laure was as greedy and deceitful as you had always suspected, and instead of transferring the latest half a million you had dumped into her account to this Zafran person, she had kept it for herself, to fund her new life in America with Jem McMorran. In short, she had stolen from you.'

Shocked, Magnus opened his mouth to speak, but Bryn shook his head slightly, signalling the barrister shouldn't interrupt. Obediently, Magnus kept quiet, and even sat back down on the sofa to allow Bryn all of the spotlight.

Opposite him, Ellington looked similarly stunned, although something about the hardness of his expression suggested he was less surprised by what Bryn was saying than the fact that he was saying it. As though reaching for a lifeline, Ellington picked up his glass of whiskey — which was almost full to the brim — drank its contents in a few glugs, and then wiped at his thin lips with a sleeve.

'I don't see why you're interrogating me about this alleged theft,' he said eventually, his voice quiet and cold.

'Well we can hardly interrogate Anne-Laure, can we?' Bryn shot back.

'I haven't done anything wrong,' growled Ellington, slamming his tumbler back onto the coffee table and almost breaking the fourth glass of the evening.

'Haven't you?' said Bryn, thoughtful now. 'Tell me, Lord Ellington, what do you know about Anne-Laure's death?'

'Nothing.'

'Nothing?' Bryn repeated, disbelievingly.

Magnus looked between them, feeling as tense as though he were watching a real courtroom drama unfold.

'You don't know anything at all about how Anne-Laure Chevalier died?' Bryn continued, leaning down and resting his hands on the back of the sofa, so he could look Ellington straight in the eye. 'You didn't read anything about it in the papers, you didn't see anything about it on the news, you didn't go to any trouble at all to find out what happened to your *rabbateur*?'

Ellington shifted in his armchair. 'Well, no, of course I know a little. I understand she died of natural causes. Which was obviously very... *unfortunate.*'

Magnus was surprised he hadn't choked on this last word, he seemed so reluctant to say it.

'Natural causes, yes, that was the official story,' said Bryn. 'But what wasn't reported in the news was that Anne-Laure Chevalier's body was significantly bruised. I happened to see her on the morning after her death, so I can tell you she had some very ugly-looking marks here... and *here.*'

He gestured to his wrists and then his hands lingered around his own neck. Ellington stared at him, momentarily transfixed, and then shook his head.

'The whole business is very unfortunate, as I said,' he whispered. 'But I don't see what any of this has to do with me...'

'Don't you?' said Bryn, sharply. 'Come on, Ellington, stop playing games. Stop pretending you're not responsible for some of those bruises.'

'I'm not!' Ellington cried, jumping in his chair as though he had received an electric shock. 'I'm not, I swear it! I never touched her!'

'Oh, I never said *you* touched her,' said Bryn. 'I didn't think someone like you would do your own dirty work. And besides, I doubt you have the strength to bruise someone so badly. But your bodyguard does — don't you, Gregor?'

Bryn looked suddenly to the corner of the room and, dumbfounded, Magnus followed his gaze. Gregor was still stood by the door, only now his large blank face was crumpled with anguish.

'Oh no,' he moaned, pulling at the sleeves of his ill-fitting suit, 'oh no, oh no, oh no…'

'*Gregor*,' said the politician in a warning voice, '*shut up.*'

But the big man didn't appear to hear him. His trunk-like legs were shaking, and he stumbled to the nearest chair and threw himself into its cushions. There followed a great crack as the chair then collapsed under his weight and Gregor dropped to the floor. But even this didn't seem to have much of an effect on the bodyguard, whose head was now in his enormous hands.

'*Gregor!*' exploded Lord Ellington, and Magnus wasn't sure which he was angrier about, the destruction of the chair, or his employee's indiscretion. 'You stupid fool, you great imbecile — just — just *stop*! Stop talking!'

'Thee was my friend,' Gregor wailed, beginning to cry as the vision of Anne-Laure swept to his mind, 'thee wath my little bird, and I hurt her…'

'*Gregor!*'

Lord Ellington started to pull himself up from his own armchair, but froze when he saw Bryn crossing the room and heading towards his bodyguard. Then he slipped back down, as though he were afraid of getting too close to the former policeman. Bryn, meanwhile, laid a hand on one of Gregor's massive shoulders, which were shuddering with grief, and said, 'Gregor, why don't you tell me what happened, that night at the Royal West Hotel?'

But it seemed Gregor was too overcome with emotion to speak, and perhaps because his lisp made him difficult to follow at the best of times Bryn said, 'All right, why don't I tell you what I think happened, and you can nod if it's correct. How does that sound?'

Gregor's square head bobbed up and down. 'Yeth pleathe.'

'I think Anne-Laure Chevalier was kind to you,' said Bryn. 'I think she always had a smile and few words for you every time she came in and out of this flat, and you liked her for it, didn't you, Gregor? Maybe you were even a little in love with her, because she was very pretty, wasn't she?'

Gregor nodded dolefully.

'But Lord Ellington didn't like her, did he? Everything I said earlier was true — he thought she was greedy and he didn't trust her. I think what happened is that one day Lord Ellington came to you, Gregor, and he told you Anne-Laure had stolen from him. Is that right?'

Another nod.

'*Gregor!*' hissed Ellington, but nobody in the room paid him any attention.

'He was angry, wasn't he, Gregor? He wanted the money back from her as fast as possible, and so he told you to threaten her, just as you've threatened other people for him in the past. He wanted you to scare her, didn't he? Perhaps he even instructed you to knock her around a little, so she would know Lord Ellington meant business.

'So you went to that party at the Royal West with Lord Ellington,' continued Bryn, not bothering to wait for a nod this time, 'and you managed to get Anne-Laure on her own. You confronted her with Lord Ellington's accusations, which she denied, and then things got a bit out of hand, didn't they?'

Gregor looked up from his hands and turned his tear-stained face to Bryn.

'Thee was acting tho thrangely,' he said. 'I'd never theen her like that before. Thee wath jumpy, thee talked and moved too quickly, thee wath trying to get away from me…'

'Probably because you were threatening her,' pointed out Bryn, reasonably. 'Also, she had just snorted a line of cocaine in the bathroom with Jem McMorran, so I suppose she would have been acting a bit oddly, come to think of it.'

'*What?*' piped up Lord Ellington.

'Oh, shut up,' Magnus snapped.

'For now, I'll give you the benefit of the doubt, Gregor, and venture you didn't intend to hurt her,' said Bryn. 'Or at least, you didn't intend to hurt her badly.'

'I didn't!' insisted the bodyguard.

'But you panicked. She was jittery, she was denying everything you were accusing her of, and she was trying to give you the slip, so you seized her by the neck and you squeezed. I imagine she's not the first person you've tried to strangle, but she might have been the first woman, and Anne-Laure was a slight thing, wasn't she? To use your own word from the last time we were here, she was *fragile*.'

Gregor stared at his enormous hands, the fingers of which were flexing as though he had no control over them.

'Thee was my friend…' he whimpered. 'I didn't mean to —'

'But you did,' interrupted Bryn, his tone suddenly stern, 'and from the look of those bruises you nearly crushed her windpipe and killed her.'

At this sudden loss of sympathy, Gregor let out a howl like a wounded dog and began to cry again.

'Thee's dead!' he sobbed. 'Thee's dead, and it'th all my fault!'

'Actually, it's not your fault,' said Bryn. 'It's not even Ellington's, although, between you and him, you managed to terrify and physically assault her on the last night of her life, so who knows what effect that had on her actions later on?' He turned to Magnus. 'Perhaps, because of them, she wasn't as on guard as she should have been, when she accepted a drink at the end of the night.'

'Wait,' said Magnus, who had been listening to this whole story unfold with horrified fascination, 'so you're saying Ellington *didn't* kill her?'

'*Kill her?*' exclaimed Ellington, looking outraged. 'Who said anything about killing her?'

'Don't you think Anne-Laure Chevalier's death was rather suspicious, given the circumstances?' said Magnus.

But Ellington only laughed. 'What good was she to me dead? She had my money, remember? I can't tell you how annoyed I was the next day when I heard she'd keeled over.'

'Yes, I imagine it's especially grating you can't go to the police or the bank about your missing money, considering your whole enterprise is so shady,' said Magnus.

Ellington, pretending he hadn't heard this, merely snorted, 'Kill her indeed! I've never heard anything like it in my life...'

Gregor, wiping at his streaming nose, said, 'Thee wath alive when I latht thaw her. I mean, thee wath coughing and thpluttering a bit, and thee wath angry and upthet with me, but thee wath alive.'

'What time was that, do you think?' asked Bryn.

'Almotht eleven o'clock. I remember, becauth we came home afterwardth.'

'So she had already gone out to the garden...' mused Bryn, more to himself than anyone else.

Magnus, who was trying to keep up with everything that had just been revealed, assumed this meant that Bryn had ruled out Lord Ellington as both the murderer and the shadowy figure in the garden. But it left a bitter taste in his mouth, to know that even though their host was such a despicable character there was little they could pin on him. He was involved in all sorts of dodgy deals, he had dispatched his brainless bodyguard to beat up a defenceless woman, and yet he seemed to be getting away with it all. Suddenly, Magnus couldn't bear to be in the same room as the vicious and hypocritical old politician for a minute longer.

'I think we're done here, Bryn,' he said, standing up and not bothering to hide the disgust from his voice. 'Let's go.' Then, as he passed the still-weeping bodyguard, Magnus added, 'Gregor, I hope after what's happened here tonight, you rethink how much this job means to you. I'm sure there are better people out there who could use a loyal bodyguard, so I'd advise you hand in your notice before you're further tainted by your association with this appalling person — and perhaps it wouldn't be a bad idea to sign up for some anger management classes while you're at it, eh? Before someone else gets hurt?'

'Yeth, Mr Walterthon,' murmured the enormous man.

Ellington, on the other hand, did not seem quite so humbled. 'That's it?' he cried, waving Anne-Laure's bank statements at them in anger. 'You come into my house, you accuse me of all sorts of nonsense, and then you just *leave*?'

'You're lucky that's all we're doing,' said Magnus, through gritted teeth.

'And thank you, I almost forgot about those,' said Bryn, snatching the documents from the politician's long, bony fingers. 'You know, you never asked me how I knew the name Zafran.'

'What?' Ellington snapped.

'Zafran. The name of the minister or official who told you he hadn't received his half a million dollars.'

'Because that sly, deceitful girl stole it!' snarled Ellington.

'Actually, she didn't,' said Bryn, 'and the reason I know Zafran's name is because it's right here on her bank statement. She transferred the money, Lord Ellington, just as you told her to, but Zafran pretended she hadn't, presumably in an attempt to extract a bit more money from you. And it worked, didn't it? I bet you've already paid him another half a million, because you believed some corrupt stranger you'd never met over your own employee. So you see, even though she needed the money, even though you bullied her and sent your bodyguard to beat her up, Anne-Laure Chevalier was loyal to you until the very end.'

They took a moment to appreciate the mixture of shock, rage and even a little regret in Lord Ellington's expression, and then, in the absence of an operational butler, Magnus and Bryn let themselves out.

CHAPTER THIRTY-SEVEN

'My goodness,' said Magnus, as soon as they were clear of Lord Ellington's house. 'That was — I mean to say — *my goodness.*'

Bryn nodded sympathetically. 'It's a lot to take in,' he said.

'How on earth did you work all of that out?' asked the barrister, who had a newfound appreciation for Bryn's way of thinking.

'By reading over all of my notes several hundred times,' admitted his friend. 'We knew Ellington was keeping secrets, we knew his dealings were probably on the border of the law, and the bank statements confirmed he'd been using Anne-Laure as a kind of go-between, although obviously I needed you to explain exactly what was happening there. As for the rest of it, I couldn't get out of my head how much Ellington seemed to have viciously disliked her, when nobody else had a bad word to say about Anne-Laure — well, except for Hilda, who has a bad word to say about everyone.'

'Apart from her new friend, *Brian,*' grinned Magnus.

Deliberately not acknowledging this, Bryn continued, 'So I began to think there must have been some bad blood between Anne-Laure and Ellington, most likely something involving money, seeing as they were both so keen on it. The bank statements proved she hadn't stolen anything, but what if Ellington thought she had? And when I looked back on the extent of the bruising around her neck, I knew it had to be the work of someone fairly big and strong — someone, in fact, exactly like Gregor. He, if you remember, had seemed particularly upset by her death when we last spoke to him, and when I tried to think back to what he had said, all I recalled was him staring at his hands...' Bryn shrugged, suddenly modest. 'But really, it was all speculation.'

'Speculation that turned out to be entirely correct,' said Magnus, both taken aback by the revelations of the meeting and thoroughly impressed by Bryn's detective work. 'And something tells me that's not all you have up your sleeve. You still know far more than you're letting on to me, don't you?'

'Maybe. But as I said, it's all speculation...'

Yet Magnus was now inclined to believe that's Bryn's version of 'speculation' was rather more than that.

'All right,' he said, 'I don't want to interfere. I'm loath to interrupt your trains of thought when these speculations of yours seem to be so on-track. But let me know if there's anything I can do to help, won't you?' Then, with a sigh, he added, 'I must admit, I'm completely invested in all of this, against my better judgement...'

'Actually,' said Bryn, 'you can help me right now.'

'Sorry?'

Magnus had been concentrating so intently on their conversation he had failed to notice that Bryn had led them beyond Westminster Square and into Westminster Row, where they were now standing outside the smart terraced house they had visited a few weeks earlier.

'Really?' he said doubtfully to Bryn. 'Morris?'

Magnus didn't exactly agree with Juliana, who thought that Morris Springfield was a sweet and sensitive figure. In fact, he thought the writer a socially-awkward intellectual snob who deliberately distanced himself from those around him for the sake of his so-called art. But the idea that Morris Springfield might have killed Anne-Laure Chevalier was absurd, especially as he had hardly known her. Hadn't the writer said they had been for coffee once, and it had not gone well?

Magnus was about to remind Bryn of this fact, but the former policeman was already pressing the buzzer of the building, and instead he was forced to explain via the intercom why they were there, making the usual vague excuses about Westminster security.

'It's a bit late for this, isn't it, Magnus?' asked Morris, peering around the doorframe so they could only see a sliver of his pallid face and greasy hair.

Magnus opened his mouth, but before he could make some excuse or apology, Bryn stepped forward.

MYSTERY IN WESTMINSTER SQUARE

'Actually, Mr Springfield, I'm afraid I have an ulterior motive for coming round here today.'

As he reached into his bag, Magnus wondered whether Bryn might be speaking a little too soon here; surely if he started talking about Anne-Laure Chevalier, Morris would simply close the door in their faces? But then, to the barrister's surprise, it wasn't bank statements or any other damning evidence Bryn withdrew from his rucksack, but a paperback copy of *Vacant Shadows*. The writer regarded the edition of his first novel being waved under his nose with mild suspicion.

'I was talking to my mum on the phone the other day,' said Bryn, 'and she told me she'd just read this amazing book, *Vacant Shadows*. She absolutely loved it, and she couldn't believe it when I said its author lived just round the corner from my work. So I was wondering, if it's not too much trouble, perhaps you could sign this copy for her? I know it's a bit cheeky to come round here and ask you like this,' continued the Welshman apologetically, 'but it's her birthday next week, and it would be the *perfect* present…'

'Of course,' said Morris, flinging open the door. 'Come in, I'll fetch a pen.'

His demeanour of distrust had vanished in an instant, and he now looked completely delighted at the prospect of scribbling his signature for Bryn's mother. Perhaps, Magnus thought, Morris didn't meet many of his fans — if indeed he had any.

The writer's flat looked much the same as it had the last time they'd been there, for the poky attic space was still dominated by piles of books, newspapers and manuscripts, as well as a few boxes, which presumably contained yet more literature. Morris skirted around these obstacles with a practiced air as he searched for a pen, while Magnus and Bryn stood patiently by the kitchenette.

'Ah, here we go!' said the writer, finally locating a pen from the pot of a long-dead plant and reaching out for Bryn's copy of *Vacant Shadows*. 'What's your mother's name?'

'Mairwen,' said Bryn, before spelling it out for Morris. 'And perhaps you could write her a message too? Just something like, *Many happy returns from your favourite writer*, that sort of thing.'

'Favourite writer, eh?' Morris tittered, lowering himself onto one of the boxes to pen the message.

Magnus smiled: he wasn't entirely sure what Bryn's plan was here, but he seemed to be doing a good job of buttering up the young intellectual.

'There you are,' said Morris at last, handing the book back to Bryn and replacing the cap of his pen. 'I hope she likes it. Has she read my second novel, *Splinters of Innocence*? It's a more experimental, *avant-garde* work, but a better book for it, in my humble opinion. I might have a spare copy here somewhere…'

'Oh, that's all right,' said Bryn quickly, 'one of my sisters is buying it for her. But thank you very much for this,' he added, looking at the signed book as though it were a great treasure. 'She'll absolutely love it. I'll be in her good graces for months.'

Magnus frowned: perhaps this wasn't an act; perhaps Bryn was in earnest after all. Then, recalling what Juliana always told him about the writer, he asked, 'How's *your* mother, Morris? Has she recovered?'

'Sorry?'

'I thought Juliana said she fell ill back in June?'

'Oh yes, yes,' said the writer. 'Oh, she's much better now, thank you. And she's always cheered up by Juliana's flowers.'

'I'm not surprised,' said Magnus, 'Juliana does the best arrangements… Well, her and your Daisy, of course,' he added to Bryn.

He expected his friend, who was tucking Morris's book back into his bag, to object to being teased again about Daisy, but for some reason Bryn was chuckling to himself.

'What are you laughing at?' asked Magnus.

'Oh, just Mr Springfield here saying he sends flowers to his mother.'

'What's so funny about that?' asked Morris, a little defensively.

Bryn looked up, his expression suddenly hard. 'Because it's not true, is it, Mr Springfield? You weren't sending flowers to your mother, at least not before June you weren't — you were sending them to Anne-Laure Chevalier.'

MYSTERY IN WESTMINSTER SQUARE

The sudden silence in the room, especially after the jovial atmosphere of a few moments ago, was striking. Magnus watched two blotches of colour appear in Morris's pale cheeks like ink on blotting paper.

Eventually, the writer asked, 'What on earth are you talking about?'

'The flowers,' said Bryn. 'The ones you were buying every week from The Station Garden. The ones you refused to let Juliana send out on your behalf, because you wanted to add jam or chocolates or whatever else to the package. But they weren't for your mother at all, were they, Mr Springfield? They were for Anne-Laure Chevalier.'

Magnus, almost as taken aback as Morris by Bryn's sudden offensive, stared at the writer, who seemed completely tongue-tied.

'Anne-Laure — *what*? That's completely — Those flowers were for my mother!'

'So why have you stopped visiting The Station Garden since mid-June?' asked Bryn. 'And why did I find loads of flowers with the Station Garden's purple ribbons in Anne-Laure's bin?'

'In her —?' Morris shook his head. 'This is nonsense! Where I buy my flowers is no business of yours! Perhaps I found somewhere I liked better than The Station Garden? And why on earth would you assume that the flowers in that woman's flat were from *me*?'

But Bryn, ignoring the question, asked one of his own instead: 'Where are you from, Morris?'

'Excuse me?'

'Where did you grow up?'

'East Sussex.' Morris looked at Magnus with a pleading expression, as though the barrister could exert some control over Bryn. 'Magnus, I really don't see why —'

'Whereabouts in East Sussex?' interrupted Bryn loudly.

'Brighton,' snapped Morris. 'But I can't understand what —'

'Like Anne-Laure Chevalier,' said Bryn. 'She was also originally from Brighton.'

Morris stared at him with his large pale eyes, and then attempted a smile. 'So you're saying I was secretly sending flowers to this Anne-Laure person because we were both from Brighton? Don't you remember what I told you last time? We went for coffee once — and yes, that was because she had found out we both grew up in the same city — but it didn't go well. We discovered we had nothing in common. She wasn't —'

'Your intellectual equal,' said Bryn, finishing Morris's sentence for him. 'Yes, I remember what you said. I also recall you telling us you'd never met her, back in Brighton; that you'd only encountered Anne-Laure Chevalier in London. But that's not true, is it, Mr Springfield? That — along with almost everything else you've told us — is a complete fabrication.'

Morris sprang from the box on which he had been sitting. 'Who do you think you are, coming into my flat and accusing me of — of whatever you're accusing me!' he cried. 'Don't you know who I am?'

'You're a liar,' said Bryn, calmly. 'You lie for a living and you're lying to us right now.'

'Magnus!' exclaimed the writer, his voice loud and shrill. 'This is totally unacceptable! I'm going to have to ask you to leave, and take this insulting person with you!'

But Magnus merely shrugged: having seen his friend at work on Hilda Underpin and Lord Ellington, there was no way he was going to stop him mid-flow now.

Emboldened, Bryn said, 'Both Agnes Chambers and Dame Winifred Rye told us Anne-Laure had had a boyfriend back in Brighton, before she moved to London at seventeen years old. A teenage sweetheart, if you will. Magnus, that boyfriend was Morris Springfield.'

'*What*?' cried the writer. 'This is — I can't believe I'm hearing — Do you know what a coincidence that would be? That, out of the whole of London — the whole of the UK, the whole of the *world* — I would end up living in the next street to my teenage sweetheart? Ridiculous!'

Coincidence or not, Morris's blustering was unconvincing. Magnus, whose judgement was refined from years in the courtroom, found himself far more drawn to Bryn's firm, unruffled demeanour.

'Go on,' he said, nodding at the former policeman.

'*Magnus!*' cried Morris again, looking outraged, but with both of them against him now there was little he could do.

'It's not a coincidence,' said Bryn, looking coldly at Morris, 'but we'll get to that later. We should begin at the beginning — like in any good book. In fact, why don't I tell you both a story, and then Mr Springfield here can tell us whether or not it's true?'

Neither Morris nor Magnus spoke, although the latter once again reflected that perhaps Bryn was wasted in the police force, when apparently he had the mind of a barrister.

'So, once upon a time in Brighton, a boy met a girl,' said Bryn, starting to pace up and down in front of the kitchenette. 'They fell in love, and he probably couldn't believe his luck: after all, she was smart and beautiful, and he was an ungainly oddball who probably spent his evenings shut up in his bedroom writing indecipherable prose.'

Morris made a noise of protestation at the back of his throat, but this did not stop Bryn from talking.

'I can't quite see what drew her to him,' continued the Welshman thoughtfully. 'Perhaps she was a little taken in by his pseudo-intellectualism, or perhaps she was drawn to that sensitive young man because she was still suffering from the loss of her parents, and prone to melancholy. Maybe she was just lonely. Whatever the reason, they became sweethearts for a while, maybe for a summer or two, until the day she announced she had been offered an incredible opportunity by a kindly benefactor, and was leaving Brighton in order to start her adult life in London.'

Morris was quiet now, but he was watching Bryn with a kind of horrified fascination, hanging off his every word.

'So they split up,' said the former policeman. 'Or rather, she ended their relationship, presumably because she wanted a fresh start, and perhaps her heart hadn't really been in it after all. But his had, and when she left him that heart was broken — he was broken — and he never quite got over it. No matter how much he wrote, no matter how successful he became, no matter how much time passed, he couldn't stop thinking about this girl, his first and only love.

'Years went by,' continued Bryn, warming to his narrative, 'and the boy — who was now a man — still harboured these intense feelings for his teenage sweetheart, so he decided to look her up. He tracked her down to London, and discovered that she, along with her name, had changed. She was not the naive little girl she had been before — the capital had transformed her into someone more worldly, a glamorous and sophisticated woman.

'Still, for old time's sake, she agreed to go for coffee with him. But it wasn't the same — *she* wasn't the same. She had seen a bit of life now, and she was no longer taken in by his cerebral posturing, no longer tolerant of his patronising manner. She made it clear to him she had moved on long ago, and told him kindly but firmly there was no hope of any romantic reconciliation.

'But the man didn't accept this. Seeing her again had had a strange effect on him: it should have given him closure on their fleeting adolescent relationship, but instead it deepened all of the feelings he had been harbouring for her over the years. He had to have her — he thought she was his.

'So he set up in Westminster Row, just a street behind his former sweetheart's flat, and though he told everyone he was there for the area's literary heritage, in reality he had moved for her, and her only. He tried to declare his love to her, but he was rebuffed — first gently, and then with growing impatience. But he didn't give up. The man was determined to win her, and so he started to keep a closer eye on her — too close an eye on her. He followed her in the street, he stood outside her house at night, he kept track of everything she did, everywhere she went, and everyone she spoke to until —'

'I can't listen to this anymore!' burst out Morris. 'Magnus, you can't believe any of this — this *fairy tale*! It's madness!'

But the barrister, who seemed to have been cast in the role of judge that evening, was recalling something from a few weeks ago.

'When we went to Hilda Underpin's flat the first time,' he said to Bryn, 'we asked her whether she had seen anything or anyone unusual, and she said she'd seen *him*, didn't she? Loitering around?'

As Bryn nodded, Morris cried, 'So what? You're taking the word of that old bag over *me?*' He turned back to Bryn. 'This is ridiculous, you've made it all up! You don't have any proof!'

'Actually, I do,' said Bryn, reaching into his bag and withdrawing the old notebook that Juliana had dug up in one of Westminster Square's Gardens. 'Because you kept a record of all of her movements, didn't you, Mr Springfield? You tracked her, drew her, took photographs of her, you even wrote bits of poetry about her. And you put it all in here.'

He handed the notebook to Morris, who turned the pages slowly, his eyes wide with horror.

'This isn't mine,' he said at last. 'I don't even — I didn't write this.'

'Yes, you did,' said Bryn, with the weary patience of someone talking to a very obstinate child. 'That's your handwriting.'

'How do you know that?'

'Because it matches the handwriting in my book,' said Bryn, drawing out *Vacant Shadows* from his bag once more.

Magnus stepped forward to look at the words Morris had so eagerly scribbled out not ten minutes beforehand: *Dear Mairwen, Many happy returns on your birthday from your favourite writer! With best wishes, Morris Springfield.* It matched the small, scrawling handwriting of the notebook exactly.

'You tricked me!' gasped Morris. 'You didn't want my autograph at all, you just wanted to catch me out.'

'I'm afraid that's true,' said Bryn. 'Still, it's not really on a par with stalking, is it? So out of the two of us I think I can retain the moral high ground.'

'I wasn't stalking her!' said Morris. 'I was in love with her!'

'The two aren't mutually exclusive,' said Bryn. 'Now, I presume this is yours as well?'

He produced the plastic wallet containing the engraved ring from his bag. Once more, Morris looked astonished to be presented with the object, although his silence told them all they needed to know about whether or not it belonged to him.

'I must say, it stumped me for a while, who would buy such a cheap ring for someone like Anne-Laure Chevalier, especially as everyone around here is so well-off,' said Bryn. 'But then, you're living at the edge of your means here in Westminster Row, aren't you? As I said before, you only moved here for her, so I expect this is all you could afford. And, of course, now I understand why the engraving says *A.C.* and not *A.L.C.* Because you didn't know her as Anne-Laure Chevalier, did you, Mr Springfield? To you, she was always little Annie Chambers.'

Morris looked between the notebook in his hand and the ring in Bryn's several times, as though the two incriminating objects were attached by an invisible string. Then, silently, he sank back down onto the cardboard box on which he had been sitting before. It wasn't an admission of guilt, Magnus noted, but the writer had stopped objecting to all of the accusations Bryn was levelling at him.

'If you don't mind, I'd like to talk about the night of Dame Winifred's charity party at the Royal West,' continued the former policeman, with ruthless purpose. 'At some point before that evening, I think you'd found out Anne-Laure was going to leave Westminster Square, hadn't you, Mr Springfield? Or at least, you'd guessed that was her plan — after all, you'd been keeping track of everything she'd been up to, and she had no reason to disguise what she was doing. So I imagine you were very upset about the prospect of losing her. She'd now told you to leave her alone on several occasions, but you hadn't quite got it into your head that she wasn't interested. So you decided to make one last-ditch, desperate attempt to make her yours.'

Magnus found he was holding his breath: were they at last going to learn the truth behind Anne-Laure's mysterious death?

'We know from the guest list you weren't at Dame Winifred's party,' continued Bryn. 'You weren't rich enough to be invited. But, as usual, you were hanging around nearby in the hope of seeing Anne-Laure. And, on this occasion, your persistence was rewarded, because at around ten o'clock she appeared on Westminster Square. I presume she was taking a break from the party, and perhaps trying to clear her head, because she'd taken cocaine half an hour beforehand in a bathroom with Jem McMorran.'

At the mention of the actor's name, Morris let out an involuntary, snake-like hiss. Taken aback, Magnus stared at him. Bryn, however, didn't seem fazed by the odd noise; it was almost as though he had expected it.

'So you grabbed your opportunity, didn't you, Mr Springfield? As well as that: you grabbed *her*. You pulled her into one of Westminster Square's gardens — perhaps you thought it was a romantic setting — and you began to profess your love for her all over again. She tried to calm you down — she always did — but this time you thought you could convince her, because that night you had a ring. You asked her to marry you. You asked her to stay in Westminster and become your wife. But it didn't work. When you tried to force the ring onto her finger, she threw it into the earth and tried to walk away. And that made you angry, didn't it, Mr Springfield? All you wanted to do was make her see how much you loved her, and make her realise you were meant to be together. So you seized her by the wrists to stop her from leaving you, and you held her tight while you tried to explain what she meant to you.'

Morris stared up at Bryn, his mouth agape. 'How do you know all of this?' he whispered.

'Because there was someone else in the garden that night,' said Bryn, 'a doorman stealing roses for his wife. He witnessed the whole scene: you grabbing Anne-Laure, her wrestling herself free, not to mention the way she turned back at you and shrieked that she was leaving Westminster Square to get away from you.'

Magnus knew Bryn had not been able to get any kind of description of the shadowy man from Inacio the doorman, but his small bluff didn't seem to do any harm: Morris had all but confessed now.

Bryn stood over the writer, his expression stony. 'How did it feel, Mr Springfield, to know that Anne-Laure was moving to the other side of the world to get away from you?'

Morris hunched over and buried his head in his hands. Magnus thought he looked, somewhat ironically, just like Jem McMorran had the other day.

'It felt like the worst thing I had ever experienced,' murmured the writer. 'But then, the next day, I saw the news, and for the first time I realised what true pain was. Only then, when I discovered she was gone, did I understand what it felt like to have your heart ripped out, your whole soul snatched clean away...'

And then he broke down into dry sobs, more like coughing than crying. Magnus raised his eyebrows: what with Jem McMorran and Gregor the butler, it seemed as though Anne-Laure Chevalier had left a trail of weeping, broken-hearted men in her wake. Then he looked over the top of Morris's head at Bryn.

'So he didn't do it, then?' he asked.

'I don't think so, no,' said Bryn. 'It wouldn't have been easy for him to get into the Royal West without an invite, and I highly doubt she would have accepted a drink from him if he had. In fact, she probably would have called the police. Besides, he didn't want her dead, did he? He just wanted... *her*.'

Morris looked up, his face wet with tears. 'What are you talking about?'

'Never mind,' said Bryn, clearly not wanting to get into the ins and outs of the case with the writer. 'But tell me, Mr Springfield: why did you bury the notebook? Was it because we almost found it, the last time we were here? Was it because, when Magnus started opening one of these boxes, he almost laid eyes on it?'

Morris looked at his feet and, once again, his lack of response was enough to implicate him.

'When Magnus opened that box, you nearly jumped out of your skin,' Bryn recalled, 'and you realised, after we had gone, you had to get rid of it. What if we came round again? What if I came back with a search warrant? You had to get it out of your flat, but you couldn't bear to throw it away, not this detailed record of your beloved. Most people would have put it in a safe deposit box or something like that, but you're not most people, are you, Mr Springfield? You have rather more artistic flair than that. I imagine you thought it would be poetic, to bury this account of your affection in the place you had last seen Anne-Laure — excuse me, Annie Chambers. So you hid it in one of the flowerbeds in Westminster Square Gardens, not banking on Hilda Underpin's dog digging it up, because presumably you were going to go back for it at some point and...' Bryn trailed off, appearing to falter for the first time since they had arrived. 'Actually, I have no idea what you were going to do with that horrible book, and I'm not sure I want to.'

Perhaps he meant to crush Morris with this comment, but his words had the opposite effect: once again, the writer leapt up from his cardboard box, only this time he cradled the notebook against his chest.

'I'm going to write about her, of course!' he cried. 'I'm going to preserve our romance in prose. It'll be my masterpiece — far better than *Vacant Shadows,* and even more nuanced, even more beautiful than *Splinters of Innocence!* It'll be a bestseller, it'll be translated into fifty languages, it'll make my name across the world!

'Who could resist it?' Morris continued, jabbering now, as though he himself were high. 'Who could resist the great love story of Morris Springfield and Annie Chambers? I'll keep us alive — I'll keep *her* alive — and she'll never really die, because she'll live forever in the pages of my book.'

He's mad, thought Magnus, suddenly. *He's totally mad.*

Bryn, however, seemed unintimidated by Morris's senseless outburst.

'You still don't understand, do you?' he said, with a bite of impatience. 'You didn't have a great romance with Annie Chambers. Oh, you might have loved her — although in truth it sounds like more of a dangerous obsession to me — but she didn't love you back. She was in love with Jem McMorran.'

Once more, the mere mention of the Hollywood actor sparked a dramatic reaction from Morris.

'Jem McMorran!' he cried, spitting the name like an angry cat. '*Jem McMorran!*'

'I notice you didn't include him in the book,' said Bryn. 'That confused me too, for a while, because you were keeping such a close eye on her you must have seen them together, even though they were sneaking around. But Jem didn't fit into your little fantasy, did he? How could you pretend she loved you, if she was running around with him?'

'*She was mine!*' shouted the writer suddenly. 'She wasn't his, she was *mine!*'

'That's enough,' said Magnus, firmly. He had watched Morris Springfield unravel with mounting disgust, but this was the last straw. 'Anne-Laure wasn't yours,' he went on. 'She wasn't anybody's. What a way to talk about a person. You need help, Morris.'

The writer, who had moved to the other side of the flat, slid down the wall until he was sitting on the floor and said, quieter now, 'She was mine.'

Magnus looked to Bryn. 'If there's nothing more we can learn from him, I'd like to go. My dinner will be ready, although he's rather put me off my food.'

'All right,' said Bryn. 'But just a minute…'

Striding towards Morris, he tried to seize the notebook from his hands. The spurned lover, however, gave a yelp of alarm, and held on fast to the paper shrine to Anne-Laure Chevalier he had created.

'Leave it,' said Magnus. 'He can't harm her anymore.'

'He might harm others, though,' said Bryn, finally wrestling the book from Morris's grip, 'so I don't think it would be a bad idea to show this to the police.'

Still on the floor, Morris gave a low moan and buried his head in his hands again, although whether this new wave of anguish was caused by the loss of the book or the mention of the police Magnus didn't know.

'And besides,' Bryn added, dropping the jotter into his bag and carelessly tossing the signed copy of *Vacant Shadows* towards Morris as a replacement, 'I have a feeling we might still be needing this notebook.'

CHAPTER THIRTY-EIGHT

'Magnus? Are you with us? *Magnus?*'

Magnus blinked, surprised to find himself sat at the table in his kitchen with his family. His fork was halfway to his mouth, and apparently he had been holding it at an angle, because the mince it had recently contained had dropped back onto his plate.

'Do you not like your shepherd's pie?' Juliana demanded, looking accusingly at his almost-untouched food.

'No, I love it — *mmm!*' said Magnus, scooping a loaded forkful into his mouth as though to prove this, although — to his disappointment — the meat and potato was now rather cold.

Juliana watched him suspiciously. 'You've been staring off into space for the last ten minutes,' she said.

'Have I? Sorry, dear…'

'Did you even hear Rosanna saying she got twenty out of twenty in her spelling test today?'

'Did you?' said Magnus, turning to his daughter with a smile. 'Twenty out of twenty? Well done, darling!'

Perhaps in punishment for his lack of attention earlier, or perhaps because she and Lee were engaged in a furious kicking match under the table, Rosanna ignored him.

'What words did you spell?' persisted Magnus.

Rosanna shrugged, still concentrating on searching for Lee's leg under the table. '*Unusual, daughter, poison…*'

'*Poison…*' repeated Magnus vaguely, thinking of the little pill that once might have been hidden in Tarquin Underpin's commando jacket.

'And *tough!*' said Rosanna, finding Lee's foot and bashing it with her own.

'That's enough!' Juliana snapped suddenly. 'If you can't behave at the table, you can get down — no pudding!'

They gaped at her. 'But *Mum!*'

'No,' she said firmly, 'and I'm not sure some of those words are entirely appropriate for ten-year-olds, even if they are difficult to spell.'

Realising they had been defeated, Rosanna and Lee slipped from their chairs and stomped out of the kitchen, presumably to continue their fight in another room, and out of earshot. With a huff, Juliana stood up and began to clear the table, despite the fact Magnus had not finished eating.

'I'm sorry you're under a lot of pressure at work,' she said, not sounding sorry at all, 'but perhaps you could give your family at least a few minutes of your attention each day? I'm beginning to think we're not as interesting or important as *arbitration cases…*'

She said this in the manner of someone who hadn't a clue what an arbitration case was, but disliked it nonetheless.

'You know you are all far more interesting and important than my work,' said Magnus firmly, 'you're a hundred times more interesting and important.'

'Hm,' said Juliana, looking a little mollified, but still dodging his attempt to reach for her hand.

Magnus turned back to his cold shepherd's pie with the impression he had somehow managed to diffuse a potential argument, but feeling a twinge of guilt nonetheless. Juliana was right: his mind had been elsewhere, and he had been ignoring his family, albeit accidentally. But worst of all, he hadn't been dwelling on work, as Juliana seemed to suspect, and as perhaps he should have been; instead, he had been thinking about the events of the last few hours.

He could not get his head around what Bryn had uncovered, first about Lord Bevis Ellington and then about Morris Springfield. It seemed unbelievable these two neighbours — neighbours he considered, if not friends, at least familiar acquaintances — could be so duplicitous, even dangerous. Or was it really so farfetched? They were both eccentrics, that was for sure, but Magnus had always regarded Ellington's snobbery and hypocrisy with amusement, and Morris's social ineptitude with patience and pity. Knowing now what they were really like was going to take some mental readjustment.

He wasn't even sure which man was worse. He thoroughly disapproved of Ellington's dodgy dealings, especially as it was likely they involved armaments, but it was the callous way he had dispatched his bodyguard to threaten — no, to attack — Anne-Laure that was so disturbing. Magnus had not seen her bruised body, but he could well imagine the damage Gregor had inflicted without even really trying, and it seemed very likely the vast man had no idea how strong he really was.

Then there was Morris, who had stalked Anne-Laure since he had arrived in London — who seemed to have thought he'd had some right to be with her, no matter how many times she had rejected him. Even if the writer was, as Magnus suspected, suffering from some mental health issues, it was still difficult to forgive him for the way he had followed, photographed, drawn and generally pursued Anne-Laure, especially when Magnus thought about how Morris had grabbed her in the garden.

So while Lord Ellington and Morris Springfield might not have killed her, there was now no denying both men had caused Anne-Laure Chevalier considerable emotional and physical distress, particularly on the last night of her life. Magnus didn't know how he was going to ever look either of them in the eye again, and he still hadn't ruled out going to the police, although he doubted Barry Boyle would do much about it, especially if he discovered Bryn was involved.

Magnus drifted through to his study and began to leaf through his paperwork without taking in a single word of it, because his mind was still full of the Anne-Laure Chevalier investigation. The notebook and ring might now be accounted for, but what of Bryn's theory of the poison pill? And what about the meeting Anne-Laure had tried to set up with Darren Dodge of *The Dawn Reporter*? It was beginning to look a little unlikely Anne-Laure had been killed by a jealous lover or ex-lover, even though they had a candidate for each of these roles in Jem McMorran and Morris Springfield. But what about his and Bryn's other theories that she had been killed for money or information? Why had she made that appointment with the journalist? Had she really been intending to sell a kiss-and-tell on Jem McMorran, or expose his drug-abuse — it seemed unlikely if they had been planning on running away together — or was she intending to expose an even bigger story than even that?

Magnus gave up trying to read the document in front of him and stared out of the window above his desk instead. It looked out onto the garden at the back of the building, but as it was now night and he hadn't closed the curtains, all he could see was his own reflection, which looked especially old and tired in the dark glass.

Bryn seemed to be happily compiling evidence and theories on his own, but Magnus could not help but think that even if he identified the murderer — assuming there *was* a murderer — it was very unlikely his young friend was going to be able to prove how they'd done it when the body had been cremated, and when Hilda seemed to have no idea the poison pill had been stolen from Tarquin's jacket. With this in mind, Magnus thought it would be far less hassle to simply convince themselves that Anne-Laure had died of a freak heart attack or brain haemorrhage after all; that it would be far easier to pretend that the 'natural causes' line peddled by the police and reported in the press was, in fact, the truth.

'But then,' Magnus murmured to himself with a grim smile, 'where's the justice in that?'

* * * *

'I do wish, every so often, you'd fill me in on what you're up to,' Magnus grumbled, as he and Bryn crossed Westminster Square together.

He was referring to the fact that Bryn had told him very little before they had spoken to Lord Ellington, and absolutely nothing before they had been to see Hilda Underpin and Morris Springfield. This evening, they were on their way to see Sheikh Hazim bin Lahab and, once more, his young friend was keeping him well and truly in the dark.

'I thought you were taking a step back from the case?' said Bryn lightly.

'Well, it's a bit difficult to keep my distance when you're divulging everybody's secrets and revealing scandals left, right and centre. No, I'm beginning to feel a little foolish, Bryn, not knowing what's going on.'

'Not as foolish as I'd feel, if one of my theories turned out to be completely wrong,' said Bryn. 'No, I think I prefer to work through the last few details myself, and have you there for moral — and legal — support.'

As Bryn pressed the buzzer of Hazim's Westminster Square house, Magnus stared at his companion: it was almost difficult to believe he was the same person he'd had to rescue from a pushy reporter outside the Royal West on the morning after Anne-Laure's death. Now, Bryn carried himself with far more confidence, far more authority, and the way he had tackled Ellington and Morris in particular had been almost pitiless. This new Bryn was going to take to a bit of getting used to, but if Magnus ignored his slight resentment at being left out, he felt oddly proud of the former policeman's progress. After all, he suspected the person from whom Bryn had learned all of this self-assurance was, in fact, he himself.

'Well, can I at least guess that we're here because you've finally figured out the connection between Anne-Laure and Sheikh Hazim?' said Magnus, in a last-ditch attempt to extract information from Bryn before they entered the house.

But before his friend could answer, the door was opened by Sheikh Hazim's butler, Steve. The pale, ginger-moustachioed man was still wearing elaborate Eastern robes, a headdress and *babouche* slippers, and therefore still looked rather ridiculous, framed as he was by the very English portico of a Westminster Square property. But, as he led them once more through the gallery of Oriental art and into the tent-like *majlis* beyond, he began to melt into his surroundings, and it was Bryn and Magnus, in their Western attire, who looked more out of place.

Sheikh Hazim's living area looked much the same as it had last time Magnus and Bryn had visited: it was still festooned with Persian carpets, *majlis* cushions and hanging lanterns, and two television sets were still blaring out rival football games. The floor was also covered in various half-touched plates of stuffed lamb and other unidentifiable chunks of greasy food, which meant, once more, there was a cloying aroma of meat in the makeshift tent, mingling with Hazim's strong perfume. The major difference from before, Magnus observed, was that the sheikh was not alone this time: two young women, a brunette and a redhead, scantily clad in belly-dancer outfits, were lounging over several cushions chatting to one another quietly, while a blonde girl was sat on Hazim's lap, feeding him lumps of cheese while his hand ran up and down her leg. In fact, Hazim was so engrossed in her that he completely failed to notice Magnus and Bryn entering the *majlis*, and Steve had to clear his throat loudly to get his attention.

'Ahem, Mr Walterson and Police Constable Summers to see you, sir.'

Hazim finally tore his gaze from the girl on his lap — and the cheese she was offering him — and noticed his guests. His fat face broke into a wide smile.

'Gentlemen!' he cried, apparently delighted to see them, even though — to Magnus's knowledge — they had arrived without invitation. 'Come in, come in! I'm afraid you've missed dinner, but there are plenty of leftovers, or you could join me in the dessert course.' He gave them an exaggerated wink and then pointed a fat finger towards the girls on the cushions. 'And look at that, there's a portion for everyone!'

The two belly dancers looked up listlessly at Magnus and Bryn.

'I want the young one,' announced the brunette girl.

The redhead scowled at her. Magnus, trying not to feel insulted, looked to Bryn, expecting to find him blushing and stuttering, but the former policeman ignored the women completely.

'We were wondering whether we could have a word, Sheikh Hazim?' he said, before adding significantly, '*Alone.*'

Hazim, looking a little disappointed, pushed the blonde girl off his fat legs and waved all three women away. The little bells on their costumes jangled noisily in their eagerness to escape the *majlis*. Then Steve, with a little bow in the direction of his employer, also departed.

'And perhaps we could put off the televisions too?' Bryn suggested. 'Or at least mute the volume.'

Hazim greeted this idea with even less enthusiasm, and frowned as he directed a remote control at each TV, turning the sound right down, but leaving the football playing on in silence.

'How can I help you?' he said, indicating that Magnus and Bryn should sit down on the cushions next to him. 'It must be serious, if it doesn't involve sport or girls...'

Magnus, who was waiting for Bryn to start his questioning, was rather surprised when the former policeman asked, 'Where do those women come from?'

He was looking at the gap in the material walls, beyond which the three belly-dancers had disappeared, a slight frown on his features. Hazim shrugged.

'We don't really spend a lot of time talking,' he said with a grin. 'One's from the UK, one's from somewhere in Eastern Europe, I think, and —'

'No,' said Bryn, 'I mean, where do you find them? How do they come to be here?'

Hazim gave a dirty chuckle. 'Why, do you want me to pass on your details? What are you interested in, Summers? One? Two? Fat? Thin? British? Or something more *exotic*?'

'I'm not interested in anyone,' said Bryn, calmly, 'I'm interested in how you get hold of these women.'

Hazim looked suddenly suspicious. 'You're a policeman, aren't you?'

'Yes.'

'Are you trying to get me into trouble?'

'That depends on how helpful you are. I'm here for a bit of information, you see.'

Magnus looked between them: he wasn't quite sure what was going on, but then he hadn't known why Bryn had buttered up Hilda Underpin either, or why he had taken a copy of Morris Springfield's book for him to sign.

'What sort of information?' asked Hazim, wary now.

'Well, how does it work?' asked Bryn. 'Do they come from an agency, or is it a private arrangement? Is it different places for different services? Enlighten me.'

'Enlighten you…' Hazim repeated, and then was silent for a few moments, apparently weighing up what to say next.

'I assume those three ladies we just saw *are* escorts?' prompted Bryn.

'Erm, yes — yes, they are,' said the sheikh, who looked a little abashed to be confronted like this, causing Magnus to wonder whether anyone had ever directly questioned the presence of all these women in his *majlis* before.

'So, what, did Steve just call up an agency?' persisted Bryn.

'Erm, yes, I suppose so…'

'Which one?'

'I don't know, there are several. They're all over London.'

'For example?'

'Everywhere! Park Lane, Piccadilly, Hyde Park… They're filled with escort agencies — discreet ones, of course.'

'So, did he just request three random girls? Or do you have favourites?'

'It depends,' said Hazim.

'On what?'

'How I feel, whether I have company, which girls are available… I like a mix of girls, a mix of nationalities and — well, I suppose I do have my favourites, yes.'

Magnus looked to his friend: was this all strictly necessary? He could think of a hundred things he would rather be doing with his evening than listening to Hazim talking about his sordid habits.

'It's not just men who use these services, you know,' Hazim said. 'It's women too. Especially rich, older women. I've even heard of some titled and regal ladies who are lonely, and who have missed the boat when it comes to making a good marriage, so they hire a nice attractive young man for the evening.'

'So these agencies,' Bryn interrupted, apparently not interested in Hazim's salacious gossip, 'I'm assuming they have your name, your details… Do they ever call you up?'

'Yeah,' said Hazim. 'But, as I said, they're very discreet. One of them, a smaller, private agency, keeps our contact details in a little black book

— I've seen it — and sometimes they'll open that up and give me a call.' He narrowed his eyes. 'Are you sure you don't want me to put in a word for you, Summers? I can probably get you your first girl cheap, I'm a valued customer at these places, you know.'

'So I gather,' said Bryn, 'but no thank you, I'm not asking all of this for fun, you know.'

A tinge of annoyance crossed Hazim's features. 'There's nothing shameful in it.'

'Isn't there?'

'No,' he said determinedly. 'This is high-class stuff. The girls are beautiful, sophisticated, and well looked-after. It's —' he searched for the right word, 'it's a *privilege*, for those of us with enough disposable income to afford it, not to mention those of us with a healthy sexual appetite.'

'It's abhorrent,' said Bryn bluntly. 'They might be beautiful and sophisticated, but you can't guarantee those women are well looked-after, and don't try and convince me any of them would be doing what they do if they had much of a choice.'

For perhaps the first time in their acquaintance, Magnus thought Hazim looked genuinely angry. 'Who are you to come in here and judge me?' he demanded.

The barrister agreed with Bryn in principle, but he thought Hazim had a point here.

'We're not judging you, Hazim,' he said quickly and somewhat untruthfully. 'Bryn's just asking questions, that's all.'

'But why?' asked the sheikh, his irritation melting into bewilderment. 'What's all this about, Magnus?'

This, Magnus thought, was a good question, and one he couldn't answer, given he was still in the dark as to what Bryn was up to. But the former policeman, it seemed, was ready to be direct with their host.

'We want to ask you about Anne-Laure Chevalier,' he said.

'*Again?*' Hazim cried, throwing his chubby hands into the air in frustration. 'Did you not understand what I told you last time?'

'You told us she planned a couple of parties for you, years ago, and that was the extent of your connection,' said Bryn.

'Well, there you go!' said Hazim. 'You must realise it's unlikely she's done any more work for me since I told you that…'

Bryn, ignoring this poor attempt at a joke, continued, 'You denied knowing her because you had forgotten about her, is that correct?'

'Yes,' said Hazim staunchly. 'But listen, Steve sent you that invoice from her, did he not? So you can see that she did a party here, and you can tell it was years ago.'

'That invoice is fake,' said Bryn. 'It bears absolutely no resemblance to the invoice we found in her flat, which was addressed to Vasyl Kosnitschev, and the bank details are completely wrong. No, I think you asked Steve to mock up that invoice, didn't you, Sheikh Hazim?'

'And why would I do that?'

'You're not really known for your big parties, are you?' Bryn went on, ignoring Hazim's question. 'You don't hold big networking events like Vasyl or charity fundraisers like Dame Winifred Rye. From what we've seen, your parties are smaller, more *intimate* affairs and, from what you've just said, it's Steve who organises those on your behalf. So I think you're lying about the party-planning. But then why was your name in Anne-Laure's address book, and why did you pretend not to know her? What were you covering up? And then I realised, if we take out the party-planning, there's only really one thing you would have wanted from someone like Anne-Laure Chevalier — and it's the same thing you want from all the women who come in and out of this house.'

'*What?*'

The exclamation was out of Magnus's mouth before he could stop himself. Because this, more than the stalker's notebook, the dodgy deals in the Far East, and even the poison pill — this seemed the most outlandish of all Bryn's theories.

'Think about it, Magnus,' said his friend, calmly. 'Throughout our investigation, Anne-Laure Chevalier has been a hard character to pin down — there's always been an air of secrecy about her, perhaps even a kind of shame. According to Vasyl, Lord Ellington and Dame Winifred, she was very guarded about her personal life. Even Jem McMorran didn't seem to know the first thing about her, and they were in a romantic relationship for a couple of years.'

'Were they?' cut in Hazim, looking amused. 'Lucky boy.'

'Don't forget she was good at charming people,' Bryn continued. 'Almost everybody we've spoken to has told us that. And Hilda Underpin practically spelled it out for us, but I was too biased in Anne-Laure's favour to listen.'

'But Bryn,' Magnus sighed. 'Being charming and secretive and dressing provocatively is hardly evidence of being a — a —' He tried to think of the politically correct term. 'A *sex worker*. This is mad! You just said no woman — no person — would do that if they had much of a choice, and Anne-Laure *did* have a choice, didn't she? She was working for Vasyl, she was working for Ellington, she was in a relationship with a Hollywood A-lister, albeit one who was terrible with his finances... My point is, nobody does that kind of thing for *pocket money!*'

'Oh, I'm not suggesting this was recent,' said Bryn quickly, 'not at all. I think Anne-Laure Chevalier — or rather, Annie Chambers — moved to London at seventeen years old full of dreams. But this is an expensive city, and dreams weren't going to buy food or pay the rent. It was a way of making money for a couple of years, while she found her feet, and perhaps she told herself that because it was — how did you put it, Sheikh Hazim? — *sophisticated,* because it wasn't standing on street corners and getting into strangers' cars, it wasn't that bad. But I think she *was* ashamed. Don't forget, we've never really questioned why she changed her name.'

Magnus, who was still struggling to digest all of this, glanced at Hazim. 'Is this true?' he asked.

The sheikh looked between them, and then picked up a chunk of cold meat from one of the plates on the floor, and popped it into his mouth. He chewed for a few moments, evidently enjoying keeping them waiting.

'*Hazim!*' prompted Magnus.

'Oh, yes, it's true,' said their host, a lascivious smile spreading over his fat face. 'It was a long time ago now, but yes, she was an escort.'

'How long ago?' asked Bryn.

'Ten years? I think you're right, she'd just moved to London, and she was gorgeous, she was magnetic, she was sexy without even knowing it, she was —'

'Young,' interrupted Bryn. 'Ten years ago, Anne-Laure Chevalier was seventeen years old.'

Magnus was beginning to feel a little sick at the thought of a barely-legal Anne-Laure sleeping with this gluttonous old man before them, but Hazim shrugged, as though her age were no concern of his.

'You were right earlier,' he told Bryn, 'I do have favourites, and she was one of them. In fact, she was probably my favourite of all of the women I've ever been with — and there have been a lot,' he sniggered. 'There was something about Anne-Laure. I asked for her again and again...' He seemed momentarily lost in lewd memories, and then, looking a little less lecherous, he added, 'I was very disappointed when she left the profession.'

'Which was?'

'Oh, years and years ago. She managed to talk Vasyl into giving her a more reputable job and that was it. I don't think he realised what she had been,' he added, before Bryn could ask, 'or maybe he did, but it didn't bother him. Vasyl's a man of the world, after all. Besides, it's easy to reinvent yourself in London, and she'd done it before, hadn't she?'

'Did you ever see her again?'

'A bit, but only at parties. Sometimes I would tease her about her past — not so anyone could hear, you understand, just as a little joke between us.'

'And how did she take that?' asked Magnus, thinking he probably already knew the answer.

'Not well. I was only messing about, but she would always shut me right down. She did not like it at all. It was as though, in her head, that part of her history did not exist.'

'And did she ever come round here again?'

MYSTERY IN WESTMINSTER SQUARE

'No.'

Bryn fixed Hazim with a stern expression. 'Are you sure? Because I have it on good authority that Anne-Laure briefly called in at this house a week or so before her death.'

Hazim's eyes widened. 'How do you know that?'

'Let's just say someone went to the trouble of keeping a close eye on Anne-Laure Chevalier's movements over the past couple of years,' said Bryn. 'She asked you for money, didn't she? Just before she died? She was desperate for cash to fund her new life in America, and neither of her employers were willing to part with their cash, so she asked you for a loan — for old time's sake.'

Hazim nodded slowly. 'I've no idea how you know all of this,' he said.

'Did you give her the money?'

The sheikh looked a little uncomfortable. 'I told her if she wanted it, she would have to earn it, the old fashioned way. But that did not go down very well. She lost her temper with me, called me every name under the sun. I grew bored with her then, Miss Prim and Proper — she was not fooling me. I told her she was not half as fun as she used to be, and then she stormed out. I felt bad about it afterwards, though — when I heard she was dead. I was only joking. I would have given her the money if she had really needed it — no strings attached. For old time's sake, as you say. For my favourite girl.'

Despite the fact he felt roundly sickened by everything he'd heard, Magnus thought Hazim might be telling the truth: he looked genuinely regretful.

Perhaps Bryn thought so too, because he said, 'I'm not sure the money was essential. She just wanted to get away from Westminster Square, away from the bad memories it held, and away from a particularly obsessive admirer.'

'Jem McMorran?' asked Hazim.

'No, not him. She was in love with him, I think, so I doubt she would have taken you up on your offer. They were leaving together.'

'Jem McMorran,' repeated Hazim. 'Well, it makes sense, I suppose. They were probably as bad as each other.'

'What do you mean?' asked Magnus, curiously.

'Come on, you know what Hollywood's like! Everyone there is selling themselves all of the time! If you tell me he has never debased himself to get a part, I'll call you a liar. They all have. Everyone has!'

He helped himself to more food, shovelling it into his mouth with his fingers while he laughed and laughed.

'I think,' said Magnus, feeling his patience wearing thin, 'if Sheikh Hazim has told us all there is to know about Anne-Laure's past, perhaps we can call it a day, Bryn?'

But the former policeman held up a hand. 'Just two more questions,' he said, not taking his eyes from Hazim. 'First, which escort agency did Anne-Laure work for? Can you give us a name?'

'I do not remember,' said the sheikh, and his response was so automatic that Magnus suspected he was observing some code of honour. 'Like I said, this was years and years ago…'

'But if she was your *favourite*…?' pressed Bryn.

'I do not remember.'

The Welshman looked as though he wanted to argue, but then he continued, 'All right, second question: can you think of anybody from this specific area of Anne-Laure's past who might have held a grudge against her? Somebody from the agency, perhaps — a rival girl, a pimp she'd somehow wronged?'

'They are called *protectors* in this class of the profession,' Hazim said loftily. 'And no, I cannot. As I said, she left that life behind her long ago.'

'But somebody might have caught up with her. Somebody might have tracked her down for —'

'For what?' Hazim tossed a piece of cheese into his mouth. 'For *what*, Summers? It was almost a decade ago, she will be long forgotten in those circles. They always are, the ones who get out — or the ones who disappear. And you know why? Because there are always more girls.' He spread his arms wide, as though to embrace the whole *majlis,* and began to laugh again. 'That is why it is still going, the oldest profession in the world: there are *always* more girls!'

CHAPTER THIRTY-NINE

'Magnus, I think I've solved it. Can I come over?'

The barrister gave his head a little shake against the phone, trying to rid his mind of legal work and focus on what Bryn was telling him on the other end of the line.

'Solved it?' he repeated.

'Yes. I think I've finally fitted everything together...'

'And?' Magnus prompted.

'And what?'

The barrister sighed. 'And I don't suppose you're going to enlighten me over the phone, are you?'

'I'd rather explain it in person.'

'You just want to keep me in suspense... Oh, all right, when will you next be in Westminster?'

'I can be at your flat in half an hour?'

'Wait, you're coming round *now*?' exclaimed Magnus, looking at the piles of paperwork on his desk. 'Bryn, I've a lot on here...'

But he knew why Bryn was rushing: since being dismissed from the Victoria Police Station, this was all the Welshman had had to focus on; the Anne-Laure Chevalier case had become his entire life. If he thought he had made significant progress, it made perfect sense he would want to discuss it immediately.

'Magnus, I really think I've solved it,' said Bryn again, sounding serious. 'In fact, I *know* I have.'

'Well, if that's the case, I suppose you better *had* come around in half an hour,' said Magnus. 'I'll see you then, Bryn.'

It was not in Magnus's nature to be unduly expectant, but as he replaced the receiver of the phone he could not help but feel slightly excited: what if Bryn *had* solved it?

MYSTERY IN WESTMINSTER SQUARE

Magnus pictured the beautiful blonde woman at the centre of their investigation, realising he was not conjuring her from his own memories, but from the images splashed across the front pages of the tabloids following her death. The media had had a field day reporting on the sudden demise of the striking young socialite, and they hadn't known even half the story.

It had been a couple of days since Bryn had wrested the latest piece of the puzzle from Sheikh Hazim, and Magnus was still reeling from the revelation of how Anne-Laure had made money when she had first arrived in London. It was not that he judged her, exactly — Magnus was only too aware of how easy it was for people, especially young, vulnerable people, to fall through the cracks in a big city — but it did change the way he thought about her. Until now, Anne-Laure had seemed to him a commanding, magnetic figure, one who reduced besotted grown men to tears and always took charge of her own fate. But the sickening idea of her being Hazim's 'favourite girl' at seventeen years old reminded Magnus that her life had been difficult, full of tragedy, and that underneath it all she had not been as poised and powerful as people might have believed (although Magnus suspected, if she were alive, Anne-Laure would have scorned his pity).

The other consequence of the meeting with Sheikh Hazim was that, perhaps contrary to whatever Bryn was thinking, they now had a far bigger pool of suspects. Hazim had seemed to think that nobody from Anne-Laure's escort past would have even remembered her, but Magnus wasn't so sure: wasn't it far more likely that a figure from that murky world — a violent pimp, perhaps — would have had a motive to kill her, rather than an upstanding member of Westminster society? Maybe they had been looking in the wrong place all of this time. Because they had ruled out everybody else, hadn't they? Hazim, Morris and Ellington had confessed to their various crimes against her, while Jem McMorran and Dame Winifred Rye seemed to have only been guilty of loving her too much — and being blind to the complex and damaged person she had truly been. Hilda Underpin had not been so naïve, and perhaps the absent Vasyl Kosnitschev hadn't been either, but Bryn seemed content to score them off the list as well.

Which left — who, exactly? The people they had encountered on the fringes of the investigation? What about Edwin Brackenwell, the manager of the Royal West Hotel? What about Barry Boyle himself, who had ordered her body to be cremated and been so cagey about Bryn's digging? Might one of them have been moved to drastic action to protect the reputation of Westminster Square? And what about all of the doormen and chauffeurs and neighbours and everybody else Anne-Laure had encountered on a daily basis? Once more, when Magnus really thought about it, identifying a potential killer was like searching for a needle in a haystack. So how on earth did Bryn think he had solved this case?

After about half an hour or so of turning this over in his mind, Magnus was beginning to develop a headache, and decided to stretch his legs and get a glass of water before Bryn's arrival. But as he headed out of his office and towards the kitchen, he heard female voices in the living room, and soon found Juliana, Daisy and Dame Winifred sat around the coffee table, peering at a catalogue of flowers.

'Oh, hello,' said Magnus, nodding towards the two guests. 'I didn't realise we had company.'

'Never mind us, never mind us,' trilled Dame Winifred, who looked a little like a tropical cocktail that afternoon, dressed as she was in clashing hot pink and bright orange. 'The Little Flower and I just popped by to talk to Juliana about the arrangements for my next party.'

Daisy, presumably the 'Little Flower' in question, gave Magnus a rather restrained smile. The barrister wondered idly what Bryn would do, when he discovered the object of his affections was also here.

'What sort of party are you throwing?' Magnus asked Dame Winifred, more out of politeness than any real curiosity.

'A garden party,' replied the aristocrat, with a beam. 'I've managed to convince Central Square Properties to let me hire one of the gardens — and it took some convincing, let me tell you — so we can make the most of the end of the summer.'

Magnus, looking down at the catalogue, said, 'Erm, don't the Westminster Square Gardens already have flowers?'

Dame Winifred chuckled, as though he had made a great joke, and Juliana sighed and said, 'Dame Winifred wants flowers for decoration, Magnus! To drape over the railings, to wind around the poles of the gazebo, to furnish the tables…'

'Oh, I see.'

'But now you come to mention it, I might ask my dear girl here to have a look at the flowers in the garden,' said Dame Winifred thoughtfully, patting Daisy on the knee. 'I always thought the Westminster Square gardeners were rather good, but the other week I came across the most appalling mess in one of the flowerbeds. It looked like all of the pansies had been dug up and then planted again in a most haphazard way. Yes, petal, perhaps you could be a sweetheart and check on everything *within* the garden some point?'

'All right,' said Daisy quietly.

'Oh, isn't she just a *darling*?' Dame Winifred announced to the room at large.

Magnus was spared from responding to this, for at that moment there was knock at the door of the flat.

'That'll be Bryn,' he said.

'Bryn?' Daisy sat up a little straighter.

Magnus nodded and then, pleased to have a reason to excuse himself from the flower discussion, went through to the hallway to answer the door.

'Hello,' said Bryn, shaking Magnus's hand and kicking off his shoes next to the mat. Then, hearing voices in the other room, he asked, 'Are there other people here?'

'Oh, yes,' said Magnus. 'Juliana's with Dame Winifred, picking flowers for her next party — and your Daisy's here too.'

The barrister expected Bryn to grow flustered at the mere mention of Daisy's name, but instead he nodded, as though he wasn't at all surprised by her presence, and then wordlessly headed towards the living room.

'Actually, I thought we could discuss the case in my study!' Magnus called, not wanting to be drawn back into conversations about gazebos and pansies.

But it was too late: summoned, no doubt, by the knowledge that Daisy was just next door, Bryn had disappeared, leaving Magnus no choice but to follow. He arrived back into the living room just in time to see Daisy look up at the former policeman. She wore an oddly tense sort of expression, which was far from the shy smile Magnus would have anticipated. Perhaps, he thought, things were not going well between them. Maybe their budding romance had ended before it had even started.

'Hello, Bryn,' said Juliana, smiling at him with far more warmth than Daisy. 'Would you like a cup of tea? I suppose we should move all the flowers in here, shouldn't we...'

'Oh, that's all right, I've taken an antihistamine,' said Bryn, with a nod at Daisy. 'Those little pills are like magic.'

'Also, we're going into my study,' chipped in Magnus, 'which you will be pleased to know is a safe haven from pollen.'

To his slight annoyance, everybody ignored this comment. Dame Winifred, who had been watching Bryn with pursed lips and narrowed eyes, said, 'Is this your *innamorato*, Daisy?'

'My *what*?'

'Oh, don't tease them, Winifred!' pleaded Juliana.

'Your *boyfriend*, dear.'

'Oh!' Finally, Daisy was reddening. 'Well...'

'Bryn, why don't we go through to my study?' suggested Magnus.

He assumed his friend would jump at the chance to escape this embarrassing scene, but Bryn didn't move, and seemed surprisingly unabashed by Dame Winifred's line of questioning.

'I've met you before, haven't I, young man?' continued the aristocrat, her tone one of mock-firmness, as though she were playing the part of Daisy's overbearing mother. 'You came round to my flat that time with Magnus, didn't you? To check I was all right after that terrible break-in? I've only just made the connection: you're the policeman!'

Bryn, who still looked unbothered by being the centre of attention for so long, said, 'Actually, I'm the *former* policeman.'

Dame Winifred and Juliana, the latter of whom Magnus had not thought to tell about Bryn's dismissal, looked surprised. Daisy's expression, on the other hand, was unreadable.

'Oh!' said Juliana, frowning slightly at Bryn. 'Did you decide you wanted a change of career?'

'Not really,' said the Welshman. 'In fact, I didn't want to leave at all: I was sacked.'

'*Sacked*!' Dame Winifred squawked, and Magnus too was startled: he wasn't aware Bryn had decided to start announcing his unemployed status to all and sundry.

'Oh dear, I am sorry, Bryn,' said Juliana. 'Are you all right?'

'I'm fine,' said Bryn, and in that moment he did seem fairly cheerful. 'I should have seen it coming, really — I was warned.'

'Warned?' repeated Juliana.

'Yes, I was told to stop asking questions about Anne-Laure Chevalier's death, but I didn't,' said Bryn.

As usual, the mention of Anne-Laure's name had a dramatic effect on the room, in spite of Bryn's matter-of-fact tone: Juliana gave a little gasp and Dame Winifred clutched at her chest as though her heart were causing her physical pain. Only Daisy's expression remained sphinx-like.

'Anne — Anne-Laure?' said Dame Winifred, edging away from Daisy on the sofa, as though she expected her former protégée to suddenly enter the room and grow upset at the sight of her mollycoddling this new girl. 'What — what do you mean, questions about her death? Do they finally know how she died? Was it some kind of aneurism? Oh, I can hardly bear to think about it, even now!'

She buried her overly made-up face in her chubby hands. Bryn, who had been standing since entering the room, lowered himself onto the edge of a sofa and addressed her quietly.

'It wasn't an aneurism. In fact, it wasn't natural causes at all.'

'Do we really need to go into all of this again?' said Juliana, looking significantly at Dame Winifred, clearly worried about further upsetting her.

'At first, it looked as though it *had* been accident, though,' said Bryn, pretending not to hear Juliana. 'It looked as though Anne-Laure had overdosed on cocaine —'

'*No!*' Dame Winifred looked up, and although her make-up was slightly smudged from fresh tears, she looked suddenly fierce. 'No, I don't believe that — I *won't* believe it! Anne-Laure never would have touched drugs, *never*! She was a good girl. A sweet, hard-working, lovely girl!'

Bryn said nothing. Magnus, who wasn't sure what his friend was up to, but was fairly certain it involved trying to pull the wool from Dame Winifred's eyes said, rather tentatively, 'Dame Winifred, I'm not sure Anne-Laure was quite as innocent as you might have thought. I know you two had a very close relationship, and I don't mean to speak ill of the dead, but Anne-Laure was involved in more than a little shady business in her time.'

'Like what?' asked the aristocrat, looking up at Magnus with wide eyes.

'Like the fact that she was an escort,' said Bryn bluntly.

'A *what*?' Juliana cried.

Magnus frowned at his friend: he thought Bryn could have built up to this bombshell, perhaps via dodgy *rabbateur* work and drug dealing at parties, rather than just casually dropping it into the conversation.

'An escort,' said Bryn, responding to Juliana's question. 'A high-class sex worker.'

Dame Winifred stood up, looking angrier than Magnus had ever seen her.

'How dare you!' she said to Bryn, her voice quivering with rage. 'How dare you talk of that beautiful, tragic girl in such a *filthy* way? You're depraved! Come on, Daisy, we're going, and I'm not sure you should see this young man anymore...'

'Anne-Laure *was* beautiful, and she *was* tragic,' said Bryn, unmoved by Dame Winifred's fury. 'But she was also shrewd and ambitious and secretive. She wasn't the little angel you're making her out to be.'

'She was!' said Dame Winifred, almost petulant in her denial. 'She *was!*'

'No she wasn't,' said Bryn. 'Shortly after Anne-Laure arrived in London, she started working as a high-class escort for a private agency that provides sophisticated girls for wealthy clients — all very discreet, of course.'

There was a click as Juliana, who had crossed over to the other side of the room, closed the door, presumably so the children wouldn't overhear this conversation. Her face was very white.

'You're lying!' Dame Winifred told Bryn, tears spilling down her cheeks now. 'You're making all of this up, you have to be!'

'Sheikh Hazim bin Lahab has confirmed it for us,' said Bryn. 'Anne-Laure Chevalier was, by his own admission, one of his favourite girls.'

'Well then, he's lying too!' cried Dame Winifred, wiping a pink sleeve over her face and streaking her make-up. 'You're *all* liars! I don't understand this, why would you say these things? Why would you slander that poor, dead girl? What's the matter with you?'

She picked up her handbag and made to move towards the door, but Bryn stood up, blocking her path. In that moment, Magnus was suddenly aware of how tall his young friend was: Dame Winifred might have been a large woman, but Bryn towered over her.

'Sit down,' the Welshman commanded, and his voice was so sharp that, instinctively, she obeyed.

'I won't listen to any more of this!' said Dame Winifred, tears still pouring down her cheeks. 'Daisy, cover your ears! It's sordid! It's disgraceful! To say such things about someone who was so good, so pure, so —'

'Oh, shut up!' snapped Bryn.

He sounded so harsh that all four of them looked up at him in shock.

'Um, Bryn,' began Juliana, hesitantly. 'Would you mind watching your tone, please? Dame Winifred's had a bit of a shock, remember…'

'She hasn't had a shock,' said Bryn, with confidence. 'But she's a good actress, I'll give her that. All the tears and the denial and the outrage, it's very convincing.' As though to demonstrate his appreciation of her dramatic prowess, Bryn clapped slowly and sarcastically as he lowered himself back onto the arm of the sofa. 'I must say, Dame Winifred's done a far better job of lying to us than any of the others. But it's time to stop pretending now.'

The aristocrat stared at him with her leaky eyes and said, 'I really — I don't know —'

'I said, *it's time to stop pretending*,' said Bryn. 'Because Anne-Laure is not the only one who acted as though butter wouldn't melt in her mouth, is she, Dame Winifred? You might be able to turn on the waterworks at will, but you're not shocked and you're not upset. You've known all along, what Anne-Laure was, what she did — and that's because you were the one who forced her into it.'

'*What?!*'

Neither Bryn nor Dame Winifred seemed to hear Magnus and Juliana's exclamation: their gazes were locked on one another, almost as though they were having a silent conversation to which the rest of the room was not privy.

'I don't understand!' wailed Dame Winifred after a few moments, breaking eye contact with the Welshman and looking around for help. 'Juliana, what is all this? I thought we were looking at flower arrangements!'

'Bryn, think about what you're saying,' said Juliana, whose expression was scandalised. 'Think about who you're talking to here, this is *Dame Winifred Rye*! She's a well-known figure in society, a member of the aristocracy. She's famous for her fundraising work, for goodness' sake! What you're suggesting is utter madness.'

'Yes, she has a good front,' Bryn agreed. 'The title, the status, the charity work... Who would ever think that she was anything more than a slightly silly but well-meaning old widow?'

'Please, Juliana, make him stop — I can't bear this!'

Dame Winifred reached out for her hostess's hand and, after a moment's hesitation, Juliana took it.

'I think you should go,' she told Bryn. 'I don't know what's going on with you at the moment — perhaps you're upset over losing your job and that's why you've got these funny ideas in your head — but I'd like you to leave now, please.'

But Magnus, who had been watching everything unfold in near-silence, stepped forward and said, 'No, Bryn stays.'

'*Magnus!*' protested Juliana, still holding Dame Winifred's hand.

But the barrister shook his head. 'I'd like to hear what he has to say. Bryn, go on.'

Nodding in gratitude, Bryn stood up and began his now-familiar pacing around the room. His brow was slightly furrowed, as though he were trying to work out how best to begin, and they all watched him as he walked back and forth in front of the sofas, nobody — not even Dame Winifred — daring to make sound.

'I don't know many of the details,' Bryn said at last. 'As Sheikh Hazim told us the other day, Magnus, these agencies are highly discreet. They're all over London, they provide girls for some of the wealthiest and most high profile men in the country, but they're a complete secret. Having said that, I'm entirely convinced that there is an escort agency right here, in Westminster Square, and it's being run by one Dame Winifred Rye.'

'This is ridiculous, I hardly even know what an escort agency *is*!' cried Dame Winifred.

'I thought I'd told you to stop pretending?' said the Welshman.

'Even so, Bryn, you might have to expand a little on this, erm, theory of yours,' suggested Magnus.

'All right, think about how Dame Winifred operates,' said Bryn, talking now more to Magnus than the accused. 'Think about the last time you went to one of her parties. What did you notice about the other guests?'

Magnus shrugged. 'They were mostly businessmen?'

'They were mostly middle-aged, high-net-worth *men*,' clarified Bryn. 'Dame Winifred seems to know hundreds of them, you said so yourself, and they all come to pay homage to her at these parties. Why? Why is she so chummy with people like Sheikh Hazim? They're not exactly one another's type, are they? But they go way back. He throws his gold prayer beads her way and, in return, she provides him with the pick of her best girls.'

'Lies, all lies...' moaned Dame Winifred.

But Magnus wasn't so sure: he had always thought Dame Winifred seemed to know an unusual amount of wealthy men, and had never been able to understand why they loyally turned up to her parties again and again. But if there was something in it for them... And that was to say nothing of the secret dinner parties that Dame Winifred was rumoured to hold for her most affluent donors.

'What does this have to do with Anne-Laure Chevalier?' asked Juliana, who Magnus noticed had let go of Dame Winifred's hand.

'Good question,' said Bryn. 'Let's assume, for the sake of argument, that the story Dame Winifred told us about how she met Anne-Laure — or rather, Annie Chambers — was true. Let's say for now that, around a decade ago, Dame Winifred was walking along Brighton beach, had to take shelter from the rain in a beach hut, and was shortly joined by an angelic girl of seventeen.'

'That *is* true!' Dame Winifred cried. 'That *is* how I met her!'

'As I said, I'm not disputing that,' Bryn told her. 'What I am calling into question is your motivation in inviting her to London. The way we heard it from you before, you felt sorry for this poor orphaned girl and decided to whisk her away and set her up in Westminster so she could pursue her dream of becoming an actress.'

'That's true too,' said the aristocrat.

'Is it?' asked Bryn. 'I'm not so sure. I think, when she appeared in that beach hut, you must not have been able to believe your luck, Dame Winifred. Here was the perfect girl to add to your collection: young, naïve, strikingly beautiful, and — most importantly — unencumbered by parents or any real ties to anyone or anywhere. The ideal kind of stray. All you had to do was play the fairy godmother and paint a glamorous, irresistible picture of London, of what her life could be like. Then of course she would trustingly follow you, of course she would leave the place where she had only known tragedy, of course she would abandon the aunt who had never loved her, and the boyfriend who was beginning to stifle her. That must have been all too easy.'

'I did it for *her*,' said Dame Winifred. 'I wanted to save her, my darling girl...'

'No, you wanted to use her,' Bryn said coldly. 'Perhaps you knew, even in that beach hut, that the combination of her beauty, her air of tragedy and her innocence would make her irresistible to men like Sheikh Hazim bin Lahab. So you brought her to London, you set her up in that little house in the Mews, and —'

'And *what*?' interrupted Dame Winifred, suddenly regaining a little of her spirit. 'I forced her into — into *prostitution*, did I? You're being absurd! How could I have done that? What proof do you have of this nonsense? Where on earth are you getting these ideas...?'

'From me.'

Magnus, Juliana and Dame Winifred turned to look at Daisy — because she had been so quiet for so long the barrister had completely forgotten she was even there. But, sure enough, Daisy was still sitting next to Dame Winifred, although she was wedged up against the arm of the sofa, as though trying to put as much distance between them as possible.

Only Bryn looked unsurprised at Daisy's words and continued presence in the living room, and he gave her an encouraging nod, as though inviting her to say more.

'I thought you were nice at first,' said Daisy in a quiet voice, speaking to her clasped hands in her lap rather than Dame Winifred. 'I've been lonely in London. Juliana's been very kind to me, of course,' she added quickly, darting a glance at her employer, 'but I've found it hard to adjust to living in a big city like this, and it takes me a while to make friends because I'm shy...'

'Little Flower, *sweetheart!*'

MYSTERY IN WESTMINSTER SQUARE

Dame Winifred reached out for her, but Daisy wriggled away, and was now so tightly pressed against the arm of the sofa that Magnus thought she was in danger of disappearing between the cushions.

'So I was pleased and flattered when you showed an interest in me,' Daisy continued, still addressing her fingers. 'Sometimes I miss my mum — I miss having someone to look after me — and you seemed to want to protect me from big, bad London, although now I realise it was exactly the opposite. So we became friends, and I let you take me out for tea at Fortnum and Mason's, and out shopping on Bond Street and in Harrods, even though a niggling voice in my head was warning me you were being too generous, that you might want something in return...' She sighed. 'I was stupid. Even in those early days, I was aware I was a kind of replacement for Anne-Laure, even though at the time I didn't know what that really meant. So it was my fault, really: I should have trusted my instincts, because my instincts were telling me something was wrong.'

'It's not your fault,' said Bryn, 'and you're definitely not stupid, Daisy. She's highly manipulative, and she's been doing this for years.'

'Daisy!' wailed Dame Winifred, her voice loud and high, perhaps in an attempt to drown out Bryn. 'Little Flower, I *do* want to protect you, I *am* your friend! I don't want anything in return...'

'That's not true!' cried Daisy.

She leapt from the sofa to escape Dame Winifred's attempted embrace. Her heart-shaped face was flushed beneath her freckles, and although Magnus had the impression Daisy wasn't used to standing her ground, she looked determined now.

'She started insisting I spend more and more time with her,' the girl continued, evidently deciding to address Magnus, Bryn and Juliana rather than Dame Winifred herself. 'She began to pry into my private life, asking about how often I saw and spoke to my parents, how many friends I had in London. She was particularly interested in my love life: how many boyfriends I'd had, what kind of men I liked, how experienced I was...' Her face, which had been faintly pink before, was now burning. 'When I mentioned I was interested in — in — *someone*,' Daisy went on, determinedly avoiding Bryn's gaze, 'she wasn't happy about it. She did everything she could to try and put me off him.'

'For your own good, petal!' exclaimed Dame Winifred, edging along the sofa towards her. 'You're such a dear, pretty little thing, you deserve far more than *that*.'

She gestured over at Bryn, who raised his eyebrows but said nothing.

'Who did you have in mind?' Daisy demanded of Dame Winifred. '*Sheikh Hazim*? Or one of those other disgusting old men who leered at me and tried to grope me at your parties and dinners? Because that's how it starts, I think,' she said, turning back to the others, 'she parades us girls around at her events in front of these — these *clients*, I suppose, like she's showing off her new stock —'

'Little Flower, this is *nonsense!*'

'— and things just get worse and worse,' Daisy continued. 'You know, after Sheikh Hazim tried to put his hand up my skirt, I told her, and do you know what she did? She laughed! She laughed and she said, "*Oh, don't be so silly, Little Flower, there's nothing to worry about! Why didn't you let him have a little fun?*"'

'I didn't realise you were upset!' protested Dame Winifred.

'That's how she pushes it,' said Daisy, speaking over the aristocrat now. 'She laughs and asks you all these questions, as though it's all a joke: "*What's wrong with a little flirting, petal? Why don't you wear a shorter skirt? Little Flower, who do you think is the most handsome man here? Give him a little kiss, will you?*"'

'Of course that was a joke — it was all a joke!'

'I don't know what the next stage is,' said Daisy. 'I don't know how she was planning on reeling me in for good. Bribery? Blackmail? Maybe she was going to slip something into my drink one night...'

'Oh, for goodness' sake!'

'But I talked to the other girls, I realised what was going on, and I told Bryn, who was on his way to working it out for himself. Because, of course, this is what she did to Anne-Laure, who was far more vulnerable than me. This is what she does to all of her girls.'

Magnus, who had been standing throughout this entire conversation, backed against the nearest wall, worried his legs were going to give way: Hazim's admissions had made him feel physically sick, but this was a hundred times worse.

'I must protest!' cried Dame Winifred, rising from the sofa once more. 'Magnus, Juliana, can't you see that young man has filled this girl's head with all sorts of silly ideas about me, simply because I don't approve of their relationship! And Daisy,' she said, advancing towards the girl, 'my darling petal, how can you think such things? It hurts my feelings *so* much, to hear you talk like this, when we are *such* good friends, after *all* that I've done for you...'

She reached out and clasped Daisy's hands between her own bejewelled fingers.

'Let go!' cried the girl, trying to pull herself free.

Bryn, who had been standing back for the entire exchange, started forward to recuse her, but Juliana got their first: in the blink of an eye, she had wrestled Daisy free, and was now standing between the girl and Dame Winifred, looking so fierce she might have been a tigress protecting her cub.

'*Don't you dare touch her!*' Juliana growled.

Dame Winifred, clearly taken aback by Juliana's sudden ferocity, stepped away and burst into a fresh wave of tears.

'Not you too, Juliana! Not you too!'

Magnus looked around the room: Dame Winifred was crying noisily; Daisy was holding Bryn's arm and murmuring something to him, perhaps trying to restrain him, because the Welshman was glaring dangerously at Dame Winifred; although he was not looking quite as angry as Juliana, who Magnus thought seemed primed to smack the sobbing aristocrat across the face at any moment. It was, the barrister decided, time to step in.

'All right!' he said loudly. 'Everybody calm down, please.'

'*Calm down?*' cried Juliana, her voice high and shrill. 'Magnus, have you not been listening? Have you not heard what she tried to do to Daisy, what she did to Anne-Laure and countless other girls — *oh my God!*'

Juliana's hands flew to her head as the truth of it seemed to hit her all over again.

'There's nothing to be achieved by flying into a panic,' said Magnus, although he too was struggling to keep his head. 'Let's all sit down and —'

'I will *not* sit down!' cried Dame Winifred, her voice breaking with emotion. She grabbed her handbag from the coffee table and headed towards the door. 'And I will *not* stay here another moment and be talked to in this manner! I've never been so insulted in my whole life!'

But, once more, Bryn blocked her path.

'I haven't finished with you yet,' he said, defending the door quite as much as Juliana had just defended Daisy.

Dame Winifred turned her tear-stained face to the room at large and wailed, 'So I am to be kept prisoner here, am I? I am to be interrogated by this delusional young man about some imaginary secret escort agency!'

'Oh, we're not keeping you here because you're running a secret escort agency,' said Bryn, 'although I'm sure the police will be interested in what you've been up to there. No,' he continued, keeping his voice light but his gaze hard, 'Dame Winifred, we're keeping you here because you murdered Anne-Laure Chevalier.'

CHAPTER FORTY

Before anybody had a chance to react to Bryn's extraordinary statement, there was a knock on the front door of the Waltersons' flat.

'Ah, that'll be Lucas,' said Bryn calmly.

'What?' said Magnus. '*Who?*'

But Bryn was already heading out into the hallway and, moments later, he reappeared with a tall, dark-haired man.

'Lucas Jones,' announced the newcomer to the room at large, 'Detective Sergeant, CID.'

'Excuse me!' said Juliana loudly. 'Who is this? Where did he come from? Bryn, what on earth is going on?'

'Three very good questions,' said Magnus, who, like his wife, was beginning to feel annoyed at being kept in the dark.

'Magnus, Juliana, my friend Lucas here is from the Criminal Investigation Department,' said Bryn. 'Lucas, this is Magnus and Juliana Walterson, the leaseholders of this flat, that's Daisy Fenway, who works with Juliana, and over there is Dame Winifred Rye, the woman I was telling you about.'

Remarkably, in the disruption of Lucas's arrival, Magnus had momentarily forgotten about Dame Winifred, who was still stood a few feet away from the door, looking weepy and distressed.

'*Excuse me —*' began Juliana again, but Bryn cut in with an explanation.

'Lucas is an old friend from Cardiff, and I've been talking to him about the Anne-Laure Chevalier case ever since he was kind enough to get hold of her bank statements for me,' he said. 'When Daisy told me of her suspicions about Dame Winifred's secret enterprise, when I was finally able to fit all the pieces of the puzzle together, I knew I had to have the back-up of someone still in the police force, someone who wouldn't go to Boyle to block me. And when Daisy called me to say she and Dame

Winifred were coming round here to look at flowers, I let Lucas know where we'd all be. I'm sorry for keeping you in the dark, Magnus, Juliana, but I had to act quickly — I didn't want Dame Winifred to get wind of what was happening and do a runner.'

'*Do a runner?*' cried Dame Winifred, the colloquialism sounding strange in her plummy accent. 'Why would I do that? I haven't done anything wrong — why would I go anywhere?'

'Says the woman standing three feet away from the door,' muttered Bryn.

'So that's why you were so insistent about coming over earlier?' Magnus said to his young friend. 'And you were in on it too, Daisy?'

She nodded, and the barrister didn't know whether to be annoyed or impressed that the pair of them had orchestrated this meeting behind his back.

Dame Winifred, meanwhile, was clearly still feeling betrayed.

'Little Flower, I can't tell you how upset this makes me, to know that not only do you believe these awful lies that dreadful boy is telling you, but that you're conspiring with *him* against *me*!'

From the other side of the room, her protégée fixed her with a level stare. 'You're the liar,' she said. 'And my name is Daisy, by the way. Perhaps you were intending to change it to something more exotic, like you convinced Annie Chambers to become Anne-Laure Chevalier, but I'm quite happy with Daisy, thank you very much.'

'Speaking of *Anne-Laure Chevalier*…' said Lucas, rather pointedly.

'Ah yes,' said Bryn, perhaps realising they had drifted off-topic. 'Why don't we all sit down and go over this once and for all?'

'Why don't you stop giving orders in someone else's flat?' grumbled Juliana, although she obediently perched herself on the edge of an armchair.

'I don't see why I should listen to any more of these horrible falsehoods,' huffed Dame Winifred.

But with Lucas now taking over Bryn's post in front of the closed living room door, there was little she could do to wriggle out of the conversation.

'Before you arrived, Lucas, we were discussing Dame Winifred's relationship with Anne-Laure Chevalier,' said Bryn, picking up the thread of the story once more. 'Until now, Dame Winifred here has always pretended she was a generous benefactor figure: according to her, she whisked Anne-Laure away from a miserable childhood, set her up in one of the nicest areas of London, and spoiled her rotten until she was settled and secure enough to stand on her own two feet. Whereas what we've learned this afternoon is that, after a chance meeting in Brighton, Dame Winifred groomed, manipulated and bullied this seventeen-year-old into becoming one of the top girls in the private escort agency she was running — and continues to run — out of Westminster Square.'

If Lucas was shocked by any of this, he didn't show it. Perhaps Bryn had already told him half of it before, Magnus thought, or maybe, given he worked for the CID, Lucas was simply used to hearing the details of sordid crimes on a daily basis. But Magnus, who would have assumed he too was somewhat numbed by his profession, found it was no easier to hear Bryn's accusations for a second time. He supposed, when it came to his work, the darker aspects of what he had to deal with were confined to the courtroom and his office at Grey's Inn. But this scene was playing out in his own living room with his wife present and his children in the next room. It involved people he knew and, worst of all, the accused was a neighbour — a friend, even — somebody he had always taken to be one of the gentlest and kindest of all his acquaintances.

Dame Winifred, meanwhile, was still protesting innocence.

'Mr Jones, was it?' she said, addressing the CID officer directly. 'Perhaps, since you are here, and since you are a *professional,* we can clear up this little misunderstanding and all get on with our day? This young man — who is no longer even a police officer, by the way — is accusing me of all sorts of nonsense, simply because I suggested to my dear little friend over there that he might be a teensy bit beneath her... You know, *romantically* speaking.'

Daisy scoffed in derision, but Lucas did not react. Encouraged, Dame Winifred went on, 'So he's cooked up this fanciful story about escorts and whatnot — as though I, an old widow, know anything about that sort of thing! — and he's accusing me of this and that without any evidence whatsoever!'

'He does have evidence!' burst out Daisy angrily. 'He has *me*!'

'I'm afraid Daisy over there is very young,' Dame Winifred explained to Lucas, in hushed tones, 'and I fear she has been rather taken in by Mr Summers. Well, I don't begrudge her that: she isn't the first to lose her head over a sweetheart, and she won't be the last. But I do object to these disgusting charges being made against me, especially when they involve my darling Anne-Laure. Why, she'd be spinning in her grave to hear them!'

'How can you say that?' said Bryn, looking flabbergasted. 'How do you have the *nerve*, after what you did to her?'

Silently, Magnus willed Bryn to keep calm: after all, if the Welshman was correct in all of this, he was going to have to present and prove his case as well as any barrister. Which wouldn't be easy, when Dame Winifred was demonstrating far more resolve than any of their other interviewees. Even Magnus, who trusted Bryn, and who believed what Daisy had just told them, still had some doubts.

'Why don't you go on, Bryn?' suggested Lucas. 'Leaving aside the escort issue for a moment, why don't you tell us exactly what you think Dame Winifred did to Anne-Laure Chevalier.'

'She killed her,' said Bryn simply.

'Oh, for goodness' sake!' cried Dame Winifred, clutching at the gaudy silk scarf around her throat. 'Just listen to him, Mr Jones, this is utterly absurd! Anne-Laure died of natural causes, the police said so, and it was widely reported in the press. So how on earth could I have killed her and, more to the point, *why*?'

'Let's answer that second question first,' said Bryn, jumping in. 'And to do that, let's rewind a bit. As we know — and yes, we do *know*, Dame Winifred — shortly after arriving in London, a young girl called Annie Chambers started working for Dame Winifred Rye. She spent a couple of years as an escort to some of the wealthiest men in London, which we know for a fact, because Sheikh Hazim bin Lahab confirmed it to us. And if anyone is under any illusion she was content in that situation, we know that wasn't the case, because one Agnes Chambers of Brighton received a phone call from her niece around this time, and reported that she sounded desperately unhappy. Obviously, this woman didn't know exactly what was going on and, embittered by her niece's rejection of her, had no qualms about leaving her to her fate. They never spoke again and Anne-Laure's ties to her past were completely severed. Perhaps, then, this is when and why she changed her name.

'But Anne-Laure, as Magnus and I have learned again and again, had brains as well as beauty,' Bryn went on, 'and did not intend to stay an escort forever. Perhaps she squirrelled away enough money to give her a head start, I don't know, but the real benefactor of her story, in spite of what Dame Winifred says, is a man named Vasyl Kosnitschev.' Bryn paused and turned to Lucas. 'Kosnitschev is a Ukrainian oligarch who gave Anne-Laure her first reputable work in London, as his PA. Unfortunately, he is no longer in Westminster Square so we cannot question him further, and Sheikh Hazim seems unsure as to whether Kosnitschev knew about her past. But whether he did or not, Anne-Laure had clawed her way out, and driven, no doubt, by the fear of what would happen to her if she ever fell on hard times again, she became obsessed with making money: she specialised in PR work and party-planning, but she also helped Lord Bevis Ellington organise some fairly dodgy deals, and later — when she learned of Jem McMorran moving drugs around parties — she even turned that into a business venture.'

'Lord Bevis Ellington and Jem McMorran, eh?' said Lucas, clearly recognising the names. 'It's a small world around here, isn't it?'

'You don't know the half of it, believe me,' said Bryn.

'This just gets more and more ludicrous!' said Dame Winifred. 'Anne-Laure wasn't a drug-dealer — she wasn't any of these things! She was a sweet, innocent girl.'

'As we've discussed, you destroyed any innocence Anne-Laure ever had,' said Bryn coldly.

But while Bryn had been relating these familiar details to Lucas, Magnus had perceived a problem.

'But how come she stayed in the Mews?' he asked. 'If, as you say, she pulled herself out of this escort work, why did she remain in a flat owned by Dame Winifred?'

'Yes, exactly, Magnus,' said Dame Winifred, '*exactly*. It doesn't make any sense!'

'Yes, that confused me too,' said Bryn. 'She can't have been fond of that place — remember the first floor, Magnus? How it contained two big bedrooms that clearly hadn't been occupied for a long time? I think, years ago, she entertained some of her clients there.'

'My God...' murmured Juliana, looking pained.

'The only explanation I can think of is that, when their professional relationship came to an end, Anne-Laure and Dame Winifred parted on civil terms. Maybe Dame Winifred even encouraged her to keep the flat, hoping to tempt her back one day, I don't know. But I think, at the time, Anne-Laure was too focused on getting herself established as something more reputable to bear Dame Winifred a grudge. And, after all, that flat was ideally situated for access to her new business contacts, Vasyl Kosnitschev, Lord Ellington and Jem McMorran.'

'And we know she spent a lot of time at Jem McMorran's place, once they started seeing one another,' mused Magnus.

'Seeing one another?' repeated Lucas. 'Blimey.'

'But I think Anne-Laure always hated that flat,' continued Bryn, seemingly determined not to get distracted, 'just as she always hated Westminster Square. Over the years, she made a success of herself here, and she found love, but she could never quite forget her beginnings, and the flat, along with figures like Sheikh Hazim and of course Dame Winifred, was a constant reminder of what she had been through. But the final straw, in terms of her remaining here, came in the form of her childhood sweetheart, Morris Springfield, who tracked her down to Westminster and began to show an... *unhealthy* interest in her. Then, enough was enough. She wanted to get out, and in doing so save Jem

McMorran from himself, so they hatched a plan to escape to LA together, two days after Dame Winifred's charity party at the Royal West Hotel.'

'Again, why would she agree to work with me on that party if I had forced her into *prostitution*?' exclaimed Dame Winifred.

'Well, that's another interesting question,' replied Bryn, as though he were a teacher commending a clever pupil. Then, addressing the others in the room, he said, 'A moment ago, I told you I didn't think Anne-Laure bore Dame Winifred any grudge when she left her employment. But I think that changed. As she grew older, wiser, as she was able to look back at what had happened with a bit of perspective, I think she began to realise exactly what Dame Winifred was — and exactly what Dame Winifred had done to her. And so just before she and Jem left London, just before she cut ties with her past for good, Anne-Laure Chevalier decided she wanted revenge.'

'Good,' said Daisy quietly, and next to her Juliana nodded.

'You say that,' said Bryn sadly, 'but I'm afraid her thirst for vengeance was her downfall. If she had just gone, if she had let bygones be bygones, no matter how unjust that might have been, she would probably be sunning herself on a Malibu beach right now. But, as it was, Dame Winifred got wind of what she was planning, and moved quickly and ruthlessly to put a stop to it.'

'This is something to do with the journalist, isn't it?' said Magnus, identifying one of the only remaining pieces of the puzzle. 'This relates to Darren Dodge from *The Dawn Reporter*?'

'It does,' said Bryn. 'A few weeks before her death, Anne-Laure called up this journalist promising him a scandal so explosive it would keep *The Dawn Reporter* occupied for months to come. The story was, of course, that a well-known aristocrat was using her philanthropic activities to cover up the fact that she was running an escort agency out of Westminster Square, providing sex workers to the great and good of London society — and think about the names Anne-Laure could have given them: politicians, businessmen, celebrities, even royals. But Anne-Laure didn't tell Darren Dodge this, not yet. She wanted to ensure she got something in return for the scandal, because she was after a nest egg for herself and Jem McMorran, and both Lord Ellington and Sheikh Hazim had refused to give her any extra money.

'So instead she dropped Dodge a few tantalising hints, and arranged a meeting in person, to which she told him she would bring "evidence" of this story — something to convince him she was telling the truth.'

'Oh, this should be good,' said Dame Winifred. 'Tell me, what is this so-called *evidence*, Mr Summers?'

'Again, good question,' replied Bryn. 'At first, I thought it must be incriminating photographs or some documents that detailed exactly what had been going on, bank statements perhaps. But it was actually Sheikh Hazim who made me realise. He was very loyal to you, by the way, Dame Winifred — he didn't give you up — but he did inadvertently let slip an important detail when Magnus and I went to see him the other day. When he was talking about the discretion involved in this kind of business, he said something like, "... *A smaller, private agency keeps our contact details in a little black book.*" And that was it, wasn't it?' said Bryn, addressing Dame Winifred directly now. 'That was what Anne-Laure wanted, so she could take it to Darren Dodge and he could start publishing all of the names of the men in its pages.'

Magnus waited for Dame Winifred to scoff at this, as she had scoffed at all of Bryn's accusations so far, but she remained silent.

'So is that why Anne-Laure agreed to work with Dame Winifred on the party at the Royal West?' asked Juliana. 'To get close enough to take the book?'

'I think so, yes,' said Bryn. 'But I'm not sure she was banking on Dame Winifred keeping it as close as she did. Because, in order to get hold of this explosive item, Anne-Laure had to resort to more drastic measures.'

'Like what?' asked Juliana.

'A week before Anne-Laure's death there were two break-ins reported in Westminster Square,' said Bryn. 'The first targeted the flat of Dame Winifred Rye, and the second that of Hilda Underpin. The police took it for granted that these two attempted crimes — for both women reported nothing had been taken — had been committed by the same perpetrator, an opportunistic thief who had chickened out at the last minute. But I remember thinking at the time we shouldn't assume these burglaries had been the work of the same person, and I was right. The first, the break-in at Dame Winifred's house, was committed by Anne-Laure Chevalier, and something *was* stolen: a little black book full of a private escort agency's clients.'

Bryn then reached into his bag and, somewhat incongruously, produced a pair of black evening gloves from its depths.

'I found these in Anne-Laure Chevalier's flat when we went to clear it out with her aunt, do you remember, Magnus? I thought she had intended to wear them to the party at the Royal West on the night she died, and decided against it at the last minute. But I think they were out because she had used them to go through Dame Winifred's flat, and so she was intending to destroy them before she left.

'For Dame Winifred's part, she told the police nothing had been stolen — after all, she didn't want any more people to know about the little black book, because she didn't want to the whole story coming out. But she guessed who the thief was and I think she guessed Anne-Laure was going to go to the press. And you couldn't let that happen, could you?' Bryn said to Dame Winifred. 'If Anne-Laure had gone to the papers, if she'd revealed this massive story, it would have been one of the biggest scandals this country has ever seen — not just for you, but for whoever all your clients are. You had to stop her. That, I think, is another reason you didn't tell the police about who had broken into your flat: by then, you had decided to take matters into your own hands.'

These words sent a chill running down Magnus's spine: for months, they had been searching for a motive strong enough to justify the accusation of murder, and at last they had one: Dame Winifred had acted to protect her secret, illegal enterprise, and all of the clients who had put their trust in her. And for somebody who plucked naïve seventeen-year-olds from beach huts and bullied them into prostitution, murder probably wasn't so much of a stretch.

Finally, Dame Winifred found her voice. 'Well, this fanciful story is nice and entertaining, Mr Summers — although I'm not sure why you felt you had to cast *me* as the villain — but I'm very interested to hear how you're going to explain how I killed Anne-Laure when we all know she died of natural causes!'

She tittered and looked around the room, inviting the others to share in her mirth, but was met by stony stares from all corners.

'Well, that's where this second burglary comes in,' said Bryn, 'the one at Hilda Underpin's flat. I wonder how long you knew that there was a poison pill sitting in the sleeve pocket of Tarquin Underpin's commando jacket? Hilda, as Magnus and I found out, will tell anybody who will listen about her husband's adventures in the war, and she mentioned this pill the first time I met her. So I don't think it's a stretch to speculate that you, as a fellow widow, would also have been told about its existence. And when you learned of Anne-Laure's betrayal — when you realised you had to silence her for good — that little pill would have seemed the perfect solution.

'Here's what I think happened,' continued the Welshman. 'After you had stolen the poison pill from Hilda's flat, the question was, when and where to use it? You and Anne-Laure were already working on that party together, circling one another, preparing to strike, and that party provided you with the perfect cover: not only would there be plenty of people there to distract from what you were up to, Anne-Laure was also a socialite with a reputation for drinking and drug-taking, so — with any luck — the police would put her sudden death down to excessive substance abuse and that would be that.

'So at the end of the night, when all the guests had gone, and it was just you and Anne-Laure left tidying up the mess — she was professional to the last — you invited her into the business conference room of the Royal West Hotel for a celebratory nightcap. You probably told her you wanted to thank her for all her hard work. Perhaps you even knew she was leaving, and pretended you wanted to part as friends, in spite of what had happened between you in the past. And Anne-Laure, to her cost, agreed. Maybe she thought she had got away with stealing the book, and the idea of toasting to your friendship before she hung you out to dry in the press and in court amused her. No doubt her judgement was also off, from the cocaine, from the excitement of her impending move, from the fact that she had been physically assaulted twice that evening —'

'What?' said Dame Winifred sharply.

'Did you not notice the bruising on her wrists and around her neck?' asked Bryn. 'Perhaps it was difficult to see in the gloom, or maybe they flared up later, but you weren't the only one with a score to settle with Anne-Laure that night, Dame Winifred, and I think you should have considered how those bruises would look, on a dead body. Because if it hadn't been for the marks of violence upon her, I think you would have got away with slipping that pill into her whiskey, watching her die, and then arranging her on the sofa as though she had been sleeping. As you predicted, the police assumed the death was drug-related and the manager of the Royal West was keen to keep the whole thing as quiet as possible. But those bruises looked suspicious. Those bruises prompted me to start asking these questions about her death even though, in the end, you hadn't laid a finger on her.'

As Bryn reached the end of his account, there was a long silence in the living room of the Waltersons' Westminster Square flat. For several long moments, Magnus, Juliana, Daisy, Lucas and Dame Winifred all stood or sat stock still, digesting what they had just heard.

'What happened to this book of clients?' asked Magnus eventually. 'Where is it now?'

'Gone, I suspect,' said Bryn, whose voice had grown a little hoarse from talking for so long. 'Dame Winifred would have moved it out of Westminster Square as quickly as possible, so I imagine, after poisoning Anne-Laure, she went straight to her flat to retrieve it. Perhaps it was even in Anne-Laure's handbag when she died. But you'll remember, Magnus, that when we were talking to Dame Winifred about her break-in she mentioned a safe deposit box, so I expect she moved the book there.'

Juliana's hand flew to her forehead. 'That's where you were going!' she cried, rounding on Dame Winifred. 'The Monday after Anne-Laure's death, when you called in at the Station Garden to talk about the flowers for your next party. You cried and pretended to be upset, you tried to get your claws into Daisy, and then you said you had to be off to the bank. You had it then, didn't you? You were off to stash away this book — this evidence!'

'Evidence.' Dame Winifred repeated the word very slowly, relishing each syllable. 'How interesting you bring that up, Juliana, because — from where I'm standing — young ex-Constable Summers here has absolutely no evidence at all.'

A change seemed to have come over the aristocrat. She was still on her feet by the door, but whereas before her stance had been nervy and cowering, now she stood tall and proud. She had cried away most of her make-up, especially around her eyes, and now that she was not caked in quite so much mascara and eyeshadow, Magnus realised what a cold, hard stare she had. As she imperiously surveyed each of them in turn, daring them to challenge her, the barrister felt as though he were looking at a completely different person than the one who had been there a few moments ago. The Dame Winifred he had known as a neighbour — the kindly, foolish woman who had spent all of her time and energy organising charity fundraisers — was gone. Or perhaps she had never existed in the first place. For now, Magnus saw that it had all been pretend: the trowelled-on make-up had been her mask, the garish clothes her costume, and she had played the part of the gentle, slightly pitiful and entirely ridiculous widow to perfection, so that nobody had ever thought to properly question how she made her money, why she knew quite so many men of influence, and what sort of person she really was, underneath it all.

'I'm waiting, Summers,' said Dame Winifred, her voice commanding. 'Where's your evidence? How are you going to prove I'm a murderer?'

For the first time that afternoon, Bryn seemed to falter. Dame Winifred's lips curled into a twisted smile.

'You can't,' she said, with a mirthless chuckle. 'You don't have any evidence. Stupid boy. You come in here and conduct this overblown charade, and you can't prove any of it. Dear, dear, where are your brains? No wonder they threw you out of the police force.'

In response, Magnus and Lucas began to speak at the same time, both attempting to jump to the defence of their younger friend. The CID officer then held up his hands, indicating Magnus should go first.

'Actually, Dame Winifred, I'm fairly sure we can prove quite a lot, with statements from Daisy, Sheikh Hazim, and a few of your other girls,' said the barrister.

'As a man of law you should know prostitution isn't illegal in the UK, Magnus,' sneered Dame Winifred.

'Yes, but procurement — that is, pimping — *is* illegal, especially when your charges are under the age of eighteen, like Anne-Laure was. Plus, there's the small matter that you've been owning and managing an illegal escort agency, which is also a criminal offence.'

'The existence of which depends on the word of a few idiot girls and an obese foreigner!' laughed Dame Winifred.

'And your bank statements and phone records, which are currently being compiled by my colleagues at the CID,' said Lucas. 'And I imagine there's still evidence to be found in your flat, which is being searched as we speak.'

Dame Winifred's eyes widened. 'You can't do that!' she cried. 'You don't have the right!'

'Funnily enough, as members of the Criminal Investigation Department, we rather *do* have the right.'

Dame Winifred hesitated, apparently doing some quick thinking, and then said, 'Well, so what? How does any of this matter? This wretched country is full of so-called massage parlours and strip clubs and seedy bars where goodness knows what goes on! Do you really think my sophisticated and discreet little enterprise is going to bother the police or a judge? I doubt I'll get more than a slap on the wrists.'

'Is that a confession?' asked Magnus.

She was, he thought, a monstrous woman. Even now, when she was completely cornered, she was still snapping back at them like a feral dog.

'Hold on a minute,' broke in Juliana. 'Aren't we forgetting about Anne-Laure? Aren't we glossing over the bigger crime here? The small matter of murder?'

'What crime?' cried Dame Winifred, her eyes wide and wild. 'What murder? I'll say it again: there *is* no evidence! The body's gone! That imbecilic Police Chief at the Victoria Station cremated it!' She began to laugh again. 'No jury is going to believe your cock-and-bull story about poison pills and commando jackets, Constable Summers. Anne-Laure Chevalier died from taking too much cocaine and that's that.'

'No, that's not that!' said Magnus, his temper suddenly flaring. He was furious with her for having the gall to stand there and deny everything when they all knew perfectly well she was guilty. 'That's not that by any stretch of the imagination, Dame Winifred.'

He stepped towards her, feeling as ruthless as he did when on the attack in court, and an idea suddenly occurred to him. It was a gamble, certainly, but it might just pay off.

'Earlier Bryn said that when Anne-Laure spoke to this journalist at *The Dawn Reporter*, she hadn't revealed the details of the story she had been intending to sell,' said the barrister. 'She wanted your little black book first, so Darren Dodge could see for himself the extent of the scandal and who was involved, especially before she named her price. That was why you moved to seize the book back and that was why you killed her.'

The accused neither confirmed nor denied this. She was watching Magnus through narrowed eyes.

'But you were too late, Dame Winifred,' continued the barrister. 'By the day of your party, Anne-Laure had already gone back to Darren Dodge, she had already shown him the book, and he had already taken copies.'

'No…' hissed the aristocrat, her tone half-suspicious, half-alarmed.

'Yes,' said Magnus firmly, fully committing to the bluff now. 'It doesn't matter where you've stashed that book, it doesn't matter what secret safe it lies in now, you weren't quick enough. The journalist has everything he needs to know.'

'You're lying,' said Dame Winifred, although she didn't sound sure. 'If anybody at *The Dawn Reporter* had something like that... Why, it'd be all over the news in a matter of hours.'

'Not if a court had issued a gag order to prevent anybody publishing the story,' said Magnus.

'And why would a court do that?' demanded Dame Winifred, still looking sceptical.

'For your protection, of course.'

She looked angry and confused. 'What are you talking about, Magnus?'

'Do you know there have been similar women to you in France and America? *Madames* whose whole enterprises have been exposed? I'm sure you do, and I'm sure you're well aware of the scandals they caused, for themselves and their clients. But do you also know that these women cooperated with the police? They had to, for their own sakes.

'Darren Dodge of *The Dawn Reporter* is chomping at the bit to publish all the gory details of the story Anne-Laure gave him days before her death,' continued Magnus. 'He is the self-proclaimed "best in the business" at stirring up scandals. His exposés have destroyed Hollywood marriages, politicians' careers, and everything in between. So, what do you think will happen, Dame Winifred, if he's set loose on this particular story? How much fun is someone like him going to have with all of your dirty little secrets? Your clients? They'll be exposed, every one of them. Their marriages and careers and lives will crumble as Dodge and his cronies gleefully print every salacious detail they can dig up about these men and their involvement with your agency and your girls. You'll be reviled, Dame Winifred. Your reputation will be in tatters, you'll be bankrupt, and I expect you won't survive too long after serving your time for procurement, as men of power don't take kindly to being crossed. Perhaps they'll even find a way to finish you off while you're still in prison...'

Dame Winifred swallowed. Even under her streaky make-up, Magnus could tell she had gone very white. 'But you just said he couldn't print it. You said there was a gag order.'

'For now, yes,' said Magnus, with a shrug. 'But that gag order comes with certain... *stipulations*. In particular, it will only continue to hold if the police have your full cooperation in their formal investigation into the murder of Anne-Laure Chevalier.'

Magnus looked over at Lucas, who dutifully played along by nodding, and then paused to allow himself to enjoy this moment, and especially the nauseated expression now crossing the aristocrat's features.

'In my opinion, it's far more preferable to be tried in court than by the press in this day and age,' said Magnus cheerfully, 'because at least the justice system has rules. The media, on the other hand, are vultures, and will pick at every detail of a scandal until there's nothing left. So the way I see it, you have two options, Dame Winifred. Either you continue to deny everything Bryn is accusing you of, in which case we'll let Darren Dodge and his friends know that they are free to publish everything they know about your agency and its clients — and you'll have to deal with the consequences alone, I'm afraid. Or you can be honest and open with the police on the matter of Anne-Laure Chevalier's death, and the gag order can remain; your collaboration will earn you a little protection and — what's that word you keep using? — *discretion*. You may then be able to use a psychiatric defence for a reduced or even suspended sentence. The choice is yours, Dame Winifred, but as a barrister may I strongly advise the second option?'

There was a long silence during which Dame Winifred glared at Magnus with unmistakeable hatred. The barrister, for his part, stared back: now that her jolly façade had dissolved, it was far easier to accept her as the odious person she was.

'You know, I never could see it before,' she said eventually, 'you as a barrister, Magnus. I always thought you rather a buffoon.'

'There's more to people than first meets the eye,' Magnus said pleasantly, determined not to be rattled by her, 'as we've learned this afternoon, Dame Winifred.'

'I couldn't imagine you in court,' she continued, 'not going by what I saw of you around the Square: jogging at a snail's pace, being tongue-lashed by your harpy of a wife —'

'How dare you!' said Juliana.

'— and bumbling about with that half-wit of a policeman — who, I must admit, has a few more brain cells than I gave him credit for. You always seemed so simple, so *good*. Put it this way, I knew better than to offer you any of my girls. But I think I see it now, the barrister in you. You're blackmailing me, Magnus, and there's not a thing I can do about it, is there?'

'Not really, no,' he said cheerfully. 'So, will you cooperate with the police? Will you confess?'

At that moment, there was another knock on the front door.

'Right on time,' said Lucas, heading out of the living room to answer it.

'Oh, what now!' cried Juliana. 'I think having a murderer-slash-pimp in my home is quite enough to be getting on with!'

A few moments later, Lucas returned, trailed by Police Chief Superintendent Barry Boyle and two other officers, presumably also from the Victoria Police Station. Magnus, who had only seen Boyle once or twice before, thought he too had undergone something of a transformation: whereas before he'd had an arrogant swagger about him, now he looked decidedly sheepish. He seemed to be trying to make himself as small as possible, which was no mean feat, given his immense size.

'Afternoon,' he said gruffly to the living room at large. Then, avoiding Bryn's gaze, he grunted, 'Summers.'

Bryn nodded. 'Sir.'

'Mr Boyle has been briefed on the situation by my colleagues,' said Lucas, 'and is here to relieve us of Dame Winifred Rye. Boyle, you know what to do.'

Still looking shame-faced, the Police Chief Superintendent shuffled towards the aristocrat, who regarded him stonily. The handcuffs flashed silver in the bright afternoon light as he withdrew them from his utility belt.

'Dame Winifred Rye, I'm arresting you for procuring, for operating a prostitution business, and on suspicion of the murder of Anne-Laure

Chevalier. You do not have to say anything, but it may harm your defence if you do not mention when questioned something which you later rely on in court. Anything you do say may be given in evidence.'

'Are those really necessary?' said Dame Winifred haughtily, as he bore down on her with the handcuffs. 'What on earth are the good people of Westminster going to think?'

'Probably that you're a nasty piece of work!' snapped Juliana. 'Which would be true, wouldn't it?'

'Please, Mr Boyle, can't we be civilised about this?' Dame Winifred implored him, slipping back a little into her old persona. 'I'll go quietly to the car, I promise. There's no need for a fuss, is there?'

'Cuff her, Boyle!' growled Lucas.

After looking between them, Barry Boyle closed the handcuffs gently around her chubby wrists.

'Perhaps we can, erm, disguise them a little?' he muttered.

'*What* a good idea!' trilled Dame Winifred, pulling the long silk scarf from around her neck and managing to drape it so it hung over the handcuffs. 'There now, that's better, isn't it? Now why don't you take my arm? Then we'll just look like we're having a little walk, won't we?'

'Don't worry,' said Lucas, as Boyle obediently chaperoned Dame Winifred out of the living room by the arm for a little stroll, before sharply darting into the car, 'our boys at the CID won't go as easy on her.'

'I should think not,' said Magnus, sinking into the nearest chair.

He felt utterly exhausted. The events of the last hour — no, the events of the last few weeks — had drained him completely. But as Lucas accompanied the rest of the police officers and Dame Winifred Rye out of the Waltersons' flat, Magnus summoned the energy to grin over at Bryn, who was holding hands with Daisy on the other side of the room. They had done it, Magnus thought triumphantly; they had solved the case, and in doing so they had seen a little justice done for Anne-Laure Chevalier.

'Well,' said Daisy, after a few minutes, letting go of Bryn's hand, crossing to the coffee table, and picking up the catalogue of flowers she,

Juliana and Dame Winifred had been looking at earlier that afternoon. 'I doubt The Station Garden will be getting much business from *her* for a while.'

'I think you might be right,' chuckled Magnus.

He looked at Juliana, inviting her to share in the joke, but she was frowning to herself.

'You're, erm, very quiet, darling,' he noted.

'I'm just *speechless*!' Juliana burst out, before proceeding to contradict herself with a lengthy rant. 'This place! This *wretched place*! I always told you it was dreadful, Magnus, and that was before I knew it was full of drug-dealers and stalkers and escorts and *murderers* for goodness' sake! I can't believe it! I mean, *murder*!'

'Steady on,' said Magnus, 'it's not *full* of drug-dealers and stalkers…'

'*Isn't it?*' Juliana's tone was dangerous.

'But I see your point, it is a lot to take in, isn't it?'

'Oh, I've taken it in,' she said, almost threateningly. 'I've taken *all* of it in. Every last detail, right up to the moment that great oaf — that excuse for an officer of the law — let a murderer walk out of *my* flat like Lady Muck, with her handcuffs covered up and her nose in the air.' Juliana let out a cry of frustration and rage, and Magnus had the strong impression this wasn't the last he was going to hear on the matter. 'It's unconscionable!' Juliana raged on. 'It's utterly disgraceful, the lengths people around here will go to, to protect the reputation of *Westminster Square*!'

EPILOGUE

'Well,' Magnus said to himself, 'I suppose this is it.'

His voice echoed around the empty living room. The removal men had been round the previous day to pack away most of their furniture and belongings, and now the Waltersons' Westminster Square flat looked exactly as it had a decade ago, when they had moved in.

Until now, Magnus hadn't been able to picture what the space had been like then, before it had been filled with their elegant furniture, silk rugs, and all of Juliana's plants and rural-themed paintings. But now he felt as though he were glimpsing a moment from ten years ago, when he and Juliana had been newly-married, before Rosanna and Lee had been born, and when he had still been working his way through the ranks at Grey's Inn. Now, standing here, it occurred to Magnus what formative years they had been, the ones he had spent in Westminster Square — although he was also aware of the irony of lingering here and dwelling on the past, when an exciting future was just around the corner.

'Are we done in here?'

Juliana bustled into the vast space that had once been their living room, trailed by Rosanna and Lee, both of whom were carrying small, brightly coloured plastic suitcases. In comparison to Magnus, the rest of the Waltersons were showing very little reluctance to leave Westminster Square: the children were full of questions about their new house, garden and school in Kent, whereas Juliana was sweeping around the empty flat like a victorious general who had recently seen her greatest enemy defeated.

'I think that's everything, yes,' said Magnus. 'I just need to take the safe down to the car, and then we can do a final sweep for anything we might have missed.'

'Are we not taking this?' asked Rosanna, poking an antique mirror that was still affixed to the wall by the door.

'No, that's not ours, sweetheart, that came with the house,' explained Juliana. 'And please don't jab at it like that, it's probably Grade II-listed or something absurd like that, and we'll be charged a small fortune if we damage it. Now Rosanna, Lee, why don't you go downstairs and put your suitcases in the car? It's unlocked...'

'I reckon a lot of people *would* try and take it,' mused Magnus, looking at the gilt-framed mirror. 'You know, a banker friend of mine had a client — a man not unlike Sheikh Hazim, actually — who took half the fixtures with him when he moved out of his expensive house in the South of France. And I'm talking about everything he could detach, remove and unscrew, even the toilet seats.'

'Ha, *toilet* seats!' giggled Lee, on his way out of the door.

'Well, if he was treated anywhere near as badly as we have been by CSP, I can't say I blame him,' said Juliana. 'In fact, I'm tempted to keep a few toilet seats for myself!'

She was referring to the fact that, in the end, they had been unable to convince Central Square Properties to recompense them any more than two hundred thousand pounds for the remaining half of their twenty-year lease. Considering they had paid four hundred thousand for their flat a decade ago, what they were getting back did not take into account inflation, nor the amount of decorating they had done and all the maintenance charges they had coughed up over the years. In fact, CSP had even attempted to deduct money from the two hundred thousand as a penalty for their apparent breach of the terms of the lease agreement, but Juliana had flown into such a rage at the mere suggestion of this, and threatened them with so much legal action, they had swiftly withdrawn the extra charges.

But in spite of his best efforts, Magnus had not been able to persuade CSP that they owed he and Juliana more than the relatively paltry sum of two hundred thousand pounds. In the weeks before the matter had been settled, he had pored over the lease agreement late into the night, scrutinising each of the many pages for some legal loophole, but had found nothing: apparently, whoever CSP's lawyers were, they were some of the wiliest in the business. Furthermore, to add insult to injury, Magnus had recently discovered that whoever took on the next twenty-year lease of their flat would be paying CSP 1.2 million pounds for the privilege; exactly three times as much as he and Juliana had paid a decade ago.

As Juliana continued to huff and puff about what a raw deal they had been given, Magnus tried not to feel too frustrated with her. After all, she had won, hadn't she? They were leaving Westminster Square, and so — regardless of the circumstances — she had finally got what she wanted.

Recently, though, Magnus had wondered once or twice whether they would still be moving if it hadn't been for Anne-Laure Chevalier. Juliana had always been unhappy in central London, so he doubted she would have lasted another ten years here, but after the dramatic scenes in this very living room at the end of the summer, there was no way Juliana was going to endure much longer in Westminster Square, not after everything Magnus and Bryn had discovered during the course of their investigation. In fact, Juliana now felt entirely vindicated in her belief that Westminster Square was den of vice, and given they had exposed drug-dealing, embezzlement, stalking, assault, a secret escort agency and a cold-blooded murder, Magnus now found it rather difficult to argue with her. So when, a few days after Dame Winifred Rye's arrest, she had announced her intention to move the family to Kent, Magnus had known that in order to preserve his marriage and his relationship with his children, he had little choice but to agree to Juliana's plan.

'It hasn't all been bad though, has it?' Magnus wondered aloud now. 'We've been happy here, haven't we?'

Juliana looked at him, her expression a little startled, and then she walked over and wrapped her arms around him.

'We've been happy *together*,' she said, 'the two of us, and then the four of us. But I think we'll be happier still in Kent, where the air and the water will be clean, and the grass is the greenest in all of England, and the children can play in the garden and the fields and the woods...'

'Hm,' said Magnus, who found it difficult to argue with her when she was in his embrace. Besides — although he would never tell her — maybe she was right.

'Mum, Dad — urgh, stop cuddling!'

Rosanna and Lee were back, this time empty-handed, and Magnus sincerely hoped their suitcases were in the car.

'Mum, Dad, Bryn's outside,' Rosanna continued.

'Ah good,' said Magnus, 'I was hoping he'd catch us before we went. Well, why don't we all check every nook and cranny of this place one last time, and then I'll get the safe and we'll go down together?'

Five minutes later, when Juliana and the children each had a handful of odds and ends they had discovered lying at the back of cupboards or tucked into the edge of the carpet (one of Rosanna's purple hairclips, several pens, a single earring of Juliana's) the Waltersons headed downstairs and out into the street. It was a fine autumn day, and the reds and golds of the trees in Westminster Square's Gardens were so bold they seemed to burn in the sunshine like embers. Magnus took a deep breath of the crisp air and then sighed it out heavily: autumn was perhaps his favourite season, so it made his heart ache to depart before the trees had shed their leaves onto the roads and pavements of Westminster Square.

'It'll look even better in Kent,' said Juliana, as though reading his mind.

He smiled at her. Once more, he suspected she was right.

'Urgh, *kissing*!' cried Lee.

'We're not —' Magnus began, but then he followed his son's gaze to a few doors down, where Bryn and Daisy were preoccupied with one another behind one of the pillars of the portico. Magnus shot Juliana a mischievous look and then said, rather loudly, 'You know, I've been thinking: if Bryn and Daisy get married and she takes his name, she'll be *Daisy Summers*. Doesn't that sound like a character from a children's TV programme? *Daisy Summers: florist by day, detective's assistant by night.*'

As Juliana laughed, Bryn and Daisy broke apart, managing to look simultaneously sheepish and rather pleased with themselves.

'Erm, hello, Magnus, Juliana,' said Bryn, affecting casualness. 'We came to say goodbye.'

'Got a bit distracted along the way, did you?' said Magnus, with a grin.

'Something like that...'

Bryn and Daisy joined Magnus and Juliana on the pavement in front of the car. Rosanna and Lee were already clambering inside, squabbling over toys and books.

'I can't believe you're actually going,' said Bryn.

'Neither can I,' admitted Magnus.

'We'll miss you around here.'

'Kent's not very far,' said Juliana. 'You're welcome to visit at any time — and of course Daisy can show you the sights.'

As Daisy nodded, Magnus said, 'I'm not sure Bryn will have very much time to visit us, given he's such a hot-shot detective these days.'

'Hardly,' mumbled Bryn.

'You *are*, don't put yourself down!' Daisy told him. Then, turning to Magnus and Juliana, she said, 'He's absolutely acing the training — he's top of the class!'

'Well, it helps that Lucas is acting as my mentor once again,' said Bryn, 'and that my reputation has preceded me.'

'Yes, I imagine being known as the man who solved the murder of Anne-Laure Chevalier has given you a bit of an edge over some of your colleagues,' said Magnus.

As Bryn smiled modestly, Magnus gave him an affectionate slap on the back. A month or so ago, he had been delighted to hear that not only had his young friend been reinstated into the police force, he had also been fast-tracked onto a two-year Crime Investigators' Development Programme with the CID, and was now known as Trainee Detective Constable Summers. Magnus could not think of anybody who deserved this more. Given how Bryn had handled the Anne-Laure Chevalier case, the barrister was in no doubt that he would make a very fine detective — even though sometimes, when reflecting back on how Bryn had cross-examined their various suspects, Magnus thought he could have almost been a barrister instead.

'I have a bit of news from my old station, actually,' said Bryn, perhaps in an attempt to deflect their attention from his latest achievement. 'Barry Boyle's gone.'

'Really?' said Magnus. 'He was fired?'

'Not exactly,' said Bryn. 'The official line is that he's taken early retirement. He was due to go in a few years — that's why he'd become so lax, I think — but let's just say it wasn't his choice to leave.'

'Well, at least you're rid of him,' said Magnus.

'Even if he will still get a ridiculous pension, and probably a gold watch too,' grumbled Bryn, with uncharacteristic negativity. 'He's not very popular in the CID, let me tell you. As well as the state he's left the Victoria Police Station in, they're furious with him for trying to cover up Anne-Laure's death. That autopsy he failed to order would have been very useful right now, as would her body.'

'But I thought Dame Winifred had confessed?' said Juliana.

'She did, under the proviso we continue to protect the identity of her clients, even though we have no idea who they are. You know, I still can't believe she fell for that bluff...'

'Actually, the police should probably look into getting a genuine gag order before the court case,' said Bryn, 'because if reporters like Darren Dodge *do* find out there's a secret escort agency to be investigated, they'll be no stopping them...'

'I don't really see why Dame Winifred *should* be protected,' said Juliana, folding her arms. 'Not after everything she's done.'

'Because that was the deal,' said Magnus.

'She has a couple of very powerful lawyers working for her now,' said Bryn. 'Well, we always knew she had friends in high places, didn't we?'

'They're probably ex-clients,' said Magnus.

'Goodness, I didn't think of that,' said the policeman. 'Anyway, if she turns on the tears when she pleads guilty, with her record of charity work, and with the fact that we don't have a body or even a proper autopsy, Dame Winifred will probably get a pretty lenient sentence, confession or no confession.'

'Oh, isn't that that just *typical* of this place!' raged Juliana. 'Westminster Square: where you can literally get away with murder!'

'Well, no matter how many strings she pulls, at least she's been caught,' said Daisy. 'No matter how much Barry Boyle tried to mess things up, that terrible woman *will* get a trial and she *will* go to prison, and that's because of you, Bryn.'

Under her adoring gaze, Bryn's grim expression melted.

'Yeah, I suppose you're right…'

'Of course she is,' said Magnus, giving Bryn another clap to the back. 'Because of you, there's no longer a murderer prowling around the City of Westminster.'

'That we know of,' sniffed Juliana. 'And speaking of people prowling around Westminster, what happened to that dreadful Morris Springfield?' Then, before they could answer, she shuddered and went on, 'When I think of him coming into the shop every Monday, telling barefaced lies about buying flowers for his sick mother…'

'He's gone,' said Bryn, reassuringly. 'After we'd uncovered what he was up to, I was quite worried about whether he'd try it again with some other woman, so I ended up reporting him. This is probably confidential, but it seems he's gone back to Brighton, and so the police there have his name and will keep an eye on him. I don't know, though — he was so obsessed with Anne-Laure, and for so long, I can't really imagine him directing his affections elsewhere. If he's gone back to Brighton, I imagine it's to spend his days revisiting their teenage haunts and writing strange books dedicated to his lost love.'

'*Love* has nothing to do with it,' said Juliana firmly.

'Although speaking of someone who did love her, you know Jem McMorran's gone too?' said Magnus.

'To Santa Barbara, yes,' said Daisy. Then, when they all looked at her, she blushed and continued, 'I read all about it in some trashy magazine at the hairdresser. Apparently, he's there to "concentrate on his career" but, well, he probably had to get away from here, didn't he?'

'Poor Jem,' said Juliana, who had also been informed of the actor's relationship with Anne-Laure. 'What a terrible shame to lose someone you love like that. I suppose it's for the best he won't be here for the trial, and so won't hear all the gory details of her death…'

'He didn't even know all the gory details of her *life*,' said Magnus.

'Well, that's understandable, isn't it?' said Juliana, charitably. 'Anne-Laure wanted to start again. She wanted a chance at happiness. That poor girl.'

'Well, at least out in California Jem can throw himself into his work,' said Bryn. 'You know, concentrate on his acting, focus on his career, and maybe in doing so kick some — erm — *unfortunate* habits he might have developed over the years.'

'Hm,' said Magnus. He wasn't sure he shared Bryn's optimism: after all, if Jem hadn't been able to stop drinking, taking drugs and overspending under Anne-Laure's influence, what hope did he have now?

'This magazine article I read suggested he had a couple of roles lined up,' said Daisy, 'but they didn't sound that great. One was a part in a big science-fiction blockbuster and the other was in a comedy that sounded really stupid. He needs another *Pioneer of the Past* — another hit, I mean, not one of those terrible sequels.'

'Yes, otherwise he'll be in danger of losing his A-list status,' said Magnus, feeling this was practically an inevitability. 'If only Anne-Laure was still around to sort him out. If only they'd managed to escape together.'

'Poor Jem,' said Juliana again.

Just then, so suddenly it made them start, a voice behind them croaked, 'What's happening here, eh?'

Magnus spun around: without any of them noticing her, Hilda Underpin had hobbled along the pavement to inspect what was going on.

'So you're really leaving, are you, Magnus?' she continued. 'I saw the removal van yesterday, but I thought it was too good to be true.'

'Afternoon, Hilda,' said Magnus, responding to her rudeness with a polite little bow.

'Hilda,' said Juliana stiffly.

But the old woman wasn't paying them the slightest bit of attention. Instead, she was gawking up at Bryn and pulling her lips back into what was obviously supposed to be a smile, but instead looked like a yellow-toothed grimace.

'Hello, Brian,' she said softly.

'Erm, hello,' said Bryn.

'Who's Brian?' asked Daisy, slipping her hand into Bryn's once more.

'Who's *this*, more like!' snapped Hilda, her expression blackening as she took in the sight of their entwined fingers.

'This is Daisy Fenway, my *girlfriend*,' said Bryn, emphasising the last word rather more forcefully than necessary.

Hilda scowled, and then declared, 'I don't like her, Brian. She looks like a little hussy.'

'Excuse me?' said Daisy, in what Magnus thought was a very good impression of Juliana.

'*I said you look like a little hussy!*' shouted Hilda, as though Daisy were deaf.

'Ignore her, Daisy,' advised Juliana, 'she's not worth your time.'

As Hilda prepared a retort, Magnus decided it was time to step in and change the subject.

'We were just discussing how it's all change around here, Hilda,' he began conversationally, 'what with the departures of Vasyl Kosnitschev, Jem McMorran and Morris Springfield. And now us leaving too.'

'Thank goodness,' said Hilda. 'I'll be glad to see the back of all of you.'

'Oh, charming,' said Juliana.

'I never liked any of them,' Hilda continued. 'Well, I suppose that Russian —'

'Ukrainian,' corrected Magnus.

'Same thing. I suppose he was at least quiet, even if he did do some funny things to his house, but those two young men were just *awful*. In fact, I don't know who was worse, that preening thespian roaring around in his sports cars at all hours, or that creepy writer skulking about with his notebook.'

'Morris was worse,' said Juliana, with confidence.

'Well, I'm glad to be rid of them,' said Hilda. 'And we'll be rid of that despicable Arab soon too.'

'Really?' said Magnus. 'Is Sheikh Hazim moving as well?'

'If you mean to a graveyard or whatever those heathens have, then yes, I do,' said Hilda. 'He's at death's door, Magnus.'

'Is he?'

'Probably. He had a heart attack the other week, didn't you hear? Well, I wasn't surprised. Have you seen the size of him? It's disgusting! I'd kick him out of the country if it were up to me, so his slow death won't be a drain on tax-payers' money...'

'But he's all right now?' asked Magnus, wondering why he was concerned for Sheikh Hazim of all people, considering what they now knew about him.

'For *now*, yes,' said Hilda. 'He's back at home. And do you know what I heard? He's so fat and unfit he's installed a lift in the house — CSP won't like that, will they? And apparently he has one for his private plane too. Imagine not being able to walk up a few steps! I'm in my eighties and I still walk Tam Tam every day — don't I, Tam Tam?'

As though only just remembering the dog's existence, Hilda unzipped her handbag and pulled out the fluffy chihuahua, who looked rather bedraggled and panicked from being shut away for so long.

'Well, speaking of,' said Magnus, hoping she would go away and leave them to their goodbyes, 'hadn't you and Tam Tam better get on, Hilda?'

But she ignored this hint, and instead croaked, 'And did you hear about Ellington?'

'No,' said Magnus, his curiosity piqued in spite of himself. 'What's happened to him?'

'Oh, it's *dreadful*!' said Hilda, with relish. 'He's causing quite a fuss in the House of Lords with his ranting and raving. I don't think he can cope without that bodyguard of his. I always assumed he was rather an oaf, that one, but apparently he kept old Ellington in check.'

'Gregor's left, then?' asked Bryn.

'What are you talking about, Brian? Who's Gregor?'

'The bodyguard.'

'Oh, was that his name? Well, I suppose he was Scottish, as far as I could tell with that ridiculous lisp. Yes, I heard he went back to the army — best place for him, if you ask me. They're terrible people, the Scottish: loud, uncouth, and of course they all drink far too much. But funnily enough it was Ellington who was the old soak, wasn't it? We all knew that, of course, but it seems his fellow politicians are only just finding out. Apparently he's been shouting away and embarrassing himself at work. It's shameful, when you think about it — that this is a member of the House of Lords. But then what do you expect, when this country is going to the dogs?'

Fortunately, before Hilda could continue with this rant, Rosanna wound down one of the windows in the back of the car, stuck her head outside and shouted, 'Are we going or what?'

Hilda backed away, regarding Magnus and Juliana's daughter with a disgusted expression. 'Yes, please *do* go,' she said. Then, after kissing her dog on his wet nose, she added, 'Thank goodness I have you to protect me from all of this, Tam Tam...' and began to hobble away.

'Bye!' called Magnus. 'Don't be a stranger now!' Then, chuckling, he said, 'You know, I might miss her. She's good for a laugh, is Hilda.'

'If you say so,' muttered Juliana.

'*Mum!*' This time it was Lee leaning out of the window. 'Mum, can we *go*?'

'Yes, I suppose we should,' said Juliana. 'My parents are expecting us in time for tea... Oh, Daisy!' She cried out as she reached out for the younger woman, pulling her into a tight embrace. 'What am I going to do without you?'

'What am I going to do without *you*, more like?' said Daisy, hugging Juliana back. 'The Station Garden isn't going to be the same...'

'Oh, it'll be fine without me! You were always much better at doing the books than I was, and I know you'll do a wonderful job as manager. But you know where I am if you need me —'

'Which I'm sure I will...'

'And you *must* keep in touch, and you *must* come and visit us, especially if you need a break from this dirty great city...'

While Juliana and Daisy continued their emotional and exuberant goodbye, Magnus turned to Bryn.

'Well,' he said.

'Well,' Bryn replied.

Magnus offered his hand, and after Bryn had shaken it, they too embraced, although far more quickly and formally than Juliana and Daisy. Then Magnus grinned: it seemed, for them, there was nothing else to say or do. He was quite confident they knew what they meant to one another, and he assumed a lifelong friendship was unavoidable, once you had solved a murder case with someone.

'You kids have fun, now,' he said, after he had kissed Daisy on the cheek and Juliana had made a fuss over Bryn. 'Stay out of trouble.'

He gave them one last wave, ducked into the car, and shut the door. While Juliana checked Rosanna and Lee were buckled in and unfurled the map, Magnus settled himself into the driving seat and started the engine. Then, just before pulling away, he glanced over at his wife, who was now taking one last look at the pristine porticos of Westminster Square.

'All right?' he said.

'Yes,' she replied, fixing him with an expression so full of joy that Magnus could not help but laugh. 'Now, let's get out of here, shall we?'

AIDEN PATTERSON

Aiden Patterson is a journalist who studied in New York. From his days as a trader to his time as an investigative reporter, he has an intimate knowledge of the gritty underbelly of London and New York's social scene. His reports on white-collar crimes and his involvement in various high-profile cases inspired him to pen this novel.